SEAN WALLACE is .... ne Books, which won a World Fantasy Award in 2006. In the past he w .... *Fantasy Magazine,* ...... Award winning .... d Fantasy nomin ...... for Clarkesworld magazine .... ing anthologies: ...... New Fantasy Horror The ...book, Ye .... *wocky, Japanese Dreams, The M ....noth Book of ....punk* and *The Mammoth Book of Warriors and Wizardry;* and co-editor of *Bandersnatch, Fantasy Annual, Phantom* and *Weird Tales: The 21st Century.* He lives in Germantown, Maryland with his wife, Jennifer, and their twin daughters, Cordelia and Natalie.

Recent Mammoth titles

The Mammoth Book of Warriors and Wizardry
The Mammoth Book of One-Liners
The Mammoth Book of the Vietnam War
The Mammoth Book of Westerns
The Mammoth Book of Dieselpunk
The Mammoth Book of Air Disasters and Near Misses
The Mammoth Book of Sherlock Holmes Abroad
The Mammoth Book of Insults
The Mammoth Book of Brain Games
The Mammoth Book of Gangs
The Mammoth Book of New Sudoku
The Mammoth Book of Best New SF 28
The Mammoth Book of SF Stories by Women
The Mammoth Book of Southern Gothic Romance
The Mammoth Book of Best New Horror 25
The Mammoth Book of Best British Crime 11
The Mammoth Book of Dracula
The Mammoth Book of Historical Crime Fiction
The Mammoth Book of Shark Attacks
The Mammoth Book of Skulls
The Mammoth Book of Paranormal Romance 2
The Mammoth Book of Tasteless and Outrageous Lists
The Mammoth Book of Prison Breaks
The Mammoth Book of Merlin
The Mammoth Book of Special Forces Training
The Mammoth Book of Travel in Dangerous Places
The Mammoth Book of Steampunk Adventures
The Mammoth Book of Antarctic Journeys
The Mammoth Book of Modern Ghost Stories
The Mammoth Book of Apocalyptic SF

The Mammoth Book of Kaiju

Sean Wallace

ROBINSON

ROBINSON

First published in Great Britain in 2016 by Robinson

Copyright© Sean Wallace for the selection and individual stories by respective contributors, 2016

1 3 5 7 9 8 6 4 2

The moral right of the authors has been asserted.

All characters and events in this publication, other than those clearly in the public domain, are fictitious and any resemblance to real persons, living or dead, is purely coincidental.

A CIP catalogue record for this book
is available from the British Library.

ISBN 978-1-47213-564-3 (paperback)

Typeset in Great Britain by Hewer Text UK Ltd, Edinburgh
Printed and bound in Great Britain by CPI Group (UK) Ltd, Croydon CRO 4YY
Papers used by Robinson are from well-managed forests and other responsible sources

MIX
Paper from
responsible sources
FSC   FSC® C104740
www.fsc.org

Robinson
is an imprint of
Little, Brown Book Group
Carmelite House
50 Victoria Embankment
London EC4Y 0DZ

An Hachette UK Company
www.hachette.co.uk

www.littlebrown.co.uk

Contents

Introduction:
On the Shoulders of Giants

There is something cathartic about watching giant monsters trash cities. The films that feature them are like disaster movies – visual and endlessly entertaining spectacles of uncontrollable annihilation – but with the fantastical image of a living creature at their core. At their best these cinematic tales of monstrous beings represent a profundity that is hard to articulate. Perhaps it's the morbid pleasure of seeing humanity's greatest achievements crushed underfoot and humanity itself humbled – and yet somehow, despite this imposition of out-of-control relativity, surviving.

And the purest form of this impossible fantasy of destruction is the *kaiju*.

Kaiju is a Japanese term that has been little known in the West except among aficionados of a particular tradition of monster cinema – up until recent times, that is.

The word means "monster" or "giant monster" (though more accurately it translates as "strange creature") and the cinematic tradition such monsters spawned is called *kaiju eiga* ("monster film"). As the term "*kaiju*" can refer to any monstrous creature, the more specific term "*daikaiju*" ("giant monster") is sometimes used to refer to the giant monsters of the film tradition. Either way, what we're talking about here is really, really big monsters – impossible monsters compared to which we humans are little more than insects.

Kaiju eiga as a film genre began with the creation of the now iconic giant monster Godzilla, known in Japan as Gojira, and in re-packaged form in the US as Godzilla, King of the Monsters. *Gojira* was made by Toho Studios in 1954 and directed by Ishirô Honda – a respected film-maker who was a close friend of the great Akira Kurosawa, often acting as the latter's second-unit or assistant director on movies such as *Stray Dog*, *Kagemusha* and *Ran*. *Gojira* was, for the time, an expensive film, and deservedly well thought of, though some later Godzilla films – weak in themselves but made worse through poor dubbing and cuts applied to overseas releases – tended to brand the entire genre as cheap and ludicrous in the eyes of many. The original *Gojira* itself was a relatively serious attempt on the part of director Honda to create a metaphor evoking issues raised by the nuclear attacks that annihilated Hiroshima and Nagasaki at the end of the War, and more widely to encompass the moral implications of "super-science" in the post-war world. Such thematic "discussion" was anathema under Occupation rule, but nobody takes any notice of absurd monster movies, do they?

Audiences in Japan did, in a big way, and Godzilla's iconic status developed through following decades with twenty-eight Japanese feature films (plus their Americanised counterparts) being produced, all starring the monster and assorted gigantic friends and enemies. There have been two official US Godzilla films since then, with a sequel to the 2014 *Godzilla* scheduled for release in 2018. Recently Toho announced a planned new Godzilla film of their own, thus re-igniting the Japanese franchise that had gone into abeyance after 2004's *Godzilla: Final Wars*. As a character, Godzilla has also appeared in various comic series (from Marvel, Dark Horse, IDW and others), two animated TV series, various novelizations and advertisements, and on innumerable T-shirts. Everyone knows who the Big G is, even if they've never seen any of the films nor read the comics.

But that's not the end of it. Godzilla was the catalyst for an entire genre of *tokusatsu* (live-action, special-effect driven entertainments), a genre that includes the giant-sized humanoid alien superhero Ultraman and his progeny, fighting an endless array of bizarre *kaiju*. Ultraman was originally created in 1966 for a TV series of that name produced by *Gojira* special-effects guru, Eiji Tsuburaya. The franchise has been ongoing ever since, almost without interruption, both on TV and in the cinema. Godzilla alumni Rodan (an oversized pterodactyl-like creature) and Mothra (a battleship-sized moth) also received their own spin-off movies, as Toho went on to make a horde of non-Gojira *kaiju eiga*. A goodly number of them were directed by Ishirô Honda himself. Other studios joined in the party and started making their own *kaiju eiga*, the most successful being Daiei Studios' giant fire-breathing turtle, Gamera, who has been flying around on and off since his debut in 1965.

Strictly speaking then, the term "*kaiju*" refers to monsters in this particular Japanese tradition. The tradition itself, beyond Godzilla, is characterised by a high level of absurdity, and not all of the *kaiju* concerned are even vaguely reptilian. The monsters are much bigger than is physically viable; taken literally, these strange creatures are indeed impossible fantasies, despite the frequent science-fiction trappings given them. They come in all shapes and sizes; latter-day Ultraman series have been particularly inventive in this regard, as evidenced by, for example, Gan Q from the Ultraman Gaia series of the late 1990s – a gargantuan eye with two legs, arms ending in spikes and smaller eyes scattered over its clay-like body. Weirdness is par for the course.

Kaiju origins are as diverse as imagination allows, from traditional nuclear mutation, through outer space and inter-dimensional invasion, to the incarnation of emotional and metaphysical states via the imagination of unsuspecting humans, often children. They all have names. Their favourite pastime is rampaging through cities and trashing buildings, though they're not averse to appearing at sea, on tropical islands, in space, or . . . well, anywhere really. They tend to be all but impervious to humanity's conventional military might (even nuclear) and as a result often come with science-based human nemeses in the form of anti-monster squads and huge robotic fighting machines. Whatever the imagination can come up with is likely to be utilised at some point, whether or not it makes scientific, physical or economic sense.

Interestingly enough, a detailed history of the development of Godzilla and *kaiju eiga* reveals an older ancestry for cinematic giant monsters that points outside Japan to earlier Western influences. *Gojira* itself was inspired by the US monster film *The Beast from 20,000 Fathoms* (US-1953; dir. Eugène Lourié), for which stop-motion expert Ray Harryhausen created a large, prehistoric beast known as a Rhedosaur, awakened by nuclear testing in the Arctic regions and now bent on destroying New York City. Toho executives had seen that film and, inspired by its success, wanted to make a Japanese version of it. They gave the job to Honda, little expecting he would produce something not only recognisably his own but also arguably more influential in the long run.

Of course, the non-*kaiju* rampaging giant monster tradition in cinema goes back even further than *The Beast* – and giant monsters in literature further still. The 1925 movie *The Lost World* was based on an original novel by Sir Arthur Conan Doyle, and directed by Harry O. Hoyt, with monster FX by Willis O'Brien, the "father" of stop-motion effects. It offered up the first giant monster city rampage on film, when a brontosaurus brought back from the regressive lost plateau escapes from captivity and goes on a brief but effective rampage through the streets of London.

Some years later O'Brien would create a giant monster perhaps even more iconic than Godzilla, even if this King starred in fewer movies: *King Kong* (directed by Merian C. Cooper and Ernest B. Schoedsack in 1933). This giant ape beauty-and-the-beast classic also had its own relationship to the *kaiju eiga* tradition. Initially Toho had planned on creating Gojira via stop-motion, just like Kong, but lack of available expertise and the time-consuming nature of stop-motion led him to utilise man-in-a-suit techniques and miniature sets instead. This, too, became a key component of classic *kaiju eiga*, until recent times when CGI radically changed the landscape.

Post-*The Beast from 20,000 Fathoms* and *Godzilla: King of the Monsters*, Hollywood would spend a decade or so creating a plethora of giant monsters (mostly reptilian or insectoid) that are awakened or mutated by the Bomb, though few of them display the thematic seriousness of Honda's *Gojira*. Non-Japanese giant monster films since then have rarely drawn on the full range of absurdity or revelled in the sheer delight of imaginative abandonment that true *kaiju eiga* offers. But the giant monsters have kept coming nevertheless, often totally outlandish in their own right.

There have been bipedal reptilian Godzilla-clones, of course, such as the titular monster of *Gorgo* (UK-1961), also directed by Eugène Lourié. Giant snakes have been common. Mega-sharks (and related mutant sea-life) have gained quite a fan-base, and giant spiders proved very popular (in particular, I recommend the recent *Big Ass Spider*, directed by Mike Mendez in 2013). Giant insects remain *de rigueur*, classically epitomised in *Them!* (US-1954; dir. Gordon Douglas), but more recently with *Infestation* (US-2009; dir. Kyle Rankin). Hybrid monsters, such as the self-explanatory *Sharktopus* (US-2010; dir. Declan O'Brien) or the equally ridiculous but rather cool *Piranhaconda* (US-2012; dir. Jim Wynorski) have given a B-film nod to the ludicrous side of *kaiju* design. There are even movies that offer hybrid monsters fighting other hybrid monsters (*Sharktopus vs. Pteracuda* (US-2014; dir. Kevin O'Neill). *Cloverfield* (US-2008; dir. Matt Reeves) made a decent attempt to give metaphorical resonance to an alien giant monster attacking New York City post-9/11, just as Godzilla had encapsulated the destruction of Hiroshima in 1945. Significantly, in 2013 writer-director Guillermo del Toro created *Pacific Rim*, his epic vision of a war in which a desperate humanity struggles to survive incessant attacks by giant creatures (referred to in the film as "Kaiju"). These *kaiju* arrive through a dimensional portal in the depths of the Pacific Ocean, and humanity fights them using giant mecha called Jaegers – huge robotic machines controlled by human pilots. This film more than anything else has made the word "*kaiju*" currency outside the more confined geek community. A sequel has been mooted.

As the preceding seems to indicate, the *kaiju* tradition has all along been driven by cinema rather than existing within a pre-existing literary genre. However, while that's essentially true in its purest form, giant monsters have made their fair share of appearances in other types of storytelling over the centuries. Tales featuring giant monsters go as far back as the Mesopotamian *Epic of Gilgamesh* (circa 2100 BC). Nordic myths in particular are full of giant creatures, such as Jörmungandr (the Midgard Serpent), Níðhöggr (a huge dragon), Fenrir (a mighty wolf), Ymir (the Frost Giant), or the Kraken, a gigantic octopus with a penchant for disguising itself as an island and destroying ships. Though perhaps less monster-centric than this, Greek mythology, too, has its fair share of giant monsters, including the multi-headed Hydra and Cetus, a gargantuan sea monster, but also the humanoid pre-Olympian Titans. Most mythological giants end up fighting heroes and gods, of course – and generally harken back to earlier less-civilised times. They represent primal forces, which have been, if temporarily, driven back. Even the Old Testament (Genesis 6:4) mentions that "There were giants in the earth in those days", a statement often associated with the Nephilim – whom some interpret to be large cross-bred beings, half angel, half human, who will return at the end of days.

Giant monsters, mythological and otherwise, have also had a prolific life in Golden Age comics, such as early non-superhero Atlas/Marvel lines *Strange Tales* and *Tales to Astonish*. In their heyday, Jack Kirby's eminently recognisable covers dominated the market. Like the *kaiju* of Ultraman and his ilk, Kirby's monsters were often weird, and had names such as Groot, Moomba, Fin Fang Foom, Gargantus, Grogg, and Spragg, the Living Hill. When superheroes took over the comicbook market, some of the giant monsters still remained, size being an excellent balance to the heroes' superpowers. Japanese manga has likewise included giant things, especially robots, and has burgeoned in popularity in the West over the past few decades. Meanwhile, giant monsters have appeared on and off in many of the genre and comicbook-based movies that continue to dominate the box office, mostly in secondary roles (see, for example, Guillermo del Toro's *Hellboy* from 2003 and *Hellboy II: The Golden Army* from 2008). Their presence has been facilitated by the evolution of digital animation, which allows convincing interaction to take place on screen between man and giant monster. Using modern CGI techniques, literally anything is possible, so why not giant monsters? Giant monster stories generally, in whatever cultural format, have thrived on spectacle, massive destruction and larger-than-life threats. Convincing effects have given them a new cinematic life, as impressively demonstrated by the 2014 remake of *Godzilla*.

But what about literary fiction?

In 2003 we were still in the early beginnings of the Age of the Geek, a time when pop-culture fans such as Peter Jackson, Joss Whedon and Guillermo del Toro would increasingly push genre boundaries into the mainstream. This trend has become a flood of genre geekdom over the past decade or so, thanks to super-popular TV shows such as *Buffy the Vampire Slayer*, *The X-Files*, *Battlestar Galactica*, *Smallville*, *The Walking Dead* and *Game of Thrones*, not to forget genre-based blockbuster movies and in particular such fantasy franchises as those based on the *Lord of the Rings* and Harry Potter books. The superhero movie invasion that was facilitated by the success of Christopher Nolan's Dark Knight films and subsequently unleashed in full force by Marvel Studios, beginning with Jon Favreau's *Iron Man* in 2008, is the latest incarnation of this geekification of the modern entertainment industry. These days nearly all the big box-office movies are genre-based. Comics and graphic novels are suddenly not only popular but also accepted as a valid artistic medium.

In 2003, believing there to be a lack of giant monsters in literary fiction, I decided I wanted to edit an anthology of original giant monster tales – stories featuring really huge monsters inspired by the Japanese *kaiju eiga* tradition. I corralled Perth-based film commentator Robin Pen, a fellow *kaiju* fan (that is to say, geek), into the plan and we went to work. It seemed to us that giant monsters could ride the wave of the pop-cultural renaissance, though the scale of the coming tsunami was hardly something we anticipated.

As far as Robin and I could determine, no other anthology of original giant-monster fiction had ever been produced. There were isolated stories that more-or-less fit the bill, of course – and novels, such as Herman Melville's *Moby Dick* (1851) and Anne McCaffrey's *Dragonriders of Pern* series, as well as myth-based fantasies that dealt with gods and monsters, ogres and humanoid giants. Anthologies featuring dragons, dinosaurs and largish creatures on alien planets, as for example Jack Dann and Gardner Dozois' Ace Anthology Series entry, *Dinosaurs!* (1990), had existed for some time. Assorted science-fiction tales in the pulp magazines of the 1920s onward dealt with giant otherworldly beasts, most notably the Cthulhu mythos of H.P. Lovecraft, with its huge alien monstrosities ever lurking at the edge of reality. But there seemed to have been no original anthologies of *kaiju*-like ultra-gigantic creatures.

Robin and I felt this situation was something that needed to be addressed, so we negotiated with Australian independent publisher Agog! Press and finally announced we would be putting together a collection of original giant monster stories. We had no idea what the response would be. As it happened, it was overwhelming. We received hundreds of stories from writers – both professional and newbie – from around the world. After a long reading period, intensive editing and some aggressive re-writing, we put together a collection of twenty-eight stories we were extremely happy with (plus some added haiku, or "daihaiku" as they came to be known), and the book, titled *Daikaiju! Giant Monster Tales*, was published in 2005.

Critical and reader reactions were positive, emphasising the unexpected originality of many of the stories and the diversity of tone and approach. In 2006, the anthology won the Australian Ditmar Award for Best Collection and at least one story appeared in an international Year's Best anthology. Subsequently, we decided we had so many good stories left over that we should publish two sequels over following years, soliciting some new tales from established authors to fill the gaps. These volumes, along with a second printing of the first book, were produced through a partnership between Agog! Press and Prime Books in the US: *Daikaiju! 2: Revenge of the Giant Monsters* and *Daikaiju! 3: Giant Monsters vs the World*.

I'm pleased to say that *The Mammoth Book of Kaiju* you are now about to read includes eleven stories from the *Daikaiju!* books. These stories are inventive and unusual, effectively displaying the excitement, insightfulness and diversity of giant monster fiction as a sub-genre.

Since the *Daikaiju!* books appeared, other worthy anthologies of giant-monster fiction have of course been published. Stories in *The Mammoth Book of Kaiju* have also been selected by editor Sean Wallace from the most prominent and effective of these – especially *Kaiju Rising: The Age of Monsters* (edited by Tim Marquitz and Nicholas Sharpe in 2014) and *Monstrous: 20 Tales of Giant Creature Terror* (edited by Ryan C. Thomas in 2009), with a representative from the newly released original Cthulhu-mythos anthology, *World War Cthulhu: A Collection of Lovecraftian War Stories* (edited by Brian M. Sammons and Glynn Owen Barrass). Stories have also come from more general anthologies, such as Ellen Datlow's excellent *Fearful Symmetries*, and prominent genre magazines such as *Asimov's SF Magazine*, the online *Clarkesworld* and *Interzone*.

Overall these stories by writers both well known and less well known represent an amazing wealth of monstrous goodness and ably demonstrate how entertaining a giant monster can be. They are more than worthy of bearing the name that the giants of cinema have made famous: *Kaiju!*

Read them now, and revel in the sheer joy of their awesome, and strangely meaningful, unreality!

––––––––

Robert Hood

Occupied
Natania Barron

———

Maker:

Julian moves through the narrow sewers and drainage pipes without hesitation. More a mole than a woman, she navigates with perfect precision, her thick boots trudging through every kind of detritus provided by the city. She is immune to the bloated rats, the stench, the slimy mold crawling up the side of the glistening brick. It's only the things out of place: the sound of a small gator slipping into a stream, or an unanticipated moan, that would stop her. And nothing does for quite some time.

Then, just as she is about to take the final twist toward her own alcove, near Berfa the Engine, she stops cold. Something glows. Not the light of a lantern or candle, not even the odd luminescence of the mushrooms that sometimes grow in the depths. It is something blue and cold and frosty.

Creature:

We have been asleep for so long; so long that all is dust. Our tongues. Our eyes. Our bodies. Our shrunken phalluses. These sick and sad reminders that we had bodies, once. That we felt the power of blood, felt the coursing of the Holy Spirit within us. Tasted and rutted and blazed. We were passion and power and knowledge. Too much knowledge.

A thousand thousand years, and we have suffered in the miasma of loss and excommunication and forgotten our names. Once, we were feared, favored, loved. Now, we only whisper to ourselves, with no knowledge of our names or our purposes. One among us was a healer; another a poet; another still, a guardian and warrior of a kind rarely seen. We were astronomers and visionaries and, for no reason other than our lust for life, we were cast aside. Forgotten.

We have lived without hope. What power made up our bodies has been dispersed so far and wide that we have given into the monotony. The pain. Suffering gave way to anger, and back again to suffering, and it has gone on so long that we had forgotten that once, before we had been reduced to such nothing, we had plotted. Planned. Planted seeds, however far-flung, of the hope of rebirth.

A sword. Forged from the heart of a star. Melted down and changing hands, century after century, passing borders and oceans. Coveted, cursed, stolen. Our last hope.

Maker:

Julian curses. She cannot help herself. The sudden disruption causes her to stumble, losing her footing, twisting her ankle. It cracks under her weight, sending bright sparks of pain up the side of her leg and she gasps in spite of herself, wishing she had opted for another route. The last thing she wants is dischord. Her routine is all she has – it's what keeps her from losing time, and whatever else precious she has left to her.

Part of her is sensible and tells her that she ought to keep moving, albeit it slowly, back to her enclave. It is the safest option, and safety is one of Julian's most intense concerns. She knows how difficult it is to langor in pain and suffering after safety has been ignored. With a gloved hand she reaches up and touches the stump of her ear, feeling the ragged bumps and twisted skin, hearing the strange scratching noise such a motion produces.

But the light. That blue. As she braces herself against the wall and finds her way toward breathing more regularly, she notices that it flickers and dissipates with a certain rhythm. Not quite a pulse, but it is regular. And there's a smell, too. She feels as if she can remember the scent, but not entirely – it's a distant memory. A part of her brain fires, but she can't attach any strings to the thought. It just floated a moment, and then was gone, no connection made. But the memory is not a warning. What's left in Julian's mind is something burning and bright, something strong and dangerous.

Julian slides across the grimy bricks and twists her head to get a better look. Her glasses are dirty enough as it is, but it doesn't seem to matter – her eyes are still dazzled by what she sees. The luminescence centers around the small object, half buried in the mud and mold at the base of one of the drains. The color is cold, she thinks, even though she hasn't touched it yet. As if it were ice. Which is strange, she realizes, because she is very hot and very sticky. The room is not cold. The color is cold.

Why would it be here, she wonders? Perhaps there was a deluge above, and it got knocked clean. Perhaps someone threw it down here to hide it. Or to get rid of it. Such a beautiful thing should not be let go of, Julian thinks.

Either way, Julian doesn't think much as she lunges forward to grab it. Every muscle in her crooked body twists as she moves – faster than she has moved in a decade – and as she tumbles forward into the muck, she wonders for a moment if it is pulling her. If the cold and light is reaching toward her, desiring her touch as much as she desires it.

She gasps, seized with a strange concern that someone else will take the object, and in a moment, she holds it in her hands, blinking down through grimy lenses, dazzled.

Scissors. A pair of scissors. When she touches them . . . whispers rise around her like steam.

Creature:

We all shout out as one. That touch! A touch of a human, but not entirely human. We feel her body; know her immediately as a descendent of ours. One of our children, a thousand generations removed from the perfect babes we birthed upon the earth. She is a broken, weak thing, and she has no idea what she has in her hands. No concept that we, the Watchers, are rising up from the depths in ecstasy – have waited a thousand thousand years for this moment.

It is pain and anguish and love and grief we all feel in that moment. Through that cursed, magic metal, that single touch is as powerful as the breath of life we were once given. How small it has become! How simple. What was once a flaming sword, wielded by the greatest among us, has now become a tiny thing.

The touch is enough to wake us, to rouse us. But she must do more. She must remember what she is. She must awaken herself.

We wait. We have waited long, it is true – but we would not be in existence if we had not waited so long. So, again, we pause. We draw breath. We poise on the edge and anticipate.

Maker:

The scissors are so cold, so perfectly cold, in her hands. Julian smiles, tries not to laugh as she covers them up with a piece of burlap to dampen the light. They are so beautiful. So ornate. So delicate. It reminds her of the kit her mother had, back when she lived Above. The scrollwork looks almost Eastern, and she runs her fingers along the side and smiles. She loves the cold. It's a welcome cold. A bright cold. The cold of stars in the firmament.

We are a many. We are a waiting. We are a hunger. We are a watching.

She has heard the voices before, and she is not afraid of them. In a way, she is relieved. That the whispers have intensified means she's less mad. It means that something – this pair of scissors – has been waiting for her all these years. It means her work has not been in vain. It means the years of ridicule and scorn . . .

But no one has ever understood Julian, not even Brother Barrier. No one except her companions, all awaiting her in her nook. And that is where she goes, her breath caught in her throat as she makes her way without hesitation, the scissors pressing against her breast as she navigates the sewer to the place of her own.

There are a half-dozen locks on the door of her space, and she quickly goes about releasing them, though she fails twice on the third lock. When she finally makes it inside, she is breathing so heavily that her spectacles start fogging up. Julian won't let go of the scissors, even though they bite into her hands with their unearthly cold. Her whole arm is numb now, up to the elbow, and she takes a quick stock of the room.

The specimens line the room from floor to ceiling, in jars and boxes and cans, depending on the individual situation. Arms, legs, fingers and toes are the uppermost tier, while the most easy accessible drawers and shelves are lined with the more delicate matter: eyes, tongues, and silvery webs of nerves and veins. Most are preserved, thanks to Brother Barrier's help with obtaining ingredients and fluids from above – he has always been oddly fascinated with her work, even though it has nothing to do with the steam pumps. The day he stumbled upon her, she was terrified that he would judge her, make her stop. He wore the robes of a priest, after all. But instead of fear, he was full of awe. Full of support.

What specimens aren't preserved wait in the experimental section, one level below. As Julian takes the burlap off the scissors, something miraculous happens.

The light from the scissors brightens the room, bouncing off red wet brick, and trembling through the formaldehyde, ethanol, and methanol solutions. Brilliant blue flashes across the surface, like an electric charge, and every eye turns, every finger points, every submerged ear and floating brain matter turns to focus upon her.

We are a many. We are a waiting. We are a hunger. We are a watching.

Creature:

To be awoken is an experience akin to no other. To see, however dimly, after thousands of years blind and hungry. To hear. To sense. To know. We tremble and cry out, lips making no noises, choking and drowning and screaming at once. At first, we are jubilant, in spite of the pain (for pain means life). But we realize, quickly, that in this moment of pain and awakening is confusion. Broken. Not as promised.

We are further shattered. We are fragmented. Some of us see – some of us hear – but none of us can do both. When once we suffered and dwindled as one, now we each remember and splinter. Our names come back to mind, our knowledge, but not complete. Uriel. Azazel. Samyaza. Baraquel. Kokabiel. More.

And my name. My *name*. I want to speak it. But all I am is an eye. The eye of a goat. The light from the metal of that ancient sword – no longer a sword, and much diminished – makes my existence a misery. I cannot look away from the cruelly misshapen Daughter of Nephilim, and she stares back at me stupidly. And the voices of the other Fallen pulse around me, filling the water in which I'm suspended. They are mad, trembling. Their fury will ruin this for all of us.

I panic. I am nothing but an eye. A mad, wide-seeing eye, slowly losing the only chance I have had in a thousand thousand years to breathe the air again. I do not want destruction and death. I do not want revenge. I want escape.

I know what I must do.

Maker:

Julian falls to her knees, and one cracks and shatters against the white tile. But the numbness has moved through her body so completely that she merely notes the sickening snap of cartilage, distantly. One moment her body is filled with a vibrating, orgasmic pleasure, and the next she is crawling toward a jar in the middle of her collection. She holds up the scissors and looks through the holes, as if they were another pair of spectacles. And indeed, she does see better through them. She notices that each of her specimens, now following her every breath and movement, each glow different shades. Some are the red of fresh blood; others shimmer silver and gold, tendrils of light refracting across the glass surfaces. Every color in the spectrum.

Dazzled, Julian stares for a time out of mind until she notices one different than the others. One of her favorite specimens. Not human, this one, and a rarity for that. It is the only specimen she killed with her own hands. Perhaps that is why she glances at it longer than the others, why she notices the blue hue of the dappled light – it is the only one unchanged by the view through the scissors.

She leans forward. She raises her fingers, scraped and bloody. The wide pupil regards her intently. It swims forward and backward within the glass, but it never loses focus. Julian has been a master preserver for years, and the golden goat eye is one of her favorites – she remembers well plucking it from the skull of the so recently expired creature. She'd roasted the other one. But it had been blue. This was gold, and too beautiful to be eaten.

We are a many. We are a waiting. We are a hunger. We are a watching.

Now she wants to eat it. Now she wants to touch it. To listen to it. To know it. It tells her things, whispers her name again and again.

Julian does not lower the scissors, but with her free hand she presses fingertips to the glass. She tries to recoil for the heat is overwhelming – her skin immediately bonds to the glass, and she smells burning flesh though feels nothing. A heartbeat more and the glass shatters, impaling her hand with a thousand tiny lacerations. Blood drips freely now, filling the room with a coppery, burnt scent.

She picks up the eye with her bloodied fingers and writes the word it commands her to, pressing the soft organ to the floor. On the bright white tile, Julian weeps with joy as she writes a single name: *Penemue*.

Penemue:

My name is spoken, and I arise. Unlike my fallen brothers, I am released from the nightmarish hold between life and death, animation and oblivion. It is bliss. Joy. Fury. To know my name at last is a pleasure beyond all memories. And there are so many memories.

My first thought is to take our Maker's body from her – it is not holding up well, and she may not have long in this life. But I cannot. I have ever believed in my own innocence, having been damned to eternity for loving a mortal man and bringing the gift of writing to him. Every living human being owes me a debt of gratitude for my so-called sin, but I will not make more sins out of my own hatred to God. I will not. If I am to live again, I must do it purely and without trespass. I have learned . . .

Our Maker stares at me, and I can see myself as a pillar of blue fire in her eyes. I am beautiful and horrible, but I am weak and frighteningly vulnerable in this state; this she does not know.

My brothers know, though. My hesitation to do her no harm has given them space to call her back. And I, bodiless, am powerless. I try to blaze brighter, but the voices of my brethren rise louder and louder, a dissonant clamor of commands and cries, and our Maker is frozen. Her body twitches, her neck twists, and with those delicate scissors in hand she starts to make her way toward her macabre collection – the collection she has been putting together for so long, for this purpose alone.

Maker:

Julian knows few thoughts of her own. Except a sense of gladness. A sense of purpose. The blue flame creature burns brightly, but it no longer speaks words she knows. It can no longer command her. The others, the Watchers, whom she has waited her whole life, command her steps now. Command her movements. She understands now, yes. She understands that collection around her has not been only to keep her company, it has been part of a grand plan – a plan to make her more. Greater. It's what Brother Barrier has told her, time and again. She is part of a bigger, more divine plan. And the awakened specimens, her friends, have come at last.

The scissors. She understands.

This is the blade that binds, no longer the blade that sunders. Cleave and join, Daugher of Nephilim, and give your body new life.

The first cut is the hardest, even though there is little pain. Julian has spent so much time cutting and dissecting other things, that even in her dimming consciousness, it seems wrong. But she needs another arm to do this task, and the only way she will be able to add another appendage is to make room for it on her chest.

She picks the corded arm from the sewer worker she'd harvested two months before. Or, rather, it picks her. Its container falls to the tiles and shatters, then it climbs its way up her soiled petticoat and leather vest as she leans back to accept it.

That moment of connection is a black terror, but Julian has dreamed of this her whole life. She has only not remembered the dream. Now, as it's happening, this moment of rebuilding and transformation, she recalls every detail. Of her dying. But not dying. Her ecstasy.

Again and again she plunges the scissors into her body, through cloth and skin and muscle, and again and again the specimens come to her, merging with her body. She is their mother and Maker, giving them blood and life again – saving them from death. Every step in her life has been leading to this moment – every spewed word of hate, every uttered curse below her breath. She has never believed in God, no. Julian has only relied on herself and her connection to a greater, wilder, madder design out there.

Julian plunges the scissor blades into her heart, and it is done.

And now she is all greatness and power, and mad beauty. Her body swells and grows to accommodate the appendages of her new friends, roiling and undulating, filling up the small space, pushing out that blue fire into the passageway beyond. There comes the sound of feet, but it is distant and unimportant to her now. For she is a creature of a thousand eyes and arms, a thousand voices, a thousand terrors.

And she is hunger. She is wanting. But she is no longer waiting.

Penemue:

It has gone wrong. So wrong. I should have known my brothers would never manage a peaceful entry – they are too full of fury. She has welcomed them, but she cannot see what I see. It is not that they are granting her power, but that they are fighting for it among themselves. Her humanity is swallowed up in moments as she grows beyond imagining, her form undulating like the long body of some many-armed creature of the deep, or monstrous arachnid.

My brothers fight among themselves for control of the body. Arms and teeth rend one another, and by virtue of blood and filth birth more – grow even more repulsive.

Penemue. My name still lingers on my mind and I taste something I have not in centuries: fear. I am afraid. Who am I? I have never been like my brothers. I have been outcast from heaven and hell, and now moments from my freedom, I am shoved out into the strange, dark corridor from where I was awoken, and my flame begins to diminish. Without a host, I know I will fade to nothingness. True nothingness. Perhaps that is better. I am sinless, now. I am reborn and perfect.

But I cannot. I know their hunger. Finding a host means a harsher judgement, but only I know how to stop the creature, the many-eyed beast growing fast along these strange hallways running with filth.

He stands there, clutching his heart, my blue flames flickering in his eyes. There are tears coursing down his cheeks, and his lip trembles. A priest, I can tell, even in this strange place. He wears black with a swath of white at his collar, and his bald pate reflects. He whispers ancient words familiar to me, an invocation of an angel. Of Gabriel. I remember him well. A friend in brighter times. That this man thinks I am Gabriel is a balm to me, a moment of strength in this weakened state.

"I must welcome you, messenger," the priest says, bowing his head and going down to one knee. "I am your servant, all body and soul."

I enter him in an instant. I do not think beyond that, for I can hear the walls around me shaking as the creature expands. It groans, as well, this leviathan of the deep.

I become the priest, and the priest becomes me. He is not gone, but he is no longer. I take from him his life, his memories, his intelligence, his faults. To the human eye this priest – this Brother Barrier – is like all others save for the gentle glowing of his eyes and fingernails. He tells me what I need to know of this world that has grown in my absence. I am in a sewer, where all the filth of humanity flows. Julian, the name of the Child of the Nephilim, has lived here for thirty years, since she was but a newly flowered girl, and has collected these specimens for her own pleasure, to quell the voices in her head. Brother Barrier found her fifteen years before, and helped her out of pity – but also out of understanding. He, too, has heard our voices. Not through his blood, as Julian has, but through his own preternatural abilities.

The body I have now is painfully human. The muscles are atrophied in places, the stomach soft. The heart trembles with some sort of ailment. I can heal what I am able, but there is little hope he will last beyond this task.

Creature:

The creature of a thousand corpses cries out in agony and joy, feeling the pulse of humanity above, and sensing the waters not far. The cleansing waters of the ocean. Food and drink. Revenge and lust. With nothing more than the stars to guide, the creature looks up with a thousand eyes through grates and slits in the ground, pulled toward the center of the city, along the great bend in the river.

Sliding up through the sewer, its shape changed a dozen times, rearranging its girth. Arms and legs, paws and muzzles, teeth and hooves, all slither against each other to slip through the narrow space. Up and up in an endless ladder of bodies and bones, snapping and mending over and over, dim eyes lighting up and down each unfathomable arm.

Toward the whitest, tallest building, pulled as if by magical impulse. The most holy place in the city – it must be taken down before the feeding can begin, this alone the fallen brothers agree upon. The creature of a thousand corpses knows the dark memories of their host, knows the way she had been turned away as an abomination. It feels the dead beneath the streets, smells the murder and chaos. All these beautiful and horrible gifts – they, not God, has given them to mankind. And now, it is a great reckoning.

When the creature's full girth meets the air a great fog begins, as something in the smoky atmosphere reacts against the living dead. The many fallen brothers begin to argue, surprised by the sudden pain. The creature lunges forward north, spilling white smoke throughout the streets in huge, stinking pillars. As the brothers disagree, the mass of the beast smashes left and right, crushing buildings beneath it and smothering all living things in its wake. Brick and wood and steel crumble as if mere afterthoughts, and those caught below see nothing but the massive arms casting shadows. Hands and mouths reach for any useable weapon, and so the seething creature becomes sharper and more deadly.

Penemue:

I am slow in this body, and breathing – something I had dreamed of doing so long – is an abysmal pain to me. I know where the creature is, where my fallen brothers move, but I cannot catch up to them fast enough. I pause as I exit the sewer, feeling something digging against my hip. I had not noticed it before, and I have to listen to Brother Barrier tell me about it before I throw it away. It is a weapon, which he calls a "firearm". It is intended to kill others, though I cannot imagine how. He explains it is full of ammunition. I still do not understand, so he shows me. Turning it over in the moonlight I feel the cold metal and understand better. There is a charge within, and with the proper aim, I could send a menacing bolt.

But not to the creature. Not to my brothers. Only one thing would undo them, and likely me. I pause to catch my breath and renew my focus. At my feet, fog swirls, smelling of sulphur and decay. I could see better than the other humans now running past me, away south. Some carry bodies, severed in unspeakable ways. Livestock knock over humans in their terror, trample them.

Trying to keep a distance, I make my way slowly north. I can see straight through the strange square buildings, and know immediately where the fallen brothers are going. Even though they continue to squabble, and through their squabbling grow and absorb all around them, they seek a holy place. A high, holy place. From there, they will fight. Or they will seek to storm heaven. Or they will seek more blood until they have summoned the Devil himself. Or all at once.

The skies crackle with lightning, and the fog rises. In the distance I can see the arms of the great beast limned against the dwindling starlight.

"She buried the blade in her breast," I tell Brother Barrier. He is rather quiet, and does not seem to understand. "I must reach it – I must remove it."

"Don't angels fly?" he asks slowly.

"Sometimes," I tell him. "I mostly burn."

"Seraphim," he says.

"Once," I reply.

"You were close to Heaven."

"I thought I could go back. But I see now, I cannot."

I run, now. The air smells of blood and fire. Shrill noises – sirens, Brother Barrier tells me – whine in the distance. The salt air from the sea drives tears to my eyes, remembering a life for which I earned a thousand centuries of torture. Remembering a face. Remembering hands, perfect and strong feet. A perfect human, touched by none of this terror. What became of him? We bore no children – how could we? – but his love cost me so much. Those perfect ebony hands which I loved and taught the holy marks upon paper.

The cathedral rises before me, three steeples stretching to the skies, but darkening against their white sides as my fallen brothers rise. There is no time for me to marvel in this creation of humanity, for I hear voices in the air, now. My fallen brothers. Hear their wailing cry, their furious oaths of destruction and death. Destruction of humanity, destruction of each other. They loved once, as I did. But they birthed the Nephilim. I was merely caught up.

And now. I watch in horror as I hear the side of the cathedral snap. One long tendril reaches up and squeezes, working as leverage so the fallen brothers can climb higher, that the massive creature may get a better view of the city.

In the distance I sense that the waters rise from below, Julian's steam pumps failing. Soon the city will be submerged. What does not die from the hand of my brethren will drown.

I can see the beast better now, as I come around to the square behind the cathedral. It arranges itself over and over again, the center glowing blue where the scissors lie, but never rids itself of the massive tentacles. Sometimes six. Sometimes thirteen. They lash and break and bend all around them.

I approach the cathedral at a dead run, ducking as debris falls down. There are still people inside. Many of them. No doubt they came here seeking refuge. I can smell their fear mingled with incense. The closer I get the more I see the muck and sludge the fallen brothers have dropped over the building. It hisses and oozes, stinging my face as it drips on my skin. I wipe it away, and with it comes some of my flesh. I cannot even imagine what it would do to a mortal.

Then, in a moment of sudden inspiration from Brother Barrier, I stop. I look to the heavens in between a swath of cloud. The stars blink at me. I wonder . . . the other angels. Would they hear me? Did they forget me? In this moment of need, would they heed my cry?

No. I am too afraid they will not answer. As the beast rages above me I move through from pillar to pillar around the cathedral, until I find a door unobstructed by bodies or debris. The sound from inside is somehow worse, though dampened. I do not have time to wonder at the strange symbols and drawings, so alien to me. The straining of the building rips my breath from my body, but I keep the pace while Brother Barrier sings strange hymns I do not know.

The center tower is still holding, and that is where I must go. I pass humans, many of whom recognize me as Brother Barrier until they see my eyes. Some scream, others fall into a sort of silent reverie, giving me knowing smiles. He tells me their names, and I say them aloud, and they are blessed by it.

Up and up I go, pushed ever onwards by the passing of time and the groaning of the building. On top of it all I hear the keening of the bell at the top of the tower, straining with the cries of the creature. The fighting, rending battle. It grows. More and more it grows as the fallen brothers continue their squabbling. And it will continue to swell with hatred and fury until not only this city is swallowed, but the entirety of humanity is black with its insatiable search for blood.

Just below the bells, I make my exit into the night air. My brothers feel me, but they do not yet understand where I am. Brother Barrier's body is like a blanket across their eyes. From where I stand I can see down into the gaping maws of the beast, faces and mouths open in anguish, eyes spinning in invisible sockets. They sing a thousand curses at me, but I search for only one thing. That glittering metal, stuck fast in the heart of what was once a woman.

I have never been the brave one among my brothers. My hands have rarely wielded swords, and instead have written poems and ballads and songs of old. I hesitate again, up on the ledge, and it nearly does me in. A thick cord of sinew comes up and around my ankle, snapping it but not sundering it. The pain is strange and welcome, burning with my heartbeat and the searing in my face.

Now they know.

I am a Seraphim. I am a creature of flame. With one hand I steady the pistol, with the other I draw a word in the air with blue fire: thunder. I shoot the bullet through the word as it still lingers in air, and when it hits the creature, a sound erupts from its center and shakes it to its core. Another sinew shoots out, this time around my middle, but it is with less precision. I am able to shake it off, and I can see a new fire alight down the impossible monster's gullet of a thousand mouths. Some of the pieces begin to fall, mostly those which were acquired during the creature's journey from below the city. The weapons fall, too – long metal poles, broken iron doorways. They clatter and spark as they hit the rocky ground below.

"There are only two more bullets," Brother Barrier whispers to me.

I do not hesitate with my second spell. I mark the word "silence" in the air and shoot through it again, and the whole beast shudders and stops its wailing. Now I can hear the screams from all around the city. People are dying everywhere. But if they are screaming, it also means some are living.

We are a many. We are a waiting. We are a hunger. We are a watching.

"No longer," I shout down. "Release yourselves and return to the darkness! You will win nothing by your madness!"

We are a many. We are a waiting. We are a hunger. We are a watching.

I remembered that strange liturgy. I had escaped it. But I had held out hope. That was my greatest sin. I had held out hope for myself alone, and I had abandoned them. After a hundred thousand years of suffering together, I sinned before I had even begun again.

"I am so sorry," I tell them, and Brother Barrier.

It is with that I draw the last word. I drop the gun and close my eyes. With a final, blessed breath, I dive through the word "brother" and plunge into the belly of the beast to withdraw the key to our salvation, and doom us all back to oblivion.

Titanic!
Lavie Tidhar
————

When I come on board the ship I pay little heed to her splendour; nor to the gaily-strewn lines of coloured electric lights, nor to the polished brass of the crew's jacket uniforms, nor to the crowds at the dock in Southampton, waving handkerchiefs and pushing and shoving for a better look; nor to my fellow passengers. I keep my eyes open only for signs of pursuit; specifically, for signs of the Law.

The ship is named the *Titanic*. I purchased a second-class ticket in London the day before and travelled down to Southampton by train. I had packed hurriedly. I do not know how far behind me the officers are. I know only that they will come. He made sure of that, in his last excursion. The corpses he left were a mockery, body parts ripped, exposed ribcages and lungs stretched like Indian rubber; he had turned murder into a sculpture, a form of grotesque art. The Japanese would call such a thing as he a *yōkai*, a monster, otherworldly and weird. Or perhaps a *kaiju*. I admire the Japanese for their mastery of the science of monstrosity, of what in our Latin would be called the *lusus naturae*. I have corresponded with a Dr Yamane, of Tokyo, for some time, but had of course destroyed all correspondence when I escaped from London.

And yet I cannot leave him behind. I had packed hurriedly. A simple change of clothes. I had not dressed like a gentleman. But I carry, along with my portmanteau, also my doctor's black medical bag; it defines me more than I could ever define myself otherwise; it is as much a part of me as my toes, or my navel, or my eyes; and inside the bag I carry him, all that is left of him: one bottle, that is all, and the rest were all smashed up to shards back in London, back in the house where the bodies are.

I present my ticket to the steward. There is no suspicion in his eyes. He smiles courteously, professionally, already not seeing me as he turns to the ones behind me; and then I am on board. Perhaps infected by the other passengers' gaiety, perhaps just relieved at my soon-to-be escape, I stand with them on the deck, against the railings, shouting and waving at the people we are soon to leave behind. My heart beats faster; my palms sweat; I am eager for us to depart, for our transatlantic journey to begin. I long for escape.

At last it happens. The horn sounds and the gangplanks are raised and we are off! I sigh with relief; I had not realised how tense I had been. But fear had taken its hold on me, in all the long years of living with him; his presence in my life had made me fearful; the day he would get careless, or go too far, and leave me to be captured.

No longer!

England is a cesspit of corruption. It is too small, too confining. It looks not to the future, but to the past; it is rigid and unyielding. It is time for me to look elsewhere, to the New World, where a scientist may work in peace, where there is space to grow . . . and where he, too, could roam more freely, for it is a vast land and people may disappear there more easily; and never be seen again. Yes, he could be controlled, there. But for now he is dormant within me. He will not emerge on this voyage. Not unless I will it.

A near-accident. Our huge bulk causes waves in the harbour. We nearly drown two smaller ships: The SS *City of New York* and the *Oceanic*. I watch them rise on the waves, thinking of the size and power of the *Titanic*, like the power that I, myself, hold within me. It is a power all human beings have; yet I alone have found the means of liberating it. Only in Japan, perhaps, is there science greater than mine – but that land is far and their experiments have taken them in a different direction to my own. No, I am confident in my heart, my potion is unique; and I, a true original.

The passage out goes without a further hitch. The two smaller ships are not harmed, and I feel neither satisfaction nor disappointment. I stand on the deck and watch the harbour recede from view for a long time. I watch England grow smaller in the distance. I cannot wait for it to disappear.

11 April 1912

Cork.

How I loathe the Irish!

The docks swarm with these Irishmen and their equally squalid women. They come on board, several obviously drunk and singing riotously. I stand on the deck and smoke a cigar. A man of middle years and a somewhat stooped posture engages me in conversation. "You are a doctor?" he says, on noticing my black bag (I do not dare part with it. These Irishmen may steal a doctor's bag as easily as they would slit a man's throat!). "Yes, yes," I say, "what is it to you?"

Instead of taking offence he chuckles good-naturedly. "I myself am in the medical profession," he says. I say, "Oh?" and roll the cigar in my mouth. "Yes," he says, "I am a purveyor of the snake oil cure. Are you familiar with that panacea?"

"*Enhydris chinensis*," I say. "It is a medicine of the Chinese people, is it not?" I do not tell him I had studied it intensively; my research has increasingly taken me to study the obscure and arcane sciences of the East. "Yes," he says, "it is a marvellous medicine, a cure-all."

I make a dismissive gesture and his moustache quivers at that. "Do you not agree, Sir?" he says. I tap my cigar and watch the ash blow in the wind. Will the ship never leave? I am unsafe as long as we are in these European waters. Have the bodies been found yet? Has Hyde been implicated? He is well known to the police. "Excuse me," I say. "I meant no offence."

His good humour returns. He gives me his calling card and asks me to call on him once in New York, promising me a bulk discount on his stock. It is of the utmost benefit to any doctor, he assures me. I am glad to be rid of him. At long last the ship departs. There are thousands of us on board.

12 April 1912

At last, the open sea!

The ocean is calm. The weather is mild. A sense of wild freedom grips me. The New World beckons! I have successfully avoided pursuit, capture. In New York I could start again, and the name of Jekyll will be forgotten. I pat my bag, thinking of the bottle it holds. Already I am craving it. In America I will make more of the potion. He wants to get out; I can feel him, pushing.

13 April 1912

A cold front. Strong winds and high waves. Nevertheless I brave the deck. I find being confined below excruciating, the press of people is repulsive to me. I take in the sea air but my attempts to light a cigar prove futile.

Last night I tossed and turned, the need burning inside me. I could feel Edward leering inside me, pushing to be let out. I find myself regarding women with Hyde's eyes, with his hunger. I see men and think of the blood coursing through them, and of the glint of knives. More than two decades ago when my experiments had just begun, he and I were sloppy. Jack, they had called him. I had less control of the formula then. The cold air revives me. Anticipation of the New World soothes me. I feel as though I have been given a second chance.

14 April 1912

The sea is very calm, but there is a chill in the air. It is a fine morning. I have spoken to no-one. It is a lonely life, sometimes. But I have him for company, always. The presence of the bottle in my bag reassures me. It will not be long now.

14 April 1912

An ungodly crash!

I had just been climbing up to the deck when the entire ship groaned and creaked as if hit by some vast and monstrous hammer. I fell but found my balance. My black bag was with me and I assured myself the sample inside was intact. I hurried up the stairs, finding the decks in a confusion of people. What could this mean?

"Sir?" I hear an officer speak near me, and I find myself pushed to the front, and realise the man resplendent in magnificent uniform further ahead is the captain. "Sir? We've hit something!"

"It is an iceberg?" the Captain says, his manner outwardly calm. "No, sir," the officer says. "It isn't an iceberg. It's a—"

Someone screams. It is a high-pitched scream, but I cannot tell if it is made by a man or a woman. "Look up! Look at that – that thing!"

As if on cue, the ship's powerful spotlights come on at once, piercing the night, momentarily blinding me. I hear a terrible sound, a roar as of a thousand engines cranking up to their utmost power and beyond their breaking point.

"It's a . . . it's a—!"

My God, I think, awed. How could anyone mistake this for an *iceberg*?

It towers over the ship, and the *Titanic* looks like a toy in comparison. An enormous, beautiful monstrosity, like a cross between a gorilla and a whale: it opens its mouth and roars, and a lizard's giant claws land with a deafening roar on the deck of the *Titanic*, splintering wood and cutting deep into the underlying levels. I hear screams, and see a man's head explode like a wet red balloon where the monster had crushed it in its wake.

"It's a—!"

"It's a *daikaiju*," I say, though they do not hear me. I breathe out. A giant *kaiju*! The scientist in me is enthralled. The beast within me is hungry. Hyde responds to the creature like a drunk; he bangs against the walls of his prison to be let out. Screams rise into the air. The monster, angered or afraid, lashes again at the ship. Its powerful tail slams into the side of it and the deck tilts alarmingly. Bodies fly through the air. "Abandon ship! Abandon ship!" Panic takes over the *Titanic*. "To the life boats!" A press of bodies as the people down below attempt to climb up to the open deck, to find escape. They shove and push each other in their panic. I see a woman trampled underfoot. I, too, try to make my way to the life boats, but the swell of people is too strong, and I am old; and panic rises in me as I am sidelined, pushed, shoved, hurt, and all the while the beast roars above our heads, lashing with talons and tail at the *Titanic*, ripping it slowly apart.

"To the boats!" And there they go, while, unbelievably, the ship's orchestra *plays on*, at least until the beast, annoyed, perhaps, by the noise, slashes at them with its claws and the music stops abruptly with a clatter of panicked notes. The ship tilts: we are sinking. I hear the boats dropping into the water, hear a gunshot ring out as officers attempt to control the manic passengers. "Children and women first!"

And something breaks in me. Something that has no name, no label I could easily affix to it, like to a specimen bottle, or a beaker of potion. I can escape, I realise, and yet . . .

"Doctor!" I hear the cry. "We need a doctor! Please, help!"

A woman lying on the deck, holding an injured child in her arms. Her face is panicked. There is blood on the deck.

I still tightly hold my black medicine bag. Now I open it. All of a doctor's requirements are there. I could help them . . .

I reach inside and find the bottle.

The potion. My life's work.

I could help the child, I think. Or I could let out Mr Hyde.

I stare at the bottle in my hands. To swallow its contents would liberate me, would Hyde me, would allow me to fight my way to the life boats, and to escape, to live.

I had lived half my life a monster, I realize; and that had led to my eventual ruin, and my disgrace, and finally my exile.

I look up at that titanic being towering over the ship. It is frightened, I think. Monstrous, yes: but also beautiful. And I am glad I have lived long enough to see one.

I look at it for a long moment, and then I look at the bottle in my hands.

"Please! Help him!"

I could live a monster, I realise; or I could die a man.

I stretch my arm as far back as it will go, then back, in one smooth motion, and throw the bottle as hard and as fast as I can into the roiling sea.

Now I Am Nothing
Simon Bestwick

———

May 1942

Below, a green meadow; the glittering band of a river; white-painted houses. A blue warm sky unmarked by the vapour trails of bombers. Along the riverbanks, trees burst into shocks of frothy white blossom.

Rolf surveyed it all without reaction, trod out his cigarette and went inside.

The church was pleasantly cool, also empty. He crossed to the confessional booth and stepped inside, pulling the curtain behind him.

In the cool dark, smelling of wood polish and old incense, he waited.

Footsteps clicked on the church floor. The curtain in the neighbouring booth was pulled back, then drawn across again. A soft creak came from the booth as an unfamiliar weight tested the wooden seat.

"Bless me, Father, for I have sinned," said Rolf.

"How long has it been since your last confession?"

"It's my first."

Silence. Then the man in the neighbouring booth turned his head away from Rolf and lit a cigarette. The match's glow gleamed off grey hair around a balding pate, and a green tunic with a colonel's rank.

The colonel settled back and released smoke. "Hauptmann Koenig?"

"Yes, Herr Oberst."

"You know what is expected of you."

"Yes."

"You know what will happen if you are caught."

"Yes."

"This is your last chance to turn back."

Rolf didn't answer. Behind the screen, the colonel nodded. "Very well." He took another drag on his cigarette. "The facility is a military compound in the Black Forest. A Waffen-SS garrison, near a small village called Schwartzberg."

Schwartzberg: *black mountain.* "Its purpose?"

"Unknown. Highly classified. We know only it is a weapons programme. It has been codenamed Projekt Wotan. There will be five of you. You will command. Your objective is to enter the Schwartzberg compound, ascertain the nature of Projekt Wotan. If possible, you are to sabotage it there; if not, you are to bring out any information relating to it so that alternative action can be planned. Any questions?"

"When do I meet the others, and when do I begin?"

"The others will be here in a moment. As to when – immediately. There is no time to be lost." The colonel extinguished his cigarette. "You will find an envelope under your seat containing details of where you may find the equipment you'll require. Now I must leave you."

The curtain rattled back, then was flicked closed. The colonel's footsteps clicked away into the distance, militarily precise.

Rolf reached under the seat, found the envelope. He slit it open with his thumbnail and read it.

More footsteps clicked their way into the church. Several pairs.

Rolf struck a match and set light to envelope and letter, dropping it to the wooden floor when the fire had burnt down almost to his fingers then treading it out. He stood, straightened his clothes, put a hand to the Walther pistol in his pocket and stepped out of the booth.

Four men, also in civilian clothes but standing to unmistakably military attention, stood in front of the front row of pews.

Rolf went to them. For a moment there was silence; he studied them, and they studied the lean man, brown-haired and angular-faced, before them.

"Hauptmann Koenig?" asked one, a slender dandyish man in his twenties with a neat blond moustache.

Koenig nodded, his hand still on the Walther.

The blond man nodded back. "Sergeant Mathias Kroll," he said finally. "I grew up near Schwartzberg, sir. I know the area."

"Good," said Rolf. He surveyed the others; there was a big ox of a man with a shaven head, another with cropped grey hair and an outdoorsman's tanned, leathery face, and a blank-faced boy, barely out of his teens, who didn't seem to blink.

Kroll pointed them out. "This is Mueller," he said, indicating the big man, who grinned, showing blackened, gappy teeth. "Reiniger—" the older man nodded "—and Stein." The youngster gave no reaction, just studied Koenig with the blank, incurious eyes of a fish on a slab.

Koenig looked back at Kroll. "We should get started," he said.

Kroll gave a tiny smile. "We're ready when you are, sir."

The five men filed out.

Once I was a patriot.

For God, the Fuehrer and the Reich. I believed in this. That is why I went to Russia, as a proud soldier of the Wehrmacht. As did many old friends of mine, and friends I made.

And so I saw my friends die: blown apart by shells and grenades, roasted alive by flamethrowers, torn open by bullets, gouged and hacked by bayonets, crushed by tanks and masonry.

For God, the Fuehrer and the Reich.

Once I was a patriot.

Now I am nothing.

Dawn, and a faint ground mist. Light dappling the forest floor, through the spiny branches of the fir trees. But no bird sang. Rolf couldn't help noting that.

Kroll took point. He crawled on his belly through the earth and old dried pine needles, and Rolf and the others crawled after him. Kroll squirmed down into a shallow bowl scooped into the ground and stopped just short of its upper edge, slipping a pair of field-glasses out from under his tunic and squinting through them.

Rolf drew alongside him. They were perhaps twenty metres from the edge of a clearing; from there to the main gates of the Schwartzberg camp another thirty metres stretched. And up an incline, to boot; not a particularly steep one, but still enough to slow down their approach at a time when speed would be of the essence.

Through the trees he could make out the high barbed-wire fences, the watchtower and the floodlights and the wooden huts huddled up against the flank of the stark, rock-ribbed hill behind them. Thirty metres? Might as well have been thirty kilometres; there'd be a machine gun mounted in the watchtower to cut down anyone straying near without authority.

"A little strange," said Kroll. "Don't you think?"

"What's that, sergeant?"

"You'd think they'd want us to assassinate the Fuehrer – that or one of the other Party bigwigs. Himmler, Goering – Goebbels perhaps. But instead, we're here. Undermining our own war effort. Doesn't that strike you as odd, sir?"

"We have our orders, sergeant."

"I'm not questioning them, sir. Just . . . "

"Yes?"

"The Ivans aren't going anywhere, sir. Sooner or later we'll have a big fight on our hands with them. And then there are the British. Even if they get rid of the Fuehrer, there'll still be a war to fight. Or end. So why destroy a weapon? Unless they're afraid of it too—"

"That's enough, sergeant."

"Sir." Kroll lowered the glasses. He was frowning.

"Something?"

"See for yourself, sir." Kroll passed the glasses across. Koenig raised them to his eyes and peered through them. The fence and the guard tower sprang into focus. Koenig's eyes strayed to the hill. There was very little vegetation on it that he could see, little earth to cloak the black bones of whatever odd rock it was made from. A thought occurred: "Is that the black mountain?" he asked.

"So they say."

"Not much of a mountain."

"They say it was once bigger."

Huts studded the parade ground. Accommodation, a canteen, a generator hut. Doubtless there would be an infirmary and armoury too. And at the back he saw a tall, hulking building with a pointed roof that put him in mind of a chapel of some sort – this, he guessed, would be their target, the hub of Projekt Wotan, whatever it might be. Only one thing was missing.

"Where is everybody?"

"That's what I thought," said Kroll. "No sign of anyone. Anywhere."

And then Koenig saw it, and was still. "That's not entirely true, sergeant. See? There?" He handed the glasses back to Kroll. "Look at the watchtower. Just below the platform."

A moment later he heard Kroll draw a sharp breath in, and he knew the sergeant had seen the same thing he had: the body of an SS soldier, hanging by his neck from the watchtower.

———

They crept to the edge of the wood, rising to stand as they did. All the while, from the camp there came no sound. And still there wasn't even the faintest hint of birdsong, as the sun continued to rise.

"Alright," said Rolf. "Get ready." He drew back the bolt on his Schmeisser. Kroll and Stein did the same, while Rhinemann and Mueller cocked their Mauser rifles.

"What now?" whispered Kroll.

"Might as well test the theory," said Rolf. He felt, he realized, mildly nervous. Nothing more.

"What do you m— sir!"

Rolf stepped out of the trees and into plain view. He waited in the stillness, but there was nothing. A bead of sweat crept over his temple. He brushed it away.

"Come on," he told the others, and started walking.

The ground was covered in a thick growth of grass and studded with rotted tree stumps. How long had it been since they'd cleared the area and built the camp here? He had no idea.

The gates were shut, secured by a chain. "Mueller," he said.

The big man moved forward, bolt-cutters in hand; when he drew level with the gates he stopped, stepped back. He turned and stared from Rolf to Kroll.

"What is it?" Kroll demanded. "Mueller, what?"

When the big man didn't answer, Rolf stepped past him to the gate and halted.

The floor of the parade ground hadn't been visible from their previous vantage. Now, though, it was, and clearly so.

And it was strewn with bodies.

The parade ground floor was sandy; now it was dark with dried blood. The soft buzz of flies wafted through the gate, and the reek of spoiling meat. The dead were all in uniform – SS uniform – and many still clutched weapons in their hands. Pistols, rifles, submachine guns, knives – or indeed, anything else that had come to hand.

"Get us in, Mueller," said Rolf.

"But Herr Hauptmann—"

"We are here to carry out a mission," Rolf said. "Whatever else we are, we are still German soldiers."

"Do as the Herr Hauptmann orders, Mueller," said Kroll. Mueller looked at him; Kroll didn't speak, just gazed calmly back. Finally Mueller noded, bowed his head and stepped back up to the gates.

Reiniger was looking back towards the woods they'd emerged from, his rifle's barrel moving back and forth. "It shouldn't be this quiet."

"That's enough," said Kroll.

"Let's get on with this," said Stein. His voice was jagged and grating.

"All of you," said Kroll.

There was a loud metallic snap, then a hiss and rattle of falling metal links, as Mueller cut the chain on the door. He pushed the gates wide, aimed his rifle ahead and stepped through. Rolf, and then the others, followed.

They crossed the parade ground in a loose circle, guns aimed outwards. The huts stood empty and silent, the windows – many of them shattered – like black, staring eyes. No movement. No sound.

"What *happened* here?" Reiniger muttered.

Rolf looked down. At his feet lay an SS man, both hands wrapped round the hilt of the dagger he'd plunged into his own left eye. Another lay beside him, a bullet hole in his temple, pistol still in his hand.

"They killed themselves," said Kroll. "They all killed themselves."

"Not all," said Stein. "See?" He gestured towards a dozen bullet-riddled corpses slumped on the ground. Another SS man knelt a few feet away, surrounded by empty bullet casings. He was propped into the kneeling position by the barrel of his Schmeisser, which was still wedged into his mouth. The submachine gun's butt was still braced against the ground.

"What the hell happened?" Reiniger asked again.

Mueller was muttering what sounded like a prayer.

"Shut up, all of you," said Kroll. "What now, sir?"

Rolf nodded towards the "chapel" he'd sighted before. As they advanced on it, he saw something else – a low wide heap of odd, flattened objects piled up beside its open door.

He was still trying to identify them when Mueller beat him to it. "God! Dear Mother of God!"

"Mueller—" began Kroll, then broke off as he saw too.

Rolf approached the . . . things. They'd been crushed flat, but there was no blood. It must have gone somewhere. So they must have been killed elsewhere. All the blood – all the moisture of any kind, it looked like – had been sucked or squeezed out of them. The bodies were punctured and perforated, and in places the dried, withered flesh was burned, as if by fire or some strong acid. Not all of them still had faces, but the ones that did were still screaming. Even in death.

Behind him, Reiniger vomited. Mueller was praying again, and this time Kroll didn't try to silence him. Stein drew level with Rolf and looked down at the bodies, head cocked to one side, fascinated. Only Rolf, it seemed, looked down at the corpses and felt nothing. *Nothing we haven't seen before.* Death, mutilation, agony – this particular combination of them might be new, but that was all that was. His eyes were drawn to the wrist of one of the crushed, desiccated corpses, and saw a five-digit number tattooed there. Neither the piles of corpses, or what they had once been, were new, only how they'd died.

All the same, he did not look too closely at their faces. Especially not those of the women. At last he looked away.

"Come on," he said. "We have work to do."

"Sir . . . " Kroll was pale. "Surely we should . . . "

"Whatever Projekt Wotan is, this is its work. Perhaps now we know why it has to be destroyed. We have explosive charges, incendiary bombs. We'll use them to destroy whatever this is." Rolf glared at Kroll till the sergeant looked down, then at the rest of his men, one by one. "Now come on," he said, and walked to the "chapel" door, pushed it wide and went through.

After a moment, the others followed.

Once I was a man with a family.

I was my parents' only child. They were good people, and I loved them dearly. They ensured I had a good education, was clothed and fed. I went to war to protect them from the enemy.

At the front, I received mail from them regularly, and wrote back whenever I could. Until one day, I received a letter in another's handwriting. Unfamiliar. One of the neighbours, as it proved. One of the few who had survived. Writing to tell me that not only the house I had grown up in, but the entire street was gone – blackened craters and ruins, stubs of masonry and charred timbers, all that remained.

An Allied air-raid, the letter said.

It was quick. They would have felt nothing.

The hole in the ground that had been my home, like the infected cavity left by a torn-out tooth.

I went to war to protect them.

Once I was a man with a family.

Now I am nothing.

———

The "chapel" was empty. A plain wooden building, apparently a single room. There were rows of chairs. Nothing else.

"What . . . ?" began Kroll.

Rolf raised a hand for silence and crossed the floor to the back of the "chapel", where another door was set into the wall. He pulled it open; cold dank air gusted out. Rolf stepped back and to the side, aiming the barrel of his Schmeisser into the dark.

Beyond the door was what looked like a cave – a tunnel cut through living rock. The "chapel" had backed onto the hill, the "black mountain" itself, but it was now clear that the heart of Projekt Wotan lay within the hill itself.

"Sir . . . " began Kroll.

Rolf stepped into the tunnel. Cool damp air engulfed him, fell around him like cold damp sheets. There was a faint sound in the distance. The cold air gusted into his face, and then the breeze died. A moment later the breeze blew again, but back down the tunnel, back inside the hill. Another moment of stillness, and then it blew out again.

Torches clicked on; their pale beams played across the tunnel walls. They were ribbed; the tunnel had been carved into the hill.

"Stop. Wait. Look." Rolf leant in closer to inspect the wall. The torch beam shone on something – symbols of a kind he didn't recognize. "What are these?"

"Runes?" suggested Stein, in his dead, grating voice.

"No."

"Hebrew?"

"No."

"Hieroglyphs, perhaps?" said Reiniger.

"God knows what they are." Rolf pointed the Schmeisser ahead of him and kept going. His booted feet splashed in the shallow water on the tunnel floor.

They'd gone somewhere between ten and twenty metres before the tunnel walls vanished. Their torchbeams flashed through darkness and hit wide stone walls instead. "A cavern," said Kroll.

"I know," said Rolf. He shone his own torch across the floor until it ended abruptly, dropping away into space. "Watch out ahead, there's a drop." He turned and shone the torch sideways; the light played over a blood-spattered white coat.

"There's a body here," he called, and went to examine it. The breeze blew across his face, then back again. In. Out. It made a faint noise as it blew back and forth, as if whispering over – no, not stone. What, then? The knowledge hovered at the periphery of his awareness, refusing to step into the light. Rolf tipped the body over onto its back. The dead man stared up at him with the bloody, ragged sockets that had been his eyes. His hands were red claws, pieces of tissue still clinging to them.

"There are more here," said Stein. He slipped past Rolf and played the beam of his torch over more corpses, a good half-dozen. All were in white coats. All had apparently stabbed or battered themselves or one another to death. There were tables, an instrument panel. "There are some notes," he said.

"Get them."

Stein grabbed them. "Looks like someone's tried to burn them."

"Get them."

"Yes, sir. What were they doing here . . . ?"

"Oh my God," whispered Kroll. "Sir? Sir. Here. Look."

"What . . . " Rolf heard Stein mutter, as he turned. Both Stein and Kroll were shining their torches upwards; he shone his too.

Mueller, standing beside Kroll, let out an appalled wail and fell to his knees. Rolf was vaguely aware of it, and that he should shout at

Mueller, tell him to get on his feet and act like a soldier. But he didn't. All he could do was stare up at *It*.

It filled the huge, gaping hollow in the centre of the hill, a hollow that went a long way down. Rolf looked down; the light of his torch vanished long before detecting either any bottom to the shaft or to *Its* bulk. And then he shone it up again, and *It* loomed over them, *Its* head almost brushing the ceiling of rock above them.

Was it a head? *It* was a vast, lumpy mass that crowned the pale, flabby pile that loomed above; a lumpy mass in which large black holes gaped, arranged without apparent system or symmetry. Some opened and closed; others remained fixedly open.

And that wind, that breeze, gusting in and out – yes, Rolf knew it for what it was now but he couldn't bring himself to admit it, couldn't bear to acknowledge it.

Its great, unending heap of a body glistened greasily; *Its* hide was smooth, pale and slimy, like intestine, like great sheets of gut. Pale and slimy except for dark, glistening patches that spotted it. Were there holes in the middle of those patches? And if so, what were they? More mouths? No matter. Under that hide things *moved*, like great armatures of bone. It was as if someone was trying to erect a tent from the inside; the great bulk of *It* rippled and shifted.

Mueller was rocking to and fro, whimpering, burbling out what sounded like an unending, unheeded prayer.

Across *Its* surface, tiny vestigial limbs – arms that looked almost human, insectile or crustacean forelegs, octopoid tentacles – twitched and thrashed and writhed. There were a particularly active group of them around the edge of the pit, and as Rolf watched, the reason became apparent. The bone armatures moved again; the hide in front of them stretched taut, then split bloodlessly wide. The stench that gusted out had Reiniger vomiting again.

There were sounds in the air. Were they coming from *It*? Rolf couldn't tell. It was like hundreds of tiny, twittering, chittering voices. There were words in there, sort of. He thought so, anyway. But he couldn't make them out. They were shrill, sharp, nagging, scraping at the inside of his skull, jabbing at his eyes. He shook his head, sharply.

Kroll was backing away from *It*; he was shaking his head too. From inside *Its* body slid two thick, flat . . . objects. They were on the end of limbs that glistened – *bone armatures* again, the phrase wouldn't leave his head – bone armatures coated in a thick, moving gelatine. The great flat objects on the ends of them resembled, he realised, nothing so much as huge, fingerless hands. Around their edges, thin, pale cilia stirred and began to move, dripping a colourless slime that hissed and smoked when it hit the floor.

"Kroll, get back from it," Rolf shouted. "Get back! Get back!"

The sergeant backed away, then hesitated as he remembered Mueller, still moaning and rocking before *It* and the thick, groping hands.

"Just get back," Rolf shouted, and Kroll backed away. As he did, long thin spines suddenly slid from the palms – for want of a better term – of *Its* hands. They, too, glistened and dripped. The cilia waved and tasted the air. The 'hands' shifted slightly to the side. Towards Mueller.

"Mueller!" shouted Rolf.

"Paul!" shouted Kroll. "Get up, run!"

The "hands" parted and descended. At the last second the big man seemed to recognize his danger and let out a piercing scream. He half-rose, turning to run, but it was too late; the "hands" slammed together around him. His shrieks weren't cut off, only muffled; they continued even as smoke and steam hissed out of the grip of the "hands".

"Bastard!" shouted Kroll, and opened fire, raking *It* with a long burst from his Schmeisser. The great hanging sheets of *Its* hide twitched and flapped as the bullets hammered it.

A shot rang out and Kroll staggered sideways. And then another, and another. He stumbled back and stared – at Reiniger, who'd dropped his rifle and was aiming a Luger pistol at the sergeant.

"What—" Rolf brought his gun to bear on Reiniger as the other man's third shot took Kroll in the forehead, dropping him to the ground.

"His eyes—" gasped Stein.

True enough. Blood was pouring from Reiniger's eyes, and indeed from his ears and nose. His free hand clutched at his head and a terrible keening sound came from his mouth, in the last instant before he thrust the barrel of the Luger into it and fired.

Even as he fell, *Its* "hands" opened, and a flattened, smoking thing fell to the cavern floor. Stein cried out and fled back down the tunnel. Rolf backed away, unable to look away from *It*. The thin, shrill, high chittering rose higher and higher in his ears; like Kroll before him he loosed a long burst of gunfire at *It*, then turned and ran.

Once I was a lover.

Her name was Hannah. I first met her when I was seventeen; a slender, pretty girl with blonde hair and blue eyes. Oh, so very Aryan, just the kind of girl the Fuehrer enjoined good Germans to marry.

We kissed, yes. And there were other things. And the promise of more when I returned.

I asked my parents to give Hannah my love with each letter home, even as the memory of who she was and what she meant grew more distant; even as what she waited to give me on my return became something I bought, or took.

And then the letter about my parents. And all that sustained me – all that kept me going, especially after what I saw in the woods that day – was the thought that Hannah waited.

But on my return, I could not find her. Another family lived in her house, and knew nothing of whoever had lived there before. Others, who had known us both before I went to the Russian Front, not only denied any knowledge of her fate, but having ever known her at all.

Finally, I found one friend who, braver than the rest, took me aside and whispered the truth in my ear: Hannah's mother, it had transpired, had been a Jew. And so the Gestapo had come for her, had taken her and Hannah and Hannah's brother Otto away. Never seen since. Never to be seen again.

Her name was Hannah.
Once I was a lover.
Now I am nothing.

———

In the "chapel", Rolf slammed the door to the tunnel and backed away, pulling the near-empty magazine out of the Schmeisser and slamming a new one into place.

"What now?" gasped Stein.

What, indeed? Rolf thought, or tried to. Every impulse screamed at him to run, while he still could. But—

"The notes," he said. "Did you get the notes?"

"What? Yes. Yes, I did."

The chittering – that damned chittering sound – was in the air and rising, rising. It didn't seem to bother Stein. Damn him, couldn't he hear it? "Get them out. Read them. Find out what that – thing – is."

"Yes." Stein knelt, spread out the fragments of Projekt Wotan on the bare-board floor before him. "Here. What?"

"What is it?"

"It's madness."

"Read it."

Stein nodded. "It says . . . 'The process of reviving *It* is slow but progressing. Thankfully we can ensure a steady supply of material to nourish *It* and enable *Its* revival . . .' That's all on this page, it's half-burnt. Here's another . . . '*It* was worshipped, centuries ago, by the original inhabitants of Schwartzberg, before they were burnt by the Inquisition. *It* was mighty once, but was the merest minion of an ancient race who walked the earth as gods in the time before man.' It . . . " Stein looked up. "I told you, sir, it's madness."

"So is that," said Rolf, gesturing at the door to the tunnel with his Schmeisser. *It. It.* The notes spoke of the Thing in the cavern in the same way that he thought of it. Of *It. It.* "Keep reading."

"Sir. It says . . . '*It* was left behind. The world changed. They could no longer live there. So *It*, and perhaps others like *It*, were left behind. To wait. To open the way when conditions were once more right. Perhaps to make those conditions come about. *It* was sealed inside the hill to protect *It*—' " Stein looked up, staring. "To protect *It*? What did *It* need protecting from?"

"Keep reading, damn it."

"Yes, sir . . . '*It* was sealed inside the hill and the hill was worshipped. *It* had power over the minds of men; they who propitiated *It* and served *It* would be rewarded by *Its* favours and *Its* aid . . .' " Stein looked up. "That must be it, then."

"Yes. Why try to kill the Russians when you can make them kill themselves? And if you have enemies within, something like this would be very useful." Rolf cocked his Schmeisser. "That explains why the colonel wanted it destroyed."

"Yes." Stein got up. "Sir, we have to get out of here. There's no way we can destroy *It*. I know we have weapons, explosives, but – we'd never get close enough. You saw what happened with Kroll, and Reiniger . . ."

"Yes, I did, Stein. I saw."

Stein backed towards the "chapel" door. "We have to get out, sir. Inform the colonel. We have the notes. Get him to – to bring – I don't know, we need artillery to destroy that thing, or bombers, or—"

Rolf turned and fired, emptying most of the Schmeisser's magazine in a single burst that picked Stein up and flung him back against the wall. Blood flowered out across the wood panelling. The youngster stared back at Rolf in utter shock, then slid to the ground and was still.

Rolf stumbled back, flinging the submachine gun away from him. On the "chapel" floor, Stein's body twitched a couple of times, then was still.

And the high, shrill chittering rose in the air.

Once I was a man.

I believed that humankind was glorious, not some infection on the earth. I believed that we had a purpose and a destiny. That we were great and noble and worthwhile. I believed that the good in us was stronger than . . . the other.

And then I fought in Russia.

It was ugly, brutal fighting. Friends died. I took lives, ended them with cruelty and brutality. But though vile, that was comprehensible; they were soldiers and so were we. It was comprehensible.

Until that day in the woods.

I was separated from my unit, along with several others. We tried to find our way back to German lines, and to avoid the Russians, for we knew by now we could expect no mercy from the Ivans should they take us; only a bullet, and that if we were lucky.

By the time I reached the woods, I was the only one left alive, and I was in despair. I had a pistol I had taken from a dead officer. I'd already resolved to save a bullet for myself, should the situation become hopeless; better that than starvation or capture by the Russians.

I heard the shots as I entered the woods. I froze, hid behind a tree, waited. Then, listening closely, I heard voices. They were speaking in German. They were laughing. Laughing? And all the while, the shots kept ringing out, one after the other.

I got to my feet and went through the woods, till at last I reached a clearing.

They had been forced to dig a hole. Men, women, children. Jews, I suppose. Or just Russians. Undesirables. Untermenschen. They had been forced to dig a deep hole. Around them were men in black uniforms. Einsatzkommandos: special squads. They pointed rifles and machine pistols at the untermenschen to keep them back. Three einsatzkommandos stood at the pit's edge, holding pistols. Each would make a villager sit on the pit's edge in front of them, then point the gun at the back of their heads and fire. And the men, the women, the children, tumbled one by one into the pit.

The last to die was a little fair-haired boy of about four. He didn't cry or scream. He just didn't understand. Couldn't comprehend what *had happened around him, what had become of his familiar little world.*

The einsatzkommandos *laughed and smoked, and one of them pointed his gun at the child's head.*

In the second before the shot was fired, the child's bewildered eyes met mine.

After that, the einsatzkommandos *spotted me. They fed me, gave me cigarettes, helped me find my way back to my unit.*

I broke bread with these men.

They showed me pictures of their mothers and fathers, their wives and children. Their sweethearts at home, like my Hannah. My Hannah who perhaps at that moment was being killed by men such as these. Men such as me. By men.

I believed that humankind was glorious, not some infection on the earth.

Once I was a man.

Now I am nothing.

―――――――

Rolf walked back down the stone tunnel, through the cold embrace of the clinging air.

In his head, the chittering rose: higher, higher, ever higher. He knew what it was now. Whose voice. Whose claws, seeking to gain access to whatever he might have in lieu of a soul.

Its great, heaving bulk rose before him. *Its* misshapen head stared down at him.

It *was sealed inside the hill to protect* It . . . *To protect* It? *What did* It *need protecting from?*

He knew now, of course. Just as he knew what those black, glistening patches on *Its* hide were. Not new, un-guessed-at orifices of the thing, but simply and solely patches of rot and decay.

What did *It* need protecting from? The air itself. The air of an earth that was poison to *It* and all *Its* kind. That was why *Its* masters had left, gone into hiding or hibernation, or wherever they were now. Sealed in the hill, *It* had been protected. But now *It* had been poisoned, and now *It* was dying.

And now he understood what *It* needed.

"They died because you can get into men's minds," he said to *It*. "But you don't just want to visit, do you? You're looking for a new home. But they won't let you. Barriers in the mind. Families. Faith. Loved ones. Something."

Its vast, gusty breathing filled the cavern.

"But I," said Rolf. "I am different."

Its bulk shifted, and he opened his arms to receive.

Christmas 1946

"Koenig?"

Rolf stopped, turned slowly to face his questioner.

A square in Berlin; gaunt, ruined buildings raised stark against the night sky. Snow drifting relentlessly down. Two lovers strolled back and forth across the square, arm in arm, and an off-key discordant choir of carollers regaled three American soldiers, hoping for food and drink as a reward for pleasing their audience: *Stille nacht, heilige nacht . . .*

The older man limped forward, using a stick. He was bald on top, his remaining hair white. He was thin, the flesh slack on his bones. Sick.

"It is you," he said. "Hauptmann Rolf Koenig, of—"

"Quiet," said Rolf.

The older man fell silent.

Rolf studied him. "You're the colonel from the *Widerstand*," he said. "The one who recruited me for the Schwartzberg mission."

"That's right. Schmidt. Colonel Anton Schmidt." Schmidt gazed at Rolf through the falling snow with watery blue eyes. "You were listed as missing, presumed dead after the Schwartzberg mission," he said. "Mind you, a lot of people were. A lot of explosives seemed to have been used. Far more than you and your men had with you, or should have been available at the camp."

Rolf simply smiled and shrugged.

"Where have you been all this time?"

"Is that really any business of yours?"

Schmidt stepped closer. "Don't get clever with me, Koenig—"

"Or what?" Rolf's smile stayed on his lips, but left his eyes. Schmidt blinked, wavered; a thin hand clutched at his chest. He stumbled back, looked around for help at the two or three passersby crossing the square, the carollers, still singing away.

"They can't see you," said Rolf. "Or rather, they can't see us."

Schmidt swayed, choked, fell to his knees.

"And they won't, until much later," Rolf said pleasantly. "Long after your heart has died, and I'm long gone from here. I'm rarely seen unless I wish to be. As I did with you, tonight. Tying up loose ends, you might say."

Schmidt's face was engorged, almost purple.

"I have much to do," said Rolf. "And now I have decades, even centuries, to do it in, while freely moving among your kind. A world to change. A way to open." He chuckled. "You should be grateful, really, colonel. I've ensured you won't have to see it."

With a last strangled noise, Schmidt rolled on to his back and lay still.

Rolf took a last look around the square – at the lovers, arm in arm, the American soldiers and the carol singers, all carrying on, oblivious – then, smiling, crossed the square and went out onto the main road. In the crowds and the fast-falling snow, even if anyone could have seen him, soon he would have been only a nondescript blur. And then nothing. Nothing at all.

The Lighthouse Keeper of Kurohaka Island
Kane Gilmour

———

The gray light of the morning merged with the steel color of the waves, giving Shinobi the feeling he was being tossed around in the air. He stood at the bow of the freighter, his young hands gripping the rail tightly – he'd been told and he remembered, "one hand for yourself and one hand for the ship, at all times" – and he peered into the murky shades of concrete that filled the sky and the sea. He couldn't determine where one began and the other ended.

Thick fog shrouded everything, and his one thought over and over was to wonder where all the brilliant blue had gone. From his home in Wakkanai, at the northern tip of Japan, the sea was always blue, even on stormy days. But here, in the no man's land twenty miles northeast of Hokkaido, everything looked hostile to the boy. But then, everything in the world now looked that way.

"Shinobi," he heard his father's abrupt voice from behind him. Mindful to keep one hand on the damp railing, as the massive freighter bounced in the invisible troughs of the cold waves, he turned to see his father approaching him from the starboard side of the ship. "Come inside. We are nearly there."

Shinobi walked along the railing, moving hand-over-hand lest some rogue wave slap the big ship and send him headlong into a never-ending drop through the gray moisture. "Almost where, Father? I've checked the maps. There's nothing here."

His father, a stern man named Jiro, remained quiet until Shinobi reached him along the rail, skirting the massive multi-colored metal containers that filled the center of the ship's broad foredeck. When Shinobi looked up at his father, he realized the man was not simply waiting for him or being his typical quiet self, but rather he was peering intently past the bow of the ship and into the gloom.

Shinobi knew to stay still and be quiet. His father was either deep in thought or looking for something in the fog. The man would speak when he was ready to, and not before. With nothing else to do, besides hold the railing, Shinobi studied his father's face. He quickly determined that the man was actually looking for something in the thick mist that shrouded the ship. He was just about to turn, when his father spoke.

"There," the man pointed past the bow, "Kurohaka Island."

Shinobi turned and momentarily let his hand drop from the railing in surprise. In a part of the Sea of Okhotsk he knew to be empty of any spit of land, a jagged dark shape was rising from the sea and the fog. The island looked to have strange curving towers near the center, and rough rocky shores at the edges. Finally, his eyes sought out what he was looking for – the lighthouse. It was on the end of the island, on a high rocky promontory, but its lifesaving light was absent, and its white paint made little difference in the thick fluffy coating of whitish gray that filled the air. The spire could barely be seen in all the mist.

Shinobi's father was a lighthouse keeper in the region, being paid by the governments of both Japan and Russia to ride whatever available ships were in the area, and to frequently visit and maintain the ramshackle lighthouses on the islands scattered around Hokkaido and the giant lobster-claw tips of Sakhalin, around the Gulf of Patience. Shinobi had travelled with his father to Rebun Island and Rishiri Island. He had even gone on one memorable camping trip with his father to the abandoned Russian island of Moneron, northwest of the Soya Straight. He had listened attentively to his father's few descriptions of his work on the lights. Shinobi was meant to take over his father's work some day, first apprenticing in two years' time, when he turned fifteen. He had studied hard in school, and paid special attention to the nautical maps in the library and around the house. He knew the names of every jagged rocky islet in the area, but he had never heard of Kurohaka Island.

True, his attention of late had not been on maps or studying. Instead he had been seeing things, and hoping he wasn't losing his sanity. But he had kept that information hidden from his father.

"Kurohaka?" he asked.

His father nodded grimly. "A dark place, but still part of the job. Let's go in."

Shinobi followed his father back to the ship's forecastle, wondering at the name of the island. Kurohaka. *Black tomb.* He wondered if sailors had named it that because it was such a rocky shoreline. Many times islands were given fearsome names to warn sailors off the reefs. But the name might actually stem from a true tomb.

He wondered who was buried there.

Or, considering what he had been seeing lately – *what* might be buried there.

———

The freighter had lowered them in a small speedboat with winches from the high sides of the rusting gunwales. Once in the choppy water, they had made quick time to the dark island, and his father expertly navigated them past some treacherous headlands and into a tiny sheltered lagoon. Any boat larger than their speedboat would not have made it into the small inlet. They pulled the boat up to a concrete pier that jutted an absurd four feet into the water from the wet rocky land. The lagoon looked to Shinobi to be a popped volcanic bubble more than a sandy beach. The shoreline was all dark rock, but at least here it was smooth.

Shinobi helped his father tie up the small boat to the two rusted metal cleats sunk into the concrete pier's rough surface and carry their gear ashore. When he turned to the gray sea, he could watch the freighter moving away into the distance. A different boat would swing by in two days to collect them.

"How can this island be here, Father?"

Jiro Yashida hefted his pack and began walking up the rocks, toward the interior of the island. He spoke over his shoulder to his son in short bursts. "You know the maps. Think of the shapes. A long chain of islands connects Hokkaido to Russia's Kamchatka peninsula. And Wakkanai points at the western tip of Sakhalin. Is it really so surprising to you that an island lies midway between Hokkaido and the eastern tip of Sakhalin?"

Shinobi considered his father's logic, and found that geologically, the location of the island made perfect sense. "No. I understand, but the island does not appear on the maps."

"Many don't," was all his father said.

They turned left and followed a coastal trail up along the rocks, twisting and turning through switchbacks, until the base of the white lighthouse was visible overhead. Their path, keeping so close to the shore as it did, kept the rest of the island hidden from Shinobi's view, even as the fog began to lift. What little he could see was dark brown and black rock, most of it volcanic, and fitting with his initial assumptions about the geology of the island. Shinobi was not fond of math at school, but when Earth sciences came into things, he paid strict attention.

With the base of the lighthouse just thirty feet overhead now, their path narrowed, and they needed to rely on the artificial railings made of thick heavy chains. They had been bolted into the side of the rock and painted in so many layers of heavy black paint, that even when Shinobi could see the outer layers had chipped, all he could see in the remaining holes on the links were more and more layers underneath.

Shinobi watched where his father stepped, and how the man moved his hands along the chains, as if they were the railing on the freighter – *one hand for the ship* – and he did the same. They were nearly at the top of the path, which would bring them right to the door of the lighthouse, when his father spoke.

"When did you plan on telling me? Or did you think you should keep it to yourself forever?"

The man didn't pause in his ascent, nor did he look back at his son.

Shinobi knew what his father was talking about, of course. There was just the one thing he had kept from his father in his whole thirteen years.

His father was talking about the *monsters*.

Shinobi could see them, and no one else could.

He stayed quiet, thinking how best to answer the question, as his father made it to the top of the climb and lowered his pack to the ground, just outside the door to the lighthouse. Finally, as Shinobi neared his father and the pack, he spoke, while removing his own heavy pack.

"Have I done something wrong, Father?" Shinobi hung his head as he spoke.

His father reached down and tenderly lifted Shinobi's chin, so he was looking his father in the eyes. "You have done nothing wrong, *Shino.*"

"How could you have known?" the boy asked, his eyes beginning to water.

His father quickly turned, allowing him to save face, as a tear sprang from the corner of his young eye and ran down his round cheek. The man worked a large brass key into the lock on the lighthouse door, and entered. Shinobi followed.

"The haunted look in your eyes, son. I had the same look, when I first saw the creatures."

That his father knew about the monsters was a surprise to Shinobi. That his father had seen them, as well, filled the boy with a relief he hadn't known he needed. He followed his father up the twisting iron staircase. The lighthouse was close to a hundred feet in height – Shinobi could tell by counting the stairs as they ascended in silence. He wanted to ask his father more, but he knew the man would tell him when he was ready. Probably at the top of the tower, since speaking while ascending the steep steps would require an excess of oxygen, and Jiro Yashida was a practical man of economy. Shinobi hoped to be as sensible when he was an adult.

As his father came close to the lantern section of the tower, a good twenty steps ahead of Shinobi on the cast iron stairs, he began speaking again, but softly. "Every first-born child between the ages of thirteen and eighteen has the sight, *Shino*. But only first-borns. Your brother, Naro, will never be able to see the beasts, as you do. Unless you were to die before he grows to adulthood. Most teens lose their vision as adulthood approaches, but in our family, we are unusual. We retain the sight as adults. I still see the creatures today, son."

The man stepped up off the stairs and into the service room of the lantern. Then he ascended a straight ladder to the optic section of the tower. Shinobi hurried after him, as the man stepped off the ladder and opened the door from the optic room to the gallery around the tower's top. Wind rushed into the structure and flooded down toward Shinobi. It was cold and, of course, he could smell the briny aroma of the sea, but there was something else on the wind. Something old, like dust.

Jiro walked out the open door to the catwalk and waited against the railing, as Shinobi caught up with him at last.

The fog had lifted as the day's sunlight burnt it away. The cloud cover had receded to a low blanket hovering over the land in patches and threatening possible rain, but not until later. For now the morning sunlight was piercing through the covering in spots, like samurai swords thrust downward through pillows, toward the green land spread out before them.

But the clouds did not hold Shinobi's attention.

His eyes took in the many shades of green across the central part of the land of the island, and the things that pierced the green, reaching up like clawing hands to the sky – a reverse of the angle of the beams of light slicing down from above.

They were bones.

Hundreds and thousands of *bones*.

The slim graceful towers Shinobi had seen from sea were giant rib bones, arching into the sky as high as the lighthouse. The carcasses of giant hundred-foot and two-hundred foot long strange beasts Shinobi could not recognize littered the island, and stretched as far as he could see. His father had said the island was approximately three miles long, and from his position near the top of the lighthouse, Shinobi could see most of the way to the far shore, where the green gave way to the dark volcanic rocks again. There were unnatural mounds and low hills in places, and the boy guessed they were the covered graves of yet more of the massive creatures. At the center of the island was one huge rounded hill with some irregularities and lumpy tufts of bushes and trees on it in places.

Shinobi spotted massive lobster-like claws, and desiccated snake-like twisting bodies, piled high on tangled horns and bulbous bones. Most of the creatures had decayed to the point of little more than skeletons – even though the bones were impressive at their immense scale. A few of the dead monsters still contained eyes in unusual locations, or mouths full of teeth taller than the apartment buildings back in Wakkanai.

"I see them all. This island has been a place where they come to die for centuries. Whenever one of them is injured, it comes here of its own volition. We don't know why." Shinobi's father looked gray and ashen, as if the sight of the boneyard was still unnerving to him. It did little to ease Shinobi's own tension at the sight, but the revelation that he was not going crazy and he was not the only one with the sight helped him some.

"H–how many?" was all the boy could stammer.

"We don't know. When those few of us with the sight have found these mega creatures dead in other parts of the world, it has become a tradition to bring them here. I will tell you how it began. I will tell you what happened. You are one of the rare ones, Shino. You will have the sight all your life, and like me, you must become the caretaker of this necropolis. We guard more than just the bones."

The older man fell silent as the wind ripped past the top of the tower, bringing the scent of the water and what Shinobi now suspected was the smell of the dead.

"First we will fix the light, son. It warns sailors to stay away, and that is a very good thing. Then we'll go down and have a talk. Our family first took on this bizarre appointment with your grandfather, Haruki. He was the first in our family to see that the world is truly full of monsters."

––––––––

Haruki Yashida ran for his life.

The bombing of the city had ended a few days earlier, but he knew what would come next. He had seen the hideous monstrosities with his own eyes. The war had gone on for far too long, but this new twist? He didn't know what to think. All he knew for sure was he would need to be far from Nagasaki on a ship, before they came here and did what they had to Hiroshima. The world was talking about American weapons that could level a city, but Haruki knew better.

This hell was not from the West.

The storm was approaching. Massive clouds had formed at the northern edge of the city. As the residents of the battered outskirts took shelter underground in grubby dirt tunnels and cramped wooden bunkers, Haruki raced along the broken, rubble-strewn streets, leaping trash heaps and scrambling over fallen walls, tumbled wood, shattered plaster, and the ever-present terracotta tiles that littered the ravaged city. He had been to Nagasaki once before, and loved that the old ways were still intact with regard to architecture and design. But after what he had witnessed in Hiroshima, he knew that even concrete and steel would offer little protection from what was coming.

It had taken him two days to get here from the ruins of Hiroshima on the last of the three packed refugee trains that had made it out. He had seen the final devastation, with the terrifying pink rays of death spewing from the snake-like creature's mouth. He had watched out the windows of the train, from a distance. A distance of miles, but even from that far away, he had felt the heat of the blast. Haruki understood that few would have survived the snake-beast's frantic battle with the gigantic squid-like monster. He and the others had all fled – all the way here to Nagasaki, but Haruki was one of the only people to have *seen* the beasts. The others all spoke of bombings and of some American super-weapon. Or they spoke of earthquakes and floods. Even of American troops invading.

Haruki remained silent, listening to the conflicting versions of the event. He understood that these people had seen the devastation and the destruction, but he knew they would all have different interpretations of what exactly it was that had murdered an entire city. He had lived with that discrepancy since he was a child, when he first saw the *monsters* in the world, and he had realized few others could. He came to know that only first-born teenage children could actually see the world the way it truly was. Like other teens, he should have lost his ability to see the creatures when he became a man, but for some reason, with him, the sight had never faded.

As the train pulled in to Nagasaki, he overheard some teenagers whispering quietly near the rancid stinking lavatory, which was little more than a closet with a hole in the floor of the train and the rails rushing by below. They were comparing their events of what had happened – and pouring derision over the multitudes of conflicting versions of the story they had heard the adults tell. They had seen the giant beasts, just like he had. Haruki had gone over to them and spoken softly.

"I saw what you saw. You're not crazy."

The teens had been startled by his admission, but nodded, grateful for it.

Haruki understood the haunted look in their eyes. He'd had it in his own since he was fourteen. He'd tried to find the teens again in the throngs of packed humanity swarming off the train and into the station, but he lost sight of them in the sweaty masses.

He was going to try to find a ride to the harbor, but the roads were blocked pretty heavily to the north of town, from the damage sustained days earlier by Allied bombing raids. Looking north to the approaching gray storm clouds, Haruki had opted to run for it instead. He needed to move rapidly south through the shattered residential neighborhoods, before he would pass through the industrial factories and the Allied prison camp, on his way to the southern harbor. He knew if he waited too long, any sea-worthy ships would be gone.

An underfed dog with patches of dark fur leapt out of a trash pile, snapping and barking at Haruki as he ran, but he ignored the noise, one of many sounds all blending into the hurried roar of a wartime city. As he came closer to the fence line of the prison camp, he felt a hot breeze rip into the city from behind him, and he turned to see he wasn't going to make it to the harbor in time.

The wind had blown the gray clouds filling the horizon into the city, spraying dust and small specks of debris. Flashes of pink and golden-green light erupted from within the clouds, as if mystical lightning were threatening to attack the northern edge of the town. Haruki knew that wasn't far from the truth. He turned to run again, but a shouting voice halted his run.

"Hey, mister! Over here! Quick!"

Haruki turned away from the fence line of the camp. Two of the teens he had seen on the train were hunkered down behind the low wall of a dwelling that had partially collapsed in the last bombing. Just below the line of the crumbled wall, he could see the top of a third head, with peculiarly light-colored hair. The teens he recognized waved him over, as another gust of wind carried a choking cloud of dust past his face, and he detected the scent of rotten meat on the breeze. He raced across the street and leapt over the wall, just as the two teens ducked down below the shelter of the fragmented wood and cracked plaster. A shrieking noise ripped out of the cloud behind him, and Haruki instinctively ducked down lower behind the wall with the others, just as a far stronger gust of wind rammed into the structure at his back, shaking it. A wooden food cart flew overhead, crashing into one of the few remaining walls of the vacated house, splintering into fragments no larger than toothpicks.

The force necessary to do that! Haruki thought.

He squatted lower as the wind howled and the shrieking noise grew louder around him.

"The edge of the battle . . . the debris cloud . . . It's one of the first major dangers," one of the two teens shouted at him over the roar of the wind. The boy was probably no more than fifteen, with shaggy dark hair, like most Japanese boys his age, and thick-framed glasses. The other boy Haruki recognized as older, at maybe seventeen. He had a long thin scar up the side of his face, and his countenance was grim.

"Be prepared to run as soon as the wind dies down," the older boy shouted.

Haruki just nodded. He turned to the other side of him and was in for a shock. There wasn't just one more person next to him – there were three. One was an attractive girl, probably seventeen. She had long wavy hair, and a somewhat chestnut face. Haruki had seen women like her before. She was not pure Japanese. At some point in her ancestry, she had some Pacific islander in her. Haruki found her to be stunningly beautiful. She was hunched down like he was, and holding her ears against the shrieking of the wind, as the storm found its way to where they hid. Next to her was another boy, round and chubby, at least fifteen, but possibly older. He was blubbering and crying, covered in plaster dust, and his nose was crusted with old snot.

But neither of those two held Haruki's attention long.

The third person was an adult. A man, probably a year younger than Haruki's twenty-one. But this man was not like the others. He was the source of the lighter-colored hair Haruki had spotted before he jumped the wall.

This man was an American.

Haruki stared at the man. He was wearing tan pants and a thick dark brown leather jacket. *A pilot*, Haruki realized. He was about to ask himself where an American pilot could have come from, when he realized that just across the street was the fence of the prison camp. *He must have escaped!* As Haruki scrutinized the man's face, he saw the boy inside. Then it became apparent. This pilot wasn't really an adult. He was still a teen. He had probably lied about his age to join the military. He wasn't as young as the others, but he couldn't have been much older than the girl.

The wind sped up, and more debris began to fly over the top of the small wall, crashing into the remains of the house, as Haruki hunched with the rest. He felt the wall shift behind his back, and realized how fast and strong the wind must be. Then the wind and the shrieking sound began to die down, but before it could stop completely, he felt a great tremor in the ground beneath him – not like the earthquakes he had felt near Kyoto as a child, where the ground would rumble and shake for even minutes at a time. This was an immense thud – a single impact that more closely resembled an explosion.

"Now!" the older teen with the grim face yelled.

All at once Haruki was scrambling up to his feet and running south again, with the four terrified teenagers and the brown-haired pilot. The ground shook again with another impact before they had run even ten steps. "I was heading for the harbor," Haruki yelled to them.

The American just looked at him for a moment, then turned away. The older boy grunted an acknowledgement. Haruki realized the American man might not speak Japanese.

"We are running for a ship!" he told the man in heavily accented English.

The man, running hard, turned to glance at Haruki with a half-grin. "Good plan! Those things yours?" He asked the last part with his thumb cocked back behind him.

Haruki didn't spare a glance the way he'd come. "Not ours. We are in this together."

The American nodded. They ran with the others to the end of the street, then turned onto a wide avenue that would bring them past the last factories in the southern part of the city.

"Dakota Talbott," the pilot said, his breath coming in heaving gasps.

"I am . . . Haruki."

The other teens either spoke no English, which was likely, or they were too out of breath from running. The group was no more than a mile from the harbor, but Haruki knew they were out of time.

He chanced a look over his shoulder and was glad he did.

"Down!" he shouted in Japanese and threw himself into the American's back, knocking them both sprawling to the ground. The older teens all dropped to the cracked asphalt road, as a gasoline tanker truck flew over their heads. The younger, chubby boy with the snotty nose hadn't leapt down.

He had turned to see what the problem was.

Haruki saw the boy's tear-streaked face, and knew that the boy didn't even have time to understand the threat before the truck smashed into him and swept him up the street, before it slammed though the brick wall of an armor-plating factory. A fireball erupted from the hole in the wall, sending a wave of heat and vapor back toward them.

"Stay down," he shouted. He didn't need to translate. The American had seen the fireball, too, and quickly ducked his head down to the asphalt and covered the back of his head with his hands.

Haruki did the same until he felt the wave of baking heat rip past above him.

Then he felt another stabbing thump in the earth from below, and another of the hideous shrieks occurred.

This time, he looked back.

The clouds of smoke and debris back up the street separated, as the mouth of the huge snake-creature blasted out of the center, its twenty-foot-tall teeth snapping and gnashing. Its body slithered out of the cloud like a snake, but this close up, Haruki could see that only its movement resembled that of a true snake. Its back was ridged like the bony scales or plates of some dinosaur representations he had seen in a museum. Yet the creature's skin below the bony protrusions was smooth and shiny, like that of a whale. Its head was lumpy and misshapen, not sleek like the head of a viper. But when it opened its mouth and turned its long forked tongue back at the cloud of the oncoming storm, Haruki knew it had more in common with a viper than its skeletal structure hinted at.

He saw that the creature had short fin-like legs along its length – three on each side. They didn't look functional, but as the long tube of the body, which was easily thirty feet in diameter and over a hundred and fifty feet long, slithered out of the debris and dust, it rolled on its side, and the fins scrabbled at the broken asphalt beneath the beast. Suddenly its immense bulk shifted sideways, and the creature pulled its head back to strike at the cloud.

The sharp impact to the ground came again, and then again faster.

Haruki turned away from the spectacle and saw the others all watched with him, standing limp and lifeless, looking at the gargantuan snake-beast.

"Run!" Haruki shouted.

His voice snapped the teen boys out of their stupor, and they sprinted away down the street. The American – *Dakota* – grabbed the girl's hand and ran as well, dragging her after him.

Haruki took five leaping steps, but something slammed into him from the side as the thumps in the ground increased in tempo. Then he was flying horizontally across the street, straight for a huge section of a traditional wooden wall. He crossed his arms in front of his head, as his body twisted in the air, and he saw that the giant snake creature had lunged back at the gray billowing clouds, its tail-end snapping away from the far end of the street and whipping into Haruki's body, as it crossed the road. But Haruki was confused, because the head had hit him, instead of the tail. He could see the long fangs of the creature's mouth retreating. The trail of ripped-up asphalt on the ruined street left little doubt in Haruki's mind as to the true chain of events, though.

His crossed forearms made contact with the thin wooden wall of the partially destroyed home, and the surface of it tore under the impact like origami paper. His arms barely felt it, and then he was slammed into another wall. He slid down to the floor, broken slats of wood falling on top of his head. Small pebble-like chunks of plaster rained down on Haruki, and as he stood, wobbly on his feet, he found himself looking at a completely undestroyed bathroom wall, with the mirror over the wash basin still undisturbed. Covered as he was in plaster dust and dirt, Haruki looked like a ghost.

"Haruki! You're alive!"

He glanced over to see the pilot and the girl. They were standing at the door to the broken building. Then he ran to them, shouting, "Go!"

They turned just before he got to them, and they sprinted along the street, away from the mega-snake, which was hissing and striking at something unseen in the billowing soot and dirt. Now that Haruki shot a look at the thing, he could see where his confusion had come from. He *had* been hit by the tail end. It was just that the creature didn't have a proper tail. It had a head at each end! As far as he could tell in the quick glance he had of the beast, both heads were identical.

As he and the others got several yards away from the massive beast, they found the two surviving teen boys – the one with the glasses, who had called to Haruki, and the grim-faced lad. The boys were huddled behind a pile of rocks and construction sand, which had obviously been dumped in one of the war's few lulls, in anticipation of making repairs on the ruined neighborhood. The boys were peering intently over Haruki's shoulder at the ouroboros-like thing with equally dour looks, until suddenly their faces changed. The boys began to look elated.

Dakota and the girl skirted the pile of sand to the right and Haruki peeled left, then he threw himself down with the boys and heaved, trying to catch his breath from his recent sprint. As he looked back up the street, he could see what had given the teens hope.

"Kashikoi," he said, amazed at what he saw.

He had heard tales of Kashikoi when he was a teenager. Other teens spoke of the behemoth as if it was a force of holy good in the world. Most of the teens claimed to never have seen the creature, but those few who had, spoke with a glow in their eyes, always making Haruki think they were telling the truth. Most first-borns, when they had the sight for the few years before it faded, would spot all manner of unusual monsters and creatures that existed in the world. Things from flying monkey creatures the size of a loaf of bread to human-sized monsters like a horned cyclops, and bizarre hybrid things that could barely be called animals, like winged antelope and dogs with bones growing out of their bodies. But most of the creatures the Japanese teens had seen – or at least those Haruki had heard of – were of small scale. Only a few ever spotted an omega-class creature like the massive ouroboros, or the gigantic squid that had battled it in Hiroshima, shooting purple lightning from between its long pink tentacles, out of what appeared to be its ass. Haruki had spotted something once that was about the size of a dinosaur swimming off the shore of Chiba, but until he had seen the two gargantuan creatures trying to kill each other in Hiroshima, that had been it.

Now he was seeing the omega-size beast of all beasts.

Kashikoi was something akin to a mighty tortoise. Its shell was a steeply pitched mound with lumps protruding up in steeper bursts – as if the animal under the shell were trying to force its way out in pointy places. The legs were powerful scaled things that resembled a cross between a typical tortoise's tough limbs and the leathery clawed things to be found on a massive monitor lizard. Each scale on the monster's armor was larger than a man, and standing as it was on its hind legs, the beast must have topped over a hundred feet in height. It would have been taller if its heads – the two of them on individual necks, stretching from doughy folds at the front of the shell – had been pointed upward to the sky. Instead they angled down and forward. Toward the humongous snake beast.

Each head had thick bony horns and ridges, protruding backward along the jawline, and triple fins on top of the rounded head, giving the creature more of a dragon look. The gnarled bird-beak jaws opened wide and dripped a spattering pea-green saliva that burned holes through the ground wherever it touched.

The ouroboros demon shot its head out, lancing its forked tongue at Kashikoi's belly, but the under surface of the shell was as thickly armored as the outer surface, and the snake simply bounced off, its twisting snapping body following the head in an arc through the air.

Kashikoi swung a powerful foreleg down, the jagged tips of the claws on its foot – snapped off in some long-ago battle – still tearing a gouge down the snake's side, before the wounded ouroboros skittered away sideways on its stumpy side fins. As the snake-horror blasted through the brick wall of a factory, as if the wall weren't there, masonry and smoke shooting high into the sky, Kashikoi lowered its upper body down, until its full weight slammed into the ground with the same sharp booming thump that Haruki had heard earlier.

But now the impact was much closer to him, and he was amazed as the earth shot him upward into the air from the strike, as if he had been on a trampoline. He landed in the soft sand pile, and turned to see the others all hitting the ground as well. The noise from the impact was louder than the sound of a Mitsubishi jet roaring overhead, and the sheer weight of the creature blasted a wall of air and dust toward Haruki and the others that felt like a hurricane wind.

"We can't stay here!" he shouted.

They were picking themselves up when the air shook with a trembling vibration. A powerful shriek, like those Haruki had heard earlier, ripped into his eardrums. His hands shot to cover his ears from the hideous somewhat mechanical sound.

Kashikoi was roaring!

Haruki saw that the ouroboros had lunged again, and as it had had no luck against Kashikoi's densely armored shell, it struck a rear leg this time, sinking twenty-foot white fangs deeply into the tortoise monster's scaly flesh. The blood that squirted from the wound in a gushing burst was a deep dark green. Kashikoi shrieked and focused the alien eyes of both its heads on the double-ended snake, where it was still clamped to the injured leg with one of those ends.

Golden fire ripped out of all four of Kashikoi's eyes, tearing into the snake fiend. The wave of heat rushed back at Haruki as the ouroboros instantly recoiled, releasing its grip and using its strange fins to wind its way sideways, back and away from the injured mammoth amphibian.

Kashikoi lunged fast toward the retreating two-headed snake, his immense size no impediment to his speed. The ground shook hard at each impact of the massive claws, and as Haruki fell to his side, he saw the immense tortoise creature's left head snap open and clamp down hard on the snake thing's neck, just behind one head. Steam rose from the ouroboros's body where the powerful jaw had snapped, and the snake tried to recoil, but Kashikoi's neck unexpectedly yanked backward, pulling the twisting snake into the air. As soon as its head at the other end had cleared the ground, Kashikoi swept a powerful foreleg at the monster and released his hold near the opposite head. The effect was the snake monstrosity being hurled through the air, as if it weighed no more than a fly batted away by a human hand.

But the creature was coming for Haruki and the others.

Haruki turned and moved toward the girl. Dakota was on the other side of her, having just gained his feet again. The other two teens had fled. Haruki ran into the girl and pushed her into Dakota, and the three of them tumbled down the side of the sand pile to the bottom, just as the top of the pile erupted in a spray of sand.

The ouroboros swept just barely over their heads. It flew further down the street and slammed through two buildings, twisting and winding all the way. Haruki and the other two struggled to their feet yet again, as the winding snake slithered out of the rubble and back toward them, retracting a head at one end, and then striking up and forward. It would clear Haruki's position by several feet, so his eyes naturally shot upward to watch the snake strike. Its tongue shot out, as it raced at an incline up through the air. It spewed a searing line of pink energy from its mouth, the jaws open nearly at a 180-degree angle, all fangs pointing forward. The energy beam shot across the sky and scored along the side of one of Kashikoi's two necks. The tortoise-beast started to fall backward.

Haruki turned back in time to see the other end of the snake was coming his way, and staying low, near ground level.

Dakota had seen it, too.

Haruki had just a split second for his eyes to meet Dakota's before both men were in action.

Haruki raced toward the American, but he moved instead for the beautiful girl. She was looking upward, as the mega-tortoise fell over backward onto its shell in excruciating slow motion. Haruki shifted his angle for her, as his eyes swept back toward the quickly advancing snake head. It shifted in mid-flight, its oversized eyes – larger than trucks – suddenly twitching, as its inner eyelids closed vertically before retracting open again. It twisted its head in mid-flight.

It had seen them.

Haruki lunged, just as Dakota reached the girl and pivoted. Dakota shoved the girl, throwing her directly into Haruki's arms. Haruki wrapped his arms around her as they fell to the side. He twisted so he would land on his back, cushioning the girl from the fall.

But no one was left to save Dakota.

He tried to turn at the last second, one arm cocked back as if he meant to punch the monster in the mouth. But the jaws were wide open, the immense fangs all pointing directly at Dakota as several of them skewered him from behind, right along the edge of the creature's mouth. The long fangs ripped out the front of Dakota's body. Then the huge snake mashed its mouth shut, folding Dakota's pierced corpse in half and grinding him into several pieces, some of which fell to the ground as the beast's head flew past. Haruki saw a leg and part of the pelvis still jammed between the gargantuan teeth before the ouroboros passed over him.

The girl had not seen, as her face had been turned toward Haruki's chest. And her long wavy hair had flopped over to cover her face. Haruki turned to his side and twisted to his knees, dragging the girl up. He swiped his hand across her face, pushing her hair back. Her face was gaunt and pale. She was in shock. He bent down and put his shoulder into her waist, hefting her over him like he had seen firemen carry victims.

He ran down the street, focusing on his footing amongst the rubble. When he was past the second building into which the ouroboros had crashed, he turned to catch sight of the battle one last time, before rounding a corner of a still-standing steel factory building.

Kashikoi had indeed landed on its steeply rounded bulbous back, but the beast kept rolling. Its giant back claws had dug in, the momentum carrying it around and up. The immense thing was now standing on its hind legs like a man. The ouroboros had fired its terrifying pink mouth rays again, but they appeared to do no damage to Kashikoi's armored belly. The rays shot past Kashikoi too, though, and when they did, they obliterated any man-made structure they found.

Just before Haruki rounded the building's corner, he saw the move that was coming. Kashikoi was bringing both its forelegs, and the jagged, scarred claws on their tips, inward to crush on the sides of one of the ouroboros's heads like a vice grip. The boom shook the wall of the building, as Haruki rushed past, the girl unconscious over his shoulder. He stopped only three times before he made it to the harbor and a ship that took him and the girl to Yakushima Island, south of the main islands of Japan.

———

"Who won the fight, father?"

Jiro looked out over the landscape of bones in the distance, most easy to see from their new vantage, high on the massive grassy hill near the center of the island. It was late in the afternoon, and the sun shone brightly across the strange landscape. Shinobi had been frightened by the bones at first, but upon seeing them closer, after the two had fixed the light on the lighthouse, the ever-present thick carpet of green moss that covered much of the island and the ancient bones somehow charmed the lad. Jiro stood up and stretched his lower back, then smiled.

"Kashikoi dragged the ouroboros to the sea, but the beast was revived by the water and escaped."

Shinobi stood and pretended to stretch his own back, as he had seen Jiro do. The boy often imitated his father. Jiro smiled again.

"So . . . the world believes that the devastation at Hiroshima and Nagasaki was from Atomic bombs?"

Jiro grunted. "Most people. Even many with the sight have no reason to doubt history. But history is always written by those who win in conflicts, Shinobi. The Americans claimed the credit for the destruction – who knows what *they* saw as being responsible."

The man started down the grassy hillside, and he could hear his boy following him.

"What happened to Grandfather Haruki, then?" the boy inquired.

"He and the woman married. They moved north to Wakkanai, and he took the job as lighthouse keeper of the surrounding islands. But your grandfather never lost the sight, Shino. Like you and I, he kept his ability to see the creatures his whole life. Your grandmother – my mother – forgot what she had been through just months after it happened. They were both *nijū Hibakusha*. Double survivors. Japan has officially recognized 165 hibakusha as having survived the destruction of both Hiroshima and Nagasaki, but your grandparents were actually 166 and 167. But they never told anyone. Your grandmother's memory of the event was muddled at best, and Haruki could never tell anyone what had really happened. He kept track of Kashikoi, though, as the creature moved north through the islands of Japan, in the days after the war. The beast was much more careful in its travels then, he said. Almost as if it was aware of the terrible destruction its battle with the ouroboros had wrought."

Jiro fell quiet as he descended the rest of the hillside. As Shinobi scampered down behind him, he looked again to the sky but there was no sign of another storm. Still, they would get inside the lighthouse to sleep for the night, long before darkness fell over the necropolis.

As Shinobi reached the level ground at the base of the hill, he paused and tilted his head. Jiro could see that his son was working out how to phrase his question. He waited on the boy.

"Why are there so many bones here? Why *this* island? And why is Kurohaka Island not on any of the maps?"

"This is where he took the ones he defeated."

Shinobi's eyes widened.

Jiro nodded. "Kashikoi defeated many threats against Japan, and when he killed another giant beast like the ouroboros, he would bring it here. Remember, some of the corpses here are actually monsters that were dying and came here voluntarily. Some of the bones are from creatures that died and were transported here by teens with the sight."

Jiro started walking for the lighthouse. "My father tended the light that would keep most sailors away from this island, and he received a government check from both Japan and Russia to tend to the outlaying islands as well. I took the job from him, just as you will one day take the job from me."

Jiro noticed Shinobi's absence after another handful of steps and turned to look back at where Shinobi remained rooted to the ground, at the foot of the steep hillside.

The boy had a perplexed look on his face, until he finally asked his burning question.

"What happened to Kashikoi?"

Jiro looked at the boy, then raised his eyes to the immense hill behind him. Then he lowered his eyes back to the child and raised one eyebrow.

Color drained from the child's face as realization sank in. The boy turned to stare at the side of the hill, upon which they had been perched all afternoon. The hill that was not a hill. Jiro chuckled and turned toward the lighthouse.

"We tend the light, and we protect the protector. Come now, Shino. It will be dark soon."

Breaking the Ice
Maxine McArthur

———

The footsteps stopped. Huddled under the low bridge, Kaoru stuffed his fist into his mouth to stop the whimper escaping. *Please, go on. Don't find me.*

More giant footsteps ground on the rusty girders and vibrated into Kaoru's shoulders. He was jammed into the tiny space. Surely they'd think he couldn't fit in here . . .

A shrill buzz drilled into his ears. What . . . no, it couldn't be . . . He scraped his elbow painfully against the concrete support as he jammed his hand in his pocket and thumbed the "Off" key. The thing kept ringing. Desperately he thumbed the "Receive" key . . .

A hand grabbed his sleeve. With a satisfied "Got him!" the enemy yanked Kaoru out of his refuge.

He struggled feebly against the grip on his arm. "Leave me alone."

The two worst bullies in his class: Ariyoshi and Nakata. *Bastards, oni, demons,* Kaoru spat at them in his mind. But his body just stood sullenly beside Nakata. He'd learned the futility of fighting back years ago.

Ariyoshi jumped down from the footbridge and wrinkled his nose at the mess of beer cans, cigarette butts and dried vomit in the ditch.

"Stinks down here." He slapped Kaoru casually across the head. "You stink."

Kaoru's ears buzzed and he staggered against Nakata's wide chest. Nakata shoved him back.

Ariyoshi lit a cigarette with his special silver lighter and tucked the lighter away carefully in the pocket of his non-regulation scarlet shirt. Nakata lit up, too, using an orange plastic 100-yen lighter. They grinned at each other and both blew the smoke into Kaoru's face.

Kaoru squeezed his eyes shut and tried not to cough. *They'll finish soon they'll finish soon they'll . . .*

"Where's your weekly contribution?" Ariyoshi puffed. "You're two days behind."

"I . . . I didn't get any lunch money," Kaoru heard his voice squeak. "My mum made lunch for me."

"'My mum made it for me,'" mimicked Nakata. His livid, pimple-filled face clashed with his carroty dyed hair.

A housewife carrying bulging plastic bags from the supermarket glanced over at the unused footpath and bridge, but hurried on when she saw the black uniforms. Kainan Junior High students were to be avoided.

"No excuses." Ariyoshi shoved his face into Kaoru's.

The burning eyes and nicotine-heavy breath filled Kaoru's universe. He scrambled backwards but Nakata was in the way.

"I'll get it, I'll get it. Tomorrow. I promise I will, I'll get it." He was sobbing with fear, apprehension, remembered pain.

"You better." Ariyoshi leaned back, smoothed his gel-slick hair and lit another cigarette. "Check his bag."

Kaoru choked off another cry as Nakata dragged his school bag from under the footbridge and upended it. The contents hit the ground in a shower of textbooks, notebooks, lunch box, calculator, loose paper, MD player and gym t-shirt. His pencil case burst and pencils rolled everywhere.

"Hey, that's a better calculator than mine." Nakata pounced. "The MD's too old, but . . . "

"You oughta get some new stuff, stink-arse," said Ariyoshi. "This lot's not worth stealing."

That's the point, moron. Kaoru kept looking at his feet. His pencil sharpener had come to rest beside his right toe.

"What's this?" Nakata grinned ferally. "Still playing with toys, are we?" He held up the small plastic figure of a monster, one of the daikaiju who battled superheroes of TV and manga.

"It's not mine," protested Kaoru. "It's my kid brother's." Masaki had given it to him to fix at school in his craft class, because one of the legs had snapped off during too-strenuous aerial manoeuvres between kitchen table and sink.

"Playing wiv liddle bruvver's toys, now?" Nakata cooed.

On the other side of the footbridge adult voices rose in a real altercation.

Ariyoshi's handsome face blanched and he turned away. "Let's go."

Nakata kicked as much of Kaoru's stuff under the footbridge as he could, then followed. As they sauntered away, Nakata stopped and, obviously so Kaoru could see, broke the monster figure in half. Or tried to – the hard plastic resisted. With a curse, Nakata chucked it away. The little monster hit the concrete with a crack, and ricocheted off at an angle.

Kaoru bit back his moan. At least this time he wasn't going home with half the skin scraped off his face. Coming up with explanations to fool Mum was worse than the pain.

He squatted in the ditch and collected everything, not bothering to brush off the dirt as he stuffed things back in his bag. The pencil case's hinge was broken. It didn't matter – he'd given up carrying things that mattered.

The two men quarrelling on the other side of the footbridge had calmed down a bit. One of them, a sharp-faced gangster type in a faded floral shirt, patted the other over-familiarly on the chest as he made a point. The other nodded sulkily. No wonder Ariyoshi had headed off so quickly; the sharp-faced man was his dad. Ariyoshi said he worked as muscle down at the pachinko parlour. The other kids thought he just lazed around.

The little monster wasn't there. He crawled over the stained concrete for what seemed like hours. His knees ached from crouching. He would be late for juku. Why was he bothering? He should just tell Masaki he left the toy at school. Or say it had been stolen. It was only a cheap plastic model, after all.

But in the end he found it, half inside a hollow concrete block, grey-camouflaged where once the shaggy moulded fur had been ice-white. The raised claws and snarling teeth once glowed yellow, the bulging eyes had been blood red. Three . . . four years ago, he'd wasted some of his New Year money on a "bargain bag" at the local toy store. Even though he'd bought a "12 years and over" bag, it was full of junk like the plastic monster: a leaking water pistol, and character cards he'd thrown away in grade one. He gave the monster to Masaki, who loved it.

As Kaoru picked it up, the leg fell off again. He flushed with anger at the bullies. Dickheads. Fuckwits. Now he'd have to go through all the hassle of smuggling the monster into craft class and secretly gluing it again. He didn't have any proper glue at home.

The autumn sun was already off the narrow lane and all the buildings on this side of the street. The grey canyon was damp and chilly. Most of the shop signs were old, the colours faded. Nobody shopped along this road any more, except the old people who didn't have obliging grandchildren to drive them out to the superstores.

As he climbed out of the ditch and trudged home beside the rumbling traffic, his phone vibrated in his pocket. That's right, it was because of the stupid phone he'd been discovered. He was sure he'd had it turned off all day. This call would be his mother, demanding to know where he was. Or somebody selling things.

Strange. The activate light was off but it still buzzed. He pressed 'Receive' automatically.

The screen said simply, <Do you want revenge?>.

He sighed and pressed the delete pad, then slipped the phone back into his pocket. Whatever hot new product 'Revenge' was, he didn't want any. He'd made the mistake once of answering an online sale, and they pestered him until he had to dump the phone and tell Mum he'd lost it.

At home on the ninth floor of the apartment block, Masaki played a game on the big TV screen. On the old TV, half the size, a rerun of *Ultraseven* spooled on slowly. Both the *pico-pico trrrilll* of the game and the tinny music from the TV were running at full volume.

"Where's Mum?" shouted Kaoru. She wasn't here, or Masaki wouldn't have the sound so loud.

Masaki pointed at the kitchen with the controller, his eyes not leaving the screen. His round, six-year-old features were set in concentration.

There was a note on the kitchen table beside a tray with covered bowls. The note read, 'Kaoru, I've gone to the P&C meeting. Make sure you lock the door behind you when you go out. Masaki isn't to keep watching TV.'

"Mum says turn the TV off," Kaoru yelled.

Masaki kept his eyes on the screen. "Okay." But he made no attempt to do it.

Kaoru sighed and peeked under the lids of the bowls. Hamburgers, with steamed cauliflower, potatoes and carrots. And rice. The soup bowls each held a turd-like brown curl of instant miso, ready for hot water.

He wished Mum would hurry up and finish this "home-cooked" fad. He preferred the defrosted microwave gratins and fried rice of old.

In the bedroom he shared with Masaki he took the plastic monster out of his bag and managed to prop it between two boxes of ninja cards in his desk drawer. He needed some proper tools – a clamp, for a start – but why bother? When would he build models – in his ten minutes of free time after dinner? He used some glue he'd found in the kitchen drawer and held it while the glue set. It wasn't as good a job as he'd done at school – he'd have to scrape the overflow of glue away after it set properly – but Masaki wouldn't notice. He shut the drawer carefully.

Shit. He was late for juku. He grabbed his second bag and ran full-tilt out the door, forgetting to check the lock so he had to sprint back and then missed the lift down. By the time he reached the cram school, which was in a building near the station five blocks away, sweat was stinging in the corners of his eyes and his heart pounded shamefully in the certainty of humiliation to come.

He tried to sneak into the classroom, but the teacher, a hearty bully concerned with his own popularity points, made a big thing out of his lateness.

"Perhaps our clock-reading skills need revising?" he boomed. All the students turned to stare and the two girls sitting directly in front of Kaoru's back-row seat giggled.

Kaoru sat, his face burning. *Smart quip, come on, you can think of a comeback if you try . . .*

"The elementary classes are in the next building, you know." More girls giggled.

Just as the teacher lost interest, Kaoru's phone rang. He froze in disbelief, then plunged his hand in his pocket, letting go his textbooks to do so, but the textbooks cascaded on to the floor and he had the wrong pocket and everybody was giggling this time . . .

The teacher loomed over him. "You know the rules about phones, Hoshino?"

"Y . . . yes. But I turned it off, I did . . . " he stammered, which was a waste of time and only prolonged the agony of more sarcasm.

The teacher finally turned back to the whiteboard. Kaoru stacked his textbooks, trembling. *Leave me alone, leave me alone leave me . . .*

"Don't let him get you down." The girl next to him, Emiko Tada, leaned over slightly and muttered out of the corner of her mouth, "He's a prick. And a small one, at that."

Shocked, Kaoru flicked a glance at her. Tada was known as a slob. She came to juku in old sweaters and stained jeans. She didn't style her hair like other girls, or use lip gel, or carry a fluffy phone case, or even use a phone at all. And now she'd been nice to him and he didn't know what to say, and it was too late because Tada was looking back at her books thinking he was a snob for not even acknowledging her kindness. He was hopeless.

And why had the stupid phone rung? He had definitely turned it off, but the screen still said, <Do you want revenge?>

Yes! a voice inside him screamed.

<Yes> he typed.

The screen went blank. Oh great, he'd probably accepted a virus that would screw his address file. With all of its two or three names.

The teacher's drone faded. The hunched beetle-backs of his fellow students faded. White light surrounded him.

Good, maybe he was dead.

If so, he had come to a frozen part of hell. He was striding across a plain of ice that reached to the horizon on all sides except one – when he looked behind, a jagged white mountain range pierced grey sky. A wind solid with sleet played around his ears, but it didn't feel cold. Must be a dream. His feet crunched on frozen snow . . . *his* feet? He stopped striding and looked down.

Long dark claws poked out of toes covered with a carpet of thick, yellow-white hair. The rest of the feet, the legs, the . . . he was completely covered with pelt. No wonder he wasn't cold. His arms ended in stubby fingers tipped with the same claws as his toes. It all seemed familiar.

He laughed out loud, and a roar was whipped away by the wind. The ice monster. He'd stared at that little model for so long he was dreaming about it. He started striding again. It felt good. The snow subsided like crusted sand under bare feet; when he swung those long arms his whole body rocked from side to side, and he roared again, just to hear how loud it was and then to hear how even that loudness disappeared into the frozen wasteland. Best of all, he was completely and utterly alone.

Something glinted on the ice nearby. He stopped and bent over to see better, growling in annoyance at the effort this took. Kaiju bodies weren't very flexible.

A lighter? He laughed at the incongruity. Nothing to light here.

A silver lighter. Like the one Ariyoshi used. As he stared, anger surged up in his throat in a snarl that heated his entire body. He scooped up the metal sliver with his claw and crushed it in his palm.

It was so easy.

"Hoshino-kun. Hoshino-kun!" Tada's whisper replaced the howling of the wind.

Kaoru blinked at the sight of the teacher sauntering down the line of desks, checking homework. He fumbled his notebook open and glanced at Tada.

"Thanks," he whispered back.

Tada shrugged, but her eyes laughed.

What a weird dream! Not very symbolic (he had read all the books about dreams, it was the fad-before-last, and he knew symbolic dreams should be obscure and preferably involve food or sexually significant objects), but definitely therapeutic. He felt better than he had for ages. A pity he couldn't smash Ariyoshi's real lighter.

———

"Stay away from the gang of three," warned one of the few boys in Kaoru's class who bothered to talk to him. "Ariyoshi's pissed off big time."

Kaoru nodded thanks. It was the day after his daydream at the cram school and he wanted to stay away from everyone, not just the gang. He had dutifully studied until 3am for today's math test, but still hadn't answered all the questions. He didn't even want to be a doctor, he was going to make a terrible doctor . . . Mum gave him lunch money, but not enough for the gang. And the plastic monster's leg fell off again when he took it out of the drawer. A rod would be the best way of making sure the leg stayed on, but every method he thought of required more time and tools than he had.

"What's going on?" said one of the others. "Ari's dad been beating him up again?" There was a general guffaw, hastily muffled.

"Someone smashed his lighter," said the first boy. "Ran a car over it, they reckon."

Kaoru didn't hear the rest of the conversation. A chill spread from his stomach over his whole body. It must be a coincidence. His dream couldn't possibly have picked up on an event in the real world.

I'm glad Ariyoshi's hurting, gloated a small voice deep inside him. It sounded like the ice monster's voice.

No, you're not, Kaoru shot back. *He's going to make life hell for the rest of us.* More like hell, he revised.

————

This time, the dream seemed to take much longer. Kaoru raged across the frozen land, each roar a protest at his roar-less existence in the real world. The monster's body felt comfortable to him now, and he loved the sensation of power.

The juku sign hung in the air. He didn't question why it was there. He just ran his fist through it. Didn't even sting. Crunch. That stupid teacher. Smash. Couldn't get employed at a real school, so he taught at juku. Crack. Always using the weakest kids to make himself look smarter. Splinter. Keeping us late so we have even less of a life than we would anyway . . .

The sign shattered completely.

There, that feels better, doesn't it? chuckled the ice monster.

————

"Tanaka-sensei phoned. You're to finish the workbook exercises," his mother called into his room later that afternoon.

Kaoru jumped and shoved the drawer shut on the plastic monster. He couldn't work out a way to drill a hole small enough for a wire rod.

"What are you talking about?" he yelled back.

"You know, the juku teacher." Mum stood in the doorway of his room, spatula in hand. "There's no juku tonight. Vandals trashed the place, apparently."

"What, the whole place?" Kaoru heard himself ask, and immediately wondered if she'd notice the strangeness of the question. The sign in his dream, he'd only smashed the sign.

It couldn't be another coincidence.

What have I done?

I didn't mean to.

"Kaoru, are you all right? You look peaky." Mum placed her hand on his forehead. "I'll get you some multivitamins. You know how important your grades are this year. We don't expect you to pass the uni exams first time, but you know you'll have to get into the top twenty to get into the supplementary school . . . " He tuned out, and finally she left.

He didn't mean to smash everything. What was going on? Maybe someone was playing a stupid joke on him, messing with his mind. The phone! He'd turned it off, though, hadn't he? He might have typed "Yes", drowsy and stupid, then slumped back to sleep with his head on the desk. Only for a minute or so, at the end of home-room time this afternoon. Nobody took any notice – kids stole a few minutes of sleep at school all the time, it meant they were fresh for juku in the evening.

Maybe the phone message caused the dreams. That must be it. Some company was trialling a method of implanting subliminal suggestions in people's minds. So they couldn't hold him responsible for trashing the juku.

Anyway, a sneaky thought prompted, they'd never know it was him. Nobody would suspect or be able to find out. He could get away with murder. Not literally, of course. He'd never hurt anyone . . .

He stared across the open workbook to the faded movie poster on the wall above his desk. The boy hero confronted an insect monster bigger than a house, the proboscis longer than the boy's body. Wavy lines in sunset colours surrounded the two figures, indicating the event was happening in an alternate dimension. He'd had that poster since he was in grade one. Until now, he'd always identified with the boy.

So what if his dream of the ice monster was connected with reality? It wouldn't help him keep away from Ariyoshi and his sycophants, not unless he could metamorphose into the creature when he wanted to. It wouldn't help him finish this stupid math that he couldn't understand and never would.

"I'm going out for a walk," he yelled on his way past the kitchen. The sizzle of frying onions competed with the burr of the exhaust fan.

"Take a jacket," called his mother.

Masaki waved at him from in front of the TV, eyes reflecting *Gundam*.

———

He regretted coming out as soon as he left the building. What if Ariyoshi and the gang were hanging around?

The sky was blue with coming night and the shadows between streetlights were dark. He looked up and down the street, but could see only a few people hurrying home from the station. In the park, elderly walkers chatted as they followed the path around the fenced baseball ground. Around and around they went, unworried and unflurried. Past the age of having to get family dinners, evening was a good time for them. Kaoru thought of his father, off to work before the family woke, home after they were asleep. I suppose I'll have to wait until I'm old before I can relax.

"Hey, Hoshino," a voice called from the swings.

He tensed, ready to run, but it was a girl's voice. In the gloom he could just make out Tada, rocking the preschool-low swing with her knees almost dragging on the ground. The swing creaked rustily each time she pushed it back.

"No juku, so I thought I'd get some fresh air," she said cheerfully. "You going somewhere?"

"No," said Kaoru and, greatly daring, sat on the other swing. It squeaked.

They creaked and squeaked for a while without saying anything. If this were a manga, he'd tell her his problem and she'd offer him sympathy and say something smart to solve it. But of course manga were never like real life. Who'd read them if they were?

"What do you want to do with your life, Hoshino?" said Tada suddenly.

"Wha-at?" Kaoru stared at her in disbelief, but it was too dark to see her expression. The question was so alien to his thoughts that he would have been more comfortable if she had asked him how yellow smells.

"You know," she went on in that abrupt, confronting manner of hers. "What did you always want to do when you were a kid?"

Kaoru laughed uneasily. "Same as most boys, I suppose. Be a baseball star, a pilot, game designer, I dunno." *Monster-slayer*, he added silently.

Tada's swing creaked a bit more. "What about now?"

He should get off the swing and go home. Tada was strange in the head. You didn't ask questions like this of someone you hardly knew. He never asked them of himself.

But he answered. "It doesn't really matter, does it?" He would spend the next five or six years struggling to get into a mediocre medical school because, sometime during his childhood, somehow it had been decided that he would become a doctor. He didn't even think he could pass the supplementary school exams, let alone medical school . . .

"Of course it matters." Tada stopped her swing with the scrunch of sandals dragging through dirt. "No wonder you look so wet if you think like that."

"What about you, then?" retorted Kaoru, stung by her scorn and emboldened by the darkness.

"I'm going to breed dogs," she said contentedly. "I'll get a day job, then when I've got a bit of capital I'll buy a place to build runs. It'll have to be in the country, of course, you can't do things like that in Osaka. I've got a budget and everything."

Kaoru felt his mouth opening in awe.

"It's because I like dogs," she said. "What do you like?"

Being left alone, he wanted to say, but didn't.

"What's the most fun thing you've done recently?" she pressed.

Stomp and roar and smash things, grinned the ice-monster voice inside him.

"I . . . I'm fixing a model," he said hastily, anything to avoid the thought of lighters and signs crumbling in his fist.

"There you go, then." Tada stood up, her jacket rustling. "You'll probably be an engineer or something. See you tomorrow." She ran lightly across the park and vanished in the gloom of the camellia hedge.

He was nearly asleep when the phone rang. He rocketed upright and snatched it off the bedside table before it woke Masaki. Found it, pressed "Receive", stared uncomprehendingly at the message that shouldn't be there because the battery was drained.

<Do you want revenge?>

<Who are you?> he typed. Nothing happened. He stayed hunched over the little blue screen in the dark, the only sound the *shush-shush* of the air conditioner.

<Shall I show you?>

Kaoru hesitated, then typed <Yes>

The screen's blue light flickered, then glowed brighter and brighter until it filled the whole room with blue-white radiance. Kaoru flung up his hand to protect his eyes, then realized the light didn't hurt. He *liked* the brightness. He liked being strong and fearless and invulnerable.

The wind blew across the ice plain with a wail like all the spirits of the dead. He didn't care. No wind could blow him over.

A flat rectangle tumbled over and over through the air. He reached out an arm longer than a telephone pole and caught it. Elaborate characters ran from top to bottom on one side of a wooden board. He recognized the name of the local gang. This was off the door of their headquarters, a narrow building squashed between the butcher and a funeral parlour. Ariyoshi's dad was a member. He cocked his head at the board, then, remembering the juku sign, ripped the wood in two with the fingers of one hand and flipped away the pieces. That would teach those loudmouthed bastards, always swaggering around, thinking they could get away with anything.

He noticed the ice plain nearby was covered in irregular bumps tracked through with darker lines. He peered at the bumps and saw they were snow-covered squares and rectangles. Houses? They looked like they were made of blocks or cardboard cartons, a kindergarten playscape. He remembered the daikaiju movies and roared lustily. All those boring lives: bullying teachers, moronic little brothers, nagging mums, work-sodden fathers . . . He roared again. Who needs them?

He stomped, and was gratified to see the nearest houses shudder. Stomped again, closer. The roof of one house rose upwards then broke in the middle, exactly like a cardboard carton house. He blustered and stamped his way through the town until he came out the other side, back to the ice plain. It was only a small town, he noticed with disappointment.

————

Kaoru jerked awake, sweating on top of his futon as though he'd run a marathon. The digital clock glowed 4:00. He lay there for a while, not wanting to think about the dream. On the other side of the room, Masaki lay in a mound with the futon over his head, as usual.

There was one way to find out if the dream was connected with the real world. Kaoru slid his legs over the side of the bed, tottered to his little TV and flicked through the muted channels. Porn, gossip, sport, gossip, game show repeat, porn, samurai drama . . . on the bottom of the screen, hiding the wicked merchant's dying gasp, ran a line of text: *Earthquake in Hokkaido at 0300 hours magnitude 6 town in ruins.*

The remote slid out of his palms, which were suddenly slippery with sweat. I don't want to hurt anybody, he thought pathetically. His stomach heaved and he clamped his teeth on the threat of vomit. It didn't seem like a real town, it was only cardboard . . .

The phone buzzed. He grabbed it.

<Do you feel better?>

<Go away> he typed.

<I can make you feel better>

He flung down the phone, pulled on a pair of tracksuit pants over his pijamas, grabbed his jacket and went to leave. But what if the phone kept ringing and woke Mum? Or worse, what if it woke Masaki and he answered? With a helpless gulp, he picked up the phone and dropped it in his pocket.

Outside, the cool air dried the sweat and tears on his face. He crossed the park where he'd met Tada earlier, not bothering to be nervous of the dark shadows. He trudged past the primary school, with its high open fences. Opposite the school, a light shone in the window of the newspaper delivery office. Everywhere else was dark.

What if people had been killed in the earthquake? Did that make him a murderer? But he didn't know it was real. Tears blurred the darkness.

He kept walking, around the corner and past the kindergarten. On his right, behind a wire fence, ran the railway tracks. He'd have to go to the level crossing to get onto the tracks themselves. At this time of night there'd be nobody to notice or stop him. The first train would pass through at about four-thirty.

There was someone lying on the footpath. A hunched bundle that made a snoring, slobbering sound.

As soon as he noticed, he stood still, hoping he hadn't been seen. A drunk? In case the drunk reached out to grab him, he edged past on the other side of the narrow street.

A voice wheezed, "Help me."

Keep going. He was only a kid; he couldn't carry a drunk home or go and report it to the police because they'd want to know what he was doing wandering the streets at 4am and he couldn't say, it's because I have this problem with turning into a monster, could he? It wasn't his job to clean up after irresponsible adults. He just wanted to stay out of trouble. Then he realized he knew the voice.

His heart thudding, the phone in his pocket forgotten, he edged closer. One of Ariyoshi's eyes blinked back at him. The street light on the corner gave enough light to see that the other eye was swollen shut. Most of his face was swollen or bloodstained, and he lay curled up as though it hurt too much to move. But he could still raise his head slightly and groan, "Stinky."

"What happened?" Kaoru's shocked voice sounded high like a child's.

"The ol' man . . . " Ariyoshi forced the words through cut and puffed lips. "Thought I took the gang's door . . . sign . . . "

Kaoru's phone buzzed and jiggled in his pocket.

"Go . . . 'way." Ariyoshi shut his good eye.

Kaoru didn't want to look at the screen, but his hand held the phone of its own accord.

<Get rid of him>

What?

As if he'd typed a reply, the screen said, <Everyone will think the father did it. You'll be free. No more bullying>

<I can't do that> he typed, shocked.

<I can do it for you>

The ice monster would enjoy it. The ice monster would help him get his own back for all the years of torture and misery and playing humble. Nobody would ever know. After all this time, he had power. He could destroy whole towns. He looked down at Ariyoshi, and it was as if he looked down from a great height. All around them blew wind full of icicles. All he had to do was reach out his hand and close it around Ariyoshi's neck. This time he knew what he was doing. There would be no excuses.

And when he'd got rid of all the bullies?

He'd be alone on the ice plain.

What do you want to do? whispered Tada's voice in the wind.

He looked down, this time at the phone in his hand. He didn't want to stay alone on the ice plain, even if he was the greatest monster ever.

The first train would come through at four-thirty.

He ran back around the corner to the newspaper delivery office and pounded on their door. A bleary-eyed man in layers of cheap sweatshirts opened it cautiously.

"Someone's been mugged," Kaoru panted. "On the path. Outside the kindergarten. Call an ambulance."

The man narrowed his eyes. "Is this a joke?"

"It's no joke!" Kaoru yelled.

The man flinched and turned to a phone on the wall. "Okay, okay."

Kaoru waited until he heard the man say the street number then ran again. Down the streets of sleeping houses, through the urine-dank underpass, past the shuttered grocery store to the level crossing. The barriers were raised, and he slid down the edge of the road and ran about a hundred metres along the tracks, left the phone and dashed back to the crossing.

There he waited, shuffling his feet and peering anxiously at the tracks that curved east, glinting under the line of lights. The tracks ticked. In the distance he heard the cling-clang of the level crossing in the next suburb. At the same time, the phone on the tracks started ringing, with a sound all out of proportion to the source, rising until it drowned out the clanging of this crossing, rising until Kaoru put his hands over his ears and screamed with agony.

< You can be strong >

The words glowed on the screen of his mind.

< You can show them . . . >

Under the wheels of the train green sparks flared once, then vanished. The only sound was the fading growl of the engine.

"I fixed your model."

A week later, Kaoru placed the plastic ice monster on Masaki's desk, already crowded with robots, aliens, spaceships, rangers and racing cars.

Masaki actually put down his game screen and stood up to take a proper look. "Hey, you can't even tell where it broke." His goggle eyes regarded Kaoru with new respect.

"Pretty good, hey?" Kaoru grinned, but a bit uneasily. He still felt horrible about the earthquake and concentrating on fixing the monster had been a way to forget that for a while. The wire rod idea had worked. He'd spent a week's worth of lunch money on new tools, but he still didn't have enough time to use them.

So he'd made a decision. Engineers fix things. Things like ruined towns.

"I'm not going to juku tonight, Mum." He poked his head around the kitchen door. His mother stopped in the middle of stirring a pot of stock, a recipe book held in one hand.

"Are you sick?" she said.

"No." He kept going on his way to the door as he spoke, otherwise he'd end up in a debate that would last till bedtime. He'd tell her about not going to med school later. "I'm only going twice a week from now on."

"Kaoru! Your grades . . . "

"I'll manage." As he shoved his feet into his shoes he could hear the spoon being dropped into the sink, the gas being turned off, and the recipe book slamming down on the table.

"I'll be back later," he yelled. Tada was waiting for him in the park.

Mamu, or Reptillon vs Echidonah
Nick Stathopoulos

———

Sydney sweltered in a heatwave, and with the heat came the bogon moths. The unseasonal weather had provided the perfect conditions for them as they swarmed through the city on their slow migration south, to mate and die.

Swatting one away from his sweaty face, the freelance writer descended a wide concrete flight of stairs that lead to the subterranean platforms of Museum Station. The cool tiled interior was a welcome relief from the heat and hubbub of Oxford Street.

Built in the twenties, it formed part of an underground rail network known as the City Circle, linking Sydney's central business district to Central Station and the suburbs beyond.

A blast of warm air washed over him as a train rattled onto a platform below. Brakes squealed and carriages shunted to a halt.

Today the writer had been reviewing films for an online news site, and he was particularly pleased with his latest vitriolic savaging. It was directed at a big-budget Hollywood remake of a beloved old British television show, and the results armed him with plenty of opportunities to display his wit. Somehow the Yanks never got them right. He smirked with bemused satisfaction for a moment before the mood was broken.

Oh God, he could hear *her* echoing up the stairwell. That old aboriginal woman was down there again. How he detested her stupid singing. Even though she sang in her own language – Pitjantjatjara – he could still identify the tune.

"*Jesus loves me, this I know . . . for the Bible tells me so. Little ones to him belong . . . they are weak but he is strong . . .*"

She was *so* annoying.

If he timed it just right she'd be looking the other way, engaging some other commuter, begging oh-so-politely.

"'Scuse me Sir, could you spare some change?" or "Thank you Ma'm, God bless you." Then she'd go back to her infernal singing, but he'd be safely past.

But there was no avoiding her today. Her eyes fixed directly on him as he reached the bottom of the stairs.

"Shit."

From the pre-recorded announcement he realized the train on the platform was his, so he barrelled straight past her, avoiding eye contact. He heard her pause, then sing louder. He knew it was directed at him, and didn't give a fuck.

She let him pass as she spotted a friendly young woman that was always happy to give.

"Hey lady! Don't go down there! Not today!" She held her benefactor back as she watched the critic disappear through a turnstile, and smiled knowingly.

He shimmied into the carriage just as the doors closed and the klaxon tooted. Quickly he scanned the interior, pushed past some school kids, and beat a middle-aged woman – arms full of groceries – to the only free seat. He smirked at her in triumph as he pulled out a gossip magazine from his satchel.

The woman sniffed her disgust as the train lurched forward. Madly juggling her load, she grabbed at a handrail for balance.

The writer looked up from his magazine. Something was wrong.

The train abruptly stopped, jerked forward, then stopped for good. Though the new Millennium trains were constantly breaking down, and commuters were used to the delays, a communal sigh of dismay arose from the passengers.

Strange grinding noises echoed up the tunnel, and the carriage fell silent. A bogon moth battered a light fitting.

Then, without warning, the carriage imploded.

Huge black claws tore through, then peeled back, the thin metal sheeting that formed its outer casing. A massive, fleshy appendage probed its way into the crowded compartment.

Incredulous passengers screamed as the gigantic, oversized proboscis wrenched open with a thick, liquid sound, exposing rows of needle-sharp teeth.

The woman with the groceries threw them at the maw, which, as it retracted in surprise for a moment, allowed her to dive through a gash in the floor. She crawled between the bogey and the platform to safety. But the rest of the passengers were not so lucky.

The proboscis punched deeper into the carriage, which now tilted at an impossible angle. A long sticky tongue emerged and flicked madly about, ensnaring passengers on its gooey surface, then slurped them into oblivion.

Trapped like termites, those still standing were unable to find purchase and slid towards the gnashing teeth. Others tried clambering over the backs of seats, over the passengers wedged between them, but the tongue easily located them, too.

Frozen with shock, mouth agape, the dumbfounded film critic stared in utter disbelief as the thing's tongue now flicked towards him. His magazine flew into the air as it coiled around him, dragging him screaming between its teeth – which closed on his chubby frame with a grinding delicacy.

In the nanoseconds before he died, he should have seen his life flash before him, but no. Instead, he flashed every movie character ever caught in a death throe with some nightmare denizen – aliens, mutants, behemoths, gargantuas, leviathans – now King Kong, chewing on a stop-motion native, now Gregory Peck lashed to the side of Moby Dick, now Jon Voigt swallowed alive in *Anaconda*, and finally, the penultimate moment – Robert Shaw chomped to bits in *Jaws* – except these teeth weren't rubber. He screamed out to the only woman he'd ever loved.

"*Ripleeeeeey!*"

His, and the terrified screams of other passengers, echoed up into the street, where commuters tumbled from the station in panic. Someone yelled, "Echidonah! It's Echidonah!"

The aboriginal woman was swept up with the mass, and as she reached street level, spun away from the crowd and around to the back of the now deserted café, where she paused and gulped air heavily.

"Mamu," she whispered between gulps. "Mamu."

She closed her eyes to the sounds of death, and remembered the voice of her *kami*.

OCTOBER 15, 1953

"MAMU!"

Grandmother looked up from the hole she was digging with her wira, scooping away at the dirt, and called to the tiny figure in the distance. "The mamu will get you!"

The girl didn't know whether to believe her or not, and so darted back. Like other cultures worldwide, the Anangu aborigines of central Australia used the threat of a monster to keep children in check. But that didn't mean it wasn't true.

Mamu or not, the girl preferred to follow her grandmother on her foraging expeditions than go to the missionary school. There they forced her to wear clothes that made her skin itch and to recite silly songs about Jesus. But today the girl was far from the camp, and she idly lolled behind the old woman.

Presently, they came across a sign, written in English.

"What does it say, little one? I don't understand it."

The young girl slowly made out the words, but they had little meaning to her. "I think it says to stay away," she guessed.

"Then you stay away from it! I don't trust no white fella stuff." She continued to pick her way through the spinifex, and the girl followed.

Sensing something, the old woman stiffened, sniffed the dry air, and rubbed her shoulders as the hair on her body stood on end.

The girl looked up at her grandmother quizzically.

"Kami . . . ? What's wrong?"

Suddenly a bright flash lit the entire sky beyond the low rocky hills. A low, distant rumble followed in its wake, and the thin clouds above them shuddered then were swept away with the shock wave. The ground trembled and an angry black cloud mushroomed over the horizon.

"A storm!" cried the girl.

But this was no ordinary storm, and the old woman instinctively knew it. "Quickly child! We must find shelter. Quickly!" She grabbed the girl by the arm and they ran for cover.

They were too far from camp to seek refuge there, so they dashed towards some caves in the rocky hills. Kami had often recounted how she and her family had hidden undiscovered there for many days when the white fellas first arrived, so the girl knew it was a place of safety. But as she looked over her shoulder, she watched in horror as the black cloud blanketed the hills and tumbled towards them.

The old woman dragged her behind some rocks as the churning pall overtook them, and shielded her with her own body as best as she could. There they huddled, until the blackness had passed.

The afternoon sun blazed a deep blood red as they staggered back to camp.

TWO WEEKS LATER

The Cinesound newsreel flickered in the darkened Victory Cinema on George Street. On the screen, a poisonous black and white mushroom cloud rose ominously over the barren desert. Official observers – some with berets, others with slouch hats – turned away from the blast, unprotected. Only a few scientists, in lab coats and goggles, faced the boiling maelstrom.

The voice-over had a plummy British accent.

"*Britain enters the Atomic Age with the successful detonation of its first atomic bomb, code-named Totem One, at Emu Junction in the remote and unpopulated central Australian desert. This and further tests help secure Australia's own atomic future, and the promise of unlimited clean, efficient energy."*

MEANWHILE, BACK IN CENTRAL AUSTRALIA

There were bodies of aborigines lying everywhere, some dying, some already dead. They suffered burning red skin, vomiting, dysentery. They had thought it was measles or chicken pox – there had been outbreaks of these diseases in the past – but this was something quite different.

Only a few children and a couple of the missionaries were well enough to look after the ill. The girl brought water to her grandmother. The old woman was delirious, and kept repeating, "Irati . . . irati . . . "

"What is she saying?" one of the missionaries paused to ask the girl. "What does *irati* mean?"

The little girl struggled to think of a way to describe the word. "When someone gives you a bad thing to eat."

"Poison? You mean poison?

"Yes!" she nodded. "Poison. She says the black cloud was poison."

The old woman reached out to the child.

"You must get away from here." Her eyes widened. "This land is irati!"

"But where Kami? . . . where can I go?" There was nowhere to run, no way to escape the irati.

"You must leave. Now. You must!

"No, Kami . . . I won't leave you."

"Go!" The old woman heaved an agonised last breath, and her hand fell limp.

Sobbing, the girl ran into the night.

The missionary called after her, but the child was soon engulfed by the darkness.

And when she failed to return to camp, they thought that she too had died of the sickness. Soon there would be no one left alive who even remembered her.

THREE DAYS AGO

The two black-suited men loomed over the night-duty nurse at the Harry Seidler Retirement Village. She glanced at their IDs. They wore sunglasses in the photos. She looked back up at the men. They were still wearing them. Nonplussed, she handed the IDs back and directed them to the TV room.

"That's him."

The old man fused to the battered sofa chair was totally absorbed in *Wheel of Fortune*. The ancient television screen flickered. He swore when the picture signal dropped out for a second just as the wheel slowed to a halt.

"Excuse me . . . ahem . . . EXCUSE ME."

The old man craned his neck at the two men and blinked twice.

"Yes?"

"Are you Cobden Parkes?" asked the first man.

The old man's eyes narrowed.

"You were the Government Architect in the fifties, during Premier Cahill's term?"

The old man nodded.

"And Government Architect for the Sydney Opera House . . . " added the second.

"What's this all about?" He eyed the two men suspiciously. "Who are you?"

The first man answered. "We're from the Australian Security Intelligence Organization. We . . . think you might be able to help us."

The operative crouched down to the old man's eye level.

"Daikaiju . . . what do you know about *daikaiju?*

DECEMBER 12, 1955

"*Daikaiju* – giant monsters – it's the Japanese term for the creatures."

The Premier of New South Wales, John Joseph Cahill, was a tough, pragmatic man. Hardened by too many years of politicking, he was not exactly prone to flights of fantasy. But he could plainly see the incredulity on the faces of Cobden Parkes, the Government Architect, and Harry Ashworth, the Minister for Public Works.

"Don't look at me like I'm some kind of imbecile!" The Premier puffed on his cigarette. The other two weren't so sure.

"I know what I'm talking about. The giant octopus that attacked San Francisco three years ago . . . where do you think that came from? Bloody Yanks were testing A-bombs twenty thousand fathoms beneath the ocean off the west coast. Then two years ago Japan was attacked by a prehistoric throwback that caused as much death and destruction as the two A-bombs dropped during the war."

The Premier gazed out of his office window across the city.

Parkes and Ashworth listened in silence.

"The Federal government has just granted the bloody poms full support to conduct further atomic tests in a place called Maralinga in South Australia. The Yanks are testing on Bikini Atoll. The French also have a testing programme in the Pacific . . . we're surrounded by bloody idiots."

He turned to face the men.

"Who knows what else they're about to unleash, or when we'll see the end of it?"

"Where do we fit into all this?" inquired Ashworth gingerly. "Why us?"

"We need to protect Sydney against the inevitability of a giant monster attack. It will come, gentlemen, I know it will come. And we all know the devastation wrought by those creatures when they intrude on a built-up area. Don't we?"

Ashworth shrugged uncertainly. Parkes stared at his own hands, clenched into fists on his knees.

The determination in Cahill's voice was intense. "Well, while I'm in power, I intend to do something to prepare for it. This will be a costly exercise, and controversial . . . no doubt about it. We'll probably all cop a lot of flack before it's done, but it's one form of insurance this city can't afford not to have. Maybe not today, or even in our lifetimes, but one day . . . one day . . . "

He went to his desk, opened a drawer, and pulled out a roll of blueprints, which he unfurled, balancing his cigarette on his bottom lip the whole time.

"This is what our boffins at the Commonwealth Scientific and Industrial Research Organization have come up with to stop them." He weighed down the corners of the plans with filled ashtrays.

"This, gentlemen, is an anti-daikaiju device."

Ashworth raised his eyebrows.

Parkes scanned the blueprints and tried to take it all in. "It's huge! Where do you propose we house such a contraption?"

"Good question, Parkes. The location has to be in the city, and it can't arouse any suspicion. That's why you gentlemen are here."

Ashworth cogitated for a moment, then volunteered. "Maybe it could be disguised as grain silos?"

The Premier snorted.

"Don't be ridiculous! I don't want to make Sydney any more of a target than it is. This thing has to provide the city with its major defence against daikaiju, not ICBMs."

Ashworth was somewhat more subdued this time.

"How about a new tram terminal, then? The existing terminal on the Quay needs upgrading. How about there?"

The Premier thought about it for a moment, then scrunched up his face.

"That's no good either. Sydney may not even have trams soon, if some people have their way." He shook his head. "No. This building has to last. It has to be a landmark. Something so obvious that no one would ever suspect its true purpose."

The intercom buzzed and the Premier punched the button.

"*I'm sorry, Mr Premier, it's Mr Goosens on the line.*"

"I said no calls."

"*He's most insistent.*"

"Jesus, that man refuses to give up." He tossed an exasperated glance at the two men. "Excuse me a moment gentlemen. Yes, I'll take the call."

Ashworth recognized the name. "Isn't he the conductor of the Sydney Symphony Orchestra?" Parkes shrugged.

"Mr Goosens?" The Premier knew when to turn on the smarm. It dripped from his words, just on the verge of becoming sarcasm. "*Eugene!* It's good to hear your voice, too." There was a pause as the Premier held the receiver away from his ear. "Yes, I've read your latest letter."

He listened politely for a moment, then sighed and interjected. "I agree . . . Sydney *does* need a home for your orchestra." He'd been subjected to the same lecture so often that his eyes would normally glaze over, and they did briefly. But then the glint came back and they narrowed.

He paused for barely a second.

"Yes, Eugene, I hear you. I hear you very well."

He took a deep breath. Sighed again. This time it expressed satisfaction rather than impatience.

"Eugene, before you get too carried away," he continued, with no insincerity now, "how long have you been petitioning the government for an opera house – nine years? That long, huh?"

A twisted smirk came over the Premier's face as he met the gaze of the two men in his office. They both frowned. "Well, I have some wonderful news for you. Your persistence has finally paid off. The Government Architect and the Minister of Public Works have just today come to me with a *plan* . . . and I think you're going to like it . . . "

MARCH 10, 1956

Over the centuries, the huge uplifted rocks at Emu Junction had been eroded by the elements into enormous round boulders piled precariously on top of each other.

Extremes of heat and cold had caused their rusty surfaces to exfoliate, not unlike the skin of an onion. But now they lay scattered, tossed like marbles by the force of the detonation.

The largest of the massive boulders began to radiate an eerie green glow. The sun had set, and it lit up the immediate area, casting long shadows around it.

Behind the surrounding boulders was an observer. Attracted by the glow, a young girl remained hidden, and watched, completely mesmerised.

JANUARY 29, 1957

The Premier rose to address the crowd. The gallery of the Sydney Town Hall was packed to the rafters with dignitaries and the press. A hush fell over the auditorium.

"And now, after much deliberation, I'd like to present the man responsible for the winning design – Danish architect, Jørn Utzon."

The lanky young Dane stepped forward, his grey suit draping loosely on his tall gangly frame, and unveiled a model of a building unlike anything seen before. There was an audible gasp from the shocked crowd as flashbulbs exploded about them. Everybody swarmed around Utzon and his model.

All except the Minister for Public Works, and the Government Architect – who managed forced nervous smiles over their concern – and the Premier, who was grinning from ear to ear. After all, a politician knows all too well how to hide his true feelings.

SEPTEMBER 18, 1959

The teenage girl approached the huge boulder with some trepidation. She had often frequented the site, and found comfort in the warm radiating glow, especially as she recovered from the sickness that had claimed her grandmother. But recently the glow had subsided. The surface of the rock had softened into a leathery shell, and was slightly translucent. It seemed to have transformed into some kind of egg.

As she gingerly approached, something shifted inside it. Startled, the girl darted back behind the rocks, emerging only when the movement settled. As she approached the egg again, she imagined she could make out what sort of creature lay curled inside. On closer inspection she was not only certain what it was, but also knew what she must do.

She collected the largest branches she could find and slowly levered the egg away from the cluster of rocks. Whenever she felt any protesting movement from within, she stopped and gently sang to it. The song had been taught to her by the missionaries, and this seemed to appease it. With her back against it, she then continued rolling, levering when it snagged, moving it inches at a time.

Not far from where she laboured, the termites had rebuilt their mounds. They had survived the blast, but radiation had affected them, too, and now their nests towered impressively over the landscape.

Moving the egg was hard work for one so small and sickly, and it took many days before she successfully maneuvered it around each mound and into the centre of the termite field. Once there, she rested, and waited patiently.

OCTOBER 22, 1959

The phone rang downstairs in the lounge room of the Government Architect's house. The place was conservative for an architect – right down to the chintz curtains and lace antimacassars – but then Cobden Parkes was like that, and it made him the perfect government official.

The Architect answered groggily. "Hello?" Then he recognized the voice. "Oh Harry . . . Jesus mate, it's 5am . . . what's up?"

"It's Cahill. He's dead."

It took a moment for his foggy brain to fully grasp the magnitude of the situation.

"Oh no . . . "

"There's going to be a change in government . . . and we're gonna have to go it alone."

LATER, THAT SAME DAY

The egg slowly hatched while the teenager watched with fascination. She watched as it emerged and baked in the sun, watched as its spines hardened, as it flexed long black scimitar claws that would soon begin burrowing into the giant red termite mounds around them.

Finally, the girl approached the newborn – gingerly, so as not to alarm it. Despite being blind, it sensed her presence. It raised its proboscis in her direction, smelled her, and withdrew. She froze, and softly began singing. The creature softened its stance, then slowly began rocking to the soothing, familiar sound of her voice.

She moved closer, and, unafraid, began to gently stroke its head. It nuzzled against her as she whispered, "Mamu . . . my mamu . . ."

FEBRUARY 26, 1966

Cobden Parkes rolled the tile in his palm. The milky white enamelled surface felt unusually warm. He passed it to Harry Ashworth.

Senior Professor Wraight of the Commonwealth Scientific and Industrial Research Organization pushed back his glasses.

"We've just finished testing the latest batch of tiles."

Parkes and Ashworth looked hopeful. The professor smiled grimly.

"It's not good news, gentlemen."

"What? Don't the tiles work?" Parkes' face had drained white. There had been so many problems already, now was not a good time for more of them to arise.

"Oh no. The tiles work perfectly." The professor poured them coffee from a beaker, warming on a tripod over a Bunsen burner. There was an edge to his dry voice.

"What now?" muttered Ashworth, sensing a bombshell about to drop.

Wraight plunged in. "We always knew we couldn't kill the monsters – the aim was to drive them away from the city using their own ultrasonic emissions." The professor indicated a scale model of the anti-daikaiju device on the desk before him.

"These tiles were designed to coat the entire surface of the giant dome, forming a huge mirror, as it were. They would absorb the ultrasonic pulses that daikaiju emit, the same way certain moth's scales absorb the ultrasonic beeps of bats to render them invisible. The device itself would magnify the signal as we shifted the contours, create a pulse and redirect it – luring the creatures away . . . packing them off to Melbourne, perhaps, or some equally deserving place . . . "

His attempted levity misfired, and Ashworth remained stone-faced.

"So, if the tiles work, what's the problem?"

The professor placed on the table what looked like a large military walkie-talkie with a rotary telephone dialler.

"What's this?"

"It's a mobile telephone. It works like a small radio transmitter. The US military are currently using them in Vietnam."

"Look at the size of this thing! Doesn't look too mobile to me," blurted Parkes, failing to fully grasp the situation.

"Who's going to lug something as cumbersome as this around when there's a telephone on every street corner?"

The professor tried not to sound too patronizing. "We can't underestimate the impact of this new technology in the future, Mr Parkes. There are companies already gearing up to mass-produce them. It won't be long before they're reduced to the size of a paperback."

The professor suddenly became deadly serious as he finally dropped the bomb.

"If . . . no," he corrected himself, "*when* . . . these telephones come into service, they could seriously compromise the device by generating hundreds, maybe thousands of signals. The interference would make it difficult – if not impossible – to focus and redirect daikaiju impulses."

The Minister for Public Works moaned as the full impact sunk in. "You know what this means, Cob?"

The architect knew all right – the precious design wouldn't work. He cradled his head in his hands and rocked in his chair.

"Jesus wept . . . I-am-not-hearing-this."

A defeated Ashworth threw up his hands. "How do you propose we account for future levels of interference?"

The professor's eyes widened as he rifled through the mass of plans, which spilled from the table onto the floor.

"Like this . . . "

He pointed to the plans of the hydraulic systems and already enhanced framework of the building's superstructure.

"As originally designed, the anti-daikaiju device was stationary, rotating in response to the direction of the primary source signal." The professor continued, "The roofing panels open out into huge dishes already, but with a bit of modification . . . OK, significant modification, I admit . . . we could go even further . . . "

Ashworth and Parkes listened with stupefaction as the professor's proposal assumed the implausible air of science fiction.

"Wind tunnel tests have proven that it's already aerodynamically sound, and the added offensive capability makes for a far more effective weapon."

And as he spoke, he quoted the research of Professor Hoyle from the rocket research laboratories at Woomera.

"They've just successfully tested an atomic rocket motor that could provide the initial take-off thrust. They've also secured six Rolls-Royce/ Snecma Olympus 593 engines that would take over once the device is airborne. They each give more than 38,000lb of thrust, and were specially designed for the new supersonic Concorde aircraft. These engines can position and stabilize the device, and keep it up for maybe a whole hour."

"We couldn't possibly afford all of this!" Ashworth guffawed.

The professor was more optimistic.

"They're the prototypes – gifts from the British and French governments – reparations for all the A-bomb testing in the desert and the Pacific. I'm sure with Hoyle's cooperation, these engines could be made available to us."

The professor pushed on.

"We have the technical capacity to do this. What I need to know is whether the device can be modified this dramatically – *secretly*."

Ashworth suddenly grabbed at the building plans – already a hodge-podge of additions and amendments – and began tracing their smallest details, running his finger along his own markings and scribbles.

The others fell silent, staring at his intensity with a mixture of expectation and giddy excitement.

Finally he looked up and met their eyes.

"Yes!" he cried, "it's a long-shot, but I think it can be done." He took a deep breath. "You'd better make more coffee, professor. It's going to be a long night."

The three men poured over the plans, working out the feasibility of such an audacious proposal.

As they worked feverishly into the night, the project gradually seemed salvageable to Ashworth and they all felt a new hope. Before long, it took on the appearance of an even better plan than the one they'd had before.

"There's only one major problem, as I see it," Ashworth said.

Parkes frowned. "What? You think Hoyle might not cooperate?"

"Hoyle's fine," Wraight offered. "I know him. He'll be in it like a shot."

"What then?"

"I'm thinking of someone closer to home." Ashworth pointed to the designer's name at the bottom of the plans.

"Ohhhh nooo . . . " Parkes cried. "*I* told him last time! It's *your* turn."

Ashworth's face soured.

"Bloody 'ell. These are the biggest changes yet. Utzon is gonna spew."

FEBRUARY 28, 1966

Jørn Utzon looked at the new plans with total dismay.

Behind him, huge arched concrete ribs outlined the shape of his spectacular building. Spindly cranes towered above them. The whole site buzzed with activity.

"You are not serious?"

Ashworth and Parkes steeled themselves as the Dane removed his hard hat and massaged his temple in frustration.

"How am I supposed to complete this project if you keep altering the brief? These changes do not even make sense."

Parkes remained silent. He was well aware what the Dane thought of him professionally as an architect, and now preferred the Minister to do all the talking.

Ashworth pleaded. "Please, Mr Utzon. It's only a minor alteration."

"Minor! All the machinery to elevate the sets into the opera theatre has been installed, and now you want to switch the opera theatre and the concert hall, and to introduce an entirely new infrastructure?"

"Mr Utzon. We are under instruction from the new Premier."

"And what does he know? Tell me! He is not an architect, he is a politician. I'm not concerned with your petty politics."

"Be reasonable—"

"Reasonable? REASONABLE?" The usually soft-spoken Dane began to lose his temper. "I have tried to work with you . . . I have made every nonsensical change you have requested, have I not?

"Yes, but . . . "

"But what? I design for you the most spectacular building in the world, yes?"

Ashworth grudgingly nodded.

"Then what is *this* meant to be?" Utzon slapped at the plans.

The Minister toughened. "You really don't have a choice in the matter."

"That's because you are holding me to ransom. Yes! You are

deliberately withholding funds so I will be forced to comply with your ridiculous changes."

Ashworth and Parkes exchanged glances.

Utzon had had enough. "Ugghh! This is untenable! I designed for you an *opera house*. I don't know what you are trying to build, but I want no further part in it."

And with that, Jørn Utzon walked off in disgust, tossing his hard hat into the harbour. He never set foot on the site again.

As the Minister and the Government Architect watched him wend his way through the maze of construction debris, the site around them gradually fell silent. Men downed tools, machinery ground to a halt.

Ashworth turned to Parkes and sighed, almost with relief.

"Well . . . at least it's our baby now."

Slowly overtaken by a sense of foreboding, Parkes was not so sure.

"What if we can't get it to work?"

"It'll work."

Parkes sighed. "Harry . . . they are gonna hang us up by the balls."

"Actually, Cob, it can't get any worse."

"How do you figure that?"

"Cos we're already swinging in the breeze mate, we're already swinging in the breeze."

JULY 25, 1979

At the Centre For Pacific Experiments at Mururoa Atoll, the French scientists looked on with sweaty, furrowed brows. The acrid stench of Gitanes hung heavily in the air.

The 120-kiloton weapon was meant to be lowered to a depth of 800 metres, but had become wedged halfway down the basalt shaft and could not be dislodged. After a brief consultation with their superiors in Paris, they decided to detonate it anyway.

"*Cinq . . . quatre . . . trois . . . deux . . . un . . . ZÉRO!*"

In a deep underwater trench not far from "Zone Centrale", over a million cubic metres of coral and rock slid away to expose what looked like a volcanic ledge, encrusted with eons of marine organisms.

As the debris settled, the ledge gently peeled apart, revealing a giant yellow pupil. The iris focused on a shoal of fish, which flashed silver with each instant change of direction.

Reptillon – the giant lizard – had been roused from its ancient slumber. Even at this impossible depth it could sense a distant calling. An old familiar opponent had been reborn, and was now burrowing towards the east coast of Australia.

The giant reptile knew it must challenge its nemesis once again. It shook itself free from the rocks and coral, raised its massive body from the ocean floor, and slowly began to make its way west to meet it.

TWO NIGHTS AGO

A sledgehammer fist pounded on the apartment door.

Inside, the desperation was palpable as Kenneth Wilcox frantically stabbed at the keyboard of his PC.

An honours student completing a PhD in architectural engineering, he was tantalizingly close to an answer . . . almost. Thousands of lives and the fate of the entire city depended on his results.

"Just a few more seconds."

They were now breaking down the door, and he had a pretty good idea why . . .

In the course of his research to reconstruct Utzon's original opera house designs as a virtual 3D tour, he had inadvertently uncovered an incredible secret – buried within a complex jigsaw of altered plans, and tangled impossibly for decades in a labyrinthine bureaucracy.

Thanks to recent downsizing and staffing cuts, he was able to rummage through the bowels of various government departments and examine hundreds of plans and secret documents, unchecked and without arousing any suspicion.

Or so he thought.

Just as the data he desperately sought was downloading, the door was suddenly kicked open. Two men in black, built like brick shithouses, barrelled into the room. Ken leapt to his feet, and was tossed aside.

One of them pulled the plug on the PC.

"Hey! What the . . . No! Don't!" Ken pleaded.

The other rifled through files and papers, and turned to his accomplice. "It's all here."

"No! Get out of it!" blurted Ken indignantly. "I haven't done anything illegal. Everything's declassified. It's all in the public domain. What about the Freedom of Information Act? I got rights!"

"Not since nine-eleven you don't," smirked the first man in black.

Furious, the student lunged at him, but with one deft action on the part of his target, found himself pinned to the floor by the goon, who waved a badge in front of Ken's nose.

"ASIO? Awwww, fuck."

Ken was quickly bundled out of the apartment, spirited down the lifts to the basement car park and tossed into the back seat of an unmarked car.

The first operative slammed Ken's door and jumped in the front, while the second loaded the files and PC into the boot, before climbing into the driver's seat.

A mirrored glass partition isolated Ken from the operatives. He grabbed for the door handle – missing! – and was thrown back against the seat as the car accelerated out of the car park and into the evening city traffic.

"*Who's in charge?*"

The operatives listened through hidden mics.

The student pounded the partition with his fists.

"*Fuckin' answer me!*"

They ignored him.

Stop lights magically turned green as the car wove through the traffic.

"*You don't understand. This is important. Look, I know . . . I know what it is. You have to listen!*"

A voice replied over a hidden speaker.

"What is it?"

"*It doesn't work! I've run simulations based on calibrations made by Parkes and Ashworth in the sixties – the device doesn't work.*"

"Aww, shit." The driver sighed and eyed his colleague sideways. "Do you think he's for real?"

"Yeah . . . I do."

The first operative contemplated the fate of the city as the car careered through Sydney's glittering concrete and glass canyons.

"That means the device is fucked . . . and that means the city's fucked . . . and that means we're all fucked."

"Yep. Reckon it does," agreed the driver.

The car descended into the Harbour Tunnel, heading north.

Then Ken said something that made the driver hit the brakes, hard. Cars skittled around them.

"*I know how to make it work!*"

The glass partition slid open, and the first operative looked over his shoulder at the student.

"Go on."

"I know how to make it work! You need to update all of Parkes' and Ashworth's original figures. Their data's now woefully out of date.

He definitely had the operative's full attention.

"Data? What data?"

Ben began spurting techno-babble. "It's the angle of incidence. The wings are all out of whack . . . they've got to be recalibrated. Once the angle's been determined, the correct altitude can be calculated—"

The operative shushed him. "*Altitude?*"

The two operatives exchanged astonished glances. "You mean . . . it can *fly?*"

"Uh-huh! That's the major alteration that drove Utzon to abandon the project. Parkes and Ashworth anticipated a rise in interference, though not to the extent created by mobile phones. By flying above the interference, the device can jam it, and still carry out its primary function. But it needs re-adjustment. It's just that there's no one around who remembers how to do it."

The two operatives exchanged astonished glances.

"Are you absolutely sure you can fix it?"

An exasperated Ken blurted, "Yes! In fact, I can improve it. By positioning the device above the city and angling the wings precisely, I can take advantage of all the mobile phone towers to create an umbrella shield over the entire metropolitan area. I . . . I just need my PC."

"It's in the boot," the driver reminded them.

The operative's eyebrows knitted. "You'd better be right, son."

As the car spun 180 degrees he suddenly sounded hopeful. "I think there's someone you ought to meet."

The car shot into an emergency vehicle siding in the tunnel and gunned towards the Harry Seidler Retirement Village.

MINUTES LATER

An old and infirm Cobden Parkes sat up in his new recliner in the freshly painted TV room of the retirement village.

"Who's the kid?"

Flanked between the two huge ASIO operatives, Ken sort of did resemble a kid.

"This is Kenneth Wilcox – a PhD student in architectural engineering at Sydney University."

"Well, howdya do, Kenny."

Kenny? The student harrumphed. He detested being called that. As he opened his mouth to respond, one of the operatives placed a firm hand on his shoulder and spoke first.

"He's about to do some freelance work for us."

"With your approval of course, Mr Parkes," added the other operative.

Ken's jaw dropped. It was him! Cobden Parkes! – much older, of course, but still recognizable from all the photos.

The old man looked up at Ken with disdain.

"I suppose you're another one of those arty-farty purists who thinks I'm an architectural philistine."

"N . . . No, Mr Parkes. Quite the opposite," Ken nervously stuttered. "I've studied all your work, read all your notes. Your theories – way ahead of their time – revolutionary!"

"Really?" Parkes brightened.

"Totally! The way you integrated the device into the infrastructure without compromising the integrity of Utzon's original design – sheer genius!"

The awe on Ken's face was gratifying to the old man.

The first operative interjected.

"Gentlemen, there's not much time. Mr Parkes, there's something important Ken has to tell you."

TODAY, NOW

Strategically located on an island in the centre of Sydney Harbour, Fort Denison was built during the Crimean War to defend the city against naval attack. Now its empty cannon pointed impotently out to sea where the water boiled and churned as the submerged Reptillon torpedoed towards it.

The behemoth surfaced east of the Fort.

"REPTILLON! AHHHH! REPTILLON!" The Japanese tourists on the battlements had seen this reptilian horror before. Sandstone blocks were pulverized under its weight as it pulled itself out of the foam. Shaking the water off its head, it scanned the harbour, took its bearings then tilted its head back to let forth an ear-splitting roar.

In the distance, windows in city buildings shattered and glass rained down upon the pedestrians below.

The monster launched itself back into the water sending up an enormous plume of sea spray. What remained of the little sandstone fort crumbled into the sea after it.

Tourists thought the old aboriginal woman singing near Ferry Terminal 4 at Circular Quay was just another of the many buskers that congregated there, and some even threw coins at her feet. Her quaint aboriginal Bible song bemused them.

They couldn't possibly know that the song was one of hatred, summoning the instrument of her revenge. Her voice resonated through the ages, channelling the anguished spirits of all the ancestors who had died at the hands of the white-fella.

Echidonah approached now. Through the soles of her bare feet the old woman could feel the vibration of each claw burrowing towards her. Echidonah could sense her, too, could feel her pain, and the closer it dug, the angrier it became.

She raised her arms as her chanting reached a crescendo. At that very moment, Echidonah broke the surface at Circular Quay. It crashed through the Cahill Expressway, named in honour of the once Premier of NSW. Cars and debris toppled onto the concourse, scattering tourists in terror.

The creature ignored the tasty morsels scurrying about its feet and in the tall glass mounds surrounding it – it had something bigger on its mind. Much bigger.

The aboriginal woman ran under the colonnade at the base of a building derogatively nicknamed the "Toaster". She called out to her monster from behind a column.

"Maaaaamuuuu!"

It shuffled through the wreckage and onto the wharves where ferries bashed against the piers. One capsized, hurling passengers into the glassy green water.

Unused to the sunlight, Echidonah blinked as it peered through the glare out across the harbour, where, with a mighty whoosh, Reptillon – the giant lizard – burst out of the water.

The *Eyewitness News* helicopter swung around for a better angle. The camera crash-zoomed tight on Reptillon's angry features.

Back at the retirement village, an exhausted and sleep-deprived Kenneth Wilcox entered the room, trailed by the two ASIO operatives.

Cobden Parkes looked away from the new widescreen digital television and eyed him expectantly.

"You remembered to detach all the mooring cables?"

Ken gave a satisfied nod. "Everything's exactly as you've requested."

"Well done, Kenny my boy."

This time a proud Kenneth Wilcox didn't mind being called that.

Parkes gestured to an armchair, and resumed watching the huge plasma screen. "Take a seat, sonny. The show's about to commence."

At Bennelong Point, authorities frantically evacuated the Opera House – cordoning off surrounding streets and clearing the area. Despite the danger, hundreds of people crowded the foreshore to watch the unfolding spectacle.

The two ASIO operatives stood silently at attention, on either side of Cobden Parkes, while Ken sat nervously on the edge of his armchair. Totally transfixed, they all stared at the huge plasma screen, where they could clearly see the two giant monsters facing off.

A bogon moth fluttered about their heads.

With rattlesnake reflexes one of the operatives snatched the moth mid-flight. His partner frowned disapproval as he went over to a window, opened it, and gently released his fingers. Unharmed, the moth bobbed away, and the operative closed the window behind it.

The blanket pulled over Parkes' lap had fallen to the ground, and the operative picked it up and smoothed it back over the old man's knees before resuming his vigil.

Parkes mumbled a vague thank you, but his eyes never left the television screen. The old man suddenly remembered his old friends, Premier Cahill and Minister Harry Ashworth, now long dead, remembered how they had all sacrificed for this one moment. Tears welled in his eyes. What political battles had they fought, and how much scathing criticism had they endured from the press and public!

The retired architect looked at the scene and whispered to himself. "Today we find out if it has all been worth it." The tears flowed freely now, and his bottom lip quivered. "Today my friends, we will be vindicated!"

———

Back at Circular Quay, Echidonah reared onto its stocky hind legs. Its quills bristled with expectation, while mid-harbour, the giant green lizard splashed towards its opponent. Pausing between the Harbour Bridge and the Sydney Opera House, Reptillon flexed its muscles and adopted a defiant stance as its radioactive spines began to glow ominously.

Face to face at last, the two behemoths sized each other up.

———

Before authorities could stop her, the aboriginal woman jumped a barrier and ran onto the concourse of the Opera House, where she screamed a vengeful call to attack.

"MAMU! MAMU!"

———

Cobden Parkes leaned forward, gripped the arm of his recliner tightly, and spluttered, "Now!"

The two operatives nodded to each other, then one mouthed something into his microphone.

Grinning toothlessly, an exuberant Parkes turned to Ken, and winked.

———

As the giant monsters towered over the Quay, poised for battle, a loud ratcheting suddenly distracted their attention.

Together they turned in the direction of the sound, and watched tiny white tiles fly like confetti into the air, as the glittering sails of the Sydney Opera House slowly, delicately and quite deliberately unfurled.

———

A huge exhaust rotated and locked into position above the aboriginal woman's head. She did a double-take as the engine core began to glow a radioactive blue.

A State Emergency Services recruit went to retrieve her, but was held back by his mate. The engine ignited, and the woman screamed at the top of her voice before being blown back into the dreamtime.

"*Kaaami!*"

Her shrill scream was lost as a deep, powerful roar echoed through the Harbour foreshore and the building wrenched itself from its moorings. Wings spread, it rose into the sky like a gigantic moth.

Kadimakara and Curlew
Jason Nahrung

———

"I've heard of corrugation but this is ridiculous." Steve changed down a gear as the Land Rover bumped over another waist-high furrow in the gravel road.

Sarah held on to the dash with both hands, wincing at the thought of what the jolting was doing to the equipment rattling in the back of the vehicle. "I've never seen anything like this. This could be our big break."

"We'll find out soon enough," John said, leaning forward from his cramped nest amid luggage and gear on the rear seat. "I can see Kadimakara, over there." He pushed his glasses back into position on his nose, then pointed ahead through the dusty, insect-spotted windscreen towards an ochre monolith on the horizon. It seemed to float on a bed of heat haze; the plain around it was scrunched like a tablecloth.

Sarah stared at their destination, inwardly cursing that she'd worn a tank top. But it was so damn hot, and she'd expected to be riding in the back, not having John perving down her cleavage every time he wanted to say something. Poor guy, he just couldn't help himself, however much he tried to fight it. And with those Coke-bottle glasses, he could probably see every damn freckle on her chest.

"The satellite photos didn't do it justice." Sarah retrieved a folder from a bag at her feet, doing her best to swivel away from John's telescopic lenses. "It's bigger than I thought."

"I bet you say that to all the boys," Steve said, flashing a knowing leer.

And the shorts had been another mistake, she realized, as Steve's eyes continued their roving circuit from the dirt track to her knees, thighs, chest and back to the road. "Never, unfortunately, but I live in hope."

John spluttered with laughter, spraying her shoulder with spittle.

She flinched and he fell back in his seat, stared out the window. She swore under her breath. It was like being on a high-school excursion. This was the first time she'd been out in the field with Steve since, well, that last time, but if he thought they were picking up where they'd left off, he was sadly mistaken. Hopefully, with John joining them on this trip, past errors of judgment wouldn't be repeated. Maybe it would all be worth it, if this seismic event turned out to be as unusual as she suspected. Yes, there could be a paper or two in this; a promotion, even a real job overseas where the earth really moved.

The road stretched towards the western horizon, vanishing into the haze somewhere between Kadimakara and a smaller outcrop to its north. A few scrubby wattle trees had been uprooted; others leaned at crazy angles, all facing away from the huge rock.

"Just incredible," Sarah said. "I don't think anyone's encountered anything like this before." She held up the pictures as she tried to compare the satellite images with the world around her. "It's like the rock was dropped in a pond."

The photos clearly showed the rings of disturbed earth radiating out from the monolith in rough concentric circles. They were broken only where they hit the buildings of the Aboriginal community nestled near the only other natural feature in the area, the Sentinels, whose twelve granite towers looked like jumbled flagstones when seen from above. She could just make out the wavering line of a dry watercourse jagging down the western side of the settlement from the Sentinels towards Kadimakara.

"If only," Steve said, flexing his shoulders against his sweat-soaked shirt. "I could use a dip and a cold beer about now."

Sarah swiped the air-conditioning outlet in the dash with the photographs. "I'm sure this bloody thing isn't working." Her back was stuck to the seat and her bra itched.

"Maybe it needs re-gassing," said Steve.

"Not long now and we'll be able to cool off," John added, without leaning forward. "We should be at the township well before dark."

"I hope they've got a bar." As he spoke, Steve steered off the road to avoid a particularly nasty uplift of earth. The ground didn't seem any rougher than the road as small bushes thwacked against the vehicle and rocks dinged off the underside.

John squeezed Steve's shoulder and settled back. "Sorry, mate, it's a dry camp."

Sarah sighed. "We talked about that last night." How had she ever thought going to bed with Steve was a good idea? How many days was she going to be stuck out here with these two *boys*?

"Oh yeah, I forgot," Steve said with a mischievous grin. "Better empty this then." He reached into his shirt pocket for his battered flask and let go the wheel while he unscrewed the cap.

"Steve, I don't think you should – Watch out!" Sarah shouted, but Steve was already braking hard and jerking on the wheel, the flask sloshing liquor as it clattered to the floor.

"Where the bloody hell did he come from?" Steve yelled as the Rover rocked to a stop, boxes sliding in the rear as dust billowed around them. "Jesus!" He leaned forward, fighting his seat belt as he groped for his flask.

"Did you miss him?" Sarah asked. "He came from nowhere . . . I think you missed him."

"Who?" asked John, trying to extricate himself from the avalanche of gear.

"Didn't you see him, John?" Sarah glanced back. "A blackfella . . . It must've been close." She peered out the side window, squinting through the sun and dust.

She shrieked. The men jumped.

An elderly Aborigine stood next to her window, staring at them through the glass, his wide nose twitching with dust, apparently oblivious to the half-dozen flies crawling around the corners of his moist brown eyes.

Sarah, one hand on her thumping heart, wound down her window. The fresh dirt smell rolled in on a blast of hot air.

"Jesus," she said. "You scared the shit out of me."

"Not as much as you mob scared me, missus." He smiled, revealing a few dark gaps in his wide, white grin.

"Are you all right?" Sarah asked. "We didn't even see you."

He wore faded, stained jeans and a dirty singlet. Rings of grey hair framed his dust-caked forehead. Dots of dark red paint flecked his cheeks.

"I'm all right, missus." He pointed at them with a knobby finger. "It's you mob should be worried."

"Us?" she asked. "We didn't hit you, did we? I'm sure we didn't." She looked at him more closely but couldn't see any injuries. Bare feet, she noticed, and he was thin, his skin the deepest black, and the eyes – old, but not dulled by age.

"No, missus, you didn't run into me. I come to warn you. This isn't a good place. You should all go back where you belong."

Steve snorted. "We spent three days driving out here. We're not going back now."

"'Im no good for climbin'," the man said with a gesture over his shoulder to the monolith.

"Are you talking about the climber who died last week, just before the first quake?" Sarah asked.

"We're not here to climb it, old timer," Steve said. "We're here to study it. We're scientists, from the government."

"Guv'ment? Guv'ment don't come out 'ere."

"Well, we're bloody well here now," Steve said.

"Are you from the camp?" John peered across Sarah's shoulder at the man. "You want a ride?"

The man cast an eye over the four-wheel-drive. "Better to walk, eh."

"At least tell me your name," Sarah said. "I need to talk to you about the tremors. About what you saw, what you felt."

The old man stepped even closer, staring into her eyes, and his voice dropped to a hard-edged whisper. "I told 'im, that fella that died. I told 'im, Kadimakara's no good for whitefellas to scramble on. He's no good for any mob." He wagged a finger at them. "You better stay away from 'im, missus. You don't wanna end up like that other fella."

"What are you saying?" Sarah asked. "Are you threatening us?"

"I've had enough of this bullshit," Steve said, crunching the Rover into gear. "See you there, old fella." He drove off with a lurch that sent John flying back into his seat.

"You didn't need to be so rude," Sarah said, "even if he was a bit creepy. I needed to talk to him."

"You can chat all you like when he finally gets back to the camp," Steve said, and shook his head. "Not that he made much sense. Pissed, probably." He caught a glimpse of John between jolts in the rearview mirror. "I thought you said it was a dry community?"

"Oh, it is," John said.

Sarah fired a dirty look at Steve, then reefed her gaze away. Disgusted, she bit her lip, tasting dust. Through the window, the monolith shimmered in the haze, waiting patiently.

———

The houses of the local community seemed baked in the sun. Paint had faded on the windowless walls; tin roofs wavered with the heat rising from the unsealed roads. There wasn't even breeze enough to stir the plastic bags and food wrappers that littered the bare dusty yards. People and dogs lounged under scrubby trees shading the open space in the middle of the township.

Hope hadn't died here, Sarah thought as they passed yet another rusted car body. It hadn't been game to slow down, let alone stop. No, hope had taken one look and headed for the coast where at least it could live out its old age in comfort. The urge to follow it welled inside her. Maybe the encounter with the old Aborigine had spooked her more than she realized. He'd been right on one score, though – she didn't belong here. Maybe that was what was really bugging her; the realization that her world had, to whatever degree, contributed to the state of this one.

Sarah shelved her disquiet as they pulled up outside the canteen. One thing she could be sure of – an unusual, perhaps unique, geological event had occurred here, and it held enough promise to override any apprehension she might be feeling.

She flashed a nervous grin at two Aborigines seated on a warped bench. The pair swatted at flies as they watched the three scientists get out of the four-wheel-drive.

"Uncle's inside. He's bin waitin' for you mob," one of them said with a half-hearted movement of his hand.

"Is that right?" Steve replied. "Hope it's his shout."

The man's expression didn't change, but Sarah sensed the hardening behind his brown eyes. She could've kicked Steve, she really could've.

They went in, blinking in the sudden dimness until their eyes adjusted. The screen door clunked behind them with a scratch of tired hinges and an aluminium rattle. There was the clink of someone taking a shot on the threadbare pool table, and a tinny radio played country music. A little girl in a white dress danced to it with unselfconscious grace as two others played with sticks on the floor. Everyone stopped what they were doing as the scientists entered.

"Holy shit," Sarah whispered, gesturing towards the bar.

"How the hell?" asked John.

"Tricky bastard," Steve said, and led them over. The old man leaned against the bar, his hand wrapped around a cold can of soft drink that had left a puddle on the polished timber. He raised it in salute as they reached him.

Sarah licked her lips as thirst fought with curiosity. She pulled up a stool, the cracked vinyl creaking under her, and decided she could satisfy both – if Steve would let her.

He had walked right up to the old fella and, as John asked the teenage girl behind the bar for three cans of lemonade, Steve poked the air in front of the man's face and said: "So how'd you do it, granddad? You have a bike stashed out there? A horse? What was the idea, jumping out like that? We could've hurt you."

"No bike, no fancy four-wheel-drive. I told you blokes, out 'ere, these are better, more comfy." He pointed to his bare feet. "Got good air condition' too, boss." He waved a hand, sending a few flies buzzing.

"You're crazy," Steve said, and walked back behind Sarah to get his drink.

Sarah introduced them. "And you're . . . ?"

"You can call me Jimmy Curlew. You mob shouldn't be 'ere. This isn't your place."

"Jimmy, what can you tell me about the earthquake? It doesn't seem to have damaged the community."

"How the hell could you tell?" Steve snorted behind her, and again she had to quell the impulse to slap him.

"John, maybe you and Steve should go set up the camp? Where's a good place, Jimmy?"

"Brisbane's not far, missus. Not with a good car like your one."

She laughed. "You're persistent, I'll give you that." Then she got serious. "We're here to study the rock, Jimmy, but we don't want to offend anyone. So please, where do you think is a good place for us to camp?"

He studied her, then nodded. "All right then, missus, if that's what you want. There's a little billabong, over by that creek there." He pointed out the back door. "Not much water, but he's got good shade. Close to Lumaluma. You mob will be safer there."

"Thanks, Jimmy. You boys go on, I'll catch you up."

"You be all right, Sarah?" John asked, wiping the dust from his glasses.

"Yeah, I just want to find out more about what they saw from here and how it affected them."

Sarah's teammates left, promising her a fine meal of baked beans on toast, and again she asked Jimmy about the tremor.

"Lumaluma, what your mob call Sentinels, they look after us, missus. They might look after you, too, if you don't upset 'em."

"And how would we do that, Jimmy?"

"Just keep away from Kadimakara, that's all, missus. Don't go climbin' on 'im. Too many died up there already. That fella, he's got too much blood in 'im."

"Yes, I know. The latest one only last week. A heart attack, wasn't it?"

"That's what they say, missus. But it wasn't no 'art attack."

"So what was it, Jimmy? What don't you want us here? Because we are staying. This upheaval is amazing. It could make a person's career."

Jimmy shook his head. "Could cost you plenny, this career of yours. Kadimakara is the spirit of this place, older than old. We keep 'im quiet, keep 'im dreamin'." His voice rose, so it carried through the shed, and he swept the rest of the building with his gaze. "But these young ones, they aren't innerested in the old ways." He looked over to the pool table where two young men in football jerseys had resumed playing. Sarah felt their eyes on her, measuring her like she was another ball in the game. "They don't wanna stay 'ere an' sing to Kadimakara. They want money an' them fancy cars."

One of the lads threw his cue on the table. "You're mad, Uncle. And you're mad, too, missus, if ya listen to 'is stupid old stories."

He stormed out, leaving his mate to flash an apologetic grin and a shrug before he, too, sauntered away.

Jimmy shook his head and took another swig. Sarah smiled as his throat bobbed, reminding her of a frog as he gulped down a few mouthfuls before he resumed talking.

"And the guv'ment, they aren't innerested neither. They want tourists to come an' climb 'im, carve their names on 'im, piss on 'im. They don't unnerstand it's the land, missus. People forget where they come from, people forget where they are."

"And where are we, Jimmy?"

"We're in the land of Kadimakara, missus. We're livin' in 'is shadow." He grinned, without amusement.

The ground shook. Bottles rattled on the shelf. Sarah grabbed at the bar as her stool wobbled. A pool ball bounced off the table, cracked across the concrete floor.

Jimmy grabbed Sarah's arm, so hard it hurt. He put his face next to hers so she could hear over the din. "You should go," Jimmy said; eyes hard, face set. The little girl cried and the barmaid whimpered. A dog howled. "It's not safe 'ere any more, not for whitefella or black."

————

It was almost dark when Sarah reached the camp, which the men had erected in the shade of a small tree-lined waterhole hidden in a patch of scrub within sight of the community. The monolith glowed red in the fading light, the last rays of sunset tipping the pillars of the Sentinels with pink. She identified the dry creek bed she'd seen in the photos, and could just make out where it once might have joined up with the billabong before a movement of the earth or perhaps just sediment had cut the waterhole off. Now the only thing coming down from the pinnacles of grey stone were the haunting calls of curlews, but Sarah blamed the increasingly cool night air for her goosepimples.

The men had pitched the tents. Sarah had her own, though she would be sharing it with a good deal of equipment they had unpacked from the four-wheel drive. John was squatting by the campfire he'd built inside a circle of water-smoothed stones on a sandy patch near the bank of the waterhole.

"Did you get it?" she gasped, out of breath from her stumbling jog from the township. "It had to be two, maybe three points."

John, looking over his shoulder, shook his head. "Sorry, Sarah. We were still unpacking when the aftershock came. But Brisbane will have recorded it. And yeah, I'd say around 2.5 on the Richter scale. Shook some of the dust off the Rover."

"Shit." She stood, legs apart, bent over with hands on knees, the sweat cooling on her back and forehead. "I can't believe we missed it."

"But you're just in time for dinner."

She could see he hadn't been joking about the beans. They were simmering, fresh from the can, on the fry pan.

"Where's Steve?" she asked, moving over to warm herself by the fire. She breathed deeply to inhale the fragrant wood smoke. Already, she could see through the branches stars twinkling in the clear, darkening night. Out here, with no city lights or pollution, the star field would stretch from horizon to horizon. Maybe she would go for a walk later, get out of the scrub so she could enjoy that vista.

"Watering the horse," John said, and then in a low voice: "He didn't dump the booze."

Before she could say anything, Steve stepped into the campsite, one hand still working at his fly, the other holding a bottle of rum.

"I thought we agreed to leave that at the motel last night," Sarah said.

"*You* agreed. It's almost a third full, no point leaving it for the maid." He offered her the bottle.

She shook her head. "You know they can throw us off for bringing that on to their land."

"Their land? Since when?"

She clenched her teeth, aware of John motioning with his eyes for her not to get into a brawl.

"Jesus," she muttered. "I'm going to get my coat." She rubbed her arms with anger, not cold, as she headed for her tent.

"Better get the first-aid kit, too," Steve shouted. "Get a bandage for that bleeding heart of yours."

"Fuck you," she yelled through the canvas as she angrily rummaged for her sweater.

"You wish," he shouted back. Before she could retort further, she heard John calming Steve down.

Still, she didn't go outside, just lit her lantern and started to check and prepare equipment for the next day. Damn Steve. Damn that he'd been more interested in getting pissed than setting up the equipment. Damn that they'd missed the aftershock. Their first chance to get some real data, rather than Jimmy Curlew's mumbo jumbo . . . The old man's thinly veiled warning made her shiver. Not that she thought he would actually harm them. How could he? But he had suggested that the climber had not died of a heart attack – what did he know about that? She swore again as she hauled equipment from boxes, powered up her laptop. Old Jimmy wouldn't have to poison them or arrange any accidents to end this expedition. He'd just have to catch Steve boozing.

A beep from the laptop announced it was ready. Sarah was particularly interested in downloading the latest satellite pictures, and any new data from the earthquake monitoring centre in Brisbane. She'd set up as much of her own equipment as she could tonight, to make sure she didn't miss any other aftershocks. The two men couldn't do much before morning, when they'd start taking soil samples and checking for damage as part of a safety assessment.

John brought dinner to the door and she took it gratefully. Sarah could see Steve, sitting by the fire with his back to her tent, staring out in the direction of the monolith, barely visible through the trees.

"Don't pay him any mind," John said. "He gets loud when he's on the piss."

"The arsehole will ruin our trip."

"Don't let him. It's a beautiful night, why don't you come out? Birds are loud."

"They give me the creeps."

"Just birds, Sarah. Anyway, I'm going to turn in soon. We want to do as much as we can in the morning before it gets too hot, eh?"

"Sure."

"Will you be all right?"

She smiled.

"Well, if you want anything, just holler."

She thanked him and finished her meal, soaking up the juice with a piece of bread, with a chocolate bar for dessert. John, bless him, had brought her coffee as well. His heart was in the right place. If only she could transplant it into Steve's body . . . She zipped up the tent and retreated with the brew to her sleeping bag on the camp bed. But she'd only just picked up her laptop when Steve stumbled into the tent door.

"What the hell do you want?" she shouted as he clawed at the canvas then finally found the zip. He loomed large and dark at the door, his face bright red, eyes shining in the gas light.

"I wanted to shay I'm shorry," he lisped, kneeling in the doorway, one hand on the tent pole, the other around the neck of the nearly empty bottle. "Y'know, I really like you, Sharah. Been thinkin' about you lots since that last trip."

"Well, thanks Steve." She hoped her voice was suitably sarcastic. "I'm just about to get some sleep." Then she regretted it; she didn't want to antagonize him further. "Maybe we can talk about it in the morning, eh?"

"Why not now, Sharah?" He lurched to all fours. "Y'know, it could be a cold night . . . "

She felt a chill run through her and pulled the blanket higher. "I'm sure I'll be warm enough, thanks. Why don't you turn in? Early start and all that."

"Ah, shoulda known ya wouldn't be intereshted in a real man. Not lefty enough for ya, eh?"

She flinched in the face of his sudden anger, drawing up her knees as he waved the bottle. "It was a mistake, I told you that."

John called out, his voice sounding hesitant and thin. "Hey Steve, you finished with the fire? I'm gonna put it out."

Sarah held her breath, wondering if the interruption would distract Steve or just annoy him.

"You bitch," Steve muttered, and drained the bottle.

"Steve?" John called. "I'm, ah, putting the fire out. You gonna hit the sack?"

Sarah's grip on her blanket relaxed as Steve backed out of the tent. She jumped as he whacked the bottle against the fly, then hurled it into the bush. It must've hit a rock, because she heard it smash. The sharp crack made her flinch again. "Yeah, I heard ya the firsht time. Put yaself out, why don'tcha? I'm gonna take a leak."

Then Steve was gone. She heard his shambling footfalls in the gravel, then a few cracks of branches and leaves. For a moment she thought she should go after him. Stumbling around in the dark, he could get hurt. She sighed. Serve him right if he did. A night out in the cold would do him the world of good.

John stood outside her tent. "Everything okay, Sarah?" he asked quietly, as though afraid of being overheard.

"It's fine, John. Thanks."

"Ah, okay then. I'm gonna turn in."

"Sounds like a plan."

She heard him walk away, then called after him: "John?"

He stopped. "Yes, Sarah?"

She paused, not sure what she had meant to say. "Thanks" seemed pretty weak. "Sleep tight, eh?"

"Yeah. You, too."

A moment of silence, then he resumed walking. She heard the zip of the other tent open and then shut.

Damn, she would have to go out. Her bladder wasn't letting her go to bed just yet. Maybe she could blame Steve for causing a nervous reaction.

It was cold outside, even in jeans and jumper. The fire was dead. The tent John shared with Steve lay in darkness. Poor John; he would have to spend the night with Steve's drunken snoring and bad attitude, once the obnoxious geologist returned from his nocturnal stagger.

Clutching her toilet bag under her arm, Sarah turned on her flashlight and headed down to the waterhole.

Business done and teeth cleaned, she started back towards the camp. Then she heard something. She froze. The sound of crickets rose up, and the damned curlews of course, and other birds she didn't know. Then she heard the noise again – hushed voices.

"I can take ya there," a young man said. "It's not far, boss."

"How far exactly?" Steve asked. "I'm not in the mood for a bloody midnight hike."

"Not very far, boss. Plenny of drink there. No one knows about it. Just us young fellas."

"Well, I dunno."

Sarah saw movement, a flash of pale skin as Steve ran a hand through his hair and turned towards the camp. She couldn't see the other man clearly; he was just a dark shadow among many.

"C'mon, boss, you'll be back in plenny of time. There'll be girls there, too."

"Yeah? Ah, what the hell. Lead the way, sport."

And Steve lurched off into the trees.

When Sarah was sure he was gone, she ran, fast as she dared, the short distance to John's tent. A few shouts and he came stumbling out, wiping his face and fumbling with his glasses.

"What is it, Sarah? What's wrong?"

"It's Steve. The bloody idiot's gone off with some blackfella to get drunk." She tossed her head and rolled her eyes. "Drunker," she amended. "He'll be bloody useless tomorrow. Christ, he might even get us kicked off. We can't afford to let someone else get to this, John."

"Ah, shit, all right. Let me get my boots on and we'll go get the bugger."

"Thanks, John. Hurry."

It took only a few minutes before they were both dressed and ready. She showed him the way she thought Steve had gone.

"Are you sure? That's not towards the community."

"No, it's towards Kadimakara, I know. The bar must be in a cave or something. Damn him." How typical, she thought: finally a chance to get some professional attention, and Steve was going to louse it up in a drunken fit of pique.

John eyed the Rover, shrugged, then started walking. "Steve's got the keys."

"That'd be bloody right," Sarah huffed, and trudged along next to him.

It wasn't long and they cleared the scrub and emerged onto the plain. A half moon threw everything into light and shade, making the footing treacherous, especially since the quake had thrown up deep runnels. They tried to keep their torches pointed at their feet so the beams wouldn't alert Steve and give him time to hide. They could just see his white shirt, bobbing in the wan light as he wove around rocks, spindly bushes and his own inebriated sense of direction.

Despite the cold, Sarah was sweating when they finally approached the monolith.

"For a drunk, he makes good time," she wheezed. They stopped near the base, trying to find Steve and his almost invisible guide as they gathered their breath.

"Yeah, he's a big bastard," John said, and she thought she could hear doubt in his voice. Neither had broached the subject about just how they were going to convince Steve to return to camp.

"Christ, it's big, too." She stared up at Kadimakara looming above them, silvered in the moonlight.

"Yeah," John muttered. "I would have preferred to see it in daytime. It looks a lot bigger in the dark."

"Yeah, and of course, bloody Steve has gone to the shadowed side. How the hell are we going to find him?"

"I guess we'll just have to keep looking."

Pebbles crunched underfoot, loud enough in the still, quiet night to make them wince as they worked their way around the base. An incredible lip of earth surrounded the rock. It made Sarah think someone had simply dropped the monolith from a great height. How much of it was still underground, she wondered? How deep did it go?

They couldn't hear the curlews from here, but occasionally something would scrabble in the dark, or small rocks would clatter on the stone mountain before them. She walked close to John, enjoying the sensation of another body within hand's reach, however reedy.

John checked his watch. "Christ, we've been out here for hours."

"Where the fuck could he be?"

"Oh shit," John said, and pointed up.

"Oh shit indeed." Steve and his companion were scaling the side of the rock, already half way up the slope. "I'm sure that's the boy from the canteen."

John looked at her blankly.

"Never mind," she said. "What do we do now?"

"Follow them, I suppose."

"At night? That's crazy."

"What else can we do? Look for his body in the morning and try to explain what a geologist was doing staggering around half pissed in the middle of the night?"

She trembled.

"You all right?" he asked, touching her sleeve.

"Yeah, I was just thinking about what Jimmy Curlew told me back at the canteen."

"And what was that?"

"He said the rock killed that tourist the other day."

"What the hell does that mean? You didn't believe him, did you?"

"I dunno. It's just crazy, the way the quake seemed to be centred here, and then the ground's all ruffled like this."

"I'll grant you Mother Earth's got a few tricks up her sleeve, but that's why we're here, eh? One way or the other, though, we have to get Steve down from there before we all get into serious trouble. Not a lot of jobs for washed-up seismologists these days."

They scrambled onto the rock surface. It still felt warm, as though all the heat of the day was still leaking out. The rock was pitted with age and weather. Tufts of hardy spinifex protruded from among the cracks. It was a steep climb that made their legs ache and chests heave as they fought for breath.

Sarah's apprehension mounted as they worked their way higher. She felt like a burglar, climbing across someone's roof. How long before she got caught?

"No wonder people die up here," John gasped when they called a rest stop at a place where the rock flattened slightly before curving up towards the apex. "Christ, I've got to work out more."

Sarah nodded in sympathy. Her shirt was soaked with sweat; her ankle smarted from when she had slipped. She would have felt stupid about it but John had been tripping a lot, too, as they tried to find solid footing on the smooth stone and puddles of scree. At least the moon had risen further, was giving them some extra light. They used their torches, but often the wavering beams were more a menace than a help, and in places they needed both hands to crawl up the steep slope.

Finally they neared the top, the star-filled sky arcing over them. Sarah had forgotten how many there were; how *big* the world was. A cold wind froze the sweat and made her shiver.

"There they are," John said, pointing.

"Oh Christ, he's passed out," Sarah said. "We'll never carry the bastard down."

Steve was on the ground, his guide standing over him. The teenager saw them, waved.

"What the hell happened?" John shouted as they got closer. He played his torch beam over Steve. There was a dark splash of blood near his head.

"He tripped over, boss. I think he's hurt pretty bad."

John swore as he knelt beside Steve and felt for a pulse. "He's still alive," he told Sarah, his face washed out in her torch beam. "But he's bleeding plenty." John turned back, studying Steve. The teenager stepped up behind him.

Sarah screamed. Too late. John, looking puzzled, was still turning towards her as the knife plunged into his back. She saw his face contort with pain as the blade rose and slashed down once more. He fell across Steve's body. John's torch rolled away, bouncing and flashing until it broke with a crack.

"What the hell are you doing?" Sarah tried to keep her torch beam on the teenager as she backed away. Splashes of blood glistened on his arms and face.

"Kadimakara, he needs more blood. Just a bit more. Then he will wake up and drive you mob from our land."

"That's not what Jimmy said," she stuttered as the youth approached, the gory knife held loosely in one blood-soaked hand. "He said it didn't care who it killed, black or white."

"What does that fella know? He's old an' soft."

"And you're a murdering sonofabitch," she shouted, and then cried out as the rock lurched under her. She lost her balance, fell, dropped her torch. It bounced metallically over a lip and out of sight.

The youth swayed, but kept his feet, like a surfer.

"Kadimakara awakes! Your other mate must be dead, too. All Kadimakara needs is a little more." He held his arms out, as though into a breeze. "Can you feel it?"

Oh yes, she could feel it. Trembling up through the rock, making her teeth rattle. Tears burned hot in her eyes.

The rock heaved again, even more violently, and gave a mighty crack like a glacier splitting. Sarah, already on hands and knees, fell sideways. Her head smacked on rock. She heard the boy cry out as he fell with a heavy crunch.

"No, Kadimakara," he screamed. "I'm your servant!"

A shape blotted out the moon. Dust fell over them like mist. Pebbles dinged off rock. A thundering grating sound filled Sarah's ears, penetrated by the boy's cries.

Then what seemed like a huge boulder smashed down. Sarah sprawled on her stomach. The boy flew sideways, tumbled, then vanished, flailing, into the same darkness as her torch.

Sobbing, she tried to hold on as the rock shuddered. It vibrated with the sound of a huge tree being torn from the ground, one desperately resisting root at a time. Pain shot through her fingers as she sought purchase, shredding skin and nails as the movement worsened, the rumbling increased. The moon vanished again. Shadow fell over Sarah. Something black, seeming as big as the sky, rushed towards her. She might have rolled; maybe the rock's movement threw her. The descending boulder smashed down next to her. The rock under her heaved like a bucking horse, tilting on crazy angles. Screaming, Sarah slid over the edge, plummeting, bashing into bushes and rocks, until finally a jarring thump stopped her fall.

When she could see, through the blood and fear and pain, she couldn't believe her eyes. Dust rolled from the flanks of Kadimakara; pebbles and stone cascaded down its sides. It was alive, heaving itself up on massive legs, a knobby head rearing from the south on a long, turtle-like neck. The earth trembled, jarring her broken bones. Too huge, too incomprehensible. What had been above the earth was but a piece of its armoured spine. There was so much more, still emerging, pushing the soil back in a wave that carried her, rolling her like surf. A tail of rock lashed at the ground, sending trees and boulders flying.

She dragged herself backwards, using her good arm, her good leg; tried to ignore the agony in her ribs, the myriad stabbing wounds.

Another sound penetrated Sarah's fearful daze. A whooshing sound, low and rhythmic, like a fan blade or some deep bass siren. She turned in the direction, to see Jimmy, dressed only in jeans, his scarred chest daubed with paint. He swung a bullroarer, the painted piece of timber flying around in a circle at the end of a piece of string, making that ghostly noise.

Two other men ran towards her. They too were half-naked, wearing mostly paint, but they picked her up and carried her back, ignoring her groans of pain and terror.

Jimmy started chanting, and the massive creature turned towards him, blotting out so many stars, its feet hidden in clouds of dust and soil. When it took a step, the ground quaked with a resounding crunch, but Jimmy kept his feet, and the sound of the bullroarer didn't falter.

The two men hauled Sarah back, and all she could do as she clung to consciousness was watch Jimmy facing off the beast armed only with a piece of wood on a string. She could hear the curlews, calling out in a multitude, like cicadas, and the bullroarer whining and Jimmy chanting. She could hear – feel – the thudding of the earth as the creature stepped forward on its towering limbs.

Movement caught her attention. Tearing her gaze from the spectacle before her, she saw, from the direction of the Sentinels, a flitting line of dark shapes – birds winging in the thousands from the splintered outcrop towards the monster. It turned to face them, bellowing, and again the ground shook and it seemed even the stars vibrated with the call.

The birds plunged into the rock, and Sarah screamed at the thought of them mashing on the thick, rocky hide. But they emerged unharmed from the creature's side and sped towards Jimmy. As they approached, Sarah could see a faint red glow around the birds. And then they hit Jimmy, vanishing into his body. He kept chanting, even as he jerked with each impact, and the bullroarer kept swinging, its siren call unbroken. Bird after bird, impact after impact, ploughed into him and was absorbed. And then from the bullroarer came a welter of tiny white shooting stars, shrieking like fireworks as they scribed a brilliant arc across the sky before landing somewhere inside the dark, silent spires of the Sentinels.

The beast roared, then turned and lumbered towards Jimmy once more as the incredible flock plunged into its back, then tore from its chest, only to dive into Jimmy. And the sparks flew from the bullroarer, the glimmering arch so bright it made Sarah squint to look at it.

Sarah saw Jimmy stagger, and the beast fall to one leg, and she heard it bellow one last time as her body and mind finally yielded.

———

Sarah awoke in her camp bed. Any thought, any hope, that the horror of the previous night had been only a nightmare was vanquished a moment after she opened her eyes. Someone had taken off her clothes and daubed her wounds with a chalky white ointment. Her body, what she could see of it before the pain made her rest her head back on her pillow, was more ointment than skin. One arm was tied in a splint, as were both her legs, though one not as extensively as the other. Outside she could hear chanting and the rhythmic clacking of sticks, and some murmur of conversation.

The girl from the canteen entered shortly after, carrying a bowl of brown creek water and a piece of pink-stained cloth.

"How you feelin'?" she asked.

"I've been better." Sarah risked a smile, was rewarded with only a twinge of pain from the ribs. "Thank you."

The girl bobbed her head. "The flyin' doctor, he's comin' for you. Won't be long, now. You should rest, eh."

Sarah nodded.

The girl gave her water and checked the worst of her cuts and bruises, the tightness of the splints.

"So what happened?" Sarah asked.

"Some men, they climbed Kadimakara. They fell. Maybe they were drinkin'. There's no drink allowed 'ere."

The title of a research paper flashed in Sarah's mind: *Supernatural phenomena and their causal relationship to seismic activity.* She smiled, shook her head carefully, so as not to set off any more pains.

"I do believe you're right. But what about Jimmy? The creature?"

The girl just smiled.

"Help me then."

The girl gave her a puzzled look.

"I want to see."

"You can't from 'ere, missus. Too many trees . . . "

Damn.

She heard the hum of an approaching aircraft.

"Doctor's comin'," the girl said.

Sarah nodded, the thought of being carried to the plane and then flying out not particularly appealing. Although they would have morphine. The plane made her think of something else, but she would have to hurry.

"Help me, can you please? Before the doctor gets here?"

The girl gave her a suspicious look, but nodded hesitantly.

"Great. Can you get that box? Yes, that one. Can you set it down here, so I can see it? Next to my good arm."

The girl did as Sarah asked, and then Sarah talked her through connecting the relevant wires. Fortunately she'd done most of it the night before, before Steve . . . She concentrated on her equipment, trying to fight off the sudden shaking that made her hand quiver over the laptop's keyboard.

"What time is it?"

The girl shrugged. She wasn't wearing a watch, just bangles of coloured beads and leather. "Late afternoon. You slept all day. It's good, it'll help you get better."

"Sure. Now, let's see if it works." Sarah gritted her teeth as she operated the computer. "Bingo," she muttered as the uplink finally connected.

Raised voices outside told her the doctor had landed. It wouldn't be long now, just a short drive from the bush airstrip; like the community, the landing field was also shielded from the quake by the twelve needles of the Sentinels.

Sarah swore. She needed just a little more time. There, the latest satellite photos, from this morning . . .

"I'll be damned," she said.

The girl moved around to look at the screen as Sarah zoomed in, the area around Kadimakara drawing exponentially closer.

"Jimmy," the girl said.

Sarah stared at the screen. Kadimakara was buried once more, but out of place and tilted slightly, its base still showing signs of massive disturbance. She could see the settlement, its buildings still standing. Even her campsite showed up.

"What?" she whispered. "That can't be." She panned the image and homed in on the Sentinels. She looked at the girl, who didn't seem surprised at all.

"There's thirteen," Sarah said. Outside, a curlew called.

Postcards from Monster Island
Emily Devenport

———

Sometimes people ask me, "Why didn't you run?"

"Because I had the Martian Death Flu," I tell them.

They look at me funny because they've seen the footage of people clogging the roads, and the subways and trains, desperate to get out of town the day *he* waded ashore. I wasn't in that crowd. I was flat on my back in my studio apartment, blitzed out of my mind with medicine. Two of my cats slept on top of me and my dog was snoring beside us when the whole building began to shake. Some of my books fell off their shelves, and I could hear the dishes clattering in their cupboards. I thought it was an earthquake. I considered dragging myself out of bed and crouching in a doorway.

That impulse didn't make it past the notion stage. I couldn't even muster the ambition to be worried as more books tumbled off my shelves and the windows rattled. I only managed a little curiosity when I noticed that the shaking was a side effect of slow, ponderous *BOOM*s, spaced like colossal footsteps. If the Statue of Liberty took a walk through town, she might make noises like that.

Wow, I thought. *This is the weirdest fever dream I've ever had.* And then I fell asleep again.

All night long I felt the tremors and heard the sirens. Once I awoke to a sound like ten foghorns going off at once. The cry was challenging, yet . . . oddly lonesome. That was the only time during the night when I believed something might really be going on. I thought I should at least *try* to get up. And then I passed out.

When the bombs started to drop, I pried my eyes open and squinted at the window. Morning light was trying to penetrate the dust and debris floating in the air. It wasn't making much headway.

Any normal person would have been thinking about evacuating the scene by that point. But the Martian Death Flu, though not actually from Mars, made me feel anything but normal. For one thing, when I sat up, the room started to spin. For another, my pets let me know in no uncertain terms that they were hungry. Plus my dog needed to potty.

I had to answer my own call of nature first. Halfway to the bathroom, I decided I'd better crawl if I really wanted to get there. Afterward I took more medicine, my head pounding in tune with the bombs going off outside.

The war sounded like it might be about a mile away. My apartment shook more than it had during the night, yet everything was still pretty much intact. My pets didn't like the noise, but they seemed more worried about their stomachs, so I staggered out of the bathroom and fixed their bowls.

I could barely hold myself upright long enough to do it. Once my dog had eaten, she reminded me that I needed to do something more challenging. I managed to get her collar attached and find the pooper-scooper. Then it was out into the cold, cruel world.

We passed one of my neighbors in the hall: Mr. Abé. He operated an African-clothing shop on our street. As the BOOMs and RAT-TAT-TATs shook our building, I lurched back and forth across the hall, and Mr. Abé gracefully sidestepped me.

"Sorry," I rasped.

"I hope you feel better soon, Miss Herrmann," he said. "Terrible racket, isn't it?"

"Yeah," I managed, before Peachy almost pulled me off my feet. She had her priorities, and she would tolerate no delay.

Under the circumstances it was crazy to get into the elevator, but I knew I wouldn't make it down the stairs. I don't remember how we got outside from there, but we ended up in the alley behind our building. Peachy did her business cautiously, but not as nervously as I expected she would. She stopped from time to time and perked her ears at the sounds of battle. She sniffed out her favorite spots, and I pooper-scooped. Then she pulled me back toward the alley door, and I took a moment to be grateful she wasn't going to insist on walkies. The way I was feeling, it would have been more like draggies.

Just before we got through the door, that foghorn cry sounded again. It was much louder without the walls of our well-constructed building to muffle it. Both Peachy and I were extremely impressed. Instead of loneliness, this time I heard a note of exasperation.

Peachy trotted through the door and I stumbled after her. I don't remember how I got rid of the poop I had scooped, but I can only hope I did the right thing with it. I made it back up to our floor and into our little apartment.

I *really* wanted to fall into bed. I also wanted to throw up. But I made myself grab my phone, and I also snagged the remote. All four of the cats were on the bed by then, but they made room for me once they realized I was about to fall on them.

For several moments I just lay there, the remote and phone still clutched in my hands, my stomach and my head competing for Most Amazingly Wretched Body Part. I waited until I was fairly sure I wasn't going to throw up, and then I dialed the first of my three jobs.

They were part-time jobs, the best I could find with my new bachelor's degree in library science, and I juggled them to keep myself afloat. Only one of them paid for sick time, so I had planned to dose myself with the medicine and stagger in to work, regardless of how horrible I felt. That plan had wilted in the painful (and extremely filtered) light of day. I speed-dialed the morning job.

An operator told me the number was no longer in service. I got the same message for the afternoon job. The number for the evening job didn't even connect with a recording; it just made horrible noises.

I gave up on the phone. "Guess what, gang," I croaked. "I don't have to go to work – ever again."

My building shook, the dishes rattled, and another book fell off the shelf. I should have been worried, possibly even depressed to lose my livelihood. Yet somehow I felt relieved. I knew it wasn't a rational reaction, but I couldn't help it.

I pointed the remote at the TV and pushed the ON button.

I didn't have to surf for a news channel. The story was on all of them. I hadn't seen that kind of coverage since 9/11 (though I was in the fourth grade at the time, and spent most of my time watching the Cartoon Channel, so maybe I wasn't an authority on that). Talking heads babbled about the giant creature who had waded ashore, and the bombs that didn't seem to do anything but annoy it, and the pollution and/or nuclear waste that had probably created it, and the wreckage that used to be our city, and the conference with the president that was supposed to happen any minute (but never did on that night) – and on the bottom of the screen scrolled the words: SCIENTISTS BAFFLED BY BEHEMOTH.

It was hard to get a good look at him with all the smoke, fire, tracers, exploding debris, etc. But I could see bits and pieces. He was colossal (apparently they felt *behemoth* was easier to spell). He sometimes stood on two legs, sometimes on four, and I couldn't help comparing him to a giant lemur – except that he had a thick tail that he used to bash things.

Another not-so-lemur-ish characteristic was his hide. Instead of fur, he had these triangular rocky scales that seemed impervious to everything they hurled at him. No missiles could penetrate that hide. And some of them were *really big* missiles.

They did no damage to Behemoth. But they did plenty of damage to our city. Just when I thought they would wise up and stop with the bombs, a troop of marines jumped out of an airplane and parachuted onto him. They bounced off too. When they landed, the ones who didn't get tangled in their parachutes launched grenades at him. He turned and walked away from them, toppling several buildings that had been damaged by the bombs.

"This just in," said the reporter, who sounded like he might OD on the excitement. "All troops are being withdrawn. Readings on the geiger counters are spiking. The creature seems to be generating dangerous levels of radiation."

That didn't sound good. But no one had anything very smart to add, and amazingly, the behemoth story began to suffer from the same problem every other big news story seems to have: endless rehashing of theories and footage, without anything new or intelligent to offer.

I passed out again while waiting for clarification on the radiation thing. It sounded pretty bad, and it also sounded like a good reason to clear out, assuming I could find a way to wrangle four cats and a dog. And my dizzy, flu-bedeviled ass. To where, I couldn't imagine. Because no shelter was going to take my pets; I had heard about what happened to the pets in New Orleans after that hurricane.

Maybe the radiation wouldn't reach my part of the city . . .

A few hours later I woke to hear someone on the TV saying that Behemoth wasn't radioactive *all* the time, just when a lot of missiles had been fired at him. Like maybe it was a defense mechanism or something. But then they started that old rehash again, and I stopped listening. The only thing that made my ears perk up was a rumor that another giant creature had been spotted over our city, this one in the clouds.

Yes, that was the Cloud Squid. She showed up inside a thunder storm. The rain thrashed us so long, parts of the city flooded. It did clean most of the smoke and debris out of the air, though. You've got to look on the bright side.

The bright side was pretty easy for me to see. Because, thanks to Behemoth, I wouldn't have to drag my half-dead carcass out of bed and go to work anytime soon. Sadly, it was that simple. I wondered if I might qualify for some kind of hazard pay, or even radiation disability. When I passed out again, I dreamed I was taking selfies of my new, glow-in-the-dark face, and I kept having to do it over because I couldn't quite seem to capture the pretty colors of my triangular scales.

———

When I woke up, my neighbor Frida stood looking down at me. "Bernadette – are you still alive?" she asked.

This was an ironic question, considering that Frida, who actually did look like Frida Kahlo when she wasn't in Santa Muerta drag, had painted her face to look like a flowery Dia de los Muertos skull. The effect was quite gorgeous, but it looked as if Death herself had paid me a visit. Death carrying a container of chicken soup. Accompanied by a pet ferret on a leash.

"Maybe," I croaked. I sounded even worse than the last time I had tried to communicate, but I felt better. Not great, but there was a definite improvement; my head wasn't spinning and my stomach had settled. The chicken soup smelled good.

"Can you sit up?" asked Frida. "I'll fix you a bowl of this soup and then take Peachy for her walk."

"You really are a saint, Miss Muerta." I pushed myself into a sitting position and watched her putter in the kitchen. Frankenferret sat on the foot of the bed, ignoring and being ignored by the cats while she socialized with Peachy, her best walkies buddy. Frida took Peachy out every day while I was at work, and in return she had a key to my place and unlimited borrowing privileges to my extensive library.

Frida is an artist who specializes in skeleton/calavera images, though her repertoire is much broader, including murals for businesses and private homes and illustrations for children's books. She is a *successful* artist, which in this day and age means that she barely makes a living and has to rent a studio in our odd little building. But she is living La Vida Loca, and her soup is good. She dished up a bowl and put it on a tray, then waited with her hands on her hips until she was sure I could get it down and keep it there.

"I investigated the water tank on our roof," she informed me. "I worried there might be gunk in there because of all the smoke and debris from the explosions. You know what I found?"

I swallowed a spoonful of soup and guessed, "Gunk?"

"Nope. Pure rainwater. The cleanest water I've ever seen. I have a theory about why, but I'm going to do some investigation when I take these rascals on their walk."

"Okay."

Frida herded Peachy and Frankenferret out the door and I reached for the remote. No bombs were going off, so I thought I'd better turn on the TV and find out where things stood.

Once again, the Creature Crisis dominated all stations, but now it was the Cloud Squid they couldn't get enough of. I watched some very entertaining footage of her evading air force jets and attack helicopters. Every time they fired something at her she darted away, leading them on quite a merry chase. What was *not* so entertaining was the destruction they caused when their missiles hit what was left of the city. So they weren't making any more headway against the Cloud Squid than they had against Behemoth. And I learned something else from the news ticker scrolling across the bottom of the TV screen:

DANGER ZONE HAS BEEN CLOSED . . . NO ONE ALLOWED
IN OR OUT DUE TO RADIATION THREAT . . .

Closed. Yet I still had electricity, cable, water – all the important stuff. This would make life easier, as long as it lasted. Now that the Danger Zone was closed, I couldn't leave even if I wanted to, so that simplified things. But if they were isolating us, did that mean they might drop a bomb on us? I mean a *really big bomb?* As in nuclear? Since we were already kind of radioactive sometimes?

I tried to reassure myself that they would have the common sense to realize the radiation from nuclear bombs would travel, along with dust and debris that would cause a nuclear winter. I tried and tried. And tried.

I gave that up and surfed the channels on the TV, until I found a story that was unfolding in real time. The Cloud Squid and Behemoth had discovered each other.

"It looks as though we're about to see a battle *royale* between those two monsters." The reporter was trying to sound worried, but instead he sounded like this would be the coolest thing ever.

The Cloud Squid eased herself into the airspace over Behemoth, moving almost shyly. She hovered over him, her limbs opening like the petals of a flower. He gazed up, his mouth open, revealing rows of teeth that looked like stalactites (and stalagmites).

Damn, I thought. I didn't want to see them fight. They were both beautiful in their odd ways. But then something amazing happened.

The Cloud Squid began to flash with color. I remembered the idea of bioluminescence: cephalopods communicating with each other using light and color. It was a glorious sight. Behemoth seemed to think so too, from the way he gazed at her.

And then another amazing thing happened. Behemoth's hide began to flash with color too. And why would the giant lemur with the rocky skin have bioluminescence? Beats me (though he did come out of the sea).

They flashed colors at each other for maybe twenty minutes. Reporters chattered, baffled by the scene, yet feeling compelled to make inane comments anyway. They were still hoping for a fight, but that wasn't going to happen. The two creatures stopped flashing colors, and then the Cloud Squid drifted away with her rainstorm. Behemoth sat in the rubble he had been collecting and gazed at the news cameras, and if to say, *What do you think of that?*

Reporters dutifully started their rehash cycle. After another half hour of that, I turned off the set. I was about to drift off to sleep again when Frida came in with Peachy and Frankenferret.

"Our branch of the subway line is intact," said Frida. "And as far as I can tell, so are the cables that provide our internet and electricity. If you were willing to walk, you could get from here to the edge of the Danger Zone, but you'd have to cross some flooded parts up to your chest, maybe even up to your neck."

"Are you planning to leave?" I asked.

She looked surprised. "No way. They'd have to drag me out of here."

I felt happy to hear that. I doubted anyone else would bring me chicken soup. "So – did you see anyone down there?"

"Nope. Something better." She pulled her iPad out of her backpack and called up a picture file. "I found another creature."

The picture she showed me was murky. There was very little light in the tunnel, and the water level was high enough to hide a lot of stuff. But right in the middle of it all, a face grinned at me. "It looks like a friendly dog," I said. "A giant – happy – water dog."

"He acts like one, too," said Frida, calling up more pictures. "You can't see from these pics, but he's about the size of a school bus. It's hard to tell how many legs he has, because the number seems to change – see?" She selected a picture where he seemed to have five limbs, and then another where he might have only three, though in both of them he seemed to have a vaguely tail-shaped appendage. "I call him Mega Whatsis. Sometimes he seems to be solid, but other times he's kind of gelatinous. Here's a short video I took on my iPad."

My stomach stirred uneasily at the thought of looking at something that was *sometimes kind of gelatinous*, but when I watched Mega Whatsis in the video, I saw a creature who moved confidently, even joyously, both in and out of the water. "Cool!"

"He's smart," said Frida. "Watch this next part."

Frida's hand appeared in the bottom edge of the picture. She held a cookie out to Mega Whatsis. His colossal head filled the frame until all I could see was a giant nostril sniffing the cookie. He delicately maneuvered the cookie into his mouth, using his rubbery lips, then pulled back for a moment and contemplated the taste, his happy face shifting into thoughtful lines. After another minute, he produced the cookie intact and nudged it back into Frida's hand.

"It was dry," said Frida. "No creature slobber on it."

"Wow. Peachy couldn't do that."

Frida pulled up some more pictures on the laptop. "I expected the water down there to be full of waste and toxins. But it was more like natural creek water."

I remembered what she had said about our water tank. "You think Mega Whatsis cleaned *our* water? Is that what you went down to investigate?"

She nodded. "But I don't think it was him. He likes to stay underground. And *his* water has mud and silt in it." She closed the picture files and put her pad back into its case. "I'm not telling anyone about this. If those jerks go down there to shoot bombs at Mega Whatsis, they'll cut off our supply route. And he's a big sweetheart, there's no reason to hurt him."

I decided to keep the radiation argument to myself for the time being. After all, *I* didn't have a geiger counter.

Frida undid Peachy's leash and patted her head. "She's already gone potty. I'll see you tomorrow."

"Thanks," I said.

After Frida had left, I surfed the TV stations, looking for evidence that anyone besides Frida knew about Mega Whatsis. I didn't find any – now they were full of politicians arguing about whether or not any more money ought to be spent trying to kill Behemoth and the Cloud Squid. They couldn't agree on that any more than they could agree on other stuff, so I drifted off to sleep again.

———

Sometime later, I approached wakefulness like a swimmer floating toward a bright surface. I couldn't quite open my eyes, but I felt one of the cats lying across my stomach. I petted it, enjoying the velvety feel of its fur and its plump, warm body. I heard purring, but didn't feel it vibrating in the body I was stroking.

And the fur felt too short. *Way* too short. Almost like you would expect the fur of a seal to be. I opened my eyes and saw the fat thing stretched across me. It tapered to a narrow tip that was lazily curling to and fro like a cat's tail. It widened as it crossed my body and continued off the bed, on to the floor, and out the window, most of which was blocked by its bulk.

It was a tentacle.

Two things occurred to me then. The first was that you don't expect a tentacle to be warm and fuzzy. The second was that the Cloud Squid was probably going to drag me through the window and eat me.

I lay there frozen, waiting for the Squid to make her move. When she ate me, who would take care of Peachy? Who would take care of Sheba, and Buster, and Thugly, and Jingle Monster (four more pets than I had officially declared in my lease agreement)? Would she eat them too? Jingle was grooming the tentacle as if it were another cat. Peachy had rested her head on top of it, and she was snoring again.

I'm not sure how long I lay there arguing with myself. But it was the Cloud Squid who resolved the situation. She used the tip of her tentacle like a hand and gently moved Peachy's head on to the bed. Then she patted each of the cats and the dog, and slipped away out the window.

I stayed frozen for a few more moments, but I couldn't resist the urge to look out the window to see where she had gone. I poked my head into mild morning air and the clean smell of recent rain. I saw the tentacle slipping back over the top of the roof. But why was she on the roof?

The water tank, I thought. *She's the one who put the rainwater in there . . .*

After all, she moved around in a rain cloud. Maybe the rainwater was a pleasant side effect to one of her visitations. Whatever the reason, I didn't feel like I wanted to lie in bed anymore. And I was sick of trying to get information out of the stupid talking-heads TV. Instead, I headed for my computer.

I logged onto Facebook. I wasn't surprised to see that rumors about our creatures dominated the feed. What *did* surprise me was that there were still plenty of posts about politics, religion, status reports of how people's diets were going, and pictures of funny cats. Once I got used to that, I composed my own status report and posted it.

To everyone who lives outside the Danger Zone, I said. *Please stop bombing us. Don't send any more troops. And please don't let them drop an atomic bomb. Stop attacking, period! You're doing more damage than good.*

Once I had posted that, and tweeted an abbreviated version, I got an idea. I logged onto Google Blogger and created a blog called *Postcards From Monster Island*. It was just a template, but I thought maybe I could get Frida to send me some picture files. As I was plotting and scheming over all this, I realized something.

I felt better. I could breathe. I wasn't dizzy. My head didn't hurt. I was snarf-free. And my stomach was no longer my mortal enemy.

So I fed the beasties and took Peachy out for her business. Once we were outside, we even did a little walkies. But our world looked very different now.

A sort of mountain range had grown between my street and Behemoth's battle zone. It seemed to consist of a combination of ruined buildings and actual rock. Hardly anyone was on the street, which looked largely untouched by the destruction. The temperature was mild, flowers bloomed in pots and window boxes, cooking smells tempted my starved palate, and most of the odd little shops were open, though there could be very few customers these days. The air still had that freshly washed smell, and breezes blew along the new corridor that had been created by Behemoth's Makeshift Mountains.

Call me weird, but I thought it was an improvement. The noise of traffic was gone too, though I would still hear Behemoth moving big things around, with thuds and groans as stuff fell into place. He didn't trumpet any challenges, but grumbled to himself, as if thinking aloud. Peachy perked her ears, seeming to understand every word. She even replied a few times.

Once she felt satisfied in every possible way, we came back inside and walked through the empty halls of our building. I wondered how many residents had evacuated. There weren't that many of us in the first place, maybe around ten people. Our bottom floor had been converted into shops (or maybe the top floors had been converted into apartments, I wasn't sure). We saw our super just once a month, though he did a good job with repairs. And he had put up bulletin boards next to the elevators, so I saw the note:

MEETING AT HOUDINI'S, UNIT 3C, 1:00 P.M. PLEASE
COME AND DISCUSS THE CREATURE SITUATION

The numbering in our building was as eccentric as the residents, so
Apartment 3C was on the second floor. The door stood open – someone
had stuck a sign on it with an arrow pointing inside.

I pushed the door open further and saw Mr. Abé across the room.
He waved from a wingback chair, where he nursed a cup of coffee. As
I hesitated on the threshold, Houdini poked his tattooed head around
the corner from his kitchen. "Come on in," he said, with the voice of a
carney barker.

Houdini had a magician's name, but his true passion was the classic
sideshow. He honored that tradition with the tattoos that covered him
from head to toe, and he split his time between his circus memorabilia
shop and a variety of sword-swallowing, fire-eating, knife-juggling
gigs. His apartment was dominated by his personal collection, but
everything was lovingly displayed, not jumbled together.

Over his couch hung a giant poster featuring all of the lions and
tigers in the Barnum & Bailey Circus. Beneath the leaping cats sat Beetle,
whose specialty was mounting insects for collectors and museums, and
his partner Poe, who did professional skeleton articulation. Both held
plates with orange scones made by Oskar, who perched on one arm of
the couch, sipping a cup of mint tea. Oskar owned a bakery, and seeing
the scones reminded me that my stomach was back to normal.

The gathering was completed by Frida, who fussed at the computer
with her occasional boyfriend, Gee, who was a buyer for the Museum
of Weird Stuff.

"So . . . " I took account of my neighbors. "We're the ones who
stayed. Somehow, that doesn't surprise me."

Oskar sipped his tea. "Running seemed like a hysterical reaction,"
he said. "Like lemmings jumping off a cliff."

"Yes," agreed Mr. Abé. "I've lived through much worse conflicts.

And I can tell you from personal experience that refugee camps are not necessarily better than war zones."

If you were wondering why two normal guys like Mr. Abé and Oskar would be friends with a tattooed knife juggler, a skull-faced artist, the Bug Guy, the Skeleton Guy, Mr. Weird Stuff, and Crazy Cat/Library Girl, I can only say that Mr. Abé's remark about refugee camps might explain why he's willing to look past the surface and put up with our eccentricities. And as for Oskar, baker *par excellence*, he's a very nice fellow with a flaw that was well tolerated in Germany, but is decidedly odd in the U.S. Oskar looks like Uncle Fester from *The Addams Family*. He smiles like him, too.

Houdini snagged a chair for me and for himself. "So here's why I called the meeting." His tone was so commanding, even Frida and Gee stopped surfing. "For all intents and purposes, we are now in the Danger Zone. We are stuck here, and we're the ones getting hurt by the bombs and stuff. We have to start telling the outside world what we want."

"Won't they just ignore us?" asked Beetle, around a bit of scone.

"Maybe not," I said. "We're what passes for experts now."

Mr. Abé raised an eyebrow. "Interesting. How did we pull that off?"

But Poe was nodding enthusiastically. "No, we are! I've been tweeting about it. I got the president's office to talk to me – can you believe it?"

"Good." Houdini waved a hand at Poe as if he were one of his side show performers, and he wanted everyone to step right up. "Because the biggest problem we've got is not the creatures. It's the idiots in Congress who want to drop an A-bomb on us. The only thing we've got going for us is that the president is commander in chief, and he thinks it won't work."

"But what will he think when he finds out we've got *three* creatures now?" I worried.

"There are more than three," said Gee. "I think there may be as many as seven in our city alone. *So far*. Look at the pictures we took."

Frida tapped the screen to show us action shots. "They're all doing stuff, but none of them are attacking people. See? There are people in all of these shots – some of them taking pics like we were doing, so it won't be long until the outside world finds out."

"Ah, but *what* are the creatures doing, Miss Muerta? That's what we need to prove."

Gee pushed a lock of his blue hair out of his face. "All we have is theories about most of them right now – except for Behemoth. Frida thinks he's an artist."

That remark provoked a conspicuous silence. But Frida was undaunted. "You notice he's been piling debris up? Well, he's fusing it together in particular ways. Look . . . " She found the video she wanted and hit play. We watched Behemoth shove debris into piles, then look at it critically. He rearranged things a bit, then pondered it again. When he felt satisfied, he stretched out on the pile and his underside began to glow.

When he stepped away from it, the result was an oddly pleasing amalgam of cityscape and mountain range. I had never seen anything quite like it.

"He's an artist," said Frida, with the reverence most people reserve for guys like Michelangelo.

"And I think that's why radiation levels keep spiking and then falling off. That's how he's melting stuff together."

"All well and good," Oskar said. "But that will only make people angry when we tell them. They think Behemoth is a monster, like from the movies. They see that he's giant, he waded ashore and destroyed the city. We know the military did most of that, but that will leave egg on the faces of the politicians and the generals. They will despise us if we point that out."

I heard him, but something that was unfolding on Frida's screen snared my attention. "Hey – is that footage you guys took?"

"No," said Gee. "That's from YouTube; someone took it with their cell phone the night Behemoth came ashore."

Behemoth was walking through the city, away from planes that shot missiles at him. An elevated train line stretched across his path; the train was stranded, and full of people. It looked like Behemoth was going to walk right into them, so people were screaming, trying to climb out windows. Then Behemoth paused, pivoted just as another missile was fired at him, and the bridge started to collapse.

"Wait a minute," I said. "Did you see that? Can you go back and play it again?"

He replayed the segment, then froze it at the crucial moment.

"Wow," said Frida. "Did I just see that?"

We watched the segment again.

"We've got to blitz social media with this clip," said Frida. "I've seen the early part of the footage, but they keep cutting out the end. A lot of people probably haven't seen the whole thing!"

"And there's something else we have to do," I said. "If we want to make them believe that we're experts, and they should listen to us, we need to work on our bona fides."

"But how?" wondered Houdini.

I pointed to the image on the screen. "We need to make contact with Behemoth."

———

Our trip into the Makeshift Mountains made me wonder if Behemoth and the other creatures were having some positive effect on us after all. It was a challenging climb (though a few parts of Behemoth's construct still had functioning elevators), yet I was able to troop alongside the others, despite the fact that I had just been very sick. We let Frida and Gee lead the way, since they were the youngest, and since they had also made several forays into those mountains.

For over two hours we wormed our way through mountain passages, walked single file along ridges, climbed in and out of shattered windows and across rooftops and balconies. We could hear Behemoth doing his work. We knew we were close.

"My friends," Oskar warned, "we hope Behemoth will not hurt us, but what if we're wrong? What if all those bombs and grenades have taught him to hate us?"

I didn't have an answer to that, and by then I realized I wasn't nearly as scared as I should have been. I just wanted to find Behemoth, I wasn't even thinking about *how* we should contact him. But we had to do it if we wanted a future. We were bound together with him, for better or worse.

We climbed several rows of steps, some from old structures and some newly formed, until we reached a lookout point. As we made our way around an outcrop on the pinnacle, we came face-to-face with Behemoth. He stood in the valley on the other side of the peak, not more than one hundred yards away from us – a distance he could have crossed in just a few steps. His head was almost level with us.

Those great, golden eyes rolled in our direction and focused on us.

"Oops," I said.

Yet I didn't turn to run back down the path. None of us did. And it wasn't just because we couldn't have gotten away. Those eyes saw us, and we stared back at them, but it wasn't an exchange between predator and prey. We, the Oddballs of the City, recognized Behemoth, the Oddball of the World.

We had seen it in that footage when he bumped into the elevated train. The cars began to topple from the track. Behemoth reached out and grabbed the train as it was going down. Once he had it settled more or less on *terra firma*, he shielded the people from the missiles until they could get out and flee the scene. One guy with a cell phone had caught that moment, and no one said anything about it. But we saw it. And now we were looking him right in his gigantic eyes.

Behemoth opened his mouth and emitted that cry we had heard so often in the last few days. There was no mistaking what he meant by it. I think he tempered it for us, it was gentler. It was still full of loneliness. But a new note had entered that symphony. To me, it sounded like hope.

"What should we do?" wondered Frida.

Without discussing it, we all waved at Behemoth. His ears perked.

His pupils expanded, as if he were drinking in the sight. He sighed, and settled down to contemplate us further.

We sat down and ate the lunch Oskar and Houdini had packed for us, where Behemoth could see us. When we had finished, Oskar said, "I can sit with him for a few hours. You guys go home and rest up."

"I'll spell you after that," offered Frida.

———————

And so it went. For the next few days, one of us was always where Behemoth could see us. Once we had established that habit with him, more of the creatures began to come into the open. We waved at them. Cloud Squid waved back with all her tentacles. Mega Whatsis grinned and wagged his vaguely tail-shaped appendage.

But that's not all we were doing. We started blitzing social media with our posts and pictures.

"Stop attacking!" we pleaded. "We've reached an accord with the creatures. We can manage them."

When outraged people demanded to know just where they were going to rebuild the centers of commerce and culture that had once dominated our city, we pointed out that it would be a hundred times more expensive to rebuild that stuff than it would be to build new centers of commerce somewhere else. In response, we got a lot of flack from trolls. "Do the math!" we pleaded.

Just when we thought no one was listening, the trolling stopped. And the talking heads on TV stopped speculating whether more marines were going to jump out of planes so they could bounce off Behemoth's Teflon hide. Instead, the government started to drop emergency supplies for us along the Neutral Zone. And that's when I got an email from the president.

We'll make sure you have electricity and water, he promised. *We'll keep the food and medicine coming, too. Your debts have been settled, and you won't be paying rent anymore. In return, all that we ask is that you keep managing the creatures. Keep them peaceful. Can you do that?*

Yes, I replied, though I felt a little guilty about claiming credit for what seemed more like good luck.

On the other hand, it might be something more than that. It might be the fact that even when the city seemed to be coming down around us, we didn't want to leave. The more people outside lost hope, the more we gained it. They wanted to throw bombs at Behemoth, we wanted to sit down and have lunch with him. That counted for something.

So – you remember that footage of all the people pouring out of the city the day Behemoth came ashore? Now a lot of people want to come back. Not to live – to see the creatures. So we started Danger Zone Tours. We take selected visitors to multiple stops, including the shops of Mr. Abé, Houdini, and Gee, to Oskar's bakery and Frida's gallery, Beetle's exhibit and Poe's museum, and to lots of other odd places that have sprung up. We've all got some extra cash on the side now.

We take them to see the creatures, too. Ten of them have come out into the open, so far. Mega Whatsis is the usual favorite (though he still doesn't like cookies).

The last stop on the tour is a spot where people can see Behemoth. When he looks our way, we all wave. People love that. It's the kind of reverence you would expect to see for whales breaking the surface next to a Greenpeace boat. When our visitors leave us, they talk about how glad they are the creatures showed up to teach us the error of our ways, that we were poisoning our world.

I agree that Nature has a reason for everything it does. If people who live outside of Monster Island think the creatures appeared because we abused the Earth, I won't try to tell them otherwise. Maybe they'll behave more responsibly. But I think there's another reason.

Last night, I went to sit with Behemoth, and the two of us gazed at the stars. We've done that a lot, lately. Now that the Danger Zone is dark at night, we can see the Milky Way. Behemoth usually ponders the sky with a combination of wonder and inquiry, but last night was different. Last night, he watched with a vigilance that put me on edge.

When Oskar came to spell me at midnight, I didn't leave. The two of us studied the heavens alongside Behemoth.

Then one of the stars glowed brighter. It glowed so bright, I realized it wasn't a star. It moved closer; I could see other lights on it. Behemoth stood to his full height, a low rumble sounding deep within his chest. The lights began to flash at him in patterns.

Behemoth's eyes glowed red, his brows clashed together like thunderclouds, and he fixed that bright light in the sky with his vigilant glare, opened his mouth, and sucked a colossal lungful of air for one of his fog-horn blasts.

This time his cry had no trace of loneliness in it. I wouldn't even call it a cry. This was a full-throated roar, so loud the farthest stars must have heard it. This was the sound of challenge, the promise of doom to anyone who would threaten our world.

The light flashed white-hot, then streaked across the sky and away from Earth.

"Was that what I think it was?" Oskar asked, warily.

"Yep," I agreed. "A UFO. I think Behemoth scared it away."

The creatures aren't here to destroy us. They're not even here to rebuke us for our destructive ways. They're here to defend us.

"The Creature War isn't over," I told Oskar. "This is the war that is yet to be fought."

Oskar settled down for his vigil. "Better tell the others what you saw."

I climbed back down through the Makeshift Mountains and walked up my street in our remade city, past all the odd shops, new and old, that defined the true character of the Danger Zone, until I arrived home to tend my beasties and compose a letter to the president.

One Night On Tidal Rig #13
Tessa Kum

———

With the moon long gone, the night ocean was very, very dark.

Against an overcast sky, empty of stars, the lights of the tower room appeared to float in the darkness. It should have been dwarfed by the beacon light fixed above it, but these nights the beacon was rarely lit. There wasn't enough oil to keep it from squeaking, and Thirteen was fond of her sleep.

Not that sleep was easy to come by on a tidal rig.

It was a great hulking mess of machinery, towering out of the water like some bad-tempered god, making toy ships out of the massive cargo freighters that passed it by. Calling it ugly didn't do it justice. Pipes thicker than subways tangled themselves chaotically and cogs with teeth a storey high spun with only metres to spare. Nestled deep amid the pistons in the heart of the rig lay an arcane generator, one of the last of its kind. Drawing on mysterious and not entirely understood energies, it drove the engines that laboured endlessly to turn the wings. A regular procession of sparks and power arcs lit up the rig's bowels in enchanted colours. Usually her iron behemoth shuddered and roared as it worked. The pop and sizzle echoed clearly; this close to the turning of the tide it was relatively quiet. The engines were winding down and the wings merely rolling with the powerful current they'd created.

Just as long as the number five valve didn't start venting at the wrong time, again, Thirteen paid the workings of the rig no heed.

Globes thirty through to sixty-seven along the ladder were blown, shattered or simply not there. In this unlit stretch of the ladder, she paused to scrub fiercely at an itch on her nose. She shifted her tool belt, making a note to refill her oil canister. It took a moment of groping about before she found the rung again. Three supply drops ago she'd applied for a helmet light, which had failed to show up. If she hadn't climbed this ladder who knows how many times a day, half the time in starless darkness, she might have found it daunting.

"Rusty lump of crap," she muttered out of habit, and continued climbing. The dim light of the tower room glowed above her, where she would be warm, away from the wind, and with a nice big plate of sausages and mash. Only another hour, and then she could turn the tide, and go to sleep.

Thank the Ministry of Moon Loss Rehabilitation for legislating that the tide be high twice a day. She never had more than five hours of sleep in one hit, and then only if she were lucky.

Ten rungs from the top she hesitated, and then cursed, scrambling up the last part. Warm air blasted her numb face when she jerked the door open. She snatched up the ringing phone.

"Thirteen here."

White noise filled her ear. There might have been some garbled words in the hiss.

"Can't make you out, say again?"

Garble, warble, hiss.

She hung up.

"The greatest thing about manning the oldest tidal rig on the continent is that nothing ever sodding well works."

The com speaker in the wall crackled. "What?" Fourteen, manning the next rig up the coast, had a voice full of a gravel that came from a lifetime of yelling, grumbling, swearing, and generally being a grumpy old man. She loved him dearly. Not that she'd ever say it.

"It's not even my fault." She flopped down in her frayed armchair. "No matter how many times I tighten the valve, or clean the joints, or file a report. Nothing. Ever. Works."

There was a brief pause before Fourteen answered. "What the hell are you talking about?"

She sat on her hands to warm them. "My phone, actually."

"Bloody hell, Thirt," Fourteen grumbled, "We were talking about the footy."

"Well, no wonder I wasn't listening."

Fourteen sighed.

The tower room was dingy at best. The engineers who had designed and put it together hadn't gone to any effort to make it a nice place to live. The walls were iron sheets, the rivets holding them together bleeding rust down to the floor. The 360-degree windows were spotted and covered in salt scum and bird droppings. Cracks ran down most, and a couple were boarded up with soggy cardboard.

She pressed her nose against the closest window, seeking out the green and red flashing light on the northern horizon.

"Thirteen—"

"Yeah, I know, I'm a dork, now wave back." She wiggled her fingers at the light. The newer rigs had video and audio connections to the net, not to mention heating and carpet. There wasn't much that Thirteen could do to contact the outside world besides wave. She'd tried smoke signals once, out of boredom.

"What's all this chatter?" a third voice roared. The Coast Master. All belligerence and bile, that voice. Thirteen ducked at the whip-crack in his tone.

"Just passing time, sir," Fourteen said.

"Do it without clogging up the coastline channel. Where the devil is Sixteen?"

Although there was no one for miles who could see her, Thirteen straightened her back and sat to attention. "Sleeping, sir."

"What?" the speaker distorted. "The tide turns in less than an hour!"

"I believe she has her alarm set, sir," Fourteen said, acquiescent.

There was a distinct lack of input from any of the other riggers along the coast. *Cowards*, she thought at them. Quietly, she retrieved a bottle from the small fridge at her side.

"I need her now. Why isn't she answering her phone?"

"Begging your pardon, sir," Thirteen twisted the bottle cap in her hands, "but her phone broke ages ago."

"Why wasn't I notified?"

"I believe you were. Sir."

Static filled the channel as the Coast Master paused. "She's getting visitors in fifteen minutes. Some marine scientists making a lot of noise about this here hermit crab migration. They want to see it up close."

"What crab migration?"

"Don't any of you riggers watch the news?" – Thirteen refrained from pointing out she couldn't even if she wanted to – "Massive migration going all the way up the coast. Minister of Tourism is having a fit. All the beaches are closed."

"But if they're on the beaches, why does anyone need to come out here?" Fourteen sounded bemused.

"The Sea Walls are picking up multiple moving signals. Big ones. Not serpents. The pictures from the subs aren't clear, but they think they're old crabs joining in or some shit. They'll cruise past you guys within the hour."

A new voice piped up. "How big are we talking, sir?" Wheedling, needy, nasal: Nine. Thirteen wasn't fond of him.

"Big enough, Nine. Don't you worry, we've got the Navy on standby at Port Puck."

"The Navy? What? Do we need them? And Port Puck is two hours away!"

Thirteen ignored Nine's rising panic, frowning as she stared at nothing. "Sir," she interjected, "there hasn't been a crab migration since the moon closed and the Salt Fae died."

"So? Who cares? They're on the move. Now listen up, I have four marks going by Sixteen, three coming your way Thirteen, and Ten and Eleven might get a look in as well. Smaller marks going through Six and Seven. You got everything ready, Thirteen?"

She blinked. "What?"

There was muffled mumbling, as though the Coast Master had his hand over the mic, before he spoke again. "What the hell is wrong with your phone, Thirteen?"

"Nothing," she said, not trying to hide the defensive tone in her voice. "It's old, like everything else, and doesn't work so well with the wind up and cloud cover. Sir. If I had one of those new ones—"

"You're getting a scientist, too."

"Wh—"

"Don't even start. You treat the geek with respect, make sure he has what he needs, and if I get even a whiff that you're thinking about being a prick, you won't be getting the helmet light in your next drop."

"I wasn't expecting it anyway," she grumbled.

"At this point we don't know if they're likely to pose a threat, but keep your coms on. If you need to know anything else, you'll be told. Over and out."

Silence over the channel. Thirteen stared at the scotch in her lap. There was only a couple of fingers left, so she tossed it back, screwing up her face as it burned a trail to her gut.

Then she let out a long and vicious stream of the most shocking words she knew.

"Not happy?"

"No," she said tightly to Fourteen, "Not happy."

As conversation between the other riggers slowly grew on the channel, Thirteen sagged in her chair. Her reflection glared back at her in a singularly unattractive way.

Apart from the voices of the others, she spent every day alone. Even for Fourteen, who'd been on the next rig since before she'd arrived, she couldn't put a face to his voice.

At first it was hard, but everyone adapted. She might not like it, but it was *her* solitude, and she didn't like anyone breaking it without her permission. Not to mention she hadn't had the chance to request items from the continent. Such as a new bottle of scotch.

Eight, appearing now that the Coast Master was gone, sniffed. "How much damage can a crab do?" Aristocratic accent, droll, too civilized to be a rigger.

"Thought you were jerking off, Eight," Thirteen jibed, although her heart wasn't really in it.

"*Sleeping!* For crying out loud, I was *sleeping!*"

"Uh huh," Nine snickered.

"And you're a vestal virgin. What do they think these crabs can do, in real terms? Tidal rigs aren't exactly delicate machines. The worst I can see happening is one getting caught in a wing. Hardly worth the effort."

"You have a point there," Fourteen mused. "Exactly how does anyone expect to learn anything out on our rigs? It's not like we'll be able to see anything, and with the tide turning the currents will play chaos with any fancy toys they toss in."

"Hey, guys," Thirteen fished a not-quite-finished dog end from a bristling ash tray, "my history is a bit sketchy, but it was the Salt Fae who herded the hermit crabs, right?" She discarded the butt again, and pulled out a fresh smoke.

"Yeah, I think so. Why?"

"Doesn't Fifteen have net access?" she asked, patting her pockets. Her matches were missing.

"Not anymore, her dish broke. Why, Thirt?"

"Well, given that the crabs only migrated when the Salt Fae herded them, and since the faeries closed the moon the Salt Fae are mostly dead—"

"All dead."

"—shut up! So why are the crabs migrating?"

"Thirteen, just between friends, you need to stop with the Salt Fae shit," Nine snipped.

As she struggled to think of something nasty to say, Nine added, "All that crap about you being part Salt Fae and all, getting very old I must say."

"But I am!" It sounded petulant, but she wouldn't back down. "My great-great-great-great grandmother was Salt Fae!"

"That makes you . . . " Fourteen paused, "One thirty-twoth Salt Fae?"

"More like one sixty-fourth," Nine corrected.

"*Kasha ni su fakka!*"

A beat, then a bemused Fourteen. "What?"

"I said you're both arseholes! In Salt Fae-ese!"

Fourteen sighed. "C'mon, Thirt, don't shoot the messenger."

"It's not like you have gills," Nine said.

She didn't say anything.

"*Do* you have gills?"

Pouting, she shook her head. "No."

"Ha!" Nine said smugly. "See? They don't say the Salt Fae are extinct for nothing."

Thirteen bared her teeth at the speakers.

"Don't feel bad, Thirt," Fourteen said, a smile in his voice. "We love you all the same."

"Thank you. You're still arseholes." She glanced out the window, and sighed. The lights of a chopper drew near. "I'm going to go and not be a prick to the geek." So much for sausages and mash. Ah! Matches.

"Make it quick, girl, nearly time to turn."

"Yeah, yeah. I can make it to the beacon and back before you even start, old man," she mumbled around the cigarette.

Fourteen just laughed.

The curve of her hand glowed as she lit and inhaled. Cold drafts slipped under the door, breathing through her thick trousers. She grabbed her beanie and jammed it on her head.

The wind tugged her hair as she stepped onto the catwalk. She squinted against it and hastily zipped up her coat. When she swung out onto the ladder her nose was already running. Unseen in the darkness below, the waves thundered against the rig as they had for more than a century. It was, Thirteen reflected, probably a good thing that the rig hadn't had a structural survey in more than a decade. There was probably, no, definitely all sorts of wear and tear down there that would mean the Ministry would have to spend money fixing it. Which really meant shutting Tidal Rig #13 down and loading her territory onto #12 and #14.

Hell no, this rig would be standing long after the new shiny ones had fallen to scrap.

The roosting seagulls murmured and waddled out of her way when she mounted the top platform. Her pace was slow; she could barely see, and didn't want to step on any of them. Dumb birds, she thought affectionately, and exhaled away from them.

The chopper – sleek, streamlined, top of the line – circled above, spotlight wavering about uncertainly. It caught her full in the face and she cursed, waving it away.

"Attention Tidal Rig #13. Turn on your beacon, repeat, turn on your beacon."

The birds fled screeching from the blare of the loudspeaker. Thirteen waited till the angry storm of feathers around her subsided before feeling her way towards the beacon station. Her night vision was shot. She ran her hand across a rusting surface till she found the handle. A couple of shoulder-wrenching yanks and it screamed open. Refill the oil pot, right. The light inside failed to come on.

"Tidal Rig #13, turn on your beacon, repeat—"

"I heard you the first time, sheesh."

By light of the chopper she flipped the switches, and as an afterthought slapped the com channel on. Familiar voices burbled in the wash of noise. When the tower began to hum beneath her feet, she straightened and pushed the door shut. After a last long drag on her cigarette she flicked the butt into the wind.

"Tidal Rig #13—"

"Sweet friggin' . . . . it takes a while to warm up, alright!" Exasperation made her gestures sharp. The pilot didn't speak again.

Spider legs uncurled from the chopper's belly, the hinges snapping open with scissor-like snicks. Thirteen raised her eyebrows. Only military choppers were licensed to use spider legs, the very useful toy that they were. The mechanical arms snaked down and clamped the catwalk around the beacon, forming a temporary dome frame over Thirteen's head and anchoring the chopper safely. She held her breath, face averted, as the downdraft was full of fumes, too strong for someone used to clean sea air. The floor rattled with the equipment being unloaded. When the direction of buffeting changed, she looked up. The chopper was retreating into the darkness, spider legs curling away.

Amid the sudden mound of boxes atop her rig hunkered a figure in a much cleaner coat than hers. He scurried over, and in the growing light Thirteen made out a clean face, cheek bones to cut diamonds on, a neat hair cut, glasses, and a smile that had to be surgically perfected.

"Hello, my name is Lloyd Doyer. I'm with the Coastline Rehabilitation Organization. They sent me out here in such a rush, I was never told your name."

His was a voice that had been raised on airconditioning and assumed it would be heard without being raised. Prior to this, she'd never found the nerdy librarian look particularly attractive, but it had been a long time since she'd seen another human being, let alone a good-looking one.

It had also been a long time since she'd talked face-to-face, and to her horror she realized he could see her quite blatantly checking him out.

"Thirteen," she said, and shook his hand quickly, too aware of the sweat and rust and grease coating her palms.

He gave her an adorable quizzical look. "I'm sorry, I thought that this was the thirteenth—"

"It is. The numbers tend to stick, Mr Doyer."

"Call me Lloyd, please. I must apologize for arriving with such short notice. Unfortunately we didn't detect these larger crabs till very late. My uncle was a tidal rigger, and he was very clear about the etiquette of visiting a rig."

"Really? What generation rig did he have?"

Doyer shrugged, "I really don't know, but it was along the northeast coast of Nova Mentus." He unslung his bag and fished around in it. "He always said to come bearing gifts. I didn't get much time to shop before they flew me out, but I did grab this."

Thirteen laughed, covering her mouth to hide her delighted grin.

"Is that scotch single malt? Yes? Okay, we like you, you can stay." He's pretty! He comes bearing presents! Oh, she liked him a lot.

"I'm glad it's appreciated," he said, seeming much more relaxed. "So, this is the antiquated tidal rig #13." He looked about the platform, taking in the rickety grid underfoot, the salt- and rust-encrusted beacon mounded high with leavings from the birds, and the single cannon mounted facing the ocean. None of it inspired awe in his expression.

"Um, where do I attach myself?"

Thirteen stared at him blankly before noticing the safety harness strapped around his waist, somewhat lost in his bulky coat.

"'Antiquated' is a fancy word for 'old', and in this particular case, 'old' means piece of junk built before the words 'safety' and 'regulations' met and shook hands." At the dismayed look on his face she chuckled. "It's not that bad. Look, the wind is coming from the west tonight. Just stay away from the east side of the platform and you'll be fine. It isn't even blowing that hard."

He gave her another doubtful look.

"Really. It took a class 3 gale to blow the last rigger off. Stop looking like that. You'll be fine. I'll be back when I'm done."

"Wait!" Doyer clutched her arm. "You're going? Where? Why?"

She gave his hand a comforting pat. "The tide doesn't turn by itself." This close he smelt of aftershave, curry, fuel and earth. Rare and exotic scents. A step back and they disappeared, clearing her mind.

"Now? Oh."

She paused with one foot on the ladder. He was afraid of heights. Typical. "Don't worry if the place starts shaking like a jackhammer. It's always quiet like this, just before a turning."

"This is quiet?"

Her top lip peeled back and she dropped out of sight swiftly. Scotch, yes, pretty, yes; however, it was one thing for her, whose life rotated around this clunky iron behemoth, to bad mouth it, and another thing entirely for him to. Geek. Nerd. Toff.

When she passed the tower room she could hear the com buzzing with talk. The ladder shook and rattled with every step. The metal coils and angles of the rig rose up around her, and even at the end of the cycle the throb and crunch of the engine drowned out the sound of the ocean. The rig never truly slept.

Far below she could make out the dim light of the switch room, a dirty yellow smear in the darkness.

This far down the ladder vibrated constantly. By the time her feet touched the bottom her palms were numb. She slapped on the com and clapped her hands to drive some feeling into them. Sixteen's voice came on loud, clear and distinctly pissed off. The com on the beacon was still turned on; drat. Hopefully Doyer wouldn't be able to hear it over everything else he wasn't used to. Thirteen elected to remain silent until Sixteen had finished her rant, and flicked the safety systems off. Uninvited guests were not the best way to wake up.

"Buck up," Thirteen said, when Sixteen's steam seemed low, "They might be pretty." She bit down on "too" before it left her mouth.

"Oberon's arse, they're here to look at *crabs*, Thirteen, doesn't that say something?"

There was a rare moment of silence on the channel as all contemplated the many quips that sentence prompted.

"Sod it," Sixteen spat. "I'm starting the count. All ready?"

A chorus of affirmations.

"Three . . . two . . . one . . . Turn!"

Thirteen grunted as she put her shoulder against the lever. With a screech it clunked into place. A series of clangs and thunks followed, moving deeper into the engines. A single massive shudder shook the entire structure. Thirteen sucked her cheek in, and watched the machinery around her.

The slow roll of gears was barely perceptible at first, and she squinted until she was convinced they were turning. A sudden snake of energy discharge slithered up the pipes. The platform began to shiver with the strain of the engine turning the wings. Pushing an ocean around was not easy business.

"Hold together just a little longer." She patted the wall beside her. "Mr Doyer," she raised her voice, "can you hear me?"

"Yes, Miss, uh, Thirteen."

"What, you left your guest all alone? For shame, Thirt!"

"Shut up, Nine. Doyer, I'm on my way back up. Any idea when this crab of yours is going to appear?"

"Setting up the tracking now."

The rig groaned and pinged as she flipped the intercom off and began the long climb up the ladder.

She frowned as she ascended, staring up at the sky. The beacon wasn't turning, only pointed towards land. Bloody useless. Why on earth was it blue – oh, yes. The Blue Moon Festival two weeks previous.

The wind grabbed her as she rose out of the shelter of the rig, and she halted to clutch at her beanie. Perhaps it was the remnants of chopper fuel, but something smelt off. Rank. She struggled to brush her hair out of her face, anywhere that would stop it tickling her nose. A snatch of garbled sound made her tilt her head. After a moment she resumed her climb with haste. As she drew towards the tower room, her mouth tightened. The phone, again. Some people never learned. She ground her teeth, scrambled off the ladder, wrenched the door open, and lunged for the phone.

"Thirteen here."

"Where the fucking faeries have you been?"

She flinched away from the Coast Master's bellow, half imagining spit in her ear. "Turning the tide, sir," she said, thinking that should have been obvious.

"You h . . . inc . . . —d me . . . oming—"

"You're breaking up, sir."

A savage burst of distortion blared in her ear, and although most of his words were eaten by interference, she knew she heard him utter "serpent cannon".

"Say again, or get on the coast ch—"

Without missing a beat the com speakers roared. "I said you have incoming. The biggest mark on the screen altered course to get around a rock outcrop and is now heading straight for you. The Navy have scrambled two combat moths, but they won't arrive for another half hour—"

"Half an hour?"

"Till then you're on your own. Get the cannon loaded. I don't want this thing getting tangled in the rig. The gods know how many parts we don't manufacture any more. Move it!"

"Tangled? How big is this thing? I mean, is it seriously going to be big enough for me to see?"

"I said move it, rigger!"

Thirteen growled at the Coast Master. His orders unsettled her more than she liked to admit. Only twice in her time on the tidal rig had she needed to use the serpent cannon, and she considered herself lucky to have only had reason two times. It was more than a little terrifying to go up against a serpent, a creature large enough to deal some real damage to a tidal rig. In the migration years the coastline was constantly patrolled by Navy ships, for the rigs' protection. At least the newer rigs had defences more adequate than a single unautomated cannon.

She unlocked the ammunition cabinet. The shells inside were designed specifically for use against serpents. They had so many enchantments of death, bad luck, pestilence, and destruction laid on them that the cupboard itself had to be enchanted as well, to keep it from disintegrating. The amount of arcane energy saturated into it all would fetch a disgustingly high price on the black market, what with enchantments becoming increasingly rare since the moon closed. She pulled out an iron case, flipped it open to check it was full, then shouldered it. The straps dug deep.

Outside was nothing but darkness. She strained until her eyes ached as she scaled the ladder, but the night revealed nothing, least of all giant crabs.

Something squawked when she stepped onto the landing. Bloody birds. She waded around the beacon.

The gods knew what Doyer had set up. Cameras, sensors, expensive-looking machines that went "ping!" when he touched them, and something that looked like radar.

"Can you see it?"

He whirled around, flashing a pocket torch in her eyes. "Oh! Sorry, you startled me. What did you say?"

Thirteen pointed her chin, blinking her dazzled eyes. "Tracking. Can you see it?"

Doyer shook his head. "No, something from the rig is interfering. The vibrations, maybe the arcane energy, I don't know. All I get is a big blurry blob. I thought the tidal rigs had shock absorbers built in."

"The second generation, yes."

"How do you sleep? I mean—" he blushed, "What with all the noise and bouncing. Er."

Thirteen raised an amused eyebrow. "You get used to it." Carefully she sank to her knees and pulled the ammunition case from her shoulders. Everything felt a lot lighter without it. "Did you hear the Coast Master over the com?" she said, crawling over to his side.

"No, sorry. It got so loud up here, I couldn't make anything out."

The tracking was as useless as he said. Ghost images flickered around the edges. "Apparently it's coming right for us. I'm going to turn on the beacon. He didn't say if we'd be able to see it, but given he told me to load up the serpent cannon . . ." she trailed off and shrugged. The Coast Master was probably over-reacting. "What are you trying to get anyway?"

"Anything. Everything! This is a phenomenon unheard of since the closing of the moon. There have been some claims of smaller migrations, but to have the elder crabs from off the continental shelf join in, why, it's just amazing. Imagine what we could discover! This is going to be one of the most exciting nights of my life."

Thirteen ducked her head and slunk over to the beacon station. His fervour was cute, but she had to wonder about anyone who thought an exciting night involved crabs. Marine type crabs, anyway. The control panel grudgingly opened.

"But this isn't just about crabs, is it?" She stabbed the rotation button. It did nothing. Cursing, she began spinning the winch furiously. "Hermit crabs don't get together of their own accord. That's why they're called 'hermit' crabs."

The beacon began to turn with a squeal. The blue light lit up the seething waters, showing up little flashes of silver as fish darted about. It turned slowly.

"Well, it is highly irregular—" Doyer, Thirteen decided, would be perfect to play poker with. He had no bluffing skills.

"I'm part Salt Fae, you know." The com chattered quietly, something about growing up in a trailer park, and she hit hard enough to make some nasty feedback. "My great-great-great-great grandmother lived in the reserves."

"One sixty-fourth?" he snorted laughter, which became a choke with the dead stare she levelled at him. "Well, I mean, you know, that's not, that's really not a lot. Um."

With pursed lips Thirteen turned back to the winch. If she ever met someone whose first reaction wasn't to laugh at her heritage, she'd marry them.

"I'm sorry, I didn't mean to offend you." His coat rustled as he moved. "It's just that I've never come across anyone who was actually proud of having faery blood."

Thirteen couldn't remember the last time anyone had apologized for getting her back up. "When you grow up in a caravan with an alcoholic mother and clinically depressed father, pretending you're a special faery princess has its appeal." Honesty made her tone raw.

"Oh," Doyer said, taken aback. He was quiet for a moment. "Do you know much of the history of the Salt Fae?"

"I know they shepherded the crab migrations, and I know that's the real reason you're here."

This time his silence was heavy with tension. "I see," he said. His voice was a closed book, and she could read nothing in it.

The beacon was nearly turned now, and her arm muscles were tiring. "Can you see anything yet?"

His coat rustled again, and there was a strangled gurgling noise.

"Doyer?"

She turned.

It was bigger than she expected.

Crabs had always been cute little scuttling things with googly eyes, irritating but harmless pinchers, and great-tasting with a bit of ginger and lemongrass.

She'd never realized how hideous they really were.

It towered above them; her thoughts stuttered at that. It dwarfed her rig, her enormous tidal rig, which she had always likened to a beast risen from the murky depths. Now she faced the real thing. The bloat of its shell was mottled brown. Barnacles and growths ruptured its surface like rancid pustules. Seaweed of all sorts hung from it in fat greasy clumps.

Something even bigger than the crab had left that shell behind.

Thirteen let out a little squeak.

The com crackled. "Thirteen, you okay?"

Like normal hermit crabs, its legs clustered to the front, bony, covered in short red bristles, and stiff and sharply segmented. It was too big for her to comprehend; she couldn't fit it all inside her head. So many legs! One rose, slow and ponderous, and reached forward. The water surged as it plunged down. Thirteen thought she felt the rig tremble, and couldn't help imagining that she could hear the terrible shell, dragging along the sea bed.

"Doyer?" she said softly, as if afraid speaking would attract the monster's attention. The scientist was frozen, a conflict of horror and delight on his face.

Beady black eyes stood high on thin stalks. It had no face to speak of. Little arms grew where the mouth might have been, and feelers flowed out among them, flicking about heavily in the open air. Her stomach lurched as though a trapdoor had opened in it, and Thirteen closed her eyes, unable to look any longer.

The sea churned as the crab took another step forward. This time she was sure the rig shivered.

It was unstoppable. The realization hit her and the world tilted sickeningly. She steadied herself on the beacon. The sodding idiot creature was going to walk straight into her rig.

"No! You went around the rock! Go around us, too!"

"Thirteen!"

She jumped at her name over the com. "Sorry guys." She patted around the deck until she found the ammunition pack, and dragged it over to the cannon. "I, ah, can't quite talk right now. Doyer!" The harshness in her voice snapped him out of his daze. "Whatever it is you're trying to do, do it now." Looking at the shells, covered in sigils and hexes, a twinge of doubt made her hands shake. How much effect could they have against a creature covered in its own armour?

Doyer crouched low over one of his consoles, hammering away on the keyboard. He glanced over at her, face pale and a faint sheen of sweat on his brow. "What are you doing?"

"Loading the cannon."

"What? You can't!"

"Cannon? Thirteen! What's going on?"

She turned to the huge clunky gun mounted on the platform. From the crash of the sea she knew the crab had taken another step. Its stench filled the air; rotting seaweed and mud that had never known open air. Her hands shook as she pushed the shell into the chamber and locked it in.

"You're going to shoot it?" Doyer was aghast. "But you can't! I, we, you can't do that! We have to study it, there's so much to learn, why would you do such a thing?"

He wasn't so cute now, and the look she shot him said as much. Taking hold of the trigger grips, she swivelled the gun around till the barrel pointed straight at the crab's mouth. She was unlikely to miss.

"Mr Scientist, you do what you do. I'm trying to stop it from trampling my home. Kindly shut up."

What if shooting it made it angry? Before her courage left, she pressed the triggers.

Whumpf! The concussion left her ears ringing. Doyer shrieked and flung himself flat. Leaving a curling trail of smoke and resonating with the now active enchantments, the shell spiralled through the air.

The crab lifted a leg to take another step, moving it into the path of the round. Without waiting to see the shell hit, Thirteen broke the barrel. The empty casing popped out and lay smoking, unheeded, as she pushed another into place. There was another crack of noise, barely heard, as the first round impacted on the crab's heavily armoured leg. Doyer yelled something incoherent at her.

She turned and realigned the crosshairs. This time she would get the timing right.

"Come on," she muttered, gnawing her lip. Her pulse throbbed in her fingertips. She could smell her own rancid sweat. A small blackened crater was the only evidence of her first shot.

And . . . now.

She felt rather than heard the shot, which blew the last of her hearing away. In total silence she watched the shell curve through the previous trail of smoke. Her breath caught in her throat.

The shell hit. Bullseye.

She let out a whoop. It felt wrong not being able to hear it. The crab was so close it filled her vision. It stopped and pulled its horrible beady eyes inside its shell. The little arms around its mouth waved in panic. One of them hung limp.

Doyer grabbed her shoulders and spun her round. He shook her violently, his glasses skewed, spittle flecking his chin, mouth open and teeth flashing as he screamed soundlessly at her. Thirteen shoved him. He clung to her like a mad man.

"I can't hear you!" she cried, "I can't even hear me! Let go!" She hooked her leg around his shins and swung him down. He grappled with her coat, expression gone from fury to shock. The platform jumped with his impact. The man had clearly never been in a bar brawl in his life.

Thirteen stepped back from him as he scrambled to his feet. He slowed, the rage slipping from his movements, and stared over her shoulder.

Not again.

She half turned. One of the crab's eyes slunk out from the shell. She was positive it stared straight at them.

Then it started moving again.

Thirteen closed her eyes briefly. It had taken a shell right in the kisser. Why hadn't it stayed hidden in its shell? She would have. Despite a growing sense of helplessness she grabbed another round. The spent casing dropped on her foot and rolled across the platform silently. She snapped the barrel back into place without a sound, and took the triggers again.

Doyer grabbed her around the waist and flung her from the cannon. She landed hard. Something crunched beneath her. One of his gadgets. Good, she hoped it cost a lot.

She scrambled clumsily to her feet, unable to find her balance. Her shoulder throbbed. Doyer crouched suspiciously, hands in weedy little fists, and obviously had no idea what he was doing. His lips moved around clenched teeth.

Thirteen stepped up smartly, batted his punch aside, and slammed her fist into his gut. The scientist doubled over and fell to the decking, curled in a tight ball of private agony.

"Stay down." She stepped over him and took the triggers. The crab was too close and its head too high; she couldn't lever the barrel up enough to target it. Her mouth filled with bloody tang. She bit her cheeks too hard. It was too close, too late. Not caring where it hit, she fired.

The impact knocked her off her feet. Smoke drifted over her, dense, caustic, and fishy smelling. Her throat burned and her skin prickled. She covered her face, coughing.

It kept coming, it just kept coming.

Okay, plan B. Think. It was too late to abandon the rig. The life raft was at the bottom, which was a half hour climb on a good day. Death by giant crab. It didn't seem fair. Or reasonable. They weren't even supposed to be migrating, only Salt Fae directed migrations. Crabs didn't have initiative. Bloody crabs!

It took another step forward. The rig shook as gargantuan waves crashed against it, totally unheard.

"You can't do this to me! I, *I* am Salt Fae! My great-granny was a Salt Fae! *You can't do this to me!*" What was the Salt Fae word for "stop"? She knew it, she knew she knew it.

"*Kavara! Kavart! K'vart! Kavara . . . kavarna . . . KAVADA!*" She leapt up, punching her fist at the crab. "*Kavada*, you stupid animal, *kavada!*"

Doyer stepped up.

"What the . . . ?" Thirteen stared at him, incredulous.

For someone who couldn't throw a punch, he sure knew how to hold a gun.

Movement caught her eye, and she glanced up at the crab. Something on its head. It was dark up there, but it almost looked as though someone was moving about. On a crab? On *this* crab?

Doyer gestured with the gun and Thirteen raised her hands quickly. He breathed hard and his face was red with fury.

For a moment the world was crystal clear; the chill wind at her fingertips, the smell of stagnation in the air, the way the gun glinted in the blue light.

In surreal silence, the crab crashed into the rig.

It knocked her flat. She felt the structure scream and buckle, reverberating through her body. The platform dropped down, or she fell upwards and was thrown against the beacon station. Not being able to hear her rig tearing itself apart made it worse. The acrid smell of hot metal filled the air, sharp against the soft smell of rotting fish.

After an aeon of waiting for the whole thing to topple into the sea, she realized the tremors in the rig had subsided, were nothing more than the comforting shakes of the tide turning.

Without opening her eyes, she took inventory of herself. Bruised, battered, still largely deaf. Her knee hurt more than a little from where something, probably one of Doyer's sodding boxes, had hit her. She'd bitten her tongue. Other than that, she didn't appear to be dead, and couldn't help feeling that this was something she was going to regret.

Cautiously, she opened her eyes. The panelling of the beacon station looked battered, reassuringly so. Gingerly, she looked about.

Doyer lay propped against the station, eyes squeezed shut. Blood matted the hair at his temple. His lips moved in nervous little stutters, almost as though praying.

The gun lay between them.

Thirteen rested her head on the hard grid. Normally, scientists didn't carry guns, right? It was all wrong, but given the dive the night was taking, she shouldn't have been surprised. Just her luck that it was one of the few things that hadn't been thrown from the platform.

Slowly, she reached towards it.

Perhaps her coat rustled, maybe a button scraped against the catwalk, but Doyer heard something. He snapped out like a spring and snatched the gun up, levelling it at her head before glancing about.

It was the way he went rigid that sent shivers down her arms. She rolled over.

The crab was much, much closer than she liked. It slumped against the rig, its rigid legs resting against the platform mere metres away. At first it seemed dead it was so still, until it heaved, and the rig rocked violently. The catwalk thrummed painfully beneath her. Doyer grabbed her arm in panic, and she didn't let out the breath she held until the crab subsided. Even then, its little mouth legs and eyes whipped about manically. The crab wasn't happy about it either.

Thirteen tried to remember the structure of the west side of the rig. There wasn't much call for her to go down there. The crab was well clear of the wings, but several of the pistons were partially exposed there. She turned to Doyer.

"I think it's stuck." She almost heard her voice, a hazy mumble.

The scientist jumped. Thirteen felt a thump of air hit her face as he shot the crab in fright. She raised her hands without further prompting.

"I've already surrendered!"

Doyer scowled at her, shifting his grip on the gun. Leaning close he yelled in her ear. "On what!"

Thirteen tried to swallow. Her mouth had never felt so dry. The muzzle of the gun was inches from her face, out of focus. "Could be anything. Can hermit crabs reverse?"

The crab thrashed again. They stared at each other until it calmed. Thirteen specifically did not think of the damage being inflicted on her rig.

"It's out of the water! Not enough buoyancy! Shell too big! How did it even get this far into the shallows?"

"You're the 'marine scientist', you tell me." There were little scratches around the gun's mouth that no amount of polishing could hide. It was a gun that had been used before. Don't think about it. "We need to get off the rig."

Doyer shook his head once.

"Look, this isn't personal, I'm not trying to be a prick here, but you don't seem to be seeing the whole picture. That crab is going to tear the rig apart, and if we don't get off, we're going down with it."

He tapped her nose none too gently with the gun. "More important things here than your rig."

"Yes, our lives! Please, just listen a moment. There are a couple of combat moths en route, but I don't know how long—" The crab flailed, and the groan the rig let out echoed in her bones.

His mouth shaped the words "combat moths" as though they left a bad taste in his mouth. "Call them off!"

"I wouldn't know how. The Coast Master called them in. Er," she licked her lips, "could you maybe not point that thing so close to my face?"

"Coast Master! You're sure?"

Thirteen nodded. Doyer relaxed visibly. He slumped against the station and adjusted his glasses with a little smile. She didn't know how he could stand waving the gun so close to his own head. He adjusted his glasses again.

Maybe, if she jumped him now. He wasn't paying attention to her; in fact he stared open-mouthed over his shoulder. Cautiously, she leaned around him.

There was someone else on the rig.

Doyer reached around until he felt Thirteen's knee, and squeezed it with excitement. Tears sprang to her eyes. That was her busted knee. With blurry vision she studied her second unexpected visitor for the night.

She lay awkwardly against the beacon station, flung there by the impact. Her skin was an unhealthy shade of grey and her round head smooth and bald. She wore a strange get-up, a dress that was almost indecent, and wet and rubbery looking. Kelp, Thirteen realized, the woman was wearing kelp.

Her mouth formed an "O" of realization. A *real* Salt Fae!

For a moment, she forgot the crab trashing her rig and the gun in Doyer's hand. When he turned to see if she too saw it, they shared a giddy grin. Wishes had just come true.

Doyer scuttled over to the Fae. He reached out, but stopped just short of touching her, as if afraid she would vanish.

He said something. Thirteen shook her head dumbly. The Salt Fae was *beautiful*. The scientist beckoned her over.

Roaring agony exploded in her knee when put her weight on it. Dropping instantly she wheezed, cheek pressed against the cold metal of the catwalk until the knifing pain lessened. No left knee. Got it. She dragged herself over.

"You spoke Salt Fae!"

"Kind of. Not really."

He dismissed her uncertainty with a wave and leaned close to the Fae's face. A gleeful smile lit his expression. The Salt Fae was alive.

"Fantastic! Do you know what this means? They must have adapted. Ring in the choppers, we need to get her to a lab."

"What?"

"Need to get her to a lab!"

"She needs a hospital, not a lab. Why on earth do you want to take her to a lab?"

"She's waking up!"

Both of them sat back as the Salt Fae stirred. The clean smell of salt water drifted through the air, something Thirteen hadn't been able to smell for years. This close, she could see the gills in the Fae's ribs rippling feebly. They oozed wetly as the Fae breathed through her flattened nose.

Nine would eat his words. So would Eight. Even Fourteen. And that jerk of a bartender at the Sunflower. And her sixth grade teacher, Mr Evans. And—

It was all too much. Giant crabs, pretty scientists, her home destroyed, and her own personal fairy tale come true. She didn't know what to think anymore, so she didn't.

Doyer tugged her sleeve. She looked at him blankly.

"Speak to it!"

"No!" Not since high school had she felt this shy. For the life of her she couldn't remember how to say "How are you?", the second piece of Salt Fae language she'd learned after "Hello".

"You have a satellite phone, yes? Good! Call Major Trent Necrat, of the HNS Dogmatic! Code 573-53-acrobat. Top security. Must keep this news secret. Who knows what enchantments she has access to!"

Abruptly, the world reasserted itself, and she shifted from overwhelmed Thirteen back to standard cynical Thirteen.

New enchantments. That's what this was about. Very naïve of her not to have realized. From this, it would grow into every one of the bigger crabs being hijacked, any other Salt Fae taken prisoner, and from there to military labs and questioning, and then deep sea expeditions to find the rest of them, all for a new flood of enchantments. Science, her arse. It was nothing but a cash cow.

Doyer frowned at her. There was a syringe in his hands, and as she watched he squirted the needle clear. "Get going!"

"Can't," she said, "knee is busted."

He sighed, exasperated. The Salt Fae stirred again.

"Listen, Thirteen! I need your help here. I'm sorry about the gun and all – I really didn't want to hurt you, but you didn't give me a choice. This is important. You can be a part of this." He touched her hand, his own still miraculously clean. "After this, no one will ever laugh at you again."

He looked like he cared, and he knew he was right. Damn him.

Yes, damn him.

Thirteen wouldn't have long. It surprised her to realize she'd already made her decision.

She was going to be in so much trouble.

The Salt Fae opened her eyes.

The tidal rig heaved as the crab struggled. Doyer flung himself flat. Hold together, baby, Thirteen thought at her rig, not thinking about the gun, anything except the gun. She pulled a wrench from her tool belt, and as the platform beneath her surged upwards she clonked the scientist behind the ear. A moment later she was knocked flat. The wrench skittered across the catwalk and bounced over the edge. It took a long time before the crab settled down again. The smell of cooking fish drifted up. Something was overheating below, something close to the crab. All this being tossed about was making itself known in her stomach. She concentrated on not throwing up.

When the rig was still, Thirteen checked Doyer's pulse. She'd never knocked anyone out before, well, not intentionally. There was a lot of blood. Gods, she was going to be in so much trouble. Forget the Coast Master; if this one really was a military scientist, she was screwed. "Don't die."

A hand on her arm made her jump. She looked up, into the Salt Fae's eyes.

They were dark, strange, flat, like a fish's. The hand on her arm glowed with a faint luminescence.

The woman surveyed the rig with bemusement. Thirteen had the feeling she hadn't even realized it was in their path, and now that she had crashed her crab into it, didn't care much.

She said something incomprehensible. Thirteen looked at her helplessly. The Salt Fae stood and faced the crab. She sang a piercing note that even Thirteen could hear, and wove a complex pattern with her hands. It might have been the glow of her skin, or the toll of the night, but Thirteen thought a faint trail of light followed her movements.

The crab responded to the Fae, no longer twitching, its eyes drooping slightly.

"Can you make it go backwards?" Thirteen asked, doubtful. The Salt Fae gave her a scornful look, and the rigger clamped her mouth shut. Right. Don't disturb the Salt Fae.

The Fae dropped her eyes from Thirteen to Doyer, and gave the scientist a hard nudge in the ribs. She snorted, a surprisingly inelegant gesture for such a creature, her nostrils flaring wide. Thirteen cringed away when she reached out, but the Fae only patted her head.

"You're welcome. I think."

The Salt Fae scrambled up the crab's leg, using the warty growths as handholds. At its head, she stood, and made a sweeping motion in Thirteen's direction. They were going around.

"Oh. Good. I mean—" Thirteen nodded vehemently, and then, without quite knowing why, bowed. When she straightened the Salt Fae was gone.

Ponderously slow, the crab began to move again, shuffling

backwards and turning as it did. Three point turn. Perhaps it was the Salt Fae's enchantments that let it get so close to shore in the first place. Perhaps now she had placed some spell that lightened the crab's load.

It seemed a lot of effort for not much in return. In fact, she couldn't see anything the Salt Fae could hope to accomplish from this exercise at all.

Thirteen propped herself against the station. The rig shuddered as the crab backed away, but failed to collapse. She wasn't sure whether to laugh or cry.

The Salt Fae appeared again, waving for Thirteen's attention. Thirteen waved back. The Salt Fae smiled, and raised a finger to her lips. She might have winked.

Slowly, Thirteen nodded again. "Not a soul," she murmured.

Especially not after assaulting a military scientist.

Later, when the combat moths arrived, more of her hearing returned. There was a constant muffled buzzing from the com which she had turned to full volume, and when she leaned close to those birds that had returned, within pecking range, she thought she could make out their indignant caws. They hadn't appreciated their sensational eviction.

She sat with Doyer's head pillowed on her lap, partly out of guilt, but mostly so she could tell him what happened as soon as he woke. She was certain there were some details he'd need correcting on.

The moths alighted on the side of the rig, pilots peering around for somewhere to dismount. She peeked over the edge of the platform. Giant moths, she decided, were just as ugly as giant crabs. Leaning back, she finished her fourth smoke, and started her fifth.

The pilots brought more scientists with them. She was happy to play up her lack of hearing, and watched them with amusement when they attempted to mime their questions to her. She told them that Doyer had been struck by one of his boxes in one of the crab's convulsions, and that was all. They left shortly after, taking Doyer with them. Good riddance. He wasn't that cute anyway.

Later still, with the sun high in the sky and her hearing fully returned, the phone rang. She eyed it sceptically. The Coast Master never had anything nice to say, and would probably be exceedingly incensed that she'd gone and got her rig banged up.

"Thirteen here."

"Ah, so you are alive!"

She hunkered down behind the bench. "You're not supposed to use this line, Fourt. The Coast Master will yell distortion at you."

"Eh," he said, clearly not caring, "you've been silent for ages. What happened?"

"Saw one of those crabs up close. Not cool. Blew my hearing, too."

"Mmm," Fourteen hesitated, then said, "You had your com on, remember?"

"Vaguely."

"While you and your scientist were yelling at each other, I thought I heard another voice. Some of the others did, too."

"I told you my hearing was shot. I couldn't hear shit."

"Mmm," he said again, "I think Nine is going to be nicer to you now."

"I don't know what you're talking about."

"Uh huh. You take care of yourself."

"Talk to you later."

Thirteen smiled, and hung up. With her feet on the table, she poured herself a double, no, a triple of scotch. It seemed a paltry consolation, given everything she'd gone through to get it.

She took a sip.

It was worth it.

Show Night
Steve Rasnic Tem

———

Every night from the time he was six or seven, Henry's single mother would wake him up, invite him into the walk-in closet at the back of the upstairs hall, and together they would watch the tiny people stream out of the auditoriums and theatres of the entertainment district a few blocks away, their eyes glassy as dolls'. "Look at all the rich people in their fancy clothes," she would say. "Wouldn't it be grand to dress up and go to shows?" She'd fall silent then, and he'd wait, and then she'd say, "But frightening, too, don't you think? All those people rubbing up against you, and you'd never know what any of them are intendin'. The city is such a lovely place, but such a dangerous place as well. Remember that, won't you, Henry boy? But what am I thinking of? You're just a little boy needing his sleep for a big day of learnin' tomorrow!" And she'd seem so flustered and surprised with herself, even though she said more or less those same words every night. So she'd hustle him off to his bedroom next door, retiring to her own large room with a window that bulged out over the porch like a traumatized eye – to do whatever it was she needed to do.

More than a few nights Henry had waited until she thought him safely asleep, then crept down the hall in his footed pajamas whose worn soles made a pleasing *whisper-whisper* on the old carpet, and cracked open her door just enough to see her gazing out that window, at the hill that rose like a great amphitheater across their street, tier upon tier stacked with houses and traced by narrow lanes meandering to the top. This was where many of those rich theater-going people lived, and she would not go to bed until the last of their grand cars delivered them safely back into their even grander homes.

"The richest live nearest the top, I hear, and don't they have a long way to travel up those narrow roads? Their kids must be nigh exhausted, don't you think, after such a trip?"

Henry had never understood her sympathetic tone. They were rich, weren't they? They had the grand cars and the grander homes, and they went to shows whenever they wanted. All he and his mother had were these windows, and a largely unobstructed view.

Some days she would keep him home from school and they would each pick an outfit from the dusty clothes hanging in that back closet. Even then these clothes had been ancient, smelling of dead people. He imagined he was being swallowed up in their dead skin, wrapped inside their unnaturally preserved carcasses.

But he said nothing. He did it for her, because she was his mother and because she was the saddest person he ever knew.

"Another cookie, my dear?" She passed the pewter plate his way, homemade cookies arranged into a flower shape on the yellowing bit of doily. He forced his hand out of the enveloping sleeve of the scratchy houndstooth coat and took a cookie with a polite "thank you". It would taste like cardboard, but he bit into it anyway and smiled at her until she turned back to their program for this evening: an old Dick Powell movie on their battered black-and-white console television. As soon as her head turned he crumbled up the rest of the cookie and let it fall down inside the sleeve. Later he would shake it out into the sink before he gave the coat back to her.

His reserved seat for the evening was the broad Queen Anne chair that used to belong to Grandmother Emily. It was a faded grayish brown color, the front edge worn almost to transparency by thousands of pant legs and dresses. If he looked closely he could begin to see the chair's collapsing guts inside the thin material. It had a slightly sour, cheesy smell from a succession of buttocks and sleeping cats. "Buttocks" was one of those words he'd never been allowed to use in his mother's presence, so he thought the word as much as possible.

By his side the scarred mahogany end table was layered with other people's thrown away ladies' magazines, strategically placed to cover the missing veneer. He wasn't allowed to move them, but he was allowed to use them as a drink coaster on Show Nights. A tall glass of cloudy lemonade sat there, whose bitterness he nursed for the duration of the performance. The cheesiness of the atmosphere, combined with the dryness of the cookie and bitter lemonade, made him queasy. Too-bright, blurry figures gyrated across the screen. Henry had always prided himself on never throwing up before the Show was over.

"This may have been one of your father's movies," she said, not unexpectedly. "Let's see if I can spot him. I think that may have been him at the front of that crowd scene. Oh, there he is, by the light pole. No. Well, maybe. What do you think, Henry?"

"Maybe. That could be him, I guess," Henry said for her benefit. Of course he couldn't make out the details. He couldn't make out the tiny, smeared faces of any of the extras. He could barely recognize the principal actors. In any case, he'd never believed that his father had been an actor, or a doctor, a traveling airline mechanic, a wealthy inventor, or any of the other things his mother had said about him.

———

Thirty years after his mother's death Henry lived in the same house, with much the same furniture. And that back upstairs closet contained exactly the same antique garments. Her bedroom was now his, with the same carpet, green and yellow wallpaper, and the same smell: something strawberry-like which he'd never been able to track down. Now it was his face pressed against the glass after the clubs and theaters let out, watching the constant up-and-down movements on the hill.

When they'd hauled her off to the hospital he'd been unable to make himself go. He would never forgive himself for that, but at the time, he'd been terrified. Once he was in that hospital what might they do to him? They would find something terribly wrong with him, and they would not have let him go. His mother, he was sure, would have understood. She'd always said, "I want you safe, Henry, out of the reach of strangers."

The TV he had now was color, with an impossible-to-understand remote control, although he'd eventually figured out how to power on and off, change channels, and volume. He held on to that remote tightly, ready to switch channels if anything disturbed. The faces were still on the blurry side with warring colors, the eyes strangely fixed, as if the people had been mesmerized, controlled by some hidden intelligence, some undiscovered lineage.

This perception had spoiled any entertainment value the programs might have for him; he could not lose himself in the shows as his mother had, but he still sat there glued every night of the week in the old Queen Anne chair. He sipped at bitter lemonade or at bitter tea, nibbled on stale cookies, watching, flipping the channels, making close comparisons of eyes, postures, of the relative position of arms and legs, of the overall outline of the people's forms against painted backgrounds. Obviously there was a greater intelligence at work here – these people's lives were not their own.

He began the Project when he was just a boy, working up one piece at a time. Every afternoon he sat on the front porch with battered binoculars, drawing maps of homes and utility buildings in his Big Chief tablet. One afternoon he started diagramming comings and goings, traffic patterns, the periodic appearances of this or that street beggar or pet. Sometimes he'd sneak up to Mother's bedroom for a higher viewpoint, shamed by all the old coffee cans full of her terrible cookies, and box after box of tissues to soak up her inevitable tears. He didn't really understand, except even then he knew that some people lived and breathed sadness as if it were desperately needed air.

As Henry grew into his teens his note-taking became even more obsessive. On a typical day he got up, drank a glass of foul-tasting lemonade, then immediately began work on his lists. He'd write the date at the top, some notes about the weather, perhaps some comments on what he was feeling that day. *The weather is sunny, a scattering of clouds. I went down to the store, but I felt crowded, even though there were only a few people inside. I hurried home as fast as I could.* Then he listed the comings and goings of the various families who lived on the hill, color-coding the schedules so that he could coordinate the time lines across families, comparing the lives of those at the bottom with those at the top, who he had come to refer to as "the upper crust."

Mr. Balding-with-Red-Suspenders who lived in a large white house approximately a third of the way up the hill, where the lane took some nasty turns (leading to a higher percentage of traffic accidents than anywhere else on the hill), left his home at 8am every morning. Since he did not work (disabled or independently wealthy?) his trips were circumscribed, apparently being more of the errand variety. But every other day or so his car would disappear behind a cluster of trees in the top quadrant of the hill at the same time Ms. Lemon-Dress-with-Pink-Shoes (named so because that's what she wore three days out of five) left her red bungalow less than a hundred feet away. She would walk for a time toward those trees, but Henry always lost sight of her before she reached them. It didn't matter how carefully he watched, he could never track her past a certain point. Was there an assignation involved? He could not say with any precision.

He began the Project piecemeal, in shoeboxes and crates, in castoff food containers, all of it hidden from his mother. He augmented his formal schooling with trips to the city's Museum of Natural History. There he studied the dioramas.

"Nice detail, huh?" the guard said behind him.

"Oh, yes, beautiful," Henry replied, too embarrassed to turn around and look at the man, afraid he'd throw him out for leaning on the glass. "I love the faces."

"Yes. I hear some of those take hours to do."

"They make the faces a little blurry on purpose, I think," Henry said.

"It's what makes the eyes really stand out. Their faces are a little dead, but the eyes are so alive they embarrass you to look at them."

The guard laughed awkwardly. "Well, best run on. Almost closing. Feel free to come back tomorrow."

Years of notes became years of meticulous recreations, pieces of a puzzle he hid in his closet and under the bed, behind a false wall in the attic where he knew his mother would never go, in secret cavities, disguised by layers of other things, under thick hedges, beneath outbuilding foundations, inside hollowed walls.

He never understood the *why* of his Project, just that it needed to be. He knew it had something to do with his mother, her fascination with the hill, and her anxiety at being an outsider in the city, surrounded by strangers. Finally, it just made him feel more secure to watch, and to record.

His mother's death after a year in the hospital left him inconsolable. He lay on the floor in front of her old TV, his mismatched clothes snatched from the upstairs closet, still smelling of past lives and now his own pathetic stink. He interrupted his despair only with trips to the bathroom, to the refrigerator, to the basement storeroom where she'd kept foodstuffs as a hedge against the city's "criminal element."

Then one day his despair broke, pushed out by anger over what she had turned him into. He hadn't a clue what he should do with himself. All he thought he knew about was that hill they'd both been so fascinated by, and his Project. So the next day he took sledgehammer and crowbar to the floorboards in the living room, tearing a hole near the back wall of the house, widening it, adding supports where he'd severed supporting timbers, then erecting a post to support a seriously sagging portion of the floor.

He emptied the basement easily – he simply threw it all away, an accumulation of belongings he knew nothing about. The resulting space was huge, yet barely sufficient to contain the Project pieces he retrieved from all parts of the house and yard.

Molded with clays from the garden, plaster from the hardware, twigs and branches, paints and glues and buttons and shredded bits of cloth from her sheets, even from her favorite Show Night dress, the Project took its final form: a fan-shaped mound of hill beginning in his basement, rising up through the space in the floor into the living room, its upper crust of grand dwellings almost kissing the night-and-star-painted ceiling. And across that expanse he'd created the minute detail of hundreds of strangers' lives – their houses, cars, and dangerous serpentine lanes. Finally he placed the tiny effigies themselves, eyes painted and varnished and polished to a high, reflective sheen, staring, at last seeing *him*.

————————

Another envelope dropped to the carpet under the mail slot, added to the layers of bills and notices. Similar, larger notices and warnings had been plastered over the front door and windows, yellowing the light filtering through to the living room. Henry now used the back door off the kitchen, and a circuitous route down an alley to travel to his clean-up job at a restaurant nearby. His mother had left him a surprising amount of money, but not enough to last forever, and he could not bear a job of much visibility. The Project required constant updating as pets and vehicles were replaced, as buildings were repainted, burned up, torn down, defaced, and weathered, as strangers moved and strangers died. All this work required a constant expenditure of his time and money.

His mother, if she had lived, would no doubt have despaired as her grand gentlemen and ladies moved away, and middle-class families and blue-collar laborers moved in. And a new phenomenon had evolved: secreted here and there within ruined foundations, in abandoned culverts and boarded-up buildings were homeless people, beggars, and figures unidentified. From his viewpoint, and with his devotion, Henry witnessed it all.

They still held shows and concerts down in the district on the other side of his neighborhood, but the entertainment was likely to be of a more popular, cheapened variety. Sometimes they held open-air music festivals in the plaza; Henry would open his windows and listen with eyes closed.

Keeping up with the Project had become more difficult.

Every day Henry would spy some new stranger.

"So where'd you come from?" he'd say to the figure trapped inside his binoculars. "You certainly weren't there yesterday!" He pulled his tattered notepad out of his back pocket and jotted down a few particulars: relative height, weight, R for resident or V for vagrant, and some speculation about the figure's state of mind.

Down in the basement he rolled out the clay, made arms and legs, torso, a head. This all went down quickly. A half-hour in the oven and he had "Mr. Everyman." But then he brought out the paints. Three hours later he was still painting. He painted and repainted trying to get the face right, and then the eyes. The eyes were the windows to the soul, correct? But whose soul? For so many of these figures staring up at him, their eyes led to places he did not understand.

He had to keep a constant eye on their positioning, often moving a dozen or more of their effigies every evening to keep the Project properly aligned and representational.

That afternoon returning from work more tired than usual – he'd made bad mistakes, dropping a rack full of dishes and angering the new assistant manager with his clumsy attempts to clean it up – he climbed to his bedroom and collapsed into his observation chair. He wanted just to sleep, but something nagged him. He blinked a few times, trying to shake off a blurry impression . . . of what?

He leaned forward with sudden understanding, letting his eyes sweep back and forth across the hill: the high profile of the mound, spiky with eaves and chimneys, the serpentine sweep of road, streamlined for safety over the years, flowing evenly and gently down the hill, the broad scales of mown grass and removed brush, smoothing the terraced profile, the reduction of tree growth, the slopes chiseled out and walled. It had never registered with him before, so intent he'd been with the minute, specific changes occurring to the strangers, but it was so obvious in this late afternoon light: the hill had lost mass, had in fact been losing mass over a period of years.

———————

The next day Henry began removing pieces from selected portions of the Project, rearranging things in order to achieve a more accurate representation of the hill. It was a laborious task; his specific detailing was spot on – it was his scale, his relative spacing that was off. The Project was bloated and inflated by his own ego. Now he had to let some of the air out.

The dilemma was how to take things away without creating an imbalance in the entire structure, and threatening its very existence.

From repeated trips topside other things became more apparent. The city had introduced flaws into the real structure he was trying to emulate, through both poor planning and negligent maintenance. Concrete retaining walls had dangerous cracks, drainage errors had been introduced threatening the roads. On the western slope of the hill several of the houses appeared to be leaning ever so slightly.

If he were being true to the Project he would duplicate these flaws. But how could he without jeopardizing the integrity of the enterprise itself?

He had no time to consider such issues. He had to keep his hands moving, applying and taking away materials, making observations topside then implementing them on the Project below – he didn't dare stop until some sort of equilibrium had been achieved. Once on his hurried way down he bumped the post supporting the sagging living room floor. The house shuddered around him as if with sudden, appalled awareness. He halted mid-step, holding his breath. Boards whined around him. Somewhere in a distant part of the house a gathering of cookware complained.

He gathered himself together and went back upstairs and into his bedroom. Sat in his chair, his mother's chair. Looked out at the grand hillside, his life's amphitheater. And in the twilight saw that the homeless strangers had rearranged themselves, and were in fact, looking his way. Impossible as it seemed, he could just detect the whites of their eyes, feel the direction of their collective gaze.

Henry spent the rest of the night down in the basement. First he moved the strangers, repainted their eyes to match the intensity he'd sensed in their postures, then he felt compelled to repaint the eyes of all the tiny figures on the mound. Hundreds of pairs of deliberately aimed eyes. He'd been watching these strangers all of his life. Now, apparently, it was his turn.

————

By the morning Henry had completed his revisions. The strangers would move again, of course, but it comforted him that the Project at least reflected their relative positioning at some particular moment in time. All heads had been re-angled, all eyes repainted, and all looking at him.

Some of the figures lay hidden in the vegetation as these vagrants slept during the day. Some camouflaged themselves on purpose against a fence or folded into shadow – these were the strangers who did not want to be seen.

He became aware of a distant pounding, upstairs, outside the front door. He crept up to the main floor, careful not to jostle the essential, if fragile, post. Silhouettes played on the front window shades: arms waving, heads pressed against the outer glass.

He continued up another flight to his bedroom, stood in the shadows by the house's great eye of window, peered down into his front yard and street, where construction vehicles idled, several police cars pulled across the road, officers directing traffic.

Someone pounded the door and shouted his name, barely recognizable since they'd pasted "Mister" to the front of it. Of course he did not answer.

Then there was an argument, strange to his ears since he'd witnessed so few in his lifetime, except on the television where they were more physical in nature, ritualized to fit within the time slot available. Someone shouted "paper!" Someone shouted "work!" As the morning wore on he came to realize from this war of words that some essential paperwork had gone missing. Someone had forgotten to cross their "t"s. Some "i"s had gone undotted.

He looked out at the hill, watching serenely in its enormity, unconcerned.

Henry stood there and continued to listen, attempting vainly to gain some insight into the activity below, but there appeared to be too little to measure. And still the hill watched him, unrevealing of its concerns.

Finally there came a slamming of car doors. He watched as most of the vehicles left the front of his home. All conversation appeared to have stopped for the day, but several construction vehicles – some earth movers, a crane – had been left behind, doubtless gassed up and ready for the next morning.

In the graying of late afternoon the hill exhaled the tension from its system. The flowing lines of road bent and stretched.

Henry descended the steps wearily. He stopped in his living room to look at the top layers of the Project rising behind his Queen Anne chair. Eyes glowed in the dim light. A long shadow shifted across the breadth of the mound, and he stepped back, ready for some catastrophic collapse, when the tremor subsided, and all the eyes shut, leaving him alone.

Down in the basement things were quiet. He sank to his knees at the base of the thing that filled his house and laid his hands on it, in it, and found it surprisingly warm.

He leaned over without volition, then fell sideways against the mound, crushing houses, trees, cars beneath him, and untold numbers of strangers' lives. But without surprise, it seemed, or complaint. Then his own eyes winked out.

———

When Henry stood up again the house shifted with his imbalance, and in the dimness of evening the mound appeared to change position, before resettling into the same space. The low light brought into relief the muscle-like planes, the bone-like structure, spine, and ribs pushed out in sleep. When nothing else happened he climbed the stairs.

He tried the light switch but nothing happened. He attempted to turn on the TV, but again with no result. They'd cut the power. Who *they* were, he couldn't be sure, but he knew there had always been a "they", and always would be. They were the city, and the people who lived there, and after enough years had passed, they had become the same. And they were no friend of his.

He unbolted his front door and walked outside. The great expanse of hill roused itself. Thousands of eyes blinked themselves open, parasites whose lives and deaths might pass practically unnoticed, until one of them did something extraordinary, or foolish.

The hill stood up, turned around, and snapped its teeth. Behind him the house came roaring down.

Love and Death in the Time of Monsters
Frank Wu

———

We got Mom's diagnosis the day the monster came ashore in New York.

I shouldn't have been surprised. She'd been coughing for a while. The night before she'd spat up blood during dinner. She covered her mouth with a napkin, as if I wouldn't notice. She kept saying she didn't need a doctor, all the way to the hospital.

While they were examining her, I watched TV in the waiting room. New York, so many thousand miles away, was on fire. The whole city was aflame. They showed the same footage of the Museum of Modern Art smoking and collapsing, over and over. People were grabbing Picassos and de Chiricos off the walls and crashing through the glass into the streets, burnt flakes of Monet's water lilies fluttering down around them.

Why did the monster have to pick that city? I grew up in Connecticut and I loved New York. It had all the best museums and restaurants. Had.

The creature was reptilian, walking upright like an allosaurus or carnotaurus, but dragging its tail. It was huge, impossibly huge. A frantic commentator guessed it was eighty feet tall, but that seemed an underestimate. In the long shots, its stubby little forearms looked comically puny. But, considering how big its body was, these "tiny" arms were the size of boom cranes. They didn't have any problem picking up garbage trucks and throwing them through department store windows.

As it toppled smokestacks and smashed through waste disposal plants, flames reflected in its unblinking, robot-like eyes. The eyes were fixed in its head, which swiveled like a turret, scanning for new targets. Burning oil dribbled from the top of its head, cascading down the canyons ringing the jagged scales around its brow.

The reporter saw anger in the eyes, but to me the monster's expression was mechanical, almost clinical, as if it were instinctively responding to stimuli, systematically dismantling the city which urinated and defecated into its personal ocean.

They took a lot of samples from my mom. They could feel a lump when they pushed on her tummy, but wouldn't give us any final answers. They said they'd confirm or deny the preliminary results in a day or two and that we should go home. But the doctor's eyes told us what his words would not.

When we were back at her house, I put my mom to bed.

"Am I going to die now?" she asked.

"No, no, you're not," I said.

"I know it's the cancer, Bobby," she said.

"You're going to beat it." I wanted to hold her the way she'd held me when I was little.

I called my wife Janie to tell her I'd be staying the night.

As mom slept, I watched the news. We shouldn't have been surprised when the monster appeared, considering all the radionuclides and biochemicals that we'd been dumping in the water. Now they were blaming this thing for every ship that had disappeared in the Bermuda Triangle. The reporter said its fire breath was the cause of El Niño and global warming.

Next to the TV were Mom's lighter and a pack of Marlboro Reds. Janie had been telling me for years I should make her quit. How could I do that? Some things you just can't tell your mom. Like the fact that she can't sing. Or that margarine isn't really better for you than butter. Once I watched her finish one cigarette, but she didn't have her lighter. So I was relieved when she was done. Then she took the dying cigarette and used it to light a fresh one. It was a clever use of fire, but I was horrified. I was six. I decided then I'd never smoke, years before my teachers lectured us on cancer. But the notebooks I brought to school smelled of tobacco.

The summer after college, I couldn't find a job and had to move back home. One night she asked me to run to the store and get her cigarettes. I didn't know what to do. They were poison, but she said she didn't want to live alone, now that Dad was gone. She wanted to be with him. She smoked because of love.

Sometimes she'd yell at me – actually yell – for the stupidest things, like water I spilled around the sink or hair left on the bathroom floor. But not when she was smoking. I'd be upstairs working on a project, and she'd call out my name in a singsong voice. I'd come down the stairs, and she'd grab my hand and take me out to the porch. We'd sit on the concrete and talk about life and dreams, all while she smoked and I tried not to gag. She was calm – not happy, but real, and we could talk about stuff that mattered. The best times we had were when she was smoking. So I bought her cigarettes to protect myself from her fits of rage when she was in withdrawal. Is that bad?

I took her smokes and her lighter and threw them in the dumpster that night.

I threw away a little plastic monster, too. He was green, with a plump yellow belly, a jolly Godzilla. A wind-up that shot sparks from his mouth as he walked. Mom had put him in my Christmas stocking years ago. He sat on the coffee table next to the magazines. Every week I'd find him moved, facing the wrong way after she'd cleaned up. She didn't understand that he was a movie monster watching monster movies.

Fire-breathing lizards are cute when they're a couple inches tall and made of plastic with badly-painted eyes. Not when they're eighty feet tall and flattening your favorite city. I always thought the alveoli in your lungs were cool-looking. When they're microscopic, not when the mass of cells is as big as a grapefruit.

––––––––

They chop out pounds of my mom's flesh.

She makes an unexpected joke about losing weight, but mostly she complains about the chemo. It's worse than the disease. Throwing up, headaches, racing heartbeat. Did her hands used to shake like that?

The TV screen goes white for a moment as another missile explodes at the monster's feet. He emerges unscathed from a cloud of smoke. Are the missiles leveling more buildings than the monster?

"Does the doctor have to kill me to get the tumor?" Mom asks.

"No, no, he doesn't," I say.

"Do I have a pained look on my face?" she asks, with a pained look on her face.

"No, no, you look fine," I say. "You're just going through a rough patch."

"Do you believe in miracles?"

"Yes," I say, but only for other people.

As I say this, the cancer's already in her lymph system, using it like a highway to spread through her body.

They're trying some new techniques, and the doctor's hopeful. Combination therapy, he calls it. I drive her to hours-long chemo sessions. When I can't be there, I phone my mom from work to make sure she's taken all her pills. She says she has, but sounds like she's lying. I think she has trouble swallowing. She's given up. The doctor says she has a chance at recovery if she makes it through chemo and takes all her pills, but he's lying, too. Janie says we should move in with her. The hour-and-a-half drive from our house to hers is killing me, while I try to keep my job to pay her medical bills. Mom's not sick enough to be in a hospital full-time yet, but she shouldn't be in that house alone. She says she can take care of herself, but that stubbornness is going to kill her.

They try everything. Cellular toxins. DNA replication inhibitors. Antisense nucleic acids and short inhibitory RNAs. Artillery. Great bolts of lightning. Nothing stops him; it only makes the monster angrier. They try mutagens, teratogens, carcinogens, neurotoxins, hemotoxins, genotoxins – they think that toxins in the environment created the monster, and maybe toxins can kill it. Maybe two wrongs can make a right. They don't, apparently. I worry about the residues left in the ground after the monster's moved on.

Some pranksters are trying to run up, as close to the monster as they can. From behind, so he can't see them. Idiots. They're still running through that haze of toxins, and they could still get smashed by a random swish of his giant tail. Or a missile that falls short of its mark. Despite the danger, these pranksters have spawned a host of copycats.

Now the monster's going up and down the eastern seaboard. Janie talks about flying out there to help, but she doesn't want to get stomped on. Who would? A team of guys from work drive across the country to do whatever they can. They figure that patent annuities can still get paid in their absence. I want to go, but I have to stay to help my mom. That's my fight.

Our co-workers save the Liberty Bell, but nobody tries to save the black neighborhoods of Philadelphia. Boston's gone, too. Part burnt up, the rest contaminated. My grandparents used to live there, in Arlington. My grandma would give me Coke and cake, a dangerous cocktail for a hyperactive child. I used to sneak into my grandpa's basement to look at his calligraphy and the books he'd written in Chinese, which I couldn't read. That old house is gone now.

The monster's in Jersey City. Joke all you want about that state, but my God people are dying by the thousands.

Two hours after crawling out of the Hudson, the creature tilts his head, rivulets of water tumbling down his back, water falling between the rows of plates on his back. After two hours of walking among flames of his own making, the monster still carries, in the nooks and crannies of his skin, pools of sea water, bigger than bathtubs.

I wonder if he can carry tuna or salmon with him on his rampages, then gently deposit them back in the ocean when he's done.

Maybe they can figure out a way to fill those water pockets with poison, so he can't shake it off . . . but what do I know? I'm not a scientist.

Maybe those pools are the safest place to be, nestled in the hollows and pits in his own scaly skin where he can't reach. I wonder what it would be like to be carried by the monster, swept away, giving myself over to destruction.

———

Over seven thousand have died in the last four months. The monster's been ravaging the east coast for so long that people here in California don't talk about it much anymore. Raleigh was wiped out, but nobody at work even mentioned it. I heard about it on the radio, but I didn't believe it until I read it on the internet. It's not real until it's virtual.

Stanford's in the Sweet Sixteen this year and Janie's all excited about that. She says I need at least a little fun in my life or I will go insane, and that won't help anybody. If we don't go on with the rest of our lives, she says, then the monsters win. I guess.

My mom's taken a turn for the worse. She hardly eats or sleeps anymore. I bought her some fresh veggies, but a couple days went by and she hadn't eaten them and they started to smell bad.

She still won't let us move in with her, but she doesn't mind when we sleep on her sofa. We Rug Doctored the whole house, but it still smells like smoke and we can't get out the yellow tinting everything. I gave her a new cell phone, but she never answers it and forgets to recharge it. Since she spends a lot of time in bed, Janie got her some new pillows, since hers are decades old, but she never took them out of the plastic.

"Am I going to die now?"

"No, no, you're not."

"Do I have a pained look on my face?"

"No, you look fine."

"Do you believe in miracles?"

"Yes."

"Will you go and buy me cigarettes?"

"No." But what does it really matter?

Between trying to save my mom and trying to save my job, I don't have much time with Janie. Mostly we spend that time watching basketball. I never cared for it. It's boring and stupid. Maybe people like watching tall muscular guys run back and forth and back and forth. Rhythmic like the tide. Maybe it's soothing.

We watch the game together, but afterwards I can't for the life of me tell you who won. Maybe it's Stanford, because I remember Janie being all giddy. My world is happy when she smiles.

———————

I am standing at my mom's front door, and the wind brings horrid fumes. The air smells like burnt hair and pulverized concrete, and it sticks in my throat. Has the smoke and ash from the east coast actually circled the earth to reach us here in California?

Or is it just the normal pollution we breathe every day without noticing?

I push in the door, calling out, "I bought you some flowers!" and thinking, we're all going to die.

"Why did you do that?" she screams. "This won't make it all better!"

"They're yellow roses," I say. "Your favorite."

"You're just doing this to trick me into thinking you care. I can see right through you. You don't really care about me. Nobody does! All you care about is your stupid job. That's more important to you than I am."

"No, it's not," I say, pulling moldy shriveled stems from a vase and putting in the roses. "Do you want some water? It'll help clear out your system."

"You never tell me I'm pretty." Her face is twisted, wrung like a sponge of its tears. "I wish I'd never had you. I should have stuck with cats instead."

"Would you like me to make you a sandwich?" I ask. "There's some fresh roast beef."

"Why do you bother coming here?" She pounds on the coffee table and a pile of magazines slide onto the floor. "You don't love me! You've never loved me! You're just pretending, trying to trick me! Get out! Get out! Go to your stupid job that you love more than me. No, I don't want any water. The world is going to hell in a handbasket. What are you going to do about it?"

I sit down next to her and brush the back of her hand with my fingertips.

"Don't you dare touch me!" She pushes me away. "Why did you bring me flowers? They'll be dead in a couple days. But I'll be dead before they will. Why do you bring me flowers that will die in a couple days?"

I don't know why I exhaust myself driving one and a half hours to come here. Why I come here to listen to her cough for hours on end, first thing in the morning, late into the night. If I didn't come here, I wouldn't have to put up with her abuse. This is far worse than any nicotine-withdrawal tirade. Sigh. No good deed goes unpunished.

Janie asks why I put up with Mom's abuse. I'm hoping that eventually I'll do the right thing, or say the right thing, so she'll finally say "Thank you". I don't need fanfare, trumpets. All I really want is a small act of appreciation, some tiny, tiny acknowledgment that I've done someone right once in my life.

I need to stop thinking about myself.

She is dying. My mother is dying. There is no more denying it. And this lashing out is the first of the final death rattles.

———

"Honey, quick! Turn on the TV!" Janie's voice calls over the cell phone.

"I'm at work," I say. "I have a meeting in twenty, uh, fifteen minutes."

"Oh," she says, "I thought you were at your mom's . . . . OK, then, click on Yahoo news!"

Through my glass door, I hear a cheer erupt down the hall.

"Here we see the science vessel *Iverson Lord*," the reporter on my monitor says, "hauling up what appears to be a piece of the monster, possibly part of a scale." Out of the choppy, greenish water, a shipboard crane is lifting a black mass the size of a Volkswagen. "Yes, that looks to me like one of the monster's scales. And look! Another scale, bobbing in the water. Physical evidence, I think, that the monster's been hit. But we have yet to confirm that it is dead."

The crewmen on the ship are high-fiving each other through their white environmental suits.

How ironic that, on the day the monster dies, I hadn't been thinking of it all day. Probably just staring into space.

"They nuked it!" Janie screams. "Fox News is declaring it dead! They had to wait until it was done with Atlanta and had moved back to sea. But it looks like they finally got it!"

Nukes? Was that necessary? Nobody else seems to be worried, but do we want to start down that path?

"Honey? Honey? Are you still there?" Janie asks.

"Yeah . . . "

I hear a rapping on the office door next to mine, followed by a brief, muffled conversation coming through the wall.

Misty, the excitable admin across the hall, knocks twice on my door, then opens it and pokes her head in.

"Did you hear?"

"Yeah," I say.

"Why so glum? We're breaking out champagne in the big conference room!"

"What about the meeting?"

"Oh, heck, I'm sure that's cancelled."

Her head disappears and I hear her rap on the next office.

"I'll call your mom to let her know," Janie says.

"OK."

I put my head on my desk.

I'm glad innocent people won't die anymore, but I can't bring myself to celebrate. I didn't fight, didn't shoot any missiles or throw a Molotov cocktail between the monster's toes. I am as responsible for the monster's defeat as I am for Stanford's victories. Which is to say, not at all. The war is over, and I missed it.

Then I think; if the monster and my mom's cancer spring from the same well of evil, then caring for my mom was my part in the war against the monster. Maybe. Or am I just rationalizing my cowardice?

My phone rings again.

"Your mom didn't answer!" Janie says.

"What?" I ask. "You tried her cell?"

"Of course I did," Janie says. "No answer there, either." She never leaves her house anymore, unless we take her.

"Maybe she's in the yard, smoking," I suggest.

"She can hear the phone from the yard."

"Holding the cell with my shoulder, I try calling Mom on my office line. No answer.

"OK, I'm coming to get you," I say.

"All right," Janie says. "I'll call the police over there first."

When we are still a few miles from Mom's house, my cell rings. It's the cops. They say that they'd found her sitting upright, in a chair next to the phone. It was ringing when they arrived. Her head was lolled to the side, but she was still breathing, still alive.

Once we get to the hospital, they make us sit in the waiting room. For hours. The TV is showing celebrations all around the world. Some people are looting, rioting. Others are firing guns into the air. I wonder how many will die when the bullets land. The monster is gone, but the death toll keeps rising.

The doctor finally comes in, with an undecipherable expression.

"Well . . . how is she?" Janie asks.

"We checked the levels of cancer proteins in her blood, did some preliminary scans, and I think we got it. It could come back, but, for now, we can't detect anything trace of it."

"You're kidding!" Janie says. But the doctor doesn't look happy.

"We've had to excise a lot of tissue over the last few months," the doctor says. "There were also some adverse effects from the chemotherapy, permanent unfortunately, related to some of her other organs. Her stomach lining, her brain, her liver . . . "

"Her brain?" I ask.

"Yeah," the doctor says. "She doesn't seem to have any cranial nerve reflexes, or brain electrical activity. None at all, really. Some damage to normal tissue is an unfortunate but not uncommon side effect of whole-body irradiation. But her heart's as strong as an ox. Should keep beating for a good long time."

On the TV the President's spokesman is gloating that the Administration has saved Texas, as yet untouched by either the monster or the weapons used against it. Meanwhile, most of Georgia and Florida, including Disneyworld and Universal Studios, will remain uninhabitable indefinitely.

The war is over. Did we win?

———

Minutes later, we are taken to see Mom. The nurse leads us in and then immediately walks out. My mom wears an oxygen mask and foam dribbles from her mouth. Why hadn't anyone cleaned her up? I wave my hand in front of her face. No response. I move the mask and wipe her mouth. Still no response.

I can't see her like this, not ever again.

I pull from my pants a crushed, sweat-stained box of Marlboro Reds. One end I have pounded against my palm, compacting them just as she liked. On the inside of the flip top I'd drawn a dozen hearts. I'd drawn on the flip tops before, elephants because she liked elephants. The lines were sometimes jiggly, because it was hard to reach in there, but she would tear off the tops and save them. I push the pack into her useless hand and close the fingers over it. Her fingers are still fat, though most of the rest of her is devastated and shriveled. As I cover her hand with a blanket so the nurse won't see the cigarettes, Janie shoots me a disapproving look, but doesn't say anything. Mom lies there, not moving, just a smudge, only a shadow of her remaining.

A flash of anger passes through me. She will never say thank you. I am disappointed in myself for wanting so much, but her abusive words will hurt for a very long time.

Still . . . If I had my life to live over, would I do it again? Without a doubt.

I kiss her on the forehead and whisper, "I love you, Mom. Goodbye."

Then I turn to Janie and say, "Let's go."

"Are you sure?" she asks.

I have reached my limit. I have nothing left to give.

———————

As we drive away, a special report comes on the radio that explosions are breaking out in coastal cities all around the world. Giant monsters are everywhere, huge jellyfish and octopi. Some kind of animal I'd never of, called a pangolin, which is apparently a spiny anteater that looks like a giant pinecone. The monsters are everywhere. Belgium, France, Malaysia. What then, will we have to nuke those places, too?

Janie turns off the radio.

Now I am crying again.

"Janie, we need to go back for Mom—" I start to say, when sour air drifts through the vents. I cough once, twice. As I go into spasms, Janie pulls the car over.

I can't stop coughing, a shattering, deep cough that shakes the bone girders in my flesh and strips my throat.

"No," Janie says. "Not for her."

I sink into my seat, finally suppressing the hacking. My hands are speckled in blood.

"No, Bobby," she says. "We need to go back for you."

I nod.

Before she makes an illegal U-turn, Janie unhooks her seatbelt and slides it away. She lunges over the gearshift and grabs me tight, cradling me in her arms as I had cradled my mother.

When Janie puts the car back into Drive, I slide forward, the seatbelt over my tummy. Like I did when Mom gave me rides. For the first time in months I can relax. It's my turn now. I turn to Janie and say, "You're welcome."

"What?"

"Nothing, never mind," I say with a tearful smile, as she drives me through the night.

Seven Dates That Were Ruined by Giant Monsters or Why I Really Need to Get Out of This City
Adam Ford

―――

1. Katie Chambers – Saturday 27th July, 1988

I was fifteen years old, standing outside the cinema, waiting for Katie Chambers to show up. I'd just been dropped off by my parents and was nervously watching the family car drive away after managing somehow to fend off an uninvited PDA from my mother. I knew that I'd cop it when I got home that night with the "What's the matter, are you too much of an *adult* for me to kiss you goodbye anymore?" routine, but I didn't care. For the week that had passed since I had got the guts up to ask Katie Chambers – Katie *Chambers*, mind you – to the Saturday Matinee at the Odeon, I had been coasting on pure adrenaline and nothing, absolutely nothing, could touch me, except maybe the nagging fear that Katie wasn't going to show. The fear grew exponentially with each minute that passed, each nervous glance at my watch, but she finally turned up, only three and three-quarter minutes later than we'd arranged. There she was, stepping out of the passenger seat of a parental-looking station wagon that had pulled up across the road. Things were starting to look okay. The adrenaline was back and I had a great opening conversational gambit along the lines of *parents, what the hell are they good for, hey?*

All of a sudden it got dark, like a cloud was passing across the sun. I looked up and Gigantadon was swooping down out of the sky and everyone was screaming and running inside the theatre except for me. I just stood there and watched as two hundred tonnes of giant radioactive pterodactyl reached out one claw and picked up Katie's parents' station wagon and flew off. Katie started running down the middle of the road screaming, *Give me back my mum, my mum, give her back!* I waited for another half an hour for her to come back, but by then the previews were definitely over and the movie had started for sure. I could hear helicopters in the distance, and guns, and that weird high-pitched screaming sound Gigantadon's sonic-wing-attack makes, so I walked to the phone booth on the corner and called Mum and asked her to come pick me up.

2. Megan Lan – Thursday 18th October, 1991

I used to see Mee almost every day at uni, wandering across campus in that purposeful kind of way, striding confidently across the quadrangle on one of her various extracurricular missions. She was heavily involved in student union stuff. After six months of watching her walk past, noticing the clothes that she wore, the people she was with and the way she hooked stray loops of hair behind her ears with her pinkie finger, I decided that it was time to meet the legendary Megan Lan face-to-face.

One afternoon I saw her putting up posters, attaching them with a giant roll of masking tape to the bollards that were scattered around campus. She had dropped a pile of the posters on the ground beside her, and just as she was tearing a strip of tape with her teeth a punk on a skateboard shot past and the jet stream from his board sent the unstuck posters flying. I took the opportunity and ran over to the bollard, frantically snatching at every poster I could get my hands on. With most of them recovered, I turned to Mee and smiled what I hoped was my most self-effacing-yet-fascinating smile as I handed them back to her. She smiled back as she took them from me and tucked a stray loop of hair behind one ear. I took a deep breath and to stop myself from staring I checked out the poster she'd just stuck up. It was advertising a public lecture by Professor Jane Damage on the interface between contemporary urban planning strategies and philosophical interpretations of the role of kaiju in long-term social development. Professor Damage was Mee's honours supervisor, and she was helping out with promotion of the event to try and score some brownie points from the Prof. I offered to help Mee out with the rest of the posters, and she took me up on the offer, splitting the pile in two and arranging to meet me back at the Student Activities Office in an hour.

We had coffee that afternoon and arranged to meet at the lecture that Thursday, and then go out to get something to eat afterwards. Though it was great to be hanging out with Mee, I didn't enjoy the lecture very much. Professor Damage's theories were a little old-fashioned, which is something that often happens with tenured academics – they tend to carve out their niche at their institution and dig in, ignoring any developments in their field that post-date their appointment. The Prof. was just about to demonstrate one of her theories when the containment unit short-circuited and the three juvenile Carnivopteryxes that had been held in short-term nanostasis broke out. Within ten minutes they were big enough to fill the auditorium, and ten minutes after that they had burst through the ceiling, growing bigger and bigger as they slashed at each other with their talons and screeched telepathic war cries, shooting golden death rays at every building taller than three storeys. Mee and I were crushed up against the back wall of the auditorium in the rush to escape. When the second monster knocked over a support beam with its tail, I caught a chunk of masonry in the small of my back and a rafter came down on my right arm. Apart from some bruises and scratches, Mee was okay. Luckily, I'd fallen on top of her and most of the debris landed on me instead of her. She came to visit me in hospital a couple of times. A few weeks before I was released she started going out with a mutual friend from my botany tutorials. I hate to admit it, but they made a really cute couple.

3. Lucy Darnell – Friday 9th August, 1993

Lucy worked in the office where I was doing a three-day-a-week internship. She was always helpful when I wasn't sure who I was supposed to deliver which forms to. Her kindness made her stand out from the rest of the arseholes in the company who mainly saw me as their personal courier-slash-mailroom-slave. Lucy wasn't like that at all, maybe because she was a lot younger than most of her co-workers. She had got the job out of an internship she'd done there herself a couple of years earlier. I think she sympathized with me having to put up with all the crap I had to put up with from my superiors, which was pretty much everyone in the building, including Lucy. I would bitch to her about them when we would go to lunch at this sleazy café that served bad "modern Australian" food but made good coffee. We got close, like you do when you're having lunch together almost every day, talking about your lives and ambitions and that sort of junk.

I don't normally go out with people that I work with, but this was an internship, not a full-time job, and it was only a six-month position so I figured if it went really badly I would only have to hang in there a little while and then I'd never have to see her again. That was the worst-case scenario, though, and didn't seem too likely because we got along really well and had a lot in common. One day I asked Lucy if she wanted to go out after work some time. She smiled a coy little smile and told me she had been wondering how long it would take before I asked. We organized to go out that Friday night – she'd ditch end-of-week drinks and I'd come by after classes and we'd wander down to Little Vietnam and pick a place that looked good.

I left classes early that Friday so I could go home and change. I caught the bus to the office only to find that the whole building had been pounded into rubble, along with everything else within a seven-block radius, during a fight between Robosaurus and some weird bee-headed creature nobody had ever seen before. I hung around and tried to talk to some of the emergency guys, but they were pretty busy so I headed back home and started calling hospitals. Lucy wasn't in any of the hospitals that I called, and no one from the office knew where she was. She never came back to work at the relocated office, either. I couldn't call her at home because we'd never swapped numbers – we always saw each other at work. Someone told me that the bee-monster thing had been using some kind of hypno-pollen to turn bystanders into an army of zombie bee-drones, so I figured that that was probably what had happened to Lucy.

A few years later I bumped into her at a garage sale. She was there with her husband – she was married by then, to a really nice guy who worked in landscape gardening. She said she'd followed the bee monster for a couple of months until the hypno-pollen had worn off and she had come to her senses in Ulan Bator. She'd had to stow away on a Cathay Pacific flight to Townsville, and then hitch-hike back down from there. We swapped email addresses, but I never heard from her and to be honest I never sent her anything myself.

4. Serina Coustas – Sunday 26th January, 1997

I had met Serina at a party of a friend of a friend, and we'd struck up a conversation that had lasted until 4am, when we'd exchanged numbers and caught separate taxis. We arranged to meet in the botanical gardens on Australia Day, which was coming up, to check out the open-air concert that was happening that day. Serina knew someone in the headlining band, and I was just keen to tag along. We brought picnic stuff, and when it started raining we moved in under the fig trees along with everyone else who hadn't thought to bring an umbrella. The bands were pretty good. Serina's friends' band had named themselves after Doctor Malevolent, whose talk show was popular at the time among people who liked to think that their superior sense of irony made that kind of pop-culture trash actually worth watching.

Two songs into their set a scruffy, bearded, barefoot guy who had been wandering among the crowd came up to us and handed us an invitation to a march that was coming up to protest against the government's recent military action against Krigga and other offshore daikaiju. I made some offhand comment about nobody caring about giant monsters and Serina got upset. She didn't think that the government had been justified in their pre-emptive strikes, but I told her that I thought that they had done the right thing. Our conversation soon devolved into an argument, and from there it became a series of personal attacks, each of us caricaturing the other as warmongering nationalistic speciesists and naïve bleeding heart hippies, respectively. Serina got up in a huff, packed away the food she had brought and pulled her blanket out from under me before storming off into the easing-off rain, leaving me sitting by myself on the wet grass next to a soggy half-eaten baguette, with the rally invitation still crumpled into a ball in my left hand.

5. Tracy Evans – Friday 20th February, 2000

My housemate Tran set me up with Tracy. He was sick to death of hearing me whinge about my recently unsuccessful love life. I met her at one of those "hidden" bars in the CBD that everybody knows the name of, stepping over the vomit puddles and syringes that littered the obscure back-alley laneway which led to the seemingly barricaded entrance. Tracy was sitting at a corner table by herself, sipping a gin and tonic. I introduced myself and she stood up to shake my hand. Our voices were only just audible over the DJ's choice of up-to-the-minute noise. I excused myself for a moment and grabbed an overpriced beer from the bar before rejoining her. Conversation was slow-going, especially with the omnipresent beats, but she seemed nice enough.

We were both shy, and a little nonplussed about being out on a blind date, but we made an effort to entertain each other anyway. After a couple of drinks I suggested that we grab some dinner somewhere, and pretty soon we were in a cute little yakuza-run Japanese restaurant sharing bowls of agedashi tofu and nasu dengaku. I excused myself to go to the toilet and when I got back she was talking to the guy sitting at the table behind ours. Turned out he was an old friend of hers from high school who'd gone on to join the city's damage-control unit. He was charming the pants off Tracy, bragging about his close encounters with Nerodon and King Zenah, showing off in high-resolution detail about rescuing grandmothers from the claws of Batroxigon and finding children still alive in the collapsed basements of buildings destroyed by Gaijantizu and her Twelve Twin Sisters.

I took my seat after being introduced and watched Tracy's eyes sparkle and heard her make quiet thrilled noises at the back of her throat as Mister Damage Control went on and on about himself. After ten minutes I got up, paid the bill and left without either of them noticing me. On the way home the train was diverted to avoid a battle between the Neutrazilla Posse and Harmonadon. Everyone in the carriage rushed to the window to get a better look, but I pretended to be absorbed by the torn copy of *MetNews* on the seat beside me.

6. Lainie Goldberg – Thursday 8th October, 2002

It took weeks before Lainie would agree to go out with me. I'm not usually so persistent with women, but there was something about Lainie that made me decide to take each of her excuses at face value and keep trying to find a night of the week that she wasn't already doing something. Hearing about the things she would be doing instead of going out with me just made her seem more interesting: theatre, dance recitals, Vipassaña retreats, looking after guest artists from the innumerable festivals that the city hosted, gigs with her band . . . I'd gone along to a couple of her shows, but Lainie had always been surrounded by a gaggle of cool-looking hangers-on and groupies at the end of the night and I'd caught the last tram home rather than bothering to try to catch her attention.

I'm not sure what it was that changed her mind. Maybe she genuinely was free that night. I was just happy to be finally on a date with Lainie Goldberg, drummer from Retort Stand and the friendliest bartender at the Stars and Garters Hotel. We were meeting at the steps under the clocks at Central Station, so I walked the few blocks to my local station and jumped a train into the city. We were approaching the major inter-city station when a voice came over the PA system. It was an incomprehensible jumble of vowels and consonants, like all railway announcements, but among the garble one word could be heard clearly: Zillasaurus. The train slowed to a halt and the emergency lighting came on. The buzz of nervous conversation filled the cabin as people tried to work out what was going on. A guy with a walkman radio tuned into a news channel and relayed the news to us all over the continual, indecipherable chatter coming from the PA. Apparently the so-called "defender of children across the world" was being mind-controlled by his old enemy Power Outage and forced to cut the city off from outside help by destroying all major transport centres.

It took an hour before the CyberSamurai arrived with their Z-Bot Restrainivore so that they could hold Zillasaurus down long enough to deprogram the mind-control device, and another three hours before external power was restored to the trains and the doors of the carriage could be opened. I caught a taxi to Central Station, unable to help rubbernecking at all the flattened buildings and stomped-on cars. The taxi driver gave me his own personal spin on the attack, a conspiracy theory that made John Pilger and Chris Carter seem like suburban right-wingers by comparison. I paid the fare and took the steps two at a time, but I hadn't really expected Lainie to wait.

Her shifts at the pub changed soon afterwards and I didn't see much of her after that. I sort of lost interest, to be honest. The prospect of hounding a girl at least five years younger than me into giving me another chance seemed less than appealing all of a sudden. The last time I saw her was about six months ago in a Retorts clip on *Rage* late one Saturday night. She looked good. But then she always looked good.

7. Nancy Kiyanfar – Monday 12th April, 2004

I hadn't seen Nancy since uni. We had had a couple of the same history lectures, and had been part of the same study group. I'd always enjoyed her sense of humour and her insightful, intelligent way of looking at the world. At the time she had had a long-term boyfriend whose name was Jaived or Javed or something like that. I bumped into her in my local newsagency a few years later. She'd split up with the boyfriend about a year after graduating and moved out of the city to work as an environmental consultant for rural councils. She was back in town, visiting cousins who coincidentally lived at the end of my street, and was thinking about moving back permanently. We arranged to have dinner that night. Being Monday, most restaurants were shut, so I invited her to my place and promised to cook her my special vegetarian carbonara. At seven-thirty she rang my doorbell and I opened the door to the sight of Nancy dressed in a gorgeous burgundy dress, which wordlessly confirmed my hopes that the late-teenaged flirting I fondly remembered had not been purely the product of nostalgic self-delusion.

Dinner was delicious and the conversation was comfortable and continuous. We filled each other in on what we'd been doing for the last five years, which of our classmates we'd stayed in touch with, and joked about how we were dealing with the terrifying prospect of entering our early thirties. I cleared the dishes away and poured us both another glass of wine. I was just about to get dessert ready when I noticed that she was looking a little pale. I asked her what was wrong and she waved her hand dismissively. Just a bit of a headache, she said, frowning. She pushed her chair back from the table and began massaging her temples. I offered to grab her some painkillers and went to the bathroom to dig out some ibuprofen. When I came back into the kitchen, Nancy wasn't there. I could hear the sound of her voice coming from the back yard. I assumed that she was talking to someone on her mobile, but when I followed her outside I realized that she wasn't alone.

Standing in front of Nancy, dwarfing the pair of fully grown ghost gums that grew on the back fenceline, was Cygnatora, all two hundred feet of her. She had curved her snake-like neck downwards so that her head was only five feet from the ground, and was looking straight at Nancy, her jagged-toothed beak only inches from Nancy's face. As I stood there in the doorway, Cygnatora turned her massive head slightly and stared at me with her deep-red smouldering eyes. I froze. Nancy turned around and saw me standing there, then turned back to

Cygnatora. The two of them kept talking for a while, the giant creature making weird subsonic groans that I could feel in the pit of my stomach as it spoke. Nancy came over to me and explained that she had had a psychic link with Cygnatora since she was a little girl, and that she was going to have to go off and help out with a battle that was taking place on the other side of the Moon. She apologized for not mentioning it earlier, thanked me for dinner and told me how nice it had been to see me again. She stepped onto the monster's beak and climbed up to sit directly behind her head. She waved as Cygnatora spread her enormous wings and took off into the sky, leaving me with a flattened back shed, a pair of footprints in my back yard each the size of an above-ground swimming pool, and an entire black cherry cake with cream-cheese icing to eat by myself.

The Eyes of Erebus
Chris McMahon

———

The Dark is alive.

It hums with points of red and violet. Distant places of heat, sometimes teasing with the brilliance of their demise. It is filled with the silence of dumb mass; and strands of unknowable strangeness that twist out of sight within the coldness.

. . . Oooo, la, la, la, la . . .

There are senseless calls in the distance – the meaningless chatter of an empty universe.

I am lonely.

My lover has gone, worn down by my embrace, yet her memory remains in stone and flowering teeth of metal, vast cords of heavy basalt tied with my hard, desiccated flesh. Gifts of ice all but gone.

My eyes are vast and many, reflecting the tiny lights around me. So distant they are, yet I have seen them swell before, and as they do, my need grows apace.

I have taken many lovers, some wet, others as dry as dust, others frozen with an acid tongue, but all I take into me. None endure, nor remain to be part of me, to share this vastness.

I parted from my mother long aeons past. The flesh between us ripped on jagged edges. I tried to call, but my voice is a small thing, and as yet I am young. Never again have I passed her in this desert sea.

The lovers fail to satisfy, although their taste is a welcome distraction. My mother will have taken many by now, perhaps she will not even remember me.

Sleep at least is an end to the longing. And dream . . . my beautiful dreams . . . if only I were old enough to call as I should, perhaps then I would have my lover. Sleep . . .

> *. . . . travellin' down that lonely road,*
> *Oh, lordy mamma!*
> *I don't get no pork and beans.*
> *Oh, honey.*
> *I needs me a sugar-baby . . .*

A call!

Faithfully the signals are filtered through the shifting, swarming nodes of my nervous system. Thoughts. Feelings.

Strange. My Vendeth line has heard nothing like this before, but I am not discouraged. Each line has its own language.

Nothing more than a fragment, yet the first words since I ripped from my mother, long ago.

I search, spin and twirl, my senses reaching for the slightest trace, eyes fully open. If only I had not been asleep I would know the direction!

Excitement slowly leaches from me.

Was it nothing but a dream? Wishful thinking transforming the chatter into sense?

The lights are cold, and far away.

> *. . . and despite the health problems, Chuck."*
> *"Yes, Bob. We could not describe Eisenhower's return to office as anything else but a landslide."*
> *"Absolutely. What a result. Only eight holdout states . . . "*

There! Strange in its quality, yet words. Reaching toward me from a distant point of heat.

Does my lover wait for me even now?

This is the chance I have prayed for.

I let myself fall, swinging around one of the massive, silent giants. The tight manoeuvre has given me the speed I need.

I fix my vision on that one light in the dark.

I groan, despairing at my hunger and thirst. I hear nothing, and fear soon overwhelms me, but it is too late. I am truly in the void now. Nothing to speed me, or slow me in my flight.

One sign! That is all I ask.

My girl she knows how to roll,
O Betty!
You looks so sweet in my '50 Chevy.
Ooo, baby, ya' know how ta' jive!

There! Again. This time there can be no mistake. My sensitive ears have confirmed the target. My lover awaits! Who else could be talking such as she? Here amid the terrible emptiness of my Universe.

Soon . . .

———

"And of course, here is the man who needs no introduction. The man who saved Earth from the threat of Nemesis. Director Matrick Keterson."

Applause filled the room, the dim, cold corners cut by bright staccato flashes as photographers surged against the red-roped barriers.

Mat stepped up from the stage onto the tiny platform to join Vice-President Linten and Hari Wottard, NASA Director of Space Sciences. His head swam with the view. The Caltech lecture theatre was packed with press, suit-clad men and women in sombre power-dress. He looked across an auditorium jammed with students, all in awe as they stared up at him on the podium. Scattered amongst them were the members of his own team. Jereece, unshaven as usual, gave him a languid wave.

The applause became deafening as he took the lectern, and he unconsciously gritted his teeth. His hair was steel-grey, as it had been since his early twenties, neatly trimmed around a long, serious face.

He tried to smile and raised his hands to still the applause, his two lanky arms like a crane's wings fanning out beside him.

"Please . . . please . . . "

Gradually the applause subsided.

"Thank you. But first of all, diverting 2047KW13 was a joint effort, a team one. And equal praise must go to Director Yo Tein of the Peoples Republic of China and Vladimir Rotanski from the Russian Space Directorate." Mat turned to nod at Tein and Rotanski. "Without their help, and the help of their governments, this . . . this incredible achievement would not have been possible." Tein nodded back with polite reserve, while Rotanski merely glared.

"The list of all those who contributed is just too long. Both here at JPL and throughout NASA, where I have been lucky enough to be part of this extraordinary program."

He took a breath and looked at the crowd.

"Ladies and gentlemen. This is truly an historic time for Mankind. For the first time we have been able to protect our home, Earth, from an asteroid impact of devastating proportions.

"The revolutionary NTRs – Nuclear Thermal Rockets – now installed on 2047KW13 have already pushed it out of a collision course with Earth, using ice from the asteroid itself as propellant."

Mat stopped and scanned the crowd. They were quiet, expectant. The sound of a stifled cough from the back of the auditorium filled the room.

"There were some who said the task of diverting a 123 kilometre-long asteroid was impossible. But thankfully advance warning from our Near-Earth Object program, along with our NTR technology, meant that we got the crucial lead time we needed to meet the beast head on."

"We beat Nemesis!' screamed out a man in the front row.

The room broke into applause again.

The news was really months old. But now that the huge asteroid was less than one day away from its fly-by of Earth, the whole world was on watch – and the PR geniuses at NASA had judged it the ideal time for this event.

In the rush to divert the massive asteroid, no one had thought to name it, but that had not stopped the press. "Nemesis" was irresistible, and that name had been splashed in heavy black across media headlines for the last seven years.

"Ah, ladies and gentlemen, please . . . please! And I must correct that gentleman in the front row, and all the members of the press here please take note. 2047KW13 is not called Nemesis. There is already a minor planet called Nemesis, 128, which bears no resemblance to 2047KW13."

"When will it be named," yelled back the man, his press-tag glistening in the lights as he rocked on his heels excitedly.

Mat smiled and looked across to Hari, holding up his palms in a silent question.

Hari whispered to the Vice-President, who nodded and flashed a bright row of Texas teeth.

Hari stepped up to the podium beside him and leaned across to the mike. "One of the announcements we have for you today is the naming of 2047KW13. Usually these things are named by the astronomer who first discovered the object, but in view of the circumstances we thought it only fitting that Director Keterson have the honour."

The room erupted in applause again, and Mat looked across to the doorway to see Jereece leaning against the sill, his eyes slightly mocking as he took in the scene. Jereece had been one of the key people on Mat's team, a team leader in the NEO program and the man who first identified 2047KW13. It seemed a lifetime ago – those heart-stopping months when they realized its orbit would swing it past Jupiter and send that massive lump of ice, carbon and rock heading straight for Earth.

Hari raised his hand to the crowd then waved at Mat, clapping above his head as the room went wild.

Camera flashes stabbed into his eyes, and suddenly the empty, blank lenses were filling his view. He felt himself staring at the beginning of a vast, unstoppable future.

"It *is* an honour, and one that should not be mine."

Calls came from the room, demanding the name.

"Very well, ladies and gentlemen . . . I will keep you waiting no longer." He raised his hands once more for silence.

"I have decided to name 2047KW13 . . . Erebus."

There was silence as the room took in the name, a sense of confusion, perhaps even disappointment.

"Erebus is a deity from Greek mythology – always an old favourite for planets." That had been his ice-breaker joke, but it went completely flat.

"Erebus arose from Chaos, and was wedded to the darkness of the night, but also represented an infernal region, through which souls had to pass to reach Hades. And this – this whole project – has been a test and a challenge for Humanity. But we have passed through it, to a place where we are one step closer to controlling our wider destiny in this beautiful but deadly Universe."

There were more camera flashes, then Mat was being ushered away from the podium, displaced by Linten, who raised his hands to the crowd and began a prepared speech that highlighted the foresight and good sense of the Yerry administration. He was soon finished and people surrounded Mat, shaking his hand, patting him on the back. Everyone was talking at once, and a dense wall of expectant eyes pressed in on him.

Mat rose onto the balls of his feet to look over the heads of the crowd. He spotted Jereece and the other members of his team and waved them over. If he was going to share this moment with anyone, it would be them. They started moving toward him, but the packed crowd was swarming toward the stage now and they were pushed back.

The reporters arrived. Microphones and cameras were pushing into his face.

"Mr Keterson, what are your plans now . . . "

"Are you staying with NASA?"

"Here, Mr Keterson!"

"Mr Keterson, you have any comment to the rumours . . . "

Mat surveyed them coldly, wondering how he could extricate himself without seeming rude or aloof.

Hari appeared and took Mat by the elbow. As Director of Space Sciences he had a more public role than Mat's, and seemed at ease negotiating the aggressive crowd of TV-jockeys.

"Thank you, ladies and gentlemen. There will be more opportunities for questions after the reception," he said.

Rapid-fire questions trailed after them.

Hari nodded and four secret service agents neatly surrounded them, cutting off the press. They followed the Vice-President's entourage into an adjacent hall, which had been decked out in silver service for the grand reception. Mat was in the VIP section. By design, he and the other dignitaries were scattered through a crowd of wealthy supporters, multi-millionaires who had invested in the NTR technology. Without them, Erebus would still be hurtling toward them on its deadly course.

He dreaded the dinner, and was longing for the blessed silence and comfort of his small apartment. No doubt he would be saddled with some boorish oil billionaire whose thirty-year-old engineering degree and avid reading of the *Wall Street Journal* qualified him as a space expert.

Mat was relieved to take his seat, and eagerly accepted a cool lager from the waiter, drinking it down greedily before the press of the crowd forced social niceties on him. His face flushed with heat as the alcohol began its work, and his body relaxed. He loosened his top button and tie, and was about to lounge back in his seat when he caught sight of her.

"I believe this is my seat, Mr Keterson?"

Mat almost choked on his beer, but managed to swallow and straighten in the same motion.

She was tall and elegant, her wavy yellow-blonde hair matched perfectly to her long golden dress, which shimmered in the soft overhead lights.

"By all means, allow me . . . " said Mat, leaping up to make the suave manoeuvre of taking her chair out for her. Unfortunately his long legs caught under the table, sending the silver service and precisely laid glassware skittering across the heavy linen. He looked across at her, but only the merest tension at the corners of her mouth hinted at a suppressed smile. He was grateful for her tact.

"Why, thank you." Her accent was Southern, and delightfully sexy. "I am Athy Jates." She held out a soft yet strong hand for him to shake.

"Matrick Keterson. Pleased to meet you."

She smiled, her soft brown eyes lighting up in her rounded, beautiful face, offset perfectly with shades of subtle makeup.

He felt a little foolish introducing himself – half the world must know his face – but she seemed genuinely pleased.

Mat waved for the waiter, unobtrusively straightening his tie as Athy turned her head to watch the waiter approach.

She scanned the tray and looked back at the waiter. "Do you think you could find me some of that champagne?"

The waiter nodded, and Mat took another beer before he disappeared. He knew he should slow down – didn't they always say not to get too smashed at these things? – but after the stress of the last few months, he just needed to let loose.

He put down his empty glass and saw Athy smiling at him.

"You know, I have always wanted to meet you, Matrick. We were all so lucky to have someone like you in control of that project."

The waiter arrived with Athy's Moët. Mat took another beer and smiled, feeling relaxed and happy with the world for the first time in . . . well, seven years.

"Cheers," said Athy, holding up her glass.

He looked right into her eyes and felt a jolt of excitement. She seemed cool and collected, but Mat could not help noticing the heave of her chest above the low neck-line of the off-the-shoulder gown, or the slight tremor in her hand as they clinked glasses.

She smiled.

"Cheers," he replied.

The table filled up around them, but Mat did not take his eyes off Athy.

The waiter arrived once more, and they eagerly reached for the tray.

———

Jarry Twine pushed himself carefully across the tiny cabin of the NTR control unit. Even after almost a year in the micro-gravity of 2047KW13, he was still overbalancing. It was a tiny space, no bigger than a small trailer, yet was packed with electronics and process control equipment. The air was rank with body odours and the stale, artificial flavours of their ration-packs.

"Vapour flow on ejection port five sub-optimal, Ranky. I'd get on it," said Jarry.

"Roger, control," came the reply from Ranky, who was EVA at NTR#3, six hundred metres away.

Jarry felt a slight tremor under his feet.

"Oh, boy."

He raised the radio mike to his lips.

"Ranky! Tie yourself down! We've got another one!"

Despite the analysis of 2047KW13's structure, and all the modelling, the whole rock had been shaking like a Turkish apartment block.

They'd had seven tremors in the last shift alone. Big ones, too.

"Roger, Control. Going for tie-down."

Each of the EVA rigs carried an explosive spike for emergencies, allowing the operator to tie themselves securely to the deep-frozen ice and rock of the surface in less than a minute.

The floor surged up under Jarry's feet and his porta-screen shot across the room. He made a grab for it, but a drinking tube slammed into the side of his head.

"Fuck!"

Loose papers and equipment shot around the cabin, tossed like greens in a salad shaker as the thin walls trembled. Soon the whole thing was shaking, the big alloy casings of the monitors banging together violently.

Multiple alarms blared.

He tried to brace himself and access the console at the same time. It was useless. The keyboard was moving too much.

He pushed across the cabin and hit the view-port release. The hydraulics whined and the heavy shield shot back from the window.

"Holy mother—"

The whole surface of the asteroid was rippling, waves passing through it as though it was a fluid. He could see two of the big NTR installations being literally shaken loose.

Cries for help came from everywhere.

"Jarry! I need help. I can't hold—"

"This is NTR#1, we have systems failure—"

"Control! *Control!*"

"*Oh, mother of Christ!*"

He felt one of the big mounts on the control shack break. Then another. A wave lifted him up, tilting the whole space.

The NTR#1 control unit smashed into his chest. Pain flared from his right side.

Jarry looked out through the window.

The rough surface of ice and rock was gone. In its place was a strange, patterned expanse of bulging hemispheres, perfectly regular, as though the whole thing had been constructed by forcing dark spheres together until they joined without a gap.

A crack appeared across the middle of each bulging section.

Jarry screamed, his hands bloody as they beat at the weight of the casing that pinned him.

Another ripple swept through Erebus.

This one ripped the control room apart.

Jarry's breath was sucked from him, his whole body swelling with red-hot pain as he decompressed, tumbling out into space.

The surface of each hemisphere drew back.

He tried to scream, but the greedy emptiness sucked even harder at his vital fluids. Then his eyes exploded, leaving him in agonizing blindness.

————

Mat woke suddenly, desperately thirsty, and with a thumping headache. He felt a soft warmth against his side and the night came back in a rush.

He looked down to see Athy, her naked body curled into him, her large breasts and small pink nipples pressed into his thin chest, wavy yellow-blonde hair tumbled across his shoulder. Even through the pain he smiled, remembering the fun they had had playing cat and mouse with the media, giving the paparazzi the slip somewhere between Caltech and Athy's suite.

But something was not right.

There was an angry rhythmic sound pulsing in his ears. It sounded like traffic. No. Not traffic.

Mat groaned and shook his head.

He delicately extracted himself from Athy, covering her gently with a sheet. Then he rummaged around in the mini-bar to find the headache tablets, washing down three with a Coke, wincing as the ice-cold carbonated mixture hit his throat.

Athy had a huge suite, and he moved into the lounge room and flicked on the television.

News.

He flicked again.

News.

Again.

News.

News. News. News.

It was on every single channel.

His eyes widened and he turned up the volume on a chat show.

" . . . some are calling it incompetence, others scientific error. But all agree we have been betrayed at the highest level," said the host.

"But the thing is. How can a mistake like this be made?"

The camera swung. The man was red-faced, obviously sweating in his cheap suit. He was so angry he was almost rising from his chair as he spoke. "How can an organization like NASA, with all the resources at their command, make a mistake like this?"

The camera returned to the host. "How indeed?" he said solemnly.

"But the real question is, where the Hell is Matrick Keterson?" said an older woman.

"My God, it's Marjorie Heters," said Mat, recognizing a highly respected astronomer that had worked alongside his own team.

There was a thumping on the door, growing louder.

The camera swivelled back to the host.

"Just to recap. Australian astronomers tracking Erebus have this morning confirmed the massive asteroid is back on a course for Earth. Despite the best efforts of NASA and co-operation . . . "

Mat could not take it in. The words washed over his sleep-deprived and alcohol-sodden brain, refusing to register.

The thumping on the door was violent now, and he could hear the roaring again, growing louder.

"Who is it?"

He looked up to see Athy, tying a patterned silk gown of blue, yellow and red around her as she headed for the door.

"I . . . "

He realized he was completely naked, and he had time only to gather a pillow from the lounge to cover his privates when Hari Wottard burst into the room flanked by six secret service agents and three aides.

"Mat. Where the Hell have you been? I have been trying to reach you since 3am."

"I . . . " He had turned off his cell even before he left the reception.

Mat looked across to the clock on the wall. 4:17pm. *Christ!*

Hari pushed into the room and drew the heavy drapes, letting in the harsh afternoon sun.

"Look down there, damn you! *Look!*"

Mat stumbled toward the window, shielding his eyes from the painful glare with one hand while he held the pillow with the other. He knew nine men would be staring at his white, skinny arse.

An angry crowd, swelling by the moment, packed the courtyard and entrance of the hotel.

Mat squinted, trying to read the placards, but his eyes were still too fuzzy.

"What on earth do they want?" asked Mat.

"Want? They want to know how the *fuck* you got it wrong, Keterson. We all want to know!"

Mat's hands went slack, the pillow dropping to the rich carpet. He felt himself shrivel to the size of a pin-prick.

"You mean . . . ?"

"Erebus is still headed for Earth. *Still headed for Earth.*"

"Excuse me, gentlemen."

It was Athy, polite to a fault; and not the least bit intimidated to have ten angry strangers in her room while she was a good as naked.

"I think you should leave. Matrick will attend shortly."

"He'll be coming with us. Even if I have to drag him," snapped Hari, his face flushing red.

Athy took a small cellphone from her gown and hit a speed-dial button.

"Afternoon, Mr Kalls. Would you be so kind as to come up to the main suite with your staff?"

About ten seconds later four extremely tough-looking bodyguards moved into the room, flanking the other secret-service agents.

"I believe you are in my private quarters, Mr Wottard."

By now, Mat had collected his thoughts. If what they were saying was true, he needed to assess that data straight away. It made sense. Only the stations in Australia would be in position to track Erebus right now, but that would be changing within hours. When the US stations came on-line he wanted to see that data first hand.

"Wait outside, Hari," he said. "I'll be right out."

Hari glared at Athy, then stalked out of the room, followed by his men.

"Miss Jates?" said Kalls.

"Thank you, Mr Kalls. If you would be so kind as to wait outside for me. Perhaps you could keep those other gentlemen company?"

Kalls smiled, revealing two golden teeth amid a row of chipped neighbours.

"Yes, Ma'am."

As the room emptied, Matrick walked across to Athy. He stopped a few paces away, unsure.

"I have no idea what's going on, Athy. But I'm sorry to bring this down on you."

She smiled and closed the distance between them, rising up on her toes to plant a soft, warm kiss on his cheek.

"Now, don't you go worrying about me, Matrick. You just take your time. No need to rush into that shark's den out there. Erebus is still more than twenty hours away, and you know as well as I do the US stations will not be on-line for hours."

The smell of her soft skin and hair sent a thrill through Mat, and she smiled mischievously, sweeping her eyes down to his stirring member. She untied the front of her gown and leant in closer. He could feel the soft warmth of her skin pressed against his. She tilted her head up and kissed him passionately before pushing away and retying her gown. He had one last fleeting glimpse.

"Business before pleasure, Mr Keterson."

She took a breath, her eyes growing more serious.

"Now. You can use the other bathroom. I will have some fresh clothes brought up for you."

She smiled once more then disappeared back into her suite.

Mat felt foolish standing in the middle of the vast sitting room alone, and walked across to the other side where a set of sliding doors gave access to an unused apartment that was the twin of Athy's.

He went straight to the shower, his headache now compounded by nausea as the effects of the night caught up with him.

He needed to break down events, analyze them, but he hardly knew where to begin.

He let the hot stream wash through his hair and down his back. The citrus smell of the hotel shampoo refreshed him as he worked it into his hair.

How could 2047KW13 – *Erebus* – change orbit? Every calculation, every projection they had made had been broken down and checked to the last line, the last constant. Double-checked. Triple-checked. Ratified and cleared by five teams of independent experts. They had even surveyed the huge body before installing the NTR thrusters and the automated mining plants. They knew the density, the composition. The rest was mechanics – and the basic laws of physics did *not* change. So assuming Erebus had flipped, how could it happen? Sabotage? A nuclear strike on the body itself? Some unforeseen geological event? Impossible. Nothing that small could be geologically active – not even the Moon was. Collision with another body? Also impossible. The nearby space was mapped down to objects the size of a pebble.

He turned off the shower and dried himself, marvelling at the softness of the towel. He was surrounded by luxury. Which suddenly reminded him where he was: in the suite of Athy Jates, one of the wealthiest female industrialists in the USA.

He walked back into the bedroom of the twin apartment to find clothes laid out on his bed along with his personal effects. He felt mildly unnerved he had not heard anyone enter. He dressed quickly, checking his watch with concern as he pulled the expanding band over his wrist.

And what about his people on Erebus? Had no one heard from them?

"I've got to get to JPL. *Fast.*"

He combed his hair quickly, hardly sparing a glance for his drawn, ashen face in the mirror. His mind was already in hyperdrive, flashing ahead, running down alternate paths of investigation. If Erebus was headed for them, they had little time. None of it could be wasted on navel-gazing or over-analyzing the errors. The effort to re-divert that monolith *must* come first.

He swept into the sitting room, ready to call a quick goodbye to Athy on his way out of the apartment, but was brought up short.

A huge dining table had appeared in the middle of the room, its gleaming surface reflecting the last, glaring rays of the LA sun as it dipped in the West. A vast breakfast, all on silver service platters, was laid out on the table.

Seated at one side, with a place set up beside her, was Athy, now in a long dress of dark grey, her hair pulled back in a single ponytail.

"Athy, I need to get to JPL."

She smiled. "Of course you do. But after you've eaten. If this crisis is as big as it looks, you may not get another decent meal for days."

"But, Hari is outside—"

"Let him wait. I insist." Her voice had taken on an edge of steel, and for the first time Mat fully registered the change in her demeanour. She had transformed herself from Southern Belle to Corporate Executive.

He stepped toward the table and pulled out a chair.

At the table beside her, until now concealed by a silver candelabra, were two top-of-the-line laptops, one of which was split into six small screens.

"I have had Dajourie scanning the airways for us. This story has gone worldwide. But nothing of substance so far, just rumours and panic. It will be more than half-an-hour before the US tracking stations are online." Athy reached over and closed the media screen.

A smartly dressed woman in a red skirt and jacket entered the room.

"Ah, Dajourie. I want you to rustle up a secure phone for Mr Keterson. I think his standard link will be useless."

"Yes, Miss Jates."

Mat cursed himself, realizing he had still not turned on his cell. He pulled it out of the pocket of his coat and switched it on. Within seconds it gave an insistent *beep* and loaded with no less than one hundred and thirty-eight messages, then abruptly began to ring. Startled, Mat answered.

"Hello, erh—"

"*Mr Keterson, this is Twal Chen from* the New York Times. *Would you be able to comm—*"

Mat switched it off and laid it gently on the table. What sort of a shit-storm had he landed in?

Athy lifted one of the silver food covers, which rang with a soft *ting*.

"Greasy bacon and eggs, it's a patented hangover cure . . . Well, that and these." Athy slipped two small white pills across the table to him.

He raised one eyebrow.

"Anti-nauseant and pure codeine. Definitely not over-the-counter. But, this is an emergency . . . " She reached over and poured him an orange juice.

He swallowed the pills, wincing at the brief bitterness on his tongue – they were not sugar-coated, but then nothing today would be. It would be the truth, the whole truth, and nothing but the ugly truth.

Gritting his teeth, he took some of the bacon and eggs. He began eating methodically.

"Well, Matrick. The timing is hardly conducive, but I must admit to having an ulterior motive."

Mat was about to smile at what he thought was sexual innuendo, when he saw how serious she was. Any lover's playfulness had long vanished.

"As you know, the world headquarters for Jates Industries is in Hong Kong. I have strong business interests in China. That was where we manufactured most of the reactor components for the NTRs in your Erebus program."

Matrick poured himself a coffee, hardly taking his eyes off Athy.

She seemed suddenly unsure.

"Hell, Matrick. It was no accident I was sitting next to you last night. My Chinese associates and I wanted to offer you a job heading up our asteroid mining program. The Chinese have already committed heavily, with the government in as one-tenth partner. We have the full support of Director Tein, who will be giving us priority use of Chinese space assets."

Matrick felt the ground shift beneath his feet. It had seemed a carefree accident – a delightful night of magic – but was it nothing more than manipulation?

"Then, last night . . . "

Athy's eyes blazed. "How dare you even suggest that! What do think I am?"

Matrick dropped his fork and rubbed his temples. "I'm sorry . . . I . . . it was wonderful."

Athy took a breath and pushed her plate away from her.

"We wanted to offer you a job, Matrick, leading the program for the consortium. The rest was . . . well, unplanned. I . . . "

Mat wanted desperately to heal things between them. His first wife had left him six years ago, accusing him of . . . how had she put it? "Being an insensitive, over-analytical robot with the tact of a Nazi". He had tried hard to improve, but it seemed he still had a disastrous talent for ruining relationships.

He looked at her hopefully, searching for any sign that he had not destroyed their intimacy utterly, but she had receded into an impenetrable corporate shell. He knew then that what they had shared was something rarely given. Something quickly withdrawn.

"I see now that . . . well, with recent events it is completely impractical," said Athy.

She pushed back her chair and rose.

"Good day, sir."

She walked back into her apartments, her stiff manner the only hint at how deeply he had wounded her.

"Blast."

He turned his phone back on. It rang immediately, but this time he recognized the ring tone. He had it set to recognize Hari's cell.

"Keterson," he answered.

"Mat, finally. Look, are you coming or what? Jates's goons won't even let us ring the doorbell."

Hari sounded more relaxed.

The drugs Athy had given Mat were killing the pain, and the nausea had vanished. Suddenly he was ravenous.

"I'll be right out."

He wolfed down two helpings of the rapidly cooling breakfast, then stood, sweeping his eyes across the table setting and running his hands down the fresh, new suit Athy had provided for him.

She had been wonderful, and kind; and he had repaid her with accusations.

"Damn it!"

Dajourie appeared.

"Here, Mr Keterson."

She handed him a slim video-phone, the casing metallic and reflective.

He tapped it with his fingernail.

Dajourie turned to go, but he halted her with a light touch.

"Could you please thank Athy for me?"

Her eyes were cold and she pushed his hand away. "You can thank her yourself. Her number is programmed into the cell." Then she was gone.

Outside he pushed through Athy's guards to see Hari and all three of his aides busily talking on mobile phones.

Hari ended his call and nodded to the agents, who ushered Mat down the hall and into an elevator.

"Has the team been assembled?" asked Matrick.

"Yes, they have been working the problem, but without data . . . ," said Hari.

"When do we come online?"

"In twenty minutes. We should make it to JPL in fifteen."

"I would love to know what the hell is going on," said Matrick.

Hari simply stared at him, and Mat had the uncomfortable feeling he was measuring his neck for a noose.

————

Pestilence!

Worse even than the Seekers of the cold clouds.

Parasites of hot, flaming breath, breathing radiation like a distant sun, and yet so small and cold.

I roll again to shake off the last and the wound rips open even further.

They have torn into me! Ripping the skin and stealing the frozen blood from my outer segments.

What are these biting pests? Like all Vendeth I have the memories of my ancestors, yet nothing in that blurred landscape prepares me for this.

My sleep had been long, a blissful silence to fill the years of darkness. Lost in beautiful dreams of my lover, all skin, hot magma, steam and ice.

Slowly my blood heats, my massive body still leaking a trail of vapour into space behind me. Instinct guides me; I know my course. I pump my thinnest blood through the deep, hot chambers of my insulated heart, through funnelling veins of diamond to the rigid skin of my wings.

I unfurl, even as the rock-like skin of my lids draws back across my length. At last I take my first glimpse of this new solar system.

A cool yellow sun, triumphant in its middle years, and before me, the scent of my quarry. My ears grow sensitive once more as my blood flows and warms. Jets of superheated steam build in my outer jets, the strain against my inner walls welcome after such a period of dormancy.

> *. . . like a cold stone rapper,*
> *street hard,*
> *I don't take no fall.*
> *You can't take my grill,*
> *No, sucker.*
> *Can't take my grill . . .*

. . . . and today on the Yopa Linfey show we have a special guest, someone who has . . .

. . . . the news today, Tuesday 23 May, 2054, headlining today's stories, are the rumours true, will Erebus . . .

> *. . . Yeah, red hot!*
> *I'll burn you, baby.*
> *Ahhh! I gotta get this!*
> *Got to,*
> *Gotta, get me some . . .*

I scream and block my ears from the torrent of noise. It has been a trick. A ruse. No Vendeth mate awaits me. My heart tears with loss, then rage.

I am too small? My song too weak to attract a single lover?
Mother!

Before me lies my greatest disappointment, nothing but a planet. A cold planet, and yet . . .

I send huge jets blasting into space, stabilizing me, correcting my course, wasting vital, precious fluids; but I have no fear, no.

Even through the disappointment I feel a jolt of excitement, of lust. Many are the empty, cold lovers I have taken, yet this would be my greatest conquest.

My eyes swell with greed at the feast before me.

Oceans of precious water. Surfaces swelling with organic carbon, neatly organised into easily digested pieces by the processes of slow, gravity-bound life. With this feast, I would be mighty. My song would resound with the vast chambers of magma I could harness from this sparkling planet of blue and green.

Yes, I could truly grow.

My fins unfurl, flexing and expanding, hardening. I will need them soon, to break my fall as I surrender to the embrace of this world. This cold, mindless lover.

Oh, I hunger for your embrace.

Feel me swell . . .

———

Matrick checked his models one last time, re-running the test cases through his programs. There was nothing wrong with the modelled scenarios, although he knew that already.

The Erebus mission room was packed. His team, led by Jereece, crowded the big monitors of the darkened room, the ghostly light of the screens making their drawn, hungover faces as pale as ghouls.

Jereece could not sit still. Wired on caffeine, he paced from one station to the next, talking rapidly. He leant down to one monitor then looked back up to Matrick, where he sat with Hari and a small team of rapidly assembled experts led by Terry Kones, a presidential advisor Mat had never seen before. He was waiting to call President Yerry, a secure cell link placed with perfect symmetry on the desk in front of him. None of the "experts" had said a word, Mat's small talk met by stony, slightly terrifying silence.

Mat had asked that Rotanski and Tein attend with their teams, but he was overruled. In less than a day his project had been turned from a shining example of international cooperation to another national security project that shut everyone out except NASA and the military. Rotanski was furious, and was downstairs with his team, periodically demanding access. Tein was already back in China.

"Three minutes to tracking feed," called Jereece.

"Let's get ready, gentlemen," said Kones.

On cue, the three advisors flipped open their own heavy-duty laptops.

A dull, heavy feeling settled into the pit of Mat's stomach.

"Hari, what is going on here? I thought they were observers," said Mat.

Hari looked uncomfortable. "They *are* here to observe. Directly, for the president."

Kones looked at Mat, his eyes briefly contemptuous before becoming guarded once more. His jaw was clenched. "We are here to observe, and to take direct control of this program."

The other men, who were dressed in identical black suits with closely shaved haircuts, were busy on their laptops, and were ignoring the exchange.

Mat's heart began to hammer in his chest, and his hands came down protectively on the keyboard of his laptop.

"Hari?" asked Mat, his voice shaking with outrage.

"I'm sorry, Matrick. The president's own team have always been closely monitoring the program. With the current situation . . . we felt a change was needed. The public needs reassurance."

"What about the Russians and the Chinese?" asked Mat.

"That is being handled at the diplomatic level," said Kones.

"But this is a scientific project . . . " Then it hit him. They were not talking about another intervention. They were planning a nuclear strike on Erebus.

"Hold on a minute—" started Mat.

"No, you listen to me!" snapped Hari, his face flushing a dangerous red. "You had your chance. How you managed to *fuck* this up, I don't know. But you and your people are to give Kones and his team your full cooperation, understand me? They have a mandate from Yerry himself."

Mat was shaking not only with anger – but with fear. Time was running out, and the wrong move could spell the end for all of them.

"But, Hari," said Mat, pleading with his boss. "Surely you know that a full strike will not prevent impact. That thing is not a metallic body. Even with penetrators it will just shatter into fragments."

"Oh, we will smash it alright," said Kones. The men at his side laughed coldly.

Mat's eyes flashed down to the laptops they were using. Heavy duty. Military. They were inputting launch codes. This could not be happening. This was everything he and his team had tried to avoid.

"No, I can't let you do this."

Kones's eyes flickered to two heavy-muscled, armed MPs who had been standing guard unobtrusively at the door. They were behind Kones' chair in an instant.

Mat's jaw went slack and he looked across to Hari in disbelief.

"I'm sorry, Matrick. National security."

Kones motioned with his chin, and the two marine MPs returned to their position.

Jereece, oblivious to the whole thing, turned toward them and held up his hands, counting down with his fingers.

"Feed in ten, nine . . . "

They all looked up to the huge screens above the room, now displaying the NASA logo.

" . . . three, two, one."

One of the screens flickered, went dark then filled with an actual magnified view of Erebus, coming in from their advance observation satellites. The asteroid was a tiny blip against a field of bright stars.

"Jereece. Anything from Control on Erebus?" asked Mat.

Jereece's face was grim. He shook his head. Seven astronauts. His people. Gone.

Mat's attention went to the second screen, which had a bright set of orbital schematics set against a light blue background. A heavy black line denoted the corrected orbit Erebus should have taken, while a red line showed another trajectory entirely, one with multiple, irregular changes to speed and direction. It looked like a joke. Something concocted by a team of drunken NASA scientists after the Christmas party. Asteroids just did *not* behave like this.

But Mat did not draw any conclusions; he was too well trained for that.

"Jereece. Feed the trajectory information over the network," called Mat.

"OK. Should be coming across . . . now."

The raw data loaded into Mat's program and he initiated an interpretive scenario. The fast little machine spat the results out in less than ten seconds.

His breathing grew fast and shallow as he looked over the results. His hands began to shake, his fingers tingling with hyperventilation.

"Work the results," he muttered to himself. "Work the results."

The room was full of raised voices on the edge of panic.

He forced his breathing to slow.

"Quiet down, people. Focus on the job." His voice was stern, but controlled.

The noise receded.

"We only need the current orbit for the targeting satellites, gentlemen. Let's not waste any time," said Kones.

Mat could hardly believe the insanity that was taking place here. Any nuclear strike – however massive – would leave myriad smaller fragments to rain down on Earth. Not only that, Erebus was now too close for even the most massive of explosions to divert. He had to shut Kones out of his mind. He needed to understand what was happening.

Based on his modelling, it appeared that somehow Erebus had flipped itself, not once but seventeen times until every one of the four NTR mounts and the Control base had been dislodged, along with the automated ice-miners. Then it had changed its own orbit by applying thrust. There had been no collision; no explosion. It had been a carefully controlled orbit correction. Erebus was acting like a spaceship. A spaceship under the control of some sort of intelligence. There was no other explanation.

But the surveys? Multiple sample points, taken randomly, some at depths of up to ten kilometres below the surface. They revealed nothing but carbon, ice and rock, all mixed like a pudding across the surface of the body. The composition had been remarkably consistent – yet they found nothing that would suggest an artificial construct. Their high-energy scans of the internal structure had been designed only to determine if it had enough integrity to take the applied thrust of the NTRs without fracturing.

The secure cell on the desk in front of Kones rang. He swept it up and answered it with machine-like precision.

"Lieutenant-Colonel Kones here, sir. Everything is ready. Do we have the Russians and the Chinese on board, sir?"

Mat could hear Yerry's voice, small and mouse-like across the link, but could not make out the words.

"Yes. We have relayed the targeting information," said Kones in reply.

"Wait!" yelled Mat. "Stop! Erebus is some sort of spaceship."

Suddenly Mat was lifted from his feet and dragged away into the corner of the room, one MP on either arm.

Jereece watched it happen with incomprehension, the pen in his mouth falling to clatter on his desk. The other members of Mat's team had ceased work, some standing up from their seats.

"Get back to work! All of you," yelled Hari.

Reluctantly they re-took their seats, but their eyes were glued to Mat. Not a single one of them was moving.

"The feed, Jereece! Crank the magnification on Erebus to max!" yelled Mat.

Jereece worked his terminal furiously.

Mat did not struggle. He would win this only by convincing Hari and Kones what they were dealing with. If he was right, if Erebus was a spaceship on its way to visit Earth, then it would already be shifting into position for an orbital insertion but it was not. It was on a collision course.

The tiny image of the asteroid increased in size until it filled a quarter of the screen, then magnified again.

Gone was the irregular shape, crusted with ice and debris from its long journey through the Oort cloud.

What they saw now was a long segmented form, like a string of pearls, flanked by six wings of reflective material that drew together at ninety degrees to the body like the petals of some enormous flower. Each spherical segment was faceted, like the featured surface of a geodesic dome. The wings were supported by wedge-shaped structures that emerged from the central segment, darker in colour than the bright wings themselves.

"Jesus, those sails must be more than a hundred kilometres square," said Jereece.

"They are symmetrical," said Mat in wonder. "This has to be an artificial structure. Hari! Kones! This is a ship. A spaceship."

Kones looked at the image without emotion. Beside him Hari's mouth was open, his eyes fixed on the screen.

"Is it still on a collision course for Earth?" said Kones.

"Yes," said Jereece. "It's accelerating."

No. This cannot be right.

"Jereece. Its course must be consistent with some sort of orbital insertion. Check it. Quickly!"

Jereece rapidly worked the data. He paused, shook his head then tried a different approach, then turned to Mat.

"Whatever this thing is, Mat. It will impact on its current course."

Mat could not understand. If it was some sort of a ship, perhaps driven by an automated system, was it possible that it had been damaged by their efforts to divert it? No. Its orbital corrections had been too precise. The conclusion was inescapable. The intelligence that directed Erebus meant for that thing to hit them.

The panic rose again, and this time Mat did nothing to stop it. What could he do?

As they watched they could see jets of material shoot in unison from it segments.

"It's increasing speed."

The huge, gossamer wings fell away, leaving only the stubby support structures. The whole body was becoming streamlined, the segments drawing together and flattening out.

Kones lifted the cell link back to his ear. "The object is still on collision course and is accelerating, Mr President," said Kones. "Acknowledged, Mr President."

"Kones! Tell your men to release me," said Mat.

Kones gave Mat a level look, then nodded to the MPs, who let him go and marched back to their station at the door.

Mat took his seat and watched the screen, fighting a sense of unreality. It was as though he had left the world he knew and stepped through into somewhere else – somewhere utterly alien. He knew a nuclear strike would not avert the threat. Yet as furiously as he considered the problem, he could provide no alternative. How could he have foreseen this? *This!* Perhaps Rotanski's people could think of something.

Kones looked across to his men. "We have the Russians and the Chinese on board. Let's proceed with the strike."

"Mr Kones," said Mat.

Kones looked across at Mat, his eyes intense.

"Is there any way we could delay the strike? Get Rotanski's people in here? There may be something else we can do."

"Negative," said Kones, continuing as though Mat had said nothing.

Mat pushed his palms into his eyes, trying to stifle the impulse to scream at Kones. He had to seize control of the moment – to think of something. But it was too late.

"Gentlemen. Target locked. Satellite online. Initiate on my mark. Three. Two. One. Mark."

Kones and his team hit their keyboards in unison. Four soft taps, and their fate was sealed. Seconds later there was a series of snaps as the lids shut.

"What are you hitting it with?" said Mat.

"This has all been modelled by our own people," said Kones, reopening his laptop. "I've sent the data through your network. We have one hundred and twenty-five warheads converging on Erebus. More than a thousand megatons of firepower. Seventeen will penetrate the asteroid itself; the rest are programmed to detonate at the surface."

Mat plugged the data into his own model, but he already knew the answer. Finding those launchers at short notice was impressive. Even so. Ten years ago, with Erebus so much further from Earth, a strike like this might have made a difference, but not now. His own model confirmed his fears.

It would be more than seventeen hours before the missiles closed on Erebus. For now he needed a strong coffee, and to collect his thoughts.

He pulled out his cell to check his messages, but before he could even turn it on Kones snatched it from his hands.

"No private communications allowed."

Mat glared at Kones, but he seemed invulnerable to any protest.

Kones waved to the two MPs.

"Sweep everyone. No communications are to go in or out. The network is already sealed to the outside."

Mat looked over at Hari. "What the hell is this?"

Hari shrugged, and for the first time Mat saw defeat in his slumped posture.

"I'm sorry, Mat. They've taken mine as well. This is being controlled by the military now. Orders were to keep a lid on developments – God knows how they can hide more than a hundred simultaneous launches. Any tin-pot country with a satellite and space program must know what we are trying to do."

"And how futile it will be," said Mat.

Kones eyes swept over to lock onto his, then Hari's, his gaze determined. "I will only say this once. If we are facing a global crisis, this needs to be coordinated from the top down. The President and his staff are already secure. Other preparations are being made for the impact. Your only job, Keterson, is to tell us exactly where those fragments are going to land after the strike on the body."

Mat was roughly pushed to his feet. One MP stood by impassively while the other swept him with a portable metal detector.

He could feel the small, heavy lump of Athy's cell in his pocket, and was resigned to giving it up. But the hand-held swept over it without registering a blip. Then he remembered the sleek, metallic casing. It was shielded!

Bless you, Miss Jates.

————

"We're getting something."

Mat jerked awake, scattering the greasy cardboard relics of yesterday's dinner onto the thick grey carpet of the Erebus mission room along with a very cold, very ugly brew of coffee that was more than seven hours old.

His head pounded and he focussed on the big display with difficulty. There were no magic pills to help him this time. He rubbed his stiff neck while he took in the images. He felt as though he had been watching that huge plasma rectangle his whole life.

The view of Erebus was better than ever. The petal-like wings were long gone now, the segmented body flattened, the six stubby support structures now woven together beneath the flattened under-surface like the wings of a hypersonic aircraft. The whole structure seemed so rigid it was hard to believe it had re-shaped itself at all.

The surface of the body comprised multiple elements, each of which now glittered like lenses. Like eyes.

Its whole structure was baffling.

"One of the forward observation posts has taken a spectral reading of the gases being ejected by Erebus," said Jereece.

Mat looked down into the central part of the room. Like the main desk above, the consoles were scattered with the remnants of takeaway meals and Styrofoam coffee cups. Yet where before – over a thousand long nights – these had been an integral part of the feeling of camaraderie within the 2047KW13 team, now they were like the remnants of prison food. The whole atmosphere in the room was oppressive.

Three more agents had joined Kones, along with five more MPs. They were in danger of outnumbering the scientists. Hari had lost his seat on the upper table, evicted by another "specialist", and had been forced to take a vacant seat in the main room below. It seemed the NASA hierarchy had been temporarily voided. No one had been allowed to contact friends or family. "Arrangements have been made," was all Kones would say.

"What have you got?" asked Mat.

"The gases are mostly hydrogen, ejected at very high speed, followed by a trail of water vapour."

The views flickered and changed. A one-minute countdown started in the corner of the screen.

"This is it, gentlemen," said Kones, pointedly ignoring the four female members of Mat's team who were busily working on the floor below.

They saw an actual view of Erebus on one screen, with a schematic of the incoming trajectory on the other.

Mat's heart was hammering so violently it shook his whole chest. The headache, his aching neck – all was forgotten.

"There they are," yelled Jereece. The chemical boosters on the nukes were powering up for the final strike, standing out like a forest of fireflies before the leviathan of Erebus.

One of the women cried out, and one of the others reached across quickly to put an arm around her. At some unspoken signal, most of his team left their seats and crowded together before the screen. He should have been with them.

Then, just before impact, something incredible happened.

Erebus applied a massive thrust away from the detonation coordinates.

"Sir! Sir! All 125 warheads have missed the target," yelled one of Kones's men.

"Get control of yourself!" snapped Kones.

The picture went suddenly white, then dead. The screen with the tracking information displayed a large red "ERROR". The nuclear detonation had obliterated the forward observation posts.

Hari rushed toward Kones.

"What the hell just happened?" demanded Hari.

A marine MP blocked him.

Kones was sitting silently, collecting himself. He reached forward and shut his laptop.

"Most of the warheads were programmed to detonate at fixed coordinates. That was what blew out your satellites."

"But they missed."

Kones nodded. "Yes. But the seventeen penetrators were smart-bombs. Our own," said Kones with a touch of pride. "They will have tracked the target. Of that you can be sure."

Mat rose unsteadily to his feet.

"How can we track the debris field now?" yelled Hari, his voice breaking as he pushed against the MP. "The NASA satellites are gone. That thing was due to impact in less than four hours."

"You and your whole team are to relocate with us," said Kones.

"Where?" demanded Mat. "These people have families. They might all be dead in a few hours. They deserve their own freedom, Kones."

Kones merely returned Mat's gaze. "You will all be moved to a secure location. As for your families, they will be taken care of."

Mat stepped back, and collided with the bulky MP behind him.

God help them.

He reached down and touched the solid shape of the secure cell in his pocket.

"I need to go to the toilet," said Mat.

"We will wait for you downstairs," said Kones. "Don't worry. We won't leave without you."

———

Pain.

Red hot, searing pain. My body has been ripped asunder.

Magma. The glowing, lifeblood of my body, splashes cooling into space, spilled from the fractured tubes of my diamond chambers. One of my segments has been obliterated, the eyes shattered.

But I am more than the sum of my parts. Each tiny cell of my outer body speaks with its own tiny song; and is a seed of rebirth. Enough of me remains to rebuild; to reform.

Enough of my mind remains to know from where those pestilential bringers of fire arose. I, at one with orbits and bodies of mass, traced their approaching vector back to their source. The dumb little comets, they were easy to escape. It is the smarter comets whose mother I need to punish.

It seems gravity-bound life can bite.

Have no fear, my lover.

I am strong.

———————

The tall glass windows of the atrium seemed to magnify the harsh sunlight as they pushed through the doors under guard.

Outside a swelling crowd was screaming for news, behind a cordon of soldiers five deep, each holding a submachine gun levelled at the demonstrators.

At a command from Kones, the ranks parted.

A line of six black Humvees with darkened windows awaited them.

Suddenly there was an explosion behind them.

The crowd screamed and ran as five of the big glass windows shattered with the impact, big fragments of glass crashing nosily to the tiles.

The soldiers swivelled, and a group of press suddenly pushed toward them, surrounding Kones and the rest of Mat's group of bewildered scientists.

There was confusion and shouting, and without warning the crowd surged back, breaking the ranks of the waiting soldiers.

People screamed.

Mat saw others fall, to be trampled by the mob.

A man waving a microphone seized Mat and pulled him away from the group. Mat started to struggle until the journalist leaned in toward him and whispered in his ear, "Athy sends her regards."

Mat took another look at the man. At six-four, with a livid scar down his left cheek, he did not look like your regular TV prop.

He took Mat by the arm and started pushing roughly through the crowd. Five other large men joined them, forcing a path.

Mat could hear Kones yelling orders at his men.

Within seconds they were inside a nondescript Ford and screaming through the back lots of JPL.

"You're going the wrong way. This won't get you out," said Mat.

The man who had rescued him just smiled.

Three turns later he saw a civilian helicopter sitting in a deserted rear carpark, the rotors turning with angry determination.

They abandoned the car and ran.

Mat was bundled inside, and almost fell across the lap of Athy when his long, awkward legs tangled with the cramped seating. A slight smile played on her lips, which she quickly banished. Her eyes were coolly assessing.

He sat beside her, trying to collect his thoughts, unsure about the ethics of abandoning his team, and yet convinced that Kones was leading them down a useless path. Erebus would hit them, of that he had no doubt; either the asteroid itself or the fragments left by the strike – either way the total incoming mass was the same. If they survived the plasma wave of the impact, what then? He did not want to spend years locked in some secure underground haven along with the President and a thousand hard-case military types like Kones.

"Take it up, Mr Kalls."

"Yes, ma'am," replied Kalls from the cockpit.

"Athy, I'm sorry for my hasty words this morning," said Mat, laying a hand on her shoulder. He felt awkward talking like this in front of a cramped helicopter full of Athy's men, but time was running out for all of them.

"That is quite alright," said Athy coolly, pointedly brushing his hand away. "This is strictly business, Mr Keterson. We need your expertize."

Mat felt his heart go cold. It seemed adolescent, even infantile, to care so much about a casual affair, but the loss of intimacy between them disturbed him more than he could say. For just a few brief hours it had seemed as though the world was his. After years of awkward and ill-fated relationships, years of dedication to the Erebus project, it seemed that at last the world – and Cupid – had smiled on him.

Seconds later they were racing through the sky.

LA was burning.

Whole districts were ablaze, the streets filled with people running, fighting, dying. Below him Mat could see the highways were choked to a standstill. Kones would never get out in time.

Mat swallowed and turned to Athy. "Where are we heading?"

"I have a rocket-plane at the airport, fuelled and ready to go."

"Where?"

"Gansu province. Northwest China."

"Jiuquan Space Centre," whispered Mat. "We can't be in the air when the plasma wave hits."

"We don't plan to be," chimed in Kalls from the cockpit.

———————

Mat's eyes adjusted slowly to the cavernous situation room at Jiuquan.

"This was where we centred the NTR project," said Athy beside him. "And, as you know, most of the launches were from here."

Mat nodded impatiently. "But most of the technology was American."

Athy smiled. "This is China, Mat. Do you think a few patents are going to stop them?"

Mat's head jerked around at her.

"That's right. Our syndicate has been manufacturing the NTR drives as fast as we can for five years. We already have hundreds of them up in L_1."

"So the asteroid project—"

"A whole colony, Mat. That's what we were planning. A whole self-supporting community that lives off the raw materials available out there. A true space colony." Her eyes were glowing with the fire of her vision, and just for the moment, the awkwardness between them was forgotten.

"That's why we wanted you. No one alive knows the asteroids like you do, or the best way to survey and approach them. Plus you were already a leader in the application of the NTR technology."

There was a babble of excited voices, all in Chinese.

Athy walked quickly over to the terminals and interrogated a technician. Mat was shocked to hear her speak fluently in Cantonese, and was reminded yet again how little he knew about her. The seemingly innocent Southern Belle who took him to her bed was long vanished.

She turned toward him.

"Erebus is entering the atmosphere. It's still intact. There are a score of minor fragments, but they will not survive re-entry."

"But that's impossible. It was hit with ground-penetrating nukes. With its composition it should have broken up."

The technician spoke rapidly then pointed at the big screens above the room.

"This is historical footage. A fast-forward of images collected after impact from long-range spy satellites," said Athy.

Mat could hardly believe his eyes.

The massive body – smashed to pieces and leaking hot fluids into the darkness of space – slowly reformed itself, once more taking the long, streamlined form it had before the nukes hit it.

The images flickered and changed. Now there was a shaking video feed, a real-time view of Erebus itself as it plummeted through the atmosphere, superheating the air, surrounded by massive turbulence. It had flattened even further, and was coming in like an antique shuttle, heating up along the leading edges of the huge flattened underside.

"How are we getting that feed?" asked Mat.

"Tein has fighter craft tracking it."

Mat shook his head. It was suicide. Even so he could not tear his eyes away from that image.

"It's trying for atmospheric entry. I was right. It *is* a spaceship."

Athy's eyes were flickering from screen to screen as the image grew. She was shaking, and Mat knew it was not from the cold.

He reached down and placed an arm around her shoulders, and she did not protest, letting him draw her into an embrace.

All around the room, a deathly quiet had settled.

It must have been only a matter of minutes, but it seemed like they watched that massive, alien thing plummet down toward them for an eternity.

A single voice barked a command, and suddenly the room was in motion again.

Mat looked across to see Tein on the floor of the room. He nodded gravely to Mat, before continuing to work.

One of the big screens flickered again, and they could see the trajectory of re-entry. An elegant curve, that would put Erebus down in the North Atlantic, less than three hundred kilometres from mainland USA.

"Oh my God . . . " said Mat.

He felt Athy tremble in his arms, and looked down at her, but her features were composed, her eyes focussed with intelligence.

"The East Coast. It cannot possibly survive. Not even with the aerobraking that Erebus is applying," said Mat.

He felt a guilty relief, a hidden, exultant joy, that *he* was safe. That he would survive the initial impact of this massive body.

Tein marched up to them, and Athy disengaged herself from Mat, looking up at him with a mixture of longing and anger on her face.

He was more confused than ever.

"Good evening, Mr Keterson. I trust your flight over was pleasant?" said Tein in English. His British accent was strong, a relic of his Hong Kong education.

Mat gritted his teeth. Tein always treated him with excessive good manners that were aggravating at the best of times. Now with billions of tonnes of rock, ice and God-knows-what hurtling down toward them it was downright infuriating.

"Very pleasant."

"Good to hear it." Tein smiled at Athy, who turned back to the screens.

"I would like to give you a tour of our facilities – a full briefing on our proposed projects. Then I would like you to go back to the US."

"Back?" said Mat.

"Yes. If this is as serious as I fear, we will need to bring to bear all the resources of the developed world. Our government is already making diplomatic moves with the Russians and others, but we need you to convince President Yerry of the absolute need to assist us."

"Assist? With what?"

"The evacuation of Earth, Mr Keterson."

The babble of excited voices rose on the floor below.

Erebus was glowing red hot, the streamlined edges below it shining with the fires of Hell itself.

Below the huge, red-hot form they could see the ocean – a peaceful flat expanse, shimmering in the sun. It looked impossibly tiny beneath the bulk of Erebus, as though the vast Atlantic had shrunk.

Impact.

For a brief moment they could see a vast spout of water rising to the sky, then a white-hot, rushing wall of superheated gas, vapour and sediment.

The screen went blank.

Silence.

Tein gave a quick command and the feed switched to another aircraft, now heading out of the area as fast as it could fly. Its rear-mounted camera showed a wall of fire expanding from the crash site like the ring of a huge atomic bomb. A column of material rose into the sky, and yet below this the Atlantic seemed still and calm. The blast wave, and the oceanic surge that would follow, were still on their way.

Tein looked silently at the screen and chanted something in Chinese.

Athy looked at him sharply, a single tear glistening on her cheek. Her eyes flicked to Mat and she wiped it away.

"Come with me, please. We have another communications centre set up inside," said Tein. "The main control room must return to space operations now. We all have our work cut out for us."

Mat and Athy followed Tein into a small room set up with banks of monitors, each showing a different video feed.

"God, that's New York," said Mat.

The streets were filled with people, climbing over cars and trucks jammed-packed in the streets. Buildings were on fire. Bodies lay on the sidewalk amid scattered suitcases and boxes of possessions, as unnoticed as alleyway rubbish.

Mat looked from screen to screen. It was the same all across the Eastern seaboard of America, yet every city in the world seemed to have been gripped by the same panic. Everyone trying to flee, yet trapped by the sheer mass of humanity.

Mat and Athy followed Tein's lead and took a seat at the bare conference table, while an assistant brought coffee in white, chipped ceramic cups. Tein gratefully accepted a steaming cup of green tea.

Mat tried to bring the cup to his lips, but his hand was shaking so badly he spilt the hot fluid on his hand. He hardly reacted, overwhelmed by a crushing sense of guilt. If only he had insisted on more detailed surveys . . . perhaps if they had used more NTRs . . .

Athy watched him with cool assessment.

"You know there is nothing you could have done to stop it," she said.

Mat's reason slowly asserted itself. It was true, given the behaviour of Erebus, and the lack of effectiveness of the nuclear strike . . . what could he have done?

Perhaps if Earth had a fleet of space-going destroyers armed with powerful energy weapons – maybe they could have outmanoeuvred and dismembered Erebus. Perhaps. Who knew what other resources that . . . alien artefact . . . could bring to bear?

Mat gave up trying to drink his coffee and used both hands to place the cup carefully on the table.

"How many hours till the blast wave hits us?"

Tein took a measured sip of his tea.

"It will hit China in seven hours, the East coast of America in less than one. The wave will have completely circumnavigated the globe in sixteen hours. But our calculations show the power is greatly diminished already. Erebus slowed its descent quite markedly prior to impact."

Tein lowered his teacup to the saucer with a soft clatter.

"So what exactly are you proposing?" said Mat.

Tein pushed his cup away from him slightly and straightened in his chair.

"The consequences for the planet will be extreme. We are facing a disaster unique in recorded history. The climate disruption will make the Greenhouse Effect look like a mild summer's day. Crop failures, agricultural impacts, storms of incredible intensity . . . how many years of this can our delicately balanced global society survive?"

Mat looked across to Athy, who was calmly sipping her coffee, a quiet determination on her soft features. She looked back at him like a stranger.

"We were already preparing for the most ambitious space project in history," said Tein. "With the impact of Erebus, the stakes are even higher.

"What we want to create is a true outpost of global civilization. Self-supporting. Big enough to survive. With a wide enough gene pool to carry on the torch of civilization if the worse should come to pass."

"But what about food? Surely you will need to be supported from Earth? How can a project like this possibly be sustained now? It might be decades before the climate begins to stabilize again."

"The asteroid colony was already designed to be self-supporting. We have identified the natural resources we will need out in space. We have stockpiled seed-stock, agricultural supplies—," said Tein.

"You mean grow your own food? To construct a rotating colony with simulated Earth-gravity?" said Mat, incredulous. Every cost model ever run had shown how prohibitively expensive this was.

"Work has already begun on stockpiling the materials in orbit. But we will need to accelerate plans. Time is short," said Tein.

Mat sat as Tein and Athy sketched out the details of the massive undertaking. Athy became animated, her eyes aglow with the dream of space colonization. He tried to focus as the time crawled forward. Finally, while Mat drank his now stone-cold coffee, one of Tein's assistants approached them and whispered something in Chinese.

The smile on Athy's face fled instantly.

Mat did not need a translation. The blast wave was about to hit the East Coast.

The views of New York, Boston and the other cities still showed the same chaos, as though people were trapped by those high walls of concrete.

First came the wall of superheated air, shattering windows and igniting anything that was exposed: wood, paper, plastic. Flesh.

The TV images were silenced instantly.

Tein switched to satellite feeds, and Mat watched, stunned as a massive wave engulfed New York. The buildings were buried under the huge swell, and the wave continued sweeping on into the interior – unstoppable.

Tein's aide reappeared.

"We have your plane ready, Mr Keterson."

Mat turned to Athy, hopeful that she would come back with him, but this time it was all business. Tein and she had needed him to bring in the US support, he could see that now. The feeling between them had been nothing more than a fanciful delusion, like a mist killed in the cold light of day.

He turned away and gritted his teeth.

"OK, Tein. I will talk to Yerry."

"Are you sure this is safe?" yelled Mat over the roar of the helicopter blades. He looked out through the window, struggling to see anything in the darkness. He had been seconded to Hari Wottard's Erebus team, and the former NASA director had insisted on this "familiarization run".

"Our people have modelled its growth. It has been predictable. We have been to the edge of Erebus more than ten times a day since it landed," said Hari. "I may need to you to supervise some of the investigations – up close."

Mat loosened his collar.

"We will be at the edge any minute, Mr Wottard," said Captain Stephenson, their pilot.

Mat looked over at Hari, but he was looking out, his gaze riveted on the view below. He was now coordinator of the President's Erebus Emergency Panel.

"Switch on the lights, Stephenson," ordered Hari.

Mat looked down.

Miles and miles of naked seabed, once beneath the vast North Atlantic, now devoid of life – dried to dust and exposed to the bleakness above.

For so long Erebus had been just a series of images to Mat. In his mind, a massive, mindless asteroid; a challenge for him to divert from its collision with Earth, yet still nothing more than a stream of data – a transmission of zeros and ones rendered to photographs and short video images. Just a concept. Even when it came alive, shaking off his nuclear thermal rockets and its layer of dust and ice, transforming into its monolithic, segmented form, it was still nothing more than a phantom on a screen, an impossible, intelligent artefact, determined on its course for Earth, undeterred by even a massive nuclear strike.

Even the footage of the impact – Erebus, glowing red-hot as it hit the North Atlantic – and the scenes of devastation from the East Coast and Africa; the blast wave and the huge swell of water that had followed, had filled him with nothing but a sense of unreality.

This was different.

Now he would see Erebus with his own eyes.

He would see what came of his failure.

They were flying over the strange, almost desert-like surface under a dark brooding sky. The only sign of the sun was a slight lessening of the oppressive dark near the zenith; otherwise they were obliged to run under lights, as though it were a night-time operation. The dust kicked into the upper atmosphere by the impact of Erebus would take years to drop out. Meanwhile the globe had been divided into hemispheres of Night and Gloom.

"We are coming up to Erebus now, sir."

Mat felt a chill on his back, even though the stuffy cabin was heated against the frigid air outside.

He had returned from China five weeks ago. As soon as he reappeared in the US he was promptly put under guard, then shuffled through an obscure string of underground military installations that no taxpayer had ever heard of. Not a single person he had seen had been inclined to listen to Tein's plan for setting up a self-supporting asteroid colony – and Mat had to admit the further he was away from it, the more absurd the whole thing seemed. It was also impossible the US could take a lead role in the enterprise, since all its major space assets had been destroyed by the Erebus tidal wave. Reports were showing a steady stream of lifts from Jiuquan. Madness or not, the Chinese and their partners were going.

The initial blast wave had been weaker than they'd feared. By the time it reached the West Coast, it was little more than a hot, biting wind that gave third-degree burns to those exposed to it. Apart from the devastated East Coast, most of the US infrastructure was intact. The Midwest was fighting fires and a flood of saltwater, surging down along the major drainage lines.

The world had been expecting Armageddon, but aside from the American continent and the West coast of Africa, it had survived the impact with little more than a scrape. In fact the panic had caused as much destruction as Erebus itself.

The long-term effects of the climate disruption would be harder to gauge. In the developed world at least measures were being taken to stockpile and preserve foodstocks, protect water supplies from contamination, even grow under artificial lights powered from nuclear, coal and gas.

"Here it is," said the pilot.

"Dear God," whispered Mat.

Well of Darkness.

Erebus had grown from a thickening across the horizon to a vast, black wall that rose more than three kilometres above them, reaching from the dry bed of the Atlantic into the upper atmosphere.

The pilot positioned the helicopter three hundred metres away and swivelled the bank of powerful halogens toward it.

The skin was dark, the whole structure composed of cells about a hundred metres across. These individual bubble-like cells were crowded together to form a compact lattice.

"It looks biological," said Mat, still amazed that Erebus had survived impact.

"It's grown exponentially over the last five weeks," said Hari quietly, his voice almost at a whisper, as though Erebus itself would hear him if he spoke too loudly. "It's absorbed most of the North Atlantic; the sheer mass of it now stretches from Newfoundland to the Straights of Gibraltar and from Brazil to Angola.

"Northern Europe is freezing solid. The poor bastards. First the dust cloud, then the loss of the Gulf Stream . . . "

"But it's halted its expansion at the land surface, hasn't it?"

Hari looked intently at Mat, his face drawn and pale. "For now. But its mass is still growing at the same rate."

For the first time the implications hit him. For it to have experienced that sort of growth in only five weeks . . .

"We have less than a month before it takes the whole planet," said Mat. The mathematics of it was chilling.

As they watched, Erebus began to bulge outward. New cells appeared, pushing apart their neighbours. Then more.

"Damn. I've never seen this sort of growth," said Hari.

The wall quivered, then began to expand, faster and faster.

"Oh, shit!" cried Hari.

The pilot did not need an order. He turned the helicopter and accelerated back towards the mainland. Behind them the whole jostling mass was accelerating, *outpacing them.*

"Turn the lights back towards it!" yelled Mat.

The co-pilot swivelled the lights back towards Erebus.

The cells were looming closer. Each one was bigger than their helicopter, and there was thousands upon thousands of them. In one moment of horrifying clarity, Mat truly understood how massive Erebus had become.

A whole section of the cells began to outpace the others, reaching out from the main body of Erebus towards them. The cells changed as they drew near, the heavy skin rolling back to reveal a curved, glistening surface beneath. Mat saw his own reflection in hundreds of these lenses, as though they were being chased back towards the mainland by the vast faceted eye of some gigantic insect.

"It's still coming! *It's still coming!*" yelled Phom, their co-pilot. She had turned in her chair, like Mat and Hari, and was watching the mass of cells close on them. Her hands were held out toward Erebus as though to ward it off.

Eyes.

Coming for them.

Thousands. *Thousands of them.* Mat was lost inside them, shrinking like a microbe falling backwards into a drop of water. He had no doubt now. It was alive. A single huge entity come to take them all.

Those eyes were chilling in their blank intensity, charged with purpose, power and merciless intent. And the most frightening thing of all: it did not see them.

To Erebus they were nothing.

Never had Mat felt so utterly insignificant. His very existence was dissolving like an aspirin tablet in the vast ocean of Erebus's being.

"It's coming down!" screamed Hari.

Mat looked up and saw he was right. Erebus was flattening out, reaching toward them. Closer.

One enormous eye was so close he could have reached out to touch it. Opalescent, dull silver with no pupil or iris.

Closer.

The helicopter shuddered then spun out of control. Eyes and darkness swept around them like a whirlpool.

Mat was aware of someone screaming, and looked over to see Hari yelling, his eyes wide, unfocussed. Only then did he realize he was screaming, too.

Mat gripped the chair and bit his lip until it bled.

"Shit, this is it!" screamed Hari.

"I can't hold it!" yelled Stephenson.

Even Mat could hear the panic in the pilot's voice. That was bad. If the pilot lost it, they were all doomed.

Hari was screaming something incomprehensible, tears squeezed from his eyes as he screwed his lids shut.

"Stephenson!" yelled Mat.

The pilot looked around, his eyes were wild, flitting from point to point.

"You have to focus! You have to get us back." Mat thought desperately for a way to reach him, then he saw the writing on the US Army jacket. CAPTAIN STEPHENSON. Military. *Just push the right button.*

The whole craft seemed to be surrounded by those huge bulbous eyes. Empty. Implacable.

Mat projected his voice with as much authority as he could muster. "Do your job, soldier! Now! Get us out of here!"

Clarity flowed back into Stephenson's eyes. His training took over.

Like a miracle the helicopter slowed its hurtling flight and stabilized. Mat could see a thousand tiny reflections of the chopper. He looked closer into the eyes. Beneath the tough outer cover they were perfectly smooth, reflective, yet there was a long line through the middle of each round surface. Perhaps a second eyelid? They glistened wetly, and stank of salt – the rank, rotting smell of the sea.

"We're gaining," yelled Phom with relieved elation.

Mat let out a long breath, conscious for the first time of the throbbing pain in his lip and the taste of blood in his mouth. He forced himself to let go of the seat arms.

Phom was right. They were leaving Erebus behind. The acceleration caused by the collapse of the wall was slowing. One by one the lids were closing over the eyes. The whole thing was becoming a featureless expanse once again, nothing more than the bumpy wall of darkness they had first observed.

"Hari . . . " Mat looked across at his former boss. The man was still crying, yet he was wiping the tears away from his face as though they were acid, burning his skin.

"What?" snapped Hari.

"Hari, we have got to stop that thing." Mat's voice sounded weak, at least to himself, and he cleared his throat.

"The President has authorised a full-out nuclear strike. No other nuclear power is joining us. Even with the growth, no one else wants to risk adding a nuclear winter to the climate disruption."

"A strike!' said Mat, his heart hammering. "A nuclear strike could not destroy it in space, how do you think that will help now?"

"What the hell else can we do? What can we do?" said Hari.

"There has got to be some other way. Nerve agents. Viruses. Attack it biologically. Analyze its structure."

"We've tried, Mat. We have tried it all. It's not like anything we've ever seen. It's got nothing like DNA. The whole thing is some sort of distributed nervous system. Parallel processing across the whole structure. Anything vulnerable is buried under a trillion tonnes of flesh and water. We took samples straight away. But it does not respond like Earth-bound life."

Mat suddenly knew what he had to do. After all, Tein and his associates, including his beautiful Athy, had been right. There was no way they could have known about the real threat Erebus represented, yet they had embarked on the only course that would save them. It was not a matter of saving civilization, but of saving Mankind itself.

"Take me to President Yerry, Hari. I know what we need to do."

Hari looked at Mat suspiciously.

"What? If you have any ideas, you tell me. I will take it to the Erebus Panel."

Mat shook his head. He might have bowed to Kones, letting that military jerk bombard Erebus with nukes in space, but never again would he stand by while idiocy was given free rein.

"I need to see Yerry. Straight away. In person."

Mat looked straight into Hari's eyes, saw the fear and uncertainty there, and held his ground.

"OK, Mat. You win. But you'd better not be wasting everyone's time. In case you haven't noticed, we have more than fifty million dead and a whole country in ruins."

Mat said nothing. Instead he looked out across the dry, dark expanse of the ocean floor, back at the dark line of Erebus.

Time truly was running out.

"This is your plan? *This is your plan?*"

Mat was deep inside the Nevada Presidential bunker. They had taken his blindfold off a few minutes ago. It was Cold War paranoia at its best. He could hardly believe it; after all, it was not the Russians who had flooded the Eastern seaboard from the Great Lakes to Florida, and who was slowly expanding over the bulk of mainland USA.

"Mr President. We need to help Director Tein. We need to get our best people *off* this planet. We need to move our key resources while we can. Get everything into orbit with whatever we have, then get away from Earth."

"To go where? To live in space? *With the little green men?*" screamed Yerry. Mat have never seen the man so livid. He had put on weight since he'd last seen him, the rotund belly held back by the stretched buttons of his fine Italian suit. His round fleshy face, topped with short, grey hair – so familiar from a thousand broadcasts – was bright red.

"Mr President, I think we need to consider hard options. Tein at least has the infrastructure in place . . . "

"I am minutes away from sending a nuclear strike into that *thing* out there. I am trying to defend what is left of this country. And you are telling me to forget that? To let it just keep expanding across the Midwest?"

Yerry, almost a foot shorter than Mat, was literally jumping up and down on the spot, using his finger like a skewer to punctuate his points.

"Yes. That's exactly what I am saying. Those ICBM boosters could shift valuable material into low-Earth orbit for Tein's project. We could lift maybe another hundred of our people – people who will otherwise die." Mat was beyond any worry about offending Yerry. He could not let them waste their last chance.

"We want to *kill* the fucking thing," screamed Yerry. "That will save millions. Thousands of millions."

Mat shook his head, retaining his calm.

"Yes, Mr President, I know your intentions. But the strike will have no effect. Those weapons could not destroy Erebus in space, and now it has thousands of times its starting mass."

Yerry rubbed his eyes with his fingers then took his hands away, shaking his head sharply, as though to clear it. He turned away from Mat and motioned to his men.

"Get him out of here," he snapped.

Two aides shuffled Mat out of the office, under the implacable gaze of four secret service agents. Linten, who had watched the whole exchange, followed Mat out.

As the door shut with an angry thud, Mat heard Linten's Texas drawl behind him.

"It's too late for a change of policy now. Everyone from the Joint Chiefs down is pressuring Yerry to act. This was unavoidable."

Mat and Linten were alone in the corridor. The Vice-President motioned for Mat to follow him and they walked down the hallway into a deserted conference room that smelt of old coffee and faint solvents from the hasty construction.

"Take a seat," said Linten.

Mat was exhausted. He had not slept in almost two days. His mind had been working feverishly throughout his journey and the interminable delays as he waited again, and again, for Yerry. He'd known he would have only one chance to sway him, and yet there had seemed little he could construct in the way of an argument, little he could add to what Yerry's own advisors had already presented to him. Each appointment had been rescheduled without notice. Today he had been given one minute.

"Yerry has never been a supporter of the space program. He was elected on other issues."

Mat smiled at that. Everyone knew Yerry had been elected on a strong ethical ticket. *Moral Revival*. The Bible Belt had put him in office. The space program had been on his hit list for cutbacks, and Linten had backed him all the way.

"But there are other people inside and outside the administration who want to be involved in Tein's program," Linten continued.

This sparked Mat's interest.

"We have been in communication with Tein and the consortium in China, and I have been coordinating a group of wealthy industrialists who want to take part. It may not be government support, but resources are resources. Tein needs everything from high-tech alloys and electronics to seed-stocks and rocket fuel." Linten took a breath; his eyes were serious. "I can not leave the President, or his team, but I need someone to represent the US in Tein's group. I want you to be that man."

Mat felt his heart accelerate. He nodded slowly, his mind suddenly full of possibilities. This was more than he had hoped for. The fact that Linten had made the offer in an empty conference room meant that it was off the record, but this was no time to quibble.

"Yerry wants you locked down with Hari and his team of advisors, but I can get you to Jiuquan in a few hours."

Linten leaned forward. His face was pale, his hands shaking slightly as he pressed them together. A small muscle ticked beneath his right eye.

"Something of us must remain," said Linten.

"I'll do my best, sir," said Mat.

––––––––

Oh, the joy of the feast!

Sweet, sweet waters – deliciously warm – nothing like the frozen, dusty drink I am used to, with its taste of sulphur and metal.

Wonderfully digestible organics! How I swell with this carbon, but I need heat. I must dig deep to reach the hot, precious fluids of this tiny world. It is these I need to warm my inner segments, to truly gain the power I need to grow.

At last I shall reach my prime. A fully realized Vendeth of heroic proportions. My call shall reach to the dark centres of galaxies. My lovers shall come, and I shall take them into me.

But the taste of this world! It is as sweet as nectar.

Mmmmm . . .

Something approaches.

I open eyes across vast sections of my Westward length.

Tiny lights. I know these. The bringers of fire. The hot weapons of the parasites.

In my desiccated, starved form I feared them, but these cannot harm me now; I have grown too vast on sweet water, methane hydrates and the bounties of gravity-bound life.

What I need now, they bring.

––––––––

The compound surrounding Jiuquan had become a huge, complex city of tents, portable offices and hastily erected industrial buildings, their zinc coatings gleaming dully under the heavy sky.

A mass of power cables threaded through the site and emergency power had been channelled from the local grid. Huge lights illuminated every inch of ground. The nearby airstrip had been expanded, and everything from rocket-planes and passenger jets to huge, prop-driven transports were touching down and lifting off every few minutes. The pace had become frantic since the failure of the nuclear strike on Erebus.

Mat had been here a week. Tein had set aside one precinct for the American contingent, but so far they had done little but stockpile a hopelessly uncoordinated flood of raw materials, technology and fuel in the vast network of storehouses.

He was on his way back from a briefing with Tein. Many of the components were already in orbit, but they needed more, so much more, before they even stood a chance of surviving. He turned into the narrow alley formed by two towering industrial buildings and pushed through the busy mass of people, carefully stepping over a mass of cables.

He had tried more than twice a day to reach Athy, but she never answered his calls. It infuriated him that he could not control his impulse to be near her. He was being a fool. Miss Jates had finished with him – she had made that plain before he left for the US. So why could he not put this obsession out of his mind? Why did those few hours they spent together – the sound of her laugh, her eyes, the softness of her hair – keep flooding back into his mind when he had so much more to think about? When they would all soon be dead and every minute wasted was another score of lives lost?

Once more Mat pushed Athy out of his thoughts and concentrated on the logistics of the project. There was much to be concerned about, yet most disturbing was the trend that Mat was seeing.

He had expected Linten to send scientists and engineers, but what he was getting was a mass exodus of America's rich and powerful and their families and advisors, every one hoping to barter a place on the asteroid colony with badly needed supplies. It seemed Linten was busily repaying his election contributors. It was insane.

The reports from the US were bad. Initially the strike seemed to be effective. Whole sections of the advancing wall had been obliterated and Erebus withdrew – but only temporarily. It soon began advancing again, faster than ever. Soon they would have another type of refugee – the politically powerful. *They* would be entirely more difficult to shut out. President Yerry and his ilk still controlled enough firepower to wipe Jiuquan off the face of the Earth.

In less than a week Erebus would have covered the whole of continental USA, a little more than that and the whole continent of America, along with Africa and most of central Europe. The mass of the thing was destabilizing the Earth's spin. Every few hours brought another tremor, and major earthquakes around the globe were being reported every hour. Earth was shaking to pieces.

Mat wove through another narrow alley and walked through the huge gaping doorway of US#28, a big industrial building he had been using as his headquarters.

He could see Trill Bates, with two aides, outside the door to his office, trying to force their way past the two Chinese guards that Tein had assigned to him. Trill saw him coming and immediately set off to intercept, his men close behind.

Trill was a large man, bald now, with thick growths of wavy grey hair on either side of his shiny dome and a paunch that pushed out across his designer belt.

"Keterson. I have been trying to see you for two days."

Although probably the richest man on the planet, the software trillionaire had become just another face in a sea of self-important men and women, all trying to get inside – to be where the decisions were made, and guarantee that *they* and not the others would take their place among the precious few leaving Earth.

They all knew that Erebus was coming.

"We received all the components, and the software, Mr Bates, and we thank you. They will be invaluable."

"But what's going on? What is the schedule? My family and I have been completely left in the dark."

His two advisors, who had not been included in Bates's impatient demand for safety, exchanged a concerned glance.

"*No one* has been told. You will be informed along with everyone else when the time comes."

Mat walked towards his offices.

"Hold on a minute!" blustered Bates, his face flushing red. He reached out to grab Mat's hand, but the tall scientist easily evaded him.

The two Chinese guards instantly levelled their rifles, barking out a command.

Bates did not need to be a linguist. One look at the steely resolve in their faces was enough. Hundreds of people had been shot at Jiuquan. Without ceremony. Without explanation. Tein expected, and received, complete obedience. So far order had been kept, but Mat suspected it would get a lot worse before the end.

Bates took a breath.

"I expect to be told as soon as you know anything," said Bates, although his voice was weak, almost asthmatic as he backed away.

Mat walked past the two guards and into his office with a sigh of relief. He dumped his notebooks and slimline reader and walked through into his communications room.

One of the concessions he had been able to wring out of Linten had been the release of his NASA team and their families. Not one of them had been happy at the treatment, but he was sure glad to have them here. Most had been dispersed through Tein's organization – sorely needed space scientists on a base swarming with non-specialists.

"What do you have for us, Jereece?"

The astronomer looked up from his monitor and smiled at Mat. Two other women from his old team were here as well, Yath and Lane. All three were busily analyzing the orbital insertion of a continuous stream of materials, as well as undertaking an overall scenario analysis of the construction in orbit. They needed to know the major problems *before* they tried to assemble the main colonies. There would be no resupply from Earth, of that there was no doubt. Whatever they got into orbit, they were stuck with.

"Erebus is still expanding at the same rate, but there is something else. Satellite photos show that it is developing cylindrical growths along its equatorial length. They look hollow," said Jereece, pointing at the screen.

Mat leant forward, concerned.

"They must be hundreds of metres across."

"And there are thousands of them."

Mat nodded. "Anything else?"

"It looks like Erebus's metabolism is starting to change the atmosphere. The good news is that the increasing carbon dioxide will offset the cooling."

"And the bad news?"

Jereece grimaced.

"At the rate the oxygen is dropping, we could not survive another month, even if it stopped growing."

Mat nodded, resolutely pushing away the slightest trace of emotional reaction. There would be time enough for that when he watched the last rocket blast away from Jiuquan.

"Oh, one more thing," said Jereece, brightening.

"What?" said Mat, cheered to see more of the old Jereece.

"You have a visitor. She's waiting for you inside."

Jereece jerked his head toward the conference room.

A few heartbeats later, Mat pushed open the conference room door to see Athy sitting alone inside, an untouched coffee on the table in front of her, busily steaming the room full of enticing volatiles. The no-nonsense outfit was gone in favour of a loose dress of light apricot, patterned with abstract shapes. A long coat was draped across the table.

The smell of coffee mixed with her faint perfume, and Mat's breathing grew rapid as he gently closed the door.

"Athy, I . . . " said Mat. *I didn't expect to see you again.*

Athy turned and smiled. Her eyes were framed with dark rings of exhaustion, her face pale and without the slightest hint of makeup, as though she had been stripped down to her essential self. Her blonde hair was tied back in a single ponytail, but roughly, with wisps escaping the temporary bondage. He was shocked to see streaks of grey. She looked thin. Stress had wasted away the beautiful curves he remembered so well.

"Mat, I have been meaning to . . . come and see how you are going."

Her hands were shaking, her eyes glassy.

She laughed self-consciously. "I know. I look a mess. Too many all-nighters. Too many drugs. But who is going to worry about health effects now, hey?"

The shaking in her body grew worse, until it was a tremor that shook her whole chest.

Mat was drawn forward. He took her hands, all caution thrown to the wind. "What is it, Athy? What's wrong?"

She leapt from her chair and hugged him fiercely, her body fitting neatly into his. "It's all coming apart. The future, everything . . . I can't believe it's come to this."

The tremors finally gave way to tears.

"I'm sorry. I didn't want to burden you with this, but none of my family got out, Mat. My mother. Father . . . I'm all that's left. I have been just holding myself together."

Mat held her, thinking of his own distant cousins and relatives, most of whom had died in the first hours after impact. They too were gone. Thankfully he was an only child, and had buried his own parents years ago. He had been spared that shock.

Athy pushed away from him.

There would never be another time to say the things he wanted to say. He wanted her desperately, for whatever time they had left.

"Athy, I love you. I'm sorry if I treated you poorly; you were kind to me."

She smiled and wiped her tears away. "And damn my Southern pride. I love you, too, Matrick Keterson." She frowned, her brow creasing with concern.

"What is it? What's wrong?"

She took a breath and fished a small flash drive out of the pocket of her coat.

"This is the final cut," said Athy. "Tein wanted to send it with one of his aides, but I wanted to see you."

"Are we . . . ?" *Are we on the list?*

Athy shook her head. "I didn't look, Mat. I don't want to know. Not yet." She smiled. "Say, does that door have a lock?"

Mat was at the door in one stride, fiddling with the tiny mechanism. There was a satisfying click.

For once Mat's dexterity did not desert him.

———

Ecstatic growth.

My sharp, tentacle roots have smashed down into the mantle now, piercing the oceanic crust and tasting the delicious magma below. It surges through my diamond veins, a flood of warmth bringing a rich soup of minerals and metals.

I take up the last of the oceans, filling the cooler chambers of my vastness; I roll across the dry lands, consuming all, taking the precious carbon into my structure. I could not grow without it.

Strange it is, this planet-bound life. How it flees before me; myriad images flood back through my senses of it running before its own destiny. What thoughts do they have, these little parasites? Do they mourn the loss of their world? Even if they did, should I feel compassion for something so microscopic?

There are no more hot comets. But I no longer need their warmth to fuel me.

Nothing can slow me now.

This world is mine.

———

Tein barked an order, and the bunker's huge blast-shield began to open.

"When are we being taken to the launching area?" demanded President Yerry.

Tein turned and smiled genially, but said nothing.

The room was packed with political leaders and the mega-rich of Earth, all suited for launch. The crowd looked slightly ridiculous in their space suits. Thankfully there had been a surplus of those.

"Director, Tein, I demand an answer!" shouted Yerry.

Tein's guards tensed. Even his own aide, Lieutenant Yoshi Chan, whom he prized for her self-control, reached down to the holstered pistol at her side. Tein caught her eyes and shook his head. His guards took the same cue and relaxed back to attention.

"President, Yerry, I apologize for the delay. But as you know, to coordinate so many launches simultaneously is an extremely complex enterprise."

"Tein. My people tell me that the advance wall of Erebus is less than twenty minutes away from Jiuquan."

Tein smiled. "My information gives us more than a comfortable hour to launch. Please relax."

Yerry seemed convinced, but Hari Wottard, who had become the President's chief advisor on Erebus, whispered urgently in his ear. Tein had little time to spare for their feelings. He nodded to Lieutenant Chan, who surreptitiously left the room. She would be back soon.

He walked confidently through the crowd, greeting leaders and other self-important figures with quiet words of praise and encouragement.

They were in the forward launch bunker, a massive structure created in concrete and steel. Originally it had been a construction area for the old-fashioned chemical boosters, and more recently had been used for launch preparation. Its size, and proximity to the main launch field, made it ideal for his purposes.

The huge blast-shield – designed to withstand the accidental detonation of a nuclear device being sent into orbit – fell back into place with thud, giving them an excellent view of the launch field. No less than seventy-three heavy-lifters waited outside for departure.

Tein had completed his circuit of the room and was approaching the US President once more. "President Yerry. I want to thank you and your countrymen for the invaluable assistance you have given. The men and materials you provided have enabled us to meet, and exceed, our goals for the asteroid colony."

Yerry nodded in acknowledgement as Tein walked back to the main control panel. He checked his watch. It was time. This had to be timed precisely.

He stepped up onto a small platform and raised his voice.

"Through your efforts," said Tein, waving his arms to include the whole group of multi-national leaders and wealthy capitalists, "you have enabled the survival of Humanity."

There was a loud detonation, then another, and then a continuous roar as one by one the massive boosters lifted from the steel platforms of Jiuquan.

Tein turned to watch, but the light was blinding, pouring in through the big window in a blaze of chemical fire.

Behind him, Tein could hear the panic, but he shut it out of his mind. Would there be time for one last cup of tea?

"What the hell is this?" screamed Yerry.

Tein shielded his eyes against the glare and watched as Chan re-entered the room with hundreds of Chinese infantry. He held back tears as he watched his men and women. Not a single soldier lost composure.

Tein nodded to Chan, who gave an order in Cantonese.

Five hundred sub-machine guns were cocked in perfect unison. The panic in the room was replaced with a shocked silence.

Above them, disappearing like fairy-lights into the gloom of the darkened sky, were the last spacecraft to leave Earth.

Tein cleared his throat.

"All I ask for now, ladies and gentlemen, is decorum."

Yerry's jaw was slack.

"But, but . . . you are remaining behind."

Tein smiled. He had read Yerry and the others like a book. They had been so sure that he would secure his own place of safety – so sure that he would insert himself in the place of another, more deserving, younger candidate – that they had allowed themselves to be blinded to the truth.

He looked up at the disappearing lights. His own nephew, Twang, only twenty-three but already a brilliant biologist, was among the chosen few. Tein would survive – at least through him. He only hoped that Twang would honour his memory.

"Mr President, T-minus thirty seconds," whispered Hari Wottard.

Through the huge window, there was a gust of rank, rotting air. Tein tasted salt on his tongue. It filled the air, stinging his skin.

Erebus had sucked up every drop of the world's oceans. It now *was* the sea of Earth, transformed into one massive, rolling wave of rock and flesh.

People screamed and pointed out the window.

A huge, dark wall was approaching them, coming fast. Within seconds it was close enough for the powerful lights of the launch field to catch on it. Tein had heard reports of it from all around the world, so he was ready when it happened.

All along its length, tens of thousands of lids opened. Suddenly the lights were reflected by a galaxy of eyes, all suspended in that wall of darkness.

Death was coming, in the myriad guise of their own reflection.

"And so we kill ourselves," he muttered in Cantonese.

"Sir?"

He looked down to see Chan at his elbow with a cup of tea.

"Oh, thank you, Chan."

Tears glistened on her cheeks as she carefully handed him his plain, yet much-loved cup and saucer. She bowed deeply.

Tein frowned. "Stand straight. You know I dislike such imperialist traditions, Chan."

"Yes, Director. I know."

They turned to watch Erebus approach.

"The eyes! *The eyes!*"

The civilians were screaming.

Indeed the eyes were frightening, sweeping down to engulf them. But was this any less frightening than a life spent without purpose? Without moral principle?

As Tein sipped his green tea he watched the assembled crowd carefully. How very few had cultivated *peace of mind*. How easily they gave in to panic.

The saucer clattered softly as he put down his tea cup.

Erebus was closing on them.

"Wait," said Yerry. "They aren't eyes! They're *mouths!*"

All along its length, the opalescent eyes split across the middle, the upper and lower membranes drawing aside to reveal an awesome set of metallic teeth, grinding together in hungry anticipation.

Thousands of teeth, each big enough to swallow a multi-storey building.

"Fascinating," said Tein.

Then the Eyes of Erebus were upon them.

———

Lover, feel my embrace.

———

"Mat, we're receiving a feed via satellite."

Mat gave a gentle push and drifted across the cabin toward Jereece's workstation.

"My God."

Erebus had circled the globe. The long cylindrical tubes that had grown up all along the equator were erupting regularly now, shooting up vast sections of digested mantle and waste material.

"Do you have an analysis of those gases from the tubes?"

Jereece nodded. "Yes. They're the same as the jets we observed incoming, hydrogen and superheated steam. The whole mixture is igniting in the atmosphere. There are more than fifty thousand launches a day. Billions of tonnes, all breaking orbit and heading out into space."

Mat snapped his fingers, the sudden movement sending him crashing into the metal hull of the capsule. He stabilized himself with a light touch.

"It's a Light Gas Gun," said Mat. Erebus was digesting the planet, flashing water into steam to super-pressurize a chamber of hydrogen and fire chunks of Earth out into space along those massive tubes. It took a light gas like hydrogen to produce the high muzzle velocity.

"Do you have anything else?" asked Mat.

"Yes, there seems to be some sort of radio communication emanating from Erebus into space. I can't make any sense out of it, but it's incredibly powerful, and increasing in strength."

Mat rubbed his tired eyes.

"Didn't the lab boys in Hari's team say something about that?"

Jereece nodded. "Yeah, that's right. It seems that it communicates with itself using various wavelengths of electro-magnetic radiation. That's how it coordinates its own structure and nervous system through all those disconnected elements."

"Well, no point getting too concerned about the damn thing's biorhythms," said Mat.

Jereece smiled, but did not laugh.

The usually cheerful astronomer was subdued, his eyes haunted.

"What's wrong?" asked Mat.

Jereece tried to smile but failed. He took a deep breath, then turned back to his monitor, his eyes glued to the image of Erebus, swarming and rippling over Earth.

"I've been thinking," said Jereece. "The Missing Mass. I think it's biological."

"Missing Mass?"

"You know – the missing mass of the Universe. Some cosmological models say it should be much more massive than the observed visible mass."

"Ahh," said Mat. The last few weeks, getting all their materials safely away from Earth orbit to their new base in the asteroids, had been hectic. It had been a long time since he could amuse himself with cosmological speculation.

Jereece turned to Mat.

"I think the Missing Mass is Life. *Enormous* Life. And if that's true – it makes us look like microbes . . . molecules. Who knows what is out there? I mean, what eats Erebus? Where does the food chain end?"

Mat's tired brain chewed over Jereece's theory then he pushed it out of his mind. It did not matter what was out there, for now they simply needed to survive.

"Call coming in," yelled Yath from the other side of the small cabin.

Mat floated back to his station.

"Afternoon, Mr Keterson."

Mat smiled as Athy's face filled the screen. She was dressed in a grey, workman-like uniform crumpled with weeks of neglect. Her hair was greasy and unkempt, with long strands fanning out around her head in the zero-g. A knot of desire tightened low in his stomach. For a second he just looked at her, marvelling that they had found each other and survived through it all – the arrival of Erebus – the slow destruction of Earth.

"You're a sight for sore eyes," said Mat.

"How long till you reach the construction zone?" she asked.

"Only ten hours now. Time to let someone else have a turn watching Erebus."

Athy leant forward toward the video camera.

"Come home, Mat. I need you," she whispered.

His breathing accelerated, blood pounding in his temples.

"I'm on my way," he whispered hoarsely.

He smiled as he cut the link.

———

My need grows apace. This lover, however sweet, will shrivel beneath my embrace, leaving only its hot core to power my heart.

My voice is growing stronger, the call insistent, yet I must wait. Again I must sleep, and dream.

Soon another *must* answer the call, and at last I will have a true lover. This time, a Vendeth.

Our brood will be strong, of that I have no doubt – and will awaken hungry, tearing their way free of our bodies with savage determination.

But for now I am alone, and the heartbreak is still hard to bear. I had so hoped this lover would be the one. Those strange snatches of song I first heard, I now recall like a broken promise.

Is love truly so hard to find?

Running
Martin Livings

———

The three of us sit on the beach, keeping a keen watch over the Indian Ocean; the waters are grey, of course, reflecting the grey skies above. I've seen photos of Mauritius before, with clear azure skies and crystalline oceans, the sand a brilliant white beneath a blazing sun, but I'm assured that those days aren't as common as the advertising would lead you to believe, even when there isn't a major storm brewing off the coast. The gusting winds and occasional smatterings of rain are deceptively subtle reminders that Tropical Cyclone Katrina is on its way, sweeping in low across the ocean, a wall of foul weather rising from the sea to the clouds. But it isn't the cyclone we're waiting for, watching for, rather something which is travelling with it, behind it, inside it. Something far more destructive, and far more attractive.

I glance over to my left, where Belinda sits with her long legs stretched out on the pale sand. She's a statuesque woman in her mid-thirties or so, judging by her background at least. We must look a little like reflections in a funhouse mirror; her hair is cropped short the same as mine, and we're dressed in similar clothes – black motorcycle leathers with boots and gauntlets. Mine are brand new though, virgin-smooth, untested, while hers show signs of previous use, previous runs: patches repairing tears, edges frayed, the leather as rough as sun-aged skin. I know what to wear from reading about it, seeing videos; she's simply wearing what she's always worn. That thought alone makes me feel very humble.

I look away from Belinda, to my right. Ryuichi is there, sitting cross-legged, eyes closed, wearing only a tank top and shorts, his feet dirty and bare. He looks very old to my eyes, though I know he's only in his sixties; his bare limbs are wrinkled and sunken, but wiry and muscled beneath the sagging skin. His worn face is placid; he barely seems to be breathing, as if meditating. I wonder if he's asleep. Sitting here next to Ryuichi makes me feel like a baby in the presence of a god; he's a genuine legend in the field, arguably the first runner, and easily the oldest still participating. When I'd heard he was heading here, I knew I had to come as well. It was probably the only chance I'd have to meet the great man. If the next run didn't kill him, old age eventually would.

As if he feels my gaze, he opens an eye and looks at me. A smile flitters across his lips like a blown leaf. I blush and look away, further to my right, behind us. There's a grassy area back there, set up with umbrellas and chairs for those who simply want to enjoy the views of the ocean without getting their feet sandy, lined with palm trees that are swaying quite violently in the growing wind. A Japanese film crew is there, frantically setting up cameras and barking incomprehensible orders to one another. They are understandably excited, of course. In their own way, they're as eager as we are, perhaps even more so. Beyond them, framed against the dramatic green-coated mountains that jut out at random points throughout the island, the seaside town of Flic en Flac is hunkered down, low and spread out, almost as if it knows what's coming. Its inhabitants certainly do; most have fled into the ocean in rough fishing vessels, or travelled by any means available into the centre of the island, hoping to avoid the worst of the damage. And not from the cyclone; they'd withstood hundreds of those over the years. No, they're running from something else entirely.

Running from, running to, running with. One way or another, we all run, sooner or later.

I'd been incredibly lucky to get a flight here earlier in the day, an eight-hour stint from Melbourne, arriving at Sir Seewoosagur Ramgoolam International Airport just shy of noon. The plane had been virtually empty, only the flight staff and myself. It was the first time I'd ever flown, and in other circumstances I might have enjoyed the experience. But I never even looked out of my window, instead using the hours of bumpy flight to re-read everything I'd brought with me in my carry-on luggage, the books that covered sixty-odd years of history, theory and practice. I didn't even notice that we'd landed; the stewardess had to call me three times before I looked up from my studies. We'd disembarked pretty quickly, heading into the airport, whisked through customs, then I'd walked calmly through the doors that open into the main airport proper, into chaos. Hundreds of people trying desperately to get seats on flights out of the country, screaming children, natives shouting in French and Creole, angry and frightened. I'd never seen anything like it. Luckily Belinda had been there to meet me, holding a sign high over her head with my name on it. She'd freed me from the jostling crowd, and taken me to the deserted town, the quiet beach. To the man who would lead us in our run.

"How long?" Belinda asks, her voice barely louder than the wind around us. I turn to her reflexively, ready to answer that I don't know, but realize a moment later that she isn't addressing me, of course she isn't. Why would she? How could I possibly know?

"Soon," Ryuichi replies calmly.

"Can you see it?" I ask, nerves making my voice crack a little. "Where?"

The old man smiles slightly. "Right there," he says, pointing to the shore, not twenty metres from our feet.

I look, but don't see anything, just water licking the sand like a cat drinking. I hear Belinda take a surprised breath, so I know she's figured it out. I feel stupid and young. Again.

"The tide," she whispers, and I see it. The waters are receding visibly, pulling away from the beach, leaving seaweed and tiny panicked sand crabs exposed to the open air. I see this happening, and in my mind I picture the implications, extending into the ocean, towards the horizon. A dip here means that there's a bulge out there somewhere, a bulge that's headed our way at a rate of knots. The thought both thrills and terrifies me.

Soon, Ryuichi had said, and he knows about these things. Soon, then. The waiting is nearly over. It's almost time to run.

I get to my feet and stretch, my leathers cracking along with my joints, both stiff from disuse. Belinda does the same, almost a foot taller than me. She catches my eye and winks, grinning.

"Ready, kid?"

I nod, trying to smile back, though my guts are telling me fairly forcefully that I'm not ready, not by a long shot. I need more time. Minutes, hours, days. Years. I won't admit it though, not in this company. This is the opportunity of a lifetime, and I'm not going to let it escape me, no matter how scared I might be. I've prepared as well as I possibly can, given the circumstances; I've worked out religiously for years to increase my fitness to its optimum, studied hundreds of videos and written accounts of previous runs, even learnt to surf to get a feel for the general dynamics, though nothing can really simulate the real thing with any degree of accuracy. If I'm not ready now, I never will be. I nod again, more forcefully this time, mainly to myself.

Belinda speaks again to Ryuichi, who's limberly getting to his feet, showing no sign of discomfort or difficulty. I hope I'll be as fit as he is when I'm his age. Hell, I wish I was that fit now. "Where should we start?" she asks, almost reverentially.

The old man thinks for a moment, rubbing his stubbled chin with his fingers. Then he turns and points behind us, past the picnic area where the film crew are still frenetically preparing their equipment, active and noisy as a bag of popcorn in a microwave. "On the street, back there. By the shops." He seems to be visualizing it in his head, seeing the patterns of possibility, imagining the unimaginable. "Yes, right there should be fine. Yes." His Japanese accent is faint, eroded by decades of globetrotting, but still there. I guess you never really lose your heritage, even if you lose pretty much everything else.

Belinda nods. "Okay, let's do it."

We walk up the beach, Belinda and I leaving deep imprints of our boots in the sands, Ryuichi barely leaving a trace of his passing. As we reach the grass, Ryuichi veers away from us for a moment, crossing to the film crew. They all fall silent as he approaches them, looking at him with a peculiar mixture of pity and awe. Mainly awe, I like to think. He says a few words softly in Japanese, and the crew members look out towards the ocean suddenly. Ryuichi turns away from them, and the film crew's chaotic bustle returns and redoubles, as they grab their equipment and begin to retreat with an air of relaxed panic. I look out to the ocean as well; it's a reflex, I can't stop myself, any more than I could stop myself from flinching if someone faked a punch at my nose.

Is part of the horizon raised now? I can't tell, not really, but I suspect it is. The other half of the wave is approaching, the peak that matches the dip that's pulling the ocean back behind us. I turn away, concentrate on putting one foot in front of the other. Focus on the moment, that's the advice Ryuichi himself had written in his book, *Life on the Run*, a combination autobiography and instruction manual. I've read it at least a dozen times. I'm always amazed by how he could talk about his life with such candour, especially about his childhood, about the loss of his family and his first run. *The* first run.

"There," Belinda says, pointing back, excitement making her voice tremble a little. "Here it comes."

I look back over my shoulder again and look at the ocean. Yes, it's definitely there, cresting the waves. My stomach lurches at the sight of it, even though I'd already seen it in news reports as helicopters followed its path through the shallower waters a few days earlier. It's faint and blurred, seen through a curtain of distant rain, but it's there alright. Somehow the sight of it makes it abruptly real, makes everything real. My heart pounds so hard it hurts, and the breath is sucked out of me like I've been sucker-punched in the stomach.

They say that everything looks smaller on television, somehow, even with other objects to offer some helpful perspective. I've never really paid much attention to that until now. The thing is *huge*, rising from the waters, still only visible from its massive shoulders up. Even through the distant rains offshore, I can see the long, curved spines that run along the length of its head, from its snout up its face and beyond, looking incongruously like a mohawk haircut. Its eyes are shaded by a heavy brow, but I can make out a faint red glow there, like a campfire deep in a cave. Its mouth is closed for the moment, a fact for which I'm profoundly grateful. Its neck is almost nonexistent, its head joining straight up to a barrel chest, only a little of which is visible yet. Its skin is rough, covered with oddly shaped scales that fit together like a three-dimensional jigsaw puzzle. Each one must be the size of a car, and I can already see dozens, hundreds of them. At the point where it emerges from the sea, the water is bubbling and roiling like an overexcited jacuzzi. It must be doing forty, fifty nautical miles an hour, pushing up massive amounts of water as it goes. Pushing it towards us.

I'm frozen in my tracks, a pillar of salt in the shape of a man who foolishly looked back.

Belinda's gloved hand touches my shoulder. "C'mon!" she hisses, and I'm restored to life in a heartbeat, my limbs suddenly obeying my commands again. I turn away from the ocean once more, concentrate on moving. Belinda and Ryuichi are still walking calmly, and I attempt to do the same. *Dead man walking*, I find myself thinking, imagining myself on death row in prison, heading for my own execution. But it's not that at all. Not dead man walking. Live man running.

I watch Ryuichi's back, remembering the story in his book about his experience in Nagasaki. It was a matter of days after America had dropped the second atomic bomb on the city, setting a tiny sun ablaze over its streets, levelling it in a matter of moments. Some of his family had lived there, an uncle and aunt, and his parents had gone looking for them amongst the rubble, blissfully ignorant of the dangers of radiation. They'd brought their child with them, only three years old, holding his hand tightly and trying not to let him see the twisted figures amongst the debris, arms curled by the intense heat, fists raised. The pugilist stance, it was called, a classic indicator of death by burning. Ryuichi had broken free of his parents and went to play, the ruined landscape a gigantic playground in his three-year-old eyes.

Then it had appeared, the first one seen in modern history. Until that day, we'd believed them to be legends, dragons and wyrms of myth. Figments of superstitious imaginations, primitive fears manifesting in exaggerated tales of giant beasts. We'd been comfortable in our modern, clinical, rational world. Safe from monsters.

Until that day, when the first *daikaiju* appeared, a hundred metres tall, crashing through what was left of Nagasaki, flattening what remained. It resembled a gigantic lizard raised on its hind legs, though its face was more ape-like in shape, and it had jagged plates lining its back like a stegosaurus. Later on, they would give it a name that became legend, a combination of the Japanese words for "gorilla" and "whale", in an effort to describe something that was, in essence, indescribable. But on that day, in Nagasaki, nobody thought about what it was, or what to call it. They were too busy. Busy running. Busy dying.

Ryuichi saw his parents crushed beneath one enormous foot, mercifully vanishing into its shadow an instant before the impact. It was headed towards him, as unmindful of the child as we are of the insects we crush as we walk here and there. Moving with deceptive slowness, each step like walking through water, but crossing twenty or thirty metres each time. It approached like an avalanche, like a tidal wave.

The boy turned and ran.

We step off the grassed area, the hard leather soles of my boots clumping on the rough black bitumen. The road here is uneven and crude, but better than many of the roads we'd driven on earlier in the day to get here. One had been barely more than gravel, a long stretch of straight but hilly road, blocked off at one end with a gate that probably would have been manned any other day. Today it had been deserted, and we'd opened the gate ourselves, granted ourselves access.

On this day, the island of Mauritius virtually belongs to us. At least for the moment. But in a few minutes, I suspect that ownership will be transferred to the gargantuan creature ploughing towards us through the Pacific. Another glimpse over my shoulder reveals more details, as it grows nearer; its shoulders are clear of the waters now, and instead of arms there are maybe half a dozen enormous tentacles on each side, whipping around in slow motion. They must be as long as the creature is high, at least a hundred metres, possibly more. And it continues to rise from the sea, as it pushes a wall of water in our direction. I hope Ryuichi has calculated this correctly, otherwise our run could be over before it's even begun.

After the first appearance of the *daikaiju* at Nagasaki, encounters grew more and more common. At first only one would appear at a time, then two or three, coming together as if drawn to one another, battling amongst the cities and towns of men. The devastation was staggering; thousands killed in a matter of minutes, then they would retreat once more, into the mountains and valleys, oceans and lakes, and not be seen again. Expeditions were sent after them, armed with everything from prayers to nukes, but there was no trace of them. They appeared when they chose, and disappeared just as readily. And on those occasions when we had the chance to organize a military response while they were still there, we found that weapons had little or no effect on them, apart from enraging them even further. Slowly but surely, mankind began to adapt: setting up early detection systems, preparing evacuation plans and drills, organizing shelters. Humans are pretty flexible, really. We just learned to run. Mostly away, but not entirely. To begin with, a few film studios realized the amazing potential in these giant monsters, and risked life and limb to capture their rampages on celluloid. These *daikaiju* films found instant popularity in their home country of Japan, and over the decades they gained a cult following overseas as well. It was the thrill of the danger, without the actual danger accompanying it.

But for some, that wasn't enough. Some wanted the real thing.

We walk a little while longer, passing a few touristy shops on either side of us, until we reach an intersection. Here the road joins a larger road, on one corner of which is a decent-sized grocery store, not dissimilar to the ones back home, apart from the unfamiliar name, "Cora". Beyond this road, the area becomes more residential, ramshackle houses mingling with newer tourist villas. A lot of the older buildings look like they've been added to repeatedly over the years, mixing styles and materials, never quite finished. I read once that the native Mauritians often extended their houses piecemeal as the money was available, resulting in an architectural style I'd categorize as "hodgepodge". Here, at this intersection, Ryuichi stops.

He nods. "This will do." He looks back over his shoulder, and I do the same. The film crew has vanished, presumably retreating to a safe distance, safer than ours at any rate. All I can see is the beach, and the ocean, and the monster. It's almost clear of the water now, its hindquarters splitting into four enormous legs, like roman columns covered in barnacles, and I realize that it looks a little like a centaur at this point. I can hear its passage, a dull roar like an airplane heard from a distance, and something else below that – a deep hum that I can't identify. The wind is picking up, but I don't think it's the cyclone yet, just the rush of air that the creature is pushing in front of itself.

Then the wave at its feet hits the beach and explodes, spraying water high into the air, and for a moment I can't see it anymore. My heart feels like it's trying to smash its way through my ribs, as the deep guttural crashing of water fills my ears. I'm certain we're going to be engulfed, swept away by the agitated sea, crushed against the rough walls of some Mauritian house before getting sucked back across the grass and sand and towed out to sea, pulled underwater to a tropical ocean grave. I can see it in my mind, clear as a photograph, clear as a premonition.

It doesn't happen, of course. The wave gurgles across the grassed area, foaming like detergent, and then washes weakly around our feet. It barely passes our ankles. I look over at Belinda, recognize a hint of the same fear that I'd just experienced, though she covers it up with a thin, tight smile. Ryuichi, on the other hand, looks as relaxed as a yogi.

"Get ready," he murmurs.

Then there is the first tremor, a minor earthquake, and I know without looking that the creature has reached the land. The sand on the beach is muffling its massive footfalls for the moment, but that won't last long. Soon it will hit solid earth, not that far behind us. Soon we'll start to run. My first run. I've dreamt of this almost my entire life, and now that it's actually happening, I'm having trouble believing it's real.

The road beneath my feet lurches, almost tipping me over, and I yelp once, surprised. It's real alright. "Be ready!" Ryuichi calls, bending his knees and touching his spread fingers against the rough bitumen. I do likewise, though it's harder to bend in these damn leather pants. I'm starting to think Ryuichi had the right idea. After all, if something goes wrong, I might as well be naked for all the protection these leathers will offer me. I close my eyes, feeling the vibrations in the street beneath me, trying to see what is happening in my mind. See the centaurine behemoth galloping towards me, each step covering hundreds of metres, each footstep crashing into the ground, sending plumes of dust into the air, and pushing dirt forward, forward, until . . .

"Now!" Ryuichi cries, but I'm already moving, as the ground beneath me rises sharply. It feels like being in an elevator, my weight suddenly increasing. I spring up and begin to run.

We all run, one way or another.

Ryuichi was the first. In his late teens, a little younger than I am, he travelled to the site of a *daikaiju* encounter. It was an enormous pig, but with a mane like a lion and tusks the size of city buses, and it was ravaging a small city in the south of Japan. He sought it out, while everyone else was fleeing. He remembered the sensations he'd felt as a small child, his experiences then, and somewhere inside those terrifying memories he found something wonderful. Watching footage of subsequent monster attacks over the years that followed, he barely saw the creatures themselves, majestic and huge, towering above the buildings like gods. No, what he saw was the ground that supported them, and what it did beneath their weight, their power. How it reacted. How it *flowed*.

That day, that young man did the unthinkable, the unbelievable. And since then, a small group of crazed enthusiasts have followed, quite literally, in his footsteps, seeking adventure or adrenaline or even some kind of enlightenment at the pounding feet of these monsters. Most everyone else ran away from them, and the maniacal film crews ran to them. But we don't run away, or run to.

We run *with* them.

This is the most bizarre feeling I've ever experienced, a surreal dislocation. It's a little like riding on an escalator, being pushed upwards and forwards, but the speed of the journey varies quite wildly. It's considerably less smooth than surfing, but the sensation isn't completely dissimilar to that nonetheless. As I run, the road begins to fracture and break beneath my feet, pulling off in different directions. I don't have time to think; I step hurriedly from the chunk of bitumen I'm riding onto another in front of me, then another, each one falling by the wayside as I pass it. Somewhere behind me, I can hear the creature, its breath hot and wet on the back of my neck like a tropical breeze. Droplets of water splatter on my shoulders, and I hope it's the cyclone catching up with us, rather than monster slobber. That would be kind of disgusting.

I catch sight of Belinda on my left. She's running like Hermes himself, winged heels masked by knee-high leather boots. I'm momentarily hypnotised by the fluidity of her run, moving from platelet to platelet like a gymnast, never pausing, never faltering. Never stopping. When you're running, as the old saying goes, he who hesitates is lost. I can't see Ryuichi; I don't know whether he's behind or in front of us. I hope he's okay.

The piece of road I'm riding lurches suddenly to one side, and my balance begins to falter. A burst of cold fear splashes up my back, and I react without thinking, quickly shifting my weight and leaping forward, leaving the crumbling bitumen behind me. I hear it collapse, crashing into a thousand pieces of rubble, and I realize how close I was to joining it. I have to concentrate, stay focused. Live man running, or dead man falling. It's up to me and God to decide which one I am. And the monster, of course.

To my right, I can see the town begin to fade, or what's left of it at any rate. Flic en Flac has been shaken, flipped upwards on a wave of rock, and then dropped back down in its wake. What remains looks more like a rubbish dump than a seaside tourist town, wreckage and debris spread surprisingly evenly across the ground. Beyond the town, we begin to enter more rural surroundings, huge expanses of sugarcane stretching for miles ahead of us. I hope that the creature sticks to the roads, where the solid ground will help us keep our footing, stay ahead of it, like riding a stormfront. But I know I can't rely on that. I've seen footage of runners getting caught in a tidal wave of soft earth, feet stuck in the sucking mud, dragging like ploughs, until they're finally pulled beneath the monster's feet and crushed into the dirt, just messy smears left in its wake. This is an extreme sport, often a death sport. But I feel I have to do it anyway, despite the risks. After all, you're never as alive as when you're close to death.

The rock I'm running on begins to list to one side, the left, and I realize that the creature is turning slightly. I don't need to see it to know this; I can picture the shockwave of earth, imagine its alignment. I know that the front of the wave will always be angled away from the direction it's moving, whilst it veers off to the sides the further around you go. I'm still travelling forward, but I'm leaning left, so my position on the wave is too far to the left of the *daikaiju's* path. I'll have to sidestep in order to continue running. Of course, I could always allow myself to slip off the wave on this side, ride the ever-decreasing ripples of rock back down to ground level, and end the run here and now. It's a tricky manoeuvre, but hardly impossible.

Ah, the hell with that. I didn't wait this long and come this far to wimp out now.

I start stepping across, my legs pumping, my breath burning my lungs. I'm starting to tire, I have to admit, and it's only been a matter of minutes. Running is incredibly demanding both physically and mentally, and it's starting to take its toll. I ignore the fatigue though, ignore the pain, and continue to run, cutting across the creature's path.

This is where it could go horribly wrong; a miscalculation, a misstep, and I could end up beneath the feet of the beast, monster toe-jam. I can see it to my right now, from the corner of my eye, its breath steaming in the air around its maw, tentacles flailing like an underwater anemone. Its legs swinging back and forth, so slowly, so deadly. The ground is rising higher and higher beneath my feet the closer I get to it. Alarm bells start to ring in my head.

Turn.

Turn.

Turn!

I turn left and redouble my efforts, trying to get some distance between myself and the monster. My legs are steel springs, my arms pistons in a perfect engine, my brain a supercomputer. I focus utterly on what's in front of me, striding from rock to rock. I am a legend, a superman, a godling. Invulnerable. Invincible.

A noise to my left catches my attention. I glance across and see Belinda stumble, crying out as she rolls from her platform, head-sized chunks of rock and soil tumbling with her as she vanishes, her yelps of pain cut off suddenly. I watch the spot for a moment longer, horrified. Frozen.

I'm just a man. Barely more than a boy. Flesh and blood, same as Belinda. Less. Vulnerable.

I'm going to die here.

"Go!" a voice behind me screams, and without thinking I obey. My legs work independently, pushing me forward, and after a few stumbling staccato seconds I find my rhythm again. The ground underneath my feet is softening, long broken stalks of sugarcane whipping past me like slalom flags, and I have to dodge left and right to avoid being hit in the face. But it's still solid enough to support my weight, thank heaven.

"Thought we lost you for a second there," the voice calls out again, and I glance to my right. Ryuichi is there, further back, closer to the creature, but running almost casually, not a worry in the world. I can't understand his attitude to the monster at his heels, despite reading his memoirs. If my family had been killed by a monster, I'd hate them, fear them, keep the hell away from them. Instead, Ryuichi seeks them out, not to try to hurt or kill them, but to share an experience with them. To run with them. It makes no sense to me.

"Belinda?" I call back to him, legs moving automatically, boots slapping the mud beneath them fast and loud enough to sound like a drum beat, or a heartbeat. Life signs.

He nods in an exaggerated fashion, almost theatrically. "She'll be fine," he yells, barely audible over the rumble and roar of the beast's rough progress.

I relax a little, relieved both for her and for myself by proxy. I've seen videos of runners doing what she'd done; it's similar to a surfer's ignominious exit from a particularly large wave, painful and dangerous but not often fatal. She'll be battered and bruised, perhaps even a little broken, but she'll live. I hope that's the truth, at any rate. We believe what we need to believe, in order to keep going.

The wind whistles over my buzz-cut hair, my eyes watering a little. I'm keeping a close eye on the ground just in front of my feet now, stepping left and right, back and forward, depending on where the heaving earth is carrying me. And always I'm acutely aware of the massive presence behind me driving me on, and the smaller one to my side sharing the experience. I wonder for the thousandth time why Ryuichi does this. In his book, he spoke of his reasons, but they were masked by rhetorical questions, so there were no easy answers. The one that's always puzzled me was simple – six ordinary words – but the old Japanese man seemed to find something more in them, a philosophy that I didn't understand.

His question was, *Why are there no daikaiju fossils?*

Ryuichi is waving to me, grinning. I wave back with a smile. He continues to wave, more animatedly than before, and with sudden dread I realize that he's not smiling, he's grimacing. And he's not waving, he's gesturing. Gesturing ahead at something. I raise my eyes from the undulating soil at my feet, knowing it is dangerous to do so, but suspecting that it would be even more dangerous not to.

I'm right. Worse luck.

We're headed directly for a mountain. Mauritian mountains aren't like the gentle slopes back home, where you can often barely notice the incline as you climb one. No, they are acute lumps of stone, easily taller than they are wide, jutting defiantly at the sky. The one in front of us looks suspiciously like a pudgy finger carved in rock, covered by a thick blanket of dark green vegetation. It must be four or five hundred metres high, dwarfing even the behemoth at our heels. For a moment I'm caught in its majesty, its beauty, its grandeur. Then I snap out of it, and see it for what it really is.

A wall. A huge stone wall. And we're hurtling towards it.

I look left and right, hoping for a way off the earthwave before we hit, but both Ryuichi and I have been too skilful in our placement; we're right at the tip of the arrowhead, which is aimed directly for the centre of the mountain. Even if we skipped to the sides, we'd still be smashed against it. I look to Ryuichi for some kind of comfort, some hope, but his posture doesn't offer much of either. He's almost back-pedalling, as close to panic as I've ever seen him, in all the years of watching the movies of him running. Between us, we've had a deadly combination of inexperience and overconfidence. *He who hesitates is lost*, they say, but they also say *look before you leap*. And *pride cometh before the fall*.

I look back over my shoulder, fear falling away from me as if caught in the slipstream. The creature continues to advance, not slowing at all, perhaps not even noticing the mountain. I still can't see its eyes, just the dull red glow from beneath its brow, but I suspect that even if I could, I'd see nothing there, no intelligence, no will. Looking at it this close, it's somehow less monstrous, less bestial than from afar, or on a television screen for that matter, stripped of dramatic music and editing.

. . . no fossils . . .

Turning back, I see Ryuichi signalling me again. I'm not certain what he's trying to tell me, so rather than attempting to interpret his motions, I pay attention to his actions. He's allowing himself to fall back, closer to the creature, and this time he appears to be doing it on purpose. I blink a few times, trying to both clear my eyes of tears and to comprehend what he's doing.

Then the penny drops. The closer we are to the creature's feet, the more force will be behind us when it hits the mountain. Too far forward and we'll be dashed against the rock. Too far back and we'll be caught between it and the monster. But if we get it just right . . .

Goldilocks never played for such high stakes.

I slow the pace of my run, feeling the earth under my boots start to jerk and wobble more violently as I do so. We're closer to this moving epicentre now, and the Brownian motion of the ground is become more pronounced and chaotic.

I just hope we have time before . . .

The outskirts of the wave ahead of us crash into the mountain, sending a wall of dirt into the sky. Like a wave breaking on rocks, the soil is scattered into a million directions, raining down on us in large sodden clumps. I have to dodge desperately in order to keep my footing on the ground, which is starting to tilt upwards, rising ominously. I look over at Ryuichi one last time. He gives me a thumbs-up signal. I return it, though I wish I was as confident as he is. I hear the monster behind us bellow, just once, as if thwarted by this gigantic rocky finger in its way. I can sympathize.

Then we hit, and I'm flying.

At first the ground is still beneath my feet, pressing them hard as it accelerates into the sky carrying me along with it, rising on a column of soil and sugarcane. Then it falls away, and I'm running in thin air. The gap between me and my footing widens, ten metres, twenty, fifty. In front of me, the vegetation cloaking the mountain speeds past my eyes. It's impossible to judge how close I am to it. Too close, I'd wager. Any moment now, it'll slap me hard in the face, and then I'll be scraped along it like an insect hitting a sloped windscreen, leaving a long smear behind me as I'm sanded into oblivion on the rough shrubs.

Suddenly, the mountain is gone, and all I can see is grey cloudy sky, and distant vistas of fields and roads below me. I realize I was right about how useless my leathers really are.

My stomach turns over, and I realize I've stopped ascending, gravity finally taking a firm grip on my ankles. And slowly, almost reluctantly, I begin to freefall. I don't even think to scream; the sensation is both exhilarating and terrifying, and between the two emotions I'm struck completely dumb. My muscles have gone dead, arms and legs flapping in the wind like a paper doll's. I look down and see the mountain again, the finger pointing up at me. Now it doesn't look defiant. It looks accusing. *You*, it's saying, *you human, you proud, stupid human. This is what happens. Icarus flies too high, Pandora opens the box. Now reap what you have sown.*

Then there's an impact, a tumbling, and everything goes green, then grey, then black.

I'm not certain how long I'm out for. It can't be long, maybe a few seconds. Still, for a short time I'm floating in the dark, warm and safe and numb. It's bliss. Then there's water splashing on my face, and I come to. I'm sprawled in the bushes on my back, bent in an uncomfortable position, a warm barrage of huge raindrops splattering on my forehead and cheeks, running into my nose and mouth, choking me a little. I try to sit up, but a sharp pain in my back persuades me to stay put for the moment. Instead, I raise my head and look down myself.

It's nowhere near as bad as it could have been, I have to admit. My leathers are looking pretty torn and tattered, and there's a reasonable amount of blood coming from a dozen or so minor wounds that I can make out, but I seem to be pretty intact, no obviously broken bones. I turn my head painfully to the side, and see that the shrubs I've landed on cushioned my fall quite effectively, still green and springy despite the sunless skies. All in all, it could have gone much worse for me. I'm alive.

"Ryuichi," I croak, then again, louder this time. "Ryuichi?"

There's no answer. I try to sit up again, this time ignoring the sharp recommendations of my bruised coccyx, and manage to reach a sitting position without fainting, though my head is spinning like the clouds above me. They catch my eye for a moment, and I look upwards. We're in the midst of the cyclone now, though I've landed in a shallow depression in the peak of the mountain so I'm shielded from the worst of the winds. But over my head, I can see Katrina venting her fury, the clouds streaming in enormous circles across the sky. It looks like we're almost in the storm's eye.

"Ryuichi?" I call again, and look around carefully for the old Japanese man, my idol, my hero, my teacher *in absentia*.

I see him, maybe ten or fifteen metres away from my position. He's landed in the vegetation as well, though he landed face down. Unfortunately, the tree hasn't saved him; it's bare of leaves, a jagged lightning bolt of wood standing upright on the top of the mountain. He isn't moving, and I know he never will again, not of his own volition. The branch he's impaled on, through the chest and out of his back, is a darker shade than the rest of the tree, and I realize it's Ryuichi's blood staining it almost black. Blood also streams from the old man's mouth, pooling on the ground beneath him. He has that posture, that near-indefinable body language that speaks of death; I've seen pictures of corpses, and of unconscious people, and there's something about the dead that silently screams out, tells you that the person, perhaps the soul if it exists, is no longer present. Something has departed.

Ryuichi's life has ended, his long and tumultuous life. I feel tears begin to burn the corners of my eyes, but I blink them away, determined not to cry. This was exactly how he always said he wanted to die, in books and interviews. You really are never as alive as when you're close to death. And before he died, he truly lived.

I feel a burst of hot, moist air against my back, through the rips and tears in my leathers, and I turn my head and look up. And up. And up.

I almost forgot about the *daikaiju*. How strange is that?

I'm not afraid, not anymore. If I die here, then this is where I die. I'll be proud to share a grave with the grand master. But somehow I don't think that's going to happen; the monster isn't even looking in my direction. It's raised up, its tentacles stretched to the skies, like a footballer about to take a mark, or an evangelist beseeching the Almighty. And it's so *still* – just a slight waving of its serpentine arms in the gale force winds that must be whipping around them. It's as if it's waiting for something. I look up as well, follow its gaze.

And then I see it. Right above the mountain, hovering like a halo. At the centre of the storm, the point around which the angry grey clouds are rotating, I can see it, just barely through the rain that's pouring into my face.

The eye of the cyclone. It's the purest blue I've ever seen.

A tiny hole in the clouds has formed there, opened up by the tremendous forces unleashed by the storm. It's fragile, and fleeting, but it's there. The eye blinks, once, twice, then closes for good. I'm blinking back tears and raindrops, wiping my own eyes desperately, hoping to catch sight of it again. But it's gone. It takes me a while to accept this. Once I do, I lower my eyes again.

The creature is gone as well.

I clamber to my feet, my knees trembling violently under my own weight. I stagger to the edge of the mountain, where the *daikaiju* had been just moments before, and look over, but there's no sign of it, apart from the enormous trail of destruction it has left in its wake. I see that now, from high above, and find it hard to believe that I'd been riding that wave. Running with the monster.

Why are there no monster fossils? There must be a thousand answers to that one, from biodegradable skeletons to ancient animals predating the fossil record. But standing here on shaky legs, hundreds of metres above the torn fields, I can only think of one that seems plausible to me, and I suspect it's what Ryuichi believed as well.

These creatures, these *daikaiju*, leave no fossils because they're not animals, not even alive as such. They're forces of nature, like the cyclone that still roars around me, or an avalanche that swallows a dozen daring skiers whole. Ryuichi couldn't hate the monster for killing his parents, any more than he could hate a flood or a drought. Some people might, but not him. All he could do was try to understand it, get close to it. Run with it.

Down below, picking its way through the torn earth, I can see a figure limping, tiny as an insect. I can make out black clothing and short hair. It's Belinda, making her way painfully towards me. Behind her, driving up in the distance in some kind of open-topped four-wheel drive, comes the film crew, cameras still pointed my way despite the lack of a *kaiju* to film, *dai* or otherwise. Belinda waves to me, and I wave back tiredly, leaning on the rocks on the edge of the mountain, ignoring the wind and rain. We'll do this again, her and I, and perhaps others will join us, new blood to replace the old that's been spilled.

I smile at this thought, finally understanding Ryuichi's attitude, his serenity. I don't know if I'll ever be as sanguine as he was, but at least I'm on the path now. To be a part of something like this, something so magnificent, that was enough, and it will continue to be enough.

We all run, one way or another.

With Bright Shining Faces
J.C. Koch

———

"You can't draw monsters!"

Mrs. George looked up from her lesson plan. It was Quiet Time and her first graders were normally quite good with coloring quietly for a few minutes, especially because Story Time came right after.

Cody, the boy who'd just broken the main Quiet Time rule, glared at Sukie, who sat next to him.

Sukie was busy drawing. She didn't look up, just shrugged. "Can too," she said mildly.

"Can *not*," Cody insisted. "Especially not like those." He punched his finger onto Sukie's drawing. Sukie shrugged again and moved her paper further to the left, away from Cody.

Sukie was a small, quiet girl with straight honey-brown hair, big, bright blue eyes, and a serious demeanor. She normally kept to herself, and this should have made her the class outcast. But it was quite the reverse. As opposed to being shunned by the other children she was always invited to play with them, and most of the class wanted to partner with her whenever a buddy was required.

Whether it was because she didn't like any of her classmates more than the others, or because she knew she was popular without seeming to try or care, Sukie never chose the same partner twice in a row.

But other than when she was required to be a part of a couple or a group, Sukie kept to herself. The other children were respectful of her apparent wish to be solitary, and none of them ever mocked her.

Cody wasn't normally a belligerent little boy, and the other children were rarely this confrontational with Sukie. Mrs. George could reprimand him, and her first instinct was to do so, lest whatever hold

Sukie had over the other children be broken and she be turned into the class victim and, by extension, Cody into the class bully.

However, there was something in the way he was upset – there was fear in the little boy's tone, easily as much as there was anger.

Mrs. George got up and went to see just what Sukie was drawing and to provide the calming influence the teacher standing next to a student normally enforced.

Cody looked up at her, eyes wide. "Make her stop it, Missus Gee. She's drawing bad things." Yes, he was frightened.

"May I see, Sukie?" Mrs. George asked gently.

"Sure." Sukie moved her drawing back to the center of her desk.

Mrs. George was prepared for something horrible – many times students drew things they experienced at home, terrible things, and part of her job was to determine if the drawing was real and, therefore, if the child needed to see the school psychologist, nurse, or on-campus police officer.

Sukie's father was an oil rigger and her mother worked as a cocktail waitress in one of the more popular casinos in Gulfport. Those professions didn't necessarily provide a stable home life, though most of the children in her school had parents working on the rigs and/or in the casinos.

Sukie's grandmother took care of her and her older brother, Spradlin, and Mrs. George had met her when she'd had Spradlin in her class. Mrs. Selwyn appeared normal, but she'd always made Mrs. George nervous, even though the older woman really just liked to talk about how Spradlin was named for his mother's family and how the oil rigs were destroying the ecological balance of the world, her son working on one or no.

However, Mrs. George had a hard time determining what about this picture was upsetting Cody so much. It was a rather crude drawing of what looked like a fatter version of a Tyrannosaurus Rex. It was a little early for it, but because of a traveling exhibit, they'd done a whole week on dinosaurs last month, culminating in a school field trip to the University of Southern Alabama Archeology Museum when the dinosaur exhibit was there. All the school had been involved, so Sukie still being interested in the ancient creatures didn't seem out of the ordinary.

However, Mrs. George had been teaching for many years now, and Cody's reaction felt quite real, not made up to get Sukie in trouble or draw attention to himself.

"Sukie's just drawn T-Rex," she said reassuringly, as she patted Cody's shoulder. "And very well, too," she said to Sukie. This wasn't a lie – most first graders weren't going to take the art world by storm, after all – and this was a serviceable rendition of a giant lizard. "And she's allowed to draw whatever she wants, just as you are."

"But *look* at it," Cody said. "*Look.*"

She did. It remained a fat, crude rendition of a T-Rex. "Cody, you know that monsters aren't real, don't you? Besides, Sukie's drawing a dinosaur."

"No," he insisted. "She's drawing monsters." His voice dropped. "*Real* monsters. And monsters aren't supposed to be real. My mom said."

"My grandma said monsters *are* real," Sukie replied calmly. "And she's right. You're just afraid."

"My mom said that we *should* be afraid," Cody muttered. "She said that no one should ask them to visit."

"It's okay. They're my friends." Sukie reached out and patted Cody's hand. "But don't worry – I won't let them hurt you."

Mrs. George expected Cody to pull his hand away. Girls still had cooties at this age, and the boy was so upset with Sukie that she didn't expect him to be pleasant.

But instead of belligerence, Cody relaxed. "You promise?"

Sukie nodded. "I promise." She looked up at Mrs. George. "I won't let them hurt you, either, Missus Gee."

"Well, thank you, dear. That's very brave and kind of you. Now, Cody, are we all alright here?"

He nodded. "Yes. I'm sorry, Missus Gee."

She squeezed his shoulder. "It's okay. We all get scared sometimes."

She headed back towards her desk, but as she did, something moved in her peripheral vision. It was Sukie's picture – it still looked like an over-fat T-Rex, but it no longer looked crudely drawn. Now it looked filled-in and real. And she could have sworn that she'd seen it move.

But when she looked at the drawing directly, all that was there were the green and brown crayon scribbles Sukie had done.

Mrs. George shrugged and went back to the front of the room. "Class, are we ready for Story Time? Today we'll read *Clifford, The Big Red Dog.*"

The children all cheered, Cody included, and Mrs. George went happily back to the normal routine of her day.

———

The normal routine lasted until recess. Sukie wasn't playing with the other children. She was off in a corner, under a tree, crayons and paper with her, busily drawing. Her face was wrinkled in concentration and her crayons moved swiftly over the paper.

Mrs. George wondered if she should reprimand Sukie for bringing the art supplies outside – the children weren't supposed to do this. However, the girl wasn't bothering anyone, and she was taking good care with crayons and paper both.

Mrs. George looked around. There was a belligerence in the air that wasn't normal. As she watched, several small scuffles broke out, between children who normally didn't fight with anyone, let alone each other.

She and the other teachers and aides broke these little fights up. All participants seemed on edge, which was to be expected, but none seemed angry, which wasn't. Students from her class and Mr. Crandall's upper grade glass were the most involved, percentage-wise. Spradlin was in Mr. Crandall's class.

At least one child per fight had a picture of some kind of "monster" on their person or identified as theirs. Only those from her class and Mr. Crandall's. Mrs. George looked at each drawing. Some were lizard-based, some aquatic, and a few looked like giant trees – all had a great many fangs and claws and such. She was certain they were all Sukie's work.

Each child who had a drawing was hysterical to get their picture back, either from the teachers or, in a few cases, from the children they'd been fighting. She and the other teachers discussed punishments. No one was truly hurt, and all the children were so riled up, discretion seemed the better course. A few minutes of Quiet Time to think over bad behavior was determined to be the approved course of action. In order to ensure all the children would be able to calm down, they decided full confiscation wasn't the right answer either.

So each child got their drawing back. Every one of them seemed more relieved than normal for something like this. The children who didn't have drawings seemed envious. Mrs. George wondered if the fights had started because children without drawings had tried to take them away from children who had them. Then she dismissed this idea as silly.

This excitement filled up the majority of recess time, and most of the school had come to gather around while the fights were subdued. However, a fast headcount showed there were some missing, from her class and Mr. Crandall's.

Mrs. George looked back to Sukie, who had all the missing children near her, either waiting in a well-ordered line or standing off to the side, pieces of paper held in their hands.

Sukie finished a drawing and handed it to the next child in line, who happened to be Cody. He trotted off to the other group, looking quite happy.

As the first bell rang and the children all trooped back inside, Mrs. George called him over. "What do you have there?"

The boy held the paper up for her to see, but didn't hand it to her. "My own monster!"

This drawing was no better or worse than the others Sukie had created. It was crude, and from her lizard-like group, only this one was reddish, with wings, a long sharp beak, and six claws on each foot, of which it also had six. In keeping with what appeared to be Sukie's theme, there were extra claws on the wings, as well.

"I thought you didn't like monsters." This one resembled a bigger version of a pterodactyl, with more legs, feet, and claws than a real one. "This looks a little . . . scary."

"This one's mine, so it won't hurt me," Cody said, all happy confidence. "Or you, Missus Gee," he added loyally. He trotted off, carrying his drawing carefully.

Mrs. George took a good look at the children in line. Every one was in her class. The ones in the other group were all in Mr. Crandall's class. She wasn't sure if this was good or bad, but, as Sukie handed another drawing to Lori, who took it and skipped off, the second bell rang.

Sukie said something and the other children headed for the classroom. Some looked disappointed, others crestfallen, some worried. Only Cody and Lori and the others who had drawings already seemed happy and contented.

Sukie was last in, and as she took her seat, Mrs. George wondered if she should just allow Sukie to keep on drawing or not.

"We're going to have Quiet Time because there were a lot of children behaving badly."

The children who had drawings, whether they'd been in fights or not, hunched protectively over their pictures.

"I'm sorry, Missus Gee," Sukie said. "I'm doing my best. I had to take care of Spradlin's class first because they're old and bigger."

How to reply to this? Clearly Sukie felt the fights were over her drawings. The rest of the class' expressions showed they agreed.

"Well . . . Sukie, you weren't involved in the fighting." At least, not intentionally. "Why don't all of you who weren't a part of it color? Those who were, you just sit quietly and consider why fighting isn't a good thing."

"Sometimes it's good, Missus Gee," Lori said. "Sometimes you *have* to fight. Like in the Civil War and stuff." The other children, other than Sukie, nodded. Sukie's attention was back to her drawing.

"Well, yes," Mrs. George acknowledged. "But not over petty things, children."

Cody opened his mouth, but before he could speak Sukie reached over and touched his arm. The boy shut his mouth immediately.

Mrs. George decided to let this play out.

———————

"And then, the children just acted as if everything was normal," she told her husband over dinner. "But it wasn't normal. We had Quiet Time for the rest of the day and not one of them complained or acted restless."

"Did every child get a drawing?" he asked as he cut into his steak. He sounded about as interested in her work as he normally did, which was barely. Her work was never as interesting as his.

"Yes. It just seemed . . . easier to let Sukie draw pictures for the other children."

"Then you handled it right."

"I suppose. But, how was your day?" Mr. George was a police officer, and normally he was the one with the unusual stories, not her. She didn't allow herself to feel disappointed that he wasn't that interested in the oddities of her day – she'd gotten used to it years ago.

"Something like yours. More petty crimes, increase in domestic calls, lots of fighting. Some issues on one of the oil rigs."

"On the rigs? What happened?"

"Fighting mostly. A couple of the riggers went over into the ocean. Not our problem, that's what the Coast Guard's for. We were informed because we had to notify next of kin." He gave her a comforting smile. "None of the parents at James Conason Elementary, don't worry. I always check."

"Hard not to worry what with all this . . . fighting."

He shrugged. "Full moon's coming. You know it makes the crazies crazier."

"The children didn't seem crazy. They seemed . . . scared."

He finished his meal quickly, shoved his plate back, and patted her hand. "I'm sure it's just a little fancy that will pass. Some popular TV show or something."

"Something . . . I suppose."

"Double shift time. Don't wait up." He got up as quickly as he'd eaten, eager to get back to work.

In the early days of their marriage, Mr. George had worked double shifts so he could move up and they could have a better life more quickly. Once he'd reached a better pay grade he'd stopped, so they could spend more time together, especially since they'd never had children and only had each other.

But for the past couple of years he'd started taking more and more double shifts. Mrs. George had given up asking why; she had her suspicions, and they didn't center around Mr. George trying to make a better life for the two of them. They centered around the fact that Mr. George had a beat that covered most of the strip clubs near the seedier casinos.

Mr. George gave her a quick kiss and headed out the door. Saving her from dwelling on what had happened to their relationship or having to ask herself why she hadn't mentioned the drawing Sukie had given her, at the end of the day, just before the final bell rang. She hadn't wanted to mention it, in part because she couldn't explain to her husband why she had it in her pocket, and why she didn't want to let it out of her reach.

Her drawing was of a dragon, meaning Sukie was branching out into mythology. Crude, like all the others, and, as with the other drawings, not quite like a dragon should be. Six legs, three sets of wings, with the middle set being the largest, and, as with all of Sukie's other drawings, lots and lots of claws and teeth.

Mrs. George also didn't mention that if she looked at this drawing just right, out of the corner of her eye, it looked much more real. And very much alive.

————

The next day Mrs. George noticed a change in the class. Whereas the day before they had seemed nervous, frightened and belligerent, today they all seemed expectant.

The moment everyone was seated and the tardy bell had rung, Sukie raised her hand. "Missus Gee, may we sing a song, please?"

This was an odd request, but there was nothing wrong with a little singing. "Certainly. What song?"

Sukie cleared her throat and began to sing. "Good morning to you, good morning to you . . . "

The other children joined in. "We're all in our places, with bright shining faces, good morning to you."

"Well, isn't that nice? Did you know that schoolchildren used to sing that song for their teachers about a hundred years ago? Where did you learn it, a television show?" If this was now a song from a new, popular show, then perhaps all the rest would be, as Mr. George said, easily explained.

"No," Sukie said. "Missus Gee, you need to sing, too."

"I do?"

"Yes," the little girl said emphatically. "You do. Do you still have what I gave you?"

Mrs. George looked at the class. They all looked expectant and, she realized, they all had their drawings on their desks. "Yes, I do, Sukie. I see we all do." She pulled the drawing out from her purse and put it onto her desk.

"Put your hands on your picture," Sukie said. "And then we all sing."

Mrs. George had learned how to prevent a first grader from taking over her class in her first year of teaching. However, there was something in Sukie's tone and expression that made Mrs. George do as requested.

"Now do we sing?" Cody asked Sukie.

The girl cocked her head, as if listening to something. Then she nodded. "Now."

They sang. The song ended and Mrs. George waited. Nothing. She cleared her throat. Time to take back control of the class and put them onto their regular schedule. "Well, that was a nice way to begin the day. Let's all pull out our math books and—"

Lightning flashed and, moments later, thunder rolled. The ground rumbled and shook and the windows rattled. She'd heard the sound and felt the movement before, many times. A sudden storm had arisen. Perhaps the children had picked up that it was coming, just as animals were supposed to be able to do. Perhaps that was why they'd been so strange.

Mrs. George stood up. "Class, orderly lines, please, like we've practiced." In case of hurricane, all the children were to go to the auditorium, which had the least windows and where the school could ensure everyone was accounted for.

The children all looked at Sukie. Who nodded. They got up and headed for the door. As she counted heads and ensured everyone was out of the classroom, Mrs. George happened to look down at Cody's desk. While the paper Sukie had given him the day before was there, there was no drawing on it.

It was foolish and foolhardy, but she looked at the other desks. All the children had left their papers, but all the pages were blank. She hurried back to her desk, telling herself it was to grab her purse. But as she did so, she verified that the page Sukie had given her was now blank as well.

Lightning and thunder hit again, this time with almost no break in between. The sound was louder than before and the ground shook again. Mrs. George trotted outside. There would be time to figure out what was going on later, once the hurricane was over.

But, as things turned out, what was causing the ground to shake wasn't thunder, lightning, or a hurricane. It was Mr. Crandall.

Well, it *might* be Mr. Crandall. Or, rather, it might possibly be Mr. Crandall, on a very strange and frightening day.

There was a creature – a giant creature – standing in the middle of the playground. It resembled a giant lizard, but more sinuous, and it had flippers – she realized it was much more like a pliosaur, only with many teeth and claws on the flippers which the original pliosaurs hadn't had.

It also had Mr. Crandall's face, or what was left of his face. As she watched, his face melted into the giant monster, forming a shining face shape around his eyes. The only thing that seemed to remain of Mr. Crandall were his eyes – she was very sure they were Mr. Crandall's eyes still.

There was bedlam, of course. Only not from everyone. The children in Mr. Crandall's class and hers weren't running, screaming, or crying. They were all looking at Mr. Crandall, but without fear. Just as she was.

Cody took her hand. "Ready, Missus Gee?"

"Ready for what, Cody?"

"To make things right," Sukie said, as she took Mrs. George's other hand. "We've been chosen."

A woman stepped out and stood in front of whatever Mr. Crandall had become. It was Mrs. Selwyn. She smiled, a very feral smile, and Mrs. George felt afraid for the first time.

Mrs. Selwyn raised her arms and all of a sudden, she grew. And then she changed. First there was a giant woman and then, as lightning struck and thunder rolled, there was a giant tree, with arms and legs, covered in bark that looked like sharp scales, vicious branches replacing limbs and digits, and there, in the center, Mrs. Selwyn's face.

Her face melted into the tree leaving, as with Mr. Crandall, only a shining shape of her former face around the eyes. The eyes looked human, only old – ancient really. And they looked around with clear malevolence.

The Selwyn-Tree roared something to the Pliosaur-Crandall, which in turn roared at the children who were in Mr. Crandall's class. Starting with Spradlin, the children all changed. They were lizard-like, or dinosaur-like, some aquatic, even a few tree- and plant-like creatures. None were as big as either the Selwyn-Tree or the Pliosaur-Crandall, though they were still quite huge. But all ended up with bright, flat, shining faces around human eyes – human eyes that flashed with hatred when they actually looked at humans.

The tree looked straight at Mrs. George now, and her mouth went dry. The hatred from the Selwyn-Tree was intense, almost physical it was so strong. Sukie squeezed her hand. "It's okay, Missus Gee. Grandma doesn't hate you at all. Changing doesn't hurt. And you'll be happy once it's through."

"Can I go next?" Cody asked. He sounded breathlessly excited.

The tree looked at him and nodded. "All of you . . . now." It was a horrible voice – loud, screeching, jarring, and definitely malevolent. "Sukie, lead the way."

One by one her class turned into giant monsters, just a little smaller than the monsters who'd been Mr. Crandall's class only minutes ago. Each one was a replica of what Sukie had drawn. Each one kept the shining, flat outline of their original faces along with their own eyes, but Mrs. George was sure they weren't interpreting what they saw with their childish, human minds. Whatever their minds had become, human wasn't it.

Sukie was a giant T-Rex only more so, Cody was now a nightmare version of a pterodactyl, Lori was some kind of giant squid, the other children were the same, or worse, depending on where you stood on the tentacles versus limbs debate.

The Selwyn-Tree came to her, its leg-like roots tearing up the ground as it moved. "You fear. You think you should stay. Let me show you what you want to save." A tree limb swung towards her and Mrs. George flinched. But it landed gently on her head.

She saw an image of Mr. George at work the night before. But he wasn't alone. He also wasn't fully dressed. He was making love to one of the female officers she'd met once or twice, making love in a very animalistic way he hadn't done with Mrs. George for years.

"You're making that up." But she knew it was true, had known it was true for those same years.

"You know that I'm not. He has betrayed you as they all have betrayed *us*."

"But the others . . . " Mrs. George found herself using the favored line of reasoning she'd heard from her students for years. "It's not fair."

"No. It's not fair. Join us or die. That's not fair, either," the Selwyn-Tree said. "But those are your only choices."

Sukie-Rex and Pterodactyl-Cody both turned to her. "Come with us," Pterodactyl-Cody said, voice a terrifying shriek. "We'll miss you if you don't."

"You know stuff even Grandma doesn't," Sukie-Rex somehow roared intelligibly. The Selwyn-Tree nodded.

Mrs. George considered her options, as her class looked at her with their bright shining faces.

———

"You were right," she said to the Selwyn-Tree, as she flapped her wings and landed on the auditorium roof, crushing it and everyone stupid enough to still be inside. "The change didn't hurt at all."

She was a dragon now. Well, not really. She was a combination of all she'd been and all her ancestors had been, as well as all her avatar had been in the ancient times, before the cosmos had sent a meteor into their world and left only their consciousnesses to wait millennia for the right channel to open up.

Sukie's family had been that channel, and Sukie herself would, one day, lead them all to claim not only this world, but the others out there they'd seen while waiting to come back to full life. But until then, Sukie-Rex needed a teacher, and Selywn-Tree, the one who gave All Life, needed a general she could rely on.

"Do they need us in the water?" Selwyn-Tree asked, her voice strong, bold, and beautiful.

"No. I flew over and flamed the rigs – our relations in the water will do the rest." George-Dragon laughed and enjoyed the way it sounded now – not friendly, but loud and dangerous and powerful. She enjoyed the memory of oil rigs being pulled up and dropped onto parts of the coastline, as much as the memory of those rigs pulled under the ocean. She knew Selwyn-Tree could see these images within her own mind as well – it was part of her power as the All Life; she could see all their thoughts if they wanted her to. And George-Dragon wanted her to.

"You enjoyed. That is good. But the pleasure is not yours alone."

"Oh, I know. I put some of the little ones on the islands. They're having fun with those trying to escape the mainland."

Selwyn-Tree looked quite pleased with her initiative. "Good. They should learn to enjoy this, we will be doing it for some time."

Pliosaur-Crandall joined them. "I can keep my group on the coast and in the water. I know you're moving on – where shall we meet you when we're done?"

"We will go inland," the Selwyn-Tree said. "I expect we will leave a clear trail, though it may be quite . . . wide."

Pliosaur-Crandall honked a laugh. "We'll find you. Have fun." He turned back and flopped onto what was left of James Conason Elementary, heading back to the water, as his students trampled what was left of Gulfport and, as George-Dragon looked a little farther and from side to side, Mobile and New Orleans and everything in between.

The Gulf of Mexico was on fire from the thousands of oil rigs now blown up and burning. The oil rigs that had stolen their life's blood for the weak, pathetic, and horrible humans. Seeing the thousands of those on fire or blowing up was especially rewarding.

"Lead us on the best path to destroy these humans who took our world and ruined it," Selwyn-Tree said to her.

George-Dragon nodded her head, enjoying how she could see for miles, watching her children stomping on casinos and tossing police cars like they were Hot Wheels toys. Sukie-Rex threw a squad car towards her and George-Dragon batted it with her tail. Mr. George and his lover went flying right to Pterodactyl-Cody, screaming in terror, though the sound was, like them, pathetic and weak. Cody caught their car in his mouth and chomped right through it. The human screams stopped. She really did have the best students.

She did have one worry. "Can nuclear bombs hurt us?"

Selwyn-Tree laughed. "Nothing here can hurt us anymore. We need neither food, nor water, nor sleep. We have taken all the poisons, all the chemicals, all the pollution, and made it a part of us."

"Good," George-Dragon said, as part of her class met the incoming National Guard troops. They jumped up and down on the tanks, squashing them flat. She loved seeing them enjoy themselves so. "Then I think we head right to Kansas and Nebraska and play with some things buried there in the ground."

"A fine plan," Selwyn-Tree said. "Lead on."

George-Dragon looked around. "My class, play time is over," she called, her cry echoing through the air. "It's time to learn how to blow up nuclear bombs for maximum damage."

She flew slowly northward, as her cheering students followed her, stomping on anything and everything they came across, singing all the while. "We're all in our places, with bright shining faces, good-bye to you."

Kaiju
Gary McMahon

———

Diving deep, something large moves and writhes with the currents, heading into the comforting darkness. The waters become cold, the water pressure increases. A sleek, muscled body drives on, speeding ever downwards, moving fast towards the bottom of everything.

———

Jeff pulled up at the kerb and stared out of the side window at the remains of his house. The army took down the road blocks a few days ago, the useable highways were being patrolled by the police and the Territorial Army, and things were slowly making their way back towards some kind of normality.

He didn't want to leave the car. He felt as if it offered him some kind of protective bubble from the world. Not in any literal sense, of course – nobody felt safe now, not after what happened – but inside the car, behind a layer of metal and glass, he could at least compartmentalise his thoughts.

There was no point in staying here, though. He had no choice but to get out. He needed to be sure there were no survivors.

He shifted his gaze to the windscreen and watched a young woman picking her way through the rubble a few yards up ahead. She was dressed in a blue boiler suit, like the kind worn by staff on the factory floor where he used to work, and her hair was pulled back severely from her face. Her pale cheeks were smudged with dirt. Her tiny white hands looked steady enough, but her gait was ungainly as she moved carefully through the broken bricks and shattered timbers that had once formed a home – presumably hers, or that of someone she knew.

Jeff felt like crying. He had lost so much. Everybody had. He didn't know a single person who remained untouched by the events of the past three weeks. When that thing attacked, it brought with it only destruction. Like a biblical plague, it wiped out everything in its path.

That thing . . . the beast . . . the monster . . .

Thinking of it now, he felt stupid. It was a child's word used to describe something he struggled to label in an adult world. Everything changed the day it arrived; even the rules of physics were twisted out of shape, along with the precarious geometry of his own existence.

When he was a boy, he loved reading comics and watching films about monsters. Now he was a man, and he had seen the proof that monsters really existed, he could not even begin to fathom what his younger self had found so fascinating about them.

He opened the door and got out of the car. Night was falling but it was still light enough to see clearly. There was a slight chill in the air. The woman was closer now to his position, and she wasn't as young as he'd initially thought. Middle aged: possibly in her early forties. The mud on her face clouded her features, at first hiding the wrinkles and the layers of anguish that were now visible.

"Have you seen them?" She approached him as she spoke, stumbling a little as she crossed onto the footpath. He saw that the heel of one of her shoes – the left one – had snapped off during her travels. The woman hadn't even noticed.

"I'm sorry?"

"We all are . . . we're all sorry. But have you seen them? My children?"

He clenched his fists. Moments like these, situations in which he could smell and taste and just about touch someone else's loss, made him nervous. He felt like a little boy again, reading about mythical creatures from a large hardback book.

"No. No, I haven't."

"They're still alive. Somewhere." She glanced around, at the wreckage of the neighbourhood." Her eyes were wide. Her lips were slack. "They let me come back here to try and find them. They were in the cellar when it . . . when it hit. The Storm . . . "

That's what they called it: the Storm. The name seemed fitting. He couldn't remember who first coined the term, probably some newspaper reporter.

"I . . . " He stopped there, unable to think of anything that might help the woman come to terms with her loss.

"I got out, but they stayed down there. The army truck took me away – they wouldn't let me go back for them. They were trapped, you see . . . by the rubble. The Storm trapped them inside, underneath. I have to find them."

She reached out and grabbed his arm. He could barely feel her grip, despite her knuckles whitening as her fingers tightened around his bicep. "Could you help me look for them?" Her smile, when it struggled to the surface, was horrible. Jeff thought he'd never seen an expression so empty.

"I have to . . . I have things to do. This was my house." He pointed to the pile of bricks and timbers and the scattered glass shards; the piles of earth; the pit formed by a single foot of the Storm.

"We were neighbours?" She peered at him, trying to focus. "Before it happened?"

"I guess so." He'd never seen her before in his life. This woman was a stranger but they were all supposed to be connected by their shared tragedy. Jeff had never felt that way. He was alone with his ghosts.

They stood there for another moment, as if glued together by some sticky strands of time, and then he pulled away. Her arm remained hanging there, the fingers of her hand curling over empty air

"My children . . . "

He looked into her eyes and saw nothing, not even an echo of her pain. She was stripped bare, rendered down to nothing but this mindless search for things that were no longer here. He couldn't tell her; she wouldn't be told. She needed to discover the truth for herself.

"Good luck," he said, and he meant it.

Jeff walked away, heading towards the ragged hole in the earth where his house had once stood, the great footprint of the beast that had once passed this way. He wished he'd seen it happen. It must have been an amazing sight, to see the buildings flattened by the gigantic beast as it charged through the neighbourhood and towards the city.

He heard the woman's scuffling footsteps behind him as she moved away. He wished he had it in him to help her. He hoped she would find her children alive, but doubted she ever would. Not even the bodies would remain. Not even bloodstains.

The Storm came, and that was all. There was no reason for its arrival. It wasn't like the old movies he'd seen as a kid, where an atomic detonation or the constant experimentation of mankind caused a rift in the earth or a disturbance in the atmosphere, and out stumbled a stop-motion nightmare. No, it was nothing like that. The Storm came, it destroyed whatever it encountered, and it went away again, sated.

They were unable to fight it. The authorities didn't know what to do; the army and navy and air force were at a loss: none of their weapons had any effect on the Storm. So they waited it out, hoping the thing would either wear itself out and tire of the rampage, or move on, crossing the border into another country. Fingers hovered over the buttons of nuclear launch systems. Members of parliament voted in secret chambers. The nation prepared for a great and terrible sacrifice.

He remembered those first surprisingly clear pieces of footage transmitted on the Internet, and then again on the news channels: HD-quality CCTV pictures of some great lizard-like beast emerging from the shadows on the coast, a B Movie come to life. But this was not a man in a suit, or a too-crisp GCI image. It was colossal, the height of two tower blocks, one standing on top of the other. Its arm span was a half a mile across, but it barely needed to stretch them so far to tear down a church, a town hall, a factory warehouse . . . Bullets and bombs simply bounced off its thick, plated hide to create more damage to the surrounding area. Its call was the trumpet of Armageddon. When it opened its mouth to roar, the sound was unlike anything humanity had heard before.

Nobody knew what the creature was, where it came from, why it appeared. The scientists mumbled in jargon, talked about tectonic plates, seismic events, and then finally, they went quiet. They locked themselves into deep underground laboratories to try and invent something that would kill the thing.

And then . . . then it went away, slinking back into the ocean, the waves covering it like a blanket. The sea bubbled. Ships capsized. The coastal barriers fell. The Storm passed.

But the Storm could return at any time. They all knew this, but it went unspoken. There were celebrations, the blockades came down, people started to rebuild what had been ravaged. But somewhere back in the shadows, or under the dark waters, the Storm waited. Perhaps it even watched.

Jeff walked across the roughly turned earth, his boots hard and solid as he made his way towards the hole in the ground. When he reached it, he went down onto his knees and peered over the rim. It was deep, with standing water gathered at its base, and in each of the toe prints. There was no sign of a body, or of body parts. His family were wiped out, deleted, removed without trace from the face of the earth.

He smiled, gritting his teeth.

As a boy he'd loved monsters. As a man, he wasn't so sure how he felt.

If it were not for the Storm, he would have been forced to think of some other way to dispose of them, but the monster answered his desperate prayers and came to cleanse him, to remove the evidence of his crimes.

He wondered . . .

If he hoped hard enough, wished for long enough, might it come back? There were other people he wanted to get rid of. It was a nice thought, but he knew it was a fantasy. The situation had nothing to do with him; it was simply a handy coincidence. Even now, it amused him to think something this absurd had saved him from being found out. It was as if one of those childhood comic books had come to life.

Jeff got to his feet and moved slowly away from the ruins. The breeze turned into a light wind, and it whipped up a mass of litter, sending papers and packets and scraps of material scampering into the gutter. Jeff watched them as they tussled. He remembered the way his family struggled: Katherine and the girls, fighting for their sad little lives. It was like watching a movie, only less real. The actors didn't even look like the people they were trying to portray.

They'd never looked like his family, those actors. The woman he'd married, the daughters he'd fathered, were at some point replaced by strangers. That was why they had to go. It all seemed so clear, and then, without thinking, he'd done it: he had ended them. There was no memory of planning, or running through it all in his mind. There was only the act itself, and the mess left behind.

The wind died down. The litter went still. He smelled old fires and diesel fumes. He tasted bitterness at the back of his throat. Something huge loomed against the horizon, its form unclear, fluttering and unstable.

Jeff walked back to the car, climbed inside, turned on the engine, and waited. He watched the woman as she made her way across the street, towards yet another ruined house. He smiled. Inside his head, he heard the voice of the Storm.

The roaming woman sat down in the rubble, staring at the ground. She clenched and unclenched her hands and then started rooting in the dirt, as if she might find her lost children there, somewhere beneath the disturbed top soil. He imagined her brushing away gravel to see a face staring up at her, eyes closed, lips sealed shut on a silent scream.

Clouds moved behind her, shifting across the low red sky. Something dark shimmered beyond them, like a promise straining to be fulfilled. He thought of giant butterfly wings, and then of the opening mouth of the Storm.

Jeff started the car but waited a few moments – still watching the woman – before driving away. He didn't turn on the radio. All they ever talked about was the Storm.

As he headed down the road, towards some unidentified place he'd never been before, he thought about this new world and wondered how everyone would cope with the way things were now, the changes happening in the wake of the monster. Jeff had stepped through the veil, but the rest of the world followed behind him.

He drove all night, and then he stopped the car in a lonely place to sit and look up at the sky. Trees stirred like wraiths against the breezy evening. The stars pulsed, the darkness bulged, threatening to burst open like a ripe melon, and he tried to catch a glimpse of the old world, the one they'd all left behind. After a long time, he gave up trying.

And at the bottom of the sea, curled up among the old wrecks in a long, deep, nameless trench, something yawns and blinks its eyes before drifting back into a deep, soundless slumber. It dreams of screams and bloodshed, and finds comfort in the sweet memory of Man's fear.

Whatever Became of Randy
James A. Moore

———

Have you ever wondered how much anger a person can take before they change beyond any hope of redemption? I've been thinking about that a lot lately, and the sad fact is, I still don't know the answer.

I don't think I ever will.

At any rate, I should get down the details before I forget them, before the media hype and the interviews with survivors get to be too much.

His name was Randall Clarkson. We just knew him as Randy. Randy was not the brightest bulb on the old Christmas tree, but he wasn't stupid, either. He was a good man who took care of his family even when times got very, very bad and they did, believe me.

Randy was ten when I met him. He and his family moved to the same town as me and mine. There was a new facility opening, you see, and his folks and mine were all the same sort of doctors. All they ever told me or Randy was that they worked for a "think tank". We used to get the giggles trying to draw what a think tank would look like. I think Randy came up with the best illustration. It was a giant brain on treads that was running over half a city and crushing buildings under the treads. He was a good artist, too. That's another thing most people won't remember about him in a few weeks. All they'll see is what he became, not what he was before the incident at Castle Creek.

Castle Creek is where we grew up. More accurately, the creek ran right past the town of Harts Bluff, Colorado. Tiny town. I mean that. Our closest neighbor was Summitville and that place looked huge next to us. And Summitville did its best not to even exist in the eyes of the world.

We had a private school, the best that money could buy, and we had satellite TV, and once every month, we took a field trip to a real town.

Harts Bluff was not a bad place to grow up, but with a population of only around 100 people, you could go stir crazy very quickly.

Randy was there for ten years, right alongside me. We were friends who bordered on being brothers. We had fights, we had good times but through it all we were friends. There weren't too many kids around the same age as us.

After a decade together, our families went their own ways. The project was done with, and there were new think tanks to consider on different subjects.

We stayed in touch. Not every day, but once in a while we'd call each other and shoot the breeze. Life got in the way for a lot of that, but we managed just the same. There was college to consider. I went to MIT and Randy went to a little liberal arts college in upper state New York. I went into the family business, genetics. Randy went into working as an illustrator. He made a decent living, which in hindsight was a good thing. He had his own hours as a freelancer, and that was even better. Because while I was setting myself up in the business of mapping the human genome, Randy was working his ass off and taking care of his parents.

Samuel and Myrna Clarkson both managed to come down with recurrent Glioblastoma Multiforme originating in the brainstem. Translated into simplest terms, they both developed aggressive brain tumors that were inoperable. The tumors were not only resistant to chemotherapy and standard radiation; they were also metastasizing at unholy rates and as malignant as Adolf Hitler.

Randy had just set himself up in Manhattan and was making enough money to handle his bills, just barely, when the news reached him.

He left New York the next day and flew to California to be with his parents. The good news for him was that he had talent. The better news was that he'd managed to establish a few solid contacts before he bugged out. The work followed him and he managed to wrangle new clients, even while he was spending a ridiculous amount of time taking care of his parents and their affairs.

I would have probably thought nothing of the entire situation, but believe me when I say it's a little unusual to have two people developing the exact same sort of cancer at the exact same time. In their cases it wasn't just a possibility that the diseases were related: I know, because I managed to get samples sent to me at the National Institutes of Health.

Genetics, remember? In this case I decided to study the two cancers and see if there were any genetic markers linked to them. The cancers were aggressive and not behaving themselves. I wanted to know what caused them and to help out a friend if I could. If he was like a brother to me, then his parents were an aunt and uncle. I hadn't kept up with them as well as with their son, but they were often the subjects of conversation between us.

The end result of my examination was unsettling. They didn't have similar cancers. They had the exact same cancer. Genetically speaking, they were suffering from the same organism, which was as impossible as it was preposterous. I checked the samples three times and then asked for more samples to reconfirm.

The end result was the same. Two people who were unrelated by blood were sharing the exact same disease. Which is pretty damned impressive for a disease that has traditionally only come via genetic mutation from one individual. I thought about the possibility of a contagious cancer that could spread through contact or, God forbid, through something as simple as a sneeze, and had to talk myself down from a full-blown panic attack.

Cancer is not, cannot be contagious. By its very nature it cannot be transmitted from one person to another. That's just the way it is. I came to the conclusion that there had to be another answer, and I went about trying to find it.

And while I worked on trying out every new theory I could come up with, Randy did his best to keep his parents comfortable as their lives and bodies withered away. Want to hear an irony? They were coherent through the entire process. Brain tumors. You'd have expected them to have hallucinations, or seizures, or even blinding headaches, but the worst pain was mild and they remained in control of their mental faculties throughout the wasting of their bodies and the tumors that savaged them.

Randy, on the other hand, suffered plenty. His career didn't come to a complete halt, but it slowed down a bit. He had enough money, that wasn't the issue. What he didn't have was time to himself. When he wasn't working his ass off to keep up with his orders, he was taking care of his mother and father or helping them settle affairs that needed handling. As anyone who has ever dealt with a long lingering death can tell you, it's an exhausting experience, emotionally and sometimes even physically.

I wanted to be with him, wanted to spend as much time as I could trying to give him a little back up, but I was working, you see, trying my best to understand what the hell the samples from his parents meant and how best to stop the impossible cancer from eating them alive.

Happily, Gwen came into Randy's world. I didn't meet her at the time, but I heard about her. Gwen was a hospice nurse. She came highly recommended and I managed to get a little financial aid for my friend in exchange for more samples and the promise that we would be allowed to autopsy the bodies of the decedents when the time came. Does that sound cold? I suspect it does, but I had to get those promises in order to get the payments worked out. Gwen might have been a lovely girl, but she was also a lovely girl who had to make a living in the sort of field that remarkably few people want any part of. Insurance is nice, but the provider in this case wanted nothing to do with the comfort and dignity of the patients when it cost more to have a nurse provided at home than it did to have a hospital room.

So, Randy met Gwen. She was there for him when I could not be to take care of the physical needs of Randy's parents, things like changing out their IVs, offering them pain medications and changing the sheets on those occasions when they couldn't get to the bathroom in time. You think it's a vile thought to have to change a dirty sheet for a grown up? Here's one for you: imagine being a grown up whose child has to change your dirtied linens. That was another indignity that the Clarksons were spared. At least most of the time.

I was still studying the impossible cancers when they finally killed Randy's parents. I put away my slides and my DNA reports for the funeral. The ceremony was strictly ceremonial: the bodies were taken by the NIH and kept on ice for careful examination. It was a long, long time before they were buried. Let's be honest here, most of that was my fault.

The service was simple and straightforward, exactly what they would have wanted, and as always seems to be the case, it lead to a reunion of sorts. Most of the people who had been in the think tank our parents were a part of showed at the funeral. Some of them we hadn't seen since leaving and others who had been in our lives to one extent or another for most of that time.

There were hugs and tears and a few smiles, too. Reminiscences of times long gone and promises to be better about staying in touch, most of which were lies even if we believed them right then.

And through it all, there was Randy doing his best to hold it together and the new woman in his life. Gwen was right there beside him. Randy was always one of the solid guys, one of the strongest men I knew emotionally, but everyone has their limits and his had been met and exceeded in the last few months. Having her there was like having a wall to lean on. I could see that in a matter of seconds, and I was both relieved that he had found someone to help him through the worst of it, and envious.

He'd told me about her, of course. I just didn't expect her to be so damned attractive. I was there mourning the loss of people who were all but family to me, there to comfort my best friend in the world, and all the time I had to force myself not to stare at her.

I managed by remembering the puzzles I had ahead of me when I left for home. There were a lot of them, too. My biggest obstacle was going to be separating the enigmas from my feelings for Randy and his parents.

The people who had raised my best friend were dead. They, along with my parents, had been the closest things we had to a normal life growing up and they were gone, removed from the world with little to prove they had ever been there. The work they had done was secretive at best, and in many cases classified either by the government or by whatever company had paid them for their efforts.

Somewhere between the time they had met in college and around a year before their deaths they had acquired cancers that matched in impossible ways. And there was the problem. I had to know what had caused the impossible to happen if I wanted to prevent it from happening ever again.

I spent one week with Randy, being with my friend and at the same time researching everything I could about his parents through the documents they had around their home. I examined old bills, letters to family and friends, phone records and the other flotsam and jetsam that had become a part of their world for whatever brief period of time.

I was looking for clues as to what could have given them their mutual cancer. I was searching for the cause of the impossible. If I had been dealing with two strangers, I could have probably found the catalyst with relative ease, but a married couple is expected to do a lot of things together.

One week turned up remarkably little, but was long enough for me to half fall in love with my best friend's girlfriend. Gwen was strong, and sharp and quick with a witty comment whenever the situation allowed her to show it. She was also good enough to know when Randy wasn't ready for humor.

She had known his parents long enough to get a glimmer of what they had been like before the cancer, and while the pain of losing them was at best minor for her, the empathy she had for their son was a very real and defining emotion.

She loved him and he loved her and damn it, I grew infatuated with the woman. I could spend a hundred pages waxing poetic about my feelings for her, but that wouldn't change anything that happened.

I fell for her but I was also smart enough not to fall too hard. She was with my best friend and there was no way in hell I could have lived with myself if I'd been the sort to throw myself at her. I could never be that mercenary where a friend is concerned.

We did not become lovers. She did not leave him to be with me. I never let us get into a situation where anything could have happened. Instead, I was the best man at their wedding two years later. I watched the girl of my dreams, or at least a few fantasies, marry my best friend and I couldn't have been happier about it.

I studied the strange cancer that infested both of Randy's parents with obsessive intent. Before I was done, the genome of the damned thing was mapped out as carefully as it could be. It was, not surprisingly, almost identical to the human genome. They had a similar point of origin, but somewhere along the way the changes had gotten intense.

Mutation. Depending on who you talk to, it's the cause of all evolution and all life on the planet earth. Well, that and the whole water plus breathable atmosphere thing. A few strokes of lightning in the primordial ooze, a spark of life and after that, everything comes down to evolution, mutation and survival of the fittest.

So what does it say about a cancer that decides to spread itself into human bodies without any noticeable point of origin? Simple. It says that as a species, the human race is very, very close to extinction unless something is done to find the source of the cancer and the cure for it, immediately.

Of course the same thing has been said a thousand times before, I'm sure. The difference is, cancer is harder to isolate than a virus or a germ. Cancer is a mutation, and very good at biding its time before it strikes again. Oh, and anything that will kill a cancer will normally kill the host, too. It's just a question of which dies faster.

I would have kept working on the puzzle of those cancers for the rest of my life or until I solved them, but that decision wasn't mine alone to make. There were other doctors who wanted to study what I had already deciphered and wanted to see what they could add to the equation. There were other puzzles I needed to look at as well, and so as much as I wished otherwise, I set the examinations on the back burner and got on with my life.

Eventually Randy stopped asking for progress reports. There was a short span where we were barely speaking, but he realized there was only so much I could do after a while. I suspect he had help from Gwen.

So for a couple of years we played the used-to-be-friends game. We sent cards at holidays and birthdays, etc.

Then it was my turn to bury family. My father died of a heart attack. It was unexpected. Really, I had always held a secret belief that the man would outlast me. He had always been in excellent shape. There were no warning signs that anyone was aware of. He just keeled over and died one day.

Randy and Gwen attended the funeral. Most of my time was spent being there for my mother, but we had time to reconcile.

I had time with my friend. Time enough to recognize the early warning signs that something was wrong with him.

Very, very wrong.

His face was the same as it had always been, but his expressions were a bit different. He talked the same, but enough time had passed since we'd been around each other that I could see the small things: I noticed that he spoke at a slower speed, and that he squinted a bit with his left eye when he was concentrating. None of the signs were large, but they were there if you knew how to read them. Lucky for him, I did.

I had to urge Gwen to send him in for a check-up. She in turn had to convince him. Randy had developed a dislike of medical facilities and procedures when he dealt with his parents' illnesses.

Well, I say dislike, but maybe hatred was a better term. At any rate, Gwen was the one who convinced him to take the tests. I was the one who wrangled a consult on the results.

Turned out to be cancer, the same sort that had killed his parents.

I know, because I'm the one that ran the tests confirming that fact.

He took it better than I would have had it been me when I gave him the news. Instead of breaking into tears he sat on the sofa in his living room and nodded as I explained the facts as we knew them. Then he nodded silently and asked what had to be done.

We called specialists, and like with his parents before him, I even arranged for most of his bills to be absorbed by the NIH as we looked over the results of those tests. I started making demands to see the end results of the autopsies on Randy's parents, but that proved a useless gesture on my part. The investigation was ongoing. There would be no end result in the foreseeable future, because the very thing that had scared me senseless had the same impact on others as well.

I was given more raw data to study, which I promptly set aside to work more closely on making sure that my assumptions were right. I needed to know if it was environmental, or genetic or something stranger.

And in the meantime, we treated the cancer as aggressively as we dared, using every method that had been approved by the FDA and a few that had not. When chemo failed, we worked with radiation. When radiation failed, it was time for the removal of a single mass in a relatively safe area.

When I had the freshest samples from Randy, I compared them to the notes I had made and the continued examinations of the cancer that had killed his parents.

There was something I was missing in the details, you see. I could feel it, even when I couldn't clearly see it. So I studied all of it again, desperate to understand what was happening.

Four weeks into the research and testing, Randy was looking a great deal worse for wear. He'd lost weight, and his skin had taken on a decidedly yellow tinge.

I went to visit my friend in the hospital where he was going through another battery of tests to see if anything at all had helped with the cancer. Nothing had.

Randy looked at me as I started going through the test results and shook his head. "Fuck it."

"What?" I wasn't shocked by the language. I was taken aback by the quiet venom in his voice.

"I said 'fuck it,' Alan. I'm done with the tests today. I need to get the hell out of here."

I nodded my head.

"I can probably arrange that."

"Well, that's good because I'm leaving either way." "Where are you planning on going?"

Randy looked at me for a long moment, studying me, trying, I suspect, to decide if I would aim to stop him. "Camping. I haven't been camping since before Mom and Dad died."

If ever there was a test of our friendship, that was it. Camping meant being away from the city, away from the medicines. It also meant having enough supplies to accommodate any serious changes in the weather, because the cancer had compromised his immune system enough already. A good old-fashioned cold could wind him back in the hospital for a very long stay, or in the morgue for a longer one.

"So, I'll make it happen." It was all I could say. Randy wasn't a prisoner and he didn't intend to be one. Was I opposed to his decision? Absolutely. But it wasn't my choice to make.

And in the long run, I couldn't really blame him. I wouldn't want to spend my remaining time in this world in a hospital bed, especially if that time had dwindled down to weeks.

I worked it out. We went camping. I brought along a small pharmacy to make sure Randy was mostly pain-free, and a couple of books to keep me company while he and Gwen kept warm.

And I made sure I had a medical team on standby at the local hospital, which was only fifteen minutes away by helicopter. Oh, yes, by helicopter. I made sure we had one of those waiting, too.

For old time's sake, I got us a campsite near Castle Creek, and a hotel room in Harts Bluff. It had been a long time since we'd been there, but unlike a lot of the world, little had changed in the area since we'd lived there.

It was a good time. I want that down for whatever might count for a record in the future. We had a damned fine time the first day and the first night.

We'd brought along plenty to eat, and we did everything old school. Strictly hot dogs, marshmallows and half-heated baked beans for dinner.

We talked about growing up together and Gwen drank in the details, absorbing the information as best she could between Randy and I both cracking up. We drank a few beers, but not enough to get anyone drunk. Just enough to let us get sentimental instead of maudlin, if you see my point.

Just before it was time for bed, I did a quick check of the camp to make sure everything was properly secured and that no stray embers were going to burn out the entire area, and then I headed for my tent.

Gwen stopped me outside of the tent, just as I was getting ready to climb inside. Her hand on my arm felt inordinately warm, and I had to hold back a gasp of surprise, because, honestly, I hadn't seen her there.

"Listen, thanks." Her voice was a whisper and I knew why. It had nothing to do with illicit affairs, much as I might wish otherwise, and everything to do with simply respecting the silence of the night.

"For what?"

"Being a friend, not just a doctor. For putting a smile on Randy's face and for including me." I looked hard into her eyes as she spoke, and thought about the words very carefully. Mostly because I was tipsy and I wanted to make sure I didn't do anything stupid. See, I trusted myself around Gwen, but not so much when I'd been drinking. So I studied her hard and made damned sure I was listening to her words. "He's my friend. You're my friend. It's no big deal." I felt those words worked much better than a declaration of my unrequited love ever would have.

Gwen stared long and hard at me, and I wondered for a moment if she'd expected something else to come out of my mouth. In the long run, she smiled quickly and then leaned in and kissed my cheek lightly.

I think the feel of her lips was still tingling there when I went to sleep.

A nice, if slightly unsettling end to a nice day.

The following morning everything that had been good and right the previous day went sour with a vengeance. I was just setting up for breakfast – coffee and scrambled eggs, along with flapjacks – when the couple came from their tent. Gwen looked the same as she had the night before.

Randy was a different story. His head was nearly painful to look at. The shape of his skull was wrong. His hair looked spotted and patchy, but that was only because his cranium had grown and warped out of proportion. The bones of his face were swollen or pushed aside by the cancer and I felt my blood freeze when I saw how much had changed overnight.

Randy had started off with the same cancer that had killed both of his parents, but believe me, I'd seen every report, examined the pictures of their bodies through the entire progression, and nothing that had happened to them had been as violent or as virulent as the changes he'd just gone through.

I stood quickly, ready to head for my tent and the medical supplies. Ready to call for the helicopter to take him to real medical attention.

Randy stared at me for a few seconds and then nodded his head. He understood the situation, probably better than anyone else. He'd been with his parents until the bitter end, after all. He'd watched them waste away. And something about that made me frown. I couldn't place what it was, but the thought didn't sit right with me.

"Make your call." Randy shook his head. "Get your experts up here."

Gwen was doing her best to keep him calm, to keep herself calm, but she was fraying around the edges. It's one thing to nurse somebody you barely know through bad times and something else entirely to tend for a loved one. All those phases of denial they tell you about? You go through them when you find out about your own impending death, but you do it when it's someone you love, too. I think she wanted more time, I know she wanted him better.

And I knew even as I made the call that he wasn't going to get better.

Whatever had swollen his face was too strong, too aggressive. We all knew it. We were, I think, just going through the motions.

Fifteen minutes can seem like forever. I was pacing like an expectant father and staring at the sky, trying to force the 'copter to appear through sheer force of will when Randy moved closer to me.

"Mike, this isn't going to end well." He spoke the words in a flat monotone and settled his hand on my shoulder. His fingers gave a quick squeeze to make sure he had my attention, like there was any chance at all I'd have been talking to someone else.

I shook my head and felt the sting of tears. The night before I'd been positively optimistic and even then I knew he was as good as dead. Now, with the massive pressure that had to be building inside of his skull, he'd be lucky to last a day if something drastic wasn't done to relieve the pressure. "No, Randy." I felt like a fool, damned near on the verge of blubbering and I closed my eyes for a minute to stop the flow of tears from winning their fight for freedom. "Goddamnit, it's not gonna end well."

"So relax, Mike." He tapped me on the shoulder and then sat down on one of the fold-up chairs we'd brought along. "They'll get here. Relax a few minutes, bro."

So I did. We spent ten more minutes pretending my best friend's head wasn't starting to look a bit like a pumpkin, enjoying the perfect weather and the black ink I'd made for coffee. After that it was all downhill, with a side of hell and damnation.

There wasn't enough room in the helicopter, so Gwen stayed behind and so did I. I could have argued and managed to get myself on with the medical team, but the facts were simple enough. First, I'm a researcher and not a physician and all I would have done was get in the way and second, I wasn't about to have Gwen try to drive herself to the hospital.

Even at my worst, I'm not that much of a bastard.

We watched them strap Randy in and stood side by side as they lifted off. I grabbed the medical supplies. The tents and everything else could blow away in the wind for all I cared. I was heading for the Jeep we'd come up in when I heard Gwen's gasps for breath.

I turned sharply, because the sound was unexpected, and felt the burn of a pinched nerve lance down my neck.

Gwen stood at the same spot she'd been in while we watched Randy's take off, her face twisted into a mask of tragedy for the first time since everything had started going to pieces.

It was easy to forget that she was dealing with losing her husband at the same time I was dealing with losing my best friend. Easy because I kept trying not to think of them together; easy because she was always so strong, always so good at hiding everything behind the mask of serenity almost every person in the medical field adopts after a while. With Randy away from the scene, she let down her guard and cried almost silently, her eyes tracking the horizon where the 'copter had disappeared as if she could see where he was going even past the mountains that blocked her view.

I think I loved her right then more than at any other time. I know seeing her that way broke my damned heart.

I gave Gwen a hug and pulled her to me. Part of me wanted to do more than comfort her and I think she knew it. Still, I behaved myself. The indiscretions came later.

After the funeral.

Eyewitnesses said that the helicopter was heading for the landing field behind Denver Memorial when it exploded. The fragments scarred the west side of the main building and blew out four windows. Shrapnel that went through one of the windows chopped halfway through one patient's leg and resulted in death a few minutes later. In all of the ensuing chaos, no one bothered to check on the poor bastard and he bled to death. Pretty sad; as I understand it he was there to get his tonsils removed.

Here's the thing about explosions: any way you look at it they're messy. Despite all of the personnel who were there and on call, no one could help much with the wreckage of the 'copter until it was far too late. They found Randy's body some fifteen minutes after the crash. According to the forensic reconstruction, Randy crawled away from the downed aircraft on hands and knees. They could tell because of the blood patterns on the asphalt and the markings in the grass.

Poor Randy crawled through fire and twisted metal and burning fuel and air hot enough to scorch his lungs. The autopsy confirmed every single blister and laceration. The photos documented them in color and black and white alike. I watched the goddamned footage of the autopsy on the man who was my brother, my family, and I memorized every word.

Because there were three other facts the autopsy revealed that left me numb and reeling every time I let myself think about them.

Fact one: the top of Randy's head had effectively exploded by the end of his burning, pain-wracked journey through the hellish landscape of the helicopter's remains. The top of his skull was blasted open and fragmented. His face was mostly intact, but the eye sockets were shattered and his eyes had blown out from the internal pressure. Fact two: Randy's brain was gone. Missing. Completely removed from his body. Not a single identifiable cell of his gray matter could be found inside of his cranium and believe me, they looked and then they looked again. His brain was gone, baby, gone; lost to the world and not to be found.

Fact three: the cancer that had grown and riddled every part of Randy's body was gone too. I know because they involved me in that part. Despite the possible contamination of my emotional connection, they sent me sample after sample to reconfirm what they had already discovered. Randy's body was completely cancer-free.

I still remember the comment I got from Edward Langley, my direct superior when he read my report, right before he remembered that the subject of the report was my dearest friend in the world.

He shook his head and said, "What the fuck, Mike? Did the cancer just get up and walk away?"

I wish I could have taken it as a joke.

Word got out, of course. It's impossible to avoid having someone tell somebody they shouldn't have about something that bizarre. I had endless requests for interviews and so did Gwen. It wasn't long before people were cracking jokes about brain-eating cancers and cancer-eating brains. I suppose that it was just human nature. I guess that's maybe why I've always been rather pessimistic about the human race. We buried what little was left of Randy three weeks after his body had been taken for examination. Gwen cried and I cried and somewhere along the way we wound up in my hotel room and in each other's arms. I know neither of us planned it, at least not on a conscious level.

I think we might have had a chance as a couple, but there was this ghost between us. I won't say the sex was awkward or uncomfortable for either of us because it wasn't. It's just there were too many memories associated with Randy for either of us to feel right about our sexual tryst.

We were human and it cost us a lot in the long run. Hell, it cost the world when you get down to it. You see, we both knew Randy well enough to know not only the sorts of things he would do, but where he would do them.

We could have stopped a lot of it. Not all, maybe, but a lot. The reports were sporadic at first and easily dismissed.

The first sighting that got a police report came from Denver. As the helicopter crash was still on a lot of people's minds the news brought the story to the attention of the city and condemned the caller as a sad specimen of a human being who suffered from a miserable lack of taste. That was one of the nicer comments I heard. I agreed with every one of them.

The reports grew. Several people swore they'd seen something in the woods, not a brain, but something with an exposed brain and that it was far too large to belong to a human being. Stories, rumors, suppositions and in the end they were all scoffed at as seemed perfectly normal.

I didn't pay too much attention to the stories, because I was still reeling from the death of my friend, the guilt over having slept with Gwen and the mysteries surrounding his mortal remains.

Here's a simple fact of life: cancer doesn't just vanish. Not when it's so advanced that damned near every organ in the body has been compromised. I couldn't get around that part of the equation. There was no way I had been wrong in my diagnosis. I had seen the evidence and I wasn't the only person to see it. Hell, I still had slides of the stuff on file, but there was no evidence of its existence in the autopsy reports.

There were peculiarities aplenty though, I can tell you that. Areas in the soft tissues were extremely aggravated, swollen, and distended, with no sign of what had caused the irritation. Reading those notes again and again, I came to realize that the answer to Ed Langley's question was a resounding yes.

The cancer in Randy's body got up and walked away. The points of irritation fit almost exactly with the areas where the cancer had become most aggressive. For all the world it looked like the damned stuff had pulled out of his body like the proverbial rats from a sinking ship.

I wanted to laugh, because it sounded so preposterous until I looked at the facts.

Randy died at the helicopter crash site, but his body kept moving, kept pushing him along even as he burned and inhaled toxic gases that scorched the inside of his throat and lungs. He only stopped when his head exploded, presumably from some sort of internal force. But I've never seen or heard of anyone who had his or her cranium blow itself out like a bad tire. In most any case you hear about, the only way to ease pressure from a swollen brain is by opening the skull. Here's a thought for you, what if the brain itself understood that? What if the cancerous lumps that had infiltrated the brain and the body of Randy decided the only way to survive was to get the hell out of Dodge? Where would they go?

Insanity. I knew that, but I couldn't get over the fact that the cancer vanished, along with Randy's brain. That was just as impossible and as insane.

His parents had suffered from the exact same cancer. Not one that was similar, but one that was genetically identical. Not a mutation of cells reacting in the same way, but a mutation of cells spreading between members of the same family.

I thought about that a lot, as if I wasn't already trying to make myself crazy. I thought about the impossibilities and about the possible causes for them. What did all three of them have in common? Damned near everything. They lived together for years, they ate the same foods, vacationed in the same places.

They worked in the same unusual fields, as researchers and parts of think tanks. Well, Randy's parents did. He was just along for the ride. A whole Pandora's box of possibilities lay down that path.

I'd been worried that the cancer I was studying could be virulent, but what if it was something worse? What if it was somehow sentient? What if it actually understood enough of its surroundings to pull free from Randy's body when he burned?

What if the cancer that had invaded his parents had managed to evolve and then move on to him when they died?

I was still considering every twist of that scenario I could come up with when the first confirmed sightings came in.

They were on every news station and fed across the Internet as well. I couldn't very well call it a brain in the purest sense, but it's a close enough physical description. It was huge, of course. Easily half the size of a house, and it bobbed in the air like a bad prop from a drive-in era monster show, sliding across the landscape on a thick column of black.

One look and I knew. I understood. The blackness under it was flesh or sorts, the same flesh that surrounded the gray brain in a fine run of delicate black, almost like a spider's web. It was not solid but a fall of tendrils that slithered and danced along the edge of the ground, holding that tremendous weight.

The thing was spotted moving near Interstate 70, heading for Denver. In hindsight, I suppose it had to start in Denver and then come back. But I'm getting ahead of myself.

I believe the first people who reported it must have been scoffed at, but after a highway patrol car spotted it as well, everything happened very quickly.

Despite the look of the thing, no one fired at it initially. They merely followed it and tried to warn traffic away from it. The Colorado Highway Patrol has cameras in most of their cars these days. The pictures weren't exactly crystal clear but there was a long stretch of video where you could see the thing moving along the side of the road, the fall of black matter undulating under it, the finer threads of the stuff sometimes reaching out and touching one thing or another as it moved along.

While the news cameras were on their way to catch additional footage of the giant brain, the news broke about Harts Bluff. A trucker trying to make a delivery discovered everyone in the town was dead. He was nearly incoherent with panic, but eventually the state patrol got the news out of him. Seems when he went to make his delivery the bodies were already laid out and gathering flies.

Each person in the town had been murdered; their skulls crushed and emptied of their contents. It didn't take a genius to do the math, especially when the brain moving along the side of the road lashed out at a man trying to fix a flat tire and snatched him up into that nest of tendrils.

It was all on tape; the man screaming, rising higher and then dropping to the ground, his head already opened and bleeding. The same footage showed the highway patrol driving toward the thing, climbing from their vehicle. They inadvertently recorded their own deaths on the dashboard camera.

Two men in uniforms fired up into the thing towering above them. The camera didn't show all of it, couldn't show all of it, but there was enough detail to make clear that their target was the same obscenity. They hadn't even emptied their side arms before the thing retaliated. Those seemingly thin filaments of flesh were sharp and strong enough to cut their skulls apart in seconds. The details were blurry, but good enough to show the feeding process. The cops' brains were torn free and lifted up to the creature's underside, to vanish into that thick array of seething black tentacles.

Three people died on that film. I can't tell you how many more died when the thing hit Denver.

It was too big to miss when it was near the road, but the thing – the brain and the mass under it – hid just fine in the woods. Helicopters and planes tried to spot it, but without any luck.

For two days after the film had been released the world waited for another sighting. I did not have that luxury. I was called in immediately under the belief that there might be something that I could tell them about the thing. It seemed that they managed to get a sample of the creature as a result of a few bullets.

I studied the samples for only a few seconds before knowing the answer. It was the same cancerous mass that had riddled Randy's body. There was no mistaking the cellular design. I could damn near have identified it by scent.

I reported my findings. I had no choice. I couldn't very well let the ramifications go unexplored. Ten minutes after I'd made my report I was calling Gwen and trying to explain to her what I had discovered. I tried, but by the time I got to her she already knew. You see, Gwen had gone to Denver as soon as she saw the footage. She knew. Somehow she knew that what was left of Randy was on a killing spree.

I guess you probably know the rest of it. There isn't that much more to tell. By the time the giant brain was seen again it had evolved, or perhaps simply matured.

The shape was still the same. The basic form of a brain was still there, but the images were much clearer. I could see that the deep curls of the gray matter were filled with still more twists and turns and folds of flesh and that entire mass had to be closer to seventy or eighty feet long and easily half as wide. The black mass of cancerous material had wrapped itself around that brain, growing like roots across the surface and forming a strange black node in the front that looked almost like a gigantic eye waiting to open. The cilia that spilled down from the massive shape drifted further and further out, sweeping along streets and gathering bodies as they moved. Each person snared was lifted and then efficiently murdered. Each skull was split and opened as easily as a chef could cut a melon, and the brains were removed, and consumed, pulled into the greater mass.

It moved on cancerous tentacles that had adapted, you see, developed internal organs and a respiratory system that was unique. We'll be years understanding the mutations and how they could happen so quickly.

I remember watching the carnage on the television, the casual power it threw around, waves of force that blew police cars, military vehicles and all of the personnel trying to use them through the air and into the sides of buildings. Whether that strength was purely physical or something more is another mystery we may never fully understand.

It lifted high up into the air as it lashed out and shattered the bodies of soldiers and the buildings around them with equal ease.

I remember watching the barrages of firepower that did nothing at all to touch the thing. Bullets, mortar shells, hell, flame throwers blasting out plumes of fire that should have roasted the thing alive. Nothing so much as scratched it.

Not until the end, when Gwen stepped out into the street and called out Randy's name. I couldn't hear her, of course. No one could have. But I saw her lips move and I saw the way the gigantic thing stopped its forward progression and dropped down until it almost touched the ground and swayed in front of her as if mesmerized.

Those drifting tendrils, capable of killing with such ease, reached for Gwen and I screamed, terrified that they would carve her apart. Instead they merely touched her face. Leave it to the press to get it right. I believe it was a cameraman from CBS who zoomed in and recorded each gentle touch and the pale, terrified expression on Gwen's face as she endured the contact. Her chest heaved with a barely restrained scream, and her eyes closed as the tears started falling.

And a moment later, she stepped back four paces and then dropped to the ground as the soldiers cut loose with a final volley. Bullets, grenades, flames . . . They fired whatever they could find and, in the end, it worked. Of all the scenes they've shown again and again since the attack on Denver, the one everyone enjoys the most is the series of explosions that tore chunks out of the gigantic floating brain and the resulting rain of blood and sludge.

Gwen would have probably died in the mess, but what had been Randy once upon a time pushed her aside at the last moment. It could have easily killed her. I have no doubt of that. Instead, and if you watch the films as many times as I have you can see it for yourself, it nudged her, she was pushed through the air and drifted to the ground almost a dozen yards away. There wasn't a scratch on her when they examined her.

I barely saw her. I really never had a chance. I was called back to work, asked to examine more of the same materials I had already studied and to verify that the resulting biological stew wasn't contagious.

I spoke to Gwen once on the phone, and even then I could tell it was a waste of time. The media had noticed her and they have never been known for their gentle methods of persuasion. Overnight Gwen went from grieving widow to American hero. She had bravely risked herself to give the military their opening and no one was likely to forget that.

Because of who she was and the very likely origin of the nightmare that killed an estimated hundreds of people (no one knows for sure, because they haven't had a chance to check everywhere between Harts Bluff and Denver) and the man she married, more tests were performed before she could leave the hospital. There were blood tests, cat scans, X-rays, ultrasounds. Whatever they could think of, they did it.

I know, because I'm the one who ordered the tests. I haven't spoken to Gwen but that once. I haven't had the time and neither has she. Despite the constantly confused look on her face the press still wants to ask her the same questions again and again. There are rumors of a book deal and even possibly a movie deal. Like I said, she's an American hero.

I've got the results in front of me on my desk. I've looked at them a dozen times and then I've looked at them some more.

Just to be safe, I've gone over the video footage at least as many times, all to make sure that I wasn't imagining things.

First, a careful examination of the footage shows the giant brain reaching out with its tentacles and scaling the buildings on either side of it, lifting into the air before it took a savage barrage of fire without flinching. It also shows, if you're looking very carefully, a fine substance falling from the thing as it ascended and again as it fell down to be close to Gwen. I had to look repeatedly to confirm because there was so much already going on and I wanted to make sure my eyes weren't fooling me.

Second, close examination of the remains showed that the tendrils under the creature were damaged. What I had at first assumed were likely bullet holes and scratches from the multiple explosions were, upon a second examination, too uniform. My conclusion is that the thing deliberately released something into the air. It could have been the equivalent of shedding skin, or it could have been something far worse. It could have been, and I ask you to bear with me on this, it could have been seeds, or possibly even the equivalent of pollen.

What would bring me to that assumption?

Simple: Gwen has cancer. Not just any cancer, but recurrent Glioblastoma Multiforme originating in the brainstem. It is identical to the cancer that killed every member of Randy's family.

I made a few calls. Currently there are three teams from the CDC on their way to Denver. They're going in full HAZMAT suits and they're going to take samples from every solider and police officer that was at the site when Gwen became a hero.

Another team is on the way to pick up Gwen. If we're lucky, it's just her. It's just Gwen and we can possibly contain this before it gets too big to ever recover from.

If we're less fortunate then the black substance I saw falling from the thing that had been Randy's brain was a spore and the cancer has become airborne. It was windy that day. I remember that.

An airborne cancer would be bad. Worse than most people can imagine. But an airborne agent that mutates people into what Randy became? That would likely be the end of the world.

I hope we're lucky. I really, really do.

Attack of the Fifty-Foot Cosmonaut
Michael Canfield

The desert shimmered.

Most people in Henderson, Nevada, ignored it – as Jack had been advised bluntly to do. He would've ignored it too, if he hadn't been, as Sheriff Hubbins put it, "damned contrary by nature."

That, and maybe if his dad hadn't shot and killed himself in his patrol car one night seventeen years ago, out there investigating the glowing hills.

Jack stood in the front room of their mobile home, watching the glow and thinking about these things. The glow seemed to get bigger every summer, and every summer he went out to investigate – or try to anyway, stopped by electrified fences and heavy security patrols surrounding federal lands.

That night the glow was brighter than ever before. The horizon seemed to pulse with it so strongly and rhythmically the hills might have been breathing. The moon basked in its green reflection.

His old mom came in out of the kitchen, looking drawn. "Why are you just standing there – gazing out the window again? What are you always dreaming about?" she said.

He shook his head. School would start pretty soon. Other concerns would take priority. If his next season's performance was even *close* to matching his previous season's he was sure to win a scholarship somewhere. And he was probably supposed to marry Janniffer eventually. The next few years were mapped out for him based on the expectations of others . . .

Jack went outside and put on his track shoes. He sensed his mom behind him.

"Where are you going?"

"To run, Mom," he said seriously, and of course that wasn't really a lie as far as it went.

As he trotted off he looked back at her, pretty sure that she knew the truth, and sure she didn't like it.

Their mobile home was the last in the row and beyond it lay nothing but the desert, or as Sheriff Hubbins would say, "Nothing that's nothing to nobody."

Jack moved into the darkness, picking up a little speed – not too much, as he didn't want to get winded before he reached the green foothills.

————

Janniffer answered the phone and it was Mrs Jaffe calling for her dad. It was about Jack, of course. Janniffer turned down the television. The news was over anyway; Ted Koppel announced that tomorrow night Peter Jennings would broadcast live from Berlin. Her friend Paige and Paige's idiot boyfriend Doggart, who were over to watch TV with her, howled in protest.

"Shut up! It's Jack's mom on the phone!"

"It's always Jack's mom," whined Doggart, cranking the television volume back up, "I wanna hear the *Nightline* theme. I love the *Nightline* theme." And he was supposed to be Jack's best friend.

Janniffer put a hand over her ear. "I'm sorry, Mrs Jaffe, could you say that again?" Apparently Jack had gone out running about six and still wasn't back. "No, he hasn't been over here . . . do you think he . . . ?"

Doggart and Paige turned their attention from the TV to Janniffer.

"My father's not here, Mrs Jaffe," said Janniffer, "but I can beep him . . . " She hung up after promising to call Mrs Jaffe back if she heard anything, and getting Mrs Jaffe's promise to do the same.

Doggart raised his arm. "Not this time. He's on his own – I'm through getting busted by the feds."

And then Paige, who was supposed to be *her* best friend, said: "Don't you think Jack's caused you enough trouble already, Janniffer?"

Janniffer looked out the picture window. It was a clear night and she thought maybe she could see a little something different, way off there, over the blocks and blocks of suburbs. Maybe. "It's getting brighter lately, don't you think?"

"No," said Doggart with conviction. "You're imagining that. It's the reflection of moonlight off black sand. If it were radiation, the anti-nukers would have some evidence by now. Which would be okay with me, 'cause I wouldn't say no to a fat settlement. But it just didn't turn out to be anything. So don't worry, girls," he added typically, "you won't have no two-headed babies."

"Not if we stay away from you, you inbreed." Janniffe picked up the phone again and dialed her father's pager.

Paige looked up seriously. "You just gonna call your dad, and that's all. Right, Janniffer? Janniffer?"

She said nothing, just stood thoughtfully, waiting for her dad to call back. True, she hadn't seen much of Jack lately, and probably he didn't like her any more, but if he got into trouble again his friends should be there.

"Doggart," she said, "I need to borrow your jeep."

"No way," said Paige, jumping in before Doggart could say anything. "I thought we agreed not to chase after these sexist losers."

"He might get busted—" And anyway, she thought, looking at Doggart, Paige had no call to talk about losers.

"And maybe he's not even *in* the foothills – did you even think of that?" said Paige.

Janniffer paused. "Well, where do you think he is?" she said defensively.

"That's not the point and you know it."

The phone rang.

Janniffer filled her father in and he told her he would take a run out to look for Jack. He made her promise to stay put. "I don't need more than one crazy teenager running around a one-time H-bomb site," he said.

She hung up the phone. "My dad's gonna look for him."

"That's good, isn't it?" said Paige.

"Doggart," Janniffer said, "I can't take my Honda into the foothills – I need the keys to your jeep."

It surprised her how easily he gave in, reaching into his jeans to pull out his keyring.

"Doggart, what are you doing?" said Paige.

"She's made up her mind," he said coolly, moving the keys away as Paige tried to take them from him.

Janniffer almost grabbed them from the opposite direction, but Paige yanked Doggart's arm away.

"Girls, girls, *please*," said Doggart and everything stopped. "Don't fight over me!"

Paige slapped Doggart on the shoulder and Janniffer took the opportunity to snag the keys. She bolted out the front door. "See ya!" she yelled triumphantly.

Paige chased her. "Hold up! We'll come with you."

"We will?" said Doggart, surprised.

"Yes, stupid. Still think you're so funny?"

That was good, thought Janniffer, who, having jumped into the vehicle, suddenly remembered she didn't know how to drive a stick.

––––––––––

Sheriff Hubbins took the patrol car and headed toward the foothills as soon he got off the phone from his daughter. He turned off the dirt access road into the sagebrush, bumping his way through the desert around the chain-linked barb-wired perimeter of government land, looking for a way in.

Damn skinny kid, he thought, just like his old man. A skinny kid could have slipped under the fence just about any place.

Hubbins looked to the foothills, only a few hundred yards off, and they were pretty damn green – greener than he'd ever seen them, and there hadn't been a night in the last seventeen years when he hadn't looked at them. No doubt about it – the kid had gone for it. Again. Crazy, contrary, inquisitive kid. Trying to get into the foothills, trying to get them to give up their secrets.

Sheriff Hubbins knew more about those secrets than most.

And he knew that it was better for it to stay that way. If anybody found out what he knew then somebody might get themselves really hurt someday. That wouldn't happen to Jack if he, as Sheriff and family friend, could help it.

Then again, there was a pretty good chance he wouldn't be able to help it. Not if Jack kept poking.

Hubbins had the patrol car's lights off – necessary in case helicopters showed up. He searched by the beam of his flashlight aimed out the window and the green glow – and that made for damned hard searching. Still, he didn't have to remind himself that he'd fifty and more years experience in these hills: three times as much as the kid.

The patrol car's tires scrunched the dry earth slowly. There was only that, and the soft rumble of the engine.

His front tire hit a rut and Hubbins directed his flashlight onto the fence. That was it. There was the spot where Jack had scooped out the dirt and slid under the fence. Damn skinny kid.

After cutting the engine, Hubbins got out and appraised the depth of the opening. It was nothing. There was no way he was going to get his fifty inches of long-accumulating gut through that mouse hole, so he had two options: either blow the whistle and radio the military – which he didn't care to do – or widen the hole.

Reluctantly, hating to break a damned sweat in the cold night air, Hubbins popped the trunk and took out a little camping spade.

There was nothing like manual labor, enforced and at a late hour, to put a man in an unreasonable mood. Especially when he hadn't had dinner yet.

Concluding the job at last, he tossed the spade aside roughly; then, head first and belly skyward, he scooted under the fence. Dirt got down his collar and in his pants.

Pushing himself to his feet again, both knees ached. That was par though. They always ached when he stood up these days. The price you paid for letting yourself get old. Old, aching, with dirt down his ass did not put him in a better mood for the hike to come.

Just as he stood there getting his wind, he heard sounds coming out of the silence.

Not the wind and not the quiet hum of nature – but some other kind of sound. A pulsing, pumping noise – deep and rhythmic. It appeared to him as he looked across the desert that the pulsing rhythm of the glow was in sync with it. Funny. The sound was new, he thought – at least he'd never noticed it before – not even that first night seventeen years ago, when he'd driven the now restricted dirt road all the way up to the foothills looking for his fellow deputy, who was hours late reporting in.

The glow had been a lot dimmer then, just a sheen on the horizon after the meteorite's bright flash. Of course, there was speculation even at the beginning that it hadn't been a meteorite, but a UFO that crash-landed. The speculating only got worse when Deputy John Jaffe turned up dead that night, a hole in his temple and his service revolver in his hand.

But then – perhaps because government was better at keeping mouths shut in those days – nothing more was heard about the incident. And what with people moving away and new folks coming in all the time, talk died out after a while.

Hubbins began walking toward the foothills. There was nothing much up there for Jack to see, even if he made it without being picked up by the military – just blackened metal. But he'd never been able to convince the kid of that, even though it happened to be true.

———

Jack's skin hadn't actually turned green, but it looked like it when he got close enough to bask in the glow.

The light permeated the wasteland, coming from everywhere and nowhere at once. He was frankly a little surprised to have made it all the way without getting caught. Probably the talk about budget cuts was true; the whole empty test site might be unguarded. It looked that way. Nothing was around. Not a thing grew above ankle height, nothing scurried across the ground or buzzed in the air. There was only the sound: the *drub drub drub*bing under the foothills. Eerie. Strange.

But it was nothing to kill yourself over, he thought harshly.

He sat there, thinking about it, for how long he had no idea. Indeed, he might have sat there all night if an earthquake hadn't hit the area.

It began as a rumble in the hills – and before he could move, the ground slid away underneath him, carrying him along like flotsam.

Then the hills stood up.

Jack grabbed hold of an exposed clump of root to stop his slide. The hills shook dirt off themselves and Jack saw what he thought was a man. A giant: fifty feet tall at least, naked – but a man nonetheless. It towered over him.

Jack realized the roots he'd clung to were snarled hairs at the base of the giant's calf. When the giant started walking, Jack didn't know whether to let go and risk getting crushed under a heel – or to hang on for the ride.

The giant took no notice of him in any case, but seemed intent on moving. With a few strides, it spanned metres and continued to quicken its pace. Displaying deliberate purpose, it headed back the way Jack had come. Jack could no longer let go even if he'd wanted to for fear of being kicked twenty feet into the air by the hurling of the giant's legs.

Dirt choked Jack's throat and filled his eyes. He tried but couldn't see the giant's head from his low vantage point – just locks of matted hair clumped with dirt hanging below its shoulders. The giant's arms swung in monstrous arcs, the monstrous fingers curled. And something else as the clouds of dust began to settle – Jack could see that the giant itself was the source of the glow.

Not that the giant's skin glowed; rather it was encased in the glow, a green aura.

The giant came up to the perimeter fence and Jack watched as the ground passed below.

He saw Sheriff Hubbins' patrol car and watched as the giant's other foot crushed it indifferently. If the Sheriff was in it – well, that was the end of him.

The giant took to the highway and moved toward town.

The ropey hair that Jack coiled himself in was cutting his flesh. If he had to hang on much longer his arms would be shredded.

Far off, Jack heard the *wupping* of helicopter blades.

———————

Sheriff Hubbins saw a figure coming out of the hills. Damn hard to miss, considering it was fifty feet tall and blocked out of good chunk of the sky.

Hubbins ran for the fence, throwing himself under it. His belt caught on something and pinned him. He struggled, finally unbuckled it, losing his holster and revolver in the darkness. A few bullets couldn't hurt a thing that big anyway, so he didn't waste time feeling around for his weapon.

Freeing himself just as the giant loomed over him, he was on his hands and knees when he saw his patrol car collapse under the thing's foot like it was made of kitchen foil.

By the time he got upright again the monster was already a half mile away. "I'll be," he said aloud. It was something his grandmother used to say. There was nothing left of the patrol car, and he was glad he hadn't been driving his own Lincoln Towncar that night.

The monster went off toward Henderson; Hubbins headed the other way, toward the Boulder City suburbs. It wasn't much closer, but there would be more traffic once he reached the interstate and he would get a quicker lift to a phone. Not that he knew whom he was going to call or what he was going to say when he did.

Anyway, the military was hardly going to miss spotting this one, and he had half a mind to just hitch home and say the hell with it. Send a tow truck and a big spatula for the car in the morning. But he couldn't do that: Jack was still running around somewhere – unless the thing had stepped on him – and he probably had more questions than ever.

Hubbins was lucky. Just as he reached the highway he spotted a pair of headlights coming his way. Then a trio of helicopters passed overhead, their floodlights illuminating the road like sunlight. He didn't bother to wave.

Jack slid down the giant's calf when it stopped moving to swat at the helicopters.

The rapid cracks of fire spat from their guns as the helicopters circled the giant in wide sweeps. It seemed more annoyed than anything else, now that Jack could see its round full face.

The giant was faster, much more limber, than the helicopters could ever hope to be. Its arms were extended, keeping the buzzing nuisances at a distance when, it seemed to Jack, it could just as easily have knocked them out of the sky. The rounds hitting the giant's arms and shoulders must have stung it, at least, as it twitched and flinched at the pelting.

The battle was moving steadily away from him now, but closer to Henderson and the trailer park Jack lived in. He had no hope of keeping pace with them, but he ran anyway, holding as much ground as he could.

He was out of breath though still running when Doggart's jeep pulled up. Doggart was inside, and Janniffer and her friend – and there was also Sheriff Hubbins, who had survived the car crushing and looked red and perturbed and dirty.

Everyone in the car shouted at Jack at once but he felt no obligation to speak to any of them. He looked at Sheriff Hubbins.

"What is it?" he asked the Sheriff.

"I don't know any more than you do, son."

Jack didn't believe him. Always he felt the Sheriff knew more about things than he let on.

"You saw it!" said Jack.

"Saw what?" said Janniffer.

The giant was far out of sight now, though the helicopters could still faintly be heard in the distance.

"You'll read about it in the morning paper, honey," said Sheriff Hubbins. "Hop in, Jack, we'll take you back to our house, call your mom from there. You know you got everybody upset again."

"We gotta try and stop it," said Jack, "It's headed right for the trailer park."

"Naw," said the Sheriff. "Never get that far, the army will stop it."

"*What's* headed toward your house?" Janniffer demanded.

Jack told her.

"I've seen that movie," said Doggart.

"It's not a movie," said Jack.

Janniffer shook her head.

"Ask your dad," said Jack.

"Well I saw *something*, that's for sure. But I wouldn't worry about it. They're always cooking up something out there in the hills. Ninety per cent of the land in this state is federal, you know."

"That's all you've got to say, sir?"

"It's probably a giant secret weapon robot that got out of control. The government wouldn't put it here if it really posed a threat to the community," said the Sheriff.

"It's a man. Human. I touched it."

"Well then, it's a man."

"And you're not going to do anything about it?"

"Nothing with a car full of teenagers, I'm not. Tell you what, Jack: let's run you kids back to my house and you can clean yourself up. I'll get on the horn, round up my deputies and we'll come back out. Probably just be in the army's way but—"

"I don't like it, Sheriff. I don't know why you're acting this way –

like all of this is no big deal. But I guess it doesn't make any difference. You're the way you are and I'm the way I am."

"Now listen, Jack—"

Jack turned his back on Sheriff Hubbins while he was still talking. He had never turned his back on an adult before.

"Jack!" called the Sheriff and Jack ignored him. He heard the Sheriff tell Doggart to pull the jeep up.

The jeep came alongside him and kept pace as he walked. They were all shouting at him. Janniffer was telling him not to be stupid. Her friend Paige was yelling at *her* not to be stupid. Finally Hubbins cried, "Enough!" He ordered the jeep stopped and got out.

Then he told Doggart to turn it around and take the girls home. His voice did not leave room for objections.

When the two of them were alone on the highway, Jack started walking home and the Sheriff kept pace with him, a few steps back.

Neither spoke for a long time.

"Must be pretty far from here by now – for it to be completely out of sight," said Sheriff Hubbins.

"You can still hear the helicopters," said Jack.

"You can hear pretty damn far out here, when it's quiet like this. There's nothing but dust and sagebrush, nothing at all to block a sound."

Jack turned to face him. The Sheriff was looking off into the distance and, not seeing that Jack had stopped, walked into him.

"Well," Hubbins said, "we're stuck out here now."

"Where'd it come from? What is it?"

"Your guess is as good as mine."

"I don't believe that, sir."

The Sheriff's mouth tightened. "That's too bad."

"Did my dad really shoot himself?"

The Sheriff sighed and dropped his head. "Now why would you ask me that? You know he did. I'm sorry for it. We're all sorry for it, but it happened, son.

"Things happen," he continued. "Things happen that're just a shame, but that don't mean there's anything more to them than meets the eye. That's not fair, it don't make it any easier to accept, but there it is. Your dad was my best friend. He was a good man. If he were still around he'd probably be Sheriff now instead of me."

"But he isn't around," said Jack. "And I want to know what happened to him. Did the government kill him?" Then he added, "Did you?"

Sheriff Hubbins suddenly looked drawn and old. "I grew up with your father, your mother. I was the best man at their wedding. And I've always looked out for you and her. John Arthur Jaffe Jr, how can you say something like that to me?"

Jack felt ashamed and cast down his eyes. "I know you cared for him," he said, without really being sure of anything. "But something strange did happen up there that night, and the giant proves it."

"A lot of rumors have come and gone about what happened and they're all bunk."

Sheriff Hubbins had told him that before, and he had heard all the rumors himself, of course: that the government had murdered his father and made it look like suicide because he had stumbled onto the test site of a new secret weapon—a weapon so terrible it made the H-bomb and the neutron bomb look like toys; or that he had come upon the crash site of a UFO, and was killed by aliens, which the government then covered up.

"It was my dad who went up there to investigate the flash in the sky – the meteorite or whatever it was – and never came back. Then all of sudden the government fenced off all that territory."

"Just coincidence, Jack. They were probably planning the fence for months before that night. No government project in history ever moved that fast."

"The giant glows green. Just like the hills do – did. And when my dad went up there it was the first night anybody ever saw them glow at all."

"They don't glow – that's an optical illusion."

Jack threw his hands up in disgust. "Is that what you're gonna say about your car? That it got crushed by an optical illusion? Don't lie to me anymore – that giant proves you wrong!"

"What difference does it make – it was a long time ago. Come on, it's late."

"Are you going to tell me what happened or not?"

Jack believed they had been building secret weapons out in the hills – or dumping radioactive crap everywhere. That was what the giant man was, the product of government testing. It was as silly as believing in the Incredible Hulk – but there it was. His father had stumbled into it and they killed him, then brushed everyone else off. Sheriff Hubbins could have been in on it, too. Maybe they fixed him up with the Sheriff's job. After all, he even admitted that his father would be Sheriff now if he were alive.

He told this suspicion to Sheriff Hubbins.

The Sheriff laughed a little. "Anybody who wants this job can have it. This ain't no glamor job. And I wouldn't take a job in exchange for any man's life."

"But you're hiding something."

"Look, Jack are we gonna dance like this all night."

"I got time."

"Shouldn't you be saving the trailer park from the monster?"

Jack said nothing.

"That was the fifties—" said Hubbins. "Well, the early sixties anyway. You didn't talk out about anything and everything that happened back then."

"It isn't the fifties anymore, Sheriff."

"Maybe not for you kids, but times don't change as fast as you think they do." Sheriff Hubbins shuffled his feet on the loose gravel littering the blacktop. "Jack I don't know what *really* happened up there that night – not much of it anyway. But I guess you're a man now and you should know what I can tell you. I don't believe your father did kill himself. But what's done is done and it can't be undone. Sometimes looks like there never will be an end to that business."

Jack listened. When the Sheriff paused he held his breath, waiting for him to continue.

Finally the Sheriff did. "The old highway used to run right through those foothills, and that night your dad was patrolling and saw a flash of light. He called it in and then went up to have a look. He called in a second time.

"The dispatcher said he sounded excited and out of breath. Transcripts of the calls were confiscated later but I had a chance to read them first; your father found some kind of wreckage up there – he estimated that it spread over half a mile at least. Thought it must be an aircraft. Turned out to be a spaceship."

"A spaceship?"

"And he found a man's body. A man in a space suit. And the space suit had those old letters on it: CCCP. We sure knew what that meant."

Jack shook his head. He didn't.

"That was USSR in Russian. The dead man was a Russian cosmonaut." He paused, seeming to collect his thoughts. "I was the first officer to get there, but by that time the place was already swarming with military from the testing base. They wouldn't let me through their perimeter, so I screamed and hollered until somebody with a lot of gold on his lapel came and told me about how they found your dad.

"They showed me the body of a dead cosmonaut. Then they brought me to your dad's patrol car and showed me his body. There was a bullet hole in his temple. They already had him in a body bag but they unzipped it enough to show me the wound. I asked to see the rest of him and they refused. I'd be lying if I said that didn't make me suspicious.

"But there was an awful lot of them and only one of me. I just nodded and held my tongue. I swore that I would do something as soon as I got away from them – but at that moment I was in no position to start an investigation. Who's to say there might not've been two suicides that night if I wasn't careful."

"You left him."

The Sheriff looked angry. "I used my head – not my smart mouth, son."

"And you are alive."

"That's right, Jack, I am. Go ahead and hate me for it – but it won't change a thing."

Jack was speechless. His head was swimming with thoughts and resentments. He wanted to be away from there – he wanted to go and never see the Sheriff or the town or anyone he knew ever again. He wanted never to think of his father again.

"They escorted me back to my patrol car and put a couple of their boys in with me. We all went to the station and they spent a long time in private conference with old Sheriff Bailey. Everybody on the force – there were about thirteen of us back then I guess – had all been called in, and we sat in the station waiting for them to emerge from the old man's office. When they did, they had my report all written out for me and ready to sign.

"I signed it," he continued, "you bet I did, or I would've never held a state or county job again. I just sort of understood that was how it was meant to be – the way you just sort of understood things back then – without anybody having to spell it out for you. Anyway, the report was just pretty much what I had seen minus the spaceship and . . . "

"And what?" said Jack.

"And one other thing I saw that they left out – they were picking through the wreckage – I saw a piece of the cockpit, or whatever you call that part of a spacecraft – the capsule. Your dad reported finding *one* dead cosmonaut and I saw one body. But there were *two* seats in the wreckage."

"Maybe the second cosmonaut was still alive." Maybe he still was, living for years off the radiation-soaked desert and growing under the hills.

"And killed your dad."

"And the government covered it up?"

"Wars start over that kind of thing. About thirty miles from the crash site they were doing underground H-bomb tests. They put out the story that radiation was detected at the site and that's how they kept people away. Cost them a lot of money settling the class action suit a few years ago – but they couldn't change their story after so many years – and anyway all the money went right back into the community. Settlement money built your new high school gym for one thing."

"And that's worth letting everybody believe my dad killed himself."

"I don't think anyone around here thinks less of him. Or your mother. You weren't even born yet, but the whole community came together during all that. Everybody liked your father, Jack."

Jack squinted, trying to prevent tears from coming. "Then why didn't they stand up for him? Why didn't you?"

"Maybe when you're older you'll understand – but nobody did anything that night just to hurt you or your dad. I think everybody did what they thought was for the best."

Jack wished the giant who had murdered his father would crush the whole town under his feet. He turned from the Sheriff and walked.

"Jack." He heard the tone of seriousness in the Sheriff's voice. "Jack, don't go that way. I mean it."

Jack ignored him and kept walking the direction the giant had gone. He didn't want to think about what he might find when he got back home; he only knew that he did not want to hide from whatever was going to happen.

The Sheriff was not following him, but back there – down the road – Jack heard trucks. A flood of lights swept under his feet and he turned.

The army rolled down the highway in full force.

———

Moments after her dad had ordered them to leave, Janniffer began to fear for him and Jack. Jack had been half-raving with his talk of the giant man, and even her father – who was never bothered by anything – seemed weird. And what had happened to his patrol car?

Paige must have picked up on her feelings because she spontaneously reached over and held Janniffer's hand. The two of them were in the back and Doggart was up front alone. He was uncharacteristically quiet – thank God.

They never got as far as home. Green army tanks and trucks were moving toward them down both lanes of the highway. Janniffer didn't know tanks could move so fast.

"What do we do?" shouted Doggart in a panic. There was no room for them on the road and the tanks weren't slowing down.

"Pull off!" cried Paige.

He swerved the wheel and they were out of the way just as the convoy reached them and suddenly ground to a halt.

A jeep slipped out of the line and came alongside them. An officer got out and motioned for them to roll down a window. He was a red-haired man who did not look much older than they were, but when he spoke he addressed Doggart as "Sir" and the two girls as "Ma'am" when he asked to see identification.

Paige and Doggart each showed him their driver's licenses.

"I don't have mine," Janniffer said. "I ran out of the house without it."

"I see," said the officer flatly. She could not tell if it meant that she were in trouble.

"She's Sheriff Hubbins' daughter," said Doggart. Damn Doggart. He went on: "We just left the Sheriff – he told us to go straight home and that's what we're doing.

"I see," said the officer again, "and where'd you leave Sheriff – I'm sorry, what was the name?"

"Hubbins. Maybe half a mile up."

"I'm going to have to ask you to leave your vehicle and step into the jeep, sir. Ladies. There is a curfew in effect."

"Woah," said Doggart. "The curfew is not active outside city limits."

Was there no end to his stupidity? thought Janniffer.

"I don't know what curfew you are talking about, sir, but *my* curfew is in effect anywhere and everywhere I say it is. This is martial law, sir."

Sheriff Hubbins would have been more than happy to have the cavalry arrive if they hadn't been hauling his daughter and her friends along with them. A captain with red hair and freckles got out of the jeep Janniffer and the others were riding in. He carried an electric blue folder – the kind with a flap over it and elastic string wrapped around it. He walked up to Hubbins who didn't give him time to speak.

"Son," said Hubbins, "what do you mean by hauling them kids back here into the fire zone?"

"Which fire zone is that, sir?"

"Don't bullshit a bullshitter. I saw the thing. If you're gonna catch it you're going about it mighty slow, aren't you?"

"I have my orders," said the captain cryptically. "Please take a seat in the jeep, Sheriff."

"It's like that, is it?"

"It's for your own safety, Sheriff. I notice you seem to have misplaced your sidearm."

"You noticed that, eh?" He turned around to say something to Jack but the kid was gone, slipped off into the darkness just as the battalion pulled up.

Hubbins squeezed into the back of the jeep next to his daughter. She looked at him after the battalion started up again and the captain and the driver were concerned with other things. He watched her mouth the words, "Where's Jack?" Hubbins shook his head briefly. For some reason the captain chose that moment to look back at them. Hubbins said to him, "You figure you got enough tanks?"

The captain got into the jeep and did not turn around again.

They drove along the road and it appeared to Hubbins they might have missed the giant entirely. Perhaps the monster had veered off the highway. Possible, especially since Hubbins could hear the whooshing of fighters jetting off into the east.

They came to the mobile home suburb where Jack and his mother lived. Hubbins himself had grown up there – lived most his life in the place until the Sheriff's job had enabled him to get a real home for his family. The giant cosmonaut had been and gone; the area was a shambles. Power lines were down and the streets were dark. Trailers had been kicked around like Lionel boxcars. It was quiet. The teenagers beside him were shocked speechless. It felt to Hubbins like everyone must be dead. The captain ordered his vehicles to fan out in a crescent across the devastation. Men picked up bullhorns and called out for survivors. Gradually a few beaten wretches crawled out from hiding places. The captain ordered them rounded up and had their names taken down. Hubbins did not see Jack's mother among the dusty survivors.

"Captain," said Hubbins, trying to sound as polite as possible, "you'll want to start digging, won't you? There must be other survivors under all this rubble."

The young officer looked at him as though the Sheriff had farted. "Thank you for the input," he said.

Once the soldiers had the survivors' names they started leading them to the transport trucks. This was no way to be doing things, Hubbins thought. Then, perhaps for consistency's sake, the soldiers decided to move Hubbins and the kids out of the jeep and into a transport. Hubbins asked a soldier if he could speak to the captain, who had wandered away, but his request was denied. He noted a masked indifference in the soldier's thin face – an indifference that denoted an attitude with which Hubbins was acutely familiar. He had taken the same attitude himself many times in his career. It was the attitude you take toward a bothersome but powerless prisoner. Hubbins didn't like how that made him feel, though there wasn't a thing he could do about it. Once inside the transport, the flaps were pulled down and Hubbins observed the attack survivors. There was no talk of the giant at all. It was late in the night now, and most of them had probably been asleep when it happened. The general impression was that the trailer park had been bombed.

"Bombed or strafed," said a man, an old retiree in a checked bathrobe. "I heard machine-gun fire." Others nodded in agreement. That was would have been the helicopters strafing the giant, but Hubbins decided not to say anything – even though some of the speculating got pretty wild. There were some that believed the attack had been nuclear.

"We wouldn't be here talking about it if it was," said someone else. "Maybe we just caught the edge of it. Maybe they're gonna quarantine us for radiation sickness."

Hubbins said, "If there was radiation danger those soldiers would be wearing special gear." And why weren't they wearing protective suits, come to think of it? That giant was glowing green. It was obviously radioactive. Maybe the soldiers knew less about what was going on than he did. "And anyway," objected another, "why did I hear shooting? No, it had to be a terrorist attack."

Hubbins saw that his daughter was shaking. Her friends, too. "Now come on," he said, "all this speculation is getting us nowhere."

"Well, what do you propose, Sheriff?" said a balding man wearing pajamas that had swords and shields printed on them. He was missing a slipper.

"I propose we take a ride and relax."

"If you haven't noticed, this truck isn't moving," the man commented. "What do they plan to do with us?"

"They'll take us into the hospital in Boulder City, I expect. They'll check us for shock and injury and when they're satisfied we're all right, they'll set out some cots in the high school gym for the folks that can't make any other arrangements."

"I don't need any 'arrangements'. I'll set up a tent in my own damn yard." The bald man stood up in the truck indignantly. "And I am certainly not in shock." He went to the flap and threw it open. He stepped over the back of the truck – bad move, thought Hubbins. But even he had no idea just how bad. The instant the bald man stepped onto the truck's bumper a burst of gunfire cut him to ribbons.

Jack had stolen off into the desert while Sheriff Hubbins was distracted by the advancing tanks and before the floodlights caught sight of him. Fortunately, and for whatever reason, the Sheriff had chosen not to reveal Jack's presence in the desert. Hubbins had always taken care of both Jack and his mother – though Jack now suspected it was out of guilt rather than kindness. Still, the Sheriff had been – had tried to be – a second father to him and he felt like a traitor running away from him into the desert. There was Janniffer to think of as well. He knew that she worried about him, feared for him. His mother, too, of course. It got demeaning, all these people always worried and looking out for you. That was why, maybe, he turned out to be a good runner – always wanting to get away. His clothes, having been drenched in sweat, dried and drenched again, were icy and chafing. He covered ground less rapidly now, alternating wind sprints, steady jogs, and long-strided marches. Anything to keep moving. With the way the highway twisted, and the slow rate the battalion moved, he thought he might beat it to the giant with a little luck. He didn't know what he would do then.

He kept moving.

––––––––

The giant was easy enough to spot again; there was a faint, gradually increasing roar of fighter jets to guide him. The giant was not able to ignore the jets as it had the gnat-like helicopters. It stopped walking and engaged the careening jets head on. They shot rockets at its massive bulk. Most missed – the giant was able to maneuver itself much faster than the jets were able to circle around for strikes. But some of the rockets found their target, drilling into the flesh of the massive torso like bullets. It bled. Jack heard the monstrous head shriek at its attackers in thundering incomprehensible syllables. Because of the sheer volume of the shrieks booming over the roar of the jets, it took Jack a few moments to understand that they were not animal noises – but words. Not English – but words certainly.

Now heavily wounded, the giant cosmonaut tried to drag itself from the fray. The jets kept coming. On the distant horizon Jack could see flames from two or three wrecked planes, but it now seemed as if the giant was too sluggish to destroy any more of them. Jack felt helpless. He was caught in the midst of a deadly ballet that he could take no part in. The cosmonaut had murdered his father years ago, the military and the Sheriff's office and even the townspeople had conspired to cover it up, and it all was going to end here, all their decades of lies and deceptions. The military was enacting the final episode in the drama and he was only a bystander. Just as Sheriff Hubbins had taken the truth about his father's death and hidden it from him – appropriated it for expediencies of his own – now the army was killing the giant. He was certain it was dying. The caked dirt over the giant's skin was awash in its own blood. It stumbled. The jets drove in, hammering the thing to its knees. The great chest collapsed to the earth, the great eyelids drooped as its head settled into the ground.

A river gushed from its enormous nostrils. The dying giant lay a quarter mile off, facing him. Jack edged a little closer as the fighters finished pumping shell after shell into its back. Once they broke off and regrouped high in the sky, Jack sprinted across the open ground. The giant still breathed; it opened and shut its eyes. Jack wanted – he needed – the thing to see him. He put both hands on the giant's eyelash and pulled. Then released and let it snap back. Both huge eyes fluttered, the giant seemed to stir, but remained unaware. It would be dead in a moment. It would be dead and Jack would never be able to confront his father's death. The fighters dove again. The giant had whiskers and Jack climbed them. High above, straddling its ear, Jack whipped off his shirt and waved it like a flag at the jets. If he could get them to stop firing . . .

They stopped. Perhaps it was the surprise of seeing a human being standing on the giant's ear – or maybe they realized that they had killed the monster – or maybe they had simply run out of ammo. Whatever the explanation, the jets veered off toward the base just as helicopters appeared over the horizon. These landed a few hundred yards away. That gave Jack only a few minutes at best.

He screamed into the giant's ear, trying to revive it. There was only this last moment . . . and if the giant could not – or would not – answer . . .

It moaned.

"Who are you?" Jack yelled.

The cosmonaut gave a long and garbled Russian name then stated its rank and serial number in thickly accented English. All Jack got was that his father's killer was a major.

There was no time. "You crashed," said Jack. He could see a phalanx of troops from the helicopters making their way from the road slowly, like shadows.

"Yasss," slurred the giant. "Pitched craft. Taken for prisoner. Political . . . "

Jack pressed on. "You killed a policeman. A deputy—"

"*Nye*— no. *Oszers* . . . "

Others? "Did the other cosmonaut do it?"

"Soldiers," it said, "soldiers kill him."

When Nikolai Petroyevich came to, the first thing he saw was a bright light – but it was not the bright light of heaven. It was a flashlight. And the figure behind the flashlight was not God, but a man – a man wearing a uniform.

The man spoke to him – and whatever he was saying it was not Russian. Gradually the haze began to dissipate and the words made sense. It was English, and he spoke a little English.

"Sir?" the man said.

"Where am I?" asked Nikolai in the best English he could manage.

"Just southeast of the base," said the man.

The base? What base? Where in the world? "What country?"

"America," said the man.

Nikolai realized there was a blanket placed over him, probably to keep him from going into shock. He had better say no more. This fellow appeared to be a peace officer of some kind, and would help him. His mission had been a secret, and this man would hardly be expecting to find a cosmonaut. He had mentioned a base – a military base perhaps? It might be better to let the man believe his flight had originated there.

"My—" he struggled for the right word, "co-pilot?"

"Let's just see about you first – help's on the way," the officer said with hesitation in his voice.

Nikolai assumed that this noncommittal answer meant that his fellow crew member was dead, and that he was alone. This would be a mess, he was thinking, but a mess for Moscow to unravel – not him. Most embarrassing for them to launch an experimental nuclear-powered spacecraft secretly and lose it on American soil. Nikolai laughed.

"Glad you've got your sense of humour, pal," said the officer. "The name's John – John Jaffe."

"Pleased." He avoided giving his own name. "I am not from here," he said, and he knew it must sound oddly redundant.

It did, and now the man called John Jaffe laughed as well.

"You're not too far from the base," the man told him.

Nikolai felt he was in great trouble. Worse than that, he felt intense nausea, a sign that the worst might have happened – the nuclear core of the spaceship may have leaked and poisoned him. His co-pilot was lucky in that case – he had died quickly.

Nikolai expected to be taken into custody but did not fear a long delay in his release. He was not on a spy mission after all, and cosmonauts like astronauts were international heroes. Nikolai closed his eyes and waited for whatever was going to happen to happen.

He was awakened by the roar of vehicles, the booming of loudspeakers and the shouts of men. There was a gunshot. Nikolai involuntarily snapped upright and his back seized into spasms. He could see the peace officer lying prone a few feet from him, and there were soldiers, sweating and cursing one another. They spoke too fast for Nikolai to follow their English, but they were clearly arguing over the slaying of the peace officer. Nikolai could not guess why they had done it – unless in a panic caused by the dark and a fear of the unknown.

A soldier noticed that Nikolai was conscious and advanced toward him, rifle raised. This will be it then, thought Nikolai. No slow death by radiation – I am to be executed by these fearful and desperate men. Perhaps they would neatly pin the murder of the peace officer on him. His troubles were at an end.

The soldier did not shoot. He merely kept his weapon trained on Nikolai and shouted for his comrades' assistance.

He was unable to control the urge to vomit and jerked his ruined body to the side to do so. *The soldier ought to shoot*, he thought. He shook and felt life draining from his body. He was going to die in some foreign desert and no one – not family, not friends – would ever hear from him again.

Nikolai felt a profound sympathy for the murdered peace officer. Did the man have a wife and children? If so, they would never see him again – and for what? For waiting with a dead man until aid arrived.

Nikolai quaked with pain as he thought of these things. It was a bad way to die.

But he did not die.

Though he would never find out what exactly happened next, he lost consciousness – slipped into a coma perhaps. Gradually, self-awareness returned. Or rather, a new awareness emerged: slow, dreamlike and housed in his very bones. He came eventually to understand that he had lain for years in a secret chamber in some forgotten underground facility under a vast desert – in a sort of American Siberia where the US had tested its nuclear weapons. Radiation from those tests fed his body.

Fed it and made it grow.

Though homesick and alone, Nikolai came to relish his peaceful limbo, content never again to witness oppression or governments. Even here, in the supposedly-free West, his last memory was of soldiers killing their fellow countryman: the peace officer whose only crime had been to stumble across Nikolai in a downed experimental craft –

merely coming to the aid of a traveler from the other half of the world.

At some point, radio broadcasts began piercing his consciousness. In time, they whispered undreamed of news: the Soviet regime that had oppressed his Russia had crumbled. Joyously, he decided to wake himself into this new world of peace.

Instead, he woke to violence.

Now, nearly two decades later I am killed by the remnants of the bipolar world for the crime of rising from the grave, thought Nikolai, watching a tiny human being shout at him and climb along his nose. Even enormous size and the fullness of time were not enough to protect a simple man from the machinations of the world.

Nikolai wondered about the small creature before him. It was hard to tell but it seemed that it was little more than a boy. What odd chain of events or quirk of personality led this boy to risk death beneath the roar of military might, to climb a giant's dying face to shout questions in his ear? He wanted to know about the man Nikolai saw murdered. He must be the officer's child then – who else would care about a single man after so long a time?

————

There was pandemonium in the truck when the bald man died. Hubbins watched as the passengers climbed over each other like animals to get away from the bullets. But the bullets kept coming. His daughter scrambled with the crowd and he did not want to watch her die. He was thinking that he was glad he had gotten so fat in the last twenty years, as he pushed through the bodies and threw his whole bulk upon her – hoping it would be enough, yet fearing that the army would send a man or two into the truck with hand guns to finish up once most of the witnesses were dead.

She was crying and he put his hand over her mouth. "Play dead, honey," he said to her. "Play dead." To gain another second or two of life.

————

Soldiers had killed his father, Jack had heard the giant say. So it had not been suicide.

He stood unmoving upon the ear of the murdered giant, while helicopters landed and soldiers poured out onto the desert sand. Jack wanted to kill them all, all the men who'd been there that night, all the men who had killed his father, or those like Sheriff Hubbins who had allowed his death to become a lie.

They came nearer in loping, strained gaits, laden with heavy packs of machinery and weapons. Jack knew he could easily outrun them, and probably lose them in the desert night – for a while at least. But he did not run; he had all he wanted to know about himself there beneath him, in the mountain of human flesh that was the slaughtered cosmonaut. Below him, the great dark cave of the dead giant's mouth gaped open.

————

As she crawled through the rubble that had once been her home, Mary Jaffe was thinking only of her son Jack – she prayed he was not in the group she had just watched being slaughtered by the soldiers. She had been trying to make her way toward them with her leg all twisted, too weak to call out, when the men started firing on her neighbors. She fell and hid, watching with horror as the murdered corpses of Tom Hubbins and his daughter were dragged onto the ground. She saw two other friends of her son as well. They, too, were dead. But no Jack. All night she had prayed that Tom would find her son, and now she thanked God that he had not listened to her.

There was chaos and an officer with red hair tried to restore order. The panicky soldier who had started the firing was unconscious – the officer had butted him in the head with his sidearm. Mary tried to make herself as small as possible in case they combed the neighborhood for witnesses.

They did not.

What they did instead seemed to her even more ghastly than what had happened already.

Quickly, his face wet and red with anger, the young officer ordered gasoline poured over the truck, and over the bodies that had spilled from it. He ordered his men back into the other vehicles and signaled for them to move out. Then, climbing aboard a tank, he tossed a match.

Mary cried.

————

Jack slipped and slid over the giant's tongue, ducking down at the back of the throat. Evidently the soldiers did not find the prospect of pursuing him appealing or – even more likely – no one had noticed his small figure against the giant's much greater one.

He turned and faced the new world before him. South to the stomach, he thought, or north to the brain?

There was light through the nasal cavity. Jack had assumed that this was light shining through the nostrils. But then he realized it was dark outside, so where was the glimmer coming from?

The light had the faintest tint of green to it.

As Jack forced his way up through the giant's head, he considered his chances. It was the brain that was glowing green. Whatever impossible force that had allowed the cosmonaut to grow fifty feet high and to rise again in the world was still alive in that brain. Perhaps he could take advantage of that fact.

They would undoubtedly want to study the body – because of its sheer size that might take years – and as he crawled behind the eyes he saw that soldiers were already applying grappling hooks to the giant's limbs. He did not know how long he would have. If they cut right into the brain he might be caught by morning – if the body lay in storage while bureaucratic infighting led to inaction, he might have months or even years.

His own skin was bathed in green light now, and he settled into the folds of brain tissue to allow the glow to do its work most effectively. With a little luck – with a lot of luck, actually – and the willingness to embrace the patience he had never had, Jack might grow into a giant like the cosmonaut. He had no idea what the process would be like: had the cosmonaut been growing steadily for twenty years? Or did he spring up from the dead that very night in a sudden cosmic growth spurt? Jack did not know.

Through the ear canal, Jack heard the *wup wup wup* and the whistling of helicopters rising into the air, hauling the giant heavenward. There was green light everywhere, heating, massaging and stretching his skin.

Jack found that by touching the right nerve endings he could see with the dead giant's eyes. What he saw was the rising sun.

Morning had come.

Kungmin Horangi: The People's Tiger
Cody Goodfellow

———

The churning black surf of the Pacific Ocean spouted fifty feet into the air as something very large stirred in the depths at the mouth of the San Francisco Bay. A news helicopter that had ventured too close got swooped up and crashed into southbound traffic lanes on the Golden Gate Bridge. Army and Navy choppers buzzed like mayflies over the geyser, dropping marker flares and spraying red fans of incendiary shells. Nothing seemed to slow the invader, which torpedoed in on a collision course with the Old Ferry Building at the head of Market Street.

All along the waterfront, crews of artillery and mobile missile batteries eagerly peered into the roiling silver mist for their first glimpse of the adversary itself. Behind them, legions of protestors filled the streets from the woodland grounds of the old Presidio Army Base to the Embarcadero and the heart of the Financial District, tens of thousands of furious, banner-waving marchers pressing against the embattled lines of riot-control police. They had come to denounce the federal crackdown on the labour unions, the withdrawal of government assistance and the twenty-eight per cent unemployment rate – but the spectacle unfolding in the water could not be resisted.

A missile battery atop the ferry terminal sparked to life with a salvo of lightning spears that turned the black surface of the bay into a dome of white-hot steam. Waves of scalding seawater swamped the docks, but then the bubbles subsided. The cheers of the soldiers spread up and down the waterfront, drowning out their CO's irate barking and the chanting of the protestors.

It was a brief victory; something exploded out of the water, and for just a moment, the entire city held its breath as it struggled, with its childlike collective mind of a half million or so, to understand just what it was looking at.

Then, amidst the massed shrieking of the sudden inferno pouring down on the flaming invader and its own unearthly howls of tormented rage, hundreds among the crowd began to cheer for the monster.

––––––––

The command centre of the Joint Forces Mobile Command fell silent as General Skilling entered with his retinue. "Get back to work!" he barked, and the airmen resumed running around as if the deck of the C-98 Supernaut cargo plane were covered in hot coals.

Skilling cast a jaundiced eye over the panorama of the big board, the global map jigsawed together from the composite vision of several hundred defense and private satellites and the exploded diagram of the world's media coverage. Most of two hundred screens played the images coming in from the flock of helicopters circling over San Francisco.

When he absolutely had to, Skilling turned to the man nearly everyone in the room had been mooning over when he entered: Commander Wesley Corben, the most visible officer in the Air Force's Special Counteroperations Detachment and the pilot of America's most closely guarded weapon. If he was on the scene, then the emergency was clearly under control.

Commander Corben ignored him, gazing out the window at the runway lights of Alameda Naval Air Station and a wing of F-18s scrambling off the flight line.

"This is everything we feared, Commander," said a voice from the speaker on the General's desk. Though he had never heard it so raw with exhaustion and nerves, he recognized it well enough.

"We're up to the task, Mr President," the pilot said, glancing at Skilling. "Both of us."

"Mr President, if I may," General Skilling broke in, "Commander Corben hasn't been fully briefed, but once he has been, I think he'll agree that the situation is under control, without the need for . . . extraordinary measures."

"Have it your way, General, but you boys swore up and down you could stop it at sea."

"Bring me up to speed, General," Corben said quietly, "and I'll decide whether turning the Army loose in the middle of San Francisco is a better idea than deploying Steve."

Skilling winced. He hated to hear the name spoken and glared down nearby technicians who had perked up at the word. "My opinion of your . . . weapons program is a matter of record—"

"General! They've got a visual!"

All eyes turned to the monitors, where a gargantuan tower of flames staggered across Market Street, kicking tanks and armoured personnel carriers out of its path like a burning drunk in a toy store. Suddenly, incredibly, the sixty-foot flaming behemoth sprang high into the air, clearing a row of warehouses, and vanished into the frothing Bay.

"This is most unprecedented!" shouted Dr Murai, the team's resident kaijuologist. "I've never seen anything so large move so fast. Only Dr Otaku could create such a weapon."

Commander Corben ran for the exit. Skilling did not try to stop him. "Well, Mr President," the general prompted, "I guess you know what this means."

"If that thing out there is the one they call Kungmin Horangi, then I guess it means we're now at war with North Korea as well. Don't these damn commies know when they've been licked? What the hell does that crazy name mean, anyhow?"

Skilling bit his lip. Half the intelligence community was listening in. "Some shitwit at the Pentagon says it means 'People's Tiger'."

The President's snorting, signal-distorting laugh turned heads throughout the command centre. "A tiger? Is that what it's supposed to be? Goddamn, those commies never get anything right."

———

Commander Corben sprinted across the runway to the enormous hangar where his team lounged, lobbing a football and watching the news. Without a word, they took their positions to prepare for the launch. Corben zipped into his flight-suit and stepped into the shadowy, cathedral-sized space. In the centre, an enormous American flag hung from the domed rafters, screening off most of the hangar.

Lt Mullin walked alongside, briefing him on the pre-flight check. "The new armaments are loaded, the new Hellfires are quicker on lock-on, like you wanted, but the blowback is worse, so don't go punching anyone with them. The armour's been overhauled, again, but that fibreglass shit's gotta go. It's giving him a rash."

"What about the approach?"

"They don't want you to cross on foot. Reckon the Bay Bridge can't take it."

"Did you show them our numbers?"

"Sure, but the Richmond Bridge is already falling apart, and they don't want to risk an accident. He's gotta go over in the harness."

Corben cursed. "And the other . . . problem?"

"Electrolytes are bumped up to optimum, but he's still running like a faucet. The doc says he'll adjust to the new diet, but they don't want to run antibiotics on him so soon before—"

"Another upgrade? He's not a goddamned machine. He's—"

"I know, Wes, we feel the same way, but to them he's a weapon. They don't even call him a 'he' anymore. And you know what they keep saying—"

"I know, I know. *He volunteered for this.* As if any of us knew what 'this' would be."

"Oh, and I tried to get *her* to leave before you deployed, but—"

Corben stopped, fussing with the readouts on his helmet. "I'll take care of it, Ben. She deserves better than to get thrown out by the guards."

Lt Mullin patted him on the shoulder, checked the optic jacks running from Corben's helmet to the CPU on the back of the suit, gave him a thumbs-up and went back to a safe distance.

Corben slipped behind the flag and stopped, as he always did, to offer a prayer for himself, and for Steve. Then he opened his eyes and ascended the stairs parked beside Steve's temple.

Steve lay on his back in the hangar. All the computers and gantries and medical equipment had been cleared out to give him room to get up.

At the top of the stairs, Laura waited, just like always, beside the open hatch bored out of Steve's right temple. The guards had orders to keep her out, but no one could look Steve's widow in the eye and deny her.

She lifted her black lace veil and poured those eyes all over him. "He's afraid, Wes."

"He's not afraid, Laura. He's—" A machine, a weapon, a meat puppet . . . "He was never afraid of anything in his life."

Laura got closer, her perfume burning in his nose. "He loved his country, you know that. He loved you, Wes. He loved me – a little bit less maybe. He wasn't afraid for himself, but now . . . "

"There's nothing to worry about. It's some mutt hunk of kaiju-shit from North Korea. It's probably already dead; this is just a photo op." He shook her off, but her real perfume – her sweat, her tears – made it hard to remember where he was.

"It's not the fighting." Laura tried to catch his eyes. "He's afraid of what he's becoming. He knew that this mission . . . doing this made him a symbol, like the astronauts. They're changing him again, aren't they?"

"They want him to win. That's his job, now. He has to adapt. We all do . . . "

He brushed past her, but her arms caught him, running over the countless sockets that would bind him to her husband. He pulled away. He couldn't make himself do it again, any more than he could forget that she wanted him for the same reason the Pentagon did.

"Try to get on with your life," he told her.

"I thought we were trying," she said, and he looked away. "The Army doesn't consider him dead, but they don't pay his salary. And – we're . . . Steve was Catholic . . . I can't even . . . "

Corben climbed in. "They'll understand when you do, Laura. Try not to be here when we get back."

"Give him my love, won't you?"

Corben slammed the hatch and initiated the pre-wake checks. Steve's EEG was a minimalist tundra of limbic activity with momentary temporal lobe storms, but nothing to worry about. Everything that was Steve had been scooped out of the front of his skull to make room for the cockpit. Cables snaked from the bulkhead and slotted into their respective ports on the suit. Corben tingled as those cables shoehorned his brain into the sleeping giant.

"Commander, this is your eleven o'clock wake-up call. The Green Meanies are waiting outside, and Steve's late for work."

Corben nodded at the marching columns of status lights on his smart visor. The phantom sensations of godlike power swept all the garbage out of his mind as he got into character.

"Roger that, Ben. Steve's online in three . . . two . . . "

He hit the switch.

———

Steve opened his eyes. Light burned until the visor calibrated his response and winched down his pupils. He rose to his feet, slowly, like a coma patient. His helmet brushed the hanging halogen lamps, forcing him to hunch over double to step out onto the runway.

The night sky was clear above, but an opaque canopy of fog enveloped San Francisco down to the double-decker Bay Bridge. From the heart of the fog came a constant flash and dull, rolling pops of ordnance being expended in an all-out war. Colt was developing a 90mm revolver for Steve to use, and a telephone pole-sized police baton that delivered a fifty-thousand-volt shock was on the drawing boards at the Pentagon, but for now, he was expected to beat whatever was raising hell over there with his hands and feet and some Hellfire missiles salvaged from a junked Apache helicopter.

Steve checked the harness on his heavily armoured torso, and hooked into the web of cables running back to two enormous cargo helicopters idling before him. At his thumbs-up, they lifted and spread out until the cables stood taut, rotors growling in mutiny at the nine-ton payload.

He braced himself and rolled his shoulders, tried to scratch the rash on his back. At last, the cables twanged and the tarmac dropped away. Aloft, the helicopters double-timed, lurching into the wind over Treasure Island and along the Bay Bridge, where hundreds stuck in traffic honked and shouted his name. The wind pried at the seams of his Kevlar bodysuit, the battlements upon his shoulders and head, seeking any path to steal his strength.

———

Wes Corben dissolved like aspirin inside Steve, shivering at the wind and straining to see out of Steve's eyes into the shroud over the battle. Even as his thermal overlays gave up on the blizzard of fire and smoke, his radiation scans fed him an outline of something larger than Steve, and faster, and – beyond that, he had no fucking idea what he was looking at.

"Have a nice day at the office, dear," a chopper pilot chirped in his ear, and the cables cut loose high above the impossible burning thing that even now looked up to watch him falling.

And then – and this always drove Corben batshit when it happened, but Mullin swore they couldn't find the bug – Steve's life flashed before his eyes.

———

When kaiju synthesis technology disseminated to all the extremist nations of the world, it sparked a renaissance of rogue state misbehaviour. If plutonium and anthrax were effective means of asserting one's will upon the world stage, then the revival of some sleeping monstrosity – or the creation of a new one – was a golden dream of random havoc.

Not to be left behind by kaiju-mongers in China and Africa, the

United States embarked on its own Megamorphic Weaponization project. No renegade sauropods or lumbering cybernetic chimerae could serve as a symbol of American military might, however – the people of the world's last great superpower would never rally behind a monster. At least subconsciously grasping the return of pagan idolatry that lay at the roots of the kaiju arms race, they strove to create a hero: to, in their own well-spun words, "put a human face, an all-American face, on the kaiju crisis". So they asked for volunteers.

Major Steve Arness had done so, as they never tired of reminding his wife, and had passed the rigorous screening process. They needed someone strong and fast, with excellent reflexes, with Golden Age astronaut looks that would translate into action figures, kid's pajamas and beach towels and shit. Steve was perfect.

Using gene therapy and nanomites, they reprogrammed Steve's mitochondrial DNA, and he grew. Within six months, he stood sixty-four feet tall.

His doctors pleaded with the Pentagon scientists to consider the potential for replication errors during this reckless growth, particularly in the brain, which stopped growing by age three in normal human development. To grow from three pounds to the volume of a V-8 engine block is traumatic enough for any organism, but how much more so for the most complex aggregation of matter in the known universe, the human brain? Very soon after his treatments stopped, Steve went totally insane. He devolved to a bestial shell of the confident test pilot who had volunteered for this project – and left them no choice.

After escaping from the Florida island where he was interred, he destroyed Cape Canaveral and twelve helicopters and a company of infantry before a TOW missile lobotomy felled him. Incredibly, he survived, though in a coma. Wheels began spinning, and the catastrophic setback became an unprecedented opportunity.

Neurosurgeons, structural engineers and computer designers flew to the island, and set about fixing him. The cavity in Steve's forebrain was filled with a mainframe that routed all his nervous impulses to a cockpit just above Steve's eyes. The man who controlled Steve would receive all the data of Steve's experience as raw reality; his reactions drove Steve's body as an amplified version of his own. That man would have to be an extraordinary pilot, as good as Steve himself had once been, for he would have to become Steve. Wes Corben had not wanted to volunteer for the project, but he did, because he could not bear the thought of a stranger inside his best friend's head.

———

Steve hit the ground and sank up to his ankles on a grassy palisade overlooking the Bay. The street was seeded with burning cars and military debris, and a fusillade of tracers sprayed out of the nearest cross-street. Protestors swarmed the sidewalks around his feet, waving banners and throwing rocks and bottles as they sought shelter from the meta-Biblical conflict raging above their heads.

A chorus of spotters buzzed in his ears that the enemy was closing in on his position, but he just stood there. The thing had been right under him when he dropped. How did something so big move so fast?

The building in front of him, an eight-storey office complex, sagged and spat glass as all its eastern-exposure windows shattered. Steve looked up at the titanic black shape perched on the roof just as it sprang at his face.

He tried to roll with the impact and throw the attacker over his head, but it slammed into his chest, crushing his lungs flat. Its talons got inside his arms and shredded his armour.

Pain whited out the scene. Corben almost succumbed before the dampers reduced Steve's pain-incentive triggers and told him what was wrong. Steve was laid out on his back in the street, armour and bodysuit torn wide open, the attacker straddling his chest like a dog about to bury a bone in his abdomen.

With a noisome trumpet blast that somehow cut through the din of war all around, Steve's irritable, bacteria-infested bowel cramped up and sounded a war charge. The monster flinched and shrank away, as if offended by the outburst. Galvanized, Steve brought one leg up as hard as he could between its hind legs, hoping the kaiju specialists had striven for authenticity, and levered its mammoth bulk up and as far away as he could.

The creature flailed at the air, sailing over three waterfront blocks, smashing to earth on an unfortunate retro diner and plowing across the street into the deserted stalls of the farmer's market in front of the Ferry Terminal. At last, Steve got a good look at it.

Even with its pelt burned off, Kungmin Horangi was clearly supposed to be a tiger, perhaps a new strain of the giant sabertooths the Chinese had revived from fossils and turned loose in Tibet. But its hide was a sickening mass of polyps and blisters, with arrays of envenomed quills sprouting in radiating patterns down its spine from its head, or where there was supposed to be a head. Nice try, North Korea.

Then it roared at him, and he understood that, blasphemy though it was, this was no mistake. It was the offspring of a fundamentally perverse union of land and sea fauna. But why? Why would anyone cross a tiger with a sea cucumber?

He soon found out. The head peeled open and splayed out like a banana, a thrashing mane of fanged tentacles around a gaping maw filled with busy mandibles. Its eyes, he saw, were everywhere, on the tentacles and all over its body, so that even as it recovered from the impact, it lashed out at a tank parked behind it and stomped its turret in, kicking it through the lobby window of a Japanese bank. Then it charged.

Steve snatched up the nearest solid object – a tour bus containing BC/DC, Canada's foremost AC/DC cover band – and hurled it at the oncoming monster. Kungmin Horangi changed course, talons digging into the solid masonry façade of the old US Mint, and vaulted off it. Steve barely dodged, then reached out and gripped one of its tentacles as it passed, making ready to whip it around and smash it into the street.

But the plan fell apart before the pain even reached the dazed synapses of Steve's pilot. The thorny tentacle razored through Steve's gloves, into the muscle between the bones of his fingers and out the other side, as the monster tore past him and took his hand with it, ripping off the flesh like a glove.

Steve stared at his naked bones and let out a yelp of confusion. The spotters screamed in his ears, but he heard only the sound of his own building agony as it roared out of him and shattered the last intact windows on the avenue.

The Red Korean kaiju skidded to a halt a block away. The street buckled under it, brown sewage percolating up out of smashed pipes around its massive paws. The monstrous hybrid relaxed, as though Steve were already dead and it could destroy the city at its leisure. It shot one paw out at the walls of a glass skyscraper and smashed something inside – a cat stalking a mouse through a dollhouse. Steve recognized the building: the Transamerica Pyramid, always a favourite with disaster movies.

Blood loss and encroaching shock made red warning lights blink all around the periphery of his vision, but Steve focused only on the enemy. "Weapons hot," he growled, raising his intact arm to point at the thing now engaged in smashing open the Pyramid's neighbours like an anteater ravaging termite mounds. "Fox one, fox two," he said, and Hellfire missiles arced out of the gauntlet on his forearm.

Where they hit, the sun seemed to peek out of a hole in the night, and then the whole avenue was awash in fire that reduced the air itself to ash.

"Fox three, four . . . " Steve emptied the remainder of his arsenal into the flaming mound, but he knew that no matter how hot he burned it, no matter how many pieces he blew it into, it would come back, and keep coming, and coming—

―――――――

And now, the news: In the wake of the disastrous San Francisco attack, the true extent of the damage inflicted upon the city is only now coming to light. While the kaiju invader Kungmin Horangi broke down the physical security systems of an undisclosed number of bank headquarters in the city's financial district, an army of hackers descended on the unprotected servers and deleted whole banks of financial records, credit reports and loan documents. An emergency meeting of the FDIC and SEC this morning was closed to the public, but critics predict that at least four major banks will be forced to freeze all holdings and declare bankruptcy, until such time as the records can be retrieved. While his press secretary delivered the painful news that the federal budget is already too tight to allow for more emergency aid, the President made this brief statement, while enjoying a round of golf with friends and campaign boosters at Cocoa Beach:

"We are at war, and the enemy is within our borders, as well as all around us. People will have to make sacrifices. Real Americans won't have to be told twice."

The President's golf game was cut short by the approaching Hurricane Manuel, but he still got to fire the inaugural round at Florida's first indoor duck hunting arena. The President and his party bagged fourteen mallards, and poked fun at his troubles by naming one of the two ducks he shot in a cage match "Kungmin", and the other, "Kim"—

It had not been Kim Jong-Il's intention to initiate a sneak attack on the United States. The last thing he wanted was for posterity to associate North Korea with the conniving cowardice of the Nipponese devils at Pearl Harbor. If only the American President had taken his repeated warnings seriously . . .

At first his plan was only a frustrated whim – to turn a kaiju loose on his decadent cousins to the south, and force the Americans to show their impotence, or their insanity . . . it mattered not, so long as something finally happened. A modest plan, but the Supreme Leader's restless dreams of even a shabby reconstituted dinosaur were out of his poor nation's reach. All this changed when he stole the inestimable Dr Otaku and set him to work; the dream had become the creation of a symbol of North Korea's adamantine resolve, an avatar of the People to shake the palaces of the world to dust. The notorious Nipponese kaijuologist only smiled and bowed and disappeared into his lab, saying, "I will hold a mirror up to your state, and give your reflection life."

The world laughed when it heard what North Korea was doing. With half of the capital in darkness, with disease and famine claiming nearly as many per annum as had the war that split their great nation in half, Kim was spending all their money on a desperate weapons project, using a kidnapped – and certifiably mad – scientist to make a monster.

But Kim had never listened to the world. If his rule, by the same rigorous Stalinist doctrine he inherited from his omnipotent father, was painted as incompetent tyranny by the chattering swine of the outside world, he would not deign to explain himself. Though Dr Otaku escaped to China only six months into the project – in a capsule within a giant earthworm of his own devising – the specimen in the brine tanks in his lab grew nevertheless, stunted and grotesque, yes, but it became more than he ever dared to imagine.

Kim awakened to a revelation, and dreamed a new dream of eliminating hunger and teaching the world about the true benefits of communism, but the world would not stop laughing long enough to listen. They cackled at the destruction of Kungmin Horangi in San Francisco, but soon they would hear, and see, and taste – and they would know.

In the heart of his palatial fortress at Pyongyang, Kim Jong-Il swilled Hennessy, raged at his PlayStation and waited for the world to apologize.

––––––––

General Skilling hated using the laser pointer, but he'd found it was the only way to keep the President's attention. "As you know, sir, one year ago, North Korea was accused by the UN Security Council of running a biological weapons program. Nobody thought they'd ever pose a threat to anyone but themselves, but there was some speculation that China had financed them.

"Kim Jong-Il refused to address the charges, but then Dr Otaku disappeared—"

"He wanted the head egghead for his monster factory."

"Correct, sir," Admiral Beecher cut in. "Kim is a freak for the old kaiju flicks, and when the Japs cracked the recombinant kaiju genome, he shit himself with envy, and went on a shopping spree. He did the same thing to get some movies made, a few years back."

Skilling waggled the pointer in the President's eyes. "Well, this morning, sir, we received this tape. It was postmarked two weeks ago, but it was sent parcel rate."

A screen lit up at the centre of the big board. A plump face filled the screen, eyes flashing like Siamese fighting fish behind the convex lenses of monumental goo-goo goggles. Pulling out in spastic jerks, the camera framed Kim Jong-Il at a podium before a window overlooking the snowcapped mountains of the Amnok-Kang river valley, near the Chinese border. Behind him, an elderly Japanese man in a spotless white lab coat smiled and nodded, his nimble fingers dancing as if they worked the strings of a marionette.

"That's Dr Otaku. Kim's people took him from his fortified lab on Mt Fuji."

For once, the President was all ears. "Was he brainwashed?"

"You be the judge of who brainwashed whom."

The dictator appeared tired, but smiled benignly at the clockwork soldiers flanking him at the podium. Though heavily sweetened with digital studio effects, his voice was still the querulous falsetto of a cat trying to frighten a rival as he squawked through the hostile English-language script. "To those who believe that communism is dead, Great Comrade Kim Jong-Il offers this lesson. Communism is sharing, no more and no less, from each according to his means, to each according to his needs. And so, people of the so-called Free World, we share the gift of the People's Tiger with you."

The video cut out.

The President pounded the table. "What I want to know is, why was this such a goddamned surprise? We knew he was cooking up something, we knew he had the know-how, and he warned us—"

"He warned *you*, Mr President, but—"

"The man's some kind of goddamned nut, with all the crazy crap that comes out of his mouth. 'The People's Tiger is coming?' What were we supposed to make of that happy horseshit?"

Admiral Beecher, reluctantly, stepped in. "It would appear, sir, that we did have some advance contact . . . "

The President smelled the fumble and pounced on it. "What? Who dropped the ball?"

"Our nuclear submarine *Akron*, on patrol in the Sea of Japan, pinged an unidentified object larger than itself a week ago. It emitted no hull or engine noise, so the captain assumed it was a hostile kaiju, and torpedoed it. The target was presumed destroyed."

"Why the hell wasn't I told?"

Beecher looked around for support, but they'd all been thrown under that bus too many times. "Well, it, um . . . it was in the daily briefings to the Joint Chiefs, but it looked like a non-starter. No action alerts, no response from your people—"

"Well, now we know different, don't we?"

"Yes, sir. We've since collected waterborne tissue samples on the beaches near Aomori and Sapporo, but it's difficult to account for all of the mass because . . . "

"Because what? Out with it!"

Beecher spent, General Skilling took back the laser pointer. "People have been eating it, Mr President."

That cracked the President up. "Lord, those Japs'll eat anything, won't they?"

"Sir, your morning briefing of yesterday details the same problem in San Francisco—"

"What? What page is that on?"

"Fourteen-A, sir, in the bright red box? Army recovery efforts were hampered by the protestors, some of whom appear to have been pinko fifth columnists, and they led a salvage of the remains."

"What do you mean, 'salvage?'"

"The protests were about federal aid, sir, about food for the poor. The meat of the kaiju was roasted by Steve's, ah, overzealous attack, and distributed over dozens of city blocks by the explosion. It is resistant to decay and, by all accounts, the flesh of the monster is, ah . . . "

"Spit it out!"

"Well, it's said to be delicious."

———

In South Korea, the US Army maintained a high state of alert, awaiting an order to begin the mad minute they'd been trained for – showering North Korea with missiles. But due to the desperate peace brokered by South Korea's president, and China's promise that any attack on her poor neighbour would draw a nuclear response, a shaky truce held. But at home, a new radical movement formed and, almost overnight, escalated into an all-out insurgency.

When the unwashed hippie hordes of the UC Berkeley student body staged a sit-in at which the meat of Kungmin Horangi was offered as a sacrament, the police cracked down, but nobody took it seriously. When the same thing happened at Stanford's crypto-conservative Hoover Institute four days later, they started to worry. Police raids on communist soup kitchens all over the Bay Area turned up a distribution network for the kaiju meat. Within a week, thirty-eight such establishments were shut down, and nearly three tons of the monster's flesh was confiscated and removed to labs across the country for study. What they learned in the next twenty-four hours made them freeze or burn all samples and order a news blackout.

When left in a medium of seawater and organic nutrients, the flesh replicated itself and grew. The proprietors of the soup kitchens – card-carrying communists all – were interrogated and extolled the virtues of the meat as an inexhaustible food staple, a gift from the peace-loving people of North Korea.

Their customers, however, were a different matter. The poor and hipsters alike, drawn to the necessity or novelty of free kaiju cuisine, reported that it had properties far beyond its flavour and astounding nutritional content. Eating the meat opened gates in the brain, boosting endorphins and serotonin output, creating a euphoric yet alert state which one imprisoned kaiju chef described as "like Christmas morning, where you love everyone and want to share everything". This witness had particular clout, as he was a decorated artillery officer and survivor of the San Francisco attack, who snatched up and cooked a feast of kaiju meat for his Army buddies as a goof. "If this is what communism was supposed to be about, then have we ever been barking up the wrong tree!" he declared, even as he was taken out and shot.

The government's aggressive publicity campaign to depict the meat as drugged, poisoned or radioactive seemed to fall on deaf ears. Spontaneous demonstrations of thousands blocked every law enforcement attempt to root out the trade in kaiju meat, and kitchens opened in Los Angeles, Portland, Seattle and Las Vegas – the latter of which suffered most grievously from the effect, as tourists discovered the futile stupidity of gambling and simply shared their money, and hotels opened their doors to the homeless.

The government tried, as well, to block the plague of websites devoted to kaiju cuisine and philosophy, most of which came not from North Korea, but from Japan, where the phenomenon had already saturated the community via the meat that washed ashore at Sapporo. In retaliation, domestic and foreign hackers alike descended on the federal servers in earnest, so that the NCIC criminal database was wiped clean of all records, and the New York Stock Exchange seized up and began rattling off kaiju recipes.

The next month saw the kaiju kitchens spread across the nation and out of the liberal underground, into the faltering middle-class mainstream. With more banks in default or freezing their accounts in the wake of the database collapse, unemployment climbed to nearly half the population, and social agencies were swamped and sank without issuing a single cheque. Employees at fast-food franchises were caught preparing kaiju meat for unsuspecting customers, and the suburban hinterlands began to simmer with political unrest and unconditional love. The news stopped showing the riots, as police clubs fell more and more on the heads of cornfed Republicans and even other cops who had succumbed to the forbidden flesh.

No matter what draconian measures the government imposed – martial law and curfews in the cities, roadblocks and roving gangs of National Guardsmen torching burger joints with flamethrowers everywhere else – the madness spread, and people pig-headedly, defiantly, continued to share.

––––––––

Commander Wes Corben spent the next month running Steve through physical therapy in Florida, and so had little time to read the news. He received the Congressional Medal of Honor from his hospital bed, recovering from a concussion and the psychosomatic shock of losing Steve's hand.

He pushed for a robotic prosthetic, but was outmaneuvered by the project scientists, who wanted to try out a sauropod regeneration virus they'd harvested from the remains of one of Japan's lesser-known kaiju plagues.

The treatment bore immediate fruit; within hours, Steve's cauterised stump sprouted with new buds of bone sheathed in noisily dividing cells, and before the week was out, a hand, of sorts, had grown to replace the one sheared off by the monster. That his skin broke out in shingles like the scales of a dinosaur only intrigued them more, and when Steve began to grow a tail, they were ecstatic. They talked about pushing the envelope – Steve Mk2, armies of dino-Steves stomping through Pyongyang, eating everything and everyone in their path on the long road to Beijing—

The only battle Corben won was over Steve's incontinence; they resumed antibiotics and stopped feeding him by stomach tubes. But Corben had to run Steve's meal each day, herding the brain-dead behemoth through whole pods of steamed orca and hockey-rink-sized portions of cornbread.

He came back to his motel room off-base to find Laura waiting for him. She still wore her widow's weeds, but she shed them soon enough even as he worked the key in the door. Too tired from days on end inside a dead man's head, too beaten down to argue, he let her in, and kept his mouth shut when she called him *Steve*. He told himself he was defending his friend's memory by refusing to do it where she really wanted to, in the cramped confines of Steve's cockpit.

Afterwards, he lay in bed, wondering what day it was. The phone rang. Laura turned over, sighed in her sleep, whispered a sibilant name. He picked up the phone.

"Scramble, code red, Commander. Steve's late for work."

Corben slid off the bed and stepped into his crumpled pants. "Steve's still in therapy from the changes. He's not ready to walk around the block yet—"

"Too damned bad is what they say. We need him. Tiger-Cucumber's back."

———

"As near as we can tell, the bastards hoarded a ton of the meat, and incubated it near Norfolk, right under our goddamned noses." General Skilling caught his breath as he paced alongside Commander Corben in the hangar at Bolling Air Force Base. As before, helicopters circled over the water outside, dogging something moving fast upstream to the confluence of the Potomac and the Anacostia rivers, at the heart of Washington, DC.

Lilliputian scientists and technicians crawled all over Steve, disconnecting catheters and hoses and running the final pre-wake check. Corben eyed Steve nervously, seeing the changes in full bloom for the first time. Steve lay propped on his side to accommodate his new tail, as long as he was tall, spilling out onto the runway. His bone structure had begun to warp, muscles to sculpt themselves into a very different kind of body. An ugly brainwave soured Corben's alert frame of mind: a drawing-board sketch of King Kong versus Godzilla in a genetic blender, with Steve's apple-pie freckled, Tom-Sawyer face slapped onto the hideous final product.

"How do you know there's only one?" Corben asked.

"We'll cross *that* bridge if and when we come to it. Those asses in Congress have finally seen the light, and they've voted the funding to expand the program. We won't make the same mistakes again."

Looking over the chainmail mesh of serrated scales spilling down Steve's oddly hunched back, Corben could only mumble: "Who wouldn't volunteer for this?"

Skilling saluted him and nudged him up the stairs. At least Laura wasn't here. She was still asleep in the motel room – and he knew what she was dreaming.

Corben climbed into Steve's head and fired it up without running through the checks. Steve lumbered to his feet, trampling a lot of million-dollar equipment and more than a few fleeing technicians. Though heavier than ever, he felt even more powerful, his centre of gravity lower and wider thanks to the balancing tail, which slashed the runway clear with a will of its own, and drove Steve in a bounding, simian gait that was only half voluntary.

There had been much wrangling, at the start of the program, over where to locate the pilot. Some had demanded that Steve be run by remote, but security concerns and human practicality had won out. Steve had been a Golden Gloves boxer in his youth, and muscle memory and superb reflexes made his head the safest place to be when he ran amok.

Though much of the data Steve's nerves poured into his brain was utterly alien, Corben became Steve like never before as he loped across the paved expanse of the airbase, skirting the waiting helicopters and running down to the river. Here, he could already see the churning waters parting as his adversary burst from the gray Potomac and waded into the Capitol on the opposite bank.

———

Steve hit the water and kicked across in twenty strokes, his tail propelling him like a speedboat to the shore of East Potomac Park. In the silvery light of the overcast morning, the obscene profile of the enemy loomed over the Capitol Mall – Kungmin Horangi, reborn.

Steve took note of how it moved among the white sepulchral houses of government. In its wake, only selected targets were destroyed: the Mint, the Federal Trade Commission and the fortress of the Internal Revenue Service were flattened, while the monster leapt high over the Smithsonian castle and gamboled across the open greensward, cutting a wide berth around the bureaucratic temples and museums, in open contempt for the helicopters raining missiles with depleted uranium shells down on it.

Then Steve came out onto the Mall, and saw that the green was packed with protesters. Hundreds of thousands of men and women of every class and persuasion shouted and sang and cheered the kaiju invader. It traipsed over their heads like their collective dream of a champion made flesh, somehow never stepping on a single tiny body.

The damage to its fiery, jet-striped pelt was hardly negligible – gigantic gobbets of flesh sprayed and spattered the Mall, and teeming hordes of protesters overran the barricades to carry them off or devour them on the spot.

Locked on the monster, Steve led it so he aimed at a projected ghost of its probable path and launched a volley of missiles. Bigger than ever, easily eighty-feet long, the monster launched itself into the air and the missiles strafed the Smithsonian and made a blazing pyre of the US Forest Service.

"Power down your missiles, Wes! Repeat, power down, you're blowing up government property!"

"Do you want to win or not?" Corben barked, and Steve rushed the monster.

Protesters milled around his feet as he strode through their midst, spearing his ankles and feet and tail with the shafts of their picket signs. Screaming, "Whose side are you on?" Steve stomped them until the lawn was a swamp of liquefied sedition, and broomed the Mall with his tail until the fortress of the Department of Justice and the marble walls of the National Archive wept blood and human shrapnel.

Kungmin Horangi met his charge rearing up on its hind legs, head splayed open and fang-studded tentacles questing for his face. Steve slipped under the wriggling worms and drove his fists into its blubbery chest. His tail darted behind and swiped the monster's legs out from under it. Dragging it off-balance as he once had his opponents in judo, Steve heaved the writhing bulk over his hip, sent it hurtling across Constitution Avenue.

Even before it landed, Steve was racing after the airborne abortion and pounced on it where it came to rest, he snatched a nosy news chopper out of the sky by its tail and smashed the monster with it until the whirling rotors broke off and the fuselage exploded like a cheap guitar on its sorry excuse for a head.

As Kungmin Horangi crumpled and lay prone against the toppled tower of the Old Post Office, great slits yawned open all down its neck and flanks and gave forth a faint but growing hiss. Cautiously, Steve crouched behind the rubble of the IRS; in stark disregard for every known principle of physics or biology, these monsters almost always had some sort of energy weapon. He waited to see what it would produce.

An eerie keening sound escaped from the gill-slits, and Steve went dead-stick, oblivious to Corben's spastic gyrations in the cockpit. Steve's nervous network broadcast only static, while sensations like fluttering moths in his stomach – feelings! – swamped the mainframe. Out of the unlovely orifices of this monstrous abomination, in the thick of a titanic battle, came the celestial sound of a chorus of children.

They sang in Korean, but the longing, loving voices sailed their message straight through the benighted backwaters of Corben's brain. These children, reared on Spartan rations and Stalinist dogma, sang of their dream of a world where everyone shared, and loved one another, as a family should. They offered this awful, awesome thing, from which the recording of their song spewed like the tune of an ice-cream truck, as a gift, and the harbinger of a new golden age of humankind.

In their thousands, the surviving protesters poked up out of the rubble like shoots of grass and took up the alien chorus.

Steve grabbed up tanks and cars and fistfuls of shrieking protesters and threw them at the crumpled form, rushed up behind it and planted a kick in its flanks. The monster was lofted high over the Capitol, flipping end over end as the crowd went wild in his ears, cheers and screams about evacuating the President—

Steve fell on the monster again, plunged his taloned saurian paw into its cratered, rubbery hide above its cartilaginous ribs. Venomous spines pricked him all over, skin going numb and swelling purple-black blisters the size of watermelons. Thrashing tentacles flayed the scales off his back and pumped a potpourri of toxins into his flesh, but he blanked it out as he squeezed something deep inside that pumped like a heart until he popped it, then slashed the muscles beneath its right foreleg.

The monster sagged under Steve, who wrenched the useless limb out of its socket like a drumstick and rammed it into the frantically gnawing mandibles. The tentacles swallowed up his arm and stripped it to the bone again, but the echinoderm mouth ruthlessly chewed up its own severed forelimb, and rivers of sweet-and-sour ichor showered the White House lawn as the colossal combatants grappled, the syrupy song of the children skipping but still burbling out of its speaker-gills.

"What do you taste like, eh, you commie motherfucker?" Steve roared.

Kungmin Horangi went limp in his arms, then swelled up like an emergency airbag. Steve struggled to get free, but his destroyed arm was still trapped in the barbed gullet of the monster. A blast of hot air and briny broth escaped, and Steve's nostrils caught it and told Wes that its aroma was not at all unpleasant.

Then Kungmin Horangi exploded.

Steve's arm ripped free amid a torrent of soft tissue; mountains of stomachs and intestines and glands the size of school buses lay out on the lawn and festooned the south portico of the White House, and still it kept coming, an endless, gory horn of plenty.

And Corben had to admit that he had never smelled anything so sweet in all his life.

With a Herculean effort of pure will, he pulled back on Steve to retreat from the situation. The Red Korean kaiju was limping away, deathly slow, towards the Potomac, and Steve had to get back to the hangar. He was bleeding, dying—

But the controls wouldn't respond. Corben felt himself go into a kind of paralysis, as Steve moved of his own volition towards the steaming pile of innards. Reaching it, he began to shovel them into his gaping mouth with his intact hand.

"Steve, for God's sake, it's communism! Stop eating it!" Corben yelled. He yanked on the manual overrides and punched the emergency sleep sequence, but to no avail. Steve went on gobbling up the monster's digestive tract, which it had expelled after the fashion of its secondary parent species, the resourceful sea cucumber.

And even as Corben fought to pull Steve back, the cables running into his suit fed him the taste and the texture, the gelatinous, spicy, tangy succulence of it, not unlike kimchi or pickled octopus, but tempered by the pleasantly gamy murk of tiger meat, and the briny, womb-like glow of collective well-being, of universal rightness, of belonging to a harmonious whole, that began to spread out from his stomach.

Corben coded the self-destruct sequence, ripped the leads out of his suit and undogged the hatch, all the while telling himself he was not hungry, he was not going to eat it—

"You're an American hero, Steve," Corben begged one last time. "You're like a god to them. Why can't you stop?"

A familiar voice pounded on his eardrums, and shocked Corben so that he threw himself head-first out of the cockpit. Though Steve was hunkered down on his knees over the diminishing pile of guts, Corben still fell thirty feet to the immaculately manicured White House lawn, the echo of that voice still ringing in his ears.

"Why can't you stop fucking my wife, Wes?"

Corben's arm folded under him and he hit his head so hard he saw stars, but he rolled to sit up at the sound of a helicopter touching down in front of the west portico.

High above him, the explosive charges embedded beneath the cockpit detonated, blowing the domed roof off Steve's skull in a furious monsoon of bone shards and hunks of flaming brain. Steve's hand stalled at his mouth, a colossal rope of intestine slithering free and draping itself across his lap.

A party of dour Secret Service agents in black suits hustled out the West Wing exit and crossed the lawn, but halfway to the chopper, their ranks broke and a shorter man in shirtsleeves came running up to Corben.

"Do I smell barbecue?" shouted the President.

"No, Mr President, it'll brainwash you!" Corben went for his sidearm, oblivious to Secret Service agents painting laser dots on him and running to shield the President.

"Naw, I'm not touching that disgusting foreign commie crap, but it does give me an idea." The President engaged that matinee-idol squint that denoted frontier grit and cowboy resolve, that somewhat alarming facial tic which, alone, had carried him in the southern states. "If that sea cucumber shit makes people turn pinko, then we just need an antidote, right? Fight fire with fire."

Picking his way across the debris-strewn lawn, the President stood in the shadow of Steve, still kneeling upright, though his convertible head belched smoke like an uneasy volcano. "Yes sir, a taste of true-blue courage, of independence and strength and faith, to remind them what it means to be Americans."

The leader of the free world knelt and scooped up a fillet of brain, still sizzling in its own juices.

"Smells like veal from my Daddy's ranch," he said, and took a bite.

Corben crawled up to the President, but a Secret Service agent stepped on his neck and pried his pistol from his hand. "Please, Mr President, don't! He wouldn't want—"

The President grinned. "Nonsense, boy, he knew what his duty was, when he signed up for it. Any red-blooded American with half the heart he had would jump at the chance. And, Jesus, take a look at him! Whatever it is, it sure ain't cannibalism . . . "

The President bethought himself a moment, then flagged down his chief of staff. "Now, get my Interfaith Council on the horn, and have them stand by for something big. And get me every cloning specialist you can, and some lab space, and some vats. And, you know, we're gonna need a helluva big grill . . . "

The Island of Dr. Otaku
Cody Goodfellow

———

"Meh," said the Prime Minister of Japan to the UN General Assembly, and dreamed of brown seas.

What, honestly, did they expect him to say, on this terrible anniversary of the Daikaiju Age? What consolation could the first victim of a rapist offer to the next? What wisdom, to a world where everyone raped everyone?

He blinked at a flash in the micro teleprompters embedded in his contact lenses, before he remembered to close his eyes to see the unfiltered feed. A little extra sexy edge the gaijin would have to pay retail for, ten years down the line, ha ha, what an empty game.

The speech – expensive and individually wrapped origami phrases, focus-group tested pro-corporate shit – did not come.

Instead, his contacts, along with the monitors behind the podium and every console in the General Assembly Hall, flash-cut to a scene that made most of the sullen ambassadors instantly sit up at attention.

A nanny-cam view of row upon row of Japanese schoolgirls. The Prime Minister's bafflement turned to heart-stopping rage as the camera zoomed in on one specific girl in the class, fidgeting and twitching in her seat. Despite the uniforms and the poor resolution, he recognized his daughter at once, and knew the media would be only seconds behind him.

"Good morning, Mr. Prime Minister-san," a sunny, smug voice chuckled in his hearing aid. A Caucasian, upper-class Australian voice. "Only you can hear me, of course, but everyone can see what we're going to discuss. If you're a reasonable man, there's no reason you can't spin this to your advantage, eh?"

The Prime Minister gave no answer but chopped, choked breathing, like a constipated swimmer entering a frozen stream.

On every screen, his daughter arched provocatively back in her seat, kicking out in *grand mal* seizures. The razor-pleats of her blue wool skirt hitched up to reveal the doubled outrage of melon-hued cotton panties emblazoned with a cuddly cartoon image of Kungmin Horangi, the infamous People's Tiger.

The General Assembly hall erupted into chaos, and the Prime Minister found his mic had been cut. His pleas for the scandalized diplomats of the United Nations to stop ogling his daughter went unheeded.

The Aussie voice in his ear resumed its syrupy purr. "I assume we may speak freely, so I'll get down to it. Your daughter has been a bad girl, eh? She and her friends are all hooked on People's Tiger jerky, did you know that? Well, we spiked her supply a bit, old son. Without the antidote, she'll transform into a full-fledged tiger-sea cucumber in about twelve hours, if the shock doesn't kill her. But chin up, mate. None of that has to happen."

All at once, the Prime Minister knew who was ranting at him. The third son of the sole owner and CEO of the world's largest media conglomerate. A rude, shrewd little shit who pissed on proper protocol in a desperate attempt to get noticed.

And, with a tremor of deeper, creeping dread, he also realized what this must be about.

"Of course, you'll appreciate our admittedly uncharacteristic restraint, at this point. We could have piped in some spectacular immersive VR stuff we got off your last Shinjuku toilet-trip. But the Old Guard thought it was best to take the high road."

The Prime Minister deliriously lost control of his bowels. The hermetically-sealed astronaut diapers under his impeccable Brooks Brothers suit contained the deluge, but cradled it deliciously close to his chafed, shameful buttocks. Of all the vices it took to maintain his flagging faith in democracy, his coprophilia, indulged in biweekly baths in untreated Tokyo sewage, was the most humiliating.

Would that he had the grace or guts to use this stage to end it all . . .

On the monitors, the classroom desk-grid dissolved in a panic of flying preteen bodies. Someone must have armed the posh private school's emergency protocols, because the girls were locked in the room with his poor Mariko, who had not begun to change physically, but was her unmistakably shy, insecure self in no other respect. Flipping desks and gnashing foaming jaws like she meant to bite her classmates, she herded them toward the windows. Screaming girls broke their nails on the latches, but safety precautions rendered them impossible for students to open, let alone climb out, especially during midterms.

"What," grunted the Prime Minister, "do you want?"

"What do I want? What does the whole world want? The answer to the question that has you here, soiling your three-million yen monkey-suit in front of the General Assembly . . . but instead of sticking to the script, you're going to tell them the truth."

"I do not know—"

"Of course you do, mate. You've been supplying and sheltering him since he defected from North Korea. Everybody knows it, and everybody knows he's up to something big . . . something apocalyptic.

"All you have to do to save your daughter – and whatever slivers of face you still have with the folks at home – is speak into the microphone, and tell the whole world where it can find the infamous Dr. Otaku."

———

The location of Dr. Otaku's latest laboratory fortress was indeed a closely guarded secret from the world at large, but hardly a mystery to the world's great powers, who were discovering that knowing something, and doing anything with that knowledge, were often worlds apart.

While the uncharted island of Dr. Otaku lay well within the Antarctic Circle, the ocean boiled.

Submarine vents in the ocean floor radiating out for miles from the tiny volcanic island gushed molten magma into the shallow Weddell Sea, fueling a violent transmutation that shrouded the region in perpetual columns of superheated steam, so that no detail of it was visible from the open sea or the air, let alone from orbit.

The aggressively secretive climate also did nothing for the island's defenses. No alarms sounded when the scalding waves parted to eject a titanic kaiju invader and fling its nuclear submarine-sized bulk onto the jagged tusks of volcanic stone that fringed the island's shore.

Two hundred feet of laser-guided mayhem from its screeching eagle beak to the Teflon tip of its parboiled tail, and the ex-Navy pilot cooped up in the cockpit hacked into its spinal cord was light years past pissed.

Commander Wes Corben had paid dearly to find this place, in every coin men and devils accepted, for the island was guarded by forces more sinister than fog, more sophisticated than any cloaking device or satellite baffler: the boundless power of international corporations to cover their fuck-ups.

A few years before, the volatile Antarctic coastal shelf was hopelessly fractured by overeager oil companies desperate to get out of the oil business. The geothermal instability accelerated the thawing of the region several hundredfold, until New Zealand-bound ocean liners took to skimming their wakes to harvest bobbing flocks of boiled penguins as a novelty entrée.

The oil companies used the same proactive strategy they brought to alternative energy research to hide the catastrophe, flooding every media outlet and science journal with doctored snapshots and cartoons featuring happy surfing penguins, many of whom were, thanks to digital sorcery, also avidly drinking Diet Dr. Pepper. But they also bombarded the government with phony satellite imagery and doctored climate research, and stymied muckraking environmental watchdog groups with rosy propaganda campaigns and unmanned kamikaze submarine wolf packs.

As a result, Dr. Otaku had selected the most dangerous and secret place in the world to set up his laboratory . . . at least since the last one.

The island's rocky shore lurched up drunkenly out of the boiling foam to join battle with the cyclone-riddled sky as a phalanx of near vertical cliffs of black lava rock. A maze of narrow, twisting canyons cut into the towering volcano were choked with a riotous jungle of colossal mutant fungi, like pulpy tenement towers. The fleshy gills underneath the mushroom domes powdered the giant monster's white-feathered head with psychoactive spores as it stealthily crept through the labyrinth, sneezing and mildly hallucinating.

Cmdr. Corben could not hope to have arrived undetected. The churning ocean was full of sea mines, drone subs, and marker buoys with depth charge launchers, and half the shrieking seabirds that hovered and pecked at the trampled fungi in his path seemed to have compound dragonfly eyes and cellular antennae for ears.

It didn't matter if Dr. Otaku knew he was coming. The world's foremost freelance kaiju-engineer was more devious than Dr. No and Fu Manchu in a three-legged race, but Wes Corben had come from the edge of the grave for revenge, and an angry, wounded, and divided nation had hurled him into the mad scientist's clutches solely to take it.

After his last piloting gig ended so spectacularly on the White House Lawn (Code Name: CUCUMBER BBQ: ABOVE TOP SECRET), Corben retired to spend more time with his family of single malt scotches. Still weeks away from hitting rock bottom, but the government had been willing to forgive and forget, just to get him back.

They promised him that they had modified the organic components, replacing unreliable neural processes with solid-state fiber optics driven by a nuclear power plant, and installing a host of no-nonsense ordnance. They reinvented the pilot interface, and totally retooled the manual override and emergency recovery protocols.

And they made a whole new monster for him to drive.

Named for the visionary worrywart who coined the term "military industrial complex," IKE (International Kaiju Enforcer) stood only a little taller than Corben's last ride, but the absurdly musclebound torso and rangy arms were pure Malaysian highland orangutan – albeit with rail gun cannons embedded in the outsized forearms – while the silicon-scaled hide, the shrimpy, talon-crazed hind legs, lashing, razor-edged tail, and lethally septic saliva came from the hotwired genome of a Komodo dragon.

A potent and adroitly engineered kaiju-hybrid, ideal for amphibious ops, the pork-barrel dipshit who chaired Senate Intel rebuked the "diabolical" design until he could insure it had a uniquely American stamp on it.

Which was why Ike had the head of a bald eagle.

The smaller brainpan forced them to relocate the cockpit between the shoulder blades, but it was much better protected than Steve's head.

Ike's scrappy, undersized saurian hindquarters had to scramble to keep up with his top-heavy forelimbs, but the monster hustled across the battlefield with a stampeding gait that looked awesome on TV with the accompanying stadium butt-rock theme music the Pentagon had commissioned for all his media packages.

"A tragicomic triumph over every sound principle of genetic engineering," said *Scientific American*, "and a perfect totem spirit for America's moribund status as a world power," added the *Washington Post*. "The most idiotic abomination to shamble out of the Beltway groupthink cuddle-puddle since the New Deal," jeered the *Wall Street Journal*. (The President took umbrage at the harsh reception of his "personal brainchild," and invited the seditious press corps to review Camp X-Ray Delta in the DMZ bayous of the former state of Louisiana, but the damage was done. Ike's reality shows, cartoons and merchandize tanked.)

At least, Commander Wes Corben told himself, they hadn't succeeded in putting wings on him. When the people who turned cloned tissue from his friend Steve Mancuso into a mystery meat served in every cafeteria in America sat down to make a monster, you had to expect some unpleasant surprises.

It seemed like he had arrived just ahead of the rush. Out on the ocean, he heard but couldn't see a massive naval battle – men, machines and monsters pointlessly blowing each other up in the fog. Approaching the island's central volcanic peak, Corben was almost disappointed at the lackadaisical resistance he had encountered. The mushroom-jungle was teeming with Otaku's recent experiments in mini-kaiju, anklebiter chimeras bred for tyrants as crowd control in Indonesia and Africa. Iguanadonkeys nipped at Ike's flanks with their toxic jaws and hurled inflammable feces at him, but Ike smashed them to jelly with his mighty fists. Scampering emulemurs proved harder to target, but their kicking spurs proved only a minor annoyance, gouging shallow, bloodless divots out of Ike's carbon-steel endodermis before he mowed them down with his rail guns.

Ike scaled a thousand-foot waterfall and bounded across an open plateau with a heliport and observation bunkers arranged around rows of open missile silos.

The ground shook, and a gargantuan shadow rose up out of the murky mists to blot out the milky light of the sun.

Ike thumped his chest and let out a shriek like a thousand eagles in a document shredder. Corben charged up the rail guns and kicked in Ike's adreno-blowers, thrilled to finally face a foe worthy of his undiluted wrath.

At first, it seemed as if a mountain of mushrooms shambled out to attack him, but the leviathan laboring underneath the shaggy carpet of parasitic fungi shook itself free and honked a defiant roar from its gaping maw and slime-choked blowhole.

Corben felt pity seep like lactic acid into his reflexes, slowing but not stilling his hand, as he spurred Ike to engage his miserable enemy.

The assholes called it Ishmael.

Bred by Dr. Otaku for an overfunded Greenpeace in a fit of grandiose pique in the late nineties, the walking mega-cetacean wiped out the Japanese whaling fleet in a month – but not before the fickle eco-activists had a change of heart, and stopped the cash transfer to Otaku's account.

Ishmael had been missing and presumed dead for nearly a decade, but now, it thundered across the helipad like something out of the Golden Age of Greece, when the earth was raped by the sky, and gave birth to monsters.

Despite his political repulsion for everything Ishmael stood for, Corben had to marvel at the workmanship. A gigantic orca on functional sauropod legs, Ishmael could have been a real threat, if it had arms. The monster's useless flukes had been ripped off, burned, or shot away dozens of times, but Otaku had finally overcome the fatal design flaw. You could hate the game, but never the player. And yet, Corben discovered new depths of loathing for the mind that could replace the hapless tyranno-orca's flapping flippers with gigantic, chrome-plated chainsaws.

The huge, ungainly lumberjack blades struck sparks off each other as they roared to rusty life, but Ishmael struggled to keep up, big black eyes bugging out in bloodshot shock at what it had become, wheezing and flinging great streamers of slime-mold from its infested blowhole. A blood-flecked yellow beard of the disgusting stuff hung from the whaler-killing killer whale's sick, toothless maw like a hillbilly patriarch's beard.

Ike ducked under the slashing blades and pivoted, clipping one rampaging chainsaw forelimb by its tender, infected organic stump, and bent it to sever its mate at the base as neatly as such a monumentally ghastly operation could be executed.

Ishmael fell with a shockwave that lofted Otaku Island spores to Manitoba, asthmatically bleating its melancholy love for its cruel, careless creator until Ike, wielding Ishmael's own chainsaw-limb, cored the miserable monster's speech center, signaling lunch.

———

With all the waste disposal paperwork the eco-activists and Right to Lifers had foisted on the mad scientists' guild, it was almost easier to clean house by provoking an international incident every so often, Dr. Otaku observed.

Ishmael and his ilk were bittersweet reminders of a simpler era, but all Dr. Otaku saw were their defects.

He never wanted to make weapons. He wanted to create life, which no one could corrupt, tame or control. Which forced him to come around to the unseemly business of the hour.

"Greetings, friends, allies and interested parties. You have been briefed on the rules. Shall we start the bidding?"

Otaku waved to cut the feed and sank into a chair to sip a restorative tonic of Tang and vat-grown human cerebrospinal fluid. Though it was like a cannon in his pygmy hands, he never put down the vintage WW2 Mauser which, the eBay seller promised him was the gun Goebbels used on himself and his wife in Hitler's bunker.

His unpaid summer interns, the Seppuku Clan, had the auction well in hand. The federation of *bosozoku* hackers who took over Mega-Ronin 1, Tokyo's old-school corporate defender mecha, and orchestrated the monster robot's spectacular *hara-kiri* in Tokyo Bay. The rusting remains of the beloved robot, still hunkered over the haft of its vibra-katana, had become Japan's Statue Of Liberty, a moving symbol of its enduring love affair with heroic self-defeat.

With their bleach-blonde mohawks and pompadours, their huge blue cybernetic anime eyes and biker gear made of cured Yakuza hitmen hides, the Seppuku Clan were laughably campy henchmen, but he couldn't argue with the results as they expertly filtered the flurry of wire transfers, Trojan horses and data packets, both overt and covert, pounding the firewalls of Otaku's network like piranha sperm trying to fertilize an egg. Every corporate bidder worth entertaining had tried to spike the experiment with its own software, hardware specs, and genetic codes. Most of them had also sent armadas of mercs and Somali pirates, drone blastboats, and mecha-kaiju swarms to shell the island and shoot expensive lasers at each other.

Bioweapon bombs hit like smoke tracers and sprayed viral mists that made the mushroom forests sprout wings, tails, and udders. Each was trying to outbid its rivals with one hand, while gaming the birth of Otaku's last monster with their own protocols, and sabotage the process in case anyone but them succeeded . . . exactly as he knew they would.

The reason the concerted intelligence forces of the free world could not shut down Dr. Otaku's control network was very simple. It was everywhere, and nowhere, at once.

The moment the auction cycle reached critical mass, the system appeared to crash, and Dr. Otaku ceased transmitting from his island stronghold. The auction had only been a ruse, anyway. Otaku had no intention of selling his masterpiece, but he had used the mountains of credit put on the block in millions of micro-transactions to finance the real project, and to focus the world's attention on his project, and thus, bring it to life.

The virtual womb in which his masterpiece gestated was buried in the Seppuku Clan's server on the Hardsoft Gaming Network, where the unborn monster would awaken in millions of households, cafes, arcades, and pachinko parlors around the world, to take control of its new body.

While Interpol, NSA, and a hundred corporate and government agencies in the United States and Europe frantically scoured the globe and the Net for his latest dastardly creation, an average of 1.2 million subscribers wasted their lives online at any given moment on the Hardsoft Gaming Network, which was unofficially Seppuku Clan's bandwidth-hogging bitch. While upwardly mobile parents tried to avert or manage or just profit off the impending kaiju holocaust, none noticed how their tween and teenaged kids stayed locked in their rooms and immersed in a marathon cooperative tournament, even after some of them started to die.

Today, the current peak audience of four million distributed across five continents worked like virtual slaves racing to build a pyramid, but also served as the surrogate nervous network of a new artificial intelligence cloud, training it to work in concert as parts of a single, unborn beast, straining to break out of its egg.

The game demanded their total concentration, as terabyte parcels of data comprising Dr. Otaku's ultimate monster were uploaded onto the net, and downloaded to a battery of masers and nanotech fabricators set up atop the NHK parking garage in the geographic center of Tokyo.

With the conclusion of the game, half a million elite survivors emerged victorious from the final level and were whisked into the synthesis of a new order of kaiju.

The inferior three and a half million gamers simultaneously choked to death on their own vomit, but moments later, their bank and credit accounts were drained and maxed out, and flurries of spam blasted out of their respective mail accounts (W3 GoT PWNED BY ZAIBATSU!!! UR NXT, NOOBZ!!!!), proving that there was life after death, if only in the belly of an unborn god.

––––––––

At the top of the highest peak on Otaku Island, the bleeding and battle-scarred Ike reared up on its hind legs and roared defiance at the last circle of security around Otaku's lair.

The lab itself was no paltry matter, a six-story geodesic dome surrounded by minefields and automated machine-gun towers, but the staging area for Otaku's final project was as absurdly oversized as a workbench would need to be, for the construction of giant monsters.

A paved, silicon-lined bowl the size of the Arecibo deep space radio telescope filled the yawning chasm where the mouth of the volcano once yawned. The vast expanse was traversed by a network of cables from which gondolas dangled over the great work. Swarms of hovering drones monitored or controlled the process, which, despite the teams of uniformed lackeys racing around in golf carts, the squads of ninjas drilling on platforms, and the flocks of white-coated nerds hassling with banks of expensive technology under the eye of tattooed Jap biker terrorists . . . had amounted to nothing much, that he could tell.

The bowl was empty.

Corben didn't take too long to puzzle it out. If you drove a giant monster around the world and smashed into nefarious assholes' hideouts for a living, then sooner or later, you might just stumble in a bit before the eleventh hour, and you'd only have to kick over a bunch of charts and nifty conceptual sketches.

He ordered Ike to take apart the lair. Shrugging off the depleted-uranium rounds the machine guns pumped into it like so many fleabites, Ike picked up tanks and tossed them into the minefields, loping across the field towards the lab dome when the debris stopped bouncing.

No more giant monsters dropped out of the sky or crawled out of cracks in the earth. No satellite death weapons or clouds of mustard gas to thwart his claws when he set Ike to pounding on the steel and Plexiglas wall of the dome. It yielded instantly, spilling him into the flimsy interior of his archenemy's lair, which looked like a gigantic Benihana steakhouse.

"Corben, what's the status of the operation?"

"There is no operation! There's nothing going on, here. I think the old geek just wanted the attention—"

Corben lost his train of thought as he saw something on the aft monitors. Disengaging Ike from the dome, Corben brought the vista of the huge, empty bowl up on his main monitor.

It was still empty, but suddenly, and vitally, full of . . . bullshit?

The concave surface of the bowl lit up and danced with weird circuit-frying waves like St. Elmo's fire, summoning and containing arcane energies that warped the air. There were no hoses or artificial womb machinery, or the small factory needed to assemble even modest combat mecha.

All in a flash, Wes Corben understood.

The project was all but complete.

The bowl was, as he originally pegged it, a satellite dish. It collected all the world's communications, filtering them to focus on the events that had the world's undivided attention: the battle here, and all the endless, airtime-eating, empty expert speculation about whatever the hell Dr. Otaku might be up to.

Psychiatrists, psychologists, sociologists, concerned parents, politicians, pundits, noted futurists, and even a few actual scientists, speculating, debating, and spitballing, molding the clay of inexplicable events into instant mythology. And all this bullshit, as well as the corporate gamesmanship to try to control the process, had created a tremendous sink of energy and wealth and consciousness, out of thin air. And somehow, Otaku's ingenious lackeys had figured out a way to harness all that hot air and bullshit, to coalesce it into a power source, and more—

Because the raw uncertainty, the yawning mass hysterical terror of the unknown that the bullshit sought to overcome, was the root chord that drove that awesome symphony, and dictated the form that the chaotic energy began to take.

The bowl was much more than a satellite dish. It was more like a laser, collecting all the world's fear and misinformation, transmitting it anywhere in the world, and transmuting it into flesh.

Corben had to hand it to the old devil. In a world so eaten up with the fear of the lights going off, Dr. Otaku had harnessed the earth's only inexhaustible power source, and turned it loose to make his monster for him.

Ike redoubled his efforts to gut the dome, which disgorged armies of antique flatbed tanks with energy projector lamps. They hardly singed Ike's feathers, but the static charge made all the cockpit monitors go to random satellite feeds of Brazilian children's shows. Blind, Corben kept smashing, hoping to somehow pull the plug, sure nobody was listening as he screamed, "Stop talking about it, you're making it happen . . . "

———

Mortified, Mariko rolled through the trendy streets of Harajuku, eating everything.

Every door was closed to her. She even tried to squirm down the storm drains, but they had been sealed. Everything organic that she touched dissolved and added to her already unbearable mass. Even the disgusting germs on every surface gave up their secrets with a toxic whimper, as they became her.

It was liberating to be free of fear of bacteria, but the shock of tasting everything she touched sent her into a panic, stampeding through the quarantine roadblocks and out into the city, seeking a huge bowl of tapioca to stand in until someone could administer an antidote that worked.

Soldiers shot at her, and with a wave of her pseudopods, she crushed and slurped them into her abominable spreading belly like so much melted ice cream. Classmates shrieked and hurled burning textbooks at her, and she wept hydrochloric acid tears, reducing them to crumbling husks while an NHK camera drone peeped it all. Lashing out at the drones only attracted a dozen more and set fire to a KFC, and all its flaming patrons leapt into her foaming flanks to put the fire out.

In her blood, the kaiju RNA-potentiator agent had triggered a chain-reaction throughout Mariko's body, causing every cell to revert to totipotency, a science word that meant every one of them could easily go its own way with no regrets. Made up of a colony of anything-goes amoebas casually dedicated to the *idea* of Mariko, if not to the form or the other dull mortal stuff, the new, mutant Mariko had cast off the uncool gene therapy scheme behind the spiked Kungmin Horangi jerky, only to regress into a blob.

When she broke out of the classroom, a team of mercs shot her with tranquilizer darts spiked with the antidote. But they didn't reckon on Mariko's spunk, or her morning diet of ginseng, black market estrogen, and Blue Otaku Ecstasy. The havoc these ingredients played in the total reshuffling of Mariko's genetics and morphology had rendered her a seething, primordial pit of awful potential.

She wept at the manga-scale irony. Once, she could not bring herself to eat anything but kaiju jerky, for fear of becoming a fat girl. Now she could eat everything, it seemed, but herself.

Slithering down the alley, she met a ragpicker woman, ancient and seemingly held together by dust and cat hair. Alone, the charwoman stood in her path, bent under a knapsack bulging with recyclables, but singularly unimpressed.

"Foolish girl, what are you making of yourself?"

"I don't know!" Mariko wailed, shocked at the clarity of her words, as well as the volume, which shattered windows and set off car alarms for eight blocks.

"Foolish girl . . . become the champion Japan needs."

Mariko tried to thank the old woman, but ended up eating her.

Perhaps it was the old woman's words, or just her gamy old body digesting within Mariko's formless new one, but a deep, cosmic serenity took hold of her, enfolding her like a cocoon, soothing her with dreams of a new shape.

———

On the verge of what he earnestly thought was victory, Wes Corben was already reaching for the emergency booze locker when Ike suddenly seized up and defied orders.

"Orders" are what they called them in the manuals, but as Ike's pilot, Corben entered commands directly into the monster's hacked brainstem. Most brain functions above the autonomic level were modeled by onboard computers, but the men who designed and modified Ike had learned from their costly previous model, Major Steve.

Ike should have shut down the moment it refused an "order," or gone to a fetal crouch until it was airlifted. There was no "Ike" to defy Corben's "orders," or so he thought, until he came within a hair's breadth of crushing Dr. Otaku himself.

Smashing away at the mad scientist's lair like a rabid badger with its snout in a beehive, Ike burrowed deeper into the lab complex, flinging crushed concrete, satellite dishes, lab equipment and flattened hordes of subhuman orderlies like so much beach sand. Corben dared to hope that he could finally exact revenge for all the awful twists Dr. Otaku had introduced into his life, when he lost control of Ike.

The renegade monster didn't run amuck or switch sides to pull Corben out of its own skull. On all fours, Ike crawled away from the gutted lair and began to dig a hole in the middle of the minefield.

The hole was wider than it was deep, and of no strategic value whatsoever that Corben could see. Yet Ike squatted over it in blithe innocence of the onslaught of bombs and lasers chopping away at its hunched shoulders.

Corben tried to harangue Mission Control, tried to raise anyone, but the airwaves were a helter-skelter of random red noises and bleeding shortwave chatter.

He watched the monitors in disbelief. *Fuck the regs*, he thought, and lit up a cigarette. He'd need at least that long to figure out what to do next, assuming he could do anything.

Ike was engineered to have no secondary sexual characteristics, no hormone arousal receptors that might make the monster hard to control in the event of a "gay bomb," or other sexual bioweapons.

So, even if he couldn't do anything about it, Corben still wanted very much to hear the guys at the lab explain how Ike could be laying eggs.

————

Of the seven million Tokyo residents who watched the newborn, nameless monster materialize in their midst, no fewer than fourteen died of heart attacks or strokes, while another hundred and twelve leapt or fell to their deaths as it passed harmlessly through their apartment blocks. A perfect self-projecting hologram, a thirteen-story ghost; when it thrust its metamorphic forelimbs through towering skyscrapers and maser-tank battalions, its tiny human victims lay quivering yet unharmed in their own urine, quite convinced they'd been crushed.

And there was no shortage of real destruction. The two Self Defense Force artillery units flanking Otaku's monster in the business district of Akasaka Chuo never particularly cared for each other. Infiltrated and thoroughly compromised by rival mystic prosperity cults, and with no enemy to fight but endless kaiju invaders, the rival tankers could be accused of little more than excessive zeal and poor hearing when reports came in that their barrages were passing through the target and hitting each other, the US Embassy, and the nearby Imperial Palace, with devastating accuracy.

"Shit," Otaku hissed, cutting a botched line of code and pasting a revised binary phrase into the command line. "Forgot to carry the one . . . "

And the monster instantly became utterly, inescapably solid.

The most coherent accounts of the monster's appearance described it as some sort of chimerical centipede, with hundreds of armored, highly articulated limbs that wrought street-level holocausts wherever the creature went, like a Rose Parade of whirling combine threshers.

Skyscrapers toppled against each other in its wake like felled stands of bamboo, their foundations whittled away as if by colossal Weed Eaters. The business end of the creature was a burly, almost humanoid thorax with a deadly array of wildly scything meat cleavers for arms. For a head, it had only a blunt, lobsterish battering ram festooned with hosts of compound camera eyes, and a freaky crown of trembling downlink dishes, radomes, and antennae, like the collected receiving arrays of the NSA and KGB, stuffed into its face.

The indestructible apparition seemed to frolic through Tokyo with the blind fury of a tsunami on two hundred dancing feet, but the civil defense authorities watching the city's transit grid saw an insidious plan taking shape behind the chaos.

As the monster rampaged through the city, it surgically cut off all bridges, subway routes, and highways along the Sumida River, severing central Tokyo from the eastern suburbs, and moving north, chopping down monorails along the narrow trash-chute of the Kanda River.

Even as Otaku's giant centipede raged through the city, it shrank, but not from the puny onslaught of the Self Defense and NATO forces. The behemoth was an Internet Worm made flesh, an apparition of pure data cast in a candy coating of wantonly destructive matter. And it was dismantling itself, shedding boxcar-sized segments of its serpentine body that in turn disintegrated into streams of data radiation that made gross matter thrum like overclocked chipsets, and hordes of giant spiders that spread throughout the island it had created out of central Tokyo, repairing damage and weaving webs of carbon-steel around the leaning skyscrapers of Akasaka, knitting them together to reinforce them against an imminent quake not even the doom-obsessed engineers of the city could have predicted.

———

Wracked with a pain like a thousand periods, Mariko cried out and shattered her cocoon.

Sure, she should feel exultation and curiosity to discover what she had become, but mostly, she just felt shame. The whole day had been a surprise final exam in degradation.

Getting dropped off at school by your shit-eater father's mistress was humiliating. Freaking out in class was lethal. Turning into some kind of giant amoeba and eating everyone in your path? Priceless.

And so, when she crept out of the crater of her rebirth in the parking garage behind Shibuya Station, Mariko did not give a shit what she looked like. Her awesome wings spreading to dry in the sun, radiant scales throwing off showers of holographic rainbows when she launched herself effortlessly into the air, all of it – totally boring.

But it got interesting fast.

Mariko took to the air, and immediately was cut down by the vibra-katana of Mega-Ronin 2, the new and improved defender of Tokyo. The crackling blade only grazed her, but its disruptor field rebooted her brain, grounding her but good. Well, her job was done, then, but the robot kept trying to cut her head off.

She only breathed on the stupid thing, and melted its knees as it charged her. Collapsing on its overloaded katana, the giant mecha-samurai cut its own head off, but kept trying to get up and spaz out on her again.

Fed up with the robot's retarded shit, Mariko flapped her wings and climbed to the top of the marine layer to survey the city.

On the smoky eastern horizon, a colossal buzzsaw chewed a southwesterly course through Akasaka's black glass towers and mowing through the shopper's purgatory of the Ginza, oblivious to carpet-bombing jets and irate giant moths. She noted with dismay that her home and the shit-eater's offices lay just inside the forty-square kilometer island isolated by the shrinking centipede's unchecked swath of destruction.

It wasn't like she could go home, even if she wanted to. Not like this.

The monster turned northeast to disable the Hibiya train line. Directly in its path, Mariko noted with a fiery squeak of panic, lay the corporate headquarters of Sanrio.

The monster was more than welcome to step on her school and the shit-eater's mistress, but she'd be damned if she'd let it fuck with Hello Kitty.

————

Millions of eyewitnesses described the epic battle that followed between the flying savior of Tokyo and the city-killing centipede. Thousands of hours of video from cameras, cellphones, and webcams made every one of them a liar.

Not a single conclusive image of any kind of monster would ever be recovered or extracted from the Tokyo Otaku Event, except for the spotty coverage of the rampaging dragon that NHK identified as the Prime Minister's academically unserious and somewhat homely daughter. The damage seems to appear spontaneously around her, as if shockwaves from her temper tantrum are spreading to slice the heart of the city free of its setting.

According to the most reliable eyewitnesses, exactly fifteen minutes and fourteen seconds after it materialized, the Tokyo Otaku Event vanished. Witnesses reported a brief vacuum when it disintegrated into clouds of civic-minded giant spiders which immediately leapt to work repairing the damage – but from there, they diverged into a variety of scenarios, from Mega-Ronin 2 beheading the monster with its sword, to the people bringing it down and ripping it apart with their bare hands until it imploded back to its home dimension.

————

Five seconds later, it appeared in London.

In the guise of a fire-breathing, hundred-headed eel, it crushed and cremated all bridges over the Thames, then turned its gnarly gnashing lamprey-mouths on the West End, vomiting napalm death with uncanny precision on banks, media outlets, and private military contractors.

Again, cameras captured only spontaneous wave attacks of panicked civilians who seemed to shiver the air and the helpless city to bits around them, and the vibrating, ballistic waves of giant spiders, spilling off the empty epicenter of the action to repair the damage. When it imploded out of existence three minutes later, shell-shocked crowds almost seemed to repent of the monster they'd created and become, but then someone preached that the monster was revenge for the rejection of England's traditional fish and chips as the national dish, and the rioting began afresh.

Thirteen breathless seconds later, it came to Moscow.

It looked like Stalin. It flattened the kleptocratic Duma and hurled Lenin's Tomb into orbit, then lobbed fistfuls of moldering Soviet public works across eleven time zones at strategic targets in the plush offices, dachas and barracks of Russia's robber-barons. It tried to eat Putin, and almost kept him down. The President was left alone, nonplussed and naked when the gargantuan phantom of communism dematerialized from the eye of the maelstrom it created, leaving legions of giant spiders to gift-wrap the Kremlin.

It struck San Francisco at 4:20pm PDT, so it was, like, gone, before anyone noticed.

Wherever they materialized, Otaku's phantom kaiju were only the thin end of the bulldozer. Underfoot, the real threat seeped like bacteria into the wounds the giant monsters inflicted: cadres of kamikaze hackers, armed with mainframes, laser projectors, truckloads of highly virulent nanotechnology and portable *karaoke*.

While the spiders toiled overhead, the *bosozoku* gangs dumped the nanomites into the sewers, and waited around, sniffing glue and belting out Motörhead tunes until the gestating city throbbed and incorporated them into its mad self-improvement campaign. Out of thousands of tons of garbage and raw sewage and even the pipes themselves, the mites forged the mighty thews of a living god amid the infrastructure of the city center.

Unseen, they spread and assimilated every communications system, every computer, every unproductive scrap of biomass, to form a new, vital body out of the old one; and out of the stink of their shit and the drone of their dreams, they conjured the sleeping soul of the city, coaxed it into that uneasy, unborn body, and goosed it up the ass with a psychochemical hot poker.

And the world, already braced for some unspeakable new menace for well over three exhausting cable news cycles, collectively shit itself.

————

When the wheel began to turn on the hatch of Ike's cockpit, Commander Corben took cover behind a bulkhead and drew his sidearm.

No new alert had sounded to drown out the systems failure claxons since Ike went back to nature.

Ike calmly watched the perimeter of the minefield, glancing every so often at the clutch of leathery speckled eggs under its – *her?* – flanks. Each egg was about the size of a minivan.

Beyond coming up with a betting pool and a lot of rotten jokes, Mission Control had been no help at all.

So, when the tiny assassin with the jet pack skulked into the cockpit, Corben was overjoyed. Here, thank God, was a problem he could lick with his own fists. He wanted to hug the little man, and he did, with chopping blows to the nose, throat, and solar plexus.

Gagging on his own blood, the intruder staggered back into the milky daylight streaming through the open hatch.

Corben was stunned. Dr. Otaku himself lurched at him, spitting blood, inscrutable black goggles telescoping out in alarm. His pipestem arms and childlike hands, so adept at perverting the miracles of nature, could barely hold the huge old Kraut pistol they tried to lift off the deck.

The dying doctor squeezed off a single wild shot before he keeled over. Had he lived a moment longer, he might have stopped his own bullet, which rattled round the cockpit for almost a full second before it hit Commander Corben in the armpit, grazing his left lung and flattening against his shoulder blade to lodge in the intracostal muscles of his back.

Corben kicked the scientist a couple times. No escape pod launched out of his head; no miniature emulemurs chewed their way out of the corpse to wreak bloody postmortem revenge. It just lay there, being dead.

He would have expected something, after all that trouble.

Corben rang Mission Control to give them the good news, but they put him on hold.

––––––––

"Anyone who thought Tokyo's real estate market could go no higher was eating humble pie with a side of crow today . . . " The bullshit news copy practically wrote itself. But this time, it literally made the monster stronger.

Fueled by the inexhaustible flood of computer-modeled, expert-vetted bullshit about its birth, the new entity that awakened beneath the center of Tokyo did not rise to destroy the city. It *was* the city, as much as the streets and buildings and helpless salarymen trapped in its legions of skyscrapers. When it awakened, the city center itself, ten square miles of the most expensive real estate on earth, including the Imperial Palace, the stock market, and the address of every major technological and financial entity in Japan, stood up.

Tired of rebuilding after an endless barrage of kaiju attacks, Tokyo's metamorphosis was the only sensible response: become a monster.

On millions of arachnid legs, the city detached itself from surviving streets, subway and monorail lines and then, to the shock of the world, it floated.

And then it flew.

Like everything for which the Japanese became renowned as innovators, it was assembled from parts built elsewhere, fiendishly practical, and not nearly as hard as they made it look.

Once the spiders had done away with the pesky Self Defense forces, they devoured thousands of tons of heavy, rigid concrete and secreted light carbon-steel webbing, replacing much of the rigid, dead weight of the city's infrastructure with a flexible, living skeleton.

The subway tunnels and parking garages were filled with membranous organs which, when inflated with hydrogen separated from the air by nanomite factories, became the nacelles of an enormous dirigible, wrapped in the musculature of something that one might describe as a giant jellyfish, if it were not flying, and didn't have the global headquarters of Sony on its back.

Venting a firewall of methane, the dyspeptic monster-city took to the skies like a plastic shopping bag in an updraft, sweeping aside a torrent of spy drones, news choppers, and the beleaguered dragon-crane protector of Tokyo, who set down alone in the vast cavity left by the city's awakening.

In the sky, the newborn monster-city seemed to drift, weightless as a cloud. Flailing bio-steel tentacles like the supports of a suspension bridge trailed miles behind the city. They radiated enormous arcs of raw electricity, which leapt out at news choppers and disabled passing fighter jets, much as the trailing stingers of a man o' war paralyze its prey.

What the fuck was she supposed to protect now?

––––––––

Tokyo floated out over the Bay, raining waste and suicides as it passed over a nakedly envious Chiba City. It followed the coastline south, like a hurricane, but its rainfall was not destructive, except for those who stood in its way. A rain of revolution, it conscripted everything it fell upon, in the factories, warehouses and fish hatcheries of Yokohama, for every droplet was impregnated with millions of greedy, highly motivated nanomites, which in turn manufactured spiders out of any raw materials they found. Within minutes, Otaku's spiders set up shop turning the Japanese coastline into a slave state of the flying city of Tokyo.

The monster-city had all but devoured or taken over everything of use around its former resting place, before it made a statement to the press.

The city spoke simultaneously over every terrestrial broadcast frequency, every satellite feed and PA system on earth, in the sonorous, gravitas-laced voice of a notable American actor who had long moonlighted doing commercials for Royal Dragon Sake. "I AM ZAIBATSU," it said. "YOU CANNOT DEFEAT MY PRODUCTIVITY."

The media attempted to commandeer the interview, but the UN Field Commander cut them off to demand a chance to negotiate for the release of the 1.3 million hostages inside Zaibatsu.

The monster-city laughed. "I HAVE NO HOSTAGES. THESE ARE THE CELLS OF MY BLOOD, WHICH FLOWS WHEN I AM ATTACKED. THESE ARE THE CELLS OF MY BRAIN, WHICH REMEMBER AND PREDICT, AND DREAM OF SUPERIOR PRODUCTS AND ENTERTAINMENTS FOR A NEWLY REVITALIZED WORLD MARKET."

It went on like this until they stopped trying to reason with it. There was no question of lobbing missiles at a populated megalopolis, no matter that its ragged borders were festooned with vast flytrap mouths, spastic radioactive anuses, and satellite dish-sized compound eyes.

"We won't negotiate with monsters," the UN field commander bravely stated for the record, but no one was listening.

"ZAIBATSU 1 WELCOMES OUR BROTHERS AND SISTERS," said the giant flying city-jellyfish, and released its grip on the global network.

———

Still stumbling to contextualize the event that had explained itself on their channels only moments before, the talking heads were ill-prepared for the plague of virtual deities hatching and rampaging across the web in search of host city-bodies, or the holocaust of awakening cities that swept the globe over the next twenty-four hours.

Moscow took swift action to stop its own transformation. Having once been the symbolic head of a monolithic monstrosity, the kleptocratic capital could not accept rebirth as a literal monster. A fire-bombing to make Dresden look like a child's EZ-Bake Oven reduced the Kremlin to ashes before the tomb of communism could rise up as a gargantuan spider-bear.

China fared even worse. For some reason the party elite refused to dignify with an explanation, the viral attack could not activate any of its centrally planned, stiflingly dull cities. Despite having more than the critical mass of human density and infrastructure in Beijing, Hong Kong, and a dozen other cities, the roving spirits of Dr. Otaku's unborn Zaibatsus balked at infusing any of their offered cities. When faced with the failure of drastic measures like building a city entirely out of the old Olympic complex and living and dead workers fused with several metric tons of meat glue failed, the last Communist superpower began building an army of giant robots to protect itself. They were still busily churning them out when the Mega-Yeti came.

Mariko flunked Western Conspiracies in grade school, but she doubted that the mile-tall golden behemoth was really the animated monastery of Shangri-La, the lair of the Illuminated Masters who secretly control the world. And yet the monster that trampled the Great Wall and left a Grand Canyon-sized swath of destruction en route to Beijing did indeed resemble a shaggy, fire-eyed, triple-tusked yeti made of living, molten gold, and the pagodas on its head and shoulders were teeming with hundreds of laughing, saffron-robed monks.

————

How overwhelming is the sight of a city at night, the combined work and worth of millions of humans reborn as a neon beast-god sleeping uneasily in the miasmic cocoon of its own pollution?

And how mind-boggling to witness titanic monsters striding through such cities, laying waste to all in their path, to forever bear the burden of sharing the world with titans?

How much more insane, when the cities themselves awaken, arise and walk upon the land, suddenly elevated and animated into a colossal tortoise, or floating overhead like a swimmer of alien seas? To witness the passage of a living city, its rainbow-scaled electric exoskeleton mocking the perpetual blackouts below, the question becomes not how to defeat the monster cities, but how to prevent, postpone, or control their worship as gods.

———————

Back on Otaku Island, one man had not given up the fight, though he was crippled, yet again, by the failure of his manned kaiju. He nervously thumbed the eject button, knowing that to do so would dump him on a hostile island rife with monsters, or out in a hostile sea rife with pissed-off corporate mercs whose checks probably just bounced.

"Ike is, uh— Well, he's not really a . . . "

"I figured that out when he started laying eggs! But why is this happening, now . . . "

"Well, it's . . . more complicated than that . . . Wes, she wasn't grown from scratch. You know that would've taken years. But they're working wonders with gene therapy, now, just little bugs. Catch a flu, and you're off to the races, you know?"

"What is it? Tell me later! For now, just tell me how to shut it off—"

"You need to know this now, Wes. She was a volunteer. Her lawyer vouched for her sanity. She was distraught, but she wanted to do something for her country—"

Wes suddenly smelled shit. "No . . . no, she wouldn't . . . and you couldn't . . . "

"She didn't want Steve's sacrifice to be in vain."

Ice filled his stomach. "She was fucking flipped out before her husband became America's Other White Meat. You let her—"

"She practically forced us. She demanded that we treat her right away, and that you be assigned to pilot her."

Corben looked around for a bag to throw up in.

"Her mind was wiped, of course. She can't possibly respond in any way. We gutted her forebrain to make room for the targeting opticals. Those eagle eyes really soak up a lot of neural bandwidth—"

"Why are you telling me this, now, Control?"

"Because we were in a hurry, and, um . . . well, the President wants you to know he's counting on you to do the right and honorable thing . . . "

"What is the right and honorable thing?"

"The eggs are fertile, Wes. And we're pretty damn certain that they're yours."

As with every disturbing new trend in America, San Francisco was first.

Mariko flew low over the city, weaving among the intertwined spines of the skyscrapers. The spiders had done their work more thoroughly than in Tokyo, and were only just retreating or withering into empty husks in the streets. In the Transamerica Pyramid alone, she saw thousands and thousands of faces, watching as blandly as if they were on an elevator, as the city of San Francisco awakened, and found its feet. The skyscrapers of the financial district quivered on the gnarled, colossal shell made of the rewired raw materials of the hills beneath their foundations, while a spade-shaped head the size of a stadium reared up out of the waterfront slime, blinked a million eyes, and bellowed a sonorous foghorn roar that shattered bay windows and knocked over bongs from Sausalito to Petaluma.

Crawling clumsily into the sea on hundreds of battleship-sized paddle-limbs, the megalopolitan sea turtle was twelve miles long. Ahead of the leviathan, the earth subsided and crumbled, water, oil, and gas lines erupting under its feet, sending it sliding into the sea.

The waves off its flanks swamped the San Francisco Bay like a fat man's bathtub, flooding Oakland and Berkeley. The leading towers on its shell drew near to smashing into the middle span of the Golden Gate Bridge, when swarms of spiders leapt out from the Pyramid to dismantle the bridge like Lego blocks. So many movies had dreamed of this moment, yet when it came, the fall of the bridge was a lame anticlimax; the spiders didn't drop a screw as they took apart the span and the adjoining towers, and returned with the famous deep bronze hardware to their nests, as the Brobdingnagian city-turtle sailed majestically out onto the open sea.

The awesome sight of the new Zaibatsu's towers adrift on the Pacific, bejeweled in light and sheathed in a fiber-optic corona of glistering holograms, inspired new apocalyptic faiths in dozens of schizophrenics, which quickly became mainstream cults with hordes of celebrity adherents.

Missile attacks were countermanded at the last instant, when the first electronic shockwave of the monster San Francisco's awakening was unleashed: millions of cellphone calls, texts, and mails from the human hostages inside its web of skyscrapers.

They were not prisoners. They were not afraid. They were employees. And they were very busy, so please stop calling them at work . . .

Deep within the Zaibatsu's bowels, an arsenal of deadly weapons was churned out and deployed by the living city's most fearsome weapon – its lawyers.

Within minutes of the city's awakening, the UN, the United States Supreme Court, the WTO, and every media organization in the world were bombarded with faxes outlining the unique legal status of the sovereign corporate entity formerly known as the city of San Francisco. All real property within city limits had been appropriated into the newly incorporated being; claimants were free to fight the grab in international court, but it would be days, if not weeks, before companies like Sony and Honda recovered from having their whole legal and bureaucratic systems, to say nothing for the Nikkei Stock Index itself, defect and sue them.

The President sat on his hands until San Francisco was safely in international waters before he dared to fulfill the wildest dreams of his heartland constituency, and pushed the button. But by then, of course, it was much too late. SAC/NORAD's mainframe computers disregarded the launch orders, locked down the command centers in the Pentagon and at Cheyenne Mountain, and filled them with nerve gas, all while blasting the Weathergirls' "It's Raining Men" in the President's ear over the secure hot line.

Mariko settled down in yet another empty crater, and pondered her impossible task.

The Zaibatsus had wreaked uncounted damage on the world in a long weekend, and utterly destroyed its communications, commerce, and economic systems.

Far from stamping out these institutions, however, the Zaibatsus had claimed full ownership and control of their daughter corporations' assets and legal status. In most developed nations, international corporations had lobbied for and received "personhood," a status equal to any private citizen, albeit one with thousands of bodies, hundreds of houses, fleets of vehicles, and armadas of lawyers to enforce patents, contracts, and options.

Building on this legal precedent, the Zaibatsus were working relentlessly to rebuild the economy in their own image. They found it very easy to do, because the remaining 99.9 percent of the real estate and population was still starving in darkness, and the monsters owned everything needed to rebuild.

It could take forever to kick all their asses. Like, she'd be in her twenties—

Somewhere, deep inside Mariko's pearl-scaled, serpentine magnificence, her Hello Kitty satellite phone meowed.

Her mercurial mind, still that of a bright, ADHD tweener several days off her meds, flicked from deep despair to insolent pique.

Her father was always bugging her, ever since Mom got incinerated at the catastrophic christening of Mecha-Ronin 1, and now that he'd lost his job, and she had become a mystical kaiju guardian of all the empty craters of earth's dead cities, he seemed to want to try to be her dad again.

He'd decided not to go back to Japan, and had taken a cushy gig golfing with the rich Americans in their walled enclaves back east. He'd pined for his beloved Shinjuku waterworks for all of a week, before he discovered New Jersey. He'd already bought a controlling interest in a sewage treatment plant in Newark for pocket Yen, but he still found time to meddle in her business.

As she unfurled her wings and whipped tornados of debris with her takeoff, she saw clusters of survivors bearing flower garlands and food offerings to the mighty (*too-late, too-small*) celestial dragon.

The bowls were full of Colonel Steve's Freedom Meat. The vat-grown clone-flesh of the dead American kaiju was marketed to instill rugged American patriotism into the basic brain functions and even DNA, but she could not look at the gibbering, three-toed mutants bowing to worship her (*morbidly obese, clad only in shredded American flags, covered in tumors gnarled with fetal GI Joe faces barking malignant orders*) without wondering about the side effects.

Merciful to a fault, Mariko circled back and roasted the crypto-fascist freaks with her napalm breath, and found their flash-blackened flesh far tastier than the tainted crap they tried to feed her.

Mariko climbed into the jet stream and broke the sound barrier so she wouldn't have to listen to the meowing phone in her gut.

———

Once, Wes Corben flew planes. He was good at it, but not as good as his friend, Steve, who volunteered for a top secret project that left him a seventy-foot vegetable. They trained Corben to "pilot" Steve, and together, they made the world safe for democracy. Until a conniving Nipponese cocksucker unleashed a diabolical communist monster that perverted everything it touched, including his beloved friend, the most expensive fighting vehicle in Pentagon spending history.

But Steve was only flesh and blood. And so was his wife, and Steve's wife was hard to refuse—

Steve's last words stung him, all over again. *"Why can't you stop fucking my wife, Wes?"*

Corben stroked the polished bone bulkhead of the cockpit. "I wish you would have told me, Laura."

With that, he holstered his own pistol and picked up Otaku's Mauser. If it looked like he was killed in the line of duty, he wouldn't forfeit his insurance.

Holding Otaku's tiny hands in his own around the trigger. Corben put the barrel to his temple. Maybe this was a mistake. This gun didn't weigh half as much as it should, and the bullet in his back hurt less than a mosquito bite.

Aw, why should everything be painful? he thought, and pulled the trigger.

Nothing.

He put it in his mouth and pulled it again.

Both times, the gun went off with a deafening report, but he felt little more than a burning in his mouth, as if he'd swallowed bees. It wasn't even a fucking prop gun, like the kind stupid action stars were always offing themselves with.

Suspicious, he broke out the magazine and popped the bullets.

They were transparent cylinders of a wax-silicon gelatin that vaporized when the gun was fired. A tiny microdot-sized dart in the bullet was the only active projectile. Corben had swallowed two of them, and had one in his back.

Then he looked at one under a microscope.

The darts were coated with a syrupy solution seeded with microscopic frogmen, sea monkeys with spear-guns, nets, and prop-driven gadgets to tow them around inside Corben's bloodstream.

Horrified, Corben turned up the magnification.

The nano-divers were all identical: the same tiger-stripe wetsuits, telescoping goggles and long, flowing white hair, but they seemed to be at odds about who was in charge. As he watched, the nano-frogmen attacked each other as viciously as wolverine sperm in a fertile uterus, severing each other's air hoses and puncturing tanks so the tiny bodies piled up before his very eyes.

"That's what happens when you look at them under a hot lamp, you idiot!"

"Oh God, what now?" Instantly, Corben deduced who and where the speaker was, and reflexively attacked the enemy.

He punched himself in the head.

If you've ever tried and failed to shoot yourself while trapped inside the monstrous head of your ex-girlfriend/best friend's widow, you know how hard it can be to think clearly under such circumstances, and are free to judge.

"My nano-frogmen have installed my wetware mainframe in your brainstem. Did you think I would foolishly attack you alone, hoping to be killed? When have the proud Nipponese people ever thrown their lives away in suicidal futility? Ha, that's a rhetorical, Yankee devil! In any case—"

"Shut up. I'm still going to kill myself."

"Fine, fine, let me help you. Just do nothing . . . act naturally for about another . . . what, thirty seconds?" The miniaturized Otaku bickered with his clones in the sub-basement of Corben's brain, all of which Corben was as unable to understand as he was unable to tune it out.

The cockpit radio squealed and triggered the subsonic buzzer in his spine, which must be what the tiny Otakus were trying to hotwire. If they could download his consciousness into his brain, they'd control Ike, the most powerful kaiju in the NATO arsenal . . .

Fine . . .

"Let him sit on these fucking eggs."

"What's that? What the hell's going on down there, Wes? We've been trying to reach you—"

"I've been right here," Corben muttered.

"Seattle is walking, Wes . . . It's a giant wooden Indian, and it says it's gonna crush every white man who ever said his name aloud . . . "

Corben bit his lip. "Figures."

"TOTALLY AWESOME!! Chief Seattle, avenging the genocide of Nippon's barbaric redskinned cousins. Your big-eyed white ape masters will shit themselves when they see what Los Angeles becomes . . . And Mexico City . . . "

"Tell me more," Corben whispered. If only his head were bugged to relay Otaku's ranting directly to the Pentagon. The buzzer in his temporal lobe was only designed to give him a fatal epileptic seizure, if he broke mission protocol. (And it had an mp3 player.)

"They're fighting for Manhattan," babbled Mission Control, "but it's dug in . . . gonna nuke it – at least, um, uptown – but they know they're too late . . . What the hell are you doing, over there, Wes?"

"*Flip him the bird, gaijin puppet!*" Otaku howled in his brain. "*No, a Nazi salute! Pick your nose and eat it! What the hell is wrong with this piece of shit?*"

Corben cut the connection. "We need to go home."

"*Hell yes! It's working! Go home to your imperialist masters and stomp them into the Stone Age! Go— Fuck, it's not . . . Maybe you should try shooting yourself again.*"

Corben felt no pressing urge to do anything but piss, smoke some opium, and retreat into catatonia, as soon as possible – but he was out of rations, and almost eager to descend into the hell a laughing yellow devil had once again trapped him.

"Here's the plan, douchebag," Corben said. "If you don't want me to get a blood transfusion or take a nap on a tanning bed—"

"*Face, honky! I have leukemia in a can—*"

"Where's my halogen flashlight?"

"*Okay, back off! Dr. Otaku is a reasonable entity. I'm all ears, cracker.*"

"We'll go back to the States, and I'll get you transplanted into the first sumo wrestler we come across, if you take care of this thing for me."

"*Take care of what, white devil?*"

"Them," he said, pointing at the monitor.

All at once, the eggs hatched.

"*I would be honored*," said Godfather Otaku.

The Behemoth
Jonathan Wood

———

Now:

Ankle deep in water, my Mech stumbles. I try to correct, overcook it. Massive, clumsy, the machine goes down on one knee. Around me, flat-bottomed fishing boats are swamped, sink with viscous gurgles. Gulls shriek angrily, billow around the Mech's knees.

I try to stand. Try to get my Mech to stand. In the cockpit it's hard to discern where my body ends, where the Mech's begins. Overwhelming reams of data push into my consciousnesses, try to push me out.

Around me, water stretches off in every direction. The Shallow Sea. I search for reference points, for reasons to be here.

Get up. Get moving. You can do this.

Do what again?

Before: A memory, already fading

The day Lila won the lottery, I vomited for almost half an hour.

I was in our bathroom, hunkered over white porcelain. She stood outside the door, tried to talk me down. That she was comforting me just made everything worse.

The lottery has been a fact of life since before I was born. It's just the way things are. The lottery is needed to select the Proxies. The proxies are needed to keep pilots safe from their Mech's operating systems. And the Mechs are needed by everyone. They keep us all safe. The loss of every memory in the proxy's head is just the price we pay. That's the undeniable truth. That got me through rehab: I am a pilot; I am needed; I save people.

My stomach was empty. I stared at its contents swirling in the bowl before me. Like my whole life floating, excised and ugly. And where there had been food, now there was just rage. I stormed out of the bathroom, snatched the lottery ticket from Lila's hand.

"It'll be OK." She looked small and delicate. After all the strength she'd shown, that little piece of paper had stolen it from her.

I screwed the ticket up, flung it away. She put her hand on my arm. "Don't, Tyler. Just . . . Maybe one won't come this year."

The Leviathans. The goddamn Leviathans.

I could still taste the bile and acid on my tongue. My teeth felt loose in my gums.

"It's bullshit." I couldn't acquiesce. Couldn't just give up. Because screw undeniable facts. Screw everything else. It was her who had got me through, who had stood by me.

"I'm a goddamn pilot," I said. "This doesn't happen to us. I will stop this."

"Tyler . . . "

I shook my head. "I'm a pilot," I told her. "If I go into a fight, I win."

Back further: a memory almost lost

I remember the first time I saw a Leviathan. I was standing on Chicago's seawall. They built it back in 2050 once they realized that Lake Michigan wasn't going to go back to its old shoreline. That was just before all the great lakes, joined up, became the Shallow Sea, swallowed everything north of the Carolinas. It had been standing thirty years or so by the time I stood upon it. I was eight. I remember that clearly enough.

The Leviathans had been coming down from the north for about ten years at that point, but this was the furthest south anyone had ever reported one.

When the poles melted the Leviathans had been . . . What? Waiting? Sleeping? I dream about that sometimes. Vast and subterranean, waiting for their cages of ice to melt away, for us to screw up enough so that they could come forth once more.

They'd ripped the shit out of Canada. A flotilla of refugee boats was tied up beneath where I stood. Families hunkered on decks, watching, working out if they should run.

The Mechs we had back then were for shit. The Leviathan had already ripped through three of them – jaws slicing armor, body crushing engines. I doubt it even noticed the pilots it consumed.

Chicago had its own Mech. The Behemoth. Its pilot, William Connor, had been doing the talk show rounds. He'd been going on about how he was going to be the one to stop it. No one believed him. The camera had done a close-up of Connor's eyes. Connor didn't believe it either.

That was why I was there. I wasn't meant to be. My parents had strictly forbidden it. They were busy prepping an emergency shelter for when the Leviathan ripped through Chicago and killed everyone dumb enough to stand up on the wall. But I had to see. I had to see Connor fight. So did half of Chicago. We all went to the seawall to see if he would save us or let us die.

Standing there, I was amazed at how small six hundred feet of steel built around a nuclear core could look.

It was the crowd's murmur that revealed the Leviathan to me. The fins of the beast slicing towards the Mech. Connor took a step. The spray was a white corona around the Behemoth's foot.

Then it began. If I had held my hand out in front of my face it would have seemed they were dancing in my palm. I remember it now as if I was standing on the Mech's shoulder.

The Leviathan reared up, eel-slick body whipping around and around its mechanical foe. A casual flexing of muscle that cracked foot-thick steel sheets and sent weapons spilling in explosive rain. Its massive head looked too big for its body. A heavy, under-slung jaw, a bony crest behind the eyes. Small, half-formed legs scrabbled at the Mech, claws carving through hydraulics.

The Behemoth's arms were pinned at its side. Missiles detonated at point blank range did more damage to machine than monster.

But then, and the how of it is lost to me now, Connor got an arm free. He swung it like a piledriver into Leviathan's right eye. The force of the creature's scream almost knocked me off the wall.

Connor swung again. The Leviathan's jaw hung loose. And for a moment we actually had hope.

Then the Leviathan's tail whipped out of the water, a hideous tumor of spikes and claws. It smashed into the Mech's arm, tore it free of its mooring. The Mech tottered, maimed, lopsided. The whole weight of the Leviathan was on it now.

It staggered, fell. The Leviathan wrapped sinuous coils around the Mech's chest. Metal folded like paper.

And then the explosion. A spot of bleach dropped onto the horizon, spreading, obliterating. The force of it driving the water in a wall towards us, exposing the seabed in the moment before the shockwave hit and bowled me over.

I lay on my back as a mushroom cloud rose into the sky.

Later

They figured out what had happened by the time they held the state funeral. Connor had sabotaged the failsafe mechanisms on his Mech's nuclear core. Transformed the machine into a walking tactical nuke. Then the fight started and the core had no cooling, no gyrostabilization. It was only a matter of time before it went critical. And when it had blown, fifty percent of the Leviathan's midriff had turned to meat paste.

Connor had even survived the initial blast. The Mech's auto-eject system. Radiation sickness did for him two days later, though.

And even though he was a corpse, even though they had to close the coffin because the sight of him was so awful, from that moment on I knew that I was going to be exactly like William Connor.

More recently, but mistier, barely grasped:

I pushed through shouting crowd around the city council halls. They weren't calling Lila's name so I didn't care. I crashed through doors, stormed down corridors, the crumpled lottery ticket in my balled fist. A skinny secretary with a skinnier mustache was the only one who had the nerve to tell me, "It's a closed-door meeting." He flinched out the way before I could shoulder check him.

Marburg, the spineless shit of a mayor I voted for, stood at the middle of a long conference table. He looked up at me. His cheeks went white.

"The hell is this?" My flung lottery ticket bounced off his starched shirt.

He licked his lips, flicked his eyes around the crowd. He knew exactly what it was. Still, he took the time to unfold it.

"I . . . " he started, pretending to read. "I am so sorry, Tyler." Another eye flick. Scared, I'd have bought, but he'd have to have try a hell of a lot harder to sell sorry.

"Look," said a large, puffy man, "this is a closed-door—"

I am not a big man. You do not need to be a big man when you fight in a two-hundred-ton suit of armor fueled by a nuclear reactor. You also do not need to be a big man to know the part of the neck to strike so that the ligaments in the first vertebrae snap, the hindbrain is crushed, and a man dies before he hits the floor. My gaze fell on the councilman and reminded him of this. His voice dried up.

"You," I pointed at Marburg. "Your piece of shit nephew." No one knows this story is true for sure. Except everyone knows. "You got him out of the lottery."

I scanned the room, spotted familiar faces. My finger picked them out.

"Your son-in-law's cousin."

"Your grandkid's best friend."

"The daughter of that janitor you were screwing."

I went round the room. I indicted them for their sins. Because everyone knows the lottery is a fact of life except these people. And I thought I was one of these people. The fights I'd won for them. I was their goddamn champion.

"It's Lila," I implored them. "It's my wife."

Adam Grant stood up. The one man in the room I respected. My old commanding officer. One of Connor's compatriots. A man I wanted to emulate. Right up until that moment.

"Tyler," he said. He pulled the ticket from the mayor's sweaty hand. "This . . . " He examined the paper, looked back at me. " . . . is unfortunate."

His voice galvanized the room. Postures shifted. And that was it. That was my reply. I could beat them all to a pulp but there was no bend in Grant's voice. Behind the fear there was steel. I've seen fights like that. The ones where the clear favorite lies beaten and bloody because the little guy refused to just lie down and take his beating. Behind the bluster and the fear, that was this room. My fists would mean nothing, in the end. I needed words and connections. And I'd cast those aside years ago.

A memory within a memory. Some distant nested thing:

My fist smashed into the Leviathan's mouth. It mewled, twisted away but my other fist grabbed it by the scruff of the neck. Snug in the Mech's cockpit the proxies filtered the raw data from the pressure sensors, translated it into something thick and satisfying in my fingertips.

Skin gave way. Blood gushed. The Leviathan tried to wrap its tail around my Mech's leg. I sent a knee into its midriff, brought it to the floor. Monstrous ribs cracked. The Leviathan smashed its tail uselessly in the water. My fist broke its teeth.

"You come to my town? My city? You think you can devour my friends?" I worked the Mech's fingers into the flesh beneath the base of the Leviathan's cracked skull. I thought of William Connor. Of the adoration of the people.

The Leviathan's head ripped free. I stood, waved my trophy, and hollered.

The shout echoed emptily around the cockpit. The proxies, my only companions – their consciousnesses as battered by the Mech's sensory inputs as the Leviathan was by my fists – didn't say a word.

A short while later, one memory running into another:

The technicians unstrapped me from the seat, unplugged the electrodes. The Mech left me sensation by sensation. My body became my own.

I couldn't stop shaking. My first Leviathan. I annihilated it. People were patting me on the back, telling me how goddamn good I was. But I already knew. I *knew*. It was how deities felt. I didn't need the Mech to have my head scrape the clouds.

I didn't pay attention to the proxies until I was in the elevator going down. Adam Grant was there, unwrapping a cigar for me. I glanced back at the technicians manning the gurneys.

The proxies lay there, all sharing the same expression: bewilderment, mild horror, as if trying to remember what exactly they'd given up.

They wouldn't remember. Everything from before their unplugging was gone. The human mind can't take the raw input of the Mech's sensors. It's too much to process. Once someone has been a proxy, who they were before is expunged. Their memories wiped. The propaganda fliers call it a rebirth.

A technician dabbed blood from a proxy's dripping nose.

Adam Grant saw my brow crease. "Don't worry about them," he said. "They'll be taken care of."

And proxies *are* necessary. If a pilot was exposed to the live feed from a Mech he would forget how to fight, why he was fighting. The Leviathans would tear him apart. And then they'd do the same to the city.

The proxies are necessary.

They're taken care of.

That night. I'm sure it was that night. The memories run into each other:

Lila stroked my arm. "I still can't believe it." She was wide-eyed, city lights reflecting in her pupils. "You did it."

I half-laughed. "You didn't think I could do it?"

She half-grimaces, half-smiles. "That's not what I meant. Of course I believed. But then . . . There's a difference between believing and actually seeing."

"So it was a religious experience?" I was cocksure, still too full of myself.

She kissed me. Her lips warm against mine. Her arms slipping around me. When it was over she pulled away. "I've honestly never been more scared in my life." In her eyes I saw her own brand of fearless honesty.

I pulled her to me. Kissed the top of her head. The scent of her filled my nostrils.

"Adam Grant wants me to go out and celebrate tonight," I said.

"You deserve it."

I shook my head, kissed her again. "I want to stay with you."

She smiled. Big and broad, and it felt good to have put that smile on her face. Almost as good as tearing the Leviathan apart.

Almost.

We nestled into each other, talked. I wish I could remember the words, that the sweetness could linger.

But then . . . We were lying down, her head snug against me. Then, she lifted it, a look of sudden sadness on her face.

"What about the proxies with you? They were OK, weren't they? I heard something on the news about some protest groups, and . . . God, it was awful some of the things they were saying."

That was it, I think. Maybe. The first bit of grit.

"They take care of them." I shrugged, wanting to move on.

"What did they do to them?"

Another shrug. "I don't know. They were on gurneys. They wheeled them away."

"Gurneys?"

The moment was shattering around me. It made me unfairly angry. It was my moment. Not the proxies. I sat up, she half fell off my chest, sat up beside me. "I don't know. One had a nosebleed. I guess they were taking them to the hospital."

"A nosebleed? What was wrong with him?"

"How the hell should I know? It was a nosebleed. Everyone has nosebleeds."

"So why do you think they were going to the hospital?" She looked like she was on the verge of tears.

That angered me more. That she cared so much when I had cared so little.

"I don't know. I just said it. They're just proxies."

She looked at me, blinked, as if trying to see clearly. "Just proxies?"

Dammit.

"That's not what I meant."

We stood there looking at each other. Both angry now. Both wishing we weren't.

"It's been a difficult day," she said. "Maybe we should . . . bed . . . rest." She shrugged.

But I still remembered the thunder of adrenaline – of being a *champion* – in my blood. "Actually, I think I might take Adam up on his offer."

I turned away from her.

The memory fades. Another comes up. Was it still that night? Or another? A memory so familiar it's worn a groove in my mind. Something repeated over, over, over so all that's left is one homogenous whole:

You think, by now, we'd have invented something more glamorous.

In the nightclub bathroom, I bent over the white porcelain of the sink. I pinched off one nostril, inhaled the line of white powder.

And then . . . just once? Just many times? Was this even me?

"Jesus, look at the state of him."

I don't remember who said it. It was hard to concentrate on things like that. My attention jumping from shining object to shining object. The straps on the pilot's seat. A pretty technician's face. The beeping of a cockpit dial. The desire to punch that man right in his eye.

"Screw you, you pen-pushing prick. I'll kick its ass." No idea who I was yelling at.

"He'll be fine." Was it Adam Grant who said that? Lila? Did I know who was there propping me up even back then?

"Jesus. Just strap him in."

I don't even remember the proxies I had fighting those Leviathans. They were there to stop the Mech from pushing me out of my own skull, and I'd already done the job. Some chemical substitute of me that ripped and kicked and split skulls.

I remember reaching my fist down one Leviathan's throat, turning its head inside out. I remember stomping, stomping, stomping one into paste on the seabed. I remember them quoting how much damage the waves I made did to the seawall. I don't remember caring. The crowd still cheered. For every crash there was another high.

I loved fighting monsters while I was high. Truth be told, I miss it now, even after all the rehab and the therapy. I don't do it any more. But I miss it.

More recently again. This is important. I want to get this right:

Adam Grant caught up with me in the council hall lobby.

"Jesus, Tyler." He shook his head. "That was not the smart play. You have to understand the situation."

I cocked my head. "Really?" I asked him. "What the hell do you think I don't understand about them scrubbing my wife's memory clean? About her not knowing who I am? What part am I missing, Adam?"

"Jesus." He shook his head again. Looked out at the crowd surrounding the building. I thought I could see the word "Lottery" on a placard. "Not here," Grant said. He dragged me to a bar.

"It's over." He was intense over a tumbler of whiskey. "The party is done. No more free drinks. No more getting people out of the lottery."

I felt the urge to punch him again. Add to his scars. "You're telling me that if Marburg's daughter gets a ticket, he won't get her out of it?"

"I'm telling you that if he does there will be riots. There'll be a damn revolution. The lottery . . . the proxies . . . it's a damn mess. There's too many people who don't remember the world we're fighting for any more." The creases in his brow deepened. He glanced at the back of the crowd, still visible through the glass in the bar's door. I looked too. They did not seem like happy people.

"The council have to appease the mob, Tyler. They've drunk too deep from the well, and now they need to make a sacrifice to fill it back up again."

And then I saw. There in that shitty little bar. It wasn't random chance. That ticket had been signed and sealed and addressed to Lila. They'd decided to do this to me.

I realized then the fight I was in.

"You have to help me. You have remind them of everything I've done for them."

"Remind them?" Incredulity broke his stony façade. "Your show just now reminded them all of why they picked you. You've pissed off too many people. And you know as well as I do that you fight for shit now you're clean."

A dirty truth. An ugly truth. But a truth. It left me with nothing else to say.

"Hey," he offered the thinnest of smiles. "If you're lucky one won't come this year. She'll be clear of it."

"They come every year."

He nodded. "Go home, Tyler," he said. "Enjoy the time you have left together."

Drifting back in time again. To one memory that still shines bright:

I'm a teenager. Fourteen years old. Sitting in the bleachers while the football team runs its drills. Watching old Bruce Lee flats and trying to memorize the moves.

"Hey."

She startled me. I almost dropped the screen. I spun around.

"Sorry." She was half laughing, half nervous. Embarrassed maybe.

The new girl. Transferred in. I didn't know from where. Kind of pretty. Dark hair that she wore long, and a red shirt she wore loose.

"Studying?" she asked.

"Erm . . ." I wasn't sure why she was talking to me, not sure what angle to take. "Kind of."

She shrugged, sat down on the row of chairs behind me. "I feel so behind. You guys are all so far ahead of my old school. It's all so different here."

She looked more frustrated than anything else. Her honesty disarmed me. I ventured some of my own.

"I wasn't studying, like, school stuff," I say. I show her the screen.

"Who's that?"

"His name's Bruce Lee. He was, like, this actor back a hundred years ago or so. That's why it's a flat. But he was amazing. It's all wires and special effects now, but back then it was real. He did all this stuff." I let the flat play for a minute. She watched without comment, without judgment.

"You like fighting?" she asked when I paused it.

"Erm . . ." I hesitated. This was where conversations usually went wrong. "Kind of," I said.

She nodded. "My dad does thai-jitsu, or something."

"Tae Kwon Do?"

She smiled. "Yeah, that's it."

She was prettier when she smiled. "I do that too," I said. "That and a bunch of others."

"What others?"

I listed them. After the third, she counted off on her fingers. "So," she said from behind eight raised digits. "Kind of?"

I was sheepish, felt some explanation was required. "I want . . . " I almost balked, it was like saying I want to be a movie star, but her eyes didn't let me go. "I want to be a pilot. Of, you know, a Mech and stuff. I want to fight the Leviathans."

I regretted it as soon as I said it. I tried to read the emotions on her face, to work out if she'd laugh at me or walk away.

I didn't expect what she actually did. She asked, "What about the proxies?"

"What about them?" I was off guard, still not seeing the angle.

"It seems sad." She kicked at a pebble perched on the metal seats. "What happens to them. They don't even know what they did to make themselves forget."

That seemed like an irrelevant fact. "We have to fight the Leviathans," I said, "or they'll kill us. We have to have the proxies. It's four memories of everyone's lives." I shrug. It was the simplest of math.

She shrugged. "I guess. It just seems sad."

I didn't know what to say to that. She just sat there next to me. And it was nice actually.

"Hey," I said after a while. "I'm Tyler."

She smiled that pretty smile of hers. "I'm Lila."

Closer. Approaching the now. Trying to hold the pieces together:

Lila was watching TV when I got home from the bar and my talk with Adam Grant, holding her knees to her chest.

"I was worried you weren't coming home."

The drugs. It seemed almost laughable that she was worried about that.

"I'm clean." I sat beside her, leaned in. "You know that."

"This is a lot of stress."

"I'm clean," I promised.

She put a hand on my cheek. "I need you to survive this fight, Tyler. I need you to be there to talk me back to myself."

I ran a hand over her cheek, through her hair, round to rest on the back of her neck. I pressed my forehead to hers. "Don't think like that," I told her. "One might not even come this year."

She let out the smallest, saddest laugh in the world as she pulled away. She pointed to the TV. "One already is."

And after that:

I slipped out of bed when Lila's breathing grew deep and regular. There was one other solution perhaps. Adam's talk about riots and revolution had made me think. I've seen the downtown slums on the news. I've seen the refugees.

I took the car north, close to the seawall. A foot of water swilled around my tires. Everything smelled rotten or worse. Fractured light from neon signs painted the waterlogged streets – logos become abstract and obscure. Street vendors marched around in thigh-high waders. Ragged men stood on floating platforms screaming about the lottery, about the man keeping them all down. Small crowds cheered them on. Deeper in, I watched a man reel out of a bar, drunk, fall into the swill. He emerged with an enormous leech clinging to his cheek. He ripped it away in spray of blood, staggered off.

I couldn't understand how people could live like that. Then I remembered they didn't really have a choice.

I try to keep the thread, keep ahold of my reasons, my history,
but it's gone again, and I'm falling back into older times:

"Tyler?" It was some talkshow host whose name I couldn't remember. "Are you OK?" she asked. She's didn't look concerned.

An audience stared at me. Grinning idiots. Screw them. My high was burning out. I felt like shit.

"I'm fine." Even I could hear that I was slurring. "Can you repeat the question?"

There was a time when I loved this, the attention, the presenter's bated breath. I would talk and talk, and they would love it. Stories of violence. Stories of me saving them all.

This time I just wanted painkillers and a warm bed.

"I was asking about the proxies in your Mech," the presenter asked. "Do you ever talk to them? Or their families?"

There was something in the way she asked it. Accusatory.

"Look," I said, "I didn't come up with the system. I just fight. If you want to have some Leviathan come take a shit on this city, just so everyone can remember it clearly, then that's your priority."

A mass inhalation of breath. The presenter's elegantly plucked eyebrow rose.

"Not a popular opinion," she ventured.

"Oh screw you," I spat. "We all know how this works. We messed up the earth, now we pay the toll. Four memories at a time. You don't want to be a proxy, get on the council and dodge the lottery. You want to be able to sleep at night too, become a pilot. It's worked out for me just fine."

Not an inhalation this time. A hesitation.

There was a time when I loved these things. When audiences cheered me. It was as big a high as the drugs.

Even the drugs didn't do much for me by then.

Then darkness descending, a gaping hole of memory.
And then, on the far side:

Lila woke me. I didn't recognize her at first. Later, when I saw myself in a mirror, I was surprised she recognized me.

"Three days this time," she told me once I'd washed the vomit, and blood, and shit off myself. She didn't cry. She never cried. Just that same frustrated look she'd given me in the bleachers all those years ago.

"It was those assholes on that TV show," I said. I was full of excuses back then.

"You missed a fight, Tyler."

I was at the closet door, hand on a shirt. Something I could wear to my dealers. And that stopped me. The whole system shut down around those words. I tried to form a response. A question. A denial. An excuse.

I had nothing.

"They sent Lowry," she said. I pictured him. Young kid. Scrappy. He was good. He would have fought and won. The city wasn't in ruins. Of course he'd won.

But no thanks to me.

I still wanted to be a pilot. Beneath everything, beneath even the want for the drugs, there has always been that. Ever since I saw Connor's Mech go critical and wipe out the horizon that has been the underlying, undeniable truth of my existence.

"It's time to get clean, Tyler," Lila said. "No more bullshit. No more excuses. Or you'll never pilot again. You get that, right?"

I did. I got clean.

Swimming back to the present. Back to the slums, car parked, water swirling, a lottery ticket in my hand:

I picked a bar at random. The place was crowded, the music loud. People partied with a sense of desperation. Drinking until they could forget that tomorrow was coming – implacable as any sea monster.

I stood in the center of the room. It took a minute before someone recognized me. He stared, pointed. The woman he was with turned and looked. Soon they were all looking.

Apparently I wasn't popular in that bar. Not in many bars, I suspected. I couldn't even blame them.

But I didn't need to be popular. I just needed to be rich.

I held up the ticket.

"How much?" I asked, clear and loud, finally putting all the media training crap they'd sat me through to some use. "How much do I have to pay one of you to take my wife's place on the lottery?"

From the look I got, my popularity wasn't going up.

"Five million," I said. "I'm good for it. Five million and get you and your family out of this life." I nodded at the water currently ruining my socks and shoes.

The room was very quiet. The music had died. Grim faces all around me. Folded arms. The smell of the wooden bar slowly rotting away.

One man, shorter than me, wider though, tattoos up his arms and neck, maybe in his fifties – he walked towards me. A few rumbling paces. "I think you want to get out of here."

"Ten million." Just one greedy soul. Just one. That's all I needed.

"You ain't listening."

"Twenty million." It would leave me with a pittance, I would have to move, but it'd be worth it. "You won't care what you forget with twenty million."

It was the wrong thing to say. Adam Grant had been right. The lottery was a tipping point.

I didn't recognize the signal, but suddenly eight of them rushed me. More than one held a beer bottle in his hand.

I remembered Adam Grant saying I don't fight as well now I'm sober. He was right. Still, I can hold my own.

I ducked the first blow, jabbed a fist up under the guy's jaw, into the soft part of the palate. I spun as I did it, slammed my foot into another man's groin, sent him crashing to the floor. I came out of the spin, slammed my fist into another man's nose, dodged a bottle, clotheslined his friend, then slammed my elbow back into the neck of the idiot trying to sneak up behind me.

Three left. One got in a good blow to my kidneys, sent me to my knees, spitting a curse. Another lined up a blow to my jaw. I snatched his arm, slammed a palm into his elbow, watched the joint snap.

The kidney puncher grabbed me behind the arms. I swung my head back, shattered his nose. Then I crushed his kneecap for good measure.

One left.

But the crowd was not cowed. And I was breathing hard, and my hands hurt, and the pain in my kidney was like a lance of fire. And then they went from one to forty-one.

I got lost in the violence. I took men down with short efficient blows, but for every six or seven I landed, they landed one of their own. A bottle shattered over my skull, blood ran into my eyes. An elbow slammed into my ribs.

I needed to get out. I recognized my actions as a mistake too late. I stopped fighting to win. Started fighting to escape.

It cost me. Two ribs. And I couldn't lift my left arm above my shoulder any more. But I made it out. It took me two blocks before I realized no one was chasing me.

I remember that fight. For a moment the pain in my side makes sense. And then it drifts away again. Just is. Then something else swims up.

After the fight:

Lila fetched a fresh ice pack for my ribs.

"You're an idiot." The way she said it made it sound like a compliment.

"I have to fight," I told her. "It's who I am."

She smiled. "There's no winning this, Tyler. It is what it is. You fight that Leviathan. You bring me home. And I get to meet you again. Fall in love with you again."

I swallowed. "What if you don't?"

She shook her head. "All the shit you've done, I've stuck with you. You really doubt me now?"

She almost managed to make me laugh. The moment passed. "Maybe afterward you'll be smarter," I said.

She kissed me on the forehead. Snuggled in beside me.

They showed the Leviathan on the news that night. It had destroyed three townsteads on its way south. Casualties in the thousands. They said it would be visible from the seawall in two days. They said it might be the biggest in a decade.

They questioned whether I could stop it. For the first time in a long time, I did too.

Almost here. Almost at this moment:

In a vast hangar near the seawall, I stood before my Mech. The Behemoth II – named after Connor's machine. But I had always been safe in the knowledge it outranked its predecessor in every regard. It could tear a Leviathan apart. The original could only explode.

It still demanded the proxies to operate, though. Connor, who thought up a way to win an unfair fight, he couldn't think his way out of that. They all died when his Mech blew.

If I went out there without proxies the sensory overload would wipe out my memory. I would forget to fight. The Leviathan would tear me apart first, then the city.

And then, staring up, up, up at the distant cockpit, almost hidden beyond the curve of the reactor in the machine's chest . . . the faintest stirrings of an idea.

The Behemoth II. The clue was in the name.

All Connor could do was explode.

The Leviathans always initiate the fights. And a walking bomb doesn't need to know how to fight. It just needs to go off.

But would I remember what I was doing for long enough to get clear of the city?

Maybe . . .

I would die. There was that.

But the auto-eject . . . No, Connor died.

But hadn't they improved the radiation seals? Some distant memory of joking with Adam Grant after some tech demo where they talked about it. Not really believing it. Because when would that ever be an issue?

When would any other pilot be that desperate again?

When . . .

Now. Now is exactly when a pilot would be that desperate again.

An elevator ride up to a door in the Mech's midriff marked with a radiation warning. I remember that sign clearly:

The failsafe mechanisms are well designed. There are back-up systems of back-up systems. All are carefully programmed.

They are beyond my understanding. I was not a careful student at school. I was never a jock, never quite a geek, that awkward middle position of being nobody in particular.

But then Lila.

It wasn't a revolution. There was no astonishing makeover. It was simply that being nobody to everybody else didn't matter if I was somebody to her.

Love is a slow creature. It isn't like a Leviathan. There is no sudden violence. Rather it wraps its tendrils around you slowly. By the time you are aware of it, it has already won.

Or maybe I was as slow at grasping the concept of love as I was at understanding the complexities of a programming language.

In the end, I reprogram the machine with a ballpoint hammer. That seems to suffice.

The cockpit. Closer to the now:

Mech's aren't meant to work without proxies. Some inputs require needles pressing deep into muscle. They sample DNA. They demand diversity.

But I remember once – a proxy, an older woman, she had a heart attack on the elevator ride up to cockpit. The Leviathan was already visible. There was no time to call in a back-up.

Adam Grant showed me the trick.

"Give me that damn thing." He'd grabbed the needle from a panicked technician. "DNA is everywhere." He wiped the needle along the crevices of the seat. Dirt, lint, and hair clinging to it. They never really cleaned the cockpits.

Grant rammed the filthy needle into the arm of a proxy already getting input from other sensors. The technician looked appalled.

Grant shrugged. "He's a proxy. He won't remember."

It worked. That proxy took input from two sensors. I don't know what happened to him. Maybe nothing. Maybe he was fine. Maybe the poor bastard died of septic shock.

It was harder jamming the dirty needles into my own flesh. But, I reasoned, it wasn't like I'd remember.

Closer:

They tried to stop me leaving. They sealed the city gates against me. I could hear someone raging through my headset but her voice was overwhelmed by the data pouring into me. Heat readings, pressure sensors, gyrostabilizations, revolutions per minute.

I fired missiles. I felt them leaving my body. I felt the heat of their burning fuel burn inside of me. And worse. I could feel pieces of me leaking out with each projectile. The taste of strawberries carried away in a burst of flame. My father's name. What I'd eaten last night. All the inconsequential minutia that we're made of.

But I had sabotaged a nuclear reactor. I had re-engineered hardwired failsafes. Mere doors and words couldn't stop me. I blew my way out of the city. I marched on, marched out. I went to face my Leviathan.

One final memory:

"What do you think?"

Lila on the doorstep of our apartment. And she had redecorated. Repainted. New furniture. New art on the walls.

They'd not allowed her to go to the rehab facility to pick me up. A driver had dropped me off at the curb. She'd been waiting when the penthouse elevator doors opened. She looked perfect and anxious in equal measures.

I hesitated, trying to work why she was worried. I was the one who should be worried.

But she misread my hesitation, thought I didn't like her work. And I could see how much she had wanted me to like it. But she just nodded and bore it. She didn't bend, didn't break.

All I had done to her. And she thought I was doing it again. But she remained undefeated. All the monsters I had beaten, but she was the one thing I could never conquer. And I loved her for that. So deep and so strong.

"You made it beautiful," I said.

She smiled. The sun banishing clouds. "Good."

Now:

Ankle deep in water, my Mech stumbles. I try to correct, overcook it. Massive, clumsy, the machine goes down on one knee. Around me, flat-bottomed fishing boats are swamped, sink with viscous gurgles. Gulls shriek angrily, billow around the Mech's knees.

Get up. Get moving. You can do this.

Do what again?

I make it to my feet. And for a moment memory bubbles up, surrounds me. For a moment I remember everything. Lila. Grant. The people down in the slums of Chicago. The broken ribs. The sabotaged core at my Mech's heart. I know exactly who I am and exactly why I am here.

Then it's all gone.

Later?

I stand. I wait. I marvel at the world. The water is so beautiful. I wonder how it got there.

Movement on the horizon catches my eye. Something cutting through the water. I stare at it. Red signs flash in the corner of my vision but they are just one more confusing detail in the mass of data piling into my head. I want to ignore them. There is peace in that line of water as it races towards me.

I watch it. The efficient beauty of it. It distracts me from the wrongness in my limbs. From the foreignness of my body.

It is almost on me. I want to see what it is. I am curious.

And then – rearing out of the water – a vast unspooling nightmare of flesh. And God. Oh God.

Peace is gone. I scream, flail. And the wrongness of my limbs can't be ignored now.

Why am I made of metal? Why are my thoughts numbers?

The monstrosity's jaws smash into me, tear pieces from me. I can feel teeth in skin that is not my skin. Coils ensnaring me. Sensors scream in my head. A strangely remote disemboweling of my electronic innards. Reams of my coolant system spilling out onto the ground.

Why am I made of wires and metal? Why am I dying?

Warning sirens split my skull. And heat. A jagged spike of heat in my chest. Building unbearably.

What is wrong with me? Why am I wrong?

Jaws, and claws, and teeth, and scales, and death and crushing and heat and everything caving in caving in and heat *ohgodtheheat Iamgoingto*—

And then the heat in my chest crescendoes, swells, consumes.

Everything is eclipsed. Pain, and heat, and light, and the world, and memory. All reduced to single point and blown away.

Afterward:

A voice. A voice brings me out of the darkness. It repeats the same word over and over. There is something familiar about the word. I grasp at it for a moment, but cannot place it.

Where am I?

Somewhere dark. I am strapped in. Wires cover my body. I work one hand free, pull at them. They come away with small wet sucking noises.

The voice is getting nearer.

How did I get here?

Light bursts into the room. I blink, try to shield my eyes with my free hand.

When I can see again, an open door floods the room with light. It is small, full of smashed screens, cracked dials, and trailing wires. I am strapped into a chair in the middle of it all.

A woman stands in the doorway. Tall. Dark hair worn long. A muddy red shirt worn loose. She stares at me.

"Hello," I say when the silence becomes as strange as everything else about this situation. "Could you please help me?"

The woman starts as if breathed into life that very moment. She crosses the small room, pulls at the straps holding me in place. Halfway through she stops. I look at her face, and I almost believe she is going to cry.

"Are you alright?" I ask. She closes her eyes. When she opens them they are clear. She nods, resumes her work. While she frees my legs I massage life into my arms.

"I'm sorry," I tell her, "but I think I took a bump on the head. I really don't remember where I am."

She nods, frees my legs. She lets me lean on her shoulders as we cross the room's sloping floor.

Then, as we reach the doorway, I stop, stare, gasp. In the distance there is the wreckage of a massive robot lying half drowned in a shallow sea.

The woman grabs my head, pulls it around, studies me carefully.

"Are you alright?" They are the first words she's spoken to me. They are full of concern.

I turn to stare again at the fallen machine. I point. "What is that?"

Her eyes cloud again. She hesitates before she answers. "It was called the Behemoth," she says.

The name rings some deep drowned bell. I try to put a finger on the swirl of emotions. Something is wrong with my memory. Is that what's upsetting me?

The Behemoth. I shudder. "That sounds like the name of a monster."

She nods. "It could be." Then, after a hesitation. "But it was a savior too." She smiles suddenly. And it strikes me that is a very pretty smile. "It could do terrible things, but it was beautiful when it did them." A second smile. "When it fought, it always reminded me of Bruce Lee."

I don't recognize the name. "Who's that?"

Another smile. *Like the sun through clouds*, I think. She lets go of my head, takes my hand instead. "Why don't you come with me," she says, "and let me show you?"

The Kansas Jayhawk vs.
The Midwest Monster Squad
Jeremiah Tolbert

————

> *JOHN QUIÑONES: "Did you ever imagine that you would make it this far, Mr. President?"*
>
> *PRESIDENT POINDEXTER: "John, you would be surprised how often I'm asked this question. Certainly, there was a tongue-in-cheek element to our party in the beginning, but I truly believe in our ideals. To answer your question, I never had any doubts. And does the Christian Bible not say, 'The geeks shall inherit the Earth?' "*
>
> *JOHN QUIÑONES: "I believe it says 'the meek,' Mr. President, but given your success, that may have been a typo."*
>
> *20/20 Interview, December 3rd, 2028*

————

"Big . . . smackdown . . . comin'."

We'd been watching a cheap Taiwanese dino hack-job butt heads with a gigantified gibbon on TV – some territorial battle in a West African country with "New" and "Republic" in the name – when Scooter had run into the room, skidded to a stop between us and the vid-wall, and made his pronouncement.

"Oi, get the fuck out," Toni shouted and tossed a throw pillow at him. This was hardly unusual behavior, seeing as how she believed throw pillows existed solely for that purpose.

I should explain that Toni is my girlfriend, and a "right proper" British gal. Me, I grew up in the wilds of Western Kansas – in an agrarian commune, actually – and if you're wondering why she was with me, you wouldn't be the first. She joked it was the folksy accent, but that was just a dig because my attraction to her was about seventy percent accent, thirty percent hips. I always figured the real reason Toni liked me was because I was the only guy in our BFM chapter that didn't have crippling body odor.

Scooter – he's a big feller in all three dimensions, and that means he never runs unless something momentous is about to happen. He was most wired guy I knew and spent most of his time up in his room chatting with other Daij-heads around the world, so if he pried his ass out of his two-thousand-dollar maglev Aeron, you knew there was something major brewing. Presently, he dodged back and forth on his pudgy legs and tried to catch his breath as Toni continued to pelt him with cushions. A pile deep as his knees had collected at his feet already.

"Spit it out, man," I said. Eventually, we were going to convince him to go with some body-thinners, but his self-esteem was so low that he didn't believe they'd be an improvement.

"Big smackdown comin'." Scooter said again.

Toni rolled her eyes. "Jesus, mate. Ping us with an IM next time."

"No! We need to get on the road!" Scooter said. I'd never seen him so flush with excitement, except the time he scored one of the Big Guy's scales off eBay Japan. "You know how the Missouri Tiger's been marking territory over on our side the border?"

"You think we live in a cave?" Toni took a glance around, smirked, and corrected, "A cave without 'net feeds?"

"No, yeah . . . I mean . . . anyway, it's shaking everything up, just like Kilroy predicted! The Jayhawk's on the move, and monsterologists are tracking the Nebraska Noog – he's headed right this way – and Iowa's Cornfed Carnage is moving in as fast as he can. We're talking the perfect monster storm here, guys, and it's supposed to hit *five miles* north of Overland Park in the next twenty-four hours!"

Toni's eyes were wide and dancing around the room as she took in the news. I'd be lying if I said I wasn't excited myself; it was all I could do to keep from flying out of my seat and hooting like a happy owl. Here was the key to my senior thesis, unrolling a week before the due date. The Jayhawk's moping was creating a low monster pressure system which was drawing in the others like a vacuum. This was a gift from the Daij-Gods. The old Toho Men were smiling down on us.

"Toni, go get the gear!" I said, and she was up the steps before I finished the sentence. Ordinarily, a guy can't just boss his girl around like that (at least not without giving up his nookie privileges), but in this instance I was issuing a direct order as President of the KSU chapter of the Big Fuh-reaking Monster Fan Club, and our charter specifically forbade violent retaliation (thank Heinlein).

I tossed the keys to my van to Scooter. He fumbled and bent over to collect them from the floor, but I was already headed out the door and didn't have time to give him hell. "Warm up the Battle Wagon. I'll raid the pantry."

Scooter giggled. "Pantry raid."

---

poiNd3x+3r roxorz by 1@Nd$1id3. +3ch $+oxorz uP 30 poiN+z. dood!

NYTIMES.COM Headline, November 8th, 2028

Westbound traffic on I-70 was heavy – damn near everyone east of Topeka had decided to take a spur-of-the-moment Rockies vacation. Seeing as how we were headed in the direction from which everyone was fleeing, I caught the occasional "are-you-that-stupid" glance from passing motorists. I just nodded and smiled back.

I tried to get some shut-eye while Toni drove, but she kept joking about swerving into the wrong lane, and I kind of believed she'd do it.

I gave up on sleep and started going over the maps with Scooter. He'd pulled them down onto digiflex pads from the MTC site just before we left. Toni fiddled with the sat-radio until she hit a station that provided regular rampage updates: The Mech Division of the National

Guard was on highest alert readiness; the governors of Missouri and Kansas were on non-stop flights to Washington to accept Daikaiju Act reconstruction checks from President Akira; construction contractors from Des Moines to Denver were drinking heavily in anticipation of new contracts.

"It's a good thing the big guys move so slow," Scooter said. "The MTC estimates this battle will do seven billion in damages. It sure would suck to be at ground zero."

"Anyone still at ground zero right now is already dead or is so bloody stupid they deserve to be," Toni said, passing a rental car full of Japanese tourists with gear I would have died for. Hopefully the tourists would upload their data to the 'net afterwards. I was going to need everything I could find to prove my theory, which concerned using predictive weather modeling as a basis for daikaiju behavior modeling. Creatures their size were not subject to ordinary animal behavior principles, I believed, but were real forces of nature. I figured I could get twenty pages out of it, easy, if things went the way they looked like they would.

I whistled at the red lines painted across the smart map. "Highfill wants primary sources, I'll give him primary sources. He can't give me less than a B with this brewing."

"What was it you needed to pass the class?" Toni asked sweetly.

"At least a B+," I grumbled.

Scooter snerked. "Too much time chasing BFMs," he faux-whispered to Toni.

"Nah, too much time in the sack with me, love." Toni looked back to leer, and the van drifted over onto the wake-up strip. I flushed; I wasn't as comfortable with that kind of talk as she was, me being an innocent farm boy and all.

Scooter shot me a you-lucky-bastard look, and I rolled my eyes. "We need to figure the best vantage point. Did you pull topographies?" He nodded and the map reloaded. We set to examining the landscape, arguing over which bump might provide marginally better views of the battle, and Toni drove on through the night.

The big guy had been sulking down in the southeast corner of the state around Coffeyville when Tiger had made her move. It'd taken a while for the big cat's pheromones to waft south, but as soon as the 'Hawk had caught a whiff, he'd perked right up.

I was most happy about that. I knew the monsters were dumb as a fish (hell, a few of them, like Mississippi Mal, *were* fish), but the three of us had a theory – an anthropomorphic one that would have never flown in Highfill's class: the Jayhawk was *disappointed* with his territory. Scooter's personal belief was that our Jayhawk must have caught a glimpse of Manhattan Island from the BFM labs before being shipped out for release, and had been longing for a real metropolis to stomp ever since.

I wasn't so sure. Sometimes, you just *know* that things are better elsewhere. Grass, fence, other side, etc. Toni, meanwhile, had wagered that Jayhawk had a severe case of blue balls. That was impossible, of course, given we only called it a "he" because it was convenient. The BFMs were gender neutral.

"All this moving around means he's coming out of it," I said. "His funk. I was starting to think he never would."

"You'd be demoralized too if a ten-story tall Tiger laughed at your most powerful attack," Scooter said.

"Face facts, boys. He's a pathetic one, he is," Toni said. "I mean, it's cute that you care so much, but there's no way he can win this."

"Shut up!" "Can too!" Scooter and I said simultaneously. Toni laughed at us.

Truth was, neither Scooter nor I wanted to admit it, but the Jayhawk was lame by most standards. New Jersey had its Devil. Her flame-strike could light up the sky for miles and miles around. Oregon's Sasquatch was so powerful it set off a 4.1 miniquake when it battled the Californian GoldFist with his super-pummel attack!

And what was the Jayhawk's special power? The Sunflower Burst, a theta-radiation blast – which had never worked right, not even in the earlier clones.

In this Jayhawk's first tangle with the Tiger, he'd triggered his Burst too early. He glowed green for a second, but nothing happened. The Tiger had laughed and walked away. *Laughed!* Well, it looked like laughing anyway.

I sighed, and leaned back into the seat. Toni was right; Jayhawk was the worst of underdogs. We might as well have been rooting for the Delaware Credit Beast.

––––––––

Much like the New Republican Party, the Otaku Party (formerly known as the Geek-Nerd Party) began as a joke in a North Western dorm room between party founders F. Darin Fitzgerald and Lewie Brown. Spreading rapidly across the 'net through chat rooms and pop-blogs in the year leading up to the primary season in February of 2016, the party quickly become an in-joke among the nation's youth. It would have remained a joke if not for Generation Z, who had been raised on the magic ingredients of Japanese video-games, comic books, science fiction, and political activism. Generation Z's ideas of a better future were distinctly different . . . and more fun, to say the least.

AHHH, Godzilla! How the Otaku Movement Crushed U.S. Politics Second Edition, 2030.

––––––––

This close to the monster rampage the only traffic we saw was cops. We were speeding but had no worries – the club decals on the Battle Wagon kept them from pulling us over. One swarthy-looking cop even pulled up parallel to the van and gave us the peace sign. It was good to see fellow Otaku serving the public like that.

"There's a lot of visual clutter up here," Scooter said. The area homes were built nearly touching in Tokyo-chic, and they blocked out the view to the east.

Toni pulled over next to a two-story ultra-modern and turned off the car. "That one looks as good as any, yeah?"

I nodded. "Sure. Come on, Scooter. Help me with the ladder."

Toni waited by the van in case the cops came by while we were setting up and mistook us for looters. We'd taken to the rooftops during the Wichita Wreck last year, and the cops were real old-school over there. They'd arrested us and impounded the van for a week while they "checked out" our credentials. Unfortunately, finals had been that week. Scooter's parents almost didn't let him come back in the fall, and Toni had lost her scholarship. Technically, she wasn't supposed to be in the country, but nobody was about to turn a body like that into Immigration.

Up on the roof, we could see the seven or eight other chapters who had set up watch posts in the neighborhood. There were even a few teams set up down below – the only lights that didn't run in neat little lines along the highways.

"Look at those wankers," Toni said, staring through a pair of infospecs. I brought mine up and registered the others' data tags. The Independence chapter was set up less than a mile from ground zero on the roof of a grade school. "Why aren't we down there with them, eh?"

"They're monster chow," Scooter said. "I hope their clone policies are up to date."

I shuddered. I was a little bit old-fashioned when it came to full-body cloning. I'd never died. Scooter neither. Sure, I kept my policy up to date and my backups fresh, but I still believed in a soul. My parents did too, and, well, it's hard to shake those kinds of beliefs. I'm not too sure about Scooter – I think maybe he was just averse to any sort of pain. Toni had died five or six times, chasing Euro-monsters.

"Heh." Toni tilted her head, staring off into space. "Slashdot2 is calling the opposition the 'Midwestern Monster Squad.'"

"That's going to piss off folks back East who think we're part of the 'Plain States,' " I said. "Hey, Scooter. What's the latest tracking info?"

"Jayhawk is seventeen hours out. The Tiger is . . . " Scooter flipped his specs down and scanned. "There! I've highlighted him on your fields." A tiny red speck appeared on the horizon to the north.

"She's in Missouri?"

Toni was mumbling into her subvocal microphone, using it to order info from her specs. "She's coming back from a cattle yard. Impressive little minx! She did fifty grand in damages for a snack."

"Too bad 'Hawk's a vegetarian," Scooter lamented.

"Seventy percent of the state grows corn, wheat, or soybean," I said. "He wouldn't do any refundable damage if he was a meat-eater."

"I guess that's true," Scooter said. "I think I'm going to get some sleep. You guys want the van? I can sleep up here with the instruments if you want."

"You're a saint," Toni said, leering again in my general direction. BFMs always made her hot, for which I thanked Miyazaki, Iwata, and Kurasawa every night.

———————

As Levinson predicted, there was a surplus of human labor during the transition to a post-scarcity economy. Otaku Party founders developed the daikaiju economic stimulus plan to produce demand for labor and raw materials. The gengineered giant beasts, harkening back to the radiation scare films of the 1950s, struck a chord with voters. Two years after President Poindexter's inauguration, New York and New Jersey passed bills authorizing the construction of the first state-funded daikaiju, and other states soon followed. Before the end of Poindexter's first term, the first generation daikaiju were stomping their way to millions in federal funds.

Monster Economics, G. D. Levinson, Richard Tenn, et al.

———————

Sunlight streamed through the van's rear window and burned through my eyelids until I finally gave up pretending to sleep and slipped out to check on Scooter and the gear. I about fell over when I saw the pretty twenty-something with blonde pigtails chatting him up at the foot of the ladder. Oh, no, I thought. *Her.*

"That's so clever," she said, giggling.

Scooter noticed me and waved me over. "Hey Kilroy. I was just telling Lohusa about our theories."

"Oh, 'Lohusa' is it?" I squinted at her. "Hi there. Boy, you're pretty brave to still be around here."

She smiled. "You think?"

"Which chapter are you with now?" I said, not smiling.

"Independence," said Lohusa, whose real name was Allison. "I thought I should come up and deliver the news personally. We're going for a quad-state record today."

I laughed so hard I must have woken up Toni. She groaned something obscene in the van. "What a waste of clone stock," I said. "Shame you have to go and spend your parents' money like that."

"Kilroy—" Scooter stammered and turned red.

Her smile faded and was replaced with a cold glare. "At least we've got the *tanukis* to try. Your chapter's just a bunch of *boushounen*. Well." She looked over to Scooter. "Some of you."

The ground rumbled. All three of us froze. Toni even stumbled out of the van, looking every which way, about to give herself whiplash.

"Tiger," Allison said with a sneer.

"No," I said. "Jayhawk. Tiger's sig is a four-part patter. Jayhawk makes short air hops. Single boom."

Allison blushed. "I hope you kids enjoy the show from the nosebleed section!" She turned and fled downhill.

"Good sig ident, Kilroy," Scooter said. He avoided looking me in the eye.

"Thanks." I should have scolded Scooter for talking to the enemy, but they'd exploited his weakness for somewhat cute women. "What's the status of our friends?"

"Did I hear that right?" Toni asked, pulling up the zipper on her pants. "They're going for a simultaneous distance record on all four?"

"Yeah, I guess so," Scooter said. "Jayhawk is ahead of schedule. You were right about that. He's closing in quicker than we figured. Tiger is holding. And get this: The Noog and the Cornfed Carnage are traveling together. They're headed straight south from Omaha. ETA of six hours."

"What are we going to do while we wait?" Toni asked, sidling up to me with one of her grins.

"You might want to update your backups. We're moving camp in twenty minutes."

"I think I'm rubbing off on him," Toni said to Scooter, laughing.

Toni took the wheel again as Scooter and I conferred on our plan of action. The sat-radio was abuzz with talk of the smackdown. Las Vegas had odds on the Jayhawk sixteen-to-one. "Love, you want me to place a bet for you?"

"Nah," I said. "I can't take sucker money like that." It was a lame attempt at false bravado. The Jayhawk was going to get *creamed*. Even so, he was *our* BFM, and that meant something.

"Do you think this is such a good idea, moving in closer?" Scooter asked.

"Do you want to lose our record?" I countered. "You weren't scared the last time."

"But . . . well . . . Scooter hedged. "He's all riled up now," he finished lamely.

"We have a chance for a four-monster record here," I said.

"This is about that girl, isn't it?" Toni called from the front. "You know her."

"You do?" Scooter looked at Toni, then back at me, curious.

"Let's talk about something else."

"Oh no. I don't think so. An ex-girlfriend?" Toni said.

I nodded reluctantly.

"I guess the break-up didn't happen on good terms?"

"The only reason she's a chaser is to get back at me," I said. I wasn't interested in talking about my past, what there was of it anyway.

"She was kind of cute," Toni said. "She could do better than you though."

"Ha ha."

"What did you do to her?" Scooter asked.

"What?" I pretended to be confused.

"Why does she want to get back at you?" he pressed.

"She talked to you for ten minutes and you're taking her side?" I massaged my temples and closed my eyes. "Forget about it. We need to find a safe place to set up, closer than the Independence team."

Scooter grumbled and turned away to look at the maps. It was just like my ex to get her talons into my best friend like that. What was supposed to be a simple four-BFM smackdown had suddenly gotten complicated. Times like this, I wished I had taken up pocket monster breeding instead.

"My fellow Americans; I believe it is time to stop living in the Twentieth Century. There is no reason for the senseless loss of life that occurs in our country every day. Medical technology has come a long way. We can rebuild you; bigger, faster, stronger! Under my administration, medicine will be free of the shackles of superstition and fear. Regenerative cloning is just the first step. Our goal will be nothing less than the abolishment of death.

"America, I will give you save points.

"Also – bionics are really cool. Cyborgs will get more girls. And ladies, I have two words for you: 'it vibrates.'"

Presidential hopeful Alfred Poindexter, Presidential Debates, 2028.

We parked on Overland Park High's football field and took to the bleachers. It was too soon to guess where the monsters would clash, but we needed some perspective on the situation. Once we'd climbed up high, we spotted him. The colossal blue and red bird was gliding down gracefully from one of his hops. It was a minute before we felt the aftershocks of his landing.

Toni shook her head. "I've been meaning to ask you guys something."

Scooter rigged up the mini-Doppler and flicked at the monitors until they lit up. "What?"

"Don't you think . . . " Toni giggled.

"Think what?" I had nearly shouted that. Scooter flinched away.

"Never*mind*," she said. Oh great. Now she was going to pout.

"OK, fine." I didn't have time for this. "He looks like a chicken. It was the best base stock to match the mascot."

Toni cocked her head and squinted. "Yeah, hey. You're right. I would have never noticed that if you hadn't pointed it out."

Scooter coughed hard. It sounded a little like "dumbass."

I sighed. "Will the gear be safe here?"

He nodded. "They're going to clash a mile north and three miles east, I think. But we're going to need a tarp. Looks like a storm is coming in." Black thunderheads were gathering to the west. Jayhawk was passing by a couple of miles east. He was hopping and gliding faster than I'd ever seen him move. I wasn't sure about Scooter's estimate, but he'd never been wrong before.

"Let's set up and get moving on foot."

Scooter groaned, and Toni did runner stretches. I scanned the horizon with my specs, tracking the Independence team's tags. Already, there was the smell of ash on the wind.

I took a walk down the bleachers to clear my head, but I didn't have much luck.

"You're getting a bit snippy, love." Toni could be quiet when she wasn't running her mouth, and she startled me. I smiled sheepishly.

"Sorry."

"That girl. Allison? What's the story?"

"Do I have to tell you?"

"If you don't, I'm withholding sex for a month. It's your call."

I flopped onto a bench and rubbed my temples. "I told you we dated?"

She nodded. "Stop stalling."

"Okay, okay. Well. I dumped her. Er, stood her up."

"And now you're arch-enemies? How American."

"No, there's more. There was this dance."

"Ooh, I've seen this movie."

"I'm trying to be serious here. I was supposed to take her to the harvest dance. We never talked about it, but it was assumed. Only, the night of the dance, the Texas Twister was rampaging through Amarillo, and it was only a seven-hour drive."

"Pff. Typical. And you didn't even call her to cancel." Toni bit her lip and shook her head, mocking me.

"Yeah, well. She was cheating on me anyway, not that it matters. When I didn't show up, she marched over to my house. I used to have this collection of action figures. She torched them. Even Boba Fett."

"Torched?"

I grimaced. "You could see the bonfire four blocks away. She was arrested for arson, and then resisting arrest. But, you know how small towns are. She got off on community service."

"Don't tell me any of this came as a surprise. A woman scorned, and all that," Toni said.

"It was just a dance. Those action figures were the most important thing I'd ever owned. I still miss them." I hastened to add, "Once in a while, anyway."

Toni rolled her eyes. She was a champion at rolling her eyes; a silver medalist at least. "You are so clueless."

"What! I was going to make it up to her. She didn't have to get all *drastic*." I was annoyed that not even Toni understood the seriousness of Allison's betrayal.

"I'm going to say this once, love. If you ever leave me waiting in a prom dress while you go off to chase BFMs, the nicest bloody thing I will do is set fire to your prized possessions."

I blinked. "You'd wear a prom dress?"

Then she slugged me on the shoulder, and it really hurt. I had a bruise for days, honest.

"Finally, DARPA had been given the license to do in reality what we had been doing on paper since the beginning; create our dreams. Under Poindexter, our budgets quadrupled. The halls of our research facilities rang with laughter that would not have been out of place in a 1950s Sci-Fi movie. It was disturbing at first, but you eventually became accustomed to it. You were too busy trying to perfect a mobile weapons platform or grey-goo nanobot swarm of your own."

Portrait of a Fevered Mind, Emmit Haines, PhD

We waited atop the bleachers and watched the Noog and the Cornfed Carnage come in from the north. The Noog looked lame, kind of like a giant purple booger (actually modeled on the Blob, only they couldn't get the rights to the name) and Carnage was essentially a giant ear of corn atop a writhing mass of tentacles. Silly looking, but both were formidable foes. Noog engulfed anything in its path and Carnage's Rocket Kernel attack could take out a small town.

The National Guard was keeping pace with them in their gleaming gun-metal 'mechs, trying to limit the innocent casualties and helping with evacuations. Some hotshot was pulling in close, drawing fire from Carnage, and peppering him back with anti-BFM rounds. The network feed drones were zipping all around, eating up the footage. Toni was fuming; BFMs were supposed to be left in peace to battle with other BFMs.

"It's the bloody law," she said, and strung together twenty obscenities for good measure. Just then, Carnage *nailed* the hotshot with a volley of missiles and the mech went up in a puff of titanium vapor. That had to hurt so bad the guy's *clone* would feel it. The other Guardsmen drew back quickly.

"That was cool," Scooter whispered, forgetting for a moment that we would be within range of that same attack soon.

"Hey . . . " Toni said. She turned away from the battle towards the east. "Where did Jayhawk go?"

"What?" I searched the horizon myself. He had been less than a mile away a few minutes before. "How did we lose a two-hundred-foot-tall red 'n' blue chicken?"

Scooter scrambled over to the equipment. "I've got nothing."

"Can he teleport now?" Toni asked.

"Not that I know of," I said. The storm front from the west was moving in fast. Some of the rumbling rolling across the plains was actually thunder. It looked as if things would be turbulent in all kinds of ways.

"Okay, let's get moving. I taught Allison everything she knows about BFMs, and if I know her like I think I do, she's going to make her attempt while the BFMs size each other up. That's our chance too."

"Love, do you know the records for the others?"

I shrugged. "Scooter?"

Scooter pulled down his specs and accessed his records. "Carnage: twelve hundred meters. Noog: eight hundred meters. Tiger . . . oh, held by Allison and friends at seven hundred meters. They'll ignore her until after we make a pass." Scooter grinned. "And Jayhawk," he said, beaming, "four hundred meters."

"Right then," Toni said, cracking her knuckles just because the sound irritated me. "I say we go for Carnage first. Then Noog, then Tiger, and then we'll get even closer to the 'Hawk." It annoyed me that she was trying to call the shots, but I'd started thinking about Allison, and that was the kind of thing that had gotten me into trouble with her.

"Okay, sounds like a good plan," I said. "Let's move."

"We still going to do this on foot?" Scooter said, eyes wide. He sighed. "I had better take a power-up then." He retrieved an empty-seeming vial and dermal injector from his belt pouch and socketed it to his neck. It made a soft hissing sound as it injected its contents.

"Little Fast-Twitch to get me going," he said. Already, I could see his arms rippling with the quickly replicating nanites. He was going to be one sore bastard in the morning.

"Got any more?" Toni asked hopefully. He shook his head. "Right then." She turned to me. "Lead away, stud."

———

"A predicted side effect of the BFM economic stimulus project was the financial failure of several entertainment sports leagues. Frankly, there was no way two greasy men pretending to wrestle could compete for viewership with twenty-story tall behemoths doing it for real in lower Manhattan."

Monster Economics, G. D. Levinson, Richard Tenn, et al.

———

The BFMs hadn't done much damage yet, just what we called locomotive damage. Once the fighting started, Overland Park would basically cease to exist. Not that many would miss it.

We hopped a fence and jogged double-time on a path toward Carnage. My specs were set to auto-track the Independence team. Their team waited half a mile off, and still the Jayhawk was nowhere to be seen. Allison's plan had to be the reverse of ours. One way or another, someone was going to lose a record tonight.

"How far do you want to push it on Carnage?" Scooter asked between wheezes.

"Minus fifty," I said.

"Minus hundred?" Toni gave me puppy-dog eyes.

"Let's not get greedy," I said. "We don't keep the records if we turn chow."

"Fine then," she growled. "Race you there!" And she was off. Just then, the Independence team headed for the Tiger. Odd.

Scooter was too out of breath to talk, even with the boosters, so he sent me a spec-to-spec instant message.

Scooter: *What are they doing?*

Kilroy: *No idea. Try to keep up. Toni's going wild again.*

Scooter: *Screw that. Carnage isn't going anywhere.*

He was right. The BFMs were in position and they'd started checking one another out. Tiger was sniffing the air and growling a sound like twin 747s taking off. The Noog was shivering all over, twitching and sending off pseudopods to taste the air. Carnage's tentacles were digging in for the fight, kicking up a fog of dirt that rolled out into the streets. I was starting to lose sight of Toni, so I sped up.

Toni: *You don't think 'Hawk turned and ran, do you?*

Kilroy: *Nah. He's around here somewhere. I can feel it.*

Just then, I felt a familiar boom and shake from the direction of the Tiger. In the dust, it was hard to make out, but a flash of lightning illuminated the sky . . . just as a certain blue and red bird landed *right* on top of the Tiger.

"Holy shit!" shouted Scooter.

"Woot!" Toni was doing a dance in the debris just ahead of me. "He was using the storm for cover. Cheeky bugger!"

A burst of pride welled up inside me, and the tears I had to rub away weren't just because of the mess in the air. The Independence team had veered off from Tiger and Jayhawk well outside their record ranges and had turned toward Noog.

The ground rolled and I nearly lost balance. Behind me, Scooter bit it, and Toni just barely managed to stay upright.

"What the hell was that?" I asked. The dust had kicked up and I couldn't see anything more than ten meters in front of me.

"Tiger's down!" Scooter shouted. "The 'Hawk walloped him good."

"Shit! Where's he going now?" The air overhead filled with explosions. Popcorn, magnified five hundred times. "Never mind, I can guess! Turn back, now!"

We stumbled and staggered through the falling debris. Rain began to fall hard then, and thunder mixed with the sound of Carnage's missiles going off. None of them sounded like a hit, however. *Go boy, go,* was my only thought as we high-tailed it back south.

Kilroy: *Regroup on the bleachers. Copy?*

Scooter pinged back a second later. I waited for Toni's. Nothing. I kept running.

Kilroy: *Scooter, have you seen Toni?*

Scooter: *No. Y?*

"Shit."

I scanned for her tag, but the dust was so thick that the satellites had lost all tag signals. The explosions suddenly grew quiet. The only sound was that of debris and rain drops falling down all around, and klaxons, far off toward K.C. I nearly choked on all the smoke hanging in the air.

Kilroy: *I'm going to go back and look for her.*

Scooter: *It's your cloning. Good luck!!*

I stumbled through the rubble field, calling out Toni's name, and listening for movement overhead. For whatever reason, the BFM battle had stalled out, thank Toho.

"Toni!"

"Over here," a faint voice answered. I ran as fast as I could on the uneven terrain. I nearly knocked Allison over.

"Shit," I started to say, just before she clocked me. I don't think I got the word out before I hit the ground.

"'Genetic engineering will save the world by creating super-productive crops and eliminating diseases.' We've all heard these promises before, but I ask that you open your minds to other possibilities of this wonderful science. My opponent would claim that we shouldn't play God, that we should 'play it safe.' Nonsense. The great Sid Meier taught us that playing God is totally sweet."

Presidential hopeful Alfred Poindexter, Presidential Debates, 2028.

Funny thing was, Toni found *me*. She'd taken cover from heavy fallout in a Denny's and her signal had been muted out by all the bounce. I came to while she was pulling me out of the dust-fog.

"You need to stop trying to match Scooter's eating habits," she said, huffing.

"What the hell happened?" Then it came back to me. "She knocked me out!"

"And took three of the records too. But you still have the 'Hawk," she said, anticipating my question before it reached my lips.

"Who won?"

"Shouldn't you be saying things like, 'How much blood have I lost?' and 'Thanks for saving my superstitious ass instead of leaving me to be cloned?'"

"Well—"

She laughed. "That was hypothetical."

"Stop torturing me," I groaned. I felt light-headed, like maybe I *had* lost some blood. "Who won?"

"Your boy, of course. You sure know how to pick them, love."

"The Jayhawk's absence from the northern part of the state clearly created the equivalent of a low pressure system, drawing monster aggression from neighboring territories. The resulting clash of BFMs resulted in an exponential increase in damage, similar to the effect caused by a super-storm. Naguchi's hurricane damage predictive modeling deserves serious consideration as a tool for estimated future BFM damages. In conclusion, I would like to add that the Jayhawk totally kicked ass and the smackdown was the most awesome thing I have ever seen."

A New Method for BFM Behavior Modelling, *Senior Thesis by Kilroy Ackors*

I had an e-mail from Allison waiting while I recovered. She flaunted her new records, each one-hundred meters under the previous, and generously informed me that we were "even now." I had something to say about that, but it would have to wait until later.

I managed to get my paper in on time, and Highfill grudgingly gave me a B+. Come graduation, I actually had to make plans. I hadn't really been figuring on making it out of school that year.

Toni convinced Scooter and I that we needed to look for work in Europe. The EU has been adopting the BFM economic stimulus plan too, and they were going to need experienced monster chasers. I've got some applications out over the 'net. I'm looking forward to seeing Transylvanian MegaBat's drain attack. They say it's unstoppable! Yeah, well, we'll see about that when they send the Jayhawk on tour like the Governor is talking!

But enough about us. You want to know what happened to the Jayhawk.

The running theory is that he wasn't sulking all that time. He'd planned the whole thing as an *ambush*. The gene jockeys are scanning his make-up looking for an explanation for his unusual cunning. Whatever the case, he's got the run of four states for about six months while the others recoup on Monster Island. He made a mess of St. Louis and the MTC forecasts "some stormy weather" for Des Moines next week. I always knew he had it in him!

While I've been convalescing, I've watched every video I could find of the now famous battle. There was just no contest. Jayhawk used wing-beats to deflect Carnage's missiles back at him. Too bad Iowa's gene jockeys never thought to proof the Carnage against his own attack. That took him out, and Jayhawk went straight for Noog, didn't even stop to gloat over the slaughter.

For a few minutes, it looked like the Noog was going to get the best of our boy. The Noog had him engulfed from beak to toe, and then there was a flash of light inside, and the Noog disintegrated.

The problem with the Jayhawk's Sunflower Burst wasn't the power.

It was range. I can't tell you much about what happened after that. Every time I watch the replays, I get a little misty-eyed. I'm man enough to admit it.

As I filed this report with you folks at Club HQ, he's on the main feeds right now. He's developed a strut, and it's a real crowd pleaser. Merchandising rights are through the roof. And I know giant mutated chickens don't have lips . . .

But I swear that big chicken is *smiling*.

The Black Orophant
Daniel Braum

—————

From the bones and loam in a remote elephant graveyard the Black Orophant rose as prophesized.

Young Edu, just five years old and one thousand pounds, his new white tusks gleaming in the light of the half moon, watched as another star fell from the sky. A shiver ran from the tip of his trunk to the soft padded bottom of his round foot. As his mother had told him, and as her mother had told her before, the Black Orophant would come to lead the herds when the stars forming the little gazelle in the sky cried fire.

It was the hour of need, Kula, the herd's matriarch, had said. Strange creatures, demons she called them, fell from the sky and crawled from the caldera lakes. She had dispatched Edu and the other young ones to the graveyards to await a sign from the Black Orophant.

Standing in the circular clearing in the trees among the curved rib cages and bleached bones half buried in the ground, Edu heard a sound – a powerful trumpet both dark and hopeful, the battle call of no elephant, yet the cry of every elephant at once. Then a rustling in the darkness. Slow, sure steps. Above, another silent shooting star crossed the sky. A hulking form, more massive than the largest male Edu had ever seen, stepped out of the dark into moonlight. Tall as a giraffe's shoulder; skin, tusks, toes, and eyes black as a starless sky; the Black Orophant, paying no mind to Edu, nudged the bones at the edge of the clearing.

Where dark tusk touched bone, a faint shimmer lingered. Flesh sprang from dust, forming muscle and skin around the ancient skeletons. In the shadows where the great black one first emerged, rough elephantine forms now lumbered.

The Black Orophant turned to Edu. A line of bumpy ridges like a croc's ran up his back and covered his head. Edu felt a tingle of fear in his spine. The Black Orophant smelt heavily of mulch and kind of like an elephant, but the elephants behind him smelt like nothing at all and this made Edu afraid.

"Do not fear us, though the time to be afraid has come," the Black Orophant said in a combination of gesture, breath, and grunts.

"Who are they?" Edu asked, stepping away. Locusts crawled all over the Orophant's back.

"They are the elders of herds long gone."

"That doesn't make sense," Edu said.

"You are going to see much that doesn't make sense, young one, but I need you to go now. Tell the herds the Black Orophant has come. Azilba, Lord of Lions, must know I am here and our plan is ready. Tell her that Phoenix is coming. I must stay to wake the rest of our warriors from slumber."

Edu doubted Azilba of the Lions could be real, but here he stood in the presence of the Black Orophant and his herd. Things didn't make sense, but still he felt inspired.

The Black Orophant touched a bleached bone with his long curved tusks and another elephant rose as Edu ran from the graveyard.

———

Edu did not stop running as the morning sun burned away the night and the long shadows of the banyan trees that peppered the dry plains. A group of impala trotted towards a nearby watering hole. Small songbirds flitted by, filling the air with color and music.

"It would be nice to stop by the water," he thought, but he was almost to where the herd waited – the edge of their world, near the south barrier wall. It towered over the tallest of trees, an endless monolith of gray and white stretching out to the horizon.

Kula had taught him that men built the barrier wall long ago to keep the herds and the animals isolated and safe.

Edu stopped in his tracks. The breeze brought the smell of men and something oily to him. The impala bounded away, white undersides of their flicking tails revealed in warning. The songbirds went silent and landed in the trees. A tall white stork in the upper branches of a big banyan turned its slender neck, looking for danger. Edu walked up a grassy hill to look.

A creature like none he had seen before scuttled across the brush towards the stork resting in the big tree. Its diamond-shaped, crystalline body, perched atop four spidery legs, turned and rotated while it crawled. Gracefully balanced on the tapered tips of its legs, it moved over the dry brush and low grass noiselessly.

"This must be a demon," Edu thought. "This is what Kula warned me of."

The stork took flight with a disturbed squawk. Edu noticed three men hiding behind the big tree. In Edu's language there were no words for the body armor, big weapons, and power cells the men wore; but as he gazed upon them burdened with these things, he knew they looked bigger and bulkier than other men.

The demon neared the tree. Dozens of thin, fleshy, almost transparent tendrils snaked out of its crystalline body and waved in the air. Red flashes of light arced from their sparking tips, and sped to the banyan tree. The red light passed through the thick trunks as if they weren't there and engulfed the crouching men behind in flame. They slumped forward against the tree and the wind carried the stink of burnt flesh to Edu.

From behind him, another group of men appeared and fired on the demon. Crackling blue beams, like focused lightning, arced over Edu and bounced off the demon's crystal body. Electricity crackled down its long legs, dissipating into the ground.

Legs planted, it rotated the top of its body. Red light raced at Edu from its tendril tips. He braced for pain but felt nothing as the beams passed through him. The firing from the men stopped and he turned to look. Gray and red smoke wafted from their slumped-over, lifeless forms.

"The red fire only hurts men. It passes right through trees and elephants," Edu thought.

The spidery demon scuttled halfway up the hill, then stopped a few yards from Edu. It had no eyes he could see, but he felt it watched him. The Black Orophant's voice echoed in Edu's head along with Kula's. "The time of need has come." Seeing this creature for himself gave meaning to the warning.

More writhing tendrils slithered from the crystalline body. Edu's heart raced and his bowels emptied. He looked around, but there was nowhere to run. Too young to vie for a bride, Edu had never fought before, only jousts and sparring with his brothers and cousins. Red beams filled the air again, passing through him harmlessly. The demon rotated its top, tendrils waving frantically. Edu decided he would fight. He would not fight for the fallen men, but for his herd and the message he carried for the Black Orophant.

The demon lifted its front leg menacingly. Not waiting for an attack, not thinking, Edu rushed down the hill. His tusk hit the crystal body with a scraping sound. I'm too young to have a broken tusk, he thought.

The raised arm's sharp tip sliced his side. Pain spread across his skin like dried cracking mud worn too long.

Edu backed up and charged again. His forehead hit solid crystal and his vision blurred. Sliding his head down the demon's angled side, his tusk found the opening where its leg protruded from its body. Edu pushed and his tusk pierced something soft.

The demon scuttled back and raised another leg. Knowing the sharp leg tips would find him, Edu charged but stopped just before impact. As the demon raked him, Edu snaked his trunk around its back leg and pulled. The thing toppled. Tendrils flayed madly, and red fire sprayed in a frightening but harmless display. Edu's tusk found the soft spot again. He jerked his head harder, this time ripping something. As Edu stomped on the fallen thing, the last tendril sputtered red sparks and slumped to the ground. Heart racing, Edu shuffled away.

An hour later, Edu moved into the outskirts of the circle of big males guarding the herd. Comforted by the closeness of so many elephants, many his uncles and cousins, he allowed himself to trumpet a wailing cry.

His young cousins followed in a line as he passed the young, the old, and his many aunts on his way to see Kula, the herd's matriarch. Kula stood tall and regal, surrounded by old wise females. She watched him approach, her eyes bright and alert.

Edu grunted and traced patterns in the air with his tusks which meant, "The Black Orophant has appeared. I bring his message to the herd."

More elephants gathered round. Edu's aunt Zheve touched her trunk to the scrapes in his side.

"Edu, is this true? There is no time for foolishness," the old matriarch said.

"I saw him myself," Edu responded. "I promised I would tell the herds and Azilba of the Lions that he is here and that Phoenix is coming."

"This is the Black Orophant's message? Azilba is just a tale to scare young elephants so they will not stray when lions are about."

Before Edu could answer, a big male sounded a warning call. Edu's young cousins moved close to their aunts' sides. Even they could smell lions on the wind.

Bellies low to the ground, a dozen lions crawled down the hill Edu had passed only moments earlier. The big males trumpeted again, asking for instruction from their matriarch. Old Kula's eyes looked to the sky, as she did when contemplating where to graze next or the proper time to visit the graveyards.

"Let the lions come," Kula responded.

The males trumpeted again, this time in protest.

"Let the lions come to me."

The big males parted, opening an unobstructed path to Kula. The lions cautiously entered the circle, heads moving back and forth, watchful eyes scanning elephant feet and the fascinated faces of the tusk-less little ones.

A lioness strained her head up to look into Kula's eyes.

"Azilba, Lord of Lions, wishes your permission to speak with the herds of the Black Orophant," she said, a guttural sound rolling from her throat.

"How is it that I can understand you? Elephants cannot speak with lions."

"It is the hour of need," the lioness responded. "Times are strange, strange things gather behind the barrier wall, and Azilba has returned to us."

High on the monolithic, gray barrier wall, Edu watched a spider thing wave its tentacles and scuttle away.

"If Azilba is real, I will see her," Kula said.

The lioness roared and as if on cue hundreds of lionesses crested the hill.

One big cat stood in front the rest, golden fur glowing in the hot orange sun.

Walking unguarded and holding her belly high, the big cat strode into the circle of elephants.

"Azilba," the lioness proclaimed. She and the other lioness backed up and stood side by side with the encircling elephants as Azilba approached.

Azilba, tall as a zebra, humbly stopped before Kula. Her eyes met Edu's.

"This little one is brave and a great benefit to your herd," Azilba said, gesturing to Edu with her head. "I watched him kill a demon unaided."

"You know of these things?" Kula asked.

Azilba turned her head to the barrier wall. Kula looked just in time to see another spidery form disappear over the wall.

"They come from the fires falling from in the sky. The world outside the barrier wall has changed. They hunt the last of men, as men once hunted us."

"How can a lion know this?" Kula asked.

"I am more than lion just as the Black Orophant is more than elephant."

This seemed to satisfy Kula, but not Edu.

"Isn't the enemy of men our friend?" Edu asked.

"You are brave," Azilba said, "but remember you are little and the world is big. Since the building of the barrier wall, men have let the herds and the prides flourish in peace. They were close to fulfilling their duty as caretakers."

Kula glanced sternly at Edu.

"His reluctance is important to address," Azilba continued. "The barrier wall encloses much of the land that was once called Africa by the men. Outside men once lived in homes they called cities. " She nodded to a shimmering area of air high above the trees.

"There, that is where the last of the cities will appear. It is a city called Phoenix from a place once known as Arizona. War with the demons reduced the world of men and their homes to rubble. With great effort, the men ripped one of their cities from the earth, and hid in time to escape destruction."

Edu did not fully understand the meaning of "time". He knew he would grow tall and his tusks would lengthen and curve. That was time.

"Why do they fight? Surely they do not vie for each other's brides?" Edu asked.

"I do not know how the war started, young one, but perhaps men roused the demon's anger. Perhaps the demons pursue the men for reasons that make no sense. Now it is only important how this will end."

"I still don't see why we should fight for them," Kula said.

"You remember much in the tales and stories you pass to your children. Would you have your children know men only in stories like the rhino and the leopard?"

Kula shuffled in place. Edu recognized the thoughtful faraway look in her eyes.

"You owe men nothing," Azilba said. "But would you make the same mistakes as they almost did and stand idle in the face of a threat when you could render aid?"

Kula squinted and looked at the shimmering air. "How can this be? Men don't have wings. These cities don't just appear. Do they?"

"The Black Orophant said I would see things that don't make sense," Edu said.

"The young one is right. What matters now is that the demons have come for the city. We must be ready to help the Black Orophant in the coming battle."

"The Black Orophant will fight for the men?" Kula asked.

"The Black Orophant will fight, but more importantly he has something for the men of Phoenix. We fight so he may reach them." Azilba turned to Edu. "You have seen the Orophant, young one. What did he tell you?"

The herd, Kula, and the thirteen lions listened raptly. A shiver ran through Edu as he lifted his trunk to speak.

"The Black Orophant said tell the herds that he has returned. He is coming with an army of the great leaders of the herds of old."

Edu looked at the silent and confused herd. His young cousin squeezed through two pairs of legs to get closer. He understood their confusion. When an elephant fell, they became bones and nothing more. He would not believe otherwise had he not seen the Black Orophant raising the fallen himself. Edu knew the herd wanted more, but he had no more to tell.

"What would the Black Orophant say now?" Edu thought. He looked at Azilba. She seemed to know what he would say next.

"My herd," Edu trumpeted, "the Black Orophant says not to fear."

Azilba and the lions retreated to defensive positions in the low hills. She instructed Kula and the herds to do the same.

Above the trees, the shimmering air where Phoenix was to appear spat a bolt of blue electricity. It fizzled to the ground like lightning as the sky exploded into a cloud of blue sparks. Edu watched Kula flick her tail nervously and he felt afraid.

"It is Phoenix," Edu grunted. "Just as Azilba told us."

The city of Phoenix, an island of rock and dirt, floated over the hills. A mass of buildings, tall silver shapes – crowded each other right to the edge. The overwhelming smell of exhaust and the waste of men wafted to the animals waiting below.

As if responding to a silent cue, the demons on the wall moved to attack. Hundreds of red beams of light raced to Phoenix but were absorbed by a shimmering blue cloud that surrounded the city at the last instant before they hit. Edu saw the city through the cloud, though hazily, like a reflection in water.

A smaller cloud of sparking blue appeared on the barrier wall. Six bulky men emerged, almost identical to the ones Edu saw earlier except they were silver from head to toe.

The demons atop the wall attacked. Their red beams reflected off the silver men as they fired back. A spray of blue from a silver man's weapon hit a demon and for an instant it froze, then it moved backwards in a perfect mirror of its approach, before simply vanishing.

Hundreds of demons crowded the wall, surrounding the men holding them off with their strange showers of blue. Then one demon floated up, like a spiderling caught in the wind and began to drift towards Phoenix. Three more, then hundreds of the spidery things silently took to the air, floating slowly but steadily to the city. Bolts of blue arced from the floating piece of Arizona, pushing the attackers backward before they vanished.

"Phoenix's weapons send them back in time," Azilba said to Edu.

"I don't understand."

"Just lead the young ones away if the fighting gets too rough."

Edu shuddered as another wave of demons took to the air. As the demons floated up, a crack spread across the wall beneath them. The crack opened into a fiery hole, collapsing the area where the silver men stood.

Spider demons and men alike toppled and were crushed by rubble. As the dust began to settle, a giant shape emerged from the smoking hole. It resembled a spider demon, but ten times as large. Shiny protrusions jutted from its segmented body.

Explosions tore more holes in the barrier wall and more giants crawled through. Azilba raced up and down the line of lions and elephants, calming and readying them. Edu feared they were too greatly outnumbered.

A giant spider thing spat an orange fireball that streaked past the floating demons and penetrated the shimmering cloud around Phoenix. Dirt and rock rained upon the herd.

Edu heard a growing rumble and a buzzing hum as a black cloud obscured the sun. The colored bolts flying back and forth glowed brighter in its shadow. The black cloud, a swarm of locusts, flew into the crossfire, protecting Phoenix by absorbing the demon's red blasts.

The locusts coated the floating demons and crawled into the soft places where their legs met their bodies. Demons dropped from the sky and crashed to the ground.

Azilba's ears stood straight up. The rumbling shook the dry earth. A cloud of dust moved towards the battle.

"The Black Orophant, the Black Orophant has arrived!" Edu cried. A line of gray elephants with the Black Orophant at their center stampeded towards the fight. Eyes black and trained forward, the Black Orophant's herd charged with no indication of fear or emotion Edu could see. He smelled nothing on the wind.

Azilba roared, sending the prides and herds to join the Black Orophant's attack. Tusks gored and trunks swept slender legs. Lions jumped atop the giants and ripped whatever they could.

The demons shot red fire in all directions. A tuskless one shuddered.

"Don't worry, their fire doesn't harm us," Edu said to him.

The fight erupted into a cry of snarls and trumpets as the red beams ripped into the lions and elephants. The tuskless one next to Edu turned his head away.

"They burn us now," Edu thought as he gagged from the stink of flesh and locusts.

Edu wanted to fight, but did as he was told and ran back to the hill to move the group of young ones away. Edu looked up at Phoenix and saw a silver craft emerge from a small cave in the floating rock. It sped to the ground like a hunting bird. The Black Orophant veered toward it, a swirling cloud of locusts surrounding him.

"Why is the Black Orophant running?" Edu thought.

The Black Orophant stopped in Phoenix's shadow. Edu noticed a little man-child holding onto his back. The silver craft touched ground and a door in its side slid open.

A fireball raced across the plains and slammed into the Black Orophant, sending the man-child flying off his back. The Black Orophant fell to his knees and rolled on the flattened grass. The orange fire burned him, and did not extinguish no matter how he writhed.

The man-child flattened to the ground, avoiding beams of red fire. Without thinking, Edu ran towards him. Another fireball exploded somewhere nearby. Edu felt its heat on his side. In Phoenix's shadow, Edu lifted the boy with his trunk and placed him into the waiting arms of a silver man. With the boy safely in the man's arms, the door closed and the craft sped back to Phoenix.

The demons fired at the ship. Edu thought for a second it might fall from the sky. When it disappeared into the rocky cave, Edu turned to the Black Orophant. He smacked at the flames with his trunk but they still burned. Edu felt sick as he recognized the look of resignation in the Orophant's dark eyes.

"What can I do?" Edu cried.

"What you were born to do," the Black Orophant answered, the flames running up his trunk.

"Who was the man-child?" Edu asked.

"All animals have their prophecies and leaders, even men."

The blue sparking cloud around Phoenix changed to silver and then the city of Phoenix faded and vanished with a pop and hiss of rushing air, just as quickly as it had appeared. The Black Orophant trumpeted a powerful cry, a sound both dark and hopeful.

"They are gone now," the Orophant said. "The last of men. The demons will go now."

With Phoenix gone the demons no longer fought. Edu thought they could have easily slaughtered the entire herd, but instead they crawled their way back to the breaches in the barrier wall.

Azilba ran to Edu and watched as the flames consumed the Black Orophant.

"What will happen?" Edu asked.

"The world will go on. With the men gone the demons will not return," Azilba said, with a mix of sadness and hope. She shook her head and turned to where the lions were licking their wounds.

Edu watched the Black Orophant roll until he moved no more. Upon the Black Orophant's last twitch, the herd of reborn elephants lumbered away, the fury of their stampede gone. Their lack of an odor and dullness in their eyes still made Edu's spine tingle.

Edu nudged the smoking mass that was the Orophant with his tusks.

"You are special, little one," he heard the Orophant say in his head.

Edu heard another voice, and then another and another. Thousands of voices, the thoughts of all the elephant leaders echoed in his head. At that instant he knew that the Black Orophant could never die – that the Black Orophant was reborn in him and would be reborn in another should he fall.

Edu felt himself growing larger and stronger. He knew Azilba was right.

The world would go on. It would be a world without men. A world of elephants and lions, living beyond the barrier wall.

The Unlawful Priest of Todesfall
Penelope Love

————

The two travellers, exhausted from days without rest, stumbled out of the unclean wood onto the brow of a desolate hill. Their clothes, reduced to filthy rags, were sodden with sweat in the afternoon's heat. The rains were close but it was not their time yet. The whole landscape sweltered in the oppressive humidity, and pleaded mutely for release. Olan Season haze softened distances and rose in long lazy wreaths of clouds that hid sight of the sky. Before them swept a wide vale of tawny cropland descending to the city state of Uerth on the shores of the Lake Everlasting, created long ago by the damming of the Uerth river. The travellers' cracked lips pursed with thirst at the sight of the water. But on that blue and placid surface no sails showed.

The city-states of Uerth were once a collection of isolated, fortified towns, but now they were all grown together. The huge city bristled with towers of the nobility, and was generously slabbed with the fat full squares of warehouses and crammed granaries. But there was no movement, no clamour of people and animals, no reassuring, living stink. No smoke rose to soil the soft haze. The city-suburb of Zaijian, the last and least of the city-states of Uerth, lay before them, abandoned mute and defenceless to its last agony.

"Where is everybody? Has Todesfall arrived and gone already?" cried Asneath, sick with dismay. She was a small, bony, plain, fair-haired woman, her large green eyes grey-ringed with weariness, her white face taut with strain. She wore torn and stained rags, once Frir's robes of gold-trimmed green. Around her neck hung Frir's amulet, a small greenstone with the circle and the sickle carved on it.

"No. There! Look!" Baoqian exulted. He was tall brawny bronzed man, twice his companion's size, with a slab face and shaved head. His muscled body was naked to the waist, covered in Olan's blue tattoos, and an immense axe was strapped on his back. He pointed with a thick finger at a dark shape that filled half the horizon, the merciful haze a veil between the living and full sight of Todesfall's face. It was so large, Asneath had simply missed it, assumed it was a mountain or thunder cloud. She felt despair seize her as she realized for the first time how colossal Todesfall was. She strained her eyes to pierce the haze, even though she dreaded what she might see. She had so hoped, so hoped, for she knew not what, some gift or freak of the gods that would save them – but what could save them from this? Todesfall was immense, beyond mortal hope of moving.

Then Asneath screamed, for the shape lurched nearer, all at once, tearing aside the haze like a veil and for a moment giving them clear sight of all except its face. Baoqian seized hold of Asneath, reflexively, as a vast tremor shook the ground. In the city below, paving stones gaped like lover's lips. Stone walls rippled like water, water reared into walls and some fair towers fell to ruin, with distant, pitiful roars.

An immense statue of black obsidian strode through the lake towards Zaijian. Yet, for all the terror of its unimaginable height and inconceivable weight, the statue had chubby arms with the useless plump little fingers of infancy. It had dimpled knees, and above a babe's adorable penis rose a curved soft swell around the bulging belly button – all clearly visible, even from this distance, because of vast size in which they were etched in unyielding obsidian. The face hidden by haze was undoubtedly chubby, too. The watchers could imagine the rounded cheeks and soft features, the dimpled nose and double chin. Imagination pictured the face more vividly than the real thing.

The statue moved slowly, so each footfall took hours, so slow that it threw mere human watchers into an agony of impatience to watch it. Yet each step took it countless miles. When a footfall landed, the land ran like water and the water reared like land. The statue stepped, the towers fell, the aftershocks tumbled one after the other like echoes. The travellers neither moved nor spoke until all was still again.

"Let go of me," Asneath said then, in a voice that cut ice blocks from the summer heat.

Baoqian let go at once. "Todesfall is much bigger than I thought," he said, weakly.

"Of course, idiot," Asneath snapped. Baoqian had saved her life, but his insistence that they echo the ritual relationship between Olan and Frir grated away her gratitude. Now he voiced her fears exactly and in that moment she hated him. "That's what they all said, all of them that are dead. He *grows*," she said.

"If all is as they said, there is still hope." Baoqian dealt with dread of death better than Asneath. He was trained to deal with it, and meditating on Olan kept him calm and inspired within the world wreck. Besides, once the statue stopped the haze blurred its dreadful outline once again. He remembered his god could deal with everything, even this. "One day Olan went hunting—" he began.

"Can't you do anything besides tell stupid Olan stories! Can't you actually say something comforting for once!" Asneath shrieked.

Baoqian subsided, hurt.

Asneath closed her eyes, each freckle standing out like a scream on her white face. She remembered Baoqian had saved her life. She remembered she needed his help. She remembered that he had tried to sleep with her only once, and given up when she resisted. She murmured a prayer to Frir, and Frir gave her strength. She opened her eyes. "I didn't mean to be rude. I'm sorry. When do you think Todesfall will arrive?" she resumed, on a calmer note.

"Soon. Tomorrow or the next day," Baoqian guessed.

"He must not. He must not!" Asneath choked.

All the world was wrong, and some said the Great Ending was at hand. The gods had deserted them. Olan and Frir had answered prayers for help only by saying the right aid would come to the right souls at the right time and place. Rimbaud the bat, Rimbaud the crone, bringer of rebirth, was gone from her moon-roost. At night the moon's face shone broad and white, with no shadow upon it. That was bad, for Rimbaud left the living only in times of great death, when many souls needed her help on their way through the dying lands to new life. And all because Todesfall walked where he should not.

Todesfall was the son of Olan and Frir. He had killed his mother when he was born, and cost his father much trouble to fetch her back again. Todesfall, the Dark Child, kills all he touches and knows not why for he has no more understanding than a day-old child. His father had to banish him to his own realm of Dying for the sake of the world.

In the Dying lands, you must wait until Todesfall comes for you, until you see his face. The sight wipes all memory away, and then you are on to your next life and the lonely land of Dying is behind you till next time. Although it is said that sometimes he will relent if you appeal to him in his mother's name, even though she left him alone in a strange land. Only Todesfall dwells in the realm of Dying, alone and forever, forever and alone. And that is where he is supposed to remain.

"We must find the well in the north square, as we were told," Asneath said, trying to be brisk. "Then this will be over, one way or another."

Baoqian nodded. But he did not step forward. The city below would hold many dead. The dead were born of the Dance of Death, and they wanted you to join in. There lay the problem.

The Dance of Death was simple, a half-dozen steps. A child could learn it. You danced and whispered your enemy's name, and in the night your enemy died. The Dance started in Zaijian some months ago, and spread from there to the rest of the world. It brought on a terrible time, a dying time, when many were found to have enemies that deserved none. But then this statue of Todesfall started to walk and the Dance of Death ceased to work, so all saw the dance was a spell created for the statue's benefit.

The statue was far away then, in the north, in the Vale of the White Shang. It had been smaller then, much smaller – no bigger, it was said, than a baby. It was hidden in a temple of the lawful priests of Todesfall, those who ease the path of the dying into Todesfall's dark land, who lay out the dead, and guard their graves. No one outside the temple knew of the statue, for it is forbidden to make an image of Todesfall for fear the god will like it and will walk. Instead, by law, the priests are compelled to worship a block of obsidian.

The statue grew as it walked. At first it was slow, a step a day. At first the growth was not large, one inch, two, three. The lawful priests of Todesfall tried to keep it hidden. But one day its head broke through the dome of the temple and they could keep it secret no more. Then those that were killed by the Dance of Death came back. They found their slayers and carried them away.

The living tried to break the statue and could not. They tried to wall it in. That failed. Every night the dead returned and danced around the statue with their murderers still living in their arms, murderers who called for help until they died themselves, then fetched their families and friends to join their merry jig. The more that died, the bigger the statue grew. The only way to slay the risen dead was to chop off their heads, and they came in such waves that even the stoutest warrior could only slay so many before being seized by eager hordes and whirled away.

By then the statue had passed from the White Shang, where it caused much distress, through the Moon marshes to the city-states of Uerth, which rose in horror and dismay. The living fled. The Lady of Frir of the White Shang, and Lord Utan of the Five Duchies summoned a great assembly of the most powerful lords and warriors to decide how to deal with it. The Lady of Frir had seen the statue depart. Her gentle soul craved to heal all, even Todesfall. Lord Utan was the most powerful lord of the Five Duchies to the east of Uerth. His lands lay next in the path of the statue's advance. The assembly had the lawful priests of Todesfall brought before them, in chains for their treason in making such a statue when its dangers were so well known.

The lawful priests of Todesfall pleaded for their lives. They had not made the statue, they said. It had been made by their most hated foe, the unlawful priest of Todesfall. Centuries ago they had taken the statue from the unlawful priest to destroy it, but could not and so decided to keep it hidden. None in the assembly had heard of this unlawful priest and the lawful priests were put to sore trial. But they held fast, and at last the assembly saw that only raw fear had induced the priests to tell of their ancient and bitter and secret enemy.

The lawful priests said the unlawful priest dwelt in Zaijian, the last and least of the city-states of Uerth as he had since centuries past when once that city-state was rich and great. He did not live in the way of common men, but lived in death. For that reason he was constantly in sight of Todesfall's face. They said this with great malice and deep grievance, and the assembly saw that the lawful priests hated their unlawful fellow for his constant state of bliss. *That which is dead should stay dead*, the lawful priests said. It was he who made that statue, long ago, they vowed, and he who had sent the Dance of Death, *to fetch the statue back*.

Everyone knew the statue was heading straight to Zaijian. And also the Dance of Death had spread from there, as all could well remember.

The lawful priests told all they had learned of the unlawful priest. He was carefully hidden by his zealous followers, the best assassins and poisoners and embalmers in the world. They had learned the way to make contact with his followers, and the answers to the three questions his followers asked before they welcomed any guests. The lawful priests said the only way to stop the statue was to kill the unlawful priest. They would not reveal the three answers, for they hoped to use them to bargain for their lives. Instead they appealed to the White Lady, the beautiful, the good, the merciful.

When Lord Utan saw they would speak no more, he had all but one of the lawful priests executed. The White Lady pleaded for their lives, but Lord Utan told her to obey him in this, as a wife does a husband, and she bowed her head. Lord Utan took the last lawful priest with them on their journey, to show them the way to the unlawful priest and give the three answers. He assembled a host of his finest warriors, and the Lady of Frir took dozens of her priestesses to tend to the wounded. The world's greatest assassins and poisoners, they reasoned, would not give up their priest without a fight. They marched quickly for Zaijian.

Asneath and Baoqian were with the company, but neither had an important part to play until Lord Utan went mad. Green pus came from his mouth and he killed the Lady of Frir and her priestesses. His own men killed him. They set him on a bier in due mourning, with his battle-axe in his hand, but that night he rose up again. All that were killed by him rose with him and attacked the living. The living wasted time in their confusion before remembering the only way to kill them was to lop off their heads. It is not easy for an Olan warrior to slay a Frir-maid, even when green pus drips from her lips and her hair flies bristling and her hands are claws. Asneath lived only because Baoqian and some of his companions found her early and set her between them.

At first the men fought in fierce disorder, shouting to Olan for aid, until Olan aided them. Their tattoos writhed. Blue aurochs of attack raged through them. Blue dragons of defence reared over them. They fell into the battle trance, their blades singing sweetly, their eyes vacant of all but Olan's blessing. They felt neither pain nor despair nor fear of dying. The battle raged fiercely, the balance see-sawing between the living and the dead. Horses and people screamed in darkness.

Asneath knew the smaller spells of healing, although not the great spells that return life. They were Rimbaud's alone. As her first stark terror ebbed, she held Frir's amulet in her hand and meditated upon the circle and the sickle. She felt strength and certainty return to her. Murmuring Frir's chants she touched the men's wounds. Their wounds mended. She saw when they were flagging and gave them fresh strength, until it seemed to them, in their battle trance, that Asneath *was* Frir, and to fail her meant the death of Life itself. But Death and Dark were strong and terrible, while Asneath's powers were weak and mortal. She could not save them. As the night lengthened, the men staggered and wearied and foamed at the mouth. The blue aurochs and dragons turned to pale ghosts, then ebbed entirely, and the men fought on with only their devotion to Olan to sustain them. And that was not enough. Gaps were torn in the ranks around Asneath. Finally only Baoqian remained. Then, at last, dawn saved them. The dead screeched when first light touched them. Their flesh hissed and smoked. They fled into the woods.

Baoqian leaned on his battle-axe amid the carnage. He and Asneath looked around at the camp, with tents fallen and fires smashed and scattered with corpses. They saw they were the only ones still living. All that great quest had fallen on them.

"But we do not know how to find the followers of the unlawful priest, or the three answers to give them," Asneath wailed.

The sound of her voice woke movement beneath a fallen tent. They pulled the fabric aside and saw the lawful priest of Todesfall beneath. His feet were still bound, but he had one hand free, clenched tight around a small crystal vial. Nothing living or dead had touched him, but he was hurt to the death. In the desperate fight the tent pole had snapped and pierced his chest. Yet he smiled sweetly, not at them but beyond them, as if behind them he saw an old friend, long cherished in absence, coming towards him again. Asneath shivered and turned around, but there was no one there. No one living. She gathered courage and knelt beside him. She murmured a prayer and touched her amulet. She felt Frir's holy strength pour through her, banishing her mortal weariness. She touched the wound in his chest. She felt Frir deny her. She rocked back on her heels in amazement. "Frir refuses to heal you," she exclaimed. "You must have done a great wrong."

His smile broadened. He released his grasp on the crystal vial. It spilled green pus that sizzled and killed the grass it soiled.

"That is the poison that killed Lord Utan," Asneath cried, amazed.

"He should have let my brothers live," he mumbled.

"You dog! You die!" Baoqian howled. He whirled his axe around his head.

"Hold!" Asneath cried. She threw herself between the lawful priest and the blade. "He is dying now," she cried. "He will see Todesfall's face soon enough, with or without your help. He can tell us how to find the unlawful priest, and the three answers," she explained.

Baoqian considered, then let her have her way, although he spat upon the dying man's upturned face before he strode away. Asneath knelt by the priest again. She saw by the look in his eyes that his friend behind her was very close and very welcome. She did not have much time. She asked him where the unlawful priest of Todesfall could be found. He told her that a follower of the unlawful priest always waited by the well in the north square of Zaijain.

"Will killing the unlawful priest stop the statue?" she pleaded.

"If you do not kill him before the statue reaches him, then the lands of living and dying will become one," he gasped. "Then we face the Great Ending whose coming has many times been foretold but has always been held off somehow." He never took his eyes from that invisible one so uncomfortably close behind her. "In the Great Ending all who die will be reborn only in death. There will be no living soul left to worship, so even the gods will die. The dead will dwell in darkness that has no end."

She saw he dreaded that Great Ending, and she believed him. Yet also she saw laughter lurking in his eyes as if at some private jest. She wondered what this meant and concluded he was not telling the entire truth about the unlawful priest. But she had no time left. She asked him for the three answers.

He spoke thin but clear. She had to bend close to hear. He told her the first question and the first answer, the second question and the second answer. He told her the third question and she waited a long time for the third answer before realizing it would never come. For his smile became fixed and his gaze cleared. She screamed and snatched her hands over her face so she did not catch any glimpse of that Other face in the mirror of his eyes. At her cry, Baoqian came running. He had searched the camp and found some unspoiled supplies. So they journeyed on, pursued always by the dead who had once been their friends. They came at last to Zaijian.

They entered the city by the north gate in the late afternoon. The north square was immediately inside the gates; Zaijian was not a large city. A four-sided well stood in the centre, slab-roofed, with steps to the water. No doubt in normal times a man could linger here long, unnoticed, in the bustle of the crowd, but now the man sitting by the well was the only living soul there. They hurried to meet him.

Asneath had told Baoqian she did not have the answer to the third question. They had decided on a plan.

The stranger rose as they approached and removed his hat, showing himself a long lanky individual with sandy hair, a beaked nose and mild eyes. He was wearing rags that had once been fine clothes and still had a certain air of shabby finery about him. Anything less like an embalmer, assassin or poisoner they could not expect to find. A well-to-do pickpocket perhaps. They drew to an astonished halt before him.

"You are alive," Asneath blurted out, before she could think of anything sensible to say.

He bowed, doffing his hat. "As you see. You must be thirsty." He offered them each a bowl of water to drink. The travellers licked parched lips, but hesitated. "It is not poisoned," he smiled.

Asneath murmured a Frir-prayer over the water that would discolour it if it were tainted. But the water stayed clear. The thirsty travellers drank deep. "I am sorry for doubting your word," she said, setting the bowl down at last.

The man waved a dismissive hand. "You have reason. You are sent, I suppose, by the lawful priests to kill the proper priest of Todesfall."

Asneath stared in astonishment. Baoqian put his hand to his axe.

"I have expected you a long while. You are almost too late," the acolyte said. He turned to the statue that loomed over the city and blotted out the sky. Its foreshortened raised leg and foot approached, agonizingly slowly. It made the travellers fidget to look at it. Beyond, its torso reared into the clouded sky that hid sight of its head.

"Do I kill him?" Baoqian mouthed at Asneath, puzzled.

She shook her head, as the acolyte turned back to them. "Sir," she addressed him. "It is true that the lawful priests of Todesfall sent us here, but they betrayed us and killed our lord and lady. We seek to stop this statue before it brings about the Great Ending and we believe the unlawful priest was the one who started it walking. Will you not let us speak with him to find out the truth?"

The acolyte smiled at them, benevolently. "Of course, but first you have to answer three questions," he said.

"I am ready," Asneath said.

"What is the great poison, that is colourless, odourless and tasteless?" he asked.

Asneath felt a gush of relief. This was exactly as the lawful priest had told her. "Aqueta or little-water," she said, confidently.

The acolyte clapped his hands. "What are the seven noble poisons?" he asked.

Again relief filled her, for she knew the answer. "The seven noble poisons are aquafortis, arsenic and mercury, powder of diamonds." She paused, for she had heard the list but once, and memory groped for the next answer. As soon as she stopped, the acolyte started forward. She met his eyes and saw he was full of joy, of fondness for all life, that he bore not the slightest ill will to any living creature in the world, yet he would kill her if she forgot. It mattered not to him if he ended this life for her, when she had another, and another, an endless, inexhaustible supply to go on. Sweat sprang upon her skin, sweat that had nothing to do with the heat, and raw fear jogged her memory. "Lunar-caustic, great spiders and canthirides!" she gasped to the end.

"Two out of three. Well done. Here is the last. What is the name of the nameless god?" he asked.

Asneath's heart hammered even as she smiled and tried to look confident, for she knew not the answer to the third question. Her plan seemed a feeble one now it was embarked on. "I am afraid I am feeling the heat," she said, apologetically. "It is on the tip of my tongue. I just cannot remember."

Out of the corner of her eye she saw Baoqian start to manoeuvre.

But there was no need, not then. The acolyte threw up his long arms. "I am sorry to be so rude. I wouldn't be surprised if you had sunstroke," he said, and shot her a pleased look, as if wondering if she would die of it. "Come to our hall. You can sit in the shade and recover your wits. Then you can give your third answer."

She felt hopeful that her ready answers had dulled his suspicions.

He stepped back and whistled, high and shrill. A dozen shabby figures appeared from the surrounding streets. Baoqian stepped back against the well, axe raised. "Peace, friend," the acolyte said. "You have no need of that. We can kill you any time we like."

The men were a shabby bunch of outcasts whose belts were hung with swords and daggers and garrottes, with poisons and darts, with brain hooks and canopic jars. They swept Baoqian and Asneath through a broken grate into a low sewer on the south side of the square. The outcasts shot regretful looks over their shoulders as the statue disappeared from view, but Asneath and Baoqian were glad to leave it behind. They were glad too for the shade and coolness of the thick stoned sewer, even though it stank. They splashed through fetid stormwater with a crust of filth, but the outcasts were beyond noticing and the travellers past caring. Asneath soon gave up the idea of trying to retrace their steps. She saw a dozen places where traps were set, some to stop entrance, some to stop exit, and she had no doubt that many more existed that she did not spot. Fear seized her as she realized she was going to die, that she was being hurried to no good ending. She prayed to Frir for strength. "I am not afraid of death," she told herself. She did not realize she spoke aloud, until the acolyte of Todesfall smiled.

"I do not fear death either," he encouraged her. "It bores me rather. On and on, life after life. No true end. Pointless, isn't it." She realized that in his own way he was trying to cheer her. "Even the gods are trapped in it. Frir gives life, Olan guards it, Rimbaud will keep pushing souls on to rebirth, whether they want it or not. Only Todesfall had the right idea and look what happened to him. We followers of the proper priest seek the End to rebirth."

"Then this statue is doing what you want, by bringing on the Great Ending," she said, remembering the words of the lawful priest.

"No, the statue does not bring the End. We will die but there will be no peace for us in Todesfall's dim land. Rimbaud, that blind old bat, will hunt us out and hurry us on, whether we would or not, but there will be no life to be born into. We will be reborn into death, and there is no second death from that. Then the gods will fail us. Even this present mindless dance is a better fate."

"Then why does your priest do this? Why did he start the statue on its course?"

"He did not start it," the acolyte said. "The lawful priests started it when they stole it. They feared his power. But they have made him a thousand times stronger." He jerked his chin in the direction of the invisible statue, as they entered a large open space beneath the city. Tall pillars dwarfed the ragged band that splashed beneath the fluted ceiling. It was no sewer, Asneath realized, but a long disused cistern from the days before the Uerth river was dammed into a lake, when Zaijian was far from the shore and still needed a water store. A smaller area, like a stage, was raised at one end. It was lit with candelabra holding dripping candles of what she hoped was pig fat. Beyond the lit stage a tunnel disappeared into darkness. The acolyte saw her looking.

"That is where our priest dwells," he explained.

Asneath winced at the thought of living in that dank hole. "Don't the dead come here?" she asked.

"They know we are as they are, and leave us be," the acolyte said, which didn't comfort her terribly.

She wondered if the unlawful priest watched from the darkness – a man who did not live as normal men, but lived in death. Her imagination fired, picturing a green zombie with putrid flesh, or a skull with jewelled eyes. She shuddered.

What was the name of the nameless god? The question hammered in her head as it had all through this short, doomed journey. It was ridiculous. How could a nameless god have a name? And besides, what did a nameless god have to do with Todesfall? Unless, the thought occurred to her, the nameless god had something to do with the End that the followers of Todesfall sought? Also, she was puzzled by the casual nature of the unlawful priest's acolytes. They had led them straight here, on the flimsiest of pretexts. They had let Baoqian keep his weapons. They did not fear for their priest. This was wrong. She glanced at Baoqian.

He nodded, once, thinking she was signalling to him to start his advance. He slipped to the side. The ragged men let him go. Yet something held him back from vaulting onto the stage at once, and charging into the dark tunnel with raised axe. Something terrible but helpless, like the ghost of a child, tugged at him with futile, fearful persistence. Something nagged at him about the nameless god, as it had since he had first heard of it. Something he almost but not quite remembered. It hovered in the shadows on the edge of his mind, watching him with bright eyes. He tried to banish the muddled image by concentrating on present danger. He hefted his axe, framing a prayer to Olan.

The acolyte sat casually on the edge of the raised stage. "Are you feeling better?" he asked Asneath. The others grouped around her.

"Yes, much better now I am out of the sun," Asneath said. She resisted the impulse to glance one last time at Baoqian. All of a sudden, now she was going to die, she was very fond of him. She did not wish she had slept with him, but she did wish she had been kinder, more patient, that she had not snapped at him, and that she had thanked him. She fixed her eyes on the acolyte, willing him to look at her, not at Baoqian. She clasped her amulet in her hand. Beneath her breath she murmured a very foolish, little spell of Frir, beloved of young women, that makes them more attractive to men.

Baoqian hesitated, not because he thought they would die. He might kill the unlawful priest, but he was sure his followers would not let him escape. He faced his fate squarely. He prayed to die unflinching, with Olan's name on his lips. But what secret kept the unlawful priest of Todesfall so safe that his followers did not fear for him? He glanced back, and was caught by Asneath's spell. She looked like Frir, white and slim. He did not know what to do. "Olan help me," he prayed.

And Olan gave him aid. The nameless god stepped from the shadows of his mind, bright and vivid, and bowed its antlered head. "I know! I know the answer!" He started back, then spun around and stared into the dark tunnel as a cry rang out of it.

"Dada, are you there?" The voice was high and shrill, not a man's, and held a careless edge of command. "You can't hide. I heard you. Come here now. I'm bored!" the voice called.

"In a moment, dear heart," the acolyte called back, casually. "I have guests." He stared at Baoqian, appraisingly. "What is the name of the nameless god?" he asked him.

"It is dead and its name can be said only in the dying lands. We who still live cannot name it," Baoqian said, confidently.

Dada clapped his hands. "Only Olan himself could have given you that answer. Congratulations," he said, dryly. "Here is our priest," he added.

"One two three, coming ready or not," a voice said from the dark tunnel. And then a white, white child stepped out. His hair was black as night, his eyes burned and his lips were red as blood. He was five years old and dead as stones. He stared in surprise at Baoqian with his big axe. "I don't like you. Go away!"

Baoqian did not budge.

"Make him go away," the child said to Dada, crossly.

"Remember we can make him go, but even you cannot bring him back," Dada said, gently.

"Oh he can stay then. I don't care," the child said. He turned his burning eyes to Asneath. A pleased smile flitted over his lips. "Ah, she wears a necklace like mama's," he said. He ran towards her, chubby arms outstretched. As he passed Baoqian the man gave a great gasp and called on Olan for strength. He raised his axe.

"Stop!" Asneath screeched. All her Frir-soul revolted at killing a child.

Baoqian froze, mid-swing. The child stopped and turned on Baoqian, hands on hips, without the smallest flicker of fear on his small, dead, imperious face.

"I really don't like him," he said to Dada. "He's mean. Like the men who made mama and I drink that nasty drink."

"He means the lawful priests of Todesfall," Dada explained.

"Will I dance at him?" the child asked, and none needed to ask what dance he meant.

"He made that dance up out of his own head. Just imagine," Dada said to Asneath, proud as any parent.

"He's not mean," Asneath stumbled desperately into the breach. "He was just playing. He wanted to give you a scare."

"You can't scare me. What's your name? My name is Qushi," the child said, pleased, without waiting for answer. "Do you want to meet Mama? She's just in here."

"Just a moment," Asneath said. She turned to Baoqian in appeal, hoping he understood how she felt, her horror and her pity and her regret. "There must be another way that does not involve killing," she said. "And – and – how did you know the third answer?" she asked him, softly.

He stared at her in pure horror then bowed his head and whispered. "One day Olan went hunting. His hounds started a stag with a human face and they hunted it through the world. It turned at bay at last in the poison wood, but as Olan raised his spear to slay it, it spoke to him with human tongue. 'Kill me,' it said, 'And the Great Ending is at hand.'"

"'Liar and coward,' Olan called it. 'What is your name?'"

"'Except in the dying land I have no name,' it answered. Then Olan saw it was a dead god living and stayed his hand."

She waited a long moment, but there was no more. He shuffled his feet, apologetically. "You can tell me more Olan stories anytime," she whispered.

This was so different to the rebuke that he expected that he jerked his eyes up to meet hers, blushed and gave her a pleased smile.

"Are you coming, hurry! Mama is waiting," the child interrupted before Baoqian could say anything more. Asneath climbed onto the stage. The child took her hand. His hand burned like cold flame.

The tunnel led to a small tomb lit by more smoking candles of pig grease. Gaily coloured toys lay in heaps of profusion, balls and drums, dancing marionettes and painted wooden animals. A woman lay on the tomb, a corpse preserved by the highest of embalming arts. She had coarse yellow hair, dressed with rich jewels, and her sharp pointed chin and nose showed her a shrew. But there were also lines of love and laughter about her eyes and mouth. One hand lay at her breast, beside an amulet of Frir, a cheap trinket. The fingers were heavy with rings, although the hand was red and chapped with toil. The corpse wore rich robes that Asneath was prepared to swear she had never worn in life. This was a poor woman who lay before her. Her other arm was outflung and a blanket and pillow lay askew beside it.

Asneath's flesh crept.

The child scrambled into his bed. "Mama has gone away and can't come back," he said. And Asneath saw the anger in his eyes, that his mother would leave him alone in a strange land.

"Believe me it was none of our doing," Dada said from behind her. "Our priest is reborn to his task, over and over. He knows who he is by his dreams. When he is grown a man he comes to us and undergoes the purification and ritual. He is with us in death until his body wears away, for all our arts. Then we store his relics with great care and wait for him to be reborn to us again. The lawful priests have always feared him but they waited their chance when he was weak. They found him when he was yet a boy and killed him and his mother, thinking that way to end his power. Did they think to fool Todesfall?"

"We all strive to be like our gods for that is the path to them. But he is too like and has opened a path for the god to come to him," Asneath said, in great fear. She saw Qushi's bafflement, his pain, his rage and his shame. She saw why he danced the Dance of Death and why the statue woke when he called it, and walked to meet him. He did not understand or care, no more than Todesfall, that he would have to kill the whole world to bring his mother back to him.

"Todesfall neither knows nor cares what he does, no more than a day-old child," Dada agreed. "But he shares our priest's pain, that he can never be with his mother again. That has made them one in spirit. When they meet in the flesh our world will join with Todesfall's. Life and death, hand in hand. Life in death, I mean. Then none will be safe, not even the gods themselves. Truly, the Great Ending is at hand."

"There must be a way," Asneath said. Her first thought, her first refuge, was prayer. Prayer to Frir. But wiser and greater folk than she had already tried that, and already failed. Prayer to Rimbaud, then? No, Rimbaud was goddess of rebirth, not death – besides, the goddess was absent from her moon-roost. Memory of the moon's blank face made her shiver. That only left Olan, the banisher, the betrayer.

"We must take him to his father's temple," she said. "The White Lady received this answer to her prayers, that the right aid would come at the right time and place to the right souls. If this is not the right time and place then what is?" she said. "We can only pray the right souls are near." She turned to the child. "Do you want to go and visit—?" She bit her lip rather than mention the father who tore Todesfall from his mother's grasp. "Someone you know," she finished.

"I will if you carry me," Qushi said. He held up plump arms.

Asneath picked him up. No heart beat beneath his breast, no breath rose and fell upon her cheek. He was cold, cold all over. She felt her skin prickle and numb. She felt her heart freeze. Yet he laughed and wriggled as if he were a living child, pleased to be carried in a woman's arms. "Faster," he called.

Then the ground trembled around them as another footfall shook their world. Overhead, towers fell. Within, the roof of the cistern groaned. Stones ground against one another. Stone dust trembled to the floor like rain.

Realizing they had little time, Dada seized one of the candelabra to light their way. Baoqian came with them on the return journey, but the other acolytes ran ahead, eager to see the statue again. As they neared the surface they had to brace themselves against a second tremble in the earth, much nearer than before.

"But that is too soon," Dada said, amazed.

One of the acolytes came running down towards them, face aflame. "He is striding towards us much quicker than before," he cried, exultant, then dashed back out again.

They stepped out into the square. It was night, warm as milk, and the blank, fearful moon shone orange and swollen through the mists. The statue loomed over the city, blotted out the sky behind it. It was walking faster now, fast enough for mortals to see. One step while they stared, then two.

"We must be on the right path, for it seeks to stop us!" Asneath cried, relieved and terrified.

"Quick!" Dada led them forward. The statue needed only one or two more steps to overtake them.

They ran out onto a broad embankment overlooking the harbour. Earth shook and buildings tumbled. They saw the dead at last, thronging the lake shore, rejoicing in the arrival of their lord. The dead turned their faces towards them as they came into view, faces as blank and horrible as the empty moon. The statue loomed over the city, as a child looms over a toy. Another step and its bulk hid the moon.

"I see Olan's temple," Baoqian shouted. A big building, that must once have been handsome, stood on a prominent spot overlooking the harbour. He recognized the two pillars that stood before all temples to Olan, the legs of Olan they are called. Even as he shouted, the statue took its last step towards them, a step in real time, a hasty lurch that splashed into the shallow shore water. They all fell over at the impact. Buildings shuddered and collapsed. A wall of water reared from its footfall.

"Run!" Baoqian shouted. He thrust Asneath before him. Dada ran at his heels. The wave swilled behind them, overwhelming the embankment, dashing the dead away. Baoqian reached the twin pillars.

He seized one, and caught Asneath and Qushi together with his free hand. Dada threw himself past them and inside the temple. The wave smashed past them, as if following him in. The wave shouldered the pillars, but it would take more than Todesfall's strength to unseat them.

Asneath was overwhelmed, baffled, deafened, blinded, choked. She was helpless against this wave, and if she had been alone it would have ripped her, flung her and dashed her senseless against the rocks. But Baoqian stood firm as the legs of Olan. Then the wave broke over their heads and the ebb began. Baoqian roared and tightened his hold. At last the wave ebbed around their ankles, spent. Gasping, Baoqian released Asneath, who set Qushi down.

Qushi was outraged. "Now I am all wet," he said, as water poured from his mouth. The flood would have killed a living child. He would not let Asneath pick him up again, but ran ahead. "Where is Dada?" he said.

Behind them, the statue, with an awesome grinding, started to bend.

Within the temple was dim and austere and empty, wet to tall windows that let the orange moonlight in. On the north wall stood the altar, with two pillars before it, the arms of Olan. "Here I am," said a voice. They looked up to see Dada perched above the windows, just above the water line, clinging to the statue of a bat.

Rimbaud has no temples for she is always wandering about and has no time to settle down. Mostly she has shrines attached to Olan's temples, for the two met on Olan's travels to find his wife and became firm friends. It was the wily crone who thought of the way to fetch Frir back again. Where there is a shrine to Rimbaud there is sure to be a statue of a bat, and a few of her beloved bats. Even now, a dozen fruit bats circled around the ceiling, shrieking, disturbed by the giant wave and Dada's mad scramble to their refuge.

Qushi screamed with laughter. "What are you doing up there?"

"Trying to get down," Dada said, promptly.

"You are silly," Qushi said, affectionately.

"We must pray to Olan," Asneath said, turning to Baoqian, for she did not know how.

"A true warrior prays with his axe," Baoqian said, gruffly.

"Here's your chance, friend." From his perch, Dada gestured behind them. "I thought they had held off too long."

Asneath and Baoqian turned to see the dead pour through the door, as the wave had done. They came in silence, arms spread wide, ready to dance.

"Get to the altar!" Baoqian directed Asneath, readying his axe.

"They will do as I say," Qushi said, cocky, and raised his arms in command. Then he screamed. "My hands! They've gone!"

Asneath screamed with him. For his hands and arms had vanished, or so she thought, until she knelt and felt them. They were still there. They had gone black, not the colour, but in absence of light. As the statue neared, the form of the child was changing to that of his god. She picked him up. He felt lighter than before, his living weight draining from him. They ran to the altar and Baoqian stood before them, between the all-guarding arms of Olan.

The outraged bats screeched in the dome. Baoqian wielded his axe, soul singing. A blue dragon spread wings above him; a blue auroch charged through him. The dead fell before him.

Dada jumped down to the ground and ran over to them. The dead ignored him. He turned cheerfully on them. "Can I lend you a hand?" he said, tearing off an arm. "Mind your head," caving in a skull. He tore a path through to the living.

Then the roof was swept away as a child sweeps his toys aside. The living crouched, hands over their heads in useless protection as boulders the size of horses rained around them. But the arms of Olan are a strong shield and no stones struck them. Then the statue looked in. The face was too far above to make out, in shadow, remote and dim, yet awe and dread froze them.

"Watch your step!" Dada said, catlike recovering his footing first, and bringing his boot down hard, on a femur. It cracked with a dry crunch.

Then the dead drew back, with a dry murmur, bowing in reverence to their lord. The dance was over.

A vast hand reached in through the roof, of black obsidian. It groped with the plump uncoordinated fingers of infancy. The child in Asneath's hold screamed as flesh swept from him. He shone darkly with utter absence of light, and he lifted in Asneath's arms. Or rather the living world seemed to bend around him, bend in to him, to oblivion.

"Mama! Mama!" he screamed.

A voice sighed with him, filled with the same feeling, a voice bigger than the world. "Mama, mama," the statue sighed, through the aeons.

"No!" Asneath cried, as Qushi rose towards the reaching obsidian hand. Or it rose to him or . . . Perspective altered in ways she could not comprehend. She clung to the dead child. She lifted with him, or the world left them behind. Dada seized her waist as she rose, and tried to hold them down.

The giant head lowered enough for them to see the face, a face larger than the city. But there was no face. There was only a frightful whirl, a vortex of power sucking life into that other place, that lonely land of Dying that lies so close to ours, marching hill to hill, dale to dale, heart to heart, skull to skull, and yet is so distant and so terrible.

"Todesfall! Lord!" Dada exclaimed in reverence, tears pouring down his cheeks. He sank to his knees, forgetting to hold Asneath.

Only Baoqian stood between them and it – Baoqian, the arms of Olan. Baoqian roared in rage and hopeless defiance. He screamed Olan's name and gave an impossible leap. A blue dragon reared over him, a blue auroch leaped through him, but he was a flea to the colossus that bestrode them. He swung his axe in a great arc. It was not a human movement, it was divine. It was a prayer. The blade shattered when it hit the obsidian. Then the hand swept him aside. He was crushed against the left arm of Olan, and slid dead and broken to the ground.

The hand seized Asneath and Qushi. Then the statue stood. They swung high, impossibly high above the world, and all the time Qushi squirmed in Asneath's arms and *changed*. Asneath clung to him, her face buried against his shoulder, hoping to shield him with flesh still human. But he was oozing from her arms and floating, and shining now, shining with blackness, drawing the world into him. "I must pray," she thought, but all she could think of was Baoqian. He was dead and she had never thanked him. The hand came to a halt. She knew they must stand high, high above the world, before the face. She dared not look. The cold breath from Dying flooded over her. "Frir! Frir!" she cried, as her last desperate grip failed. "Save us! Save him!"

And the gods answered her prayer. A voice too large to hear thundered in her ears, like the sea and sky a thousand times magnified. She was sure it spoke one slow, sure, remorseless word. "Hold."

The child in her arms grew heavy again, and ceased moving. She raised her head. She saw Qushi had taken on flesh once more, with normal pink skin. But his eyes were closed, he was limp in her hold and he was not breathing. Below the world was hidden beneath silver mist that curved to the horizon. Around them was cold darkness with the empty moon like a dead lamp lighting a cold black room.

She saw at once they had made a mistake. The statue of Todesfall had not become larger. It had stayed the same size it ever was. It was the world that had become small. Perspective had slipped, but now she saw the true state of things. For Olan restored everything. Olan towered over them, over the rim of the world. He was so large that half of him was hidden beneath the horizon. She could see only the upper part of his chest, heavily tattooed, and far above the shaved dome of his head gleamed above a face, stern and blurred. He was as large again to the statue as even the fondest father towers over his new born babe. And Olan was not fond. Olan's arms were folded. "Hold," one word, still rang in her ears, the echoes reverberating to a close.

For the right prayer had come to the right souls, at the right time and place, when Baoqian died fighting without hope, his battle axe shattered in his hand, when Asneath called on Frir instead of despair.

One glimpse. One word. Todesfall had to obey. That was all.

Perspective slipped with a sickening swoop and the world swam to its right size again. The statue was the size of a baby so there was no fall at all. Asneath knelt on the cold stones of Olan's temple with Qushi still in her arms. Dada stared at her, astonished. "Can it be? Have you won?" he asked.

"Child!" a woman called.

Asneath saw it was dawn for there was a golden light shining through the temple doors. There was a woman standing in the light, blinding, radiant. Asneath raised her hand to shield her eyes. She saw a poor woman, in rags. Her reaching hands were red and chapped with toil. She had a sharp, pointed chin and nose, that told a shrew. But her eyes were filled with all the love and laughter in the world.

"Mama!" Qushi squealed. He ran towards her, arms wide.

Then mother and child were gone. The light was gone. The body in Asneath's arms lay still, so still. Yet Asneath could not let him go, even though she knew his soul had gone on to where he so longed to go, back to his mother and better luck in his next life. But that did not help her in this one. She knelt over him and wept, wept for the living and the dead. After a long while, she became aware that Dada was kneeling next to her, that his blameless, murderous eyes were fixed on her.

She hiccuped out incoherent words, that she hoped he would not kill her.

"We are deeply in your debt," he hastened to assure her. "Look. You have returned our statue." He picked up the baby-sized statue and brought it to her to show her, cradling its heavy weight in his arms with care. But he shielded its face from her sight, so she never saw it.

"Hide it better this time, so the lawful priests will not find it," she managed.

"I don't think they will try that trick again," he said, cheerfully.

"I thought it was dawn," she sobbed, remembering. She wiped her tears and looked up through the shattered roof. She saw that the Frir-light had deceived her. It was deep night still. The moon was high, but she saw with joy that reassuring shadow was splashed across its face.

"Look," she said, swallowing her sobs. "Rimbaud has returned to her roost."

So they knew the world had come perilously close to the Great Ending whose coming has many times been foretold yet has always held off somehow, but now the danger was past, and reassurance shone in the moon's shadowed face. Asneath climbed to her feet, decided to lay the dead boy down beside Baoqian. She turned to see an astonishing sight.

A dozen confused fruit bats had flown around the dome while the battle raged and great events shook their tiny, uncomprehending animal world. Now as silence fell they grew bold. They flew down into the hall of the temple and they circled above the crushed figure of a man. The sight filled them with strong, strange elation, feeling foreign to them. A feeling neither beast nor human but divine.

One by one, they flew to the pillar and crawled down, until the bravest of them brushed the dead man's face with his soft whiskers. The touch was too much for him and he drew back with a squeak of fear. They formed a strange illusion as they huddled there, a strange shadow on the pillar, like an old woman in a cloak. And stranger still, as the echo of the squeak died, the old woman shook her cloak and stepped from the stone.

The crone looked at Asneath, and Asneath fell to her knees before the power of her bright eyes. She turned to Dada. "Blind old bat, am I?" she laughed, mockingly. He dared not meet her gaze.

She bent and touched the dead man beside her, and his crushed flesh healed. Asneath felt hope so great seize her that she thought she would choke. "Baoqian," the crone called, in a hoarse rasp. But he did not wake.

Asneath's wild hopes sank.

"No time to lie about, lazy bones," the crone scolded, and kicked Baoqian smartly in the ribs.

This time he woke, with a surprised grunt. He sat up and rubbed his face.

The shape of the crone collapsed back into bats, who flew in all directions with startled shrieks. But her voice rang out, strong and mocking as life itself. "You've traipsing enough to do yet before you earn your rest. Get up, get up, and live," Rimbaud said.

So he did.

Cephalogon
Alys Sterling

———

"What is this?" Will poked his chopsticks at a tentacle slowly writhing its way out of the mound of rice-shaped algal starch in front of him.

"Think of it as a Martian delicacy." Maura grimaced at her own plate.

"Just so long as I don't have to think of it as dinner." Will waved his arm, indicating the dining hall around them, its three long yellow-topped tables occupied by scientists of various persuasions. "My kingdom for a steak."

"It's supposed to be a horse," Maura said.

"I'd rather eat a horse than this." Will teased the tentacle out a little further. The suckers showed bright red against the orange flesh.

"If this is anyone's kingdom, it's mine." Pete picked up a slimy lump of his own dinner and shoved it into his mouth without looking at it.

"My coring rig then."

"No way," Pete said, still chewing. "That's company property."

"A whole horse would feed all of—"

A series of loud thuds rattled the plates on the tables and drowned out Will's last words.

"Do they have to do that while we're eating?" Maura shouted, as the noise of the bombing run died away.

"Of course. You know there just aren't enough hours in the day to test weapons." Will held up the tentacle, now captured between his chopsticks. "Personally, I'm more worried about things like this. I don't mind eating seafood, but this isn't even a real squid. Vern is serving up mutants again."

"It's all the bombs," Pete nodded. "There's radiation or something else they're not telling us about. That's why we're getting so many mutations."

Maura shook her head. "Nah. It's all that crap the last team kept putting on the fields to try to get crops to grow. Those chemicals just went straight into the lake."

"And they still never got anything to grow," Will said. "Some of the stuff they used, I'm surprised the rocks aren't sprouting tentacles."

"We need to get the proper bacteria in situ." Maura gestured with her chopsticks, as though jabbing bacteria into the Martian soil with them. She never seemed to lose enthusiasm, no matter how many of her experiments failed. Even her hair bristled with it, short blonde curls shooting out energetically from her head. She looked like an avenging angel in a white lab coat.

"Chemicals aren't the answer."

"I don't notice anything growing in your plots yet," Pete said.

"The soil is toxic. I just need to breed a strain that can—"

Another round of bombing cut off Maura's reply. The mess hall windows shook in their insulated frames.

"That was a little close," said Pete.

Before anyone had time to answer, another run commenced. The floor rippled. Will's chair rocked, then tipped backwards as the lights flickered and went out. His shoulders hit the metal ridge of the chair-back, and then his head hit the floor.

He woke in darkness, feeling something sticky on his cheek. A cold, writhing worm was forcing its way into his nose. He tried to breathe, and choked on rising nausea.

Beams of light cut the blackness; someone had found the emergency torches.

"Helb!" Will shouted. "I'b udder addag."

"Silly." Maura knelt over him.

Will felt her fingers on his cheek. Her nails scraped his skin as she pried at the thing stuck there. It came away in increments, trying to hang on.

"It was only your dinner." Maura dangled the red-suckered tentacle in front of him.

"No way am I eating that now," Will said. "You can have it for a specimen if you want."

Maura sighed. "If I analyzed all the mutants Vern catches, we'd get nothing to eat. Besides, my field is microbiology. Compared to what I normally look at, this thing came from a giant."

"Hey, when you two are finished discussing the food, there's something you might want to come see." Pete beckoned from the door.

Will let Maura help him up. He walked over to the door, gingerly running his fingertips over the back of his head. By the feel of it, he had quite a lump. Then he reached the open door and stood shivering in the chill night air, lump forgotten.

Between the mess hall and the lab huts, a thirty-centimetre-high escarpment now broke the once-flat ground. Looking from side to side, as Pete swung the beam of his torch, Will saw the irregularity continuing into the distance towards the lake, and on in the other direction through the rest of the Lewin Agri-Industries compound.

"That last one was no bomb test," Pete said softly.

"Bloody hell," Maura whispered. "Marsquake."

"Idiots!" Will shouted, as though he could make the managers of Conglomerated Armouries hear him across the lake. "Fools. Military-minded assholes. I told them months ago there was a fault zone here, and what do they do? Bomb the shit out of it, that's what."

———

The damage looked worse in the morning. Cracks ran across the dining hall windows. One of the oldest buildings on Mars, constructed eighty years ago by a team of terraformers, had collapsed. The Quonset hut, which housed Will's equipment, was still in one piece, but a quick look inside before breakfast revealed the equipment itself had not fared so well. Toppled shelves and broken core samples littered the floor.

Everything would be cross-contaminated now. Will groaned. Weeks of drilling wasted.

He stomped off to the mess hall hoping to find Maura, but she wasn't there. He spooned up algal porridge at several times his usual speed, his mind filled with visions of twisted metal. He had to get out and inspect his drilling rig. It would take months to get a replacement up here. Not to mention an extension on his grant. As he gulped down the last slimy mouthful, Pete came in followed by a man with a Conglomerated Armouries badge on his jacket.

"Will, a word with you." Pete beckoned him out of the mess hall, leading the way across the broken ground outside to his office. "This is Andrew Short, from Conglomerated Armouries. Will is our geologist." He waved Short through the door ahead of him. "He may be able to explain what's happened."

"What's happened," Will said to Short, "is that your bloody bombs have gone and caused a Marsquake, that's what. Don't say I didn't warn you."

Short looked taken aback. "We have yet to determine the cause of the quake. The planet may still exhibit some post-terraforming instability. Besides, it's by no means certain that our test site was the epicentre."

"Very good, Short." Will applauded soundlessly. "Look out there." He pointed back out the door, at the miniature escarpment bisecting the compound. "That says we're awfully close right here."

"In any case," Short continued after a moment, "we have a more serious problem. The lake is disappearing."

"What? You—"

"I'd like you to go have a look," Pete interrupted, before Will could decide what to call Short.

Personally, Will wouldn't mind if Lake Edgar disappeared off the face of Mars. At least then Vern would have to stop serving mutant squid. But Pete hadn't exactly given him any choice about going.

Short drove Will out to the lake in his Mars buggy, an ATV equipped with huge cleated tyres and a state-of-the-art locator system. If not for the satellite location, Will might have believed they had reached the shore of the wrong lake. Slimy patches of algae, now dying in the chill sunlight, marked the old waterline. The ancient lakebed, refilled fifty years ago by the terraformers, lay once again bare and exposed for a good kilometre before water came into view.

Short manoeuvred the buggy forward. Will felt the wheels slip, breaking through the dried crust of the algae patches and sliding on the slime beneath. He put a hand out to brace himself as they rolled down a steep incline. The vehicle bounced down a final step in the ground, and Will hit his head on the roof. It was the last straw.

"Why do you have to drop so many bombs on Mars, anyway?" Will burst out, no longer able to contain his frustration. "Isn't it enough you made the moon so radioactive no one can land on it? We've barely made Mars habitable, and now you're destroying it, too."

"Habitable? You know better than I do how many scientists have tried and failed to make crops grow here. Without a source of food, Mars can't support large settlements. We might as well get some use out of the planet. After all, we can't test these things on Earth."

"Why not? Where do you intend to use them, if not Earth?"

"Think of the damage to the environment." Short seemed honestly horrified. "We can't just go blowing big holes in our own ecosystems. These are deterrents. The government would never actually use them."

"Then why test them at all?"

Short paused for so long Will thought he finally had him stumped for an answer. "For the joy of it." Short held up a hand, forestalling Will's reply. "Because having dreamed the things up, figured them out, made the prototypes – how can I not want to see if they *work*?"

Will turned in his seat to look at Short, reassessing his opinion of the man. "You actually design them? I thought you were military."

Short grimaced. "It's an honorary rank. Couldn't have a civilian in command, even up here."

When they reached the edge of the water, Will could practically see it ebbing away in front of him.

"Shit," he said. "Must be some kind of underground fissure." He opened his door, letting in the stench of dying algae. When he stepped out, something squelched underfoot. He looked down. Dead and dying squid littered the slime-covered rock of the exposed lakebed.

Will tasted porridge at the back of his throat. He tried to hold his breath as he stacked pebbles to mark the current waterline. It didn't work. He leaned forward, spewing the contents of his stomach into the water. Behind him, he heard Short losing his own breakfast. Will spat to clear his mouth, and walked back to the buggy.

"Shouldn't have had seconds on the eggs this morning." Short slid behind the wheel.

"You get eggs? Where from?"

"Earth. Send them up dried. Army supplies." Short swallowed between words, looking like he might spew again at any moment.

"I think I should drive," Will said.

"You know why the water's gone already?"

"See there, where the fault line goes into the water?" Will pointed at the uneven seam the buggy had bounced over. "I think it opens up again under the lake. I'd have to dive to know for sure. You wouldn't have deep-water equipment on hand, would you?"

Short shook his head.

"Damn. Of all the things not to bring—" Will thought longingly of his own hardsuit, gathering dust in his lab back on Earth. There was something else he had seen gathering dust lately . . . "Wait a minute. I know where I can get an old outdoor suit that might work, but I'd need some kind of propulsion unit."

"Suit jets?"

"Yeah, if I had any."

"I might be able to help you out with that."

They detoured through Conglomerated Armouries' facility on the far side of the lake to pick up the jets, a slim, white-enamelled backpack unit with bars reaching out at hip level for control. While they were there, Will had as much of a look around as he could. He was surprised to see a number of soldiers marching in drill, on a rectangle of ground so packed down their stamping boots raised no dust.

"What's all that about?" he asked Short. "Do you really believe you'll be attacked up here?"

"No." Short glanced over as the drill sergeant shouted something. "But it keeps them busy."

Reddish dust coated what looked like a pile of junk in an old crate in the corner of Will's Quonset hut. Some of the core samples had fallen into it, but the suit's hard shell had taken no apparent damage. Will lifted out the top half of the suit and put it on the work table.

"You sure about this?" Short wiped a finger across the suit's shoulder, leaving a clean bronze-finished trail behind.

"Looks all right to me. Soon find out if it's not watertight." Will grunted as he lifted the bottom half of the suit out of the crate.

"What about air?"

"Suit has an integral supply. About enough for four hours' dive, I reckon. And it's insulated, so the cold won't be a problem." The hard outer shell, meant to protect the wearer from windblown debris, ought to protect Will from the pressure of the depths. At least, so he hoped. He didn't voice his doubts as Short helped him attach the manoeuvring system to the suit with heavy webbing straps. As a final touch, Will glued a self-rewinding reel of nylon cord to the front, just under where the straps crossed.

"What's that for?" Short asked.

"Guide-line. If there is a fissure under the lake, I'll have to go in and see how deep it goes."

"You're enjoying this. You want there to be a fissure." Short pointed a finger at him.

Will grinned. "Hell, yes. Think about it. The only unexplored territory on Mars, and I get to see it first. Imagine what it must have been like for the teams who came in before the terraformers. Every day, you'd get to see something no one had ever seen before. Now it's all mapped and gridded, and every day we change it more."

They took Vern's runabout back to the lake, towing the fishing boat. The algae along the exposed lakebed crunched under the runabout's wheels, already freeze-drying in the Martian wind. The new waterline lay a metre or so back from Will's marker.

"Looks like it's slowing down. It may reach equilibrium soon." Will hefted his helmet up. Just in case he was wrong, he wanted to dive while there was still some water left.

Short finished winching the boat out from the trailer and cast off. The water parted viscously around it as they headed for the middle of the lake.

————

Beneath the water the light quickly faded, obscured by floating particles of algae, so that Will swam through a tea-coloured murk. He switched on his helmet light, thankful the terraformers had seen a need for night-time navigation. The light made a tunnel through which bits of detritus spun aimlessly. A squid jetted through the cone of light, emitting an ink cloud behind it. Its tentacles alone stretched a metre long.

"Hey!" Will said, startled.

"What is it?" The suit radio made Short sound a thousand miles away.

"A squid nearly as big as me. I didn't know they grew that size."

"Oh, sure. They come much bigger than that on Earth. Don't worry, they didn't seed any giant ones up here."

"You don't call a two-metre squid a giant?"

Will let the weight of the suit pull him down to the lakebed, searching for the fault line. He grew used to seeing squid flit past, rippling bright red and white stripes at him, or shooting out ink.

The terraformers had covered the lakebed with a layer of finely ground Martian rock, mixed with chemicals and bacteria, which was supposed to simulate natural soil. It seemed to work better for growing seaweed than for growing wheat. Slimy green growths up to half a metre tall covered the bottom of the lake. Will poked a finger at a particularly bulbous one, meeting a jelly-like resistance. When he pulled his hand back, a small plume of green motes spun out into the water.

It took him a while to locate the fault line, due to the limited range of his light. At last, his beam illuminated a ribbon of bare red rock slashed like a wound across the lakebed. Will followed it, feeling the tug of a current speeding him along.

Suddenly, the ground beneath him opened up into a dark slit, the gap widening to ten or fifteen metres across in the centre. Will fought the current pulling him down towards it.

"Shit." He hovered above the fissure, his light failing to penetrate its depths.

"What now?" Short asked.

"I've found where all the water's gone. There's a bloody great hole in the rock here. I'm going down to take a look, see how deep it goes. Don't worry if you lose radio contact with me for a while."

Will unreeled the end of his safety line from the chest of his suit, tying the thin white cord around a projection at the lip of the fissure. He double-checked the fastening before swimming downward, into the darkness.

The fissure opened out into a cavern so huge Will's light couldn't reach the other side. He struck out from the fissure, using a slight push from the suit jets to move himself along until he came to a wall. Then he let himself sink down again, following the curve of the wall, noting red and yellow banding in the rock. A few minutes later, he found a hole. The opening, and the tunnel beyond, had five sides, smooth and suspiciously regular.

Will swam through the tunnel, his light glancing off rock close around him. It came as a relief when he finally emerged into another huge cavern.

"Short? Can you hear me?" As Will expected, Short didn't answer. The tunnel had sloped downward; the rock above him must now be thick enough to interfere with radio reception. Nonetheless, it made him uneasy to be cut off from all communication. One mistake down here, and no one would ever see him again. Will checked his guideline, took a deep breath, and went on. He had enough air for an hour's exploration before turning back, and the feeling that an hour was not going to be enough.

Will's light reached further in the algae-free water of the new cavern. He saw more openings, low in the cavern walls. He checked the suit's wrist-compass, and chose one to the northeast. He swam through several more linked caverns, one with a frozen waterfall of yellow flowstone ten metres high. From there, he entered a long tunnel. When the tunnel widened, he found himself floating in an almost spherical chamber, with tunnels leading out in all directions. Directly below him a huge tube plunged straight down. Will's light caught odd shadows on the black rock of its sides. Peering closer, he saw ridges set in semicircles covering the rock. There seemed no purpose or pattern; perhaps they were the work of some rock-adhering creature like a Martian barnacle, eons ago when these caves had formed.

Will swam down until he reached the largest cavern yet. A forest of thirty-centimetre-thick columns filled the chamber. Their surfaces exhibited the same sort of ridges as the tube above. Will jetted slowly forward, weaving his way in between them. Some distance in, he found a broken column. He searched the cavern floor for a small enough piece to take back as a sample, stirring up black sediment that glittered in his helmet light. At last, he found a fist-sized bit, one side showing the strange markings. Perhaps Maura could make some sense of them. The hardsuit had no pockets, but Will managed to wedge the rock between the crossed harness straps of his propulsion rig. The broken edges sawed at the straps as he pushed the rock under them. Odd. Will took a closer look at the stump sticking up from the floor. Conchoidal fractures. This rock looked glassy, like obsidian. What were pillars of volcanic rock doing in a clearly limestone-type cave?

He looked back through the forest of columns. Their consistent size tempted him to believe they must be artificial, but their layout followed no pattern he could discern. Surely only natural formations would exhibit such a random placement. And besides – who could have built them? No evidence of ancient Martian life larger than nano-organisms had ever been found. His barnacle ridges could make Maura famous. Will grinned. If he could get her to analyze something so large.

Will checked his guideline, making sure it had not fouled on any columns. He would need it to find his way out of this cavern, for sure. He gave it a sharp tug. The line went slack in his grip.

Will's stomach congealed into an icy lump. He knew he had tied the line securely, but what if it had caught on some sharp projection, and been cut? He forced himself to remain still; not to yank on the line again. He might still be able to follow it back to the exit from this cavern, at least. Will began backtracking along the line, swimming slowly so as not to disturb it more than necessary. He was directly underneath the hole in the ceiling when the line suddenly went taut.

The pull strengthened, yanking him through the hole. He let out a yell as he rushed upwards, unable to figure out what the hell was happening. At the top of the tube, the line jerked him sideways, through a tunnel, out into a cavern, into another tunnel. In the next cavern, lacy cream-and-red-barred fans hung from the ceiling. Will had not seen those formations before. He had never been through this chamber. Whatever had hold of his line was pulling him deeper into the labyrinth of caves.

He could see the guideline, the nylon rope glowing white ahead in the beam of his helmet lamp. It stretched across the unfamiliar cavern to a dark opening in the far side. As Will drew nearer, something moved within the darkness. Then his lamplight flashed into the tunnel, illuminating sinuous orange flesh. A tentacle at least ten metres long, and more behind, writhing in the shadows.

Will tore frantically at the front of his suit. He had attached the guide-line mounting as securely as possible, with industrial adhesive. He had known his life might depend on not losing it. Now, his only chance of survival lay in getting rid of it. He pounded it with metal-gloved fists, but it didn't budge.

Will hit his propulsion jets, twisting around to face away from the tunnel and pushing the knob to maximum. The jets couldn't out-pull the giant mutant waiting in the dark. He slowed, but the squid inexorably reeled him in. He wondered whether it would weaken before he ran out of propellant. If only he had a knife – he could cut the line. But he had not brought any extraneous attachments, except for the safety line and jet harness. The harness – suddenly, Will remembered his rock sample. The edges had been sharp enough to tear at the harness straps.

Clumsy with haste, Will pulled at the straps. He fumbled the rock free, then felt it fall from his grasp, before he could close his fingers on it. He lunged towards it, his movements nightmarishly slowed by the suit and the water around him. With his change in attitude, the jets pushed him downward, faster than the rock could fall. He reached out, and it floated into his outstretched hand. But his move down had cost him; the creature reeled him in faster, temporarily unhindered by his jets.

He sawed at the line, imagining writhing tentacles reaching to embrace him. Will never felt the line part; he only knew he had succeeded when his jets sent him shooting through the cavern, narrowly missing the fringe of rock formations overhead. He kept going, waiting for those tentacles to grab him and pull his suit apart at the joints to get at the soft, defenceless creature within, like a normal squid eating a crab. He didn't stop until he ran smack into a wall of white stone.

Will spun slowly around, shining his light. He had swum into a small chamber, a dead end. As he turned, he noticed something strange about the walls. Aside from the opening by which he had entered, they were all perfectly flat, meeting at regular angles. Ridges of shadow made patterns on the walls, as they had on the pillars. He stared at the back wall, concentrating on the pattern. Laid out flat, it looked strangely regular, exhibiting an odd sort of symmetry. As he stared at the walls, the patterns replicated outward, forming a lattice around him. Quasicrystalline symmetry. The whole damn chamber was a three-dimensional representation of a quasicrystal. Of course! The pillars had been arranged the same way, only down among them he couldn't see it. He turned slowly, positioning himself at the centre of the lattice, the point at which the pattern originated. From there, Will gazed into infinity. He felt he had only to slide a little further into the pattern, find the exact fit, and he would be able to see the future, or the past, his mind expanding until it could contain the universe.

A shrill beeping jarred Will out of his trance. It took his sluggish mind several beep-filled minutes to recognize the suit's air level warning. He had only an hour's air left.

He made himself jet along slowly, the need to go carefully, watching for any hint of a familiar tunnel warring with the knowledge that he had only an hour to find his way out. He took shallow breaths. Assuming he had jetted a fairly straight course fleeing from the giant squid, he used his wrist compass to move back in the opposite direction, praying he would find a cavern he recognized before he reached the one where the squid lurked.

When he swam into the chamber with the bore down into the pillar room, his sense of relief was as great as if he had already reached the surface. From here, he need only head southwest to find his way out. He oriented himself with the compass, and found himself faced with a choice of two tunnels.

Will floated, caught in an agony of indecision which held him as tight as any tentacles could. The wrong choice would cost him his life. He remembered all the horror stories about divers who never returned, cautionary tales his instructor had used to drive home safety lectures. He might just end up as the most gruesome example yet.

Something moved inside the right-hand tunnel. Will started, bowels clenching. A small squid, no more than twenty centimetres long, tumbled out into the chamber. Will started laughing, the sound echoing crazily inside his helmet. He knew he should try to stop, but he didn't care. The squid had shown him the way out. Still giggling, he jetted into the tunnel.

———————

Somehow, in all his panic to escape, Will had managed to hang on to the lump of rock from the broken pillar. He showed it to Pete when he made his report on the size of the rift in the lakebed. "There's something very strange going on with the geology in those caves. Formations that just can't be natural."

Pete turned to Short. "He was down there the full four hours?"

"He was practically blue when I pulled him out," Short said.

"Is that so? And do you have any idea how deep you went?"

"I couldn't find a depth gauge," Will admitted. He hadn't been able to find a waterproof camera either, a lack he now regretted even more

"And there's another thing, a chamber, with carvings on the walls . . ." Will let the sentence trail off as he saw the expression on Short's face.

"Raptures of the deep, Will. You came up laughing like a maniac and babbling about a giant mutant squid."

"The important thing is, you're fairly sure the lake won't drain much further?" Pete tried to change the subject, but Will ignored him.

"You don't get raptures in an atmosphere suit. I know what I saw."

"You saw a giant squid? How large?" Pete asked.

"I'm not sure. Big enough to think I was lunch. Twenty metres?"

"And you think it built pillars and carved things on them?"

"No." Will made an effort to keep his voice calm and even. "I don't know what made the pillars. But you know as well as I do that the squid have been mutating in that lake. Who knows what's going on down there in the depths? After all, I'm the first person who's ever been down to see."

Pete sighed. "All right. Even if there is a giant squid, it's not doing anyone any harm down there, is it? Now, I want you to let the doc have a look at you. Take the afternoon off, have a rest."

Will did go see the doctor, but not until he had taken the rock over to Maura's lab. "Have a look at this. Any idea what might have made those ridges?"

Maura ran a finger over the surface, then held the rock up to the light. "I've never seen anything like it. Where did you get this?"

"From a cave under the lake." Will didn't tell her any more; he didn't want to prejudice her judgement. More than that, he didn't want Maura to accuse him of seeing things the way Pete had.

When he walked into the mess hall at dinnertime, everyone there turned to look at him.

"Are you all right?" Maura motioned him over. "I hear you had a pretty close encounter down there." Her words expressed concern, but Will heard laughter in her voice.

Pete sat across from her, smirking. "You mean he didn't tell you about Cephalogon, monster of the deep? Will, sit down and tell Maura all about how it nearly ate you for lunch."

Will made a detour past the serving hatch, where Vern handed him a plate heaped with the usual rice substitute. Tonight, to Will's relief, no tentacles stuck out. A scatter of protein flakes decorated the top of the rice instead. Will sat and picked up his chopsticks. Then, the rice moved. The surface of the lump cracked.

"Look out," Pete said. "Ricequake."

Maura snorted.

A tentacle shot out of the top of the lump. Will slid his chair back so fast he nearly fell over again.

Pete burst out laughing. Will looked around. Everyone in the mess hall was laughing at him, even Maura. The squid made a break for the edge of the plate.

"Watch out." Pete pointed at the squid. "Cephalogon's sent its minions after you."

Will tried to poke the squid back with his chopsticks. It wrapped its tentacles around them and hung on. He lifted it up from the plate and carried it dangling over to the serving hatch.

"Vern? You've got an escapee." He lifted the chopsticks and waved the squid at the cook.

———

After dinner, Maura invited Will over to her lab.

"Watch out for Cephalogon," Pete called out as they left.

Maura grinned. "Might as well get used to it."

"I know. I'll never hear the end of it."

"Seriously though, how big was this thing?"

"The tentacle that grabbed me must have been at least ten metres long. Maybe longer; I never saw what it was attached to."

"Then it might not actually have been a squid?"

"It had tentacles. What else would it have been?"

Maura opened the door to her lab. She looked up at him, her grey eyes wide. Under the bright strip-lighting, she looked both serious and apprehensive. "A Martian," she whispered.

"Not Cepahalogon again." Will turned away. He would have gone, but Maura grabbed his arm and dragged him inside.

"Call it whatever you like." She picked up his rock sample and brandished it at him. "Something made these markings. They don't appear to be biological in origin, and they're perfectly regular in height. I think they were made deliberately. By something intelligent. And I think the patterns have some meaning, I just can't figure out what." She looked at him defiantly.

"I think so, too. I found something else down there." Will told her about the crystal room.

"So you do believe there is intelligent life on Mars."

"Was. I believe there was. Whatever made those carvings is long gone. Maura, those caves are old. Ancient. And now we've created an enormous mutant that's made its home in them. Who knows what damage it may do?"

Will sat in the mess hall slurping algal porridge and wishing for eggs when Short drove up outside, shouting at the top of his voice. Gladly abandoning his breakfast, Will went out to see what the yelling was about.

"Some kind of monster attacked the base. We felt the ground shaking last night, and this morning, we found all of our hangars wrecked. Completely flattened to the ground."

"Probably an aftershock," Will said, though he hadn't felt anything in their compound.

"Aftershocks don't leave footprints."

"We'd better bring Maura this time."

Short drove them out past the lake, skirting the old shoreline.

"Stop." Maura pointed out the window. "I want a look at those."

Red dust rose around them as Short braked. As it settled, rows of three-pronged depressions in the ground faded into view, already dust-blurred at the edges. Will got out and followed Maura as she walked along beside the prints.

"These things must be a metre across." Maura looked off into the distance, shading her eyes with one hand.

Will noticed which direction Maura faced. "They come from the lake." His stomach felt suddenly hollow. "That squid must be bigger than I thought."

Maura turned to give him a look. "Squid can't function on land. They've nothing to hold their bodies up with – no skeleton or exoskeleton for support. And they'd suffocate."

"Maybe it's mutated enough to be able to? I must have seen something, the footprints prove that."

"Cephalogon." Maura grinned at him. "I told you. It's a Martian."

"Cephalogon? Martians?" Short looked from Maura to Will. "You two are off your rockers. Come on, you're supposed to be taking a look at the hangars."

Maura paid no attention to Short. She stared out at the footprints, counting under her breath.

"What is it?" Will asked.

"The footprints. I can't make out the gait."

"How do you mean?"

"Well, look at our steps." Maura pointed back towards the buggy where Short now waited. Rows of shallow depressions in the dust marked their progress out, overlaid by Short's returning steps. "You can see there are three of us, right? Three rows of pairs of steps."

"With you so far."

"And if you saw the tracks of a horse, you'd see sets of four, all in a repeated pattern, and you could tell if it had been walking or galloping by the pattern."

"All right. So what's the problem with these?"

"Well, you can see they come out and go back. That's clear from the way the claws point. But no matter how many times I count, I keep getting twenty-five legs."

"But no animal has an odd number of legs. That's impossible."

"No animal on Earth."

"It's not quake damage." Will stood at the top of a small rise that was as close to the wrecked hangars as Short would let him get. He looked out over a scene of complete devastation. Every building had been systematically flattened. And all around them, imprinted on corrugated metal roofing sheets and crushed aircraft, circling and crossing the ground, Will saw three-toed footprints.

"Don't you see what this means?" Maura grabbed Will's arm, practically bouncing up and down with excitement. "It proves Cephalogon is intelligent. He knows what caused the Marsquake. He's attempting to stop them causing another."

"There's still no proof our tests caused the last one," Short said.

"That still doesn't prove it's an ancient Martian," Will said.

"It is. It has to be. Nothing could mutate that much, that fast."

"So how did it survive all this time? You think it's been waiting down there since Mars cooled off?"

"Must have been."

"I don't care how long it's been down there," Short interrupted. "That thing killed two of our men last night. Not to mention destroying every single one of our planes. What we need now is a plan for getting rid of it."

Maura stared at him. "That's what you brought us out here for? To help you figure out how to kill it? Don't you understand? This is a chance to study something truly unique. A totally new species. Not just life, but intelligent life."

"Dangerous life. For all you know, it intends to flatten your compound tonight."

Maura turned to Will.

"It's not a Martian." How could it be? Whatever built the pillar room and the infinity chamber had possessed enormous intelligence and a highly developed sense of aesthetics. They had been beings of great spiritual wisdom. Not squid-creatures. "It's some kind of heavily mutated squid. Probably caused by the weapons you've been testing." Will turned to Short. "So it's only right that you should be the ones to deal with it."

"At least, let's try to capture him alive." Maura sounded so desperate that Will felt a sudden pang of guilt. This was a big opportunity for her, after all. And as long as it got the thing out of his caves . . .

"It's an extremely valuable specimen," Maura said to Short.

———

Something rose, out in the centre of the lake. The dim moonlight of Phobos gleamed on a dark, rounded surface. Ripples spread as the ominous dome moved towards the shore. As it drew closer, it rose up out of the water.

"He has an exoskeleton," Maura whispered in Will's ear.

It tickled. Will held a finger to his lips, hushing her. Beside them, Short's troops silently checked their weapons. Will scanned the shore, trying to make out the hastily dug pits there which concealed the net crews. The net itself lay along the ground, looking like part of the layer of dried algae and dead squid which covered the lakebed. Flakes of algae swirled overhead on the frigid night breeze.

Short had insisted on placing riflemen close to the old shoreline, in case the nets failed to hold the creature. Will supposed the row of vehicles behind him, armoured and mounted with cannon, were there in case the riflemen failed. Unlike Maura, he felt relieved to have them. But then, Cephalogon hadn't tried to eat Maura for lunch. Will heard a splash, and turned his attention back to the lake.

The dome rose further, exposing a fringe of long, pale tentacles around its lower edge. Cephalogon had no discernable division between head and body, just the tentacle-fringed dome above, supported on a multitude of jointed legs below. By the time the creature stepped out onto dry land, it loomed thirty metres tall, at least.

Searchlights hummed into life, sweeping the monster with their beams. In the light, its carapace was smoky, translucent. Will could see the throb of organs underneath. He swallowed against a sudden surge of nausea, reliving the terror he had felt in the caves. He made himself concentrate on the creature, fighting off the memory. It was on their territory now, vulnerable.

Cephalogon stepped forward, not seeming weak on land at all. It moved steadily ahead on a forest of legs that shone with a chitinous orange covering. Behind it, the net men rose from concealment, hoisting rocket launchers to their shoulders. Hastily assembled that afternoon, the net had been Maura's idea. Will could already tell it wasn't big enough.

Rockets shot hissing into the night, carrying the leading edge of the net up and over the domed carapace. The creature stopped in its tracks. Men rushed forward to encircle it, jumping up and grabbing hold of the edges of the net to tie it down. For a moment, Will thought it had worked.

Then Cephalogon took another step forward. Anchoring ropes pulled free faster than the troops could stake them into the ground. Men still hung from the edges of the net as the creature took another step.

The net began to slip, still held by ropes behind. In front, men holding on to the net dangled ten metres from the ground. Some let go, falling and rolling away. One man stayed where he had fallen, clutching his ankle. A three-toed foot came down on him. There was a squelching sound, and a short, agonized scream.

The scream galvanized the riflemen into action. All around Will, the night erupted in a cacophany of rifle fire. Men yelled as they dropped from the net, some bleeding from bullet wounds.

"Come on!" Maura shouted in his ear. She pulled at his arm, trying to drag him away from the protection of the rifles.

Will pulled back. "You can't save it now," he shouted.

"Run!" she screamed at him. "Do you want to be trampled?"

Will felt the ground tremble, as the creature gathered speed. He remembered the crushed buildings and planes. He ran as fast as he could, with Maura right beside him. Behind them, the shooting intensified. He swerved around the nearest buggy, then crouched behind it to look back. Cephalogon had reached the riflemen, and was trampling them with all – if Maura was right – twenty-five feet.

"Pull back! Clear the field!" someone shouted over a loudspeaker.

The buggy rocked as the cannon on top of it fired with a resounding boom. Too late, Will put his hands over his ears. He peered over the buggy's hood, and saw more missiles streaking towards the creature as the other cannon fired. He watched as the missiles impacted the curving side of the dome. His hands dropped again, the noise forgotten, as he saw the missiles bounce off the shining surface without leaving so much as a scratch.

A few of them exploded on impact, but when the smoke and debris cleared, the shell gleamed whole and unbroken in the searchlights. Most simply ricocheted off, to land among those riflemen not yet trampled.

Will didn't need to see any more. He turned to Maura. She nodded, and they both ran for it. Light came up behind them, throwing their shadows long and thin over the old lakebed. At first, Will thought for some reason the searchlights were following them. Then a buggy pulled up beside them in a cloud of stirred-up algae particles. Short was driving.

They followed Cephalogon out into the desert. It quickly outdistanced them, but they followed its trail, catching the occasional glimpse of it in the distance as they reached the top of a ridge. It led them through part of the Conglomerated Armouries testing range, unimproved land that still bore the marks of old meteor hits, the craters softened into dips and ridges by a heavy layer of dust. Their progress slowed, as Short steered carefully around new pits left by recent testing.

"What about those experimental bombs of yours?" Will asked. "Would they work on it?"

"They might, if we had a plane left to drop one with."

"Ah."

"There is something else we can try. It's only a prototype, but as far as I can see, we've got no other option." Short sounded eager.

"Except leaving it alone," Maura said.

"That thing killed at least twenty men tonight. Who knows how many it will kill tomorrow?"

"It only killed your men because they shot at it."

Will could feel her shaking with fury. Reluctantly, he thought about how he had felt in the cavern when the creature tried to pull him in. Trapped, ready to do anything to try to get away. Perhaps their attack had felt exactly the same way to Cephalogon. It had only begun trampling the men in its own defence, desperate to escape. "She's right. Before they fired, it wasn't coming anywhere near them."

"I thought you were on my side," Short said. "It tried to eat you, didn't it? Isn't that proof of hostile intent?"

"I don't know if it was trying to eat me or not." Though Will hated to admit it, he *had* panicked back there in the caverns. He might have misinterpreted the situation. "I just assumed it was. It could have been attempting to communicate."

"What about our hangars? It crushed every single one of our planes. That was no 'attempt to communicate'."

"Maybe it was," Maura said. "Maybe it didn't like you bombing its planet."

Short opened his mouth to reply as the buggy crested another ridge. His mouth stayed open. There, at the bottom of a kilometres-wide crater, stood the creature. Short killed the headlights instantly, letting the buggy roll back down the ridge.

Will held his breath, watching for the reflected moonlight which would show them the creature's dome rising above the crater edge ahead.

"I don't think he saw us," Maura whispered.

Beside him, Will heard Short muttering into the buggy's radio. "Out." Short turned to them. "We've already tried to capture it once. You saw how well that worked. Now, we do things my way."

Will and Maura got out of the buggy and crept up to lie just under the top of the ridge, peering over at the creature. Cephalogon wandered back and forth over the crater floor, the movements of its legs so slight it seemed almost to float like the huge bubble it resembled.

"What's it doing?" Will whispered.

"I don't know. Dancing?"

Maura shivered. The Martian nights were cold, but Will knew it was more than that. He put his arm around her shoulders.

"We have to try to warn him," Maura said.

"How? Go down there and wave our arms at it? Shoo it away? Even if you're right, even if it is intelligent, how would it understand?"

"I don't know. But we have to try."

"What if you're wrong?" Will persisted. "What if it really did try to eat me? What if it thinks we're more soldiers? You can't go down there Maura. It's suicide."

For a moment, Will feared Maura would get up and run down into the crater anyway. He tightened his arm around her, but she merely lay where she was, watching the creature drift to and fro across the crater floor. After a while, he heard a vehicle drive up.

Will turned and saw a buggy mounted with a bizarre object he could only assume was a weapon. It consisted of three spheres that gleamed with a glassy sheen in the moonlight, linked in a straight line by metal tubing. At one end, perforated metal flanges spread out to form a half-metre-wide dish, like a flower at the end of a glass-and-metal stalk.

"You two. Put these on." Short crawled up and handed them dark goggles, donning a pair himself. "You're about to see something top secret."

With the goggles on, Cephalogon became merely a shadow among shadows on the crater floor. Then a line of light, searingly bright even through the goggles, came into being above them. The beam transfixed the creature's dome, lighting it from within.

"Is that radioactive?" Will glanced at the strange gun. The glass orbs glowed now, though not as brightly as the beam coming from the metal dish. The weapon hummed at a frequency so high Will could only just hear it.

"Classified." Short grinned at him, teeth shining in the light from the beam. "Works a treat, doesn't it?"

The monster's shell now glowed like a giant lantern. Will could see organs throbbing underneath, coloured in lurid purple. Bubbles formed, rising to the top of the dome as the creature cooked from the inside. Its guts turned from purple through orange and yellow to incandescent white as Will stared.

"Get down." Short pushed Will and Maura face down on the ground.

Will heard a tremendous boom. Then, all noise ceased. He knelt up, deafened. At first, he couldn't see anything. Then he remembered the goggles. He took them off and looked again. A rosette of legs, most still upright, marked where Cephalogon had stood. Blobs of slime and fragments of smoking carapace littered the ground around them.

Across the crater, the horizon was beginning to lighten. Will took

Maura's hand, and they watched the sky turn pink as the sun rose. Will looked down into the crater again, and felt his knees go loose. He sat down hard, still staring.

"Not dancing," Will whispered, as though the Martian might still hear him. "Excavating."

Spread out in front of him, familiar curving patterns covered the crater floor. The same patterns he had seen in the caves, only reproduced here on a gigantic scale. The rising sun threw the stumps of pillars and the remains of stone walls into clear relief. They filled the crater; the ruins of an entire Martian city.

Frozen Voice
An Owomoyela

———

They've made us speak Hlerig.

They've made us wrestle sounds slippery as fish or burly as bears through our throats. They've made us stumble through conversations, even human-to-human, that we can hardly say. We can't pronounce our names. They named me *Ulrhegmk*, which in Hlerig means *little mountain thing*.

My mother named me Rhianna.

The things that brought us Hlerig are called *mklimme*. Us humans, they call *hummke*, and all our languages share the descriptor *rhlk*, a term which means *soft* or *runny*. I use rhlk terms to describe Hlerig: *Viscous* in rhlk English, *lipkiy* in rhlk Russian, *klebrig* in rhlk German. They mean that Hlerig sticks like glue in your mouth.

We have a term for mklimme, too: *daddy longlegs*.

A longlegs came walking through my part of the city on a muggy night while my mother was gone later than usual. Thirty, forty feet above us, its eyes flashed like cats' eyes and its spindly legs crossed blocks in three, four steps. One of its feet put down right across the street, big around as a trashcan and still delicate because it was so tall, and the other two feet stood in front of the low dome of the granary and at the common park at the end of the path. Three feet, two hands. One head which descended through the air and twitched from window to window, its faceted eyes angling back and forth until it came to ours. It put its hands, wide as splayed-open dictionaries, on the sill, and looked at us and the rest of the room.

Who is watching you children? it said, in a language my mother called "whalesong." Hlerig isn't their only language, and they prefer the whalesong speech humans can't hope to pronounce. I answered in Hlerig, pushing my brother out of the way.

"My mother watches us, but she's with friends."

She shouldn't be away, the longlegs said, and its head went up and back away from our window toward the sky. *We'll find her.*

Longlegs all think they're so helpful.

I watched it walk away, and grabbed my brother. My mother had told us where she was going; after making sure we had food in the cooler, just before she walked us to class in the park two days before, she'd told me exactly where she'd be. When the longlegs went looking they wouldn't find her with friends, and then they'd look elsewhere.

I pulled my brother up to the second floor of the house, where the walls had been ripped away and rebuilt like a paper wasp nest. "We're going to find her," I said.

My brother clapped to get my attention, and then made a clumsy sign with his hands. The longlegs tried to teach him to sign like they did, with their seven digits and two opposable thumbs, but his hands were no more made for their sign language as my mouth was made for their words. I had to squint in the darkness to understand him.

"We'll tell her they're out looking and bring her into the city a back way," I told him. "We just have to make sure she's not coming over the plains."

I was young, then, and I thought that would be easy.

My brother nodded and began to prepare, picking up what he thought we'd need – scarves and a flashlight and a compass with no letters on it, only tick marks around the circumference. The needle wobbled from North to Northeast whenever we used it, but it was the only one we had.

When we were sure the longlegs wouldn't see us, we went downstairs and pushed open the door. I grabbed my brother's hand, and we ran for the edge of the city.

———

The mountain by our city is called *Etrhe*, and the rocky hills and destroyed roads leading up into them are called *ulrhe* – not foothills, not exactly, but little mountains. In the ulrhe are ruins. And the cairn.

Our mother went to the cairn whenever she could sneak out at night – whenever the mklimme in our city were few enough in number, or when the skies rumbled with thunder and crackled with lightning. Storms confound the longlegs. They can't see or hear.

She came back from the cairn with books: old books, lost books, books we hid the instant we had them.

I'd never been out to the cairn. I didn't know my way out of the city like my mother did. She knew how to evade the longlegs and their sympathizers. (*Sympathizers* have little to do with *sympathy*, and we could never tell them anything.) I just ran with my brother, past houses, past the longlegs' paperwasp structures, doing our best to look like we were on an errand whenever a longlegs turned its body and brought its all-seeing head our way.

Soon we were in the outskirts of the city, where old houses that hadn't been repopulated stood. And all the ruins began to look the same: wrecked walls, decaying doors and wooden floors, swept eerily clean of furniture and furnishings and all the detritus of domestic life. Humans had gone through, under the longlegs' watchful eyes, long ago. They'd brought everything to the cairn.

The night deepened and we were picking our way around the buildings, backtracking when roads were blocked, trying to find our way past buildings that had crumbled over their yards. Now and then shadows would move through the rubble, or seem to move, or a sound would be caught by the skeletal landscape and come twisting out at us so warped and strange that my brother had to clap a hand over my mouth to keep me from screaming. It was no wonder we got lost, and with that sense of being lost came fear. Then exhaustion.

We went into an old building. I didn't want to – the war left a lot of buildings crumbling, and every few months you'd hear about someone who got caught in one, broke a leg or their skull or their spine trying to scavenge some piece of a pre-war life. Almost without exception, those pieces were taken to the cairn anyway.

But it was cold, and we couldn't risk the mklimme finding us out there, so I smoothed the broken glass away from a windowsill and climbed inside. I told myself that when the sun rose, I'd go up to the roof and plot a course to the edge of the city. But for that night, we went up a set of groaning wooden stairs and found a bathroom – no windows – to hide in.

We didn't sleep. We huddled there for hours, my brother pressed against my side, and just as I thought he might drift off, the Hum began. The longlegs have a language for calling from city to city. Humans can't hear it but we can feel it in our bones, and certain houses amplify it. It felt like the tile floor was trying to skitter under us, trapped in the instant before the skitter, and I felt sick to the bottom of my gut.

My father used to tell us, before he was taken, that the longlegs don't sleep. They go about their business at night, walking through the cities or from city to city, with their long legs and their earth-skittering Hum. The ones inside the cities would peek in windows, make sure their humans were sleeping. And if there weren't humans sleeping there, they'd check back the next day, then look until they found them.

I couldn't understand the Hum, but I felt down to my bones that the mklimme were discussing my mother, my brother, and me.

I turned to hug my brother. His eyes were closed, his mouth pressed into a thin line that made him look much older than he was. "Don't worry," I said in pidgin rhlk. "Pretend we're playing hide-and-seek. Remember when we hid in the fireplace? Before mom brought home those encyclopedias and we had nowhere else to put them?" I brushed my hands against his hair. He has dark hair, almost black. It's a hobby in my family to name each other, because names are forbidden. Human names, at least.

When I was born, our longlegs looked from us to the mountain bordering our city and then bent down to say the words in Hlerig. *Your name is Ulrhegmk. Little mountain thing.* When I talked to other longlegs, they made noises and said my name was beautiful.

I used to stand over my brother's bed and say *Your name is Dougal. It means "dark stranger."* I'd say *Your name is Wyatt. It means "hardy" and "brave."* Or I'd say *Your name is Avalon. It's a name from a far-away place. I'll teach you to read about it one day.*

"Remember when we hid in the fireplace all day?"

The far wall of our living room was false. My mother and my father covered up the shelves along the mantlepiece. The false wall wasn't hard to get into: it was held on with construction gum, and if you knew where to look, you could slide your hand into a handhold and pull it out. Even my brother could, if he planted both feet and tugged; my mother wanted us to have access.

I hugged my brother against me. "We'll just be quiet. They can't see in."

Our fireplace had never been used for fire. No one in the city cleaned chimneys and we didn't want to ask the longlegs, so my parents called it a fire hazard and left it alone. If you were very careful, after the false wall went up, you could climb into the fireplace and ease the wall into place behind you. Sitting in the fireplace wasn't comfortable, but it was the safest place to read. You had to position yourself into a corner with your legs tucked to one side, then you could put a candle in the corner left over, and you could read.

"We'll be very quiet," I told my brother, who was always quiet. "In the morning we'll find mom, and then we'll go home."

Our longlegs, the one who caretakes our neighborhood, has a name we can't pronounce. The name it gives us in Hlerig is *Gnheg*, but in secret we call it *Eroica* because the unpronounceable name reminded my father of part of a song by that name. Eroica saw our living room before the false wall was put in, but my father wasn't worried. He and my mother painted a fireplace on the false wall when they put it up, and Eroica never noticed the difference. It was depth perception, my father explained to me; all the longlegs had problems with depth.

But their vision was fine.

They saw him running home with a book one day. A bound book, bound for the hidden fireplace, my father bounding over all the things in his path. It's funny how some things come together.

They caught him.

He must have thought he could hide the book, explain his running away, but they broke a window after he closed the door. My brother screamed, like he'd never scream again, and I held him back on the stairs. From the stairs I saw Eroica's hands (wide-open dictionaries) groping after my father (and I *hate* that word, grope, *oshchupyvat*; it's as gummy in any language as its Hlerig word *botb*, as stupid and unfeeling) until they found him, standing not quite six feet from the tip of his head to his feet on the ground, and when one of those hands wrapped around him and the other touched the book, I heard Eroica scream too.

Zenig-hrie. Frozen voices. That's the Hlerig word for books; nothing frightens them more. When they came, mother said, they stomped over our armies and our nuclear waste sites and even natural terrifying things like volcanoes and steep cliffs and the tornado alley, but on pulling a roof from a library they would scream, like Eroica screamed, and they would run away on their long long legs until certain ones, special ones, came and took the books away. Brave people, then, like fighter pilots, followed them and saw them doing strange things to the books, and later on they saw them doing the same strange things to their own dead.

You hear stories about people who tied books to tanks and cars and their own bodies so that the longlegs couldn't touch them. At first it was the big religious books, the ones that are easy to find even now because so many people hid them: the Bible, the Qur'an. Then it was anything. Then the longlegs came back with fire, and the books burned, and the people burned, and in the end (my mother used to tell me stories ending with *The End*, but this one wasn't like those; she explained to me the difference between *The End* and *in the end*) even the books didn't save them. The world lay down and we lost our voices, the frozen ones and our rhlk, our beautiful liquid tongues.

I was born later. And my brother, who snuggled into my arms in that muggy, Humming night, had been born even later than that.

I searched around in my mind until I found Aesop's fables. They're easy to remember, because as long as you know the moral at the end you can say anything that comes to mind to get you there. I told him, as I held him, about the tortoise and the hare. I told him about the ant and the grasshopper. I told him about the boy who cried wolf, and somehow, he found sleep.

Somehow I slept for a little, too, and my dreams were full of words: dancing words, warning words, words as slick as the melting wax from our candles and as dark as the fireplace in the home we'd left behind us.

————

Longlegs congregated away from the city. They liked the wide-open spaces where they could stretch their legs without worrying about where to put their feet down in the tangle of broken-down fixed-up houses.

The wide-open space east of our city in the foothills used to be part of our city, too. They tore it up. The cairn in the middle *was* the city around it: chunks of asphalt and brick wall and siding and telephone wires and telephone poles and light poles sticking out of the mess like toothpicks, a mountain among the ulrhe. Underneath that pile is where all of our books went, along with dead longlegs and the dead soldiers the longlegs took away. My mother said there were ways to get under it, using the old sewer systems, but they were dangerous and grim – you never knew when you'd find a skeleton instead of a book, and the sewers hadn't been maintained in so long that parts of them were always collapsing.

The cairn was still where they took the books and dead longlegs, but they only seemed to put them on top and pile more things on top of them. No one could tell if that's where they took the human dead; they mostly left us alone, digging graves in our usual cemeteries, unless they found corpses with no one to claim them. That didn't happen often.

No one was homeless after the longlegs took over; everyone was fed, everyone had shelter. There were even some people who loved them for that.

My mother said it was easy to feed everyone after you'd killed most of them anyway.

The good thing about the cairn was that the longlegs never went there. The bad thing was that there weren't even old buildings left; it was all torn-up ground and wild weeds, broken streets rambling through the grass. Longlegs could see you, the same way you'd see a mouse running across your floor. And sometimes you'd see movement in the grass and remember stories about wild dogs.

When we found our way out of our city in daylight, everything, even the sunlight, frightened us. Whenever we saw longlegs we hunkered down into the long grass and watched until we were sure they were moving away. Then we'd run for the cairn again, swelling larger and larger against the horizon as we neared, like a bruise rising out of the ground to overshadow us.

The sun rose too. I started calling out. My brother put his hand to my mouth but I pulled it away; even my voice sounded small in the empty hills, and the far-off longlegs didn't turn our way. Even if they'd heard me, I wonder how I would have sounded to them – maybe my plaintive rhlk cries would be no stranger than the calling of birds, out here.

We ran to the edge of the cairn, then up, into and over it, around disturbed piles of rocks, past pieces of pre-war things I could only identify because I'd read about them. After a while I got to thinking that we *were* like the birds around the mountain, and our voices were part of the world out here, speaking forbidden words in this world the longlegs built but didn't control.

Then I heard my mother's cry.

I froze. I grabbed my brother's hand, because the sound I'd heard was not language, not any language she'd taught me. My brother pulled his hand away and ran. I ran after him, tumbling rocks, scrambling over debris.

She was lying on her back. Our mother. Her head was tilted up toward the sky, and she tried to move it to look at us when we came near. When I knelt down next to her I could see a white crust at the corners of her eyes. I took her hand, and felt cold all over.

She had ink on her fingertips. Her knapsack had burst and books were scattered across the cairn with their pages flapping in the breeze. And the side of her shirt was dark with blood. I kept looking at the books, the knapsack, because I was afraid to look at the blood.

"Where are you?" she whispered, in English. It was her first language, and ours, Hlerig be damned. Then she whispered "*Non, non*," and her fingers curled around mine.

My brother put his hand on her shoulder, and she took one long, shuddering breath.

"The longlegs are looking for you," I said. It seemed like such a stupid thing to say, but I had to say something. No other words came.

She took another breath. "I fell," she said, answering what I hadn't been strong enough to ask. Her head moved, and she looked up at a part of the cairn tan with sandstone. "It was dark, and . . . "

She swallowed. It sounded like it hurt her to swallow.

"Darling, darling," she said, "they won't find me here. You have to go home."

It was in her voice, not her words, that I heard she wasn't coming with us.

I gripped her hand. "You have to show us the way back in," I said. "How to get through the old city. We'll go through the ulrhe so they don't see us on the plains."

She was quiet for a while, frowning, her eyes closed. She looked a little like my brother had the previous night; she knew, and I knew, and I think even he knew, that I was lying to myself, thinking she would come back with us.

Carefully, painfully, she raised her other hand to touch my cheek. I remember how cold her palm was. "Go back," she said. "The mklimme will take care of you."

Sometimes I wondered why my mother called them *mklimme* – that ugly, hard Hlerig word to say. She said they had the right to name themselves. Just as we wanted.

My brother was picking up the books from her knapsack, turning over the covers to see them in the full sunlight, and stacking them from biggest to smallest on the ground next to us. He was doing that not to look at her, I think.

She rolled her head to the side to watch him. Then she reached out for one of the books, and he handed it over. Her lips pressed together, and a pained noise escaped them.

"Don't bring them home," she whispered. "Let the mklimme find you."

"I want to take them," I told her. I meant, *I don't want to leave you here.*

"I want you safe," she said.

I held mother's hands on top of the book. Her skin was as cold as the cover, or the cover was as warm as her skin. I remembered when she brought my first book home, a thin volume with large illustrated pages and breaths of text on each page. It was so lively, so easy to read, that I forgot why they called it a *frozen voice.* I'd closed my eyes, and believed I could feel it breathing.

I closed my eyes, and felt my mother's hands rise and fall unsteadily with her breath.

The Hlerig word *zenig* can mean *frozen* or *dead.* "I wonder," my mother told me once, when I'd wondered why books frightened the longlegs so much, "if they don't think we've done something horrible to produce them. If when they saw us wearing books like armor, they didn't react the way we would if we saw people walking around wearing human bones and skin."

I wondered if there was a way to show them that every time the covers opened the voices lived again. Show them how to hear them, whispering stories inside you.

My mother squeezed my hand. " They think they're doing the best for us."

In Hlerig there's a word for everything, but the words don't fit us well. I can't wrestle my mouth around *chlkrig* and still think *love*, and my brilliant, warm mother, whose hand I held tight, was nothing like egg-laying *yntig*. But there are moments of synchronicity. The Hlerig word *kpap*, which means *enduring* or *venerable*, sounds a little like *kitab* in rhlk Arabic – the word for "book." And the derivation *chldn* from *chlkrig* sounds almost like *children* does. In Hlerig it means "loved."

"There will be more books, I promise you," she said.

They have made us speak Hlerig. But I wouldn't use the Hlerig words. I wouldn't speak them then.

To my mother I said *Spasibo, xie xie, thank you, d kuju*. And I held my brother's hand as he mouthed *Au revoir, annyeonghi-geseyo, má'a al-salaama, goodbye*.

Softly Spoke the Gabbleduck
Neal Asher

———

Lost in some perverse fantasy, Tameera lovingly inspected the displays of her Optek rifle. For me, what happened next proceeded with the unstoppable nightmare slowness of an accident. She brought the butt of the rifle up to her shoulder, took careful aim, and squeezed off a single shot. One of the sheq slammed back against a rock face, then tumbled down through vegetation to land in the white water of a stream.

———

Some creatures seem to attain the status of myth even though proven to be little different from other apparently prosaic species. On Earth, the lion contends with the unicorn, the wise old elephant never forgets, and gentle whales sing haunting ballads in the deeps. It stems from anthropomorphism, is fed by both truth and lies, and, over time, firmly embeds itself in human culture. On Myral, where I had spent the last ten years, only a little of such status attached to the largest autochthon – not surprising for a creature whose name is a contraction of "shit-eating quadruped." But rumors of something else in the wilderness, something that had no right to be there, had really set the myth-engines of the human mind into motion, and brought hunters to this world.

There was no sign of any sheq on the way out over the narrow vegetation-cloaked mounts. They only put in an appearance after I finally moored my blimp to a peak, above a horizontal slab on which blister tents could be pitched. My passengers noticed straight away that the slab had been used many times before, and that my mooring was an iron ring long set into the rock, but then, campsites were a rarity amid the steep slopes, cliffs, and streams of this area. It wasn't a place humans were built for. Sheq country.

Soon after he disembarked, Tholan went over to the edge to try out one of his disposable vidcams. The cam itself was about the size of his forefinger, and he was pointing it out over the terrain while inspecting a palm com he held in his other hand. He had unloaded a whole case of these cams, which he intended to position in likely locations, or dangle into mist pockets on a line – a hunter's additional eyes. He called me over. Tameera and Anders followed.

"There." He nodded downward.

A seven of sheq was making its way across the impossible terrain – finding handholds amid the lush vertical vegetation and traveling with the assurance of spiders on a wall. They were disconcertingly simian, about the size of a man, and quadrupedal – each limb jointed like a human arm, but ending in hands bearing eight long prehensile fingers. Their heads, though, were anything but simian, being small, insectile, like the head of a mosquito, but with two wide trumpet-like proboscises.

"They won't be a problem, will they?" Tholan's sister, Tameera, asked.

She was the most xenophobic, I'd decided, but then, such phobia made little difference to their sport: the aliens they sought out usually being the "I'm gonna chew off the top of your head and suck out your brains" variety.

"No – so long as we leave them alone," said Tholan. Using his thumb on the side controls of his palm com, he increased the camera's magnification, switching it to infrared, then ultrasound imaging.

"I didn't load anything," said Anders, Tholan's PA. "Are they herbivores?"

"Omnivores," I told her. "They eat some of that vegetation you see and supplement their diet with rock conch and octupal."

"Rock conch and octupal indeed," said Anders.

I pointed to the conch-like molluscs clinging to the wide leaves below the slab.

Anders nodded, then said, "Octupal?"

"Like it sounds: something like an octopus, lives in pools, but can drag itself overland when required." I glanced at Tameera and added, "None of them bigger than your hand."

I hadn't fathomed this trio yet. Brother and sister hunted together, relied on each other, yet seemed to hate each other. Anders, who I at first thought Tholan was screwing, really did just organize things for him. Perhaps I should have figured them out before agreeing to being hired, then Tameera would never have taken the shot she then took.

―――――

The hot chemical smell from the rifle filled the unbreathable air. I guessed they used primitive projectile weapons of this kind to make their hunts more sporting. I didn't know how to react. Tholan stepped forward and pushed down the barrel of her weapon before she could kill another of the creatures.

"That was stupid," he said.

"Do they frighten you?" she asked coquettishly.

I reached up and checked that my throat plug was still in place, for I felt breathless, but it was still bleeding oxygen into my bronchus. To say that I now had a bad feeling about all this would have been an understatement.

"You know that as well as putting us all in danger, she just committed a crime," I said conversationally, as Tholan stepped away from his sister.

"Crime?" he asked.

"She just killed a C-grade sentient. If the Warden AI finds out and can prove she knew before she pulled the trigger, then she's dead. But that's not the main problem now." I eyed the sheq seven, now six. They seemed to be confused about the cause of their loss. "Hopefully they won't attack, but it'll be an idea to keep watch."

He stared at me, shoved his cam into his pocket. I turned away and headed back. Why had I agreed to bring these bored aristos out here to hunt for Myral's mythic gabbleduck? Money. Those who have enough to live comfortably greatly underestimate it as a source of motivation. Tholan was paying enough for me to pay off all I owed on my blimp, and prevent a particular shark from paying me a visit to collect interest by way of involuntarily donated organs. It would also be enough for me to upgrade my apartment in the citadel, so I could rent it while I went out to look at this world. I'd had many of the available cerebral loads and knew much about Myral's environment, but that wasn't the same as experiencing it. There was still much for me to learn, to know. Though I was certain that the chances of my finding a gabbleduck – a creature from a planet light-centuries away – anywhere on Myral, were lower than the sole of my boot.

"She only did that to get attention," said Anders at my shoulder.

"Well, let's hope she didn't succeed too well!" I replied. I looked up at my blimp, and considered the prospect of escaping this trio and bedding down for the night. Certainly we would be getting nothing more done today, what with the blue giant sun gnawing the edge of the world as it went down.

"You have to excuse her. She's over-compensating for a father who ignored her for the first twenty years of her life."

Anders had been coming on to me right from the start and I wondered just what sort of rich bitch game she was playing, though to find out, I would have to let my guard down, and that I had no intention of doing. She was too much: too attractive, too intelligent, and just being in her presence set things jumping around in my stomach. She would destroy me.

"I don't have to excuse her," I said. "I just have to tolerate her."

With that, I headed to the alloy ladder extending down from the blimp cabin.

"Why are they called shit-eaters?" she asked, falling into step beside me. Obviously she'd heard where the name sheq came from.

"As well as the rock conch and octupal, they eat each other's shit – running it through a second intestinal tract."

She winced.

I added, "But it's not something they should die for."

"You're not going to report this are you?" she asked.

"How can I? – He didn't want me carrying traceable com."

I tried not to let my anxiety show. Tholan didn't want any of Myral's AIs finding out what he was up to, so, as a result, he'd provided all our com equipment, and it was encoded. I was beginning to wonder if that might be unhealthy for me.

"You're telling me you have no communicator up there?" She pointed up at the blimp.

"I won't report it," I said, then climbed, wishing I could get away with pulling the ladder up behind me, wishing I had not stuck so rigidly to the wording of the contract.

Midark is that time when it's utterly black on Myral, when the sun is precisely on the opposite side of the world from you. It comes after five hours of blue, lasts about three hours prior to the next five hours of blue – the twilight that is neither day nor night and is caused by reflection of sunlight from the sub-orbital dust cloud. Anyway, it was at midark when the screaming and firing woke me. By the time I had reattached my oxygen bottle and was clambering down the ladder, some floods were lighting the area and it was all over.

"Yes, you warned me," Tholan spat.

I walked over to Tameera's tent, which was ripped open and empty. There was no blood, but then the sheq would not want to damage the replacement. I glanced at Anders, who was inspecting a palm com.

"She's alive." She looked up. "She must have been using her own oxygen supply rather than the tent's. We have to go after her now."

"Claw frames in midark?" I asked.

"We've got night specs." She looked at me as if she hadn't realized until then how stupid I was.

"I don't care if you've got owl and cat genes – it's suicide."

"Do explain," said Tholan nastily.

"You got me out here as your guide. The plan was to set up a base and from it survey the area for any signs of the gabbleduck – by claw frame."

"Yes . . ."

"Well, claw frames are only safe here during the day."

"I thought you were going to explain."

"I am." I reached out, detached one of the floods from its narrow post, and walked with it to the edge of the slab. I shone it down, revealing occasional squirming movement across the cliff of vegetation below.

"Octupals," said Anders. "What's the problem?"

I turned to her and Tholan. "At night they move to new pools, and, being slow-moving, they've developed a defense. Anything big gets too close, and they eject stinging barbs. They won't kill you, but you'll damned well know if you're hit, so unless you've brought armored clothing . . ."

"But what about Tameera?" Anders asked.

"Oh, the sheq will protect her for a while."

"For a while?" Tholan queried.

"At first, they'll treat her like an infant replacement for the one she killed," I told him. "So they'll guide her hands and catch her if she starts to fall. After a time, they'll start to get bored, because sheq babies learn very quickly. If we don't get to her before tomorrow night's first blue, she'll probably have broken her neck."

"When does this stop?" He nodded toward the octupal activity.

"Mid-blue."

"We go then."

———

The claw frame is a sporting development from military exoskeletons. The frame itself braces your body. A spine column rests against your back like a metal flatworm. Metal bones from this extend down your legs and along your arms. The claws are four times the size of human hands, and splayed out like big spiders from behind them, and from behind the ankles. Each finger is a piton, and programmed to seek out crevices on the rock face you are climbing. The whole thing is stronger, faster, and more sensitive than a human being. If you want, it can do all the work for you. Alternatively, it can just be set in neutral, the claws folded back, while you do all the climbing yourself – the frame only activating to save your life. Both Anders and Tholan, I noted, set theirs to about a third-assist, which is where I set mine. Blister tents and equipment in their backpacks, and oxygen bottles and catalyzers at their waists, they went over the edge ahead of me. Tameera's claw frame scrambled after them – a glittery skeleton – slaved to them. I glanced back at my blimp and wondered if I should just turn round and go back to it. I went over the edge.

With the light intensity increasing and the octupals bubbling down in their pools, we made good time. Later, though, when we had to go lower to keep on course after the sheq, things got a bit more difficult. Despite the three of us being on third-assist we were panting within a few hours, as lower down, there was less climbing and more pushing through tangled vegetation. I noted that my catalyzer pack was having trouble keeping up – cracking the CO_2 atmosphere and topping up the two flat bodyform bottles at my waist.

"She's eight kilometers away," Anders suddenly said. "We'll not reach her at this rate."

"Go two-thirds assist," said Tholan.

We all did that, and soon our claw frames were moving faster through the vegetation and across the rock-faces than was humanly possible. It made me feel lazy – like I was just a sack of flesh hanging on the hard-working claw frame. But we covered those eight kilometers quickly, and, as the sun breached the horizon, glimpsed the sheq far ahead of us, scrambling up from the sudden shadows in the valleys. They were a seven again now, I saw: Tameera being assisted along by creatures that had snatched the killer of one of their own, mistaking her for sheq herself.

"Why do they do it?" Anders asked as we scrambled along a vertical face.

"Do what?"

"Snatch people to make up their sevens."

"Three reasons I've heard: optimum number for survival, or seven sheq required for successful mating, or the start of a primitive religion."

"Which do you believe it is?"

"Probably a bit of them all."

As we drew closer, I could hear Tameera sobbing in terror, pure fatigue, and self-pity. The six sheq were close around her, nudging her along, catching her feet when they slipped, grabbing her hands and placing them in firmer holds. I could also see that her dark green slicksuit was spattered with a glutinous yellow substance, and felt my gorge rising at what else she had suffered. They had tried to feed her.

We halted about twenty meters behind on a seventy-degree slope and watched as Tameera was badgered toward where it tilted upright, then past the vertical.

"How do we play this?" Tholan asked.

"We have to get to her before they start negotiating that." I pointed at the lethal terrain beyond the sheq. "One mistake there and . . ." I gestured below to tilted slabs jutting from undergrowth, half hidden under fog generated by a nearby waterfall. I didn't add that we probably wouldn't even be able to find the body, despite the tracker Tameera evidently wore. "We'll have to run a line to her. Anders can act as the anchor. She'll have to make her way above, and it's probably best if she takes Tameera's claw frame with her. You'll go down slope to grab Tameera if anything goes wrong and she falls. I'll go in with the line and the harness."

"You've done this before?" Anders asked.

"Have you?" I countered.

"Seems you know how to go about it," Tholan added.

"Just uploads from the planetary almanac."

"Okay, we'll do it like you said," Tholan agreed.

I'd noticed that all three of them carried fancy monofilament climbing winders on their belts. Anders set hers unwinding its line, which looked thick as rope with cladding applied to the monofilament on its way out. I took up the ring end of the line and attached the webbing harness Tholan took from one of his pack's many pockets.

"Set?" I asked.

They both nodded, Tholan heading downslope and Anders up above. Now, all I had to do was get to Tameera through the sheq and get her into the harness.

As I drew closer, the creatures began to notice me and those insectile heads swung toward me, proboscises pulsating as if they were sniffing.

"Tameera . . . Tameera!"

She jerked her head up, yellow gunk all around her mouth and spattered across her face. "Help me!"

"I've got a line here and a harness," I told her, but I wasn't sure if she understood.

I was about three meters away when the sheq that had been placing her foot on a thick root growing across the face of stone abruptly spun and scrambled toward me. Tholan's Optek crashed and I saw the explosive exit wound open in the creature's jade green torso – a flower of yellow and pink. It sighed, sagged, but did not fall – its eight-fingered hands tangled in verdancy. The other sheq dived for safer holds and pulled close to the rock face.

"What the fuck!"

"Just get the harness on her!" Tholan bellowed.

I moved in quickly, not so much because he ordered it, but because I didn't want him blowing away more of the creatures. Tameera was at first lethargic, but then she began to get the idea. Harness on, I moved aside.

"Anders!"

Anders had obviously seen, because she drew the line taut through greenery and began hauling Tameera upward, away from sheq who were now beginning to nose in confusion toward their second dead member.

Stripped-off line cladding fell like orange snow. I reached out, shoved the dead sheq, once, twice, and it tumbled down the slope, the rest quickly scrambling after it. Tholan was moving aside, looking up at me. I gestured to a nearby mount with a flat top on which we could all gather.

"Got her!" Anders called.

Glancing up, I saw Anders installing Tameera in the other claw frame. "Over there!" I gestured to the mount. Within a few minutes, we were all on the small area of level stone, gazing down toward where the five remaining sheq had caught their companion, realized it was dead, and released it again, and were now zipping about like wasps disturbed from a nest.

"We should head back to the blimp, fast as you like."

No one replied, because Tameera chose that moment to vomit noisily. The stench was worse even than that from the glutinous yellow stuff all over her.

"What?" said Anders.

"They fed her," I explained.

That made Anders look just as sick.

Finally sitting up, then detaching her arms from her claw frame, Tameera stared at her brother and held out her hand. He unhitched his pack, drew out her Optek rifle and handed it over. She fired from that sitting position, bowling one of the sheq down the distant slope and the subsequent vertical drop.

"Look, you can't—"

The barrel of Tholan's Optek was pointing straight at my forehead.

"We can," he said.

I kept my mouth shut as, one by one, Tameera picked off the remaining sheq and sent them tumbling down into the mist-shrouded river canyon. It was only then that we returned to the slab campsite.

———

Blue again, but I was certainly ready for sleep, and felt a surge of resentment when the blimp cabin began shaking. Someone was coming up the ladder, then walking round the catwalk. Shortly, Anders opened the airtight door and hauled herself inside. I saw her noting with some surprise how the passenger cabin converted into living quarters. I was ensconced in the cockpit chair, sipping a glass of whisky, feet up on the console. She turned off her oxygen supply, tried the air in the cabin, then sat down on the corner of the fold-down bed, facing me.

"Does it disgust you?" she asked.

I shrugged. Tried to stay nonchalant. What was happening below didn't bother me, her presence in my cabin did.

She continued, "There's no reason to be disgusted. Incest no longer has the consequences it once had. All genetic faults can be corrected in the womb . . . ."

"Did I say I was disgusted? Perhaps it's you, why else are you up here?"

She grimaced. "Well, they do get noisy."

"I'm sure it won't last much longer," I said. "Then you can return to your tent."

"You're not very warm, are you?"

"Just wary – I know the kind of games you people play."

"You people?"

"The bored and the wealthy."

"I'm Tholan's PA. I'm an employee."

I sat there feeling all resentful, my resentment increased because, of course, she was right. I should not have lumped her in the same category as Tholan and his sister. She was, in fact, in my category. She had also casually just knocked away one of my defenses.

"Would you like a drink?" I eventually asked, my mouth dry.

Now I expected her righteous indignation and rejection. But Anders was more mature than that, more dangerous.

"Yes, I would." As she said it, she undid the stick seams of her boots and kicked them off. Then she detached the air hose from her throat plug, coiled it back to the bottle, then unhooked that from her belt and put it on the floor. I hauled myself from my chair and poured her a whisky, adding ice from my recently installed little fridge.

"Very neat," she said, accepting the drink. As I made to step past her and return to the cockpit chair, she caught hold of my forearm and pulled me down beside her.

"You know," I said, "that if we don't report what happened today, that would make us accessories. That could mean readjustment, even mind-wipe."

"Are you hetero?" she asked.

I nodded. She put her hand against my chest and pushed me back on to the bed. I let her do it – laid back. She stood up, looking down at me as she drained her whisky. Then she undid her trousers, dropped them and kicked them away, then climbed astride me still wearing her shirt and very small briefs. Still staring at me she undid my trousers, freed my erection, then pulling aside the crotch of her briefs, slowly slid down onto me. Then she began to grind back and forth.

"Just come," she said, when she saw my expression. "You've got all night to return the favor." I managed to hold on for about another thirty seconds. It had been a while. Afterward, we stripped naked, and I did return the favor. And then we spent most of the blue doing things to each other normally reserved for those for whom straight sex had become a source of ennui.

"You know, Tholan will pay a great deal for your silence, one way or another."

I understood that Tholan might not pay *me* for my silence. I thought her telling me this worthy of the punishment I then administered, and which she noisily enjoyed, muffling her face in the pillow.

We slept a sleep of exhaustion through midark.

———

Tameera wanted trophies. She wanted a pair of sheq heads to cunningly preserve and mount on the gateposts on either side of the drive to her and Tholan's property on Earth. Toward the end of morning blue, we ate recon rations and prepared to set out. I thought it pointless to tell them of the penalties for possessing trophies from class C sentients.

They'd already stepped so far over the line that it was a comparatively minor crime.

"What we need to discuss is my fee," I said.

"Seems to me he's already had some payment," said Tameera, eyeing Anders.

Tholan shot her a look of annoyance and turned back to me. "Ten times what I first offered. No one needs to know."

"Any items you bring back you'll carry in your stuff," I said.

I wondered at their arrogance. Maybe they'd get away with it – we'd know soon enough upon our return to the citadel – but most likely, a drone had tagged one of the sheq, and, as the creature died, a satellite eye had recorded the event. The way I saw it, I could claim to have been scared they would kill me, and only keeping up the criminal façade until we reached safety. Of course, if they did get away with what they'd done, there was no reason why I shouldn't benefit.

While we prepared, I checked the map in my palm com, input our position, and worked out an easier course than the one we had taken the day before. The device would keep us on course despite the fact that Tholan had allowed no satellite link-up. By the sun, by its own elevation, the time, and by reading the field strength of Myral's magnetosphere, the device kept itself accurately located on the map I'd loaded from the planetary almanac.

We went over the edge as the octupals slurped and splashed in their pools and the sun flung arc-welder light across the land. This time, we took it easy on third assist, also stopping for meals and rest. During one of these breaks, I demonstrated how to use a portable stove to broil a rock conch in its shell, but Tholan was the only one prepared to sample the meat. I guess it was a man thing. As we traveled, I pointed out flowering spider vines, their electric-red male flowers taking to the air in search of the blowsy yellow female flowers: these plants and their pollinating insects having moved beyond the symbiosis seen on Earth to become one. Then, the domed heads of octupals rising out of small rock pools to blink bulbous gelatinous eyes at the evening blue, we moored our blister tents on a forty-degree slope.

Anders connected my tent to hers, while a few meters away Tholan and Tameera connected their tents. No doubt they joined their sleeping bags in the same way we did. Sex, in a tent fixed to such a slope, with a sleeping bag also moored to the rock through the ground sheet, was a bit cramped. But it was enjoyable and helped to pass most of the long night. Sometime during midark I came half awake to the sound of a voice. "Slabber gebble-crab," and "speg bruglor nomp," were its nonsensical utterances. The yelling and groaning from Tholan, in morning blue, I thought due to his and his sister's lovemaking. But in full morning I had to pick octupal stings from the fabric of my tent, and I saw that Tholan wore a dressing on his cheek.

"What happened?" I asked.

"I just stuck my damned head out," he replied.

"What treatment have you used?"

"Unibiotic and antallergens."

"That should do it."

Shame I didn't think to ask why he wanted to leave his tent and go creeping about in the night. That I attributed the strange voice in midark to a dream influenced things neither one way nor the other.

It was only a few hours into the new day that we reached the flat-topped mount from which Tameera had slaughtered the remaining sheq. I studied the terrain through my monocular and realized how the excitement of our previous visit here had blinded me to just how dangerous this area was. There wasn't a slope that was less than seventy degrees, and many of the river valleys and canyons running between the jagged rocks below were full of rolling mist. Claw frames or not, this was about as bad as it could get.

"Well, that's where they should be," said Tholan, lowering his own monocular and pointing to a wider canyon floored with mist out of which arose the grumble of a river.

"If they haven't been swept away," I noted.

Ignoring me, he continued, "We'll work down from where they fell. Maybe some of them got caught in the foliage."

From the mount, we traveled down, across a low ridge, then up onto the long slope from which we had rescued Tameera. I began to cut down diagonally, and Anders followed me while Tameera and Tholan kept moving along high to where the sheq had been, though why they were going there I had no idea, for we had seen every one fall. Anders was above me when I began to negotiate a whorled hump of stone at the shoulder of a cliff. I thought I could see a sheq caught in some foliage down there. As I was peering through the mist, Anders screamed above me. I had time only to glance up and drive my frame's fingers into stone when she barreled into me. We both went over. Half detached from her frame, she clung around my neck. I looked up to where two fingers of my frame held us suspended. I noted that her frame – the property of Tholan and Tameera – was dead weight. Then I looked higher and guessed why.

Brother and sister were scrambling down toward us, saying nothing, not urging us to hang on. I guessed that was precisely what they did not want us to do. It must have been frustrating for Tholan: the both of us in one tent that could have been cut from its moorings – two witnesses lost in the unfortunate accident – but sting-shooting molluscs preventing him from committing the dirty deed. I reached round with my free claw and tightly gripped Anders's belt, swung my foot claws in and gripped the rock face with them.

"Get the frame off."

She stared at me in confusion, then looked up the slope, and I think all the facts clicked into place. Quickly, while I supported her, she undid her frame's straps, leaving the chest straps until last. It dropped into the mist: a large chrome harvestman spider . . . a dead one.

"Okay, round onto my back and cling on tightly."

She swung round quickly. Keeping to third-assist – for any higher assistance and the frame might move too fast for her to hang on – I began climbing down the cliff to the mist. The first Optek bullet ricocheted off stone by my face. The second ricochet, by my hand, was immediately followed by an animal grunt from Anders. Something warm began trickling down my neck and her grip loosened.

———————

Under the mist, a river thrashed its way between tilted slabs. I managed to reach one such half-seen slab just before Anders released her hold completely as she fainted. I laid her down and inspected her wound. The ricochet had hit her cheekbone and left a groove running up to her temple. It being a head wound, there was a lot of blood, but it didn't look fatal if I could get her medical attention. But doing anything now with the medical kits we both carried seemed suicidal. I could hear the mutter of Tameera and Tholan's voices from above – distorted by the mist. Then, closer, and lower down by the river, another voice:

"Shabra tabul. Nud lockock ocker," something said.

It was like hiding in the closet from an intruder, only to have something growl right next to you. Stirred by the constant motion of the river, the mist slid through the air in banners, revealing and concealing. On the slab, we were five meters above the graveled riverbank upon which the creature squatted. Its head was level with me. Anders chose that moment to groan and I quickly slapped my hand over her mouth. The creature was pyramidal, all but one of its three pairs of arms folded complacently over the jut of its lower torso. In one huge black claw it held the remains of a sheq. With the fore-talon of another claw, it was levering a trapped bone from the white holly-thorn lining of its duck bill. The tiara of green eyes below its domed skull glittered.

"Brong da bulla," it stated, having freed the bone and flung it away.

It was no consolation to realize that the sheq corpses had attracted the gabbleduck here. Almost without volition, I crouched lower, hoping it did not see me, hoping that if it did, I could make myself appear less appetizing. My hands shaking, I reached down and began taking line off the winder at Anders's belt. The damned machine seemed so noisy and the line far too bright an orange. I got enough to tie around my waist as a precaution. I then undid the straps to her pack, and eased her free of that encumbrance. Now, I could slide her down toward the back of the slab, taking us out of the creature's line of sight, but that would put me in the foliage down there and it would be sure to hear me. I decided to heave her up, throw her over my shoulder, and just get out of there as fast as I could. But just then, a bullet smacked into the column of my claw frame and knocked me down flat, the breath driven out of me.

I rolled over, looking toward the gabbleduck as I did so. I felt my flesh creep. It was gone. Something that huge had no right to be able to move so quickly and stealthily. Once on my back, I gazed up at Tholan and his sister as they came down the cliff. My claw frame was heavy and dead, and so too would I be, but whether by bullet or chewed up in that nightmare bill was debatable.

The two halted a few meters above, and, with their claw frames gripping backward against the rock, freed their arms so they could leisurely take aim with their Opteks. Then something sailed out of the mist and slammed into the cliff just above Tameera, and dropped down. She started screaming, intestines and bleeding flesh caught between her and the cliff – the half-chewed corpse of a sheq. The gabbleduck loomed out of the mist on the opposite side of the slab from where it had disappeared, stretched up and up and extended an arm that had to be three meters long. One scything claw knocked Tameera's Optek spinning away and made a sound like a knife across porcelain as it scraped stone. On full automatic, Tholan fired his weapon into the body of the gabbleduck, the bullets thwacking away with seemingly no effect. I grabbed Anders and rolled with her to the side of the slab, not caring where we dropped. We fell through foliage and tangled growth, down into a crevasse where we jammed until I undid my frame straps and shed my pack ahead of us.

"Shabber grubber shabber!" the gabbleduck bellowed accusingly.

"Oh god oh god oh god!" Tameera.

More firing from Tholan.

"Gurble," tauntingly.

"I'll be back for you, fucker!"

I don't know if he was shouting at the gabbleduck or me.

———————

There was water in the lower part of the crevasse – more than enough to fill my purifying bottle and to clean the blood from Anders' wound before dressing it. I used a small medkit diagnosticer on her and injected the drugs it manufactured in response to her injuries. Immediately, her breathing eased and her color returned. But we were not in a good position. The gabbleduck was moving about above us, occasionally making introspective and nonsensical comments on the situation. A little later, when I was trying to find some way to set up the blister tent, a dark shape occluded the sky above.

"Urbock shabber goh?" the gabbleduck enquired, then, not being satisfied with my lack of response, groped down into the crevasse. It could reach only as far as the ridge where my claw frame was jammed. With a kind of thoughtful impatience, it tapped a fore-talon against the stone, then withdrew its arm.

"Gurble," it decided, and moved away.

Apparently, linguists who have loaded a thousand languages into their minds despair trying to understand gabbleducks. What they say is nonsensical, but frustratingly close to meaning. There's no reason for them to have such complex voice boxes, especially to communicate with each other, as on the whole they are solitary creatures and speak to themselves. When they meet it is usually only to mate or fight, or both. There's also no reason for them to carry structures in their skulls capable of handling vastly complex languages. Two-thirds of their large brains they seem to use hardly at all. Science, in their case, often supports myth.

Driving screw pitons into either side of the crevasse, I was eventually able to moor the tent across. Like a hammock, the tough material of the groundsheet easily supported our weight, even with all the contortions I had to go through to get Anders into the sleeping bag. Once she was safely ensconced, I found that evening blue had arrived. Using a torch, I explored the crevasse, finding how it rose to the surface at either end. Then the danger from octupals, stirring in the sump at the crevasse bottom, forced me back to the tent. The following night was not good. A veritable swarm of octupals swamping the tent had me worrying that their extra weight would bring it down. It was also very very dark, down there under the mist. Morning took forever to arrive, but when it eventually did, Anders regained consciousness.

––––––––

"They tried to kill us," she said, after lubricating her mouth with purified water.

"They certainly did."

"Where are we now?"

"In a hole." She stared at me and I went on to explain the situation.

"So how do we get out of this?" she eventually asked.

"We've both lost our claw frames, but at least we've retained our oxygen bottles and catalyzers. I wish I'd told Tholan to screw his untraceable com bullshit." I thought for a moment. "What about your palm com? Could we use it to signal?"

"It's his, just like the claw frame I was using. He'll have shut it down by now. Should we be able to get to it." She looked up. Her backpack was up there on the slab, up there with the gabbleduck.

"Ah."

She peered at me. "You're saying you really have no way of communicating with the citadel?"

"Not even on my blimp. You saw my contract with Tholan. I didn't risk carrying anything, as he seems the type to refuse payment for any infringements."

"So what now?" she asked.

"That rather depends on Tholan and Tameera . . . and on you."

"Me?"

"I'm supposing that, as a valued employee, you too have one of those implants?" Abruptly she got a sick expression. I went on, "My guess is that those two shits have gone for my blimp to bring it back here. If we stay in one place, they'll zero in on your implant. If we move they'll still be able to track us. We'll have to stay down low under the mist and hope they don't get any lucky shots in. The trouble is that to our friend down here we would be little more than an entrée."

"You could leave me – make your own way back. Once out of this area they'd have trouble finding you."

"It had to be said," I agreed. "Now let's get back to how we're going to get out of here."

———

After we had repacked the blister tent and sleeping bag, we moved to the end of the crevasse, which, though narrow, gave easier access to the surface. Slanting down one way, to the graveled banks of the river, was another slab, bare and slippery. Above us was the edge of the slab we had rolled from, and, behind that, disappearing into mist, rose the wall of stone I had earlier descended. Seeing this brought home to me just how deep was the shit trap we occupied. The citadel was just over two hundred kilometers away. I estimated our travel rate at being not much more than a few kilometers a day. The journey was survivable. The Almanac loadings I'd had told me what we could eat, and there would never be any shortage of water. Just so long as our catalyzers held out and neither of us fell . . . .

"We'll run that line of yours between us, about four meters to give us room to maneuver. I'll take point."

"You think it's safe to come out?" Anders asked.

"Not really, but it's not safe to stay here, either."

Anders ran the line out from her winder and locked it, and I attached its end ring to a loop on the back of my belt before working my way up to the edge of the slab. Once I hauled myself up, I was glad to see her pack still where I had abandoned it. I was also glad that Anders did not require my help to climb up – if I had to help her all the way, the prospective journey time would double. Anders shrugged on her pack, cinched the stomach strap. We then made our way to where vegetation grew like a vertical forest up the face of the cliff. Before we attempted to enter this, I took out my palm com and worked out the best route – one taking us back toward the citadel, yet keeping us under the mist, but for the occasional ridge. Then, climbing through the tangled vegetation, I couldn't shake the feeling that something was watching us, something huge and dangerous, and that now it was following us.

––––––––

The first day was bad. It wasn't just the sheer physical exertion; it was the constant dim light underneath the mist sapping will and blackening mood. I knew Tameera and Tholan would not reach us that day, but I also knew that they could be back overhead in the blimp by the following morning blue if they traveled all night. But they would stop to rest. Certainly they knew they had all the time they wanted to take to find and kill us.

As the sun went down, Anders erected one blister tent on a forty-degree slab – there was no room for the other tent. I set about gathering some of the many rock conches surrounding us. We still had rations, but I thought we should use such abundance, as the opportunity might not present itself later on. I also collected female spider vine flowers, and the sticky buds in the crotch branches of walker trees. I half expected Anders to object when I began broiling the molluscs, but she did not. The conches were like chewy fish, the flowers were limp and like slightly sweet lettuce, the buds have no comparison in Earthly food because none is so awful. Apparently, it was a balanced diet. I packed away the stove and followed Anders into the blister tent just as it seemed the branches surrounding us were beginning to move. Numerous large warty octupals were dragging themselves through the foliage. They were a kind unknown to me, therefore a kind not commonly encountered, else I would have received something on them in the Almanac's general load.

In the morning, I was chafed from the straps in our conjoined sleeping bags (they stopped us ending up in the bottom of the bag on that slope) and irritable. Anders was not exactly a bright light either. Maybe certain sugars were lacking in the food we had eaten, because, after munching down ration bars while we packed away our equipment, we quickly started to feel a lot better. Or maybe it was some mist-born equivalent of SAD.

An hour after we set out, travel became a lot easier and a lot more dangerous. Before, the masses of vegetation on the steep slopes, though greatly slowing our progress, offered a safety net if either of us fell. Now we were quickly negotiating slopes not much steeper than the slab on which Anders had moored the tent the previous night, and sparse of vegetation. If we fell here, we would just accelerate down to a steeper slope or sheer drop, and a final impact in some dank rocky sump. We were higher, I think, than the day before – the mist thinner. The voice of the gabbleduck was mournful and distant there.

"Urecoblank . . . scudder," it called, perhaps trying to lure its next meal.

"Shit, shit," I said as I instinctively tried to increase my pace and slipped over, luckily catching hold before I slid down.

"Easy," said Anders.

I just hoped the terrain would put the damned thing off, but somehow I doubted that. There seemed to me something almost supernatural about the creature. Until actually seeing the damned thing, I had never believed there was one out here. I'd thought Myral's gabbleduck as mythical as mermaids and centaurs on Earth.

"What the hell is that thing doing here anyway?" I asked.

"Probably escaped from a private collection," Anders replied. "Perhaps someone bought it as a pet and got rid of it when it stopped being cute."

"Like that thing was ever cute?" I asked.

Midday, and the first Optek shots began wanging off the stone around us, and the shadow of my blimp drew above. A kind of lightness infected me then. I knew, one way or another, that we were going to die, and that knowledge just freed me of all responsibility to myself and to the future.

"You fucking missed!" I bellowed.

"That'll soon change!" came Tholan's distant shout.

"There's no need to aggravate him," Anders hissed.

"Why? Might he try to kill us?" I spat back.

Even so, I now led us on a course taking us lower down into the mist. The firing tracked us, but I reckoned the chances of us being hit were remote. Tholan must have thought the same, because the firing soon ceased. When we stopped to rest under cover of thicker vegetation, I checked my palm com and nearly sobbed on seeing that in one and half days we had covered less than three kilometers. It was about right, but still disheartening. Then, even worse, I saw that ahead, between two mounts, there was a ridge we must climb over to stay on course. To take another route involved a detour of tens of kilometers. Undoubtedly, the ridge rose out of the mist. Undoubtedly, Tholan had detected it on his palm com too.

"What do we do?" Anders asked.

"We have to look. Maybe there'll be some sort of cover."

"Seeble grubber," muttered the gabbleduck in the deeper mist below us.

"It's fucking following us," I whispered.

Anders just nodded.

Then even more bad news came out of the mist.

I couldn't figure out quite what I was seeing out there in the canyon beside us, momentarily visible through the mist. Then, all of a sudden, the shape, on the end of its thin but hugely tough line, became recognizable. I was looking at a four-pronged blimp anchor, with disposable cams taped to each of the prongs. We got moving again, heading for that ridge. I equated getting to the other side with safety. Ridiculous, really.

"He's got . . . infrared . . . on them," I said, between gasps.

A fusillade sounding like the full fifty-round clip of an Optek slammed into the slope just ahead of us.

"Of course . . . he's no way . . . of knowing which camera . . . is pointing . . . where," I added.

Then a flare dropped, bouncing from limb to limb down through the vertical jungle, and the firing came again, strangely, in the same area. I glimpsed the anchor again, further out and higher. Tholan and his sister had no real experience of piloting a blimp – it wasn't some gravcar they could set on autopilot. Soon we saw the remains of what they had been targeting: an old sheq too decrepit to keep up with its seven, probably replaced by a new hatching. It was hanging over the curved fibrous bough of a walker tree, great holes ripped through its body by Optek bullets.

We climbed higher as the slope became steeper, came to the abrupt top edge of this forest of walker trees, made quick progress stepping from horizontal trunk to trunk with the wall of stone beside us. After a hundred meters of this, we had to do some real climbing up through a crack to a slope we could more easily negotiate. My feet were sore and my legs ached horribly. Constantly walking along slopes like this put pressure on feet and ankles they were certainly not accustomed to. I wondered just how long my boots and gloves would last in this terrain. They were tough – made with monofiber materials used by the military – but nothing is proof against constant abrasion on stone. Maybe a hundred days of this? Who was I kidding?

By midday, we were on the slope that curved round below one of the mounts, then blended into the slope leading up to the ridge. Checking the map on my palm com, I saw that there was likely a gutter between the ridge and the mount. I showed this to Anders.

"There may be cover there," I said.

She stared at me, dark rings under her eyes – too exhausted to care. We both turned then, and peered down into the mist and canted forests. There came the sound of huge movement, the cracking of walker trunks, broken vegetation showering down through the trees below us.

"Come on." I had no devil-may-care left in me. I was just as weary as Anders. We reached the gutter, which was abundant with hand and footholds, but slippery with rock-slime. We climbed slowly and carefully up through thinning mist. Then the blimp anchor rappeled down behind and above us like an iron chandelier.

"Surprise!" Tameera called down to us.

The mist was now breaking, and I glimpsed the lumpy peak of the mount looming to our left. Higher up, its propellers turning lazily to hold it against a breeze up from the ridge, floated my blimp. Tholan and Tameera stood out on the catwalk. Both of them armed, and I was sure I could see them grinning even from that distance. I swore and rested my forehead against slimy stone. We had about ten meters of clear air to the top of the ridge, then probably the same over the other side. No way could we move fast enough – not faster than a speeding bullet. I looked up again. Fuck them. I wasn't going to beg, I wasn't going to try to make any last-minute deals. I turned to Anders.

"We'll just keep climbing," I said.

She nodded woodenly, and I led the way. A shot slammed into the rock just above me, then went whining down the gutter. They were playing, for the moment. I glanced up, saw that the blimp was drifting sideways toward the mount. Then I saw it.

The arm folded out and out. The wrongness I felt about it, I guess, stemmed from the fact that it possessed too many joints. A three-fingered hand, with claws like black scythes, closed on the blimp anchor and pulled. Seated on the peak, the gabbleduck looked like some monstrous child holding the string of a toy balloon.

"Brong da lockock," it said.

Leaning over the catwalk rail, Tholan tried pumping shots into the monster. Tameera shrank back against the cabin's outer wall, making a high keening sound. The gabbleduck gave the blimp anchor a sharp tug, and Tholan went over the edge, one long scream as he fell, turned to an oomph as the monster caught him in one of its many hands. It took his rifle and tossed it away like the stick from a cocktail sausage, then it stuffed him into its bill.

"Keep going!" Anders shoved me in the back.

"It used us as bait to get them," I said.

"And now it doesn't need us."

I continued to climb, mindful of my handholds, aware that the gabbleduck was now coming down off its mount. We reached the ridge. I glanced down the other side into more mist, more slopes. I looked aside as the gabbleduck slid down into mist, towing the blimp behind it, Tameera still keening. It had its head tilted back and with one hand was shoving Tholan deeper into its bill. After a moment, it seemed to get irritated, and tore his kicking legs away while it swallowed the rest of him. Then the mist engulfed the monster, the blimp shortly afterwards. Tameera's keening abruptly turned to a long agonized scream, then came a crunching sound.

"It'll come for us next," said Anders, eyeing the stirring mist, then shoving me again.

We didn't stand a chance out here – I knew that.

"What the hell are you doing?"

I passed back the ring of the line that joined us together. "Wind it in."

She set the little motor running, orange line-cladding falling around her feet. I glanced at her and saw dull acceptance that I was abandoning her at last. The large shape came up out of the mist, shuddering. I began to run along the ridge. It was a guess, a hope, a chance – on such things might your life depend.

The anchor was snagging in the outer foliage of walker trees and the blimp, now free of two man weights and released by the gabbleduck, was rising again. I was going for the line first, though I'm damned if I knew how I would climb the four-millimeter-thick cable. At the last moment, I accelerated, and leapt: three meters out and dropping about the same distance down. My right leg snapped underneath me on the roof of the cabin, but I gave it no time to hurt. I dragged myself to the edge, swung down on the blimp cables, and was quickly in through the airtight door. First, I hit the controls to fold the anchor and reel in the cable, then I was in the pilot's seat making the blimp vent gas and turning it toward where Anders waited. Within minutes, she was on the catwalk and inside and I was pumping gas back into the blimp again. But we weren't going anywhere.

"Oh no . . . no!" Anders's feeling of the unfairness of it all was in that protest. I stared out at the array of green eyes, and at the long single claw it had hooked over the catwalk rail. I guessed that it would winkle us out of the cabin like the meat of a rock conch from its shell. I didn't suppose the bubble metal alloys would be much hindrance to it.

"Gurble," said the gabbleduck, then suddenly its claw was away from the rail and we were rising again. Was it playing with us? We moved closer to the windows and looked down, said nothing until we were certainly out of its reach, said nothing for some time after that. At the last, and I don't care how certain the scientists are that they are just animals, I'm damned sure that the gabbleduck waved to us.

Acknowledgements

"Introduction: On the Shoulders of Giants" © 2015 Robert Hood. Original to this volume.

"Occupied" © 2014 Natania Barron. Originally published in *Kaiju Rising: Age of Monsters*. Reprinted by permission of the author.

"Titanic!" © 2013 Lavie Tidhar. Originally published in *Apex*. Reprinted by permission of the author.

"Now I Am Nothing" © 2014 Simon Bestwick. Originally published in *World War Cthulhu*. Reprinted by permission of the author.

"The Lighthouse Keeper of Kurohaka Island" © 2014 Kane Gilmour. Originally published in *Kaiju Rising: Age of Monsters*. Reprinted by permission of the author.

"Breaking the Ice" © 2007 Maxine McArthur. Originally published in *Daikaiju! 2: Revenge of the Giant Monsters*. Reprinted by permission of the author.

"Mamu, or Reptillon vs Echidonah" © 2007 Nick Stathopoulos. Originally published in *Daikaiju! 3: Giant Monsters Against the World*. Reprinted by permission of the author.

"Kadimakara and Curlew" © 2007 Jason Nahrung. Originally published in *Daikaiju! 2: Revenge of the Giant Monsters*. Reprinted by permission of the author.

About the Contributors

Robert Hood is an Australian writer, whose long career in the speculative fiction field has been punctuated with film commentary, notably concentrating on the cinema of giant monsters. He co-edited the award-winning *Daikaiju! Giant Monster Tales* in 2005, following up with two further volumes of rampaging kaiju, and is the creator of the website Undead Backbrain. His latest book is *Peripheral Visions: The Collected Ghost Stories* (IFWG Publishing). His author website is roberthood.net.

Natania Barron is a word tinkerer with a lifelong love of the fantastic. She has a penchant for the speculative, and has written tales of invisible soul-eating birds, giant cephalopod goddesses, gunslinger girls, and killer kudzu, just to name a few. Her first novel, *Pilgrim of the Sky*, is a mythpunk multiverse adventure, and her short stories can be found in *Weird Tales*, *EscapePod*, *Crossed Genres* and many anthologies. She lives in North Carolina with her family.

Lavie Tidhar is the author of *A Man Lies Dreaming*, *The Violent Century*, and the World Fantasy Award winning *Osama*. His other works include the Bookman Histories trilogy, several novellas, two collections and a forthcoming comics mini-series, *Adler*. He currently lives in London.

Described as "among the most important writers of contemporary British horror" by Ramsey Campbell, *Simon Bestwick* is the author of *Tide Of Souls*, *The Faceless*, the serial novel *Black Mountain*, and the upcoming *Hell's Ditch* and *Redman's Hill*. Having spent most of his life in Manchester, he now lives in Liverpool with a long-suffering girlfriend.

This is taking some getting used to, but he's starting to enjoy it. When not writing, he goes for walks, watches movies, listens to music and does all he can to avoid having to get a proper job again. All donations towards this worthy cause will be gratefully received.

Kane Gilmour is the international bestselling author of *The Crypt of Dracula* and *Resurrect*. His short stories have appeared in *Kaiju Rising: Age of Monsters*, *SNAFU II: Survival of the Fittest*, and *MECH: Age of Steel*. He also writes the sci-fi noir webcomic, *Warbirds of Mars*. He lives with his family in Vermont. Find him on the web at kanegilmour.com.

Maxine McArthur has published three science-fiction novels and a number of short stories. Her first novel *Time Future* won the 1999 George Turner Prize and her third novel *Less Than Human* won the 2005 Aurealis Award for science fiction novel. Her short stories have appeared in anthologies by the Canberra Speculative Fiction Guild, *Aurealis* magazine and several other anthologies, and in Ticonderoga Press *Year's Best Australian Fantasy and Horror 2010* and *2011*. She lives in Canberra and works as an editor at the Australian National University.

Not generally known for his writing, *Nick Stathopoulos* nevertheless has had small amounts of fiction published in various publications over the years. Nick was born in 1959. The son of Greek migrants, he grew up in the Western suburbs of Sydney. A graduate of Macquarie University, he is a multi-award winning illustrator and has worked as an artist for over thirty years in fine art, film, television, animation and book publishing. He is currently a finalist in the prestigious BP Portrait Prize in London (Robert Hoge), and was a finalist in the Archibald Prize in 2003 (Mr Squiggle), 2008 (David Stratton), and 2010 (Geoff Ostling) and 2012 (Fenella Kernebone). He has also been a two-time finalist in the Doug Moran National Portrait Prize. He exhibits regularly at Sydney's NG Art Gallery. He divides his time between an inner city terrace studio and a cottage in Katoomba.

Jason Nahrung grew up on a Queensland, Australia cattle property and now lives in Ballarat with his wife, the writer Kirstyn McDermott. His fiction is invariably darkly themed, perhaps reflecting his passion for classic B-grade horror films and '80s goth rock. His most recent long-fiction title are *Salvage* (Twelfth Planet Press) and the outback vampire duology *Blood and Dust* and *The Big Smoke* released in 2015 by Clan Destine Press. He lurks online at jasonnahrung.com.

Emily Devenport has been published in the U.K., Italy and Israel, under three pen names. Her novels are *Shade, Larissa, Scorpianne, Eggheads, The Kronos Condition, Godheads, Broken Time* (which was nominated for the Philip K. Dick Award), *Belarus* and *Enemies*. Her new novels, *The Night Shifters, Spirits of Glory* and *Pale Lady*, are in ebook form on Amazon, Smashwords, etc. Her short stories were published in *Asimov's SF Magazine, Full Spectrum, Uncanny, Clarkesworld* and *Aborginal SF*, whose readers voted her a Boomerang Award. She blogs at www.emsjoiedeweird.com. Someday she hopes to get her degree in Geology and volunteer at a National or State Park.

Tessa Kum wrote her story many years ago, and still thinks crabs have mighty scary faces. Recent publications she has appeared in include the *Review of Australian Fiction* and *Baggage*, an anthology of speculative fiction. She lives in Melbourne with a small angry bird and drinks a lot of tea. Find her at silence-without.blogspot.com

Steve Rasnic Tem's latest books include *In the Lovecraft Museum* (PS Publishing) and the massive collection *Out of the Dark: A Storybook of Horrors* from Centipede. Following up his 2014 novel *Blood Kin*, in 2016 Solaris will present his dark Sf novel *Ubo*, a meditation on violence as seen through the eyes of some of history's most disreputable figures.

Frank Wu is a transdimensional interspace being, living physically near Boston with his wife Brianna the Magnificent, but regularly projecting his mind across time and space to commune with dinosaurs and energy beings. Visualizations and written accounts of these journeys can be found in *Analog, Amazing Stories, Realms of Fantasy* and the radiation-hardened memory bunkers of planet Gorsplax.

Adam Ford is the author of the short story collection *Heroes and Civilians*, the novel *Man Bites Dog* and the poetry collections *Not Quite the Man for the Job* and *The Third Fruit is a Bird*. His stories have appeared in *Daikaiju! Giant Monster Stories, This Mutant Life, Aurealis* and *Desktop*. His website is theotheradamford.wordpress.com

Being able to escape into the realm of the imagination was handy growing up as the youngest of eleven. *Chris McMahon*'s three-book fantasy series, The Jakirian Cycle, showcases his unique imagination. This is Heroic Fantasy in a world of ceramic weapons, where all metal is magical (prequel novella free website download). Chris is also a chemical engineer, and applies this specialist knowledge and mindset to his writing. He is currently working on a hard SF novel called *The Tau Ceti Diversion* – a collision of corporate-driven space exploration and alien first contact (see chrismcmahon.net for details).

Perth-based writer *Martin Livings* has had over eighty short stories in a variety of magazines and anthologies. His first novel, *Carnies*, first published by Hachette Livre in 2006, was nominated for both the Aurealis and Ditmar awards, and has since been republished by Cohesion Press. martinlivings.com.

J.C. Koch is scared by horror stories but writes them anyway. J.C.'s stories have appeared in *Arkham Tales, Necrotic Tissue, Penumbra, Kaiju Rising: Age of Monsters, The Madness of Cthulhu Vol. 1*, and *A Darke Phantastique*. In addition to writing about scary things, J.C. also likes to do scary things like pay attention to politics, keep up with the Kardashians, and play the stock market. With no time to actually do any of those things, though, J.C. tends to stay hidden under the bed, letting more of the terrors of the mind bleed onto the page, both metaphorically and literally. Reach J.C. (otherwise known as *Gini Koch*) at Going Bump in the Night (ginikoch.com/jkbookstore.htm).

Gary McMahon is the award-winning author of nine novels and several short story collections. His acclaimed short fiction has been reprinted in various "Year's Best" volumes. *Gary* lives with his family in West Yorkshire, where he trains in Shotokan karate and cycles up and down the Yorkshire hills. Website: garymcmahon.com

James A. Moore is the award winning author of over twenty-five novels, thrillers, dark fantasy and horror alike, including the critically acclaimed *Fireworks, Under The Overtree, Blood Red,* the *Serenity Falls* trilogy (featuring his recurring anti-hero, Jonathan Crowley) and his most recent novels, *Cherry Hill* and *Smile No More.* In addition to writing multiple short stories, he has also edited, with Christopher Golden and Tim Lebbon, the British Invasion anthology for Cemetery Dance Publications. His most recent novels include *The Blasted Lands* (A Seven Forges novel), *Alien: Sea of Sorrows* and the forthcoming *City of Wonders.*

Michael Canfield has published horror, mystery, suspense, fantasy, science fiction and just-plain-odd stories in *Daily Science Fiction, Escape Pod, Strange Horizons* and other places. His story "Super-Villains" was reprinted in the prestigious *Fantasy: The Best of the Year* series, edited by Rich Horton. Born in Las Vegas, he lives in Seattle.

Cody Goodfellow has written five novels – his latest is *Repo Shark* (Broken River Books) – and co-written three more with John Skipp. Two of his three collections received the Wonderland Book Award. He wrote, co-produced and scored the short Lovecraftian hygiene film *Stay At Home Dad,* which can be viewed on YouTube. He is also a director of the H.P.

Lovecraft Film Festival–Los Angeles and cofounder of Perilous Press, a micropublisher of modern cosmic horror. He "lives" in Burbank, California.

Jonathan Wood is an Englishman in New York. His urban fantasy series, which begins with *No Hero* has been described "a dark, funny, rip-roaring adventure" by *Publishers Weekly*, and Charlaine Harris, author of the Sookie Stackhouse novels described it as, "so funny I laughed out loud." His short fiction has appeared in *Weird Tales*, *Chizine* and *Beneath Ceaseless Skies*. He can be found online at jonathanwoodauthor.com.

Jeremiah Tolbert lives in Kansas with his wife and son. He is a web designer and life-long fan of all things kaiju. His son's room is decorated with pictures of baby Godzilla, and he looks forward to the day soon when they can watch kaiju movies together on Saturday afternoons.

Daniel Braum is an American author whose favorite kaiju are Gidorah, Mothra and Gamera. His science fiction, fantasy and horror stories often reside in the places between genres. More about his fiction can be found at danielbraum.com and bloodandstardust.wordpress.com.

Penelope Love is an Australian writer whose stories have appeared in Australian and U.S. anthologies. Her story, "A Small Bad Thing", was first published in *Bloodstones* (Ticonderoga Press) and was reprinted in *The Year's Best Australian Fantasy and Horror 2013*. Her work has been nominated for the Aurealis Awards 'Best Science Fiction Short Story' for 2007, 2010 and 2011, and has appeared in the award-winning anthologies, *One Small Step* (Fable Publishing) and *Belong* (Ticonderoga Press).

Alys Sterling shares a small flat in London with the Cult of Khoshek, who refuse to leave due to a prophecy that the Great One will manifest any day now, via her television set. She plays bass guitar in a band called